OLYMPUS
AT WAR

Also by Kate O'Hearn

The Flame of Olympus

The New Olympians

Pegasus

OLYMPUS AT WAR

KATE O'HEARN

Aladdin

NEW YORK   LONDON   TORONTO   SYDNEY   NEW DELHI

ALADDIN

An imprint of Simon & Schuster Children's Publishing Division
1230 Avenue of the Americas, New York, NY 10020
First Aladdin paperback edition January 2014
Text copyright © 2013 by Kate O'Hearn
Cover illustration copyright © 2013 by Jason Chan
All rights reserved, including the right of reproduction in whole or in part in any form.
ALADDIN is a trademark of Simon & Schuster, Inc., and related logo
is a registered trademark of Simon & Schuster, Inc.
Also available in an Aladdin hardcover edition.
For information about special discounts for bulk purchases, please contact
Simon & Schuster Special Sales at 1-866-506-1949 or business@simonandschuster.com.
The Simon & Schuster Speakers Bureau can bring authors to your live event.
For more information or to book an event contact the Simon & Schuster Speakers Bureau
at 1-866-248-3049 or visit our website at www.simonspeakers.com.
Designed by Karin Paprocki
The text of this book was set in Adobe Garamond.
Manufactured in the United States of America 0815 OFF
4 6 8 10 9 7 5
The Library of Congress has cataloged the hardcover edition as follows:
Kate O'Hearn.
[Olympus at war]
Pegasus / by Kate O'Hearn.—First Aladdin hardcover ed.
p. cm.
Summary: Reborn as the Flame, thirteen-year-old Emily has saved Olympus from destruction,
but when the gruesome Nirads begin a new invasion, Emily and her friends become entangled
in the conflict as old grudges are unearthed and new enemies are discovered.
978-1-4424-4412-6 (hc)
[1. Pegasus (Greek mythology)—Fiction. 2. Diana (Roman deity)—Fiction. 3. Monsters—Fiction.
4. Mythology, Roman—Fiction. 5. Fantasy.] 1. Title.
PZ7.O4137Peg 2012
[Fic] dc23
2011052026
ISBN 978-1-4424-4413-3 (pbk)
ISBN 978-1-4424-4414-0 (eBook)

OLYMPUS
AT WAR

OLYMPUS WAS UNLIKE ANYWHERE EMILY
had ever been before. It was a magical fantasyland
filled with people and creatures beyond imagination.
A place where rain didn't fall but the lush green gardens never wilted. Flowers bloomed constantly, filling the air with their intoxicating fragrances. The air
itself seemed alive. It was honey sweet and warm and
enveloped you in a blanket of peace; it was rich with
the sounds of singing birds and filled with insects
that never stung. If a bee landed on you, it was only
because it wanted to be petted.

The buildings in Olympus were as beautiful and
unique as the land itself. Most were made of smooth
white marble with tall, intricately carved pillars

reaching high into the clear blue sky. There were open theaters where the Muses danced and sang for the entertainment of all.

The wide cobbled streets were lined with statues of the strongest fighters and heroes. There were no cars or trucks pumping pollution into the air. The Olympians walked or flew wherever they needed to go. Occasionally they would ride in a chariot drawn by magnificent horses.

Then there were the libraries, more than Emily could count, containing the texts from the many worlds the Olympians visited and guarded. Some of her favorite books were in the library at Jupiter's palace, brought in especially for her.

Emily could never have imagined a more perfect place.

But living in Olympus, amid all this splendor, Emily was miserable.

She missed her father. She spent every waking moment thinking and worrying about him. He was back in her world, a prisoner of the Central Research Unit. The CRU was a secret government agency obsessed with capturing aliens and anything out of the ordinary to use as weapons. She had been their prisoner for a short time and knew how single-minded and cruel they were. But they still had her father. What were they doing to him? Were they punishing him because of her escape? Had they killed him? So many fears and unanswered questions tore at her heart that she could never be completely happy or stop worrying about him.

Even spending time with Pegasus didn't ease the pain. Emily was desperate to get back to New York to find her father, but Jupiter wouldn't let her go. He insisted her place was here among the other Olympians. And with the invading warrior race of Nirads still posing a threat to Olympus, Jupiter couldn't risk sending any of his fighters to Emily's world on a rescue mission. No matter how much she pleaded with the god, he refused to allow her to leave.

Emily paused as she walked through the gardens of Jupiter's palace. She raised her face to the sun and felt its warm rays streaming down on her. Was this the same sun that shone in her world? Was her father allowed to see it? From her own experience as a prisoner in the CRU's deep underground facility, she doubted it.

Emily felt even more determined. If Jupiter wouldn't let her go, she had no choice but to run away and rescue her father herself. Walking along the stream that coursed through Olympus, she saw a group of beautiful water nymphs splashing on the shore. They waved and called their strange greeting. Moments later they slipped beneath the surface, and the water calmed as if they'd never been there.

Lost in thought, Emily wasn't paying attention to where she was walking and tripped over a small rock. She cursed and righted herself. On top of everything else, she was still getting used to the new gold leg brace that Vulcan, the armorer of Olympus, had made for her. He had constructed it using the same gold as Pegasus's bridle. A very special gold that was lethal to Nirads. With one brief touch they were badly poisoned. Longer contact proved fatal to the ferocious warriors. With this brace Emily could not only defend herself against the invaders, she could walk and run once again.

But learning to get around with the strange device had taken time and effort. Now she could almost move as well as she had before her leg was permanently damaged by the Nirads in New York.

She walked toward Jupiter's maze, a large labyrinth built in the middle of a garden and consisting of tall green bushes grown in complicated patterns. It took a lot of practice to navigate it, but Emily and her friends had discovered that the maze was the perfect place to hold private conversations.

Emily found her way through the labyrinth, where Pegasus was waiting for her beside the pedestal at the center. The magnificent winged stallion always stole her breath. Standing quietly in the dark of the trees, he glowed brilliant white. His head was high and proud, and his coat shiny and well groomed. There wasn't a feather out of place on his neatly folded wings.

When Pegasus saw her, he whinnied excitedly and nodded his head.

Beside the winged horse stood Emily's best friend from New York, Joel. Joel's Roman features, black hair, and warm brown eyes always reminded her of the classic Italian paintings she'd seen in the art museum. He was no longer the violent, angry boy she had first met. Spending time in Olympus had softened his outer shell of rage and hurt due to the loss of his family. Now he let others see that he had a deeply caring heart and a ready laugh. Joel spent his days working with Vulcan in the Olympus armory. He had even helped design the brace on Emily's leg.

Emily looked around. "Where's Paelen?"

"He'll be here in a few minutes. He had something to pick up." Joel reached for her elbow. "Em, you're absolutely sure you want to do this?"

"What choice have I got?" Emily answered. "Joel, all I think about is saving my dad. There's nothing else I can do. We wouldn't have to sneak around like this if Jupiter would help!" She threw her hands up in frustration. As she brought them down, brilliant flames flashed from her fingertips, hit the edge of her good foot, and scorched the ground around it. Emily howled and hopped in pain.

"Emily, calm down!" Joel warned. "You know it gets worse when you're upset."

"Nuts!" she cried. "Being the Flame of Olympus is one thing. But constantly setting myself on fire is another!"

"You've got to calm down," Joel insisted. "Remember what Vesta taught you. You can control the Flame if you remain calm."

"That's easier said than done," Emily complained as she sat down and rubbed her singed foot. Ever since she emerged from the Temple of the Flame, she was discovering powers she couldn't control. Powers that continually set things alight.

Joel sat down beside her. "We'll get your dad out of there. I promise. But you can't help him if you can't control the Flame."

"Joel's right." Paelen emerged from the trees behind them. In contrast to Joel, he was small and wiry, and he was able to get into the tiniest of spaces. Paelen had a notorious habit of getting into trouble, but with his crooked grin and dark, sparkling eyes, he always found a way to make Emily smile. "And if I were you, I would lower your voices. Half the maze can hear your conversation." He sat down beside Emily and gave her a playful shove. "Set yourself on fire again I see."

"No, I tripped," Emily answered, shoving him back.

Paelen smiled his crooked smile. "Of course you

did; which is why your sandal is charcoal and still smoldering."

In the time they'd spent in Olympus, Emily had really grown to like Paelen. Between him and Joel, she couldn't have asked for better friends. Paelen was also one of the few Olympians who understood what they'd been through as prisoners of the CRU on Governors Island.

"Speaking of sandals"—Emily changed the subject—"you didn't steal Mercury's again, did you?" She noticed the winged sandals on his feet.

"Me? Of course not," Paelen said in mock horror. "You know I'm no longer a thief. Mercury just gave them to me. He is having another set made for himself." Paelen paused and frowned. "He said the sandals prefer to stay with me. I do not understand what he means, but I'm not going to say no to such a useful gift." He petted the tiny wings on the sandals. "These flying sandals saved our lives in your world and helped us escape the CRU. There is no telling what else they can do." He leaned closer to Emily and eagerly rubbed his hands together. "So, tell me. When do we leave for New York?"

Pegasus stepped forward and started to nicker.

Paelen nodded and translated for the others. "Pegasus heard Jupiter, Mars, and Hercules talking. They are going on an expedition to see if they can discover how the Nirads entered Olympus in such large numbers without being seen. Until they know and can secure the route, we are still in danger. Pegasus suggests if we are going to go to New York to rescue your father, we should leave once they're gone."

Emily rose and kissed the stallion on his soft muzzle. "Thank you, Pegasus. That's a great idea." She turned to Joel and Paelen. "It's settled, then. The moment Jupiter leaves, we're out of here!"

Quietly they discussed their plans as they strolled through the maze. Emily rested her hand on Pegasus's neck as he walked beside her.

"We'll need some human clothes," Joel mused aloud. "We can't arrive back in New York dressed like this."

"What is wrong with these?" Paelen looked down at his tunic. "I have always dressed this way."

"You're kidding, right?" Joel smirked. "Paelen,

we look like rejects from a gladiator movie! Look at me—I'm wearing a dress!"

"It's a tunic," Emily corrected him, "and I think it suits you." She looked down at her own beautiful gown made from fine white embroidered silk with an intricate braided gold belt at her waist. The material ended above the golden brace on her damaged left leg, leaving it exposed. Emily had never felt embarrassed revealing the deep, angry scars from the Nirad wounds while she was on Olympus. The Olympians regarded them as a badge of honor. She had earned them in the service of Olympus, and she had learned to be proud of them. But as she gazed down at her leg now, she realized that the deep scars and leg brace wouldn't be viewed as positively in her world.

"Joel's right," she agreed. "I can't go back there like this either. We've got to hide this brace."

Pegasus started to neigh, and Paelen translated. "If anyone should try to steal it from you, Pegasus would defend you, as would Joel and I." A playful twinkle returned to his eyes. "Of course, should that fail, you could always set yourself on fire again. That would surely scare off any attackers!"

"Thanks, Paelen," Emily teased as she shoved him lightly. Then she patted Pegasus on the neck. "And thank you, Pegs. But I still think we will need to find other clothing."

"Other clothing for what?"

Emily looked up at the owner of the new voice. Despite all the time they'd spent in Olympus, she still couldn't get over the sight of Cupid. Seeing Pegasus's wings had been strange at the beginning. But somehow they suited him. She couldn't imagine him without them. But looking at a teenager with colorful, pheasantlike feathered wings on his back was something else.

Cupid pulled in his wings and landed neatly in the maze before them. "So, where are you going that you need new clothing?" he asked.

"None of your business," Joel shot back. "Didn't your mother ever teach you any manners? It's not polite to listen in on other people's conversation."

"Of course," Cupid said. "But she also taught me that when humans and Olympians mix, there is always trouble. And what do I see before my curious eyes? Humans mixing with Olympians."

Cupid smiled radiantly at Emily, and it set her heart fluttering. She had a terrible crush on him, and he knew it. He was the most beautiful Olympian she had ever met, with fine features, light sandy blond hair, sapphire blue eyes that sparkled, and skin like polished marble. Though Cupid was very old, he looked no more than sixteen or seventeen.

Emily stole a glance at Joel and saw his temper starting to flare. The way Cupid pronounced the word "humans" was always meant as an insult. "Get out of here, Cupid," Joel warned. "This is a private conversation, and you are *not* welcome."

"Is this true?" Cupid said slyly to Emily. "Do you really wish me to go?"

The intensity of his stare kept the words from forming on her lips. Everything about him was trouble. Joel had told her some of the myths concerning Cupid. She knew that, like a coward, he had fled the area when the Nirads first attacked and had stayed away until the danger had gone. Yet despite all this, she couldn't tell him to go.

Before the moment became awkward, Pegasus stepped forward and snorted loudly.

"Trouble?" Cupid repeated as he turned and feigned innocence to the stallion. "I am not causing trouble. I just wanted to speak with the Flame."

"Her name is Emily," Paelen said defensively. He moved to stand in front of Emily to block her from Cupid. "Do not call her Flame."

"And I told you to leave," Joel added, taking position beside Paelen and crossing his arms over his chest.

"Or what?" Cupid challenged. "What will you do to me, human?"

Once again Pegasus snorted, and he pounded the ground with a golden hoof. There was no mistaking the warning. Emily saw fear rise in Cupid's eyes. Even Paelen took a cautious step back from the stallion.

"There is no need to lose your temper, Pegasus." Cupid held up his hands in surrender. "I shall go."

His wings opened as he prepared to fly. But before leaving, Cupid plucked a colorful feather from his right wing and placed it in Emily's hair. "Something to put under your pillow to remember me by," he said as he jumped into the air and flapped his large wings. "See you later, Flame!"

Pegasus reared on his hind legs, opened his own huge wings, and shrieked into the sky after him.

As Cupid escaped, he turned and waved back at her, laughing as he went.

"I came this close to hitting him!" Joel said, balling his hands into fists.

"Me too," Paelen said.

Pegasus gently nudged Emily and nickered softly.

"You must stay away from Cupid," Paelen explained. "Pegasus says he is trouble. Even more than— What?" Paelen turned sharply to the stallion. "Me? Pegasus, how can you compare Cupid to me? We are nothing alike. I may have been a thief, but Cupid is a troublemaking coward, and I resent being compared to him. And what about you?" Paelen turned to Emily. He pulled the feather from her hair and tossed it to the ground. "You should have told him to go. Cupid would think nothing of handing you over to the Nirads if it meant saving his own skin and feathers. Stay away from him!"

Emily watched in complete confusion as Paelen stormed off into the maze and disappeared. Paelen had never shown any trace of anger or raised his voice to her before. "What did I do?"

Joel looked at her in surprise. "You really don't know?"

When she shook her head, he said, "Never mind. We've got bigger things to worry about. You must learn to control those powers of yours before we leave. You've got your training session with Vesta. Keep it and learn as much as you can."

As Joel walked away, Emily turned to Pegasus and shook her head. "You know something, Pegs? The older I get, the more confused I get. Can you please tell me what just happened here?"

Pegasus gently nudged her and led her back toward Jupiter's palace to find Vesta.

Emily spent a long afternoon back in the Temple of the Flame struggling to learn how to master her powers. Vesta tried to teach her, but every time Emily summoned the powers, they became uncontrollable.

Vesta patiently explained how to pull back the Flame, to control it. But every time Emily tried, she failed, and flames shot wildly from her hands and around the temple.

"I can't do it," Emily complained, defeated.

"Child, you must focus," Vesta scolded. "I can see your mind is elsewhere. If you are not careful, you will lose control of your powers completely and hurt yourself as you did earlier today."

Emily's eyes shot over to where Pegasus stood at the entrance of the temple. He lowered his head guiltily.

"Thanks, Pegs," she muttered.

"Do not blame Pegasus for telling me what happened," Vesta said. "He cares about you and does not wish to see you harmed." Vesta rested her hands on Emily's shoulders. "Emily, you must understand. You are the Living Flame of Olympus. Your power feeds the Flame here in this temple, and it keeps us alive. Countless generations ago, I took the heart of the Flame to your world and hid it in a child. It has passed from girl to girl throughout the ages until it finally reached you. You were born with this power. I am sorry that we have had to summon it from within you to save Olympus. But the moment you sacrificed yourself in this temple you changed. Emily, you carry the power of the sun deep within you. If you do not harness these powers soon, you may do yourself and everyone around you a great harm."

Emily looked down at her burned sandal. She already knew how dangerous her powers were. She had accidentally burned up enough items in her quarters to prove it. It was reaching the point where she was running out of secret hiding places for the singed victims of her powers.

"I'm sorry," she finally said. "I'll try harder."

Turning back to the plinth, she looked into the brightly burning flames. They were fed by her and were the only things in Olympus her powers couldn't damage.

"All right," Vesta said patiently. "Look into the flames. I want you to focus on what you intend to do. Visualize yourself doing it. Then concentrate and carefully release the power within yourself."

Emily lifted both her hands and concentrated. She imagined that she was a giant blowtorch turning on the gases. She felt prickles start in her stomach and flow up her spine and flood down her raised arms toward her hands. "Come on, Em," she muttered to herself. "You can do it."

Suddenly a wide, wild stream of fire shot out of her fingertips.

"Very good. Now concentrate," Vesta instructed. "Control the stream, Emily. Make it tighter."

Emily held her breath as the raging flames shot out of her hands. Concentrating as Vesta taught her, she pulled back and refined them until they became a narrow beam of red light. But the tighter she pulled back, the more intense it became.

The beam of light shot through the flames in the plinth and across the temple until it hit the far wall. It did not stop. It burned a narrow hole right through the thick white marble and continued out into the sky over Olympus.

"Cut if off now, Emily," Vesta warned. "Just think 'stop'!"

In her head, Emily imagined shutting off the gases to the blowtorch. But nothing happened. She mentally turned all the dials and flicked all the switches that controlled her powers. But once again, the beam would not stop.

"Cut it off, Emily," Vesta cried. "You must make it obey you!"

Emily tried again and again, but nothing happened. As her panic increased, so did the intensity of the laserlike Flame. It pulsated as it tore through the skies over Olympus.

"I CAN'T STOP IT!"

A sudden blow from behind sent her tumbling forward, and she fell to the floor. With her concentration broken, the red beam stopped. She panted heavily and studied her hands. No burns, blemishes, or pain. She looked up, and what she saw made her suck in her breath. Pegasus's whole face and neck were burned bright red. Worst of all, his soft white muzzle was black and blistering. It was Pegasus who had knocked her over and stopped the flames. But when he touched her, her power had singed his beautiful skin.

"Pegasus!" Emily ran over to him. "I'm so sorry. I swear I didn't mean to do it!"

She felt sick as she inspected his wounds. She had done this to him. "Please, forgive me!" Without thinking, Emily reached forward and gently stroked his burned face. At her touch the skin started to heal. Soon Pegasus was completely restored.

"I can't do this, Pegs." Emily sobbed as she stepped away from him. "I just can't. I hurt you. What if I'd killed you? I'm just too dangerous to be around."

Emily dashed out of the temple. Tears rose to her eyes as she ran down the tall steps. She cringed as she replayed what happened and, worse still, what could have happened.

At the base of the steps, she looked up and saw Pegasus and Vesta emerging from the temple.

"Emily, stop!" Vesta called.

Emily turned and ran farther away. She couldn't face Pegasus again, knowing she had almost killed him. She ran past other Olympians on the street, ignoring their curious stares and concerned queries. She had to get away. Away from Pegasus and anyone else her powers could hurt. She was just too dangerous to be allowed in public.

Emily finally ran into the open amphitheater. The Muses weren't performing that day, so the thousands of seats sat empty and alone. The perfect place for someone dangerous. She ran down the steps, toward the center stage, and threw herself to the ground. It was over. Her life was over. There would be no trip back to New York, no rescue of her father.

All there was now was pain.

Sobs escaped her as she finally realized all the things she'd lost. She wished she'd never emerged from the flames at the temple. Olympus and Pegasus would have been better off without her.

Tears blinded Emily as she looked around in misery at the beautiful marble theater encircling her. She wiped them furiously away. As she flicked the tears off her fingers, there was a blinding flash and a terrible explosion.

Her world went black.

EMILY AWOKE IN HER BED. FOR AN INSTANT she feared she was back at the CRU facility on Governors Island. But as her eyes slowly focused, she saw that she was in her beautiful room at Jupiter's palace. All the windows were open, and the sheer curtains were blowing gently in the sweet, warm breeze.

"Welcome back."

The Great Hunter, Diana, was standing beside her bed. The two had formed a tight bond after their time together in New York. She was the daughter of Jupiter and everything Emily hoped to grow up to be like. Diana was strong, brave, and caring. She went to New York and risked her life to save Pegasus.

The tall woman took a seat on the edge of the bed

and lightly stroked Emily's forehead. "That was quite a shock for us."

Emily frowned. She was stiff and sore, with a pounding headache. She knew something big had happened—she just couldn't remember what. Finally she recalled the events at the temple. "I hurt Pegasus," she whispered miserably. "I burned him."

"Pegasus is fine," Diana assured. "You are the one we are all worried about."

Emily raised her head and looked around the room. They were alone. No Joel, no Paelen—and no Pegasus. Her friends were keeping away from her because she was dangerous. Her powers were uncontrollable, and now she had to be locked up.

"What happens now?" she asked softly, unable to face Diana. "Where are you going to lock me away?"

Diana frowned. "Lock you away? Child, why would we do that?"

Emily's emotions welled up. "Because I'm dangerous and I hurt Pegasus."

"Oh, Emily," Diana pulled her into a tight embrace. "No one is going to imprison you. Your powers got away from you, that's all. It has happened to all of us. We just did not expect to find your tears quite so potent."

"My tears?" Emily sniffed. "I don't understand."

Diana explained that the amphitheater caretaker had watched Emily run to the stage and saw how the flick of her tears had caused an explosion that shook all of Olympus. He was far enough away to be hurt, not killed. However, the blast did destroy the theater and create a huge crater. Pegasus finally found her suspended high in a tree several miles away.

"I-I don't understand," Emily said. "My tears caused an explosion?"

Diana nodded. "We do not really understand either. When the Flame emerged from you, Vesta said its full powers would be released. But she never expected them to be this potent. Even your tears are filled with the power of the sun."

She couldn't even cry without hurting herself or everyone around her! Every day was getting worse and worse. She was no longer a person, a girl with a bright future ahead of her. She had become a nuclear bomb waiting to go off.

"I don't want it," she finally said in a whisper. "I

don't want any of these powers. I didn't ask for them. I just want my old life back with my dad."

"I am sorry, but you do not have a choice," Diana said. "You were born with the Flame. It is part of you. But I promise, you can learn to control it. Do not fight your powers, Emily. Embrace them and accept them as your ally, not your enemy."

"And if I can't learn?" Emily asked.

"You must," Diana said as she stood and crossed to the door. "Rest now. You will feel better soon."

Emily doubted she would ever feel good again. She climbed stiffly from her bed and walked over to one of the windows. She sat on the ledge and quietly watched the activity below, just like she used to do in her apartment in New York.

But this wasn't Manhattan she was looking out over with its heavy traffic, police sirens, crowds, and shops. It was Olympus. The light breeze blowing through her hair was sweet and warm, not polluted like New York's smoggy air. She watched winged Olympians and large birds soaring together in the clear blue sky. Butterflies the size of cars fluttered around, playing a kind of tag with some young children. Down in the square, centaurs and giants walked and talked together as casually as people in her own world would. Everywhere she looked, Emily saw amazing things. But watching the world below only added to the feeling that things would never be normal again.

"Dad, where are you?" she said miserably. Emily no longer grieved over the death of her mother. Somehow in this strange and wondrous world, she always felt her mother's presence nearby, as though all she needed to do was reach out to touch her. It was her father who occupied all her waking moments. His rescue now seemed impossible. How could she help him if she couldn't even help herself? She was a dangerous monster—unable even to cry without possibly hurting or killing someone.

Lost in misery, Emily was unaware of time passing until she heard a gentle knock at her door.

"Emily?" a deep voice called. "May we enter?"

Emily was surprised to see Jupiter come into her room. Although she, Joel, and Paelen lived in his massive marble palace, she only ever saw him at mealtimes. But even then, those banquets were so big and noisy; she never got to speak with him. He had never been to her quarters, and the one time she did manage to speak privately with him was when she'd begged him to let her return to New York to rescue her father. That request had been denied.

"Jupiter." Emily bowed her head with respect.

"Emily, I was most disturbed to learn what happened at the theater yesterday. It seems your tears are very powerful. I hope you are all right."

"I'm fine, thank you," Emily said.

Behind Jupiter stood another man. He was equally large and had a commanding presence similar to that of the leader of Olympus. He was just as tall and had the same long white hair and full beard. But unlike the serious, somber face of Jupiter, this new man had a warm, smiling face filled with joy and mischief. The difference between the two could be found in their eyes: Jupiter's were dark and deep and seemed to hold the knowledge of the ages, while this man's eyes were so pale they were almost like pearls. In truth, to Emily he looked less like an Olympian and more like Santa Claus.

"I do not believe you have met my brother," Jupiter said casually. "This is Neptune." He turned to his brother. "And this is the Flame of Olympus. Although I have recently discovered she prefers to be called Emily."

"Emily," Neptune said as a huge smile appeared on his warm face. "My son told me what happened to you. How are you feeling?"

Emily's eyes grew wide as she remembered that Neptune was Pegasus's father. "I'm fine, thank you," she stuttered. She looked down at Neptune's strong, muscular legs beneath his tunic.

"Perhaps you expected a fish's tail?" Neptune started to chuckle.

Emily flushed and nodded. "I'm sorry, sir. I didn't mean to be rude and stare, but I'd always heard you lived in the sea."

Neptune's face wrinkled with booming laughter that seemed to fill the whole palace. "No doubt you thought I rode a chariot of shells drawn by a team of sea horses, carrying a trident in my hand as I stirred the seas into rage."

Emily's face turned redder and she nodded.

It was Jupiter's turn to chuckle. "Do not let him fool you, Emily. He does just that and more."

"But not when I am on land," Neptune finished, growing serious. As he stepped farther in the room, he turned back to the door. "Son, come in here."

Emily heard familiar and welcome clopping sounds coming from the corridor, and in moments Pegasus entered her bedroom. He was as blazing white as ever, and every feather lay smoothly on his wings. There was no evidence of the burns she had caused. Emily was grateful to find there was no trace of hesitation when he stepped up to her.

"Pegasus," she said softly as she stroked his soft muzzle. "Are you all right?"

"He is fine," Neptune said. "But he is very worried about you. After the incident at the amphitheater, he asked if I might be able to help. So I went to my most talented Sirens and asked them to weave their finest silk from the grasses that grow in the deepest part of the sea. It is my hope that this will help."

Emily watched Neptune produce a shimmering sea-green handkerchief from his tunic. It seemed to change color when it caught the light, and reminded her of iridescent fish scales. He handed it to her, and as she turned it in her hands, Emily saw an embroidered picture of her riding Pegasus in the center of the fine fabric.

"Pegasus gave the Sirens strands of hair from his tail for the embroidery," Neptune explained. "This is their best work."

"I just hope it works for the Flame's tears as well," Jupiter added. He stepped closer to Emily. "This was made with all the powers of the Sirens and the sea. Please keep it with you at all times. We believe it may be strong enough to collect and store your tears without causing any more damage to Olympus or yourself."

Emily looked at the beautiful, weightless handkerchief with the embroidered Pegasus. It was the most beautiful thing she'd ever seen in her life.

"All we need to do now is test it," Neptune said.

"Test it?" Emily said fearfully. "I'm not sure about that."

"Not today, child," Jupiter reassured as he put his arm lightly around her shoulders. "When you are feeling better. In the meantime, I want you to rest. That was a rather nasty surprise you had yesterday. When you are more recovered, ask Pegasus to take you to the new arena we are building for you. It will work as a much better training ground for your powers. Now that we have seen their extent, we need to ensure everyone's safety until you have better control of them."

Emily looked up at Jupiter and nodded. She thanked Neptune again for the beautiful gift and stood beside Pegasus as they left the room. When they had gone, Emily threw her arms around the stallion's thick neck.

"I'm so sorry I hurt you!" she cried. "It got away from me, and I couldn't stop it."

Pegasus nickered softly.

"Pegasus, what am I going to do? One more mistake like that and I could kill someone. I might do more damage to Olympus than the Nirads did."

Pegasus gently nudged her, to let her know he understood. He then invited her to stare into his eyes. As Emily locked into his gaze, a clear vision filled her mind. She was sitting on Pegasus's back, flying away from the palace—her fears and worries eased in that glorious moment.

"Can we?" she asked hopefully. Of all the wonderful things to do and see in Olympus, Emily's favorite was riding Pegasus and discovering new places she'd never been before.

Emily quickly changed and tied her new handkerchief to her braided belt. She climbed onto the stallion's back. When she was settled comfortably behind his large wings, Pegasus stepped up to one of the wide windows and confidently leaped through it.

Emily clung to the stallion's mane as they soared in the skies over Olympus. Riding Pegasus was better than all the roller-coaster rides she'd ever been on in her life! She felt safe with him, but at the same time, there was the wild exhilaration of flying high in the air with no safety harness. It was just her and Pegasus.

On the ground beneath them, people and creatures waved greetings to the Flame. In the sky around them, other winged citizens flew in formation beside them.

After some distance their escorts drifted away, and the two of them were flying alone. In no time her troubles were put aside and she savored the freedom she always felt when riding the magnificent winged stallion. As they gently glided in the thermal winds over the mountain range in Olympus, Emily could feel Pegasus's wings beating confidently.

Soon the stallion started to descend down the side of the mountain. Emily recognized the place they had gone on the very first day after she emerged from the temple. It was a private, secluded beach with shimmering silver sands beside a beautiful sparkling lake.

After he landed, Pegasus moved smoothly along the diamond-dust shore, his hooves splashing lightly in the water. Birds sang in the trees just back from the beach, and the air was rich with the smell of the lush green forest. Spending time with the stallion always made Emily feel better and cleared the cobwebs from her troubled mind.

She wasn't sure how long they'd been there when the peaceful tranquility was shattered by loud, urgent shouts from Paelen and Joel. She looked up in the sky and saw Joel clinging to Paelen's back as Mercury's winged sandals struggled to carry the combined weight of the two.

"Emily, are you all right?" Joel asked as he climbed

off Paelen's back. "Diana wouldn't let us see you. She said you needed to rest after you went nuclear and blew up the theater."

"I'm much better," Emily answered, grateful to see her friends. She reached forward and patted Pegasus's neck. "We both are."

"Good," Paelen said, "because we have a big problem. Nirads are back in Olympus."

"What?" Her feelings of peace ended with that one word: Nirads. The four-armed savage fighters who'd nearly killed her and Pegasus in New York and who had damaged her left leg.

"Where are they?" she demanded. "Is this another invasion?"

"I don't think so," Joel said. "We've heard there aren't that many."

"One Nirad is too many," Paelen added.

Emily looked at Pegasus and then her two friends. They had all thought the war with the Nirads was over. After the Flame was relit and the Olympians' powers restored, the warrior race had fled Olympus. No one imagined they would return. "So, what do we do? Get ready to fight?"

"No. Jupiter is raising the army again," Paelen said. "He, Neptune, and Hercules have gone out to where they were spotted to find out how many there are and how they are getting here. While they are gone, Mars and Vulcan are arming everyone with the same gold as your brace and Pegasus's bridle." He held up a golden dagger and pointed to the one on Joel's belt. "Apollo and Diana are organizing the remaining fighters. They've ordered us to find you and take you back to the palace. They don't want us to fight. We are to remain there with you until this is over."

Emily felt fear constricting her throat. The Nirads were back. She knew this time that she, as the living Flame of Olympus, was their target. If she were to somehow be killed or even severely wounded, the Flame at the Temple could be extinguished, and then there would be no hope for anyone's survival. She couldn't let that happen.

"We're not going back to the palace," she said, deciding. "It's too dangerous, and the Nirads are too big and strong. We'd be sitting ducks! I think we should go to New York. We were planning to anyway. When we get my dad free, I'm sure he can help." Emily looked at the stallion. "Pegs, what do you think we should do?"

Pegasus pawed the sand, whinnied loudly, and nodded his head.

Emily patted the stallion's neck. "It's settled, then. We go back to New York right now."

AS THEY PREPARED TO LEAVE, EMILY'S FEARS and doubts rose. She didn't want to stay at the palace and await the Nirads, but deep down she felt like she was abandoning the Olympians in their moment of need.

Joel settled on Pegasus's back, behind her. Emily looked over to Paelen. "You ready?"

Paelen nodded. "Let us go."

Pegasus started to trot along the silver sands, moved straight into a gallop, and leaped confidently into the air. Both Emily and Joel felt the thick, strong muscles in his shoulders and back flex as the stallion flapped his huge wings. As they climbed higher in the sky, Joel's arms wrapped tighter around Emily's waist, and she wove her fingers through the stallion's thick mane for a stronger grip.

"We're ready, Pegs!" Emily called.

The last time they had flown like this, they were fleeing the Nirads at Governors Island. This time they were fleeing Olympus for the same reason.

Pegasus flew faster and faster as they climbed higher in the sky. Emily looked back and saw Paelen using Mercury's sandals to fly behind them. Moments before they entered a thick white cloud, she thought she caught sight of something else following them at a distance. But before she had the chance to tell Joel, Pegasus prepared to enter the Solar Stream—the portal that Olympians used to travel from world to world. Pegasus moved impossibly fast to reach the speed that would open the door to the Solar Stream. Suddenly the stars around them turned into a brilliant blur, and they were gone.

Emily was certain she'd seen . . . something. She kept looking back, but within the powerful Solar Stream, with its blinding white light and the near-deafening whoosh of crackling energy, the most she could see was Paelen flying directly behind the stallion's tail.

"What is it?" Joel called.

Emily concentrated on him and had to shout to be heard over the tremendous power of the Solar Stream. "I thought I saw something following us!"

Joel quickly turned back. "I don't see anything!" he shouted.

"It's probably nothing!"

The journey through the Solar Stream seemed much longer than the last time. But then again, last time she had been traveling to her death. Eventually they burst out of the noisy brightness. The stars around them seemed to slow down to a stop, and they emerged into a brilliant, clear night sky. Emily sucked in her breath as her heart thrilled at the lights of New York City rising straight ahead.

The sense of joy and relief was a surprise to her. Emily never realized just how much she'd missed her old home.

"I thought I'd never see the city again," Joel said, as awestruck as she was.

"Joel, look," Emily called excitedly. She pointed to a tower rising majestically in the sky. "They fixed the

Empire State Building after Jupiter's lightning bolt blew the top off!"

"And it's got its Halloween colors on," Joel added as they both looked at the orange lights shining brightly at the top. The Empire State Building was unique. The colors were always changed at its top to reflect the season or special events. "It was May when we left. Now it's October? We've been gone almost six months?"

Joel's words filled Emily with dread. It felt like they'd only been in Olympus for a short time. But the Empire State Building's Halloween colors and the cold temperature of the air around them proved it true. In the past six months, what had the CRU done to her father?

Before long, they were approaching Governors Island. Emily looked down and felt sick as she remembered what had happened there. Joel's arms squeezed her tighter, and she knew he felt the same.

Pegasus began to descend, and Emily's fears increased. "No, Pegs, not here. We can't go back to Governors. The CRU are here!"

But her pleas were ignored. Pegasus was going to

land at the far end of Governors Island, a side of the small island Emily hadn't seen before. The Central Research Unit had their facility under the beautiful homes on the part of the island closest to Manhattan. There was no mistaking the military look to this area, with its several tall barracks, presumably where the soldiers stationed here lived.

They touched down in an open space between two barracks. The cold autumn wind was blowing off the water and caused Emily to shiver uncontrollably in her light Olympian dress. But apart from that, Governors Island was eerily quiet.

"Pegasus wants you to stay on his back," Paelen whispered, holding up his hand. "He has brought us back here to see if any Nirad warriors remain."

"How will we know?" Joel asked in alarm. "Stay here and wait for them or the CRU to come after us?" Joel leaned past Emily to speak to the stallion directly. "Pegasus, please, this is their base. We shouldn't be here. We've got to go."

"Joel, calm yourself," Paelen said. "I have an idea. These sandals always know where to find things I ask them for. Let me try now." He looked down at his winged sandals. "Search the island for Nirads. Are there any more here?"

Emily and Joel watched in the moonlight as the sandals obeyed Paelen's command and their tiny wings started to flutter. They lifted Paelen in the air, stopping when he was about ten feet high. They turned once, then came back down to the ground.

"The sandals have never failed me before," Paelen explained. "I do not believe they have done so now. There are no Nirads here."

"Then what happened to them?" Emily asked. "There were lots here right before we left. Bullets couldn't stop them, so what did?"

Pegasus started to neigh.

"I do not know," Paelen said. "Neither does Pegasus. He cannot smell any soldiers on this island. He believes the government has abandoned it."

"This was a huge facility. Why would they do that?" Joel asked.

Emily shrugged. "Maybe it was too difficult to explain the Nirads' presence in New York? When our picture was in the newspaper, they said we were a hoax. But maybe enough people saw Nirads and the damage they did and started to ask a lot of questions. So the CRU had to move."

"Could be," Joel agreed. "But where did they move to?"

"Perhaps to where they are holding Emily's father," Paelen suggested. "The sandals were taking me there before. I am certain they will do so again."

"Then let's go," Emily said as another shiver coursed down her spine. "There is nothing here but bad memories for all of us."

Once again Emily couldn't shake the strong feeling that they were being watched. She searched the darkened area but couldn't see anything out of the ordinary. She leaned forward and whispered in Pegasus's ear. "Pegs, I have a strange feeling. Is there someone else here?"

Pegasus lifted his head and started to sniff the air.

"What is it?" Joel softly asked.

"We are not alone," Paelen whispered as he, too, started to look around. Pegasus pounded the ground angrily and snorted. Without warning, he bolted forward. He galloped across the open area, toward one of the dark barracks. Shrieking in fury, the stallion rounded the building and charged a figure lurking in the shadows. Emily and Joel were nearly thrown off Pegasus's back as he reared and kicked out at the mysterious figure.

"Pegasus, no!" a frightened voice cried. "Please, it is me, Cupid. Please stop!"

"Cupid!" Emily gasped. Pegasus went back down on all fours and snorted furiously. He shoved Cupid brutally in the back of his folded wings to drive him out of the shadows.

"What are you doing here?" Joel demanded as he slid off Pegasus and charged forward.

Paelen poked an accusing finger at Cupid. "You have been following us! Why?"

Cupid stood before the group. "The Nirads are in Olympus."

"So you decided to follow us?" Joel challenged.

"Emily is the Flame, perhaps the most powerful of all Olympians. I thought the Nirads might come after her. So I came to help protect her."

"Liar!" Paelen accused as he shoved Cupid. "You are a coward. You came because you thought Emily would use her powers to protect you from the Nirads.

But you were wrong. Go back to Olympus, Cupid. We do not want you here."

"I will not go!" Cupid shouted back. "And you cannot force me, thief!"

"Just watch me," Paelen cried as he lunged at Cupid. Soon the two Olympians were rolling around on the ground and throwing powerful punches at each other. "Stop it!" Emily shouted.

"We don't have time for this!" Joel moved to break up the fight, but Pegasus stepped forward and blocked him.

"No, Joel. Don't," Emily warned. "They're much stronger than you. You'll get hurt. Pegs, do something. Please, stop them!"

Pegasus lunged forward and caught Cupid's wing in his sharp teeth. The Olympian howled in pain as Pegasus dragged him away. Joel caught Paelen, holding him back.

"Ouch! Let go," Cupid cried. "Pegasus, let me go!"

"Stop it, both of you!" Emily ordered as she slid off the stallion's back. She shivered and wrapped her arms around herself to keep warm. She stepped between the two fighters. "Just stop it."

Paelen tried to push past Joel to challenge Cupid again. "Go back to Olympus!"

"No!" Cupid shouted. "I will not!"

Joel caught hold of Paelen's shoulders and blocked his view of Cupid. "Calm down, Paelen," he said as his own teeth started to chatter. "This isn't getting us anywhere. We're wasting precious time."

"But he should not be here," Paelen cried. "He will get us all killed."

"I will not," Cupid said. "I can help." He turned to Pegasus. "I want to help the Flame."

Emily split her attention between Paelen and Cupid. The last thing she needed was another Olympian here to worry about; especially another one with wings.

"Cupid, please," she finally said through chattering teeth. "Go back to Olympus. We are only going to be here for a short time, then we're going right back."

Cupid turned his full attention on Emily. "You are here to free your father. I want to help."

Emily shook her head. "It's too dangerous. Hiding Pegasus's wings and keeping him from being seen is going to be tough enough. I can't see how we'll manage with you as well."

"I have done it before—I can do it again," Cupid challenged defiantly. "I used to come to this world regularly before Jupiter put a stop to all visits. I will not leave you here, Flame. If you refuse to allow me to travel with you, I will follow you anyway. You have many powers, but you do not have the power to send me home."

"Maybe she cannot," Paelen agreed. "But she can burn you to a cinder. That will stop you from following us."

"Paelen, enough," Emily warned. "I told you, I'm not using my powers again. They're too dangerous."

Pegasus started to whinny. Whatever the stallion was saying, Emily could see it was putting fear in both Paelen's and Cupid's eyes.

Paelen lowered his head guiltily. "I am sorry, Emily," he said softly as he hoisted her up onto the stallion's back. "I have been a fool. I should have seen that you and Joel are shivering and in need of protection from this cold night air. Perhaps we should go back to one of the homes and take shelter there for the night."

"No way!" both Emily and Joel said in unison.

"I don't care how cold I am," Emily continued. "I won't stay here. Maybe we can get closer to where they are holding my dad and find somewhere there."

Joel nodded quickly in agreement. "If it's not too far, let's do it."

BACK IN THE SKY, EMILY WAS NUMB FROM the cold. She could feel Joel shivering behind her. Paelen's sandals led the group north over the Manhattan skyline. Emily looked to her left and saw Cupid flying closely beside them. His wings were smaller than Pegasus's, but not by much. She shook her head in frustration as she watched him fly. How were they supposed to keep those wings hidden?

As it was, she feared they weren't flying high enough. What if someone saw them? Would they call the CRU? Would the hunt start all over again? Her simple plan of rescuing her father was suddenly becoming very complicated. She realized she hadn't considered how she was actually going to free her father once they discovered where he was being held. That had been a mistake.

It wasn't long before they were moving away from the bright lights of the city. The sandals kept them going in a steady northern direction. Emily looked down and realized that they were passing over Yonkers and, finally, into the less populated areas on the way up to the Catskills.

"I know this area," Joel said from behind her. "My parents used to take me and my brother here when we were kids."

"Really? Me too!' Emily looked back at him in surprise. "There was a great rest stop we always went to—"

"The Red Apple Rest?" Joel asked.

"Yes!" Emily said excitedly. "It's where my mom and dad met."

"We always went there too," Joel said. "Wouldn't it be funny if we were there at the same time?"

"It sure would," Emily agreed through chattering teeth. She was chilled to the bone. If they didn't get out of the night air soon, she was certain she and Joel would catch pneumonia. Paelen, Cupid, and Pegasus didn't seem to notice the cold at all.

"There it is!" Excited, Joel pointed down to his right. "Look, it's the Red Apple."

Emily leaned over and saw that the restaurant was boarded up and abandoned. "It's closed," she said sadly. "I wonder what happened."

Both Emily and Joel were too absorbed by the closed restaurant to notice that Paelen's sandals were directing them downward. But when Pegasus started to neigh, they looked forward.

"We are going down," Paelen called.

"We must be near your father!" Joel added excitedly.

"Here?" Emily said. "But there's nothing around here but mountains, forest, and the Red Apple."

"And a great place to hide the CRU," Joel said.

Emily saw bright flashing lights in the distance. But they were descending in the opposite direction and farther over a dark forest. As they came down to the level of the treetops, Pegasus whinnied and sharply veered away.

"What is it, Pegs?" Emily called nervously. She looked down and still couldn't see anything hidden in the dark trees beneath them. "Have they seen us?"

Cupid glided closer to the stallion's side. "He

doesn't want to approach, as you and Joel are too chilled to confront them. He says we must find you warmer clothes first."

Emily was conflicted. If they were close to finally finding her father, she hated to leave the area. But she was freezing. Pegasus was right. She and Joel needed to warm up soon or they'd both be in big trouble.

"I've got an idea!" Joel called from behind her. "Pegasus, get us to those flashing lights. I know exactly where we are."

Pegasus neighed once and changed direction in the sky again. He took the lead as Paelen and Cupid flew at his side.

Emily turned back to Joel. "Where are we going?"

"Down there," Joel pointed at the bright lights. "Pegasus, you'll have to land before we get there. We don't want to be seen yet."

As they approached the flashing lights, loud pounding music and screams filled the air. Emily saw the flashing lights were from amusement rides. The screaming was from people on the rides.

"Land right there!" Joel called, and pointed toward

an opening in the forest near the fence surrounding the amusements.

Once on the ground, Joel slid stiffly off the stallion's back. He called Paelen and Cupid closer. "This is perfect. A few years ago, my dad took me up there for Halloween. It's the Haunted Forest Festival. There's a big haunted house and all kinds of things to see and do."

"Joel, we don't have time to go to the festival," Emily said irritably. She was cold and worried about hypothermia. "We need clothing, and then we've got to find my dad!"

"I know," Joel shot back. "But look at us. We can't go anywhere dressed like this. And look at them." Joel pointed at Cupid and Pegasus. "Look at those wings. We've got to find a way to hide them."

"So?" Emily challenged.

"Emily, it's the Haunted Forest! Don't you get it?" Joel continued. "They have performers dressed in scary costumes. We could walk right in there and everyone would think we were part of the show. I bet we could get into the actors' trailers and find some clothing."

"Oh," Emily said, finally understanding. "I get it. But wait, we don't look scary. We still don't fit in. We're dressed like Olympians, not vampires, ghouls, or ghosts."

"I do not understand," Paelen interrupted. "In this place, people are dressed as the dead? Why would they do that?"

"To scare the people who come to visit," Joel explained.

"And these people wish to be scared?"

Joel nodded.

"I still do not understand," Paelen said.

"Neither do I," Cupid added.

"And me," Emily agreed. "I always hated the haunted house."

"Maybe," Joel said. "But right now, with all of us looking like this, it is the only place for us."

They started to walk toward the festival. In the chilly night air rose the sweet aroma of cotton candy, caramel apples, and all the other amusement-park delights.

"They have food here?" Paelen asked eagerly.

"Oh, yeah," Joel said.

Pegasus also lifted his head and sniffed in the strong fragrance of festival food.

Before long, they crept up to a chain-link fence. On the other side they saw bright flashing lights from the countless game booths as visitors tried their luck at winning large prizes. Further in, they spotted all the carnival rides. There was a tall Ferris wheel filled with excited people, while the Octopus spun its riders around in the air to the beat of music. Across from the Octopus was the Merry-go-round, its horses rising and falling in steady rhythm as they chased each other around in the never-ending race. Not far from the fence they saw the biggest, brightest ride of all—the Monster Roller-coaster. Moments later, the coaster's car whooshed down the steep tracks past them, its occupants screaming in both terror and delight. Joel was right. Emily spotted countless performers dressed in costume.

"This is madness," Paelen grew quiet as his wide eyes tried to take in all the sights of the carnival. "I have never seen a sight like this before. I must see more—"

"Paelen, wait," Joel said. "I've got another idea." He

bent down and scooped up a handful of wet mud and decaying leaves. He rubbed the mess on his face, arms, and tunic until he was covered. Joel grinned at Emily. "There, now I fit right in. I'm an Olympian zombie."

Emily laughed at the leaves and twigs sticking up in Joel's hair. "Good idea. Help me down off Pegs. I'm going to be a zombie too." She turned to Cupid. "And you. You're going to be a winged zombie."

Cupid shook his head and looked mortified. "You are not suggesting I rub that filth on myself."

Emily bent down and filled both hands with freezing, wet mud. She stepped up to Cupid. "Not at all." Before he could protest, Emily threw the mud at him. "I'll do it for you. There, now you're a zombie too."

She turned to Paelen. "What about you?"

Paelen quickly held up his hands. "I will do it, thank you. I do not understand why, but I will."

Finally everyone turned to Pegasus. In the dark cover of the forest, the stallion was glowing brilliant white. "Sorry, Pegs," Emily said softly as she stepped up to his head. "But you're glowing. We've got to make you look like an ordinary horse again. Will you let us cover you in mud?"

Pegasus gently nudged her.

"All right, everyone," she said. "Let's cover Pegasus."

A short time later they were all covered in mud and dead leaves, except for Pegasus's and Cupid's feathers. Joel demonstrated how zombies were supposed to move with a slow, lumbering walk. Emily laughed as she watched Paelen and Cupid trying to mimic him.

"And remember," Joel warned Pegasus and Cupid, "no matter what you see or what happens, try not to move your wings. They're supposed to be part of your costume, that's all."

Getting over the tall fence was a problem for Pegasus, who needed more space to launch into the air. They kept watch and waited for the area to clear before flying over the top.

Finally they were all within the grounds of the Haunted Forest Festival. Despite their disguises, nerves bunched up in Emily's stomach. She was seated on Pegasus, and even with her gold leg brace hidden under his folded wing, she still felt exposed and vulnerable.

As they walked through the early evening crowd, people seemed curious and stared at them but kept their distance. On one occasion, Emily caught two girls looking at Cupid and smiling radiantly at him. "Cute guy," she heard them say, giggling, as they walked past.

They traveled deeper into the festival. The air was filled with screaming as costumed performers crept up on people unawares and did their best to frighten them. Not far ahead, they saw the main attraction—the Haunted House. Emily saw a performer dressed as the Grim Reaper carrying his scythe. He stalked the entrance, inviting people in and doing his best to terrify those waiting to enter.

"People do this for fun?" Paelen asked as he watched the Grim Reaper driving girls into screaming terror.

"I wonder how they would react if they saw a Nirad?" Cupid added. "That would soon teach these humans the real meaning of fear."

Joel sighed. "You don't get it. People come here to be frightened because it's safe fear. No one gets hurt. It's meant to be fun."

"I still do not understand your world," Paelen said.

"You don't have to," Joel finished. "Let's just grab

what we need and get out of here before Emily and I freeze to death."

Joel led the way through the thickening crowds. Emily watched Paelen's and Cupid's faces as they stared in curious wonder at the costumed people around them.

"Over there," Joel said. "There're all the trailers. C'mon."

They approached a quieter area filled with a long line of performers' trailers. They walked past a large sign that read PRIVATE AREA. DO NOT ENTER.

"You and Pegasus keep watch," Joel said to Emily. "We'll go grab some clothes." He turned to Paelen. "I know you gave up stealing. But for now, you're a thief again."

"If I must," Paelen said in mock regret. He looked at Emily and flashed his crooked grin. "But I will not enjoy myself."

Emily shook her head and laughed. "Just go!"

Emily waited with Pegasus. "I sure hope they hurry," she said, wrapping her arms tightly around herself.

As the minutes ticked by, she heard the sound of

voices. People were heading their way. Emily looked back at the trailers and couldn't see Joel or the others. She slid off the stallion's back. "Easy, Pegs, let me handle this."

Four men in heavy makeup approached. Two were dressed as vampires; the other two were a zombie and a Frankenstein monster. "You there," called the zombie. "Can't you read? This area is off-limits to the public. What are you doing here with that horse? The costume competition is on the other side of the festival."

"I know," Emily said. "I'm sorry, but my horse was getting spooked by all the crowds, so I brought him here to calm down."

"It was stupid of you to bring him here at all," a vampire shot back. "This is no place for animals. That's why they don't allow pets."

The Frankenstein monster came forward. "What are you supposed to be, anyway?"

"Olympian zombies," Emily answered as she watched the performers start to circle them.

They all laughed. "Olympian zombies?"

"I've never seen a horse zombie before, let alone one with wings," said a vampire.

"He's supposed to be a Zombie Pegasus," Emily explained.

They came closer and started to inspect Pegasus. "Great wings," Frankenstein said, reaching out and patting the stallion's folded wing. "How long did they take you to make?"

Emily's heart nearly stopped as Frankenstein closely studied Pegasus's wing. The stallion never took his wary eyes off him and seemed to be getting agitated by the man's closeness. "Please don't touch him. He doesn't like strangers," she warned.

"That's another reason why you shouldn't have brought him," challenged the zombie.

"You're right—I shouldn't have," Emily agreed. "If you give us a few more minutes alone, we'll go."

"How about you go now?" suggested a vampire. "Or should I call security?"

The sound of running footsteps came from behind one of the trailers. Emily turned and was grateful to see Joel, Paelen, and Cupid emerging from the shadows.

"Are you all right, Em?" Joel ran up to her. Paelen was right behind him, carrying a bundle, followed by Cupid.

"What were you kids doing back there?" the zombie demanded. Then he saw the bundle in Paelen's arm. "And what have you got in your hands?"

"Who, me?" Paelen said innocently.

"Hey, isn't that Jamie's coat?" the vampire said to his friends.

"I think it is," agreed Frankenstein as they all approached Joel. "Have you kids been stealing from the trailers?"

"Not stealing," Paelen said. "Borrowing with intent to keep."

The zombie moved toward Paelen. "You've got yourself a smart mouth, kid. Give me that stuff and get out of here."

"Or you will do what?" Cupid challenged as he took a step.

"Or we'll take it from you."

"I should like to see you try, human."

The situation quickly deteriorated. Emily saw the wings on Cupid's back flutter slightly. He was getting ready to fight. Quickly she moved forward and stood between the two groups. "C'mon, guys, let's just go."

Cupid shook his head. "Flame, stay back. I will not have these humans speak to us like this."

"Okay, that's it!" the zombie said. He turned to one of the vampires. "Jimmy, go get security. We'll keep them here."

But Pegasus blocked Jimmy's path. When he moved to the left, Pegasus did the same. To the right, Pegasus moved again. Each move Jimmy made was stopped by the stallion.

"Hey, call off your horse," Jimmy said as he tried to get around Pegasus.

"Please," Emily pleaded. "We don't want any trouble. But we're freezing and need those clothes. Please just let us take them and go."

"No, Flame," Cupid said, "you must not beg. It is beneath you." He turned to the performers and opened his wings threateningly. "Now we are going to leave here and you will not stop us."

The costumed men took a nervous step back as they stared up at the large set of open wings. "What's going on here? How'd you do that?"

"Cupid, stop it! Close your wings," Emily cried. She looked at the stallion, "Pegs, tell him to stop."

Pegasus snorted, shook his head, and pawed the ground before he reared on his hind legs and spread his own wings wide. After an angry whinny, he lunged forward.

When the actors saw Pegasus and realized his wings were as real as Cupid's, they tried to run. But Paelen and Cupid stopped them. The fight was quick but brutal. Within seconds the four men were unconscious on the ground.

"Why did you do that?" Emily demanded furiously. "You might have killed them with your strength!"

Paelen pointed angrily at Cupid. "We had to because of him!" He charged Cupid and shoved him violently back. "Joel told you not to show your wings. We are trying to blend in here, not expose ourselves. Because of you, we had to hurt these innocent men!"

Once again Pegasus whinnied loudly.

Paelen turned to Emily and Joel. He took a deep breath to calm himself. "Pegasus says we must bind the men and hide them. Then we must leave before they are missed." He bent down and went through the bundle of clothes. "Here," he said as he held a full-length coat up to Emily. "Please put this on and get warm."

Emily and Joel dressed in the coats while Paelen and Cupid used the men's belts to bind their hands behind their backs. They carried them over to one of the trailers and deposited them inside.

Back on the midway of the festival, the evening was in full swing. There were even more costumed performers charging through the heavy crowds to scare the visitors. Countless people stared and pointed at Pegasus walking among them. They commented on his wings, but all seemed to accept him as part of the show.

They walked past a man dressed as a clown at a dunk tank. He was seated on a plank over a glass tank of water, hurling insults at visitors. It was his job to goad them into throwing balls at the target that would cast him down into the water.

When he saw their group, his eyes settled immediately on Paelen. "Well, folks, what have we got here?" he called through a loud microphone. "Ain't he simply adorable! What a pretty little boy walking with his pet pony. Does your mother know you're out tonight, sweet thing?"

Paelen looked at the clown but said nothing.

"What's the matter, toga boy? Don't you wanna

come over here and play? What about your friends? Hey, freaks, this is Halloween, not a toga party! Get it right."

"Are you going to accept his rude comments?" Cupid challenged.

"Yes, he is," Emily said. "We've caused enough trouble here already." She looked at Paelen. "He's only teasing you so you'll go over there and pay some money to throw a ball at the target to knock him in the water. That's how he makes his salary."

Paelen frowned at the clown above the water-filled glass tank. "He wants me to throw a ball at him?"

"Not at him," Joel said, pointing at the bull's-eye. "That target beside the tank. If you hit it, it drops him in the cold water."

Paelen walked closer to the dunk tank.

"Paelen, no," Emily cried. "Don't do anything. Please come back."

But Paelen was already standing before the line of balls to throw at the target. The clown's assistant was tossing one in the air and telling Paelen the price for three balls.

"What's the matter, toga boy? Are you chicken?"

The clown started to cluck like a chicken. "Maybe your little winged pony can help you."

"Let's go," Emily said as she caught Paelen's arm. "Please."

When they started to walk away, the clown whistled. "I guess we know who wears the pants in your relationship, huh? You gonna let a dumb girl with a bum leg tell you what to do, toga boy? Or maybe you're frightened she'll take off that brace and beat you with it!"

Paelen stopped. "He may insult me," he said softly, "but never you. That man should be taught some manners." With lightning speed, Paelen snatched up a ball and used all his Olympian strength to throw it at the target. The ball exploded on impact with the bull's-eye and shattered the target's arm. As a bell rang, the plank holding the clown split, and he was cast into the freezing water.

Paelen rubbed his hands together and smiled at Emily. "He will not insult you again."

Part of Emily wanted to scold Paelen for losing his temper. But she realized he'd done it for her, so she stayed quiet. She shook her head, "C'mon, hero, let's get going."

Before long, they were walking past stalls of food.

"I'm starving," Joel commented as he looked enviously at all the food.

"Me too," Cupid agreed. He crossed to a stall selling caramel apples and cotton candy and held out his hand. "Give me one."

"Not you now. . . ." Emily moaned as she chased after him. "Cupid, wait, you can't go around demanding things. We do things differently here. If you want something, you have to buy it."

"But I am hungry."

"Yes, so is everyone else, but we don't have any money." Emily looked apologetically at the vendor. "I'm sorry. My friend is new here and doesn't understand. We can't pay for that."

The vendor shrugged and took back the caramel apple. "With that outfit, why doesn't he enter the costume competition?" He pointed at a large, colorful tent with people pouring inside. "The prize is two hundred bucks. It's just about to get started."

"Really?" Emily looked at Cupid. "Did you hear that? Two hundred dollars!"

Excited, they returned to the group, and Emily

explained about the competition. "I know we've got to get out of here, but we need money. If Cupid won, we could buy a lot of food and more clothing."

"What would I have to do?" Cupid asked.

"Nothing," Joel said. "Just walk around the way I showed you. We could enter you as a zombie angel."

"But I am no angel."

"It's pretending, Cupid," Emily said tiredly. "You would pretend to be a zombie angel, that's all."

Cupid looked around. "Just as these people are pretending to be dead creatures to scare the others?"

"Exactly!" Joel agreed. "It's simple. Just walk in there, and with those wings, you're guaranteed to win."

"He can't do it," Paelen said skeptically. "He is a coward, too frightened to try."

"I am not!" Cupid challenged.

"Prove it," Paelen said. "Enter the competition. If you win, I will apologize."

Cupid turned to Emily. "I will do it. I will prove to you that I am not a coward or selfish. I will win the money for all of us."

Emily kept close to Pegasus as they made their way through the dense crowds and toward the tent hosting the competition. Outside the entrance, costumed contestants gathered together.

"Anyone else?" called a man with a microphone. "This is your last chance. Best costume wins two hundred dollars cash! Sign up here and enter!"

Emily stepped up to the registration table. "We'd like to enter, please."

The woman looked up at Emily, then over to Cupid. She eyed him up and down in his short, mud-covered tunic and smiled. "And what is your name, handsome?"

"Cupid," Cupid answered softly, leaning closer and smiling back at her.

"Hmmm, the god of love," sighed the woman.

"No," Emily said quickly, "not Cupid. This is Zombie Angel."

The woman repeated the name dreamily and slowly handed over a card with a number on it. "Stand over there, Angel, and wait to be called forward. Good luck."

Cupid reached forward and caught the woman's hand. He gave it a soft kiss. "Thank you."

Emily's own heart fluttered as Cupid turned on

his charm. "Um, come on, Angel," she stammered. "It's over here."

Emily stood in line with Cupid while Joel and Paelen remained with Pegasus, well away from the tent. One by one they watched the contestants being called forward. There were chain-saw killers, mummies, grotesque aliens, ghouls, and countless murder victims covered in fake blood, all climbing up on the stage to show off their costumes. When Cupid's number was finally announced, he caught Emily by the hand. "Come, Flame, I want you with me for this. Remove your coat."

"Cupid, no," Emily quickly said. "I don't want anyone to see my gold brace."

"If you wish to win this, you will do as I say."

Emily looked helplessly over to Pegasus but allowed Cupid to pull off her long coat and draw her into the crowded tent.

"Here now, number thirty-one, Zombie Angel!" the announcer called.

Cupid held on to Emily's hand as he walked zombielike up to the stage. He drew her up the steps with him.

Dressed only in her silk tunic and gold leg brace, Emily looked over the cheering crowds that greeted Cupid as he stepped onstage. It was as though she were invisible. Everyone's eyes were on the winged Olympian covered in drying mud.

"It is I," Cupid announced theatrically, waving his hand in the air and bowing dramatically, "Zombie Angel!" He smiled radiantly at the crowd, and Emily could feel them reacting to his charm. "And here now, the one who holds a zombie's heart, the Flame of Olympus!"

Cupid went down on one knee and knelt before Emily. He bowed his head and slowly opened his beautiful wings and extended them fully. The crowd roared with excitement. Girls screamed and jumped up and down, chanting "Angel, Angel, Angel" as they reached across the stage to try to touch him.

"No!" Emily cried. "Don't show your wings!"

Her eyes were wild with fear as she looked into the audience. But they were all fooled. They loved Cupid without realizing it wasn't a costume. Cheers and roars filled the tent for several minutes, until the announcer came onstage. He held up his hands, trying to calm the frantic crowd.

"Close your wings," Emily quietly ordered as she continued to nervously scan the audience.

Cupid rose and wrapped his arm and one wing around Emily. "I believe we have won," he whispered softly into her ear.

"All right," the announcer roared. "All right, calm down, everyone! I can see by your reaction we have our winner!"

Once again the cheers reached fever pitch as the announcer pulled an envelope from his pocket. "Tonight's first prize for best costumes goes to Zombie Angel and his Flame of Olympus!"

The announcer handed the envelope to Cupid. As he struggled to gain control of the screaming crowds, he pushed the microphone into Emily's face. "What's your name, sweetheart?"

"Um, Emily," she answered nervously. Her heart pounded fiercely, and she was certain the announcer was about to discover the truth about Cupid.

"And you?" he asked, moving the microphone over to the Olympian.

"I am Cupid."

Once again the girls in the tent roared with excitement in response to Cupid. Emily had never seen anything like it before. She looked across the worshipping and adoring masses in the tent, but then Emily noticed one particular pair of eyes that weren't cheering or screaming at Cupid. They were staring only at her.

"No, it can't be!" she uttered. "What's he doing here?"

"What is it?" Cupid asked.

Emily pointed at the man as he spoke urgently to some young, costumed men around him. She watched him shout into his cell phone. When he hung up, he and his men started to shove their way through the hysterical crowds. His eyes were locked onto Emily, and there was no mistaking the recognition.

"The CRU!"

AS THE CROWD SURGED AND TRIED TO GET closer to Cupid, Emily's eyes searched madly for Agent O. There was no mistaking him—Emily would remember his cruel eyes anywhere. He was one of the agents who had tortured her at the Governors Island facility and who was going to let Pegasus die when he was hurt.

"We must go," Cupid cried.

He passed Emily her coat and took her by the hand. But as they descended the stage steps, the crowd of girls swarmed around him. Emily was pushed and shoved until her hand was torn free of Cupid.

"Cupid!" she cried.

"Flame!" he called back. But it was from the rear

of the tent. The mass of girls had forced him against the canvas of the tent. Emily struggled to reach him, but the crowd was too dense. As she turned to head out, she walked straight into a nightmare.

"Emily Jacobs, what a questionable surprise to see you back here," said Agent O as he and two men dressed as aliens blocked her path. His hand closed on her arm with a viselike grip. "Or should I call you Flame of Olympus?"

"No, you can't be here," she cried as she tried to pull away. "I saw Pegasus kill you!"

Agent O shook his head. "He killed Agent J, but he left me with this," he opened his shirt to reveal a deep, angry hoof-shaped scar. "Because of you and that thing, I was transferred upstate to this boring hick town. My only escape from the monotony has been coming to this Haunted Forest with some friends. But now that I've found you, I'll get my promotion and get out of this place. You are my ticket back to New York City."

"Let me go!" Emily demanded as she struggled to pull away.

"Let you go?" Agent O repeated. "Never! You

owe me, Emily. I had a life back in the city before you stole it from me. Now I'm going to steal something from you—your freedom!" He started to haul her away.

Emily looked back toward Cupid.

"Don't worry about your winged friend back there. My men will take care of him soon enough."

As he dragged her toward the exit, Emily spotted the four costumed performers that Paelen and Cupid had attacked. They entered the tent with a group of police and security guards. "There she is," called Frankenstein as he pointed at her. "She was with the others!"

Emily was losing control. The CRU, the police—it was all happening too fast. Her inner Flame started to rumble and come to life as she began to tremble.

"Let go of me," she warned Agent O. "You don't understand. I've changed. Please, I might hurt you!"

"Shut up!" Agent O ordered, forcing her through the crowd.

As the performers, festival security, and police rushed forward, Agent O and his men pulled out their ID badges. "Back off! This is my prisoner."

"No, stop it, Em!" Emily cried to herself, fighting back the flames. "Don't do it. Hold it back!"

But her emotions and the powers wouldn't be stopped. The tingling in the pit of her stomach rose. It flowed along her arms and, finally, down to her hands. "Everyone, get away from me!" she screamed. "The Flame is coming, and I can't stop it!"

"I said shut up!" Agent O shouted furiously as he wrenched her forward. "I don't want to hear it."

Emily's powers let go.

Uncontrolled flames shot out of her fingertips and hit Agent O in the legs. He fell to the ground, rolling and screaming in pain as his trousers caught fire.

Emily pointed her hands away from the people around her and aimed the powerful flames down so that they burned deep holes in the grass and earth.

Agent O continued screaming and writhing in pain as his men tried to put out the fire on his legs. Those closest to Emily cried out in terror and ran for the exit. But the rest of the audience, those who couldn't see its origins, cheered at the unexpected fire show.

"Stop it!" Emily roared at herself. She was growing

close to panic as the flames intensified. No matter how hard she tried, she could not pull them back.

Suddenly a screaming whinny came from the tent entrance. Emily looked up and saw Pegasus rearing and spreading his massive wings. Police gathered around the stallion, trying to catch him, while the crowds roared and cheered in hysterical delight. Pegasus whinnied again and charged forward into the tent.

"Pegasus," Emily cried gratefully. Seeing the stallion coming for her calmed her somewhat and slowed the flames so she was able to regain control. Finally Emily stopped them completely.

She looked down at Agent O. "I'm so sorry! Please don't come after us. I don't have any control of my powers."

"You freak!" he howled as he clutched his burned legs. "I'm going to lock you so far underground you'll forget what daylight looks like!"

But when Agent O saw Pegasus arrive at Emily's side, his voice broke and he was paralyzed with fear. "Keep him away from me!" he squealed at his men, pointing a shaking finger at Pegasus. "Keep him back!"

As the crowd surged forward to get a better look and actually touch the stallion, Emily caught hold of Pegasus's wing and climbed up onto his back. When he began trotting toward the exit, she heard Agent O's cutting words.

"You can't escape me, Emily," he howled. "No matter where you go, I'll never stop looking for you. I'll find you and make you pay for this. . . ."

She turned back and saw the hatred blazing in his wild, frightened eyes.

From the back of the tent, girls were still chanting, "Zombie Angel, Zombie Angel!"

"Enough!" Cupid shouted, and leaped high into the air. His tunic was shredded, and it barely covered his muscular form. He was bleeding from deep scratches on his chest, arms, and face.

With wings unfurled, Cupid flew unsteadily over the heads of the cheering crowd and out of the tent. Pegasus followed closely behind. Once outside, the stallion galloped at full speed along the crowded festival midway before launching himself into the air.

Emily looked back down and saw hundreds of

flashes from camera phones as the people waved and called to them while they flew up into the night sky. Just outside the fence, in the parking area, she watched several black cars and military trucks arrive and the soldiers pour out.

"Em, are you all right?" Joel was clinging to Paelen's back as the tiny winged sandals carried them up to the stallion. "The performers broke free and called security. We had to fight the police to get away. Then we saw them going into the tent!"

"Joel," Emily cried, "Agent O and some of his men were down there!"

"What?" Joel and Paelen cried together. "Where? In the tent? Did they see you?"

"Yes," she replied. Emily pointed back to the military trucks and soldiers gathering at the festival. "They caught me, but I lost control of my powers and set Agent O on fire."

Joel punched the air in celebration. "Yes! Serves him right!"

"It was awful!" Emily cried. "He threatened me! Said he'd never stop looking for us. What are we going to do?"

"They are empty threats, Emily," Paelen called. "But we do need to find somewhere to stop and gather our thoughts."

"Let's go back to the Red Apple," Joel suggested. "It's abandoned. We could hide there and plan our next move."

Several minutes later they were landing in the dark parking lot of the abandoned rest stop. There were large, heavy boards on all the windows, and the building was completely locked up. Very little traffic was on the road, and there were no neighbors to worry about. They were alone.

"This should be perfect," Joel said, scanning the area. "No one has been here for ages."

Emily was still trembling as she slid off Pegasus and approached the rear door. "But how do we get in? We don't want anyone to know we're here."

"Leave that to me," Paelen offered. He stepped back to use his unique Olympian power. Paelen had the ability to stretch out and manipulate his body to fit into any space, even the tiniest of areas. It was very painful and noisy as his bones elongated and cracked while his body thinned. But it had saved his life on more than one occasion. He ordered the winged sandals to take him up to the roof, and they watched him squeeze into a painfully narrow kitchen exhaust chimney.

"I'll never get used to seeing him do that," Joel commented as he shivered and shook his head uncomfortably.

Moments later they heard stirring from behind the door and the sound of the locks being turned. Finally the door opened, and Paelen bowed graciously and grinned. "Come in. Welcome to my home. It is not perfect, but I like it."

Pegasus led the way in, followed by Emily, Joel, and then Cupid. They were in the gutted kitchen of the restaurant.

"I don't suppose there are any lights," Joel asked. "I can't see a thing."

"Me either," Emily agreed.

Pegasus gently nudged her. He nickered softly. "Hold on to Pegasus's wings. He will lead you," Paelen said. He closed and locked the kitchen door as Pegasus led Emily and Joel into the main seating area of the closed rest stop. It was pitch-black and cold.

"Em, do you think you could do something about the temperature in here?" Joel asked. "I'm freezing."

"Like what?"

"Like start a fire so we can see and maybe finally get warm."

"I-I don't think I should," Emily said nervously. "I set fire to Agent O's legs and nearly burned the tent down. You know I don't have any control."

Pegasus was still at her side, and he neighed softly. "You were frightened back in the tent," Paelen translated. "This is different. Pegasus says you can control it if you are calm."

Emily strained her eyes, but she couldn't see a thing. Finally she accepted that they needed light. But more than that, they needed heat. "All right," she hesitantly agreed. "But we need somewhere safe for me to do it, otherwise I could burn this whole place down."

"Come, Cupid," Paelen said as he started to move. "Help me find something for Emily to start a fire in."

Emily and Joel stood together in the dark and

listened to Paelen and Cupid go through the restaurant. They heard smashing wood coming from the kitchen and then something heavy being dragged into their area, followed by the sounds of old tables and countertops being broken up.

"All right, Emily," Paelen said as he took her by the hand and led her carefully forward. "Just a few steps and you are at the pile of wood. It is waist high. If you start with a very small flame, it should catch easily."

Emily felt the reassuring presence of Pegasus directly behind her. She tried to imagine herself back on Olympus and the lessons that Vesta had given her. She held out her hands and envisioned a small flame flowing from her fingertips down into the pile of wood.

The tingling in her stomach started and flowed up into her arms. Suddenly light and flames sprang from her fingers and shot into the pile.

"Easy," Joel warned. "That's it. Just keep it nice and small."

When the pile was burning brightly, Emily pulled back on the flames. This time her powers obeyed and the flame stopped. She saw that the pile had been built on top of an old steel stove and there was no risk of the fire spreading.

"Well done!" Paelen said as he patted her on the back. "I knew you could do it."

Emily grinned as she looked at the controlled fire. This was the very first time her powers had actually done what she asked of them. The flames drove away the darkness and were giving off much-welcome heat. She held her hands over the fire and was starting to feel warm for the first time since they left Olympus. Joel was beside her, also enjoying the heat.

Emily started to relax and looked over to Cupid. He had been silent since they landed and was standing away from the group. She left the fire and approached him. She saw the deep scratches all over his body.

Cupid was looking at the tatters of his tunic and shaking his head. "I do not understand," he said in a quiet voice. "Women used to worship me. They were shy and needed coaxing. But tonight those girls were mad. They were ripping at me. They pulled out my hair and my feathers and tore my tunic. It was as though they were all trying to steal a piece of me."

"Welcome to the new world," Emily said quietly. "Cupid, we told you this isn't the same place you used to visit. We've changed. You were like a rock star up there. Those girls wanted you."

"They wanted to kill me."

Emily shook her head. "No, not kill you. Just to touch you and perhaps have something to remember you by."

Cupid opened his wings and showed Emily the heavy damage done by the hysterical girls. She could see large holes where flight feathers used to be. "I can barely fly," he commented. "It will take ages for all these to grow back."

"Maybe not," Emily said. She reached out and stroked his colorful wings, enjoying the softness of the feathers. Wherever she touched, missing shafts sprouted and started to grow. Before long, the shafts split open and new feathers emerged.

From his wings, Emily moved to his back. She lightly traced her fingers along the deep gouges and watched them start to heal. As she worked, she looked in fascination at where Cupid's powerful wings joined his back. They seemed to be part of his shoulder blades but were able to move independently of his arms. Heavy muscles surrounded the area and gave him strength in flight. She wondered how he was able to sleep with the large, bulky wings or if he could even lie on his back. But she was too shy to ask and figured he must only sleep on his side.

Finally Emily moved to his front and healed the deep scratches on his face and chest. When she finished, she felt her own face flush. In the flickering firelight, Cupid was more painfully beautiful than she could ever imagine.

Cupid inspected his newly healed wings. He stroked the new feathers in wonder. "I had heard that you could heal Olympians," he said in awe, "but I did not believe it. Thank you, Flame."

"How many times must I tell you, her name is Emily," Paelen protested loudly as he charged over. He looked angrily at Emily. "You should have left him as he was. It might have given him some humility!"

"But he was hurt," Emily said.

"He brought it on himself," Paelen challenged. He poked furiously at Cupid. "I know what you did in the tent. You showed too much of yourself and put Emily in danger. Do you realize what might have happened if there had been more CRU people there? She would be in their facility right now being tortured!"

Cupid dropped his head in shame. "I am sorry, Emily. I was not thinking."

"No, you were not," Paelen continued. "Now the CRU knows we are here."

"All right," Joel said quickly. "That's enough. We don't need any fights in here. We've got enough problems already. What was Agent O doing there, anyway? Did you see Agent J?"

Emily shook her head. "He told me Agent J was dead. You should have seen him—he was so angry. He blamed Pegasus and me for ruining his life and said he was transferred up here because of us. But now that we're back, when he catches us, he's going to be promoted and move back to New York."

"It seems too convenient for me," Joel argued. "That he should be there the very same night we arrive."

"Perhaps they have been waiting for us," Paelen

offered. "Perhaps they have been using Emily's father as bait in a trap, knowing that she would eventually come for him. Perhaps there are agents posted everywhere around here."

"Then what do we do?" Emily asked. She started to pace the area. "We are *so* close. We can't just leave him here."

"We fight," Paelen said simply. "We are much stronger than these humans. Emily, you have your own powers. No one can stand against you."

Emily shook her head. "No way! I don't have any control. You didn't see what I did to Agent O. I might have killed him."

"I wish you had," Joel said darkly, "after what they did to us on the island."

"What did they do to you?" Emily asked. "Why don't you ever talk about it?"

"I just can't," Joel said angrily. He turned away and dropped his head. "I still see them in my nightmares. I hear myself screaming and begging them to stop. I remember the pain—"

Emily wrapped her arms around Joel and held him tight. She could feel him trembling. She had suffered at Governors Island, but she knew that both Joel and Paelen had been through much worse. They had both been tortured for information. "I'm so sorry, Joel."

Joel looked down into Emily's face. "Em, face the facts. Whether you want to or not, you are going to have to use your powers to free your father."

"I know," she answered in a hushed whisper. "But I'm so scared. What if it gets out of control again? What if I hurt you or even kill my dad? I couldn't live with myself if that happened."

Pegasus came closer and rested his head on her shoulder. Paelen and Cupid also moved forward. "We will not let it happen," Paelen said. "Emily, we will all be right with you. You are not alone. We will work together. And together we will free your father."

EMILY HAD A RESTLESS NIGHT. HER SLEEP was disturbed by terrible, haunted nightmares. There were the terrors of losing control of her powers and setting the whole world on fire. In one dream, she watched her father and Joel bursting into flame as she stood back, unable to stop the fire. In another, she was locked away in an underground laboratory as Agent O and his doctors poked, prodded, and experimented on her, trying to find the source of her powers.

Several times she awoke, gasping for air and filled with terror that she would never learn to control the fire beast that had been awakened within. That eventually it would consume everyone she cared for, leaving her alone in her misery.

The next morning Emily awoke beside Pegasus. The stallion was lying on the floor next to her, with his wing draped over her to keep her warm. She had slept but not rested. She felt tired and on the verge of tears.

"Morning, Pegasus." She patted the stallion's wing.

Pegasus reached forward and licked her cheek. She could see concern in his eyes.

"I'm fine, really," she said. "I just had a bad night."

"You sure did," Joel agreed. He handed her a plastic cup filled with orange juice. "You were crying and moaning. Those were some pretty bad nightmares. Do you want to talk about them?"

Emily shook her head. "Not really."

"Then drink your juice. That should wake you up."

Emily sat up and looked around in confusion. The fire on the stove was stoked and burning brightly. There were bags of shopping on the floor. But the biggest shock was seeing Paelen and Cupid sharing a box of glazed donuts and dressed like normal teenagers. Paelen was in jeans and a plaid lumberjack shirt, while Cupid was wearing an oversize college sweatshirt. The lower parts of his wings were tucked into his loose-fitting jeans, while the upper parts were covered by his top. From the front he looked like an ordinary seventeen-year-old. But when he turned, Emily saw the large, thick lump on his back. He looked a bit like a hunchback. But unless you knew the truth, no one would ever suspect the lump was actually wings.

She stood up and walked over to the shopping bags. "What's been going on?"

"You weren't the only one having a bad night," Joel answered, "so Paelen and I left before dawn to go check out the CRU facility. On the way back, we found a twenty-four-hour superstore on the other side of town and used the prize money to do some shopping. We got you some clothes as well."

Paelen handed her a shopping bag. "I hope the sizes are correct." He looked down at his own outfit and grinned. "So, what do you think? Do I look like a human?"

Emily was almost too stunned to speak. She smiled gently at Paelen's eagerness to blend in. "Paelen, you look wonderful." Her eyes trailed over to Cupid again. "You both do."

Cupid fidgeted uncomfortably. "I understand why I must wear this disguise, but it is not comfortable for me. I cannot sit down properly without hurting my wings."

"If you do not like it, you could always fly back to Olympus," Paelen offered. "No one asked you to come here."

Cupid shook his head. "I said I wanted to help and I will."

"No, what you wanted was to get away from the Nirads," Paelen accused. "You followed us here to get away from them in Olympus, not because you wanted to help us free Emily's father."

"All right," Emily said, stopping the fight before it got started. "That's enough." She looked at Joel. "Why did you go to the CRU facility without me?"

"Please don't be angry. It was still dark when we left," he explained. "We couldn't risk going in daylight, especially now that the CRU knows you and Pegasus are back. They don't know about Paelen and me. We figured they'd be expecting you both to show up, not us."

Emily sighed, realizing he was right. "What did you see there?"

"Not a lot," Joel answered. "It's deep in the forest, surrounded by dense trees. It's probably like Governors Island. Most of the facility is underground. There's only one small building aboveground. The rest is a large parking area and guardhouse. There's a single road going in and a tall electric fence surrounding the whole property. We saw cameras everywhere. Some were pointing down, but most were patrolling the sky. So it looks like they are expecting us to fly in."

Paelen took over speaking. "I asked the sandals to take me to your father, but they could not find a hidden way in. I believe the CRU may have discovered what I can do. They have sealed all the small entrances. There is only one entrance, and it is heavily guarded."

"With soldiers carrying big guns," Joel added. He dropped his voice. "Em, I'm so sorry. I don't think we can get to your dad. Not without help."

"But Jupiter won't help us," Emily said desperately. "Especially now that the Nirads are back. He doesn't care about my dad or the CRU. It's got to be us who free him."

"How?" Joel asked. "Em, they've got guns! None of us are bulletproof, even if you are the Flame of Olympus."

"We've got to think," Emily said softly as she started to pace. "We can't go charging in there. They'll stop us before we get anywhere. What we need is a plan."

They ate breakfast as they bounced different ideas around. It was finally Pegasus who offered the best possible solution by suggesting that they capture a couple of CRU agents and force them to describe the facility and help in the rescue.

"How?" Emily asked. "We can't just go to the facility and grab a couple of agents. We'll get captured!"

"What else is there?" Paelen asked.

Joel grinned. "I know. We go back to the festival. I bet there are still CRU agents poring over the place, looking for traces of us. What if we go see, and if they're still there, we'll grab a couple of their guys? We bring them back here and make them tell us where they're keeping your dad. Then we take their ID badges and clothing and drive right into the facility like we belong there."

Emily shook her head. "One problem: We can't drive."

"Joel can," Paelen offered. "He was driving this morning when we stole a car and bought all this food."

Emily frowned at Joel. "You did what this morning?"

"We stole a car," Joel said guiltily. "But we had to. The sun was coming up, and we couldn't risk being seen flying. Besides, we had all this food to carry."

"How could you know what to do?"

"Em," Joel said finally, "before we met, I was living in an awful foster home. I used to get very angry and frustrated. So I'd go out at night and steal a car and go driving around the city for a few hours until I wasn't angry anymore. That's how I got my criminal record."

"So, you're a car thief?" Emily said in shock.

"Not really," Joel said. "I wouldn't steal them to sell or strip for parts. I'd just drive them for a while and then return them when I was done."

Emily was almost too stunned to speak. "Joel, are you telling me that right now, right here, outside of where we are hiding from the CRU, you've got a stolen car?"

Joel nodded. "Think for a moment. We don't have a lot of time before Jupiter and the others come looking for us. We need to get your father out of there. We can't wait until night to go out. How else are we going to get around in daylight? We certainly can't fly. We need a car. Besides, we got it from a used car lot, so it's not like we're hurting anyone."

Emily looked from face to face and realized Joel was right. There was no other way for them to travel around the area. But with a car, how were they supposed to travel with Pegasus? They needed a horse caravan. When she voiced her concerns, Pegasus reached over and gave her a gentle nudge.

Paelen said, "Pegasus can't go out in daylight. It will be too dangerous for all of us if he is seen. He has asked you to stay here with him while Joel, Cupid, and I take the car and capture the CRU men."

"I can't stay here while you guys risk your lives," Emily said. "Besides, I can help."

Paelen rested his hands on her shoulders. "Emily, Pegasus will go wherever you go. If you insist on coming with us, he will not stay here. He will follow you."

Emily looked over into the stallion's big brown

eyes. Pegasus *would* follow if she tried to go without him, and to do that, he would endanger himself. She stroked his soft muzzle. "All right, Pegs," she said softly, "we'll both stay."

"And I shall stay with you," Cupid volunteered.

"Oh no, you will not," Paelen said angrily. "I do not trust you. You claim you are not a coward and followed us here to help. But you only want to stay with Emily so she can protect you from the Nirads."

"You are wrong," Cupid protested. "I will protect her should anyone come here. Besides, even dressed as I am, I do not look human. I will be a burden."

"Pegasus is here for Emily," Joel said. "And you won't be a burden. Cupid, we need your help. I may be bigger than you are, but you're much stronger than I am. If you really want to help, this is how you can do it."

"Pegasus and I are safe here, " Emily added. "Joel and Paelen need you more than I."

Emily saw fear rising in Cupid's eyes. He had heard about the CRU and what they did to Pegasus, Diana, and Paelen. She realized Paelen was right: Deep down, Cupid was frightened.

"But there may be more screaming girls."

"They'll be long gone," Joel said. "We'll just go back to the festival, grab a couple of CRU agents, and come right back here. You'll see—it will be easy."

AFTER BREAKFAST, PAELEN, JOEL, AND CUPID
left Emily and Pegasus at the Red Apple.

Joel drove their stolen car out of the parking lot.
Paelen sat in the front seat beside him while Cupid
was stretched out in the backseat complaining constantly about having to lie on his wings and all the
damage he was doing to the feathers. His fidgeting
was starting to drive Paelen crazy.

"If you do not be quiet," Paelen warned as he
turned to the back, "I will pluck out all your feathers
myself. Then you will not have anything to complain
about!"

"I do not see why you are so angry," Cupid said.
"You are not the one with your wings stuffed down

your trousers. You are still wearing Mercury's sandals and can fly anytime you wish, whereas I am burdened with this uncomfortable clothing."

"And I'm burdened with the two of you," Joel shot back. "Geez, you're like two spoiled children! Shut up so I can concentrate on driving and not getting us caught in this stolen car. Cupid, lie on your stomach and keep quiet."

"Of all the indignities . . . ," Cupid complained as he turned over.

"How far is it to the festival by ground?" Paelen asked, looking forward again. They were entering a town with a main street and buildings and houses on either side. It was still early in the morning, and people were out and rushing to get to work.

"A few miles," Joel said. "When my dad brought me up here, we stayed in a hotel. We'd eat at the Red Apple and then go to the festival. So it's all in this area called Tuxedo."

Paelen fell silent and stared out the front window. He was astounded at how different this world was from Olympus. Here the people traveled around in cars and always seemed to be in a hurry.

Above them the sky was gray and heavy as the first snow flurries of the season started to fall. "What is this?" Paelen asked in wonder as he opened the window and felt snow landing on his hand. "What is falling from the sky?"

Joel looked at him. "Haven't you ever seen snow before?"

Paelen shook his head. "It does not do this in Olympus. Until I came to your world, I had never left there before."

"Child!" Cupid yelled from the backseat. "I have been here many times and seen snow all over this world."

"I am not a child," Paelen argued.

"You are much younger than me," Cupid responded. "Younger than most Olympians. That makes you a child."

"How old are you?" Joel asked.

Paelen shrugged. "I do not know. You have lived in Olympus. Have you ever seen us measure time?"

"I never noticed," Joel admitted. "But I guess not."

"We do not," Cupid continued. "There is no need. We do not race around like you humans, trying to fill every moment of your short lives with one kind of action or another. We live, love, and enjoy ourselves."

"Until the Nirads attacked," Joel added. "I saw a lot of running around then."

Paelen heard Cupid's breath catch and knew he was terrified of even the mention of Nirads. "That is the exception," Cupid said. "Though I am certain there is not a human in this world who would not flee the Nirads."

"They'd be crazy not to," Joel agreed. "Now keep your eyes open for police, soldiers, or the CRU. We're not far from the festival."

Paelen's eyes scanned the area, searching for anything that might look out of place.

"There are a lot of extra police out," Joel muttered as they all watched two police cruisers drive past their car. "This could be a problem."

They continued out of the town and entered a wooded area. The road followed along the Haunted Forest's property. They saw the tall chain-link fence and some of the rides behind it. Finally the Haunted House came into view. In daylight there weren't a lot of festival workers about. But what they did see were soldiers and a lot of men in dark suits.

"The CRU," Joel said nervously. "Pegasus was right. They're searching for anything to tell them why we were here last night. We just might be able to capture a couple of their men."

"Do you think they will be expecting us to come back?" Paelen asked.

Cupid hauled himself up from the backseat and peered out the front window. "It could be a trap."

Joel shrugged. "It could be. I think I'll drive past the parking lot a few times to see what it's like there. Just keep your eyes open."

As expected, the parking lot was filled with black CRU cars and multiple military trucks. Several soldiers stood behind one of the trucks, taking a break. "Well, we can't drive in. I think we should abandon the car away from here and walk," Joel said.

"But how will we transport the men we are going to capture?" Paelen asked.

"We'll have to steal a CRU car," Joel suggested. "We're going to need it to go to the facility anyway. So we'll get both at the same time."

"That does not sound like much of a plan," Cupid complained.

"You got any better ideas?" Joel challenged.

Cupid fell silent and lay back down on the seat. Joel drove the car past the festival and turned in along a dirt road, heading higher into the mountains. He parked, and they abandoned the car. As they hiked through the woods, back toward the festival, Cupid continued to complain. Finally he stopped and freed the lower part of his wings from his jeans.

"Cupid," Paelen said tiredly. "You cannot show those."

"I am not going to," Cupid said. "I am going to leave my top on. But I could not walk another step with the feathers scratching against my legs. This will be fine. No one will notice."

Joel raised his eyebrows and looked at Paelen. "Is he kidding?"

Paelen finally gave up. There was just no reasoning with Cupid. "Fine, do as you wish. But if you get into trouble, do not expect us to help you."

They approached the chain-link fence and followed it until they reached the large parking area.

They ducked down behind some trees and studied the flow of men in and out of the parking lot. Not far ahead, they saw an open truck that contained scientific-looking equipment. Men were wearing white outfits that looked like space suits. They were carrying sealed containers with the word QUARANTINE printed on the sides.

"Do they think we're infectious?" Joel asked. "What could they have in there that they think is so dangerous?"

"I do not know," Paelen answered. "Did we leave anything behind last night?"

"Feathers," Cupid suggested. "The girls tore out a lot of my feathers. Perhaps they think they are dangerous."

"Maybe," Joel agreed. "Emily also set fire to the ground. Maybe they think that's contaminated as well. Whatever it is, there're a lot of men here. We're going to have to be extra careful."

Joel led the way forward as they kept low and crept into the parking lot. They crossed over to where most of the black cars were parked. When they ducked behind a large bush, Joel peered over the top. "I think these are the CRU cars," he said. "Those green trucks over there are for the soldiers. We should wait here until a couple of agents come along. Then we can make our move."

Light flurries soon turned into a full snowstorm with large, heavy flakes falling and collecting on the ground. Before long, a film of snow covered the vehicles. After what seemed an eternity, they heard the sound of muffled voices drawing near.

Paelen stole a peek and saw three CRU agents walking toward the black cars. Their heads were down against the weather, and they were talking softly. When one of them looked up, Paelen sucked in his breath. "Joel, look, it is Agent T! Do you remember him from Governors Island?"

Joel peered at the agent walking with the two others. "He was almost as bad as Agent J. He was part of the team that interrogated me. I remember his smile when they gave me those terrible drugs."

"The plan was to take two agents," Cupid said nervously. "Perhaps we should wait for others."

Fury rose on Joel's face. "No, I've got a score to settle. I want him! Let's just grab all three."

"I agree," Paelen said. "I should like to 'speak' with Agent T myself. Besides, we do not know how long it will be before more agents come, and I do not wish to leave Emily alone for very long. This may be our only opportunity."

The other two men were walking closer while Agent T stopped before another car and pulled out his keys. Paelen said, "I have an idea. Cupid, take off your top and go out there to get their attention. See if you can get them to follow you back here."

"Me?" Cupid said fearfully. "Why must I do it?"

"Because Agent T will recognize Joel and me and raise the alarm. Also, your wings will act as a diversion," Paelen explained. "Display them. Then, when the men are distracted, Joel and I can make our move."

"This is a bad idea," Cupid complained as he removed his sweatshirt and walked from their hiding spot and toward the men. Paelen and Joel crept out from behind the bush, then moved into position beside a black car.

"I am sorry," Cupid said softly as he approached, "but I am lost. Would you please tell me where I am?"

"You're gonna be more lost if you don't get out of here, kid," one of the agents said. "This is government business. Get moving."

Paelen watched Agent T step away from his car to investigate. "Look, it is working," he whispered. "Get ready."

"Please," Cupid said to the men. "There is no need to be rude. I was simply flying around and lost my way in the storm. If you could tell me where Olympus is, I will gladly go."

"Olympus?" Agent T said suspiciously. "Did you say 'Olympus'?"

It was only then that one of the other agents noticed Cupid's wings. "Oh my . . ." But he never finished the comment. Cupid struck out with a mighty punch.

Paelen and Joel dashed forward and knocked Agent T and the other agent to the ground. Joel unleashed his pent-up rage at Agent T for everything that had been done to him at Governors Island. Before long, Agent T and the others were unconscious.

Joel panted heavily as he looked up and peered around. With the heavy snow now falling, no one saw or heard anything. "Hand me his keys," he said to Cupid. "Let's get them in the car and get out of here!"

BACK AT THE RED APPLE, EMILY PACED THE
confines of the dining area, feeling like a caged animal. It seemed ages since the others left. There were
so many ways that things could go wrong. She was
afraid the police might have noticed the stolen car
and stopped them along the way. What if they'd been
arrested? Were they in a prison cell? Or perhaps the
CRU had captured them at the Haunted Forest and
taken them to the facility.

"They've been gone too long," she said as she crossed
over to the stallion and stroked his soft muzzle. "Something's wrong. We should be with them."

As more time passed, her panic increased until
Emily was ready to jump out of her skin. Finally they

heard the door opening in the back kitchen area.

"They're back!" Emily ran toward the kitchen, expecting to find Paelen, Joel, and Cupid. Instead she came face-to-face with a stranger holding a flashlight in one shaking hand and a gun in the other. Emily screamed. In that same instant the startled man's finger twitched on the trigger and fired.

The bullet hit Emily square in the chest. She flew backward and fell to the floor. It felt as if she'd been hit by a baseball bat. Her chest was on fire, and the blood was rushing in her ears. She heard Pegasus's furious whinnies as he charged the man, and then the man's frightened cries as he faced the enraged stallion.

Emily knew she'd been shot. But even as she wondered what would happen to her father without her, she felt the metal of the bullet heating up. It was melting in her body as the large wound burned itself closed. In the darkness of the unlit kitchen area she could see a bright glow rising from her chest. Her hands reached up to check and found her clothing wet from her blood. But as she poked her finger in the bullet hole, she could find no trace of the wound.

Beneath her fingertip she felt smooth, unblemished skin.

She sat up slowly. Emily looked over at the man and saw him cowering in the corner. He was still clutching his flashlight, but the gun was gone. Pegasus was standing before him, his wings open and nostrils flared in fury.

"Easy, Pegs, I'm all right," Emily said as she climbed unsteadily to her feet. She was slightly dizzy and felt strange, but other than that, she was in no pain. "I'm just a little shaken up."

Emily went to the open back door and shut it. "Who are you?" she demanded of the terrified man. "What are you doing here?"

"I-I own this place," he stuttered in fear. His flashlight was shining on her blood-soaked top, and his terrified eyes watched her as though he were seeing a ghost. "I saw smoke comin' out of it and thought vandals had broken in again. Please don't kill me!"

"Kill you?" Emily challenged. "You're the one who had a gun. You shot me!"

"I-I'm sorry," he said. "It was an accident. You came at me so fast, you startled me and my finger slipped."

Pegasus pawed the ground furiously and whinnied. He stalked forward, closer to the terrified man.

"What is that thing?" he cried in terror.

"Pegasus is not a 'thing'!" Emily said irritably. "He's a he."

"Pegasus?" the man repeated. "That the flyin' horse from them Greek myths?"

"And he's not a horse, either!" Emily replied as she stepped up to the stallion and patted his quivering neck. "It's all right, Pegs. I'm sure this was an accident. He didn't mean to hurt me." She looked at the man. "Did you? You'd better tell Pegasus the truth. He knows when people are lying."

"I swear," the man said. "It really was an accident."

Emily felt overwhelmingly tired and needed to sit down. "Come out of there and into the seating area, where I can see you better. What's your name?"

"Earl," the frightened man said as he walked cautiously around Pegasus, never taking his wary eyes off him.

"Sit down over there," she said tiredly. "Don't make any sudden movements or try to leave."

Earl sat down by the fire, still looking at Emily as

though she were an apparition. "What are you?" he timidly asked.

"You really don't want to know," Emily said. "But I can tell you this. We're here for a very good reason and need to stay hidden for a while. So please don't try to escape. I don't want to hurt you, but if you try anything, I will."

Emily felt sick threatening the man, but she couldn't have him escaping and calling the police. To illustrate her point, she stood before the fire. She called up the flames, and they shot from her fingertips into the burning wood. "I can do this faster than you can run. So just settle down and relax. When we're done, you can leave here completely unharmed."

Earl's eyes grew wide with terror as the flames moved from the raging fire back to Emily.

"Do we understand each other?" she demanded.

The man nodded. Emily patted Pegasus on the side. "Would you keep an eye on him for a while? I'm not feeling very well. I think I need to sit down for a bit."

As Emily settled down, Pegasus stood protectively beside her but never took his angry eyes off Earl.

He was still snorting and pawing the ground furiously. Emily was sure if Earl tried to move, Pegasus wouldn't hesitate to attack him. She took a deep breath and tried to relax. She was more tired than she'd ever been in her life and couldn't keep her eyes open a moment longer. Before long, she fell into a deep, healing sleep.

9

"EMILY!"

Emily awoke to Joel shaking her arms. "Em, please wake up!"

"I'm awake," she said groggily. "Please stop yelling!" Joel's frightened face hovered above her. Paelen was beside him. Pegasus was behind them, staring at her.

"Are you all right?" Paelen asked. "Pegasus told us what happened."

"It was an accident," Emily muttered, now fully awake. "We startled each other in the kitchen, and the gun went off."

"But you're hurt," Joel said as he inspected her sweatshirt. "Look at all this blood. We've got to get you to a hospital."

Emily shook her head. "No, it's all right. I don't understand how, but the bullet melted and the wound closed by itself. I'm fine."

"How?" Joel argued. "Em, you were shot!"

"She is the Flame of Olympus," Cupid explained. He was standing before their unconscious CRU prisoners. "She can heal herself as easily as she heals others."

"Yes, but a bullet in the chest should have killed her," Joel challenged.

"If she were human, it would have," Cupid continued. He approached Emily, knelt down, and stroked her cheek lightly. "Emily, the human in you died in the Flames back in Olympus. Your other life ended that day. Now you are as we are. You can no longer be killed."

Emily rose to her feet. "No way. I'll admit that something weird happened to me in the temple. But I'm still me. I'm still human."

Pegasus approached her and neighed softly as Cupid gently shook his head. "No, you are not. I know this has been a difficult transition for you, but believe me, you are not human. You are the Flame of Olympus. The human Emily died that day in the temple."

"No, that's impossible!" Emily argued. She turned desperately to Pegasus. "I still feel the same. I feel the cold and I get hungry. I can be hurt. I'm human and I'm alive."

The stallion moved closer and gently pressed his head to her. He neighed softly.

"Of course you are alive," Paelen reassured her. "You were reborn in the flames. And you feel pain as we all do. But you feel the cold only because you believe you should. Your body is Olympian, but in your mind, you still think of yourself as human. This is why you can't control your powers. You do not believe you can control them."

"But I still feel the same," Emily insisted. "What am I supposed to tell my dad? That I'm some kind of freak just like Agent O said I was?" She tried to wrestle with the truth. Tears rose to her eyes.

"Emily, don't cry!" Joel warned fearfully. "Your tears—remember what happened at the amphitheater! You could blow us all up."

Emily panicked, fearing what could happen here

if her tears fell. She reached into her jeans and pulled out the beautiful handkerchief Neptune had given her. She brought it up to her eyes and gently patted her tears.

"I can't even cry right." She sniffed and looked at the handkerchief. Her tears were beading on the surface like water on wax paper. But as she watched, a secret pocket seemed to open, and the tears slid in. Soon the surface looked as though they'd never been there at all. She looked at Pegasus. "What do I do with this now?"

The stallion nickered softly.

"He says that your tears are collected in the Siren's weave," Paelen explained. "They are not gone, nor have they been neutralized. If you ever need them, you can call them back to you. He says you must keep that with you at all times."

"What would she need her tears for?" Joel asked. "They're like nuclear weapons. They should be destroyed."

"They cannot be destroyed," Paelen said.

A sudden moan from one of the CRU prisoners reminded Emily why they were there. "I'm sorry," she said, shaking her head and sniffing a final time. "I've been thinking only about myself." She walked over to the three unconscious men lying on the floor. Agent T was starting to stir. "Shouldn't we tie them up or something? And I thought we were only going to get two CRU agents?"

"We didn't have much choice," Joel said. "The whole area was crawling with them. We were lucky we got these guys."

"There is no need for us to bind them," Paelen added. "We are stronger and faster than they are. It would be a fatal mistake if they tried to escape."

As she looked at the men, Earl approached them. "Don't kill me for talkin', but are you kids crazy? Bringin' them CRU agents here when everybody knows you're just the kinda things they're lookin' for."

"You know about the CRU?" Emily asked.

Earl nodded. "I know 'em and don't like 'em. A few years back a whole mess of them government folk moved into the area. Soon there was all kinds of crazy talk about aliens and other creatures. . . ." His eyes trailed over to Cupid, who'd taken off his sweatshirt for comfort, exposing his wings. They moved over to

Pegasus. "I also know that anyone who strays onto their property ain't never seen or heard from again."

"That's the CRU all right," Joel said. "What do you know about their facility?"

Earl shrugged. "Nothin', and I want to keep it that way. They hired a bunch of locals to build their underground bunkers. Some say the place is like a huge hidden fortress. My best friend's brother was an electrician who worked there. He talked about them deliverin' all kinds of freaky things. A few months back we were all out at a bar. He was drunk as a skunk and spoutin' stories of them bringin' in these big, four-armed gray aliens. It wasn't long after that he up and disappeared. A bunch of us tried to find him, but some agents came round and said it was best for everyone to just shut up. Not long after that, this place was condemned and my business shut down. I know it was them doin' it to warn us off."

"Nirads?" Cupid asked fearfully. "You are talking about Nirads?"

Joel snapped his fingers. "I bet those are the same ones from Governors Island. But how could they capture them? Bullets couldn't stop them." He looked at

Paelen. "Tranquilizers couldn't stop you, Diana, or Pegasus; I doubt they'd have worked on Nirads."

"Are you saying them things was real?" Earl asked fearfully. "That he wasn't tellin' tales?"

Emily nodded. "Yes, they're very real, but they're not aliens," she said softly. "They were trying to kill Pegasus."

"And you," Paelen said to her.

"They damaged my leg," Emily explained. "Now the CRU are holding my father at the same facility where they're keeping the Nirads."

"The CRU has your daddy?" Earl said. "Is that why you're all are here?"

Emily nodded.

"Where are you from?" he asked.

"The less you know, the safer it is for you," Joel warned.

"I don't hardly think so," Earl said. "The moment they find out I've been talkin' to you, I'm a goner."

"He's right," Emily said. "The CRU will kill him if they find out he's been here with us."

"I believe they already know," Paelen said as he pointed at Agent T, who was sitting up. He climbed to his feet and looked around. When his eyes settled on Pegasus, he inhaled. "It's true. You're back."

Emily looked at the man, with his black suit, perfectly groomed dark hair, and fiery blue eyes. He was tall, lean, and cruel. She instantly felt her fury rising. She remembered everything about him from Governors Island. "Yes, we're back," she responded. "We're here for my father, and you're going to help us get him out of there!"

"No, you've got that all wrong, young lady," Agent T said coolly. "You are going to surrender to *me*, and we'll all go back to the facility."

Joel stepped forward. "Do you remember me, Agent T? Because I sure remember you! The only thing keeping you alive right now is the information you've got. So look around you. In case you hadn't noticed, you're outnumbered. We've taken your weapons and phones. I'm sure you remember how strong Olympians are. Do you really want to make them angry?" Joel pointed at Paelen, Cupid, and Pegasus. "Emily and I have changed as well. Show him what you can do, Em."

Emily didn't hesitate. Talking to the arrogant agent

brought all her terrible memories of Governors Island back to the surface. She looked at the fire, held up her hands, and released the flames. They were wild and barely contained as they flashed and burned the wood in the fire to cinders.

When she looked back at Agent T, she saw a trace of fear rise in his eyes, but his shroud of arrogance quickly returned. "From what Agent O tells us, you can't control it."

"I can control it enough," Emily warned. "So you are going to tell me where my father is before I lose my temper."

"No, I'm not," Agent T responded. "We've all been trained to withstand torture. There's nothing you can do to us that will make us speak. So do whatever you like. It won't work. "

"That's right," the second agent agreed as he and the third agent rose to their feet and stood defiantly beside Agent T. "Surrender now, or this will turn very ugly for all of you."

No one expected this standoff. The CRU agents were unafraid as they faced the powerful Olympians.

"What are we going to do?" Joel muttered softly.

"Well, we can't reason with them," Emily answered. "Look at them. They don't care what we do to them." She started to pace the area. They had come so far. But it seemed everything was against them. There didn't seem to be any way to free her father.

"I know what will work." Paelen pointed at Cupid. "He can make them talk."

Cupid's eyes went wide, and he stepped back. "Oh no. I know what you are suggesting, but I will not do it."

"Do what?" Emily asked.

Paelen continued. "He can make the agents speak without the use of force. All he needs to do is use his powers."

"What powers?" Joel asked.

"The powers of love," Paelen said. "No one can resist Cupid when he turns it on." He pointed at the agents. "Not even them."

"Whatever you kids are planning, forget it," Agent T said. "Just surrender now, and no one needs to get hurt—" He looked at his men and picked up a large plank of wood from the burning pile. "Now!"

Before anyone could react, Agent T struck Joel in

the back of the head with a brutal blow. When he fell to the floor, unconscious, the agent turned on Paelen.

The restaurant erupted into fighting. Pegasus, Cupid, and Paelen had strength on their side, but the agents were better trained in combat and blocked most punches thrown at them. Despite being out-numbered, they held their own against the powerful Olympians.

Emily crouched beside Joel and watched the fight from the sidelines. Earl received a powerful spinning kick from Agent T that knocked him out while the two other agents pounced on Paelen.

She could feel her powers rising and aching to be freed. It was taking all her strength and concentration just to hold them back. She couldn't risk unleashing them and hitting those she cared for. She would only use her powers as a last resort.

Pegasus reared and kicked out at one of the agents on Paelen. But the man was quick and ducked beneath the lethal hoof. With a sudden roll, he sprang away from the stallion and was back at Paelen. As the fight intensified, Cupid was struck by Agent T's plank of wood. The force of the blow sent him hurtling across the restaurant. He landed on his wings and cried out in pain.

"Cupid!" Emily cried.

Cupid rose to his feet, his face blazing with fury. His wings flew open, and he howled in rage. Raising his hands in the air, he pointed at the agents and charged forward.

"Stop!" he ordered. "I command you to stop!"

As if they'd been suddenly frozen, the agents stopped fighting and stood perfectly still. The plank of wood in Agent T's raised hands fell noisily to the floor. They all stood unmoving, staring at Cupid, eyes wide, mouths hanging open, and arms limp at their sides. There was no mistaking that they were completely under Cupid's control.

"Go on, Cupid, finish it," Paelen coaxed as he rose from the floor and dusted himself off. "You must use your power to make them speak."

Cupid shook his head. "No, I will not. Mother always said charm is the best weapon. I believe she is correct."

The screaming girls! And her own feelings of attraction to him. It suddenly all made sense to

Emily. She had felt Cupid turn on his charm before but never realized it was an actual power he could control. She thought it was just his good looks. "So, you could actually charm them into talking?"

Cupid nodded reluctantly.

As Joel stirred and started to come around, Emily helped him to his feet. She turned back to Cupid. "Please, you must do it! If you don't, they won't talk. We need that information about my father and how they are controlling the Nirads. I'm begging you, Cupid, please help us."

Cupid shook his head. "You do not understand, Flame. Once I do this, they will love me forever. There is no going back, no reversing it."

"We don't have a choice," Emily pressed. "It's the only way we can save my dad."

Cupid hesitated. Finally he sighed and hugged Emily. He wrapped his wings around her tightly and whispered in her ear, "I will do this only for you, Emily, no one else. Not because you are the Flame and can command me, but because I choose to do it for you."

Emily's face flushed, and she felt her heart pounding as Cupid held her. "Thank you."

"That is enough," Paelen said gruffly as he forced them apart. "Save your charm for the agents, Cupid."

Everyone stood well away from the winged Olympian as he faced the mesmerized CRU agents. Cupid said nothing. But the wings on his back fluttered lightly with annoyance.

Earl had regained consciousness. Although he had a headache, he was unharmed. Standing between Emily and Joel, he tapped her lightly on the shoulder. "That there fella, is he the real Cupid? You know, the one with the bow who shoots love arrows and stuff at folks?"

Emily nodded. "But I'm not too sure about the bow. I've never seen him with one."

Earl whistled softly. "I always seen pictures of him as a chubby little angel baby with wings, not a teenager."

Joel looked at Earl. "It's amazing when you're in Olympus and see just how much we got wrong."

All eyes focused on Cupid as he stood before the agents. His head was down, and his wings drooped as his arms hung straight down. His body language showed just how much he didn't want to do this. Finally he lifted his head and faced the agents.

Emily watched the agent's faces as Cupid unleashed his powers. At first they were staring blankly. But that was soon replaced by an expression of awe, which turned into undisguised love.

"It's working," Joel said softly. "Look at them. They'll do anything for him."

"Cupid may be a coward and a troublemaker, but he does have his uses," Paelen said. He nudged Joel with his elbow. "Can you imagine what we could accomplish with a power like that?"

Joel chuckled and winced at the pounding in his head. "I can think of a few things."

Cupid closed his wings and turned back to the group. "You may ask your questions now," he said softly. "They will answer you."

Emily was the first to come forward. She stood beside Cupid and faced Agent T. "Where is my father?"

Agent T looked at Cupid and grinned foolishly.

"Answer her," he commanded.

Without further hesitation, the agent spoke. "He

is at the facility in the forest. We are keeping him on sublevel ten."

Over the next hour, the agents willingly answered every question posed to them. They gave the exact location and condition of Emily's father. They explained everything they knew about the Nirads being held at the facility. They told the group how they could enter the underground facility without being exposed. When the questions ended, Cupid ordered the men to sit down and remain silent. They obeyed the winged Olympian like eager puppies anxious to please their scolding master.

"Twenty-one Nirads," Paelen said. "I would never have thought it possible so many could be in this world."

"I still don't understand what happened?" Emily said. "Why would the Nirads surrender and become docile? Twenty-one could easily destroy the facility and go anywhere they pleased."

Paelen shrugged. "Perhaps when they failed to kill you and we left, they had nothing left to fight for, so they just surrendered."

Joel shook his head. "I don't think so. You saw

them. They were savage and uncontrolled. I don't believe they could surrender; it would mean they were thinking about it. The Nirads we saw showed no signs of intelligent thought, just animal instincts and reactions."

"Well, whatever it is," Emily said, "I hope they stay that way. I just want to go get my dad out of there and return to Olympus."

EMILY HELPED CUPID PULL ON ONE OF THE
agent's black suit jackets over his wings, then helped
him into a heavy wool coat.

"I do not know why I must dress as one of them,"
he complained as he fidgeted with the tie at his neck.

"How many times must we explain it?" Paelen
said tiredly as he dressed in one of the other agent's
suits. "You have wings. We must hide them. You do
not hear me complaining. I have had to take off my
sandals and wear these uncomfortable shoes."

Joel was doing up the shirt buttons and pulling on
the jacket of the last suit. "Will you two stop complaining? You're making my headache worse!" He
went over to Cupid and spoke to him as though he

were speaking to a troublesome child. "We've got to look like CRU agents. They dress in white shirts, black suits, and black coats, so we dress in white shirts, black suits, and black coats. It's as simple as that."

"But what about him?" Cupid said. He pointed to Agent T.

Agent T was wearing Joel's jeans and a checkered top, and his adoring eyes never left Cupid.

"We're taking him with us, since he has a valid ID badge. And he's going to wear the long black winter coat. I don't think he'll be a problem."

As Cupid protested further, Pegasus whinnied loudly and pounded the floor angrily with his golden hoof. Both Emily and Joel looked to Paelen to translate, but he said nothing. However, the look on Cupid's face was enough to say that Pegasus had lost patience with him.

"All right," Joel said to Emily, "you know the plan. We're just going to get in there. Agent T will take us to where they're holding your dad. Then we'll get right out again. I'd love to take my time and destroy the place, but I won't. With luck, we should be back here in a couple of hours."

"I really wish we were going with you," Emily said as she stroked Pegasus's strong neck.

"So do I," Joel agreed. "We could use that fire trick of yours. But I'm sure they're waiting for you and Pegasus. Just be ready to go the moment we get back."

Emily reached up and hugged his neck. "Thank you for doing this, Joel. It means everything to me."

Joel blushed. "Emily, you and your dad are the only family I've got. I don't want him trapped in there any more than you do. Just keep the door locked and say a prayer for us."

"I will," Emily promised as she watched Joel stroking the stallion's soft muzzle.

"Take good care of her, Pegasus," he said.

Cupid stepped up to the two agents remaining with Emily. They looked eagerly at him, grateful for his attention. "You two will stay here. You will do whatever Emily tells you to do, and you will protect her with your lives. If you fail her, you fail me, and I will be most displeased. Do you understand me?"

Both agents nodded and grinned foolishly at Cupid. Cupid's charm had worked too well. Emily almost felt sorry for them. The poor agents seemed to only want to serve him now. But what was to become of them once this was over?

"Be careful," Emily said for the hundredth time. "Please don't do anything foolish to endanger yourselves."

Paelen grinned his crooked grin and kissed her lightly on the cheek. "We will be careful," he said. "But you must take care also. Do not answer this door unless you hear it is us. We cannot have you hurt again."

"I won't," Emily promised.

Cupid, with his shaggy blond hair, looked painfully handsome in his long black coat. Once again her heart fluttered. "Stay safe, Cupid," she said softly.

"I will," he promised. He bent down and gave her the softest kiss on the lips. "You too. Wait for me, Flame. I will return shortly."

Emily could barely breathe when Cupid moved away.

"C'mon, lover boy," Joel said as he tugged Cupid's coat, "that's enough. Let's go."

Emily closed and bolted the door behind them. "We should be going with them, Pegs. It's not fair for them to risk their lives for my father while we sit here babysitting a couple of CRU agents."

Pegasus nickered softly. He put his head on her shoulder and pulled her closer.

They both heard movement in the kitchen and saw Earl standing there. "Are you all right?" he asked.

Emily nodded. "I'm just really scared for them. I wish I could have gone too."

"I'm sure everything will work out fine," he said. "Those boys care a lot about you and'll do the best they can."

"Thanks, Earl," she said softly. She crossed to the door and unbolted the lock. "It's not fair to keep you here any longer. You can go. But please promise me you won't tell anyone what you saw here."

"Well, now, you know I wouldn't say a word," he said as he shuffled his feet. "But if it's all the same to you, I think I'll stay a bit to keep you company."

Emily frowned. "Why would you want to do that when you could be free?"

"To tell you the truth, I want to see those boys beat the CRU and bring your father back here to you. So why don't we sit down a spell and wait for the good news."

THEIR CRU PRISONER DROVE THE BLACK CAR out of the Red Apple parking lot, through Tuxedo, New York, and toward the secret government agency's hidden forest facility. The snow that had started earlier that morning continued to fall. By late afternoon there were several inches covering the ground. The driving was treacherous and painfully slow.

Paelen sat up front in the passenger seat, while Cupid and Joel took the backseat. As they drove along the private road leading to the guardhouse, Paelen looked back at Joel. He saw deep worry lines etched on his friend's face. Cupid's face also revealed fear, reflecting his own concerns for this rescue. They were actually planning to go deep inside a CRU facility. The chances of something going wrong were astronomical.

"We're approaching the gate," Agent T announced.

"Very good," Cupid said. "I want you to say whatever you must to ensure we get in there."

"Anything for you," Agent T said as he turned back and gave Cupid a silly grin.

"And stop smiling at me," Cupid spat. "Remember how you used to be."

The agent's grin disappeared, and he nodded. But he winked at Cupid before facing forward again.

Paelen laughed. He winked and kissed the air. "Anything for you," he teased Cupid.

Cupid leaned forward and grabbed a handful of Paelen's dark hair. He yanked his head back. "If you ever tell anyone what I have done in this world, I swear I will set the Hydra on you!"

"That's enough, you two," Joel warned. "Cupid, let him go. Let's just get this done, and you can finish your fight later."

"What fight?" Paelen said innocently.

They were drawing up to a guardhouse. A heavy chain-link gate blocked the way in. There were cameras everywhere, some pointing at them and others scanning the sky. This would be the first major obstacle.

The car pulled up to a tiny window at the guardhouse. A large, angry-looking man with an even larger weapon draped around his shoulder stood inside. When he saw Agent T at the wheel, he nodded in recognition. But then his eyes found the other passengers.

He opened the door and walked toward the car as his finger rested on the trigger of his weapon. "Identification," he demanded.

They were prepared for this. Paelen and Joel both showed the identification badges from the other agents. They silently prayed he wouldn't study the photos too closely, as they were not even close to what Paelen and Joel looked like.

But as the guard noticed the difference and became suspicious, he straightened and raised his weapon. Cupid reluctantly turned on his power. They watched the same reaction as before rising on the guard's face. At first suspicion, then awe, and, ultimately, adoration.

"It will please me if you let us in," Cupid said tightly through gritted teeth.

"Of course," the large guard said sweetly. "Anything

for you." He returned to his guardhouse and pressed the button that opened the large gate. Just as the car moved forward through the snow, they saw the guard blowing kisses at Cupid.

"How precious!" Paelen howled with laughter.

Despite his attempts to hold it in, Joel started to chuckle as well.

"I am warning you, Paelen," Cupid muttered furiously, "if you say one word about this back in Olympus—just one—I will have your head. . . ."

The rest of the journey passed in silence. Everyone seemed to understand the danger they were about to face, and the laughter stopped. Agent T drove the car to the parking lot at the side of the single building.

"This is it," Joel said tightly as he climbed out of the car and stood facing the small, squat redbrick building.

Paelen looked around and noticed how quiet and calm the area was. The heavy blanket of snow seemed to still even the birds. "Is it always this quiet?" he asked the agent.

"It's the snow," Agent T said. "No one likes coming out in it. They'll all be inside."

"And you know what you must do?" Cupid asked.

"Yes, if it pleases you, I will take you all in there to Steve Jacobs."

Cupid walked beside the agent, and Paelen and Joel followed closely behind. Joel stayed particularly close to Cupid's back to help hide the large lump made by his wings.

At the front entrance of the building, Agent T pulled out his ID card and passed it through the scanner. The door whooshed opened, and they all walked in. Just inside the door was a sign-in desk. A guard was sitting and reading a newspaper. He put it down when they approached. "Some storm, eh, Agent T?"

The agent nodded. "It's getting worse out there. He turned to Cupid. "This is Agent C."

Paelen felt his heart stop as their prisoner smiled at Cupid. "He's here to visit Jacobs."

"That wasn't on the schedule." The guard said as he frowned. He reached forward and checked a clipboard. "I have no visits listed here."

"I know. Change of plans," Agent T said. "The head is thinking of moving him. Especially now that the winged horse and the girl are back in the area.

These agents here are to assess the logistics of the move and to see if Jacobs is fit to travel."

"I'm sorry, Agent T, but if it's not on the list, I'd better check." The guard reached for the telephone.

Paelen gave Cupid a shove. "Do it," he quietly ordered.

Cupid looked at him furiously but reached out and grasped the guard's hand. "It is all right. You do not need to check. We will just visit the prisoner for a moment. Then we shall leave. Please, return to your reading. Do this for me."

The guard's face turned brilliant red. He cleared his throat and shuffled awkwardly on his feet. "Of . . . of course, anything for you." He fiddled around his desk and quickly drew up clip-on passes. "If anyone asks, just show them these." He grinned as he handed them the Cupid. "Is there anything else I can do for you today?"

"No, thank you," Paelen said.

The guard gave him only a passing glance as his adoring eyes rested on Cupid. "Please have a wonderful day."

As their agent-prisoner led the way to the elevators,

Cupid dropped his head. "This is by far the worst day of my life. My mother would be furious if she knew what I was doing." He shivered visibly and looked at Paelen. "I shall never forgive you for this."

Paelen was about to say something when Joel stepped forward. "Cupid, Venus would understand. She would be proud if she knew how much you were helping Emily." The elevator arrived, and they piled in. The agent pressed the button.

"How deep does it go?" Joel asked.

"There are twelve sublevels," Agent T said.

"And what levels did you say the Nirads are being held on?" Cupid nervously asked.

"On the bottom three."

Paelen frowned. "Wait—you told us that Emily's father is on sublevel ten. That means there are Nirads on the same level?"

"Yes. But they are dormant. They spend all their time sleeping. I assure you, they will not trouble you." He looked at Cupid again and grinned sheepishly.

A heavy silence filled the elevator as they descended. Paelen felt as if they were entering the maze of the Minotaur. One wrong turn and they would come face-to-face with the beast. Only this time, it wasn't the furious Minotaur they would encounter. It would be a hoard of deadly Nirads. Dormant or not, a Nirad was a Nirad, and he wanted to stay as far away from them as possible.

They arrived on sublevel ten, and Agent T led them forward through a maze of corridors. Halfway down a long, twisting corridor, they approached a heavy metal door. It had a sliding plaque mounted on the front that read STEVE JACOBS. The door was painted shiny white and had a coded lock. It looked identical to the doors from the facility at Governors Island. The agent entered the code on the security lock and pushed open the door.

Paelen entered first and felt a shiver pass along his spine. The room was so similar to the one he'd been held in. It even smelled the same. In the center of the room was a bed with a big lump. A blanket was pulled high over the occupant's head.

"Steve?" Joel called.

The lump stirred as a muffled voice called, "Go away."

"Steve, it's me, Joel!"

"And me, Paelen," Paelen added. "Emily is safe."

"Emily?" the lump said. Emily's father pushed down the covers and quickly rolled over. His eyes went wide at the sight of Joel and Paelen.

"Is it really you?" He leaped from the bed and gave Joel a brutal bear hug, then did the same to Paelen. His eyes darted around the room. "Where is she? Where's Emily?"

"Not here," Paelen said. "We thought it best if she stayed away. She is with Pegasus. They are waiting for you."

Tears rose in Steve's eyes, and his shoulders started to shake. "Is she all right? The Nirads hurt her. What happened? The CRU wouldn't let me see her or tell me how she was."

"She is fine. Calm yourself," Paelen said. "Vulcan built a brace for her leg. She walks perfectly."

"I really began to think I'd dreamed it all," Steve said shakily to Joel. "But it was real, wasn't it? Pegasus was here. He had a broken wing, and you kids dyed him black and brown."

"Yes it was," Joel said. "It wasn't a dream."

"Wait," Emily's father said, alarm rising in his

eyes. "The war? Olympus was destroyed. What happened?"

"We do not have time to explain," Paelen said. "We must get you out of here." He noticed that Steve was wearing a hospital gown. "Do you have any clothes here? It is very cold out."

"No, they won't give me anything but this. They won't even let me shave or cut my hair." He pointed to his thick, bushy beard and long brown hair. "I guess they're afraid I'd try to kill myself—" Steve's eyes suddenly landed on their agent prisoner. "Agent T!" His fury rose, and he launched himself at the agent. Knocking him to the floor, he started to pound him. "You did this to me! You refused to tell me about my own daughter!"

"Steve, no!" Joel cried as he struggled to break the men apart. "Please, we don't have time. He's working for us now. Stop, we've got to go. Emily needs you."

The mention of Emily's name held his fist in the air. "He's working for you?"

"Yes, Cupid charmed him. Now he is ours."

"Cupid?" Steve said.

"I am Cupid," the winged Olympian said, coming

forward. "It is an honor to meet the father of the Flame."

Steve shook his head in confusion as he regarded Cupid in his poorly fitting black suit and lumpy long coat. He looked at Joel. "What flame? What's he talking about?"

Joel grasped Steve by the arm. "We have a lot to tell you." He turned to Cupid. "Take off your long coat. Steve is going to need it." Then he looked back to Emily's father. "Do you remember how Pegasus was here to find the Daughter of Vesta? Well, that was actually Emily. She's the Flame of Olympus."

"My Emily?" he said in disbelief. "But . . . but . . . Diana, she said the Daughter of Vesta had to sacrifice herself to save Olympus. She had to die."

"Emily did sacrifice herself," Paelen said gently. "You should be very proud of her. Emily saved our world, and she saved yours. She was reborn in the flames. But she has never stopped thinking about you or wanting to free you from the CRU. So we slipped away from Olympus to get you."

"But she's alive, right?" Steve asked. "Emily is alive?"

"Very alive," Joel said. "And she's waiting for you. So please put on Cupid's coat—we need to get moving."

Steve quickly put on the long black coat. But as the group moved toward the door, the loud, furious sounds of sirens suddenly filled the air.

"They've found us," Joel cried.

Both Paelen and Cupid started to sniff the air. Cupid's expression turned to terror. "No, it is not the CRU."

"What is it?" Steve asked.

Paelen groaned. He shook his head. "Not again! This cannot happen to me twice!"

"What is it? What's happening?" Joel demanded.

Everyone heard the deep, guttural roars coming from the hall and the sound of shattering doors. Automatic gunfire mixed with the screaming of men.

"Nirads," Paelen said darkly. "They are awake."

PAELEN AND JOEL LED THE WAY OUT OF
Steve's quarters. The halls quickly filled with armed
soldiers preparing to fight the Nirads. They moved
down the corridor, toward the bank of elevators.

"I can't believe this," Joel said. "It's just like last
time."

"The Nirads will kill us all," Cupid cried as his
wild eyes darted around in terror. The wings on his
back were fluttering, and he was shaking like a leaf.

"I will protect you," Agent T said eagerly. He drew
his weapon. "They will not harm you."

"No, they won't!" Joel agreed. He reached into his
suit pocket and pulled out his golden dagger. "Did
you bring yours with you?" he asked Paelen.

Paelen nodded, and held up his dagger. "If we must fight, we will."

Having Agent T with them meant the other agents did not try to stop them or block their way. But as they stood waiting for the next elevator, they heard deep growls and roars.

Everyone watched as doors along the long corridor exploded and two Nirads charged out of their rooms. They turned toward the group and lumbered forward.

Soldiers in the hall opened fire, but the bullets bounced off the Nirads' gray marble skin and ricocheted around the area, knocking out lights and hitting other soldiers. "Their weapons will not work against them." Paelen shook his head. "When will these foolish people learn?"

"We're trapped here!" Cupid cried as he frantically searched for a way out. The elevators were still several levels away. "They will tear us apart! We are all going to die!"

"Cupid, calm down!" Joel said as he pointed. "Look, there're the stairs. Let's move!"

The group entered the stairwell. From above they

heard the sounds of fighting. "We're surrounded," Steve cried as the two Nirads from sublevel ten entered below.

The Nirads were gaining on them as they dashed for the next level. They weren't going to make it. Paelen and Joel stopped running. They turned and raised their gold daggers. "Keep moving," Joel ordered Steve. "Get back to Emily. She's at the Red Apple!"

Paelen's mind flashed with the terrible memories of what the Nirads had done to him on Governors Island. Of the pain he felt when they tried to rip him apart and the sounds of his own bones breaking. His hand started to shake.

"You okay?" Joel asked quickly.

"No," Paelen admitted.

"Me neither."

Further comment was cut short as two creatures rounded the bend and faced them. The Nirads' bead-black eyes settled on Joel and Emily's father. They bared their sharp, pointed teeth and snarled with vicious rage as their clawed hands opened and closed into fists. With renewed energy, they charged forward.

Joel held up his dagger. But he'd never fought with a knife before, let alone a dagger against a Nirad. As he flashed the golden blade in the air, it nicked one of the Nirad's four arms, causing a spray of black blood. Howling in pain, the creature swung a brutal fist and knocked the golden blade out of Joel's hand, sending it flying away. The creature roared and lunged at him.

Paelen tried to reach Joel to help, but the second Nirad was moving. It swatted him aside as though he were shooing away a troublesome fly. Paelen was knocked off his feet and sent tumbling back down the stairs.

When he hit the bottom, he looked up, and his eyes went wide in horror. The one Nirad had Joel in a brutal grip and was hoisting him in the air. Without a backward glance, the creature roared triumphantly and carried him up the stairs. Despite Joel's size, he was helpless against the terrifying strength of the four arms wrapped around him.

"Paelen!" Joel cried as he was carried away from the group and up and around the bend in the stairs. "Paelen, help me plea—" Suddenly the voice was cut off.

"Joel!" Paelen shouted. He feared his best friend had just been killed by the Nirad. "Joel!"

Above him, the other Nirad was still fighting to get hold of Steve. As Paelen reached for his gold dagger, he heard Cupid order Agent T to shoot.

"No!" Paelen cried as he dashed up the stairs. He knew human weapons were useless against the Nirads. In these tight quarters, firing the weapon at the Nirad was a disastrous idea.

The agent's weapon went off. The bullet struck the creature, ricocheted off its marblelike skin, and hit Steve in the chest. The Nirad caught hold of Emily's father just as he crumpled to the floor. Paelen shouted and sprang forward. He drove his gold dagger deep into the creature's back.

The Nirad released Steve and howled in pain and fury as it tried to dislodge the dagger. But it was too late. The Olympian gold's deadly poison was already doing its job. The fearsome creature staggered on the steps as its strength ebbed. In a final, agonized cry, it swooned and tumbled noisily down the stairs.

Paelen jumped aside as the huge creature somersaulted past him. He didn't pause to check on the

Nirad. "Cupid, help Steve," he ordered as he chased after Joel.

Paelen was close to panic as he climbed floor after floor, searching for his friend. "Joel!" he howled, "where are you?" But his calls went unanswered.

Paelen finally reached the ground level. He burst through the stairwell doors and into the lobby. Destruction was everywhere. Just like on Olympus, the Nirads had left nothing standing. Bodies of CRU agents and soldiers littered the floor, and the sign-in desk was in pieces and scattered around the room. The main entrance doors had been ripped off their hinges and tossed aside.

Paelen ran outside. Large tracks were impressed in the snow. They were all headed in the same direction, deeper into the forest. In the distance, he saw the electric fence had been knocked down as the army of Nirads had torn through it.

Paelen studied the tracks. His eyes caught hold of a sight that nearly stopped his heart. Red stains in the snow. He didn't need to see more to know what it was. It was human blood. It was Joel's blood. Paelen's knees gave out, and he collapsed to the ground.

EMILY SAT WITH EARL AND THE TWO AGENTS, snacking on the last of the food supplies. The moment Cupid left, the two agents clung to Emily like bees to honey. They were anxious to please her so she would tell Cupid what a great job they were doing. But what they were really doing was driving her insane.

"Please just sit down and eat something," she said as they hovered near her. "Geez, now I know what the president goes through with the Secret Service. . . ."

Pegasus was standing beside her, enjoying the last of the glazed doughnuts Emily handed up to him. "I've got all the protection I need with Pegasus."

"What's it like on Mount Olympus?" Earl asked. "I ain't never been to Greece."

"Neither have I," Emily answered. "The real Olympus isn't in Greece. It's another world. You have to go through this highwaylike thing called the Solar Stream to get there. But it's really awesome. More beautiful than anything you could ever imagine and filled with amazing people and animals."

Earl sighed. "I'd sure like to see it someday."

"Maybe you will when all this is over."

"You could come with us," one of the agents suggested, a brilliant, almost crazed smile lighting his face, "when we go there with Cupid."

Emily and Earl looked at each other knowingly but said nothing. They lapsed into silence as they waited for news from the others.

Time seemed to stop. As each moment ticked by, Emily felt her fear growing. "How long has it been?" she finally asked.

Earl checked his watch. "'Bout an hour and a half; they should be back here any time."

Emily started to pace the area. "I just wish they'd hurry."

The two agents also stood and began pacing along with her.

"Would you two please sit down!" Emily shouted. "I'm fine. See? There's no one here to hurt me!"

The words were no sooner out of her mouth than a huge crashing sound came from the kitchen area. Pegasus whinnied loudly and charged forward into the darkness. Emily strained her eyes in the firelight but couldn't see anything.

The two agents burst into action. "Stand over there," they ordered, driving her away from the kitchen. "We'll check this out." One of them pointed at Earl. "Keep an eye on her."

Emily could hear Pegasus's shrill and furious whinnies. "Pegs!" she cried. She began to feel the Flame within her start to stir. "No!" she told herself. "Not again. Not now!"

From the kitchen came more sounds. Mixed in with Pegasus came grunting and squealing. "What the heck is that?" Earl cried as a large animal charged into the dining area, knocking aside the two agents.

After all her time in Olympus, Emily thought she had seen just about everything that world had to offer.

But now, standing before her was a massive, winged boar. It was covered in coarse brown hair, with sharp, pointed tusks curling out of its large, threatening snout. But stranger still were the wings. They were folded close to the stocky body and stuck out almost a meter past the boar's hind end. Its feathers were as brown and coarse as its hair. The raging animal charged forward but stopped just short of Emily.

Pegasus followed quickly behind. He bent his head down and hit the boar with enough force to send it rolling away from Emily.

The enraged animal righted itself and turned. It charged at Pegasus. The stallion stood his ground and lowered his head again. As the two heads met, the sound of their skulls knocking together was sickening.

"Pegasus!" Emily cried.

Earl was beside her and holding her back. "Don't!" he warned. "I don't know what that thing is, but if it's anythin' like the wild boars we got around here, it ain't no friend! We gotta get outta here!"

"I'm not leaving Pegasus," Emily said, pulling away.

Pegasus reared on his hind legs and kicked out at

the ferocious boar. Although the animal was big, it was lightning fast and darted away from the stallion's lethal hooves.

"Stop it!" Emily roared. She could feel flutters in her stomach turning into heavy tingling as the power of the Flame increased with her fear. Soon it would rise and flow along her arms, and there would be nothing she could do to control it. "Please, stop fighting. The Flame is coming!"

The fight was terrible. The boar charged forward and darted under the stallion's kicking legs. When it reached Pegasus's vulnerable underside, it threw its head up, and the sharp tusks tore into the flesh of the stallion's underbelly.

Pegasus shrieked in pain as both his hooves came crashing down on the boar's back. It squealed and darted away but then turned and faced Pegasus again. In the dim light, Emily could see blood pouring from the stallion's wounds. But Pegasus wouldn't stop. He reared again and charged the winged boar.

Suddenly, from all around the boarded-up rest stop came a sound Emily knew all too well. Her eyes flew wildly around the dining area. Thick, filthy fingers with sharp claws were tearing away the boards on the windows. As they fell away, daylight showed the horrors yet to come. An army of Nirads were outside the Red Apple and were tearing their way in.

"Nirads!" she cried, running closer to the fighting stallion. "Pegasus, stop, we've got to get out of here! Nirads are here!"

"Them the four-armed aliens attackin' Olympus?" Earl asked as his terrified eyes darted around the room. "The ones that hurt your leg?"

Emily nodded. The sounds of breaking windows, tearing wood, and roaring Nirads in the confines of the tight area were deafening. "They're here to kill us." Emily had to shout to hear herself. "Get the agents and go! Leave before it's too late!"

"I ain't leavin' you," Earl called. "You're comin' with me."

Emily's powers were rising. In moments fire would burst forth from her fingertips. "I can't. The Flame is coming and I have no control!" She shoved Earl away as the tingling rose from her stomach and moved along her arms. "Go now before it's too late!" she howled.

Just as the first Nirads touched down on the floor of the Red Apple, Emily's powers let loose. Despite her terror, she forced herself to concentrate. The flames shot wildly out of her fingertips, but as a Nirad charged toward her, she pulled back and tightened the Flame into a thin red beam.

She pointed her hands at the Nirad. The red beam struck the ferocious nightmare and burned right through the creature, cutting it in half. The air was filled with howls of pain as it fell to the floor and died.

But there was no time to celebrate. More and more Nirads were pouring into the restaurant. Emily ran forward and fired at a second Nirad and then a third. But in her panic, her aim was off, and she only managed to wound the rampaging creatures.

With the red beam still firing from her fingers, Emily's wild eyes found and shot at more Nirads. But as they went down, more and more seemed to replace them. She had no idea how many there were, except that it was countless more than they had ever fought before. Even with her powers, they were badly outnumbered.

"Pegasus!" she cried. The stallion and boar were still fighting. As she stole a glance back, she saw several Nirads joining the fight and moving in on Pegasus. Earl and the two CRU agents were taking on a single Nirad. She ran toward them.

The Nirad quickly dispatched one agent and then the second one. It turned on Earl.

"Earl, no—"

The Nirad caught hold of him and raised him in the air. Emily was there in a flash. She pointed her hands at the Nirad as it squeezed Earl in a crushing embrace. Her red beam struck the vicious creature's leg and cut it off. It roared in pain and threw Earl across the restaurant.

Emily couldn't see where Earl had landed. She didn't know if he was dead or alive. But she didn't have time to find out. She turned her hands toward the Nirads attacking Pegasus. But fear of striking the stallion kept her aim off.

As Emily struggled to control the red beam so that it would hit only the Nirads, she was charged from behind. A Nirad caught her around the waist and hoisted her easily off the ground.

Her arms flew around wildly as she lost control of the Flame. It shot in all directions throughout the restaurant. The beam burned its way through the walls, the ceiling, the floor, and any Nirads in the way. Everything the powerful red beam touched was sliced like a knife through soft butter. Soon the walls of the Red Apple blazed furiously.

"No!" she cried. As terror threatened to overwhelm her, Emily finally regained some control and pointed her hands down at the Nirad. Fire burned the creature's legs. It roared in agony and released her; they fell to the floor together.

Emily scrambled away. But the relief was short lived. Before she could raise her hands again, she was tackled and driven down to the floor. Pain exploded in her head as more arms wrapped around her.

As the brutal arms squeezed tighter, Emily continued to fight. But it was in vain. Her powers stopped, and she had no strength against the Nirads. She looked up, searching for Pegasus.

The stallion had been knocked to the ground, and his pain-filled cries split the air as the Nirads swarmed over him. "Pegasus!" she howled.

The Nirad holding Emily lifted her off the ground. But as more creatures moved forward, everyone heard the loud creaking and moaning coming from the building itself.

Emily looked up and saw the latticework of cuts and scars in the ceiling from her powerful red beam. The entire roof was a roaring flame. Then the weight of the snow above and the fire below proved too much for the weakened timbers. Before anyone had time to react, the beams broke and the entire burning ceiling came crashing down.

EMILY REGAINED CONSCIOUSNESS AND opened her eyes. A scream escaped her lips before she could hold it back. She was being carried in the arms of a Nirad. The creature looked down at her as he clamped his third hand across her mouth.

He shook his head. The message was clear. Don't scream.

Emily struggled. Yet despite the Nirads' unbelievable strength, his grip on her was surprisingly light and causing no pain.

When the Nirad was certain she wouldn't scream again, he removed his hand from her mouth. Emily nearly gagged at the taste of filth on her lips. She looked around and was terrified to discover she was no longer at the Red Apple. She was surrounded by the huge, lumbering creatures as they trudged through the deep snow of the forest.

It was only then that Emily noticed all the cuts, burns, and large tears to her clothing. She was covered in blood and smelled of smoke. But she wasn't in any pain. Her jeans were badly damaged, and most of the gold leg brace was exposed. The Nirad was being careful not to touch any part of the brace. As if it somehow knew that touching it would be dangerous.

Her hands were covered in dried blood, dirt, and ashes. But the skin was smooth and unblemished. She could also move them without any trace of pain. She suddenly realized that despite the torn shreds of her clothes, she wasn't feeling the cold of being outside in a heavy snowstorm. Cupid was right. She really was an Olympian after all.

Only then did she remember what happened. How the entire roof of the Red Apple had burned and then collapsed on them.

What about the others? Emily suddenly remembered Pegasus. The last thing she recalled seeing was the

Nirads swarming all over him. "Pegasus?" she cried as panic set in and she struggled to escape the arms that held her. "Pegs, where are you?"

From far behind the group, Emily heard the stallion whinny. Her heart filled with relief that he was still alive. "Are you all right?"

The Nirad holding her gave her a light squeeze and grunted. It shook its head again. Emily focused on its eyes. They were different from those of the other Nirads she'd seen. This Nirad appeared to possess intelligence and understanding. When it looked at her, instead of the normal glazed expression and desire to kill, it really seemed to see her. The color of the creature's skin was also different from that of the Nirads she had previously encountered. Those had a gray, marbled skin.

This Nirad had the same marbled skin tone, but the color was dark orange. Emily looked around and saw an array of different-colored Nirads—orange, gray, even lilac. Leading the group deeper into the forest was the winged boar. Bleeding hoof scars were imprinted on its back and wings from the fight with Pegasus. One of the boar's wings was held at an odd angle and dragged along the surface of the snow, broken.

"Please put me down," Emily said softly to the Nirad.

The creature looked at her but remained silent.

"Can you understand me?"

At the front of the group the winged boar stopped. It turned and trotted back to Emily. It stopped before the Nirad holding her, and Emily felt the creature react. It lifted her higher, away from the sharp tusks of the vicious animal, and gripped her more securely.

The boar squealed and fluttered its good wing threateningly at her.

Pegasus responded immediately and whinnied angrily from behind. The boar looked back, squealed again, and then returned to the front of the procession.

High in the Nirad's arms, Emily stole a glance over its thick shoulder. There were a lot more gray Nirads surrounding Pegasus. They growled, drooled, and poked him with sticks to keep moving.

Emily inhaled sharply at the sight of her beloved stallion. Pegasus was covered in deep scratches, burns, and filthy debris from the roof collapse. But worst of all were his once-beautiful wings. The fire had burned most of his feathers off, leaving only singed, downy feathers behind.

"Pegs," she whimpered. "I'm sorry."

The Nirad holding her lowered her until she could no longer see Pegasus. It looked down into her face, and for a moment Emily saw profound sadness resting there as it gave her a gentle squeeze.

"Were you ordered to capture us?" she asked in a hushed whisper.

The creature nodded slightly.

"You can understand me!"

The creature looked up toward the boar leading the group before looking back down at her. Once again it gave a slight nod.

Emily's mind was in turmoil. Ever since she'd encountered the first Nirad in New York she had thought of them as mindless creatures set on only one thing: destruction. But if this Nirad could understand her, could the others? Was there more to them than she first thought?

As she was carried deeper into the forest, she continued to study the Nirads around her. She started to notice other significant differences. It was more than just the color of their marbled skin. She observed that the gray Nirads were stockier. They drooled, shuffled, and seemed to follow the others rather than lead. The lilac Nirads appeared to be in control of the gray ones. She watched as they occasionally barked growling instructions at them.

Emily then looked back at the face of the orange Nirad carrying her and noticed a big difference. It stood taller and straighter. Although it had the same muscular build, long dark hair, four arms, and claws as the others, these orange Nirads had a presence that suggested intelligence and perhaps even empathy.

Emily stole a look forward at the winged boar before asking the Nirad carrying her, "Can you speak my language?"

The creature shook its head, then opened its mouth to reveal a row of terrifyingly sharp, pointed teeth. It had a very tiny tongue and made a soft sound, but nothing she could understand. She realized that without a proper tongue, it could never speak her language.

When she opened her mouth to ask another question, the Nirad brought its third hand down across it again. It motioned to let her know the winged boar was slowing down to listen.

Emily nodded. The creature removed its hand, and they walked on through the forest in silence. After a time, Emily saw the ground beneath them rising and realized they had reached the base of a mountain.

But instead of climbing up, they were walking to the left. Up ahead, Emily saw a dark area that could have been a cave entrance blocked by huge boulders.

The winged boar squealed, and the group stopped. The Nirad carrying Emily stood well back as the gray Nirads moved forward. Grunting and growling, they started to shift the huge snow-covered boulders away.

Emily could see Pegasus again. Several orange Nirads surrounded him, but they left him untouched. His head was down, and his eyes were closed with exhaustion. His beautiful silky mane was matted with blood. Emily desperately wished she could touch him to heal him. But she knew the Nirad would never allow it.

She was certain it was holding her at an angle so that she could see Pegasus. The way it looked at her told her so. But it would do no more than that.

"It'll be all right, Pegs," she called to the stallion, heedless of the winged boar standing just a couple of yards away. "We'll get out of this somehow."

The boar turned and squealed at her again.

"What are you going to do?" Emily angrily replied. "Kill me? Go on, then, try it. But if you dare to touch Pegasus one more time, I swear I'll unleash my powers and kill us all! Do you understand me?"

The winged boar looked at Emily and tilted its head to the side curiously. It moved closer. Once again the Nirad lifted Emily higher, out of reach. But the winged boar was having none of it. It squealed angrily at the Nirad until Emily was lowered to the boar's level.

Emily was now face-to-face with the large animal. She looked into its deep brown eyes and saw great intelligence there; it immediately reminded her of Pegasus. The boar's sharp tusks were a few inches away from her face. But Emily felt no fear for herself. All she cared about was keeping Pegasus safe.

"I don't know who you are or why you are doing this," she said, "but I mean it. If you hurt Pegasus again, I will turn my powers against you. Even if it kills me—I don't care. Leave him alone."

The boar moved even closer to Emily, until the end of its whiskered snout touched her cheek. At the moment of contact, the boar squealed in shock and jumped back. It looked down at its broken wing and moved it slightly. Then it looked over to Pegasus and grunted. Finally, it moved forward and pressed its snout against one of Emily's hands.

Against her wishes, Emily's powers healed the boar. The hoof marks on the animal's back faded and disappeared while the wing set and moved into its normal position on the boar's back.

"You're an Olympian!" she said in shock.

The boar stared at Emily for several heartbeats, until it eventually drew away. It walked over to Pegasus and squealed.

Pegasus raised his head proudly and faced the boar. He whinnied several times and pounded the snowy ground with his sharp golden hoof. She wished more than ever that she could understand him. Something very serious was happening here, and she needed to know what.

After a long exchange the winged boar looked back at Emily. It turned and walked through the deep snow to where the Nirads were uncovering the cave entrance. When it was opened, the boar entered.

Everyone started to move. They streamed one by one into the dark cave. Soon the Nirad carrying Emily stepped forward. As she looked back toward Pegasus, she struggled to see past all the Nirads surrounding him. He was being led in behind her. Emily couldn't see a thing as her eyes adjusted to the pitch-dark of the cave. She could hear the occasional grunt as the Nirads piled into the tight area. A moment later something brushed against her leg—a Nirad arm—and as it grazed along her exposed gold leg brace it howled in agony and fell to the ground, clutching its wounded arm and bellowing in pain. It rose to its feet and charged toward Emily, desperate to kill. Before Emily could react, the orange Nirad holding her struck out at the attacker with one of its strong arms. She heard the fist make brutal contact with the face of the attacking Nirad. It fell backward, roaring as it went.

As it gained its feet for a second attack, more orange Nirads surrounded Emily in protection. By the time her eyes adjusted fully to the darkness, she realized it had been one of the gray Nirads attacking her.

The shrill sound of the winged boar filled the air, and all the Nirads stopped. The animal charged through the creatures and approached Emily. It looked up at her Nirad and squealed.

The Nirad grunted and growled in response. It knelt down to show the boar Emily's exposed leg brace. It sniffed the gold, turned to Pegasus, and squealed loudly.

Emily strained to see around her Nirad to look at the stallion, but her view was blocked. She heard Pegasus pounding the stone floor of the cave, but he said nothing.

The winged boar concentrated on Emily again and grunted. It snatched a cover from the nearest Nirad and draped the filthy rag over the exposed gold. A second rag was then torn from another Nirad, and the boar ensured that all the gold of the leg brace was covered.

The boar charged through the gathered creatures and approached the back wall of the tight cave. It opened its wings and made several loud and short sounds.

Suddenly the rear wall burst to life as if there had been a silent explosion. Blinding white light poured into the dark cave, followed by ferocious winds and the sounds of crackling electricity. Emily inhaled sharply and realized this was a portal to the Solar Stream. It was how the Nirads had traveled to her world. As the winged boar entered the blinding light and disappeared, the Nirads followed closely behind.

Fear coursed through her as her Nirad approached the portal.

"No, don't," she begged as she struggled in its arms. "Please, I belong here. This is my world. I don't want to leave!" She struggled against the Nirad's strong arms, but they would not give. It held her close and grunted softly but moved forward. Moments later Emily was carried through the bright portal and she disappeared.

PAELEN WEPT AS HE KNELT IN THE SNOW.
How could the rescue plan have gone so wrong? He
cursed himself for not bringing Emily and Pegasus.
She could have used her powers. Joel wouldn't have
had to die.

His tears fell unchecked down his face as he
grieved over the loss of his best friend. Until Emily
and Joel had entered his life, Paelen had been alone,
scavenging and stealing his way through a life apart
from the other Olympians. Always on the outside,
never part of anyone or anything. But Joel and Emily
had changed all that. They brought joy and adven-
ture into his life. More than that, they had become
his family.

Now Joel was gone and Emily's father was hurt. What words could he ever tell her to make up for that? He had failed them all.

"Paelen," Cupid called. He was standing at the entrance of the building, clutching Emily's father. Agent T was beside him. "Go start the car," Cupid ordered as he carried Steve closer. "Paelen, this human is badly wounded. We must get him help."

Paelen rose to his feet and looked at Emily's father. His eyes were closed and his face pale, but he was breathing. He felt for the pulse in Steve's neck. It was still beating strongly. But for how long? Inhaling deeply, he drew himself away from the Nirad tracks and reluctantly followed Cupid and Agent T.

Paelen sat in the backseat of the car, cradling Emily's father and keeping pressure on his bullet wound. The stain on the front of his hospital gown was slowly spreading. He was losing a lot of blood.

Cupid was in the passenger seat up front with Agent T. "Get us back to the Red Apple," the winged Olympian ordered quietly. "And hurry."

While Agent T drove them away from the CRU facility, Paelen shook his head. "Why Joel and Steve?"

he wondered aloud. "The Nirads were only after Joel and Steve."

Cupid looked back. "No, they were after all of us."

Paelen shook his head. "You are wrong. That creature could have killed me. But it was as though he barely even saw me. He knocked me away as though I meant nothing and was focused only on Steve. Why?"

Cupid faced forward. "And why did the Nirad take Joel away?" he mused. "He could have simply killed him and left him behind. But he took Joel's body with him."

Paelen shuddered. Cupid had given voice to his worst fear. That Joel was really dead. "What are we going to tell Emily?"

"That Joel died bravely defending her father," Cupid said. The winged Olympian leaned forward and looked out the window at the sky above them. "The snow is getting heavier. We must collect Emily and Pegasus and leave this world soon."

They traveled in silence as they made their way along the slushy roads, back through Tuxedo and toward the rest stop. Everyone noticed a large number of fire trucks and police cruisers out on the roads. Paelen also saw several military trucks driving past.

"They must be searching for the Nirads," Agent T suggested.

Cupid shook his head. "How can they? The Nirads went in the other direction. These men look like they are heading to—"

Cupid stopped and looked back at Paelen, and they said together, "The Red Apple!" He looked over at Agent T. "Move faster."

The car sped toward their hiding spot. When they drove along the road in front of the rest stop, they saw flashing lights from fire trucks, police cruisers, and military vehicles crowded into the parking area. The building itself was all but collapsed. Part of the roof was still burning as the firemen struggled to put out the flames. Everywhere they looked, they saw destruction. Nothing of the rest stop remained intact.

"Emily!" Paelen cried.

As Agent T started to turn the car into the crowded parking lot, Cupid ordered him not to. "Continue down the road."

"Cupid, what are you doing?" Paelen asked.

"We must not let them see us. Emily and Pegasus are already lost. Why should we surrender ourselves so easily?"

Paelen's fear turned to fury. "Emily is not lost!" he shouted. "We must go back and find them!"

"Paelen, calm down," Cupid ordered. "We will. But we must not be seen. This is the time for stealth. For once in your life, trust me. I am older than you, and I know what I am doing."

Paelen was too frightened to know what to do. Steve was wounded, Joel dead, and now this. It was beyond anything he'd ever experienced.

The car continued past the Red Apple and farther down the road. Cupid instructed Agent T to pull into the empty parking area of a closed gas station. Paelen gently lowered Steve's head onto the backseat as he climbed carefully from the car.

"All right," Cupid said. "We have two choices. I can fly back to Olympus to get help—"

"No!" Paelen cut in as he brutally shoved Cupid. "You are not leaving for Olympus, you little coward! Emily and Pegasus are in that wreckage. They need us to get them out before the CRU does."

The wings under Cupid's suit jacket fluttered as he righted himself and stepped closer to Paelen. Looming above him, his eyes blazed with fury. "I am not a coward!" he shouted. "Are you so incapable of believing that I can care for Emily and Pegasus? That I would abandon them in their time of need? I do care, Paelen. And I am not going to leave them to the mercy of the CRU. I was going to say that I could fly back to Olympus for help or that we could both go over there to find Emily ourselves. I was going to suggest we stay and do this ourselves."

Paelen was shocked into silence by Cupid's outburst. In all the years he'd known him, he'd never seen him this angry. "I am sorry, Cupid. I have been unfair. You are not a coward. You have done everything we have asked you to, even though it hurt you to do so." Paelen looked over to Agent T and saw his besotted eyes following Cupid. "We could not have made it this far without you. But losing Joel and now seeing the Red Apple and knowing Emily and Pegasus are in there, I am not thinking clearly."

Cupid calmed. "I know I have not always proved myself to you and the others. And yes, perhaps I came here as much to get away from the Nirads as to help Emily. But believe me, Paelen, I do want to help. Now, let us ensure Steve is safe, and then we can walk back to the Red Apple and see about Emily and Pegasus."

They checked on Steve in the backseat. He was still unconscious, but his bleeding had stopped and he was breathing well. After they made him as comfortable as possible, they started back toward the Red Apple.

The snow was now falling heavily. The thick flakes settled on their hair and shoulders and limited their vision to only a few yards in front of them. Keeping in the dense trees that grew behind the large rest stop, they approached the area.

One of the first things they noticed was Agent O supervising the search. He was walking with two crutches, and his legs were covered in thick bandages. Yet despite his wounds and obvious pain, he was well enough to bark orders at the others working in the area, demanding they not stop until they found Emily.

"They have not found her yet," Paelen said gratefully. "There is still hope."

His eyes scanned the whole area. The destruction was all but complete. "What happened here?" he asked in a hushed whisper. "Could it have been Emily's tears again?"

They watched in silent shock as several men emerged from the wreckage. They were struggling to carry a heavy stretcher. A sheet completely covered the body. But as the men moved to put the stretcher on a truck, an arm fell out from under the cover. It was the color of gray marble.

"Nirads!" Cupid said. "While we were gone, Nirads attacked our hiding place!"

"How is this possible?" Paelen asked. "The Nirad tracks at the CRU facility showed they were moving deeper into the woods. How could they get here before us?"

Cupid shrugged. "They could not. But if it was not the same Nirads as at the facility—"

"Then there are more here in this world," Paelen finished.

As they concentrated on the wreckage, Paelen, Cupid, and Agent T crept closer, trying to see any signs of Emily or Pegasus. There were CRU agents and military personnel poring all over the area and searching through the wreckage. But there were no traces of their missing friends.

A short while later another stretcher was carried out of the smoldering debris. Paelen and Cupid could tell by the size that it was another Nirad body. But it was different. The lump under the sheet ended at the waist. Moments later, a third stretcher emerged, with an equally strange shape. The men carrying it slipped in the snow and fell. When they hit the ground, the body fell off the stretcher, revealing only a heavy set of legs and lower torso.

Paelen pointed. "Look at the cut edge. It has been burned."

"Emily can kill Nirads," Cupid mused. "It is no wonder they came after her. If they knew she and Pegasus could kill them, they would have to get them first, before completing their attack on Olympus."

"Or here," Paelen added. As he scanned the debris, Paelen shook his head. "We have seen Nirads pulled out of there, but where are the others?"

"Maybe he can tell us?" Agent T offered helpfully as he pointed at yet another stretcher being pulled from the debris. Unlike the others, the occupant was not fully covered by a sheet. He was wrapped in a blanket. His face was badly burned, but he was alive and moaning loudly.

"Earl!" Paelen said. "We must get to him. He can tell us what happened here."

They watched Earl being loaded into an ambulance. Cupid turned to Agent T. "Where will they take him?"

Agent T smiled radiantly, grateful to contribute. "They can't take him back to the facility, not with what the Nirads did to it. If it were me, I would secure a hospital and take him there."

Paelen realized if the CRU managed to take Earl away, they would never learn what happened to Emily or Pegasus. He looked at Cupid. "We must stop them."

"How?" Cupid asked. "This whole area is covered with agents. We will be captured before we get anywhere near him."

"If it pleases you, I can do it," Agent T offered. "They know me and will not suspect that I'm doing it for you. I could capture the ambulance, and we could get away from here."

Paelen looked at Cupid. "We have no choice. If he wants to do it, let him try."

Cupid said to their prisoner, "Yes, it would please me very much if you could do this. Go secure the vehicle. When you have it, take it to where we left the car. Paelen and I will join you there."

Agent T's face beamed as he stood, anxious to carry out Cupid's wishes. "I will do anything for you, Cupid."

Cupid cringed as the agent showed his undying devotion. From their hiding place they watched Agent T's demeanor change. He straightened his back and walked with the arrogance they were used to seeing. His voice was loud and commanding as he approached the group of agents standing beside the ambulance containing Earl.

They could hear him demanding a full report. Both Paelen and Cupid breathed a sigh of relief when they heard the others report that there were no traces of the girl or horse in the wreckage. Just the Nirad bodies, two dead CRU agents, and the one surviving man.

Agent T ordered them back to work in the debris. Alone with the ambulance, he secured the rear doors and stormed up front to the driver's side and climbed in. Moments later the ambulance burst to life. Agent T put it in gear and began driving away from the area.

"We must go," Cupid said as he rose and caught Paelen by the sleeve. "We do not want Agent T waiting there for us long. He may try to come back to look for me."

The ambulance was waiting for them beside the black car when they left the cover of the trees. Agent T was standing at the rear doors, bouncing with excitement.

"I told you I could do it!" He sounded like a hopeful child looking for praise. "Did I do well?"

"Yes," Cupid said. "You did very well."

They opened the ambulance doors and were immediately struck by the smell of smoke rising from Earl. His face was raw with burns, and he was moaning softly.

"Earl," Paelen said gently as he climbed in and approached the side of the stretcher. "It is us, Paelen and Cupid. Can you hear me?"

Earl's eyes fluttered open, and he turned his face to Paelen. "Thank God, it's you," he said weakly.

"What happened?"

"Monsters came. Them big four-armed things. They attacked us."

"Are Emily and Pegasus still in the rubble?" Cupid asked.

Earl shook his head slightly and moaned at the movement. "No," he choked. "I saw 'em take 'em away right after the ceilin' came down."

Paelen cursed. Then he hesitantly asked, "Was Emily alive?"

Earl took an unsteady breath. He shook his head. "No. Not at first. When the burnin' roof came down, she was buried in the worst of it. This big orange Nirad dug her out. It started to howl like crazy when it pulled her free, like it was grievin' or somethin'. I tell ya, Emily was nothin' but a little rag doll in its big arms—all burned up and broken. There was no mistakin', she was dead. But then she started to glow—you know, just like when I shot her. Right there in the Nirad's arms. After a few minutes she moved. Then the others found Pegasus and got him movin'. They left me for dead."

Paelen looked at Cupid. "An orange Nirad? We've

only seen gray ones." He looked at Earl. "This orange Nirad, was it their leader?"

Earl coughed and winced in pain. "Ain't certain. When they first got here, there was this big wild boar with wings—"

"A boar with wings? Are you certain?" Paelen asked.

When Earl nodded, Cupid cursed. "It is Chrysaor! What is he doing here?"

"It cannot be," Paelen said. "He would not betray us. Not to the Nirads." He concentrated on Earl. "Were the boar's wings as brown as the rest of him? Did they hang over his rump?"

Earl nodded. "That's him all right. Whatever he is, Pegasus didn't like him one bit. They started fightin' with all the fury they got. I couldn't see much, 'cuz this big Nirad caught hold of me. He darn near broke all my bones and squeezed the life outta me. Emily tried to help, but she lost control of the flames. Then the roof came down." Earl started to cough. When the fit ended, he asked, "You know that boar?"

"Chrysaor is Pegasus's twin brother," Paelen muttered, deep in thought.

Earl's burned eyelids shot open. "Pegasus has a twin that's a boar?"

Paelen nodded. "They have been fighting most of their lives. Now it appears that Chrysaor has sided with the Nirads against Olympus."

"But what does he want with Emily?" Cupid asked.

Paelen shrugged. "I do not know for certain, but it frightens me. Emily is the source of all our powers. Whoever possesses her could control Olympus."

Earl started to cough again.

"You need help," Paelen said. "So does Steve."

Agent T finally spoke. "If you don't want to be captured, you can't take either of them to the hospital. Once they realize Earl is gone, they will search the hospitals first."

"What can we do?" Paelen asked.

"Leave me," Earl said weakly. "Just go after Emily and Pegasus."

"You will die if we leave you," Cupid said. "Normally, as you are human, I would not care. But Emily does. So leaving you and her father is not an option."

They moved Steve into the ambulance, beside

Earl. Agent T proved invaluable with his first-aid skills. Using the ambulance supplies, he was able to treat the men. Earl remained conscious long enough to offer a safe place for them to hide. He and some buddies had a hunting cabin up on the mountain.

Agent T disabled the tracker device in the ambulance, ensuring that they wouldn't be followed, and drove up into the mountains. Just as Earl had promised, they found the small hunting cabin nestled deep in the trees. It was covered in undisturbed snow and offered them seclusion and protection from the CRU down in Tuxedo.

Once they had transferred Steve and Earl into the safety of the cabin, Cupid and Paelen built a roaring fire to warm the place. Earl was still on the stretcher, moaning softly.

"How is he?" Cupid asked.

Agent T grinned up at him before saying, "Not good. He needs a doctor. So does Jacobs over there on the sofa. Though the bullet went right through him, I don't know what damage it's done. He may be bleeding internally."

"If he needs a doctor, he shall have it," Paelen said

confidently. Then he frowned. "What is a doctor and where do we find one?"

Earl managed to tell them he knew of a doctor they could trust. He gave Agent T the telephone number before fading back into unconsciousness.

Paelen straightened and looked around the small cabin at the two wounded men. He'd never felt so helpless in all his life. He was in a strange, unfriendly world with no idea how anything worked. One of his best friends was dead, the other missing. CRU agents were hunting them once again, and everything was going wrong.

He looked at Cupid. The winged Olympian didn't show any of the fear or insecurities Paelen now felt. Cupid was calm and in control as he took notes from Agent T on how to contact the doctor. Despite everything he'd ever felt toward Cupid, Paelen had a newfound respect for him.

"So where do we find this thing called a telephone?" Cupid asked.

The CRU agent shrugged apologetically. "There aren't as many around as there used to be. Everyone has a cell phone these days. I'm so sorry, Cupid, but my phone was left at the Red Apple." The agent looked as though he were about to cry. Finally he said, "We might find one in town, though. The trouble is, by now the other agents will be on the lookout for me and the ambulance."

Cupid nodded. "You will not be going back into town. I will."

"Not alone," Paelen said. He looked out the cabin's window. "It will be getting dark soon. If you can carry me, we can fly back together. My winged sandals were also left behind at the Red Apple. I would like to see if we can get them back if they have not been discovered yet. Then we could use the telephone to get the doctor."

Cupid looked as though he were about to protest, but then closed his mouth. "I will carry you," he said softly. "Once it is dark we will leave."

While they waited for the sun to set, Paelen investigated the small hunting cabin. In the kitchen he found canned and dry food, but there was very little sugar or other food for the Olympians. Neither he nor Cupid had eaten since that morning, and he was feeling his strength starting to ebb.

In the bedroom there was a small closet with winter clothing that could help them blend in with the locals. Paelen carried a selection back into the main area. He started to check through the pockets of the CRU agent's suit he was wearing as well as the other clothing's pockets. He didn't find anything at all. He looked at Cupid and Agent T. "Do you have any money?"

Cupid found nothing. But Agent T was still wearing Joel's clothing from earlier that day and discovered almost fifty dollars left from the costume competition's winnings. He handed it eagerly to Cupid.

Paelen said, "I believe we should also buy some more food. There is plenty here for the humans to eat, but nothing for us. I do not know about you, but I am starving and getting weaker."

Cupid nodded. "Me also." He stepped over to the window. "It is dark out. We should change our clothes and go."

The snow had finally tapered off, and the clouds cleared as a cold, crisp starry night arrived. When they tried to leave, they discovered that asking Agent

T to stay behind proved more difficult than they expected. He followed them out into the snow and begged Cupid to take him with them. Tears welled in the agent's eyes when they refused.

Paelen felt his sympathy for Agent T rise. He was a wreck. Paelen now understood why Cupid had been so reluctant to use his powers on the men.

"We will not be long," Paelen reassured him gently. "And I know for certain it would please Cupid greatly if you were to stay with Steve and Earl and do your best to help them." Paelen looked over to Cupid. "It would make you happy, would it not?"

Cupid sighed and dropped his head. "Yes, it would make me very happy if you would do that for me."

That seemed to satisfy the teary agent. He sniffed and smiled sadly. "I will, just for you. You will be so proud of me. Just promise you'll come back safe."

"We will," Paelen promised.

After the agent went back inside, Cupid shook his head. "I have destroyed him. It would have been kinder to torture the agents rather than use my powers. There is nothing left of him."

"You did it for Emily," Paelen said. "She would not

have allowed us to hurt the men. I am sure when this is over we will find a way to restore him."

Cupid looked doubtful as he walked away from the cabin. The snow was knee-deep and heavy. They needed to find an area clear enough for Cupid to spread his wings and have a running start if he was to carry Paelen's weight as well.

Not far from the cabin they finally found the perfect spot. Cupid lifted Paelen into his arms and launched himself into the cold night sky.

EMILY WAS HELD TIGHT IN THE NIRAD'S
arms as they traveled through the Solar Stream. On the
two other occasions when she had ventured through it,
she had been riding Pegasus. Perhaps it was the steady
movement of the stallion's powerful wings or just
being with him that had distracted her, but this time,
with no Pegasus to reassure her, the brilliant light surrounding her and the booming sounds assaulting her
ears left Emily feeling sick and dizzy. She looked up
into the Nirad's face and could see that it was also not
enjoying the experience. Its eyes were closed and its
mouth was a tight, thin line. If the noise of the Solar
Stream hadn't been so loud, she was certain she would
have heard the creature whining.

They finally emerged in the back of another darkened cave. The Nirads filed out into the daylight, which was gray and miserable. As Emily recovered, she looked at the strange world around her and sucked in her breath. The sky was heavy with black storm clouds. Yet the air felt dry and arid. The ground beneath them was black and dusty, with every step stirring up dark gray dust clouds around their feet. There were no trees or any signs of plant life.

Not too far away she saw small animal-like creatures scurrying around on the dry ground. They were almost the size and shape of raccoons but didn't have fur. Instead they had dark gray and brown marbled skin. They showed no fear as the parade of huge Nirads, led by the angry boar, filed past them. In the sky above, large, leathery batlike creatures circled in the dull sky. Their wingspan was almost as wide as Pegasus's was. They were graceful and agile, and their wings cut silently through the still air. Occasionally they made strange calling sounds that seemed to carry for miles.

As she looked around, Emily continued to see no plant life at all. There were no trees, no grass, no weeds, and no flowers. Nothing appeared to grow in the black, dusty soil. They soon approached an area with roughly built stone structures.

The primitive stone houses had four solid side walls and a single stone slab for a roof. She almost expected to see a caveman emerging. Instead Emily was stunned to see what she realized was a female Nirad, exiting her home with a child held in her arms.

The Nirad woman was almost as big as the men were but with even longer claws and hair. She also had four thick, powerful arms, which she waved in the air threateningly at the sight of Emily and Pegasus.

Everywhere Emily looked, Nirads stopped to stare at the line of escorts around her. Most growled and shook their fists angrily at her when the group walked past, but some seemed to drop their heads and look away in sadness.

"So, this is your world," she said to her Nirad in awe.

He looked down at her and nodded.

"Do you have any children?"

The Nirad's eyes seemed to mist. Emily was certain she saw heavy sadness there as once again he slowly nodded.

"Are they in danger?"

He made several soft guttural sounds that Emily couldn't understand. His expression was pain-filled and earnest as he tried to explain.

"I'm sorry, I can't understand you," she said softly. "I wish I could speak your language. I don't even know if you have names. Do you?"

Her Nirad nodded and opened his mouth. He made a deep sound that he slowly repeated several times.

"Tange," Emily tried, hoping to get as close to the sound as possible. "Is your name Tange?"

The Nirad nodded.

Emily silently celebrated the breakthrough. She and the huge male Nirad called Tange were actually communicating!

"Do you know why I am here?" she asked.

Tange shook his head. But then he motioned toward the front of their group.

Emily strained to see around the line of Nirads blocking her view. Tange lifted her higher, and she saw their destination. It was a tall, white marble palace that looked completely out of place in the dark, mournful landscape. As she looked at the tall pillars and white marble steps leading up to the magnificent entrance, she instantly recognized the design. It was a replica of Jupiter's palace, reproduced in the Nirad world. Along the road leading to the palace stood a long line of statues that seemed to serve as an honor guard.

"That palace is from Olympus!" Emily breathed. "What's it doing here?" She looked back to Tange. "Is Jupiter here?"

Before Tange could answer, another large orange Nirad came up beside them and growled ferociously. His eyes settled on Emily, and he shook his head and barked a single harsh word to her. The message was clear. Stop talking.

Emily saw pure murderous hatred blazing in the Nirad's face. He wouldn't hesitate to kill her if he got the chance. She curled closer into Tange, wondering what she and Pegasus had done to cause such rage among the Nirads.

All along the journey to the white palace, Emily saw evidence of the Nirad hatred as crowds gathered to stare and growl at her. When some gray Nirads tried to approach, Tange and the orange Nirads drove them away with threatening growls and raised fists. The same happened when the crowds tried to throw stones and clubs at Pegasus. Only the orange Nirads prevented the stallion from being hit.

"Why do you all hate us?" Emily asked Tange softly.

Tange said nothing as he carried her steadily toward the palace. The closer they got, the more statues Emily saw lining the route. Some were back from the road, and a few had been knocked over and were lying in broken rubble. Scanning the area, she realized there had to be hundreds of these Nirad statues, if not thousands.

Whoever had carved them had put an expression of terror and pain on all their faces. Not one was smiling or standing in a normal position. They all seemed to be frozen midaction, trying to move or run, and not one of them looked happy. They all had that same horrible, pain-filled expression. Finally she had to look away. The sight of those horrible faces was making the journey worse.

Eventually they arrived at the steps of the white

palace. Emily watched the winged boar go up ahead of them. Two orange Nirads were standing guard beside the doors. At the boar's approach they hauled open the two heavy marble doors, and the group started to file in.

When Tange carried Emily up the steps, she strained to peer behind her. "Please let me see," she asked.

Tange looked down at her, then lifted her higher until she could see over his thick shoulder. The Nirad village sprawled out around the white palace. There were thousands of dark stone structures with even more statues in all directions. It was almost like a black-and-white film. There was no color, just varying shades of gray, black, and brown. The only brightness in the whole area came from the orange Nirads themselves. Even the strange batlike things in the sky were gray and black. Emily watched them circling and wondered if that was what pterodactyl dinosaurs had looked like.

Once again Emily noticed a lack of any plant life. She wondered what the Nirads ate. She remembered Tange's wide mouth and his sharp teeth and felt her first twinges of genuine terror. Were Nirads meat eaters? And if so, what or who was on their menu?

Before full panic set in, Emily was carried through the doors of the white palace. The entrance hall was huge. It was made of the same white marble as all the structures in Olympus. But, unlike Jupiter's palace, no art or anything beautiful adorned the walls. Just more horrific statues frozen in movement.

As they lumbered forward, Emily heard shrill screeching coming from one of the rooms off the entrance hall. The grating sound set her already strained nerves on edge. She didn't want to know who or what was making that awful sound.

As she was being led toward it, Emily struggled in Tange's arms. "No, please, Tange, no! I don't want to go in there!"

Pegasus started to whinny and scream behind her. She could hear his hooves clopping on the smooth marble floor as he strained against the orange Nirads who were directing him forward.

"Chrysaor, bring her in!" demanded a high, shrill voice. "We want to see the Flame of Olympus!"

Emily was carried forward. As Tange entered the

large hall, the Nirads parted in front of them and moved to either side of the room, giving her a clear view of the winged boar stepping up to the owners of the shrill voices.

Emily began to scream.

IT WAS A SHORT FLIGHT FROM THE CABIN TO
the town. Streetlights were on, and the aroma of
woodsmoke from countless fireplaces filled the air.
When they soared silently over the wreckage of the
Red Apple, Paelen was distressed to see that the
entire area was covered by a large, secure tent with
several heavily armed soldiers patrolling around it.
No light was showing through the tent, so at least
no one was inside.

Cupid glided closer and flew silently over the trees
to the back of the wrecked rest stop. He found a clearing and lightly touched down. Paelen handed him his
clothing, and he started to dress.

"I really hate this," Cupid complained as he pulled

up his trousers after tucking his wings inside. He reached for the red plaid flannel shirt. "You have no idea just how uncomfortable this is."

Paelen braced himself for another long series of complaints from the winged Olympian. "Well, it is better than letting them see you and raising the alarm. We must get in there without drawing their attention."

"I hardly believe whether they see my wings or not will make much difference. We are going to have to fight our way in regardless."

"You could always use—"

Cupid held up a warning finger. "Do not even suggest it. It is bad enough with Agent T. I will not use my powers on these men. It would be kinder if we simply killed them right now."

"We cannot do that!" Paelen said in hushed shock. "They have done nothing to us. We will do what we did at the carnival and knock them out. Emily would never forgive us if she knew we had killed innocent people."

"Who would tell her?" Cupid asked.

"I would."

"Then you are a fool," Cupid said. "For now, we will try it your way. But if they cause me any trouble, I will not hesitate to kill them."

Paelen was shocked at Cupid's ruthless streak. "I have an idea," he finally said. "I used to get into Jupiter's palace undetected all the time. I am certain I can do this. Then, once I am inside the tent, all I need to do is find the sandals."

Cupid looked doubtful, but he seemed satisfied to be told to stay behind and wait. "All right, I will give you a short time. But if there is trouble, I will fight."

This was the best he could hope for from Cupid. Using all the stealth of his thief's experience, Paelen crossed through the parking area and crept past two guards without being seen. He could feel more than see that two other guards would soon be approaching from the other side as they constantly patrolled the perimeter of the large enclosure.

After a short, silent sprint, Paelen reached the side of the tent. The main opening was around the other side. But a guard's station had been set up there, with two large, burly soldiers sitting at a table. Their weapons were drawn, and they looked ready for anything.

Paelen crouched down and tried to lift the edge of the tent. But he discovered it had been tacked down to the ground every few inches. Tearing it up would make too much noise. He groaned inwardly, knowing what he had to do.

Checking to see the position of the patrolling soldiers, Paelen used his power to manipulate his body. With each crack and pop of his bones, he feared discovery. Soon he was too thin to fit in his clothing. With a bit more stretching, he turned into the snake-like body he used to get into tight areas.

He lifted up the edge of the tent as far as it would go and slid easily inside. He returned to his normal shape and stood amid the debris that had once been the Red Apple.

Despite the complete lack of light, he was able to see clearly. He was in what had once been the kitchen area. He made his way back to where he, Joel, and Cupid had changed their clothes in preparation for their assault on the CRU facility. Paelen forced himself not to dwell on the memories of that disastrous rescue. He was here for his sandals, nothing more.

The acrid smell of recently extinguished fire stung

his nostrils as he quietly climbed over the charred debris. He cursed every time the destroyed timbers cracked under his weight but was grateful to discover that the area where they had changed look undisturbed. It had yet to be searched.

"Sandals, where are you?" he muttered softly, looking around.

There was a slight stirring in the burned debris. Paelen's sharp senses caught movement to his left. "Sandals?"

Once again there was movement. Paelen recalled what Mercury had told him when he'd given his sandals to Paelen. Mercury said the sandals didn't belong to him anymore, but to Paelen. Suddenly that comment made sense. Their initial devotion to the messenger of Olympus and now to him was because the sandals were alive. They were responding to his voice. Buried beneath the debris, they were trying to get back to him.

"Where are you, sandals?" he softly called.

Not far ahead a deep pile of rubble shifted. The sound of stirring and movement set Paelen's heart pounding. What if the soldiers outside heard it? He climbed over to the area as quickly and quietly as he could. His nerves were stretched to the limit. "Sandals, where are you?" he called softly again.

The movement was right in front of him. A large chunk of burned roof was covering the area. As Paelen caught hold of the edge, he hoisted it in the air. He peered beneath and, with a sigh of profound relief, saw his two sandals amid the ashes.

Quickly retrieving them, Paelen lowered the roof and made his way back to the side of the tent. He stretched his body and slid under the edge. His clothing was still waiting for him.

But so were the soldiers.

As he returned to his normal shape and rose, bright lights blazed to life and shone painfully in his eyes.

Two armed soldiers rushed at him. "Freeze or we'll open fire!"

Paelen barely had time to think before a soldier's rough hands caught hold of his arms and hauled him forward.

"Drop the shoes!" another voice ordered.

"They are sandals," Paelen corrected. "And if you want them, you shall have to take them from me."

As more soldiers came forward, they heard a bloodcurdling scream. Cupid dove down from the sky. His arms were filled with large stones, and he started hurling them at the unsuspecting soldiers.

After a first pass, Cupid swooped away, turned, and came at them for a second assault, throwing more stones at the men. They had been prepared for a ground attack but hadn't been warned about enraged winged teenagers coming from above.

As the soldiers scattered and tried to raise their weapons, Cupid landed and charged at them, fighting with all the Olympian strength he possessed. Paelen took the opportunity and wrenched his arms free of the man closest to him. He tackled him to the ground. With one punch, the soldier was unconscious.

Not thinking, just reacting, Paelen lifted another soldier in the air and threw him across the parking area and into the trees. The Olympians knew everything was at stake. They couldn't get caught. With Cupid fighting beside him, not one soldier had time to fire his weapon. Before long, they were all down on the ground.

"Grab your clothing and the sandals," Cupid ordered. "We must go before others arrive."

Paelen followed Cupid back into the trees. Pausing only long enough to dress, he was grateful to feel the winged sandals back on his feet, where they belonged.

"We must fly," Cupid called as he collected his own clothing. "We still need to make that phone call."

Cupid was first in the air. Paelen ordered the sandals to follow and was thrilled as their tiny wings lifted him easily into the sky.

Within minutes of their escape, they heard the sounds of sirens rising from below. Flashing lights of police cruisers, military trucks, and CRU vehicles illuminated the roads as they raced to the Red Apple. Both Olympians knew it had been a close call.

Paelen flew closer to Cupid. "They must have raised the alarm. We cannot go into the town to make the call. We should try the place where Joel and I bought food. They are always open. Perhaps we can find a telephone there."

Cupid agreed and let Paelen lead the way. He ordered his sandals to take him to the superstore.

They were both grateful to see it was on the far end of town, well away from the Red Apple and the gathering soldiers.

They landed a short distance away and walked back to the superstore. Paelen jumped when the sliding doors at the large entrance whooshed open at his approach. He still didn't understand how they knew he was there. Perhaps a small nymph controlled them?

"Come along," Cupid said irritably. "We do not have time to play. We must find the telephone and get back to the cabin."

"Who is playing?" Paelen asked as he nervously stepped through the mysterious doors, still convinced they would snap shut on him at any moment.

Inside, Paelen was once again struck by the sights, sounds, and smells of the brightly lit superstore. There was so much sugar there. But there were also a lot more people than when he and Joel had shopped. That made him nervous.

"Cupid, can you smell that?" Paelen asked softly as his stomach started to gurgle.

Cupid nodded. "We will make the call first, and

then we must eat. I have been too long without ambrosia, and I am feeling weak."

The two Olympians stood at the entrance, wondering what a telephone looked like and how they would find it.

Finally, Cupid approached an attractive young woman carrying several shopping bags and smiled radiantly at her. Paelen watched him working his magic. The winged Olympian didn't turn on his power—he didn't need to. His smile alone was enough to turn the woman's cheeks bright red.

"Can you help us, please," he said in his most charming voice. "We need to make a call, and I cannot find a telephone."

The woman's cheeks reddened further. She reached into her pocket and produced her cell phone. "You could always use mine if you like."

Cupid took the small device and looked at Paelen quizzically. When Paelen shrugged, he looked back at the woman. "Would you mind showing me how to use this?"

"Not at all," she said. "What's the number?"

Cupid handed her the piece of paper with the

doctor's telephone number. The woman dialed and held the phone to her ear.

After a moment she shook her head. "It's going straight to voice mail. Do you want to leave a message?"

"Does that mean you cannot reach the doctor?" Cupid asked.

"I'm sorry," she said. "Do you want me to leave a message? I could give them my number, and we could wait together for them to call?" There was no mistaking the offer in her soft voice. Paelen was once again struck by Cupid's power over women.

Cupid smiled. "No, thank you. Perhaps when I next visit and we have more time."

The disappointment on her face was obvious as she reluctantly put her cell back in her pocket and drifted away.

When she was gone, the smile dropped from Cupid's face. "No doctor. We shall have to manage on our own." Cupid sniffed the air again. "Come, Paelen, this place is filled with food, and I am starving. It is time we ate."

Paelen and Cupid went back to the entrance and

collected shopping baskets. Each step they took, Cupid fidgeted. "I really hate this. My feathers are poking into the back of my legs."

"It will not be long," Paelen promised. "We will just get what we need and go."

Following their noses, the two Olympians carried their shopping baskets deeper into the store. They walked down an aisle filled with chocolate, candy bars, and cookies.

As they filled their baskets, Paelen became aware of several children drifting away from their parents to follow Cupid. The winged Olympian looked back at the small but growing group and tried to shoo them away, but the children refused to go. Farther down the aisle, a boy of no more than four broke away from his mother and ran straight at Cupid. He hugged him around the legs and wouldn't release him.

Paelen laughed at the mortified expression on Cupid's face as he struggled to disentangle himself from the affectionate child. "Go back to your mother, little human," he cried. But the more he tried to push him away, the louder the child protested and refused to release him.

Paelen pulled the little boy off Cupid just as his mother arrived. The woman's face was red with embarrassment as she apologized for her son's odd behavior.

"Madam," Cupid scolded, "will you please keep hold of your child."

As she dragged her screaming son away, Cupid looked back at the group of other children pressing closer. "All of you, go back to your parents. I have nothing for you."

But they refused to leave. Paelen tore open a bag of miniature candy bars and handed them out to the children. "Go now, young ones, your parents will be looking for you. Go on. Cupid and I need to eat."

The children accepted the treats but still refused to leave. They followed at a distance, waving and calling to Cupid.

"There is only one thing I hate more than humans," Cupid complained as he tore open a bag of chocolate chip cookies and started to eat. "That is young humans."

"You do not," Paelen argued as he stuffed his

mouth full of chocolates. "If you did, you would have struck that little boy."

Cupid regarded him with a dark expression. "I did not wish to draw undue attention to us. That is all."

"Of course," Paelen said as he chuckled. "I believe you. No one else would, but I do."

The two continued to eat as they made their way down the long aisle of sweets. They were still being followed by the parade of children. Halfway down the next aisle, they were met by store security.

"You're gonna pay for all that," a guard confronted them angrily. "And for the candy you just gave to those kids back there."

Paelen's mouth was full of food, but he nodded his head. "We have money," he mumbled. "We intend to pay for everything."

"Then eat when you get home," the guard said sharply. "We don't allow grazing while you're shopping."

That comment caused the wings on Cupid's back to flutter with annoyance. He stood erect, and his pale eyes flashed. "Animal's graze," he corrected. "We are eating. There is a difference."

"Not to me, there isn't," answered the guard. "Now bring your baskets and follow me. It's time you checked out."

Paelen started to follow, but Cupid refused. "We are not finished here yet. We will leave when we are ready. Not a moment sooner. And neither you nor any other human can command us otherwise."

"Listen, kid," the guard said as he pressed closer. He poked Cupid in the shoulder with a bony finger. "You'll leave when I tell you to. And I'm telling you to go right now."

In a move too quick to follow, Cupid struck the guard with a punch that knocked him to the floor. The children screamed and ran forward. They jumped on the guard and pinned him down, ordering him to leave Cupid alone.

As the guard curled up in a tight ball, Cupid looked down on him and started shouting. "I have had it with you humans telling me what to do! I told you, we will leave here when we have finished and not a moment sooner!" He picked up his shopping basket and continued casually down the aisle as though nothing had just happened.

"We should go," Paelen said, looking at the group of children piling on the guard. Around them, other shoppers stared in shock. "People are beginning to stare at us."

"Let them," Cupid spat as he tore open a second bag of cookies. "I have not had a decent meal since we left Olympus. I am half-starved, my wings are driving me mad, and I am in no mood to deal with humans, big or small!"

Paelen looked around at the gathering crowds. Suddenly something Emily said rose to his mind. "Cupid, do you remember what Emily said? Agent O told her that since he moved up here, his only pleasure was attending the Haunted Forest Festival."

"So what?" Cupid said, spraying Paelen with cookie crumbs as he reached for more food.

"So that means he lives in this small town. It also means he would have to buy food. This is the only place to do that in the area. What if other CRU agents and their families shop here?"

Cupid stopped and looked back at the crowds gathering around the guard. Finally he shook his head. "They are far too busy with the destruction of their facility and the Red Apple to come here. I am sure we are perfectly safe."

Cupid had barely finished the comment when they spotted two men standing at the end of the aisle. They were dressed in jeans and winter coats, but they had weapons drawn and pointed right at Paelen and Cupid, despite the children hovering near Cupid. Their stance and facial expressions were immediately recognizable.

"Freeze!" the CRU agents called.

"Perhaps you were right," Cupid muttered.

"I wish I'd been wrong," Paelen said as he looked behind them and saw several armed soldiers moving into position at the other end of the aisle.

"Drop your baskets!" the lead agent ordered. "Do it now, nice and slow!"

"There are children here," Paelen warned. "Please put down your weapons and let them leave before they are hurt!"

"We give the orders here. Now, both of you, get down on the floor."

"You are making a grave mistake, human," Cupid warned. He slowly backed up toward the group of frightened children. As he moved, he pulled off his coat, tore open his shirt, and freed his wings. He opened them protectively around the children, gathering them close to him. "It would serve you well to let them leave here right now. I will not be as amiable if one of these children is hurt because of you. "

Paelen moved beside Cupid, further blocking the children from the soldiers' weapons. He could hear the shocked cries and muttered remarks of the adult shoppers around them. They all seemed to think Cupid was some kind of winged angel.

"No one is going anywhere, Cupid," called an all-too-familiar voice. Agent O moved to the front of the aisle. His legs were still bandaged from Emily's burns, and he remained on crutches. His eyes landed on Paelen. "Paelen, did you really believe we wouldn't be watching this place? We know all about your need for sugar. I'm surprised it took you so long to show up here. You are surrounded and won't get away from me this time. Now, where are Emily and Pegasus?"

"Well beyond your reach," Paelen spat as his anger grew. "You will not take us, Agent O. Not again."

Some of the children began to cry. They huddled

fearfully together behind the protection of Cupid's spread wings. "Let these young ones leave here before I lose my temper," Cupid warned. "They are not part of this and should not bear witness to what is to come."

"You care so much about human children?" Agent O challenged.

"Obviously, more than you do," Paelen shot back. "Tell me, would you really shoot at us with these children here? Are you so desperate to catch us that you would sacrifice them?"

Paelen saw hesitation on Agent O's face. There were gathering crowds of people watching. Agent O might be single-minded and obsessed, but he wasn't a fool. He motioned to the soldiers to lower their weapons.

"All right," Agent O said. "Let the children go first."

Paelen glanced back and saw the soldiers who blocked the end of the aisle following the order. He looked down at the children and pointed to the soldiers. "Go that way, children. Go find your parents."

The children hesitated and looked up to Cupid with tear-filled eyes. "It is all right, little ones, you are safe," he said kindly as he stroked a little girl's head. Cupid looked to the adults in the aisle. "Please take them to safety. Help them find their parents."

As the other shoppers approached to collect the children, Cupid shot a warning glance at Agent O. "You will let them all leave here unharmed. This fight is between us. They have nothing to do with it."

With a store full of witnesses, Agent O nodded reluctantly. He ordered the soldiers to direct the public out of the building. While the children left the aisle, Cupid whispered, "When they are gone, we must move. If we get separated, you know where to go."

"Good luck," Paelen said as the last child was escorted out of the aisle.

"Luck has nothing to do with it!" Cupid shouted as, in one swift move, he dropped his basket and ran toward the agents.

CUPID CHARGED DOWN THE AISLE. THE TIPS of his wings caught the edges of the shelves and knocked food onto the floor as he ran. The crowds behind the agents screamed when they saw the enraged Olympian storming straight at them.

Behind him, Paelen heard the soldiers preparing to fire. He turned and hurled his basket at the men.

"Sandals, take me up!"

Once airborne, Paelen ordered the sandals to take him forward. He skimmed the food on the top shelf and watched it rain down on the shocked soldiers.

Flying over the tops of the shelves and into the next aisle, Paelen found stacks and stacks of canned goods. He snatched up a handful and threw them at the soldiers. Gunfire rang out behind him, and Paelen felt a sharp stinging in his back. He turned to see two CRU agents firing their weapons at him. Their bullets did little damage. But they did hurt.

Screaming in rage, Paelen flew full speed at the agents working with Agent O and knocked them both into a tall display of baked beans, hurling cans everywhere. Paelen ordered the sandals to carry him higher in the air. His wild eyes searched for Cupid. He heard shooting to his right and saw Cupid going down. As the winged Olympian tried to rise, he was knocked over and pinned to the ground by countless soldiers.

Paelen reacted immediately. He collected several more cans of baked beans and ordered the sandals to take him to Cupid. Paelen threw the cans with the same deadly accuracy he'd used on the target at the clown dunk tank at the Haunted Forest Festival. Unable to defend themselves against the barrage, the soldiers released their prisoner and covered their heads. Cupid was on his feet in seconds and back in the fight.

Out of beans, Paelen reached for other bottles or cans to throw. Soon more soldiers ran along the aisle toward him with their weapons raised. Paelen screamed in fury and used his Olympian strength to shove the entire length of display shelves over, burying the men in all manner of items.

As he moved to get back to Cupid, Paelen heard gunfire and felt a sharp stinging in the side of his head. He turned and saw Agent O firing his weapon. The agent wasn't trying to capture him. He was trying to kill him!

The sudden pain brought back all the terrible memories of what Agents J and O had done to him at the Governors Island facility. Then he remembered they'd done the same to Joel. Those memories turned to rage.

"Sandals," he shouted, "take me to Agent O!"

The CRU agent heard Paelen's order. His eyes flew wide in fear as he struggled to run away. But the thick bandages on his legs wouldn't let him move very fast. Paelen was on him in an instant, unleashing all the pent-up anger he felt toward the evil government agent.

He was unaware of anything else. It was just him and Agent O. He couldn't see Cupid gaining control over the soldiers, nor did he see the other agents moving in to pull him off. All he knew was fury.

A loud shattering of glass finally caught his attention. Paelen lifted his head to see Cupid flying full speed through the glass of a large window at the front of the store. That sound brought him back. He looked down. Agent O was unconscious, and his men were trying to drag him off.

"This is for Joel!" Paelen shouted as he gave Agent O a final jaw-cracking punch. "Sandals," he shouted, "follow Cupid!"

The sandals reacted immediately. Despite all the men crushing him, Paelen was lifted in the air. With several soldiers dangling from his legs, he flew toward the broken window. Just as the last man released him, he passed through the opening and up into the night sky.

The urgent popping of gunfire followed as Paelen searched the air for Cupid. From above him arrived the heavy thumping sounds of military helicopters giving chase. Paelen looked back and saw the terrifying machines gaining on him. "Faster!" he cried to the sandals. "Fly faster!"

Ahead of him, two other helicopters cut through the night sky. They were moving away from him, so he knew they were chasing Cupid. He saw flashes as they fired their weapons.

Paelen had little time to worry about Cupid, because the other military helicopters were right behind him and getting closer. He turned back. "Let me see how high you can go. Sandals, take me up!"

With a sudden change of direction, the sandals shot Paelen straight up in the night sky. Beneath him, the helicopters tried to follow, but he was moving too quickly.

"Higher!" Paelen ordered. "Take me higher!"

The air became painfully thin. Paelen felt his breathing become more labored, but not so that he couldn't breathe. He looked down and saw the helicopters struggling to follow him. Eventually they gave up and flew away from the area.

"Yes!" he cried, punching the air in celebration. He looked down and followed the trail of the fleeing helicopters. They were joining the others chasing Cupid. But the first two weren't moving anymore. They were hovering in one position in the sky, over the trees. Paelen suddenly had a very bad feeling. The two helicopters that had chased him were also now hovering above one area. Their searchlights burst to life and started to scan the trees and snowy ground below. They were looking for Cupid.

"Sandals, be very careful, but get me to Cupid."

The sandals lowered Paelen down out of the sky. Well away from the probing helicopters' lights, he entered the trees. Hovering just above ground level, they carried him over the undisturbed snow, toward the area where searchlights sought Cupid.

Up ahead, he saw a large, dark shape in the snow. Even before he arrived, Paelen's heart pounded and his mouth went dry. It was Cupid. He had been shot out of the sky and crashed to the ground. Lying unmoving, in a broken heap. One wing was fanned out behind him, while the other was trapped beneath his unconscious form. The snow around his body was turning red from blood.

Above him the searchlights continued to pan the area. For the moment they couldn't see him or Cupid. But it was only a matter of time. Paelen felt Cupid's neck nervously. There was still a pulse, and he was breathing. As the ceaseless searchlights drew closer, Paelen hoisted Cupid up in his arms.

"Get me back to Olympus," he ordered the sandals. "Quickly!"

PAELEN CRADLED CUPID IN HIS ARMS AS the sandals flew toward an opening in the trees and climbed higher in the dark sky. But as they tried to gain enough speed to enter the Solar Stream, the combined weight of the two Olympians was too much for them to bear.

After several failed attempts, Paelen was forced to give up. He ordered the sandals to take them back to the cabin. When he touched down on the porch, Paelen carried Cupid forward and kicked open the door. "Agent T!" he called. "Cupid has been hurt!"

"Cupid!" Agent T screeched as he ran forward. His face was twisted in pain. "What happened to him?"

"There were these flying machines," Paelen

explained. "They had large weapons. They were chasing us. When they realized they couldn't catch us, they shot Cupid out of the sky. He hit the ground hard. I think he has broken a wing."

Agent T ran ahead and cleared the coffee table. "Put him here," he said shakily. "When is the doctor coming?"

"We could not reach him," Paelen explained as he carried Cupid to the table. "It is just us."

Paelen settled Cupid down, and together he and Agent T inspected his wounds. His back and wings were covered in blood. They found multiple deep and weeping bullet holes. Paelen had been right. Cupid's left wing was badly broken from the fall.

"Smaller weapons do not hurt us," Paelen mused as he lifted Cupid's unbroken wing to peer beneath it. "But look what those flying machines did to him. He has been torn to pieces."

"He needs a doctor!" Agent T insisted as he gathered together bandages and antiseptic for Cupid. "He is bleeding and is going to die without one. I can try to slow the blood loss, but I don't have the skills to help him."

"I cannot reach the doctor," Paelen insisted. "And a human doctor could not help him anyway. I tried to carry him back to Olympus, but my sandals could not bear the weight of the two of us—" Paelen paused. Finally his eyes went wide. "Wait a moment. Ambrosia! Cupid needs ambrosia. It is what keeps us healthy and strong in Olympus. It will help him heal." He looked back at Emily's father on the sofa and Earl on the stretcher. "Ambrosia will help everyone here heal."

"Then why are you just standing there?" Agent T shouted. He shoved Paelen toward the door. "Get out of here! Go! Fly back to Olympus and get some ambrosia. Save Cupid!"

EMILY COULDN'T STOP SCREAMING. THE
screams just kept on coming, even after Tange put a
hand over her mouth. Her eyes were wide with terror and locked on the two creatures sitting in a set of
thrones on a dais. She tried to look away but couldn't.
They were worse than anything she could have
dreamed and more horrible than any of the creatures
from the most terrifying movies she and her father
used to watch together.

They were women. But nothing like anything she'd
ever seen before. Their skin was covered in green and
gold snake scales. They had small golden wings that
constantly fluttered on their backs like humming-

birds. Their arms ended in hands of bronze, and their legs were long and bony and had lizardlike feet with long, sharp claws.

But most terrifying of all were their heads. Their green, scaly faces had no noses, just two breathing holes like a snake. They had no lips to speak of, but slits that opened when they let out their squeals. In place of hair, hundreds of green snakes grew out of the tops of their head, writhing around as their forked tongues spit and hissed.

As Tange carried her forward, Emily spotted more statues gathered around the dais. This time they weren't adult Nirads, but children. As she looked closer, her screams found renewed energy as a realization overtook her. The Nirad statues—they hadn't been carved. They were real Nirads that had somehow been turned to stone! These Nirads no longer had marblelike skin—they *were* marble. Their terrified faces revealed the final torturous moments of unbearable pain as their living tissue had turned to stone.

Behind her, Pegasus was going mad. He reared and whinnied furiously as they were led forward, until he broke free of the Nirads surrounding him and charged ahead.

The stallion stopped just before the thrones. He reared up high and opened his burned wings. His head was thrown back in fury as he faced the two snake-women. The winged boar, seated between the two thrones, rose on his haunches and squealed loudly at the stallion.

"Calm down, Chrysaor," one of the monstrous women said, stroking the furious boar's head.

"Listen to Euryale," said the other. "This is a time of celebration. We have the Flame of Olympus in our midst. We must not have her thinking ill of us, or that we do not welcome her visit." She turned to Pegasus. "So say what you will, Pegasus," she hissed through her thin, snakelike mouth, "it will change nothing. The time of retribution has finally arrived. Euryale and I will finally have justice. Jupiter and all Olympus will pay for the murder of your mother. Our beloved sister, Medusa, will be avenged!"

Emily had stopped screaming. But she trembled in terror as she looked at the two hideous women. Fear was making it hard to think clearly. But part of her almost remembered their names.

Medusa was a . . . a . . . Emily strained to recall what Joel had told her about Pegasus's mother. Gorgon! She finally remembered. His mother, Medusa, and her two sisters, Stheno and Euryale, were Gorgons. Pegasus was born when Jupiter's son, Perseus, cut off Medusa's head. Joel had also told her that the stallion supposedly sprang from the blood at Medusa's neck. But Emily never believed him. She suddenly remembered that one look at a Gorgon would turn you instantly to stone.

Emily looked at all the stone statues in the room and realized at least that part of the myth was true. But if one look at a Gorgon could turn someone to stone, why hadn't she been turned? Or Pegasus and all the living Nirads in the hall?

With Pegasus locked in a loud, furious fight with the two Gorgons, Emily took a longer look around the throne room. Her eyes fell on a large cage set up directly behind the repulsive snake-women's thrones. It was made entirely of gold, with fine, narrow braided bars that Emily knew even she could break out of. On the roof of the cage was a huge stack of more gold. The only part of the large cage that wasn't gold was the single black stone chair that sat in the very middle.

Seated in the chair was a female Nirad. She was the smallest Nirad that Emily had ever seen. She was certain if they stood together, they would have been the same size.

She looked very young, with fine, gentle features that were almost pretty. And although she still had four arms, she was a lovely shade of dark pink with darker pink marbling. Instead of wearing rags like all the other Nirads, she was wearing a gown of the palest pink, which made her skin even prettier.

Emily sensed there was something special about this young Nirad. But one thing was certain: Whoever she was, she was by far the saddest creature Emily had ever laid eyes on. Her shoulders were slumped, and her eyes were downcast as they lingered on all the stone children gathered around the thrones. When she finally raised her pale-gray eyes, Emily's heart nearly broke. The pain they held was unbearable.

Emily glanced away from the sad, pink Nirad and continued to investigate the throne room. To her right, she saw part of another large cage. Unlike the braided gold bars of the cage at the front of the room, this one had thick, solid black bars. As Emily strained to peer around Tange to get a better look at it, her eyes settled on the occupant lying on the floor of the cage. She gasped.

It was Joel.

If Joel was here, were the others, too? Emily desperately searched the room for signs of her father, Paelen, and Cupid. But all she could see was Joel. She tried to call to him, but Tange was still covering her mouth. Her hands flew up and tried to drag his away as she renewed her struggle in his arms. Yet the harder she fought, the firmer he held her.

Tange was shaking his head, trying his best to get her to stop.

But her squeals and struggle did not go unnoticed. As Pegasus stood before the Gorgons, he turned back to Emily. It was only then that the stallion also noticed Joel. He whinnied loudly and trotted over to the cage. Pegasus reared and tried to kick the large lock off the door. But even after several vicious blows, the lock remained undamaged.

"You will not break it, Pegasus," Stheno hissed. "That lock is secure. But do not fear, the human boy inside is unharmed. For now. . . ."

There was no mistaking the threat in the Gorgon's voice. Pegasus trotted back up to the dais and continued to protest loudly. But the louder the stallion became, the softer the snake-women spoke. Emily strained to hear what was being said, but she couldn't.

Joel's back was to her. She was relieved to see his sides moving with steady breathing. From what little she could see, he looked all right. Emily finally gazed back up into the face of Tange. She nodded her head, trying to tell him she wouldn't scream or fight anymore.

Tange removed his hand from her mouth. His eyes were locked on the stone children standing before the thrones. As her initial terror faded into a steady fear, another feeling started in the pit of Emily's stomach. She recalled the pained expression on Tange's face when she'd asked if he had any children. "Are those your children?" she asked him.

Tange didn't move for a long time, and she wondered if he'd even heard her. Finally he looked down at her and nodded.

Emily's eyes flashed back to the stone children. Her throat tightened when she saw the terror on their young faces. It looked like they had been running away from the throne when they were turned to marble. Suddenly a crucial piece of the strange puzzle fell into place.

"You invaded Olympus and came to New York because those Gorgons were threatening your children, right?"

Tange nodded.

"And if you didn't cooperate, they turned them to stone?"

Once again Tange gave a slight nod.

Emily looked away, too stunned to speak. She had become so accustomed to hating and dreading the Nirads that it was hard to imagine that these fearsome, powerful creatures were actually a conquered race of slaves. They deserved her pity and compassion, not fear and hatred! The Nirads were being forced to serve the cruel Gorgons or face the destruction of their children.

As she looked, she saw some of the child statues had been smashed and the pieces scattered around the room. It was bad enough that the Gorgons had turned them to stone. But to smash them as well was just too cruel.

Her eyes drifted back to the pink Nirad in the cage. "Is she important to you?"

Tange looked up toward the cage. She watched his eyes grow even sadder. He nodded his head slowly.

Before Emily could guess who the pink Nirad was, the conversation between Pegasus and the two Gorgons ended. The stallion turned away from the throne and tried to come back to her. But Chrysaor sprang forward and blocked his path.

Pegasus reared again and faced the boar. Chrysaor rose on his stubby legs and challenged the stallion. But before their fight resumed, the two Gorgons started to scream. The sound was loud and shrill and caused everyone in the throne room to cry out in pain and put their hands over their ears.

Emily had never experienced anything like it in her life. Even Tange reacted to the horrible sounds and covered his ears. His other arms gripped her tighter and quivered. When the sounds finally stopped, Emily removed her own hands from her ears and expected to find blood.

"Pegasus, enough!" screeched Euryale. She rose from the throne and stepped down from the dais, kicking aside a child statue as she went. The statue spun and fell over; one of its tiny arms broke. In the cage, the pink Nirad howled in pain.

"Silence!" Euryale warned. "Or I will destroy more." She turned and looked at the boar. "Chrysaor, we will have no more fighting between you two."

Emily tensed as the snake-woman drew near. She could feel Tange actually start to tremble. But was it fear or rage? Looking at Tange's face, she couldn't tell.

"So," said the Gorgon, "this child is the Flame of Olympus?"

The closer she got, the more Emily could hear the living snakes on her head hissing and spitting. She stood before Emily. "A human child? Vesta was a fool to hide the heart of the Flame in a human." She reached forward and stroked Emily's cheek with her cold bronze finger. "Humans are all so . . . delicate. What could she have been thinking?"

Emily felt sick at the touch. She couldn't look at the Gorgon. She kept her eyes locked on Pegasus. The stallion was pawing the marble floor and trying to get closer, but the boar squealed again.

"I told you to stop, Chrysaor," Euryale spat. "Leave your brother alone."

Emily's eyes flashed open as she looked at the winged boar. That was Pegasus's brother? She was far too stunned to be repulsed by the closeness of the snake-woman.

"What is this?" the Gorgon said as she studied Emily's face. "Did you not know that Pegasus had a twin brother? They were born when the murderous Perseus cut off our dear sister's head." She let out a horrible, harsh laugh. "See, Pegasus? See how ignorant the humans are? Is it any wonder that we used to feed on their flesh? Why you should choose to give your loyalty and time to this one is well beyond my comprehension."

Stheno flew down from the throne and approached her. Emily had to fight to hold back more screams. Her eyes were drawn to the squirming and hissing snakes covering the tops of their heads.

As she reached for Emily, Pegasus whinnied and charged forward, trying to put himself between the Gorgons and Emily.

"Hold your tongue, nephew," Stheno hissed as she smacked the stallion's muzzle. "You know we have killed for less. You will have her back. But not until she has done what we brought her here to do."

Emily grew cold. These horrible child killers expected her to do something for them? "I don't know why you brought us here. But whatever it is you want me to do, forget it. I won't do it!"

Both Gorgons laughed their terrible, screeching laugh. "Such fire!" Stheno said. "She truly is the Flame of Olympus."

Euryale drew closer to Emily and caught her by the chin in a painful and cold grip. "You are wrong, child. You will do exactly what we say exactly when we say it or you will know pain the likes of which you have never experienced before."

Emily tried to pull away, but Tange held her steady. "I don't know what you think I can do. You've got more powers than me. I'm nothing."

"True, child, you are nothing," Euryale agreed.

"But for reasons unknown, Vesta has imbued you with all the powers of Olympus. You alone have the power to do what no other being, alive or dead, past or present, could ever do."

"What's that?" Emily asked fearfully.

The Gorgons looked at each other. Then they turned together to Emily as both of their snakelike mouths spread in hideous smiles.

"Kill Jupiter."

DESPITE HIS LOUD PROTESTS, PEGASUS WAS
locked in a large cage. Emily was carried over to the
cage containing Joel. Tange lowered her to the floor
and started to close the door.

"Wait!" Stheno called. She held out her hand.
"Give me your golden brace."

Emily looked down at her leg. "But I can't walk
without it."

"Look around you, child. Where do you think you
will be walking? If you were to somehow escape that
cage and leave our palace, every Nirad in this world
would try to kill you. They know you are the cause
of all their misery."

"I didn't do anything!" Emily challenged. "It's you

who hurt these poor people. Look what you've done to their children. You're the monsters here, not me!"

The Gorgon stood erect and started to hiss. "Do not raise your voice to me. It is time you learned some manners!" She stormed over to the cage containing the pink Nirad. "Segan, call another child in here!" she ordered fiercely. "Do it now, or I will kill twenty!"

Emily watched the pink Nirad drop her head as her shoulders started to shake.

"Do it!" Stheno commanded.

The pink Nirad looked up and closed her eyes in concentration. Moments later a gray Nirad entered the throne room carrying a screaming and growling child. If it had been human, Emily would have guessed it to be no more than two or three years old. The child tried to bite the gray Nirad's arms and struck out with her clawed hands to scratch his face.

"Over here," Stheno ordered. "Put her in the cage with the humans."

The screaming child was carried over to their cage. Emily crawled closer to Joel as the hysterical Nirad was placed inside with them.

Across the room, Pegasus whinnied furiously, trying to break down the bars of his own cage.

"Silence, Pegasus!" Stheno cried. "The Flame of Olympus must be taught obedience!"

The Nirad child took one look at Emily and Joel and began to cry in terror. She stumbled back to the door and tried to get out. Her four arms rattled against the bars of the cage, and she began to howl mournfully.

"Now, Flame of Olympus, learn your lesson well!" cried the Gorgon.

Emily's eyes flew wide as Stheno's eyes turned from emerald green to a glowing gold. She looked down at the Nirad child. "You have caused this, Flame of Olympus. This child will die because of you!"

"No, don't!" Emily panicked. "Please, don't do it. You can have my brace. I'm begging you, please don't hurt her!"

"Too late, Flame," the Gorgon screeched. "Learn your lesson. You will obey us!"

The child's frightened wails turned to howls of pain as its skin darkened slowly and became solid. It tried to move, to get away from the deadly stare, but it couldn't. Each second, more and more of it was turned to stone.

"Stop!" Emily begged. "You're killing her!"

With a final agonized cry from the child, it was done. Emily was looking at a tiny marble statue. Up in the golden cage, the pink Nirad wailed in grief, and the other Nirads in the throne room dropped their heads.

"Segan, be silent," Euryale shouted at her, "or my sister will kill another!"

Emily's heart was racing as her rage toward the snake-women grew. The Flame was rising in the pit of her stomach, but she did not try to stop it. Emily rose to her knees. "I begged you to stop," she said furiously. "She was an innocent child. You had no right to kill her!"

She raised both her hands, and flames shot from her fingertips. But they did not hit the Gorgon as she intended. With her emotions running unchecked, the flames flew through the bars wildly and shot around the throne room uncontrolled. Tange growled in shock and pain as a stream of the flames glanced off his wide, muscular chest and tossed him backward as if he weighed nothing. At the front of the throne room, the pink Nirad was crying in fear as the living flames approached her cage. But before the deadly flames reached her, a gray Nirad jumped forward and sacrificed himself to save her. He howled in agony as his marble skin started to bubble and burn.

Emily panicked when she saw the pain and destruction her powers were causing. She pointed her hands down and tried to stop the flames before they did any more harm. But as the flames scorched the marble of the throne room's floor and caused the stone to smoke and actually melt, their intensity increased.

"Stop it, Em," she commanded herself. "Stop it!"

Suddenly, from the front dais, Euryale shouted, "Turn it off, Flame, or Pegasus will die!"

Emily's panicked eyes shot up to Euryale as she flew toward Pegasus. Her eyes were already glowing gold. "Do not be a fool, Flame. I will kill my nephew if I must. Turn it off now or he dies!"

"I'm trying!" Emily screeched as she fought to pull back the roaring flames. But her fear of the terrifying Gorgons was fanning the flames. They would not respond to Emily's commands. It was as though the flames had a mind and will of their own and would not be stopped.

"Must we kill again?" demanded Euryale. She turned from Pegasus and directed her deadly gaze at Chrysaor. The winged boar squealed and tried to dash away from his aunt. As his wings turned to stone he looked pleadingly at Emily.

When their eyes met, Emily saw pain and betrayal. For his final breathing moments he struggled to drag his stony body closer to her.

"Stop it!" Emily cried as her wild emotions fueled the flames further. She tried to pull them back, to gain some control, but her mind was too frightened and unfocused. "Please, you're killing him!"

"Then stop the flames!" Stheno commanded.

Emily concentrated harder than she ever had in her life. She could hear Pegasus whinnying loudly in the cage opposite her. Hearing the anguish in the stallion's voice gave Emily the power and determination she needed to finally pull back the flames. They weakened and tapered just as Chrysaor made it to the side of her cage. The boar's transformation was complete as the last of the flames died away. His dark eyes faded and turned to stone.

Stheno stepped closer to the cage and faced Emily with a cold, cruel expression. "You will control your temper, Flame, or I promise you, Pegasus and the human with you will suffer the same fate as Chrysaor."

Emily fell back to the floor, panting heavily. Her frightened eyes moved away from Chrysaor to look around the throne room at the havoc her unleashed, uncontrolled powers had wrought. Eventually guards arrived and carried Tange and the burned Nirad away. Tange was moaning softly, but his wound didn't look fatal. The other burned Nirad didn't move.

Emily sat in stunned silence at her loss of control. She was grateful Joel was still unconscious and hadn't witnessed the horror of it all. When her eyes finally settled on Chrysaor, she realized he, like the Nirad child, was dead because of her.

She watched Pegasus drop his head and paw the ground. Despite their constant fighting, the stallion had loved his brother and was grieving his death.

"I'm so sorry, Pegs," she muttered softly. Emily looked at the smooth, unblemished skin of her hands and realized that despite the damage she had just caused, she was lucky not to have burned Pegasus or the pink Nirad. This time it had been much worse than what had happened at the temple. Her powers were growing stronger, but her control was worsening.

In that moment Emily vowed never to use her powers again.

"Now will you give me your gold brace, or must we do this all again?" Stheno demanded, holding out her bronze hand. She seemed not to notice or even care what had just happened.

Emily sat beside Joel and undid the straps to the complicated golden device. She tossed it to the door of the cage, unable to look at the evil Gorgon. "Take it!"

"You are learning, Flame," Stheno said, collecting the leg brace. "Jupiter will have his proof that we possess you. He will have no choice now but to surrender to us."

The two Gorgons came together and held up the gold brace. "First we kill Jupiter; then Olympus is ours!"

ONCE THE GORGONS HAD THE GOLD LEG brace, they cackled with laughter and left the throne room. Emily concentrated on Joel. His face was bruised and covered with dried blood. His nose was broken badly, and his eyes were swollen shut. As she gently stroked his forehead, her healing powers started to work on him, and the bruises began to fade.

His eyes fluttered open.

"It's all right, Joel," Emily said softly. "You're safe."

"Em," Joel muttered. "What happened—" His eyes shot open, and he sat up. "Nirads!" he cried. "Emily, the Nirads are awake."

"Joel, be quiet!" Emily slammed her hand over his mouth. Her nervous eyes looked toward the doors the Gorgons had disappeared through. She helped him sit up and watched his reaction as he took in his surroundings. "What happened?" he asked in a whisper. "Where are we?"

"The Nirad world."

Emily explained how she and Pegasus had been attacked at the Red Apple and brought here. Then she told him what she knew about the Nirads and how it was the Gorgons who were behind the attacks on Olympus and not the Nirads themselves.

Joel shook his head in disbelief. "The Gorgons? Really? There's not much written about Medusa's sisters. Just that Medusa was mortal while they were immortal. And they were as bad as she was and could also turn people to stone."

"They're the most terrifying and hideous creatures I've ever seen," Emily said. "Much worse than the Nirads when we first saw them. Their heads really are topped with hissing snakes, and they're covered in scales."

"Just like in the myths," Joel said.

"Joel, this isn't a myth!" Emily shot back. "The Gorgons have enslaved the Nirads and are killing their children to keep them under control. When I wouldn't give them my leg brace, they turned that poor Nirad child to stone right in front of me!" Emily dropped her head. "She died because of me. Then they said they'll do the same to you and Pegasus if I don't do what they tell me to."

"What's that?" Joel asked.

"They want me to kill Jupiter."

"What?" Joel cried.

Emily wouldn't have thought it possible for Joel to look any more shocked. But when she told him the Gorgons' plans, his eyes grew as big as saucers. "You can't do it!" he insisted. "No matter what they do to Pegasus or me, you just can't do it!"

"I won't," Emily said. "I won't use my powers again. They're too dangerous. You should have seen what happened at the Red Apple and here right before you woke up. They got away from me. Joel, my powers are growing and I can't control them. I think I just killed a Nirad, and I know for sure I hurt Tange."

"Tange?"

Emily explained to Joel about the large orange Nirad and the damage she did in the throne room.

She pointed at the big burned spot in front of their cage. "It could have been even worse."

Joel tried to comfort her, but Emily was almost as frightened of her own powers as she was of the Gorgons. She was terrified that eventually she wouldn't be able to stop them, and her nightmares of burning up the whole world would come true.

"Emily, I'm sure Tange is fine. The Nirads have skin as tough as stone."

"You didn't see it, Joel. It was like a firestorm I just couldn't stop."

"But you did stop it," Joel said.

"Barely," she answered. "But what about the next time?"

"I'm sure your dad, Paelen, and Cupid will get us out of here before then—"

"My dad?" Emily cried excitedly. "Joel, you've seen my dad? How is he? Did you get him out of the CRU facility? Does he know about me and what happened at Olympus? Did you tell him how much we wanted to get back to him?"

Joel caught hold of her hands. "Emily, calm down. Your dad is fine." He filled her in on what had happened at the CRU facility. "The Nirad caught me, but I'm sure the others got away safely."

Emily sat back against the cage bars. This was the best news she'd heard in a very long time. She was glad her father had been freed from the CRU, but still worried that he might have been hurt by the Nirads. "So they brought you here alone?"

Joel shrugged. "I guess so. The Nirad hit me, and I passed out. I woke up with you here."

Emily and Joel sat together holding hands. Having him there made her feel much better. When Tange returned to the throne room, Emily tried to see how badly she'd hurt him. Tange first approached the pink Nirad's cage and then walked slowly back to his post.

His chest was covered in a thick dark-green paste, but there were exposed burn marks around the edges showing where her flames had touched him.

"I'm so sorry, Tange," Emily called. "Please forgive me. I swear I didn't mean to hurt you or that other guard. The power ran away from me. I don't have any control."

Tange didn't react to her words and stood stone-still at his post.

"Tange, please," Emily begged. "I swear I would never hurt you or your people. It was an accident!"

Across the throne room, Pegasus was pacing the confines of his cage. His head was down and he was whining softly, stopping occasionally to lunge at the bars, trying to break out.

"What happened to Pegasus?" Joel asked, seeing the burns covering his body.

"I'm what happened to him," Emily said miserably. "He was hurt in the fire I started at the Red Apple. And then the Gorgons killed his brother." Her eyes went over to Chrysaor. In his final, agonized moments, she had seen the change in him. He'd realized his mistake in siding with his aunts. That regret was now permanently etched on his stone face. She crawled over to the bars closest to Chrysaor. Joel joined her and looked at the boar.

"That's his brother?" he said in shock. "I'd read that Pegasus had a twin brother, but most of the stories say he was a giant. I didn't know he was a winged boar."

Emily nodded and reached out to stroke the boar's cold stone snout. "Chrysaor led the Nirads to the Red

Apple." She looked at the statue. "I wish you hadn't done this, Chrysaor. If you hadn't betrayed Olympus, we could have been friends."

Beneath her fingers, Emily felt the stone snout of the boar warm up. She pulled her hand back. Had she imagined it? She looked and could see the stone was fading as brown rose to the surface.

"Em, did you see that!" Joel cried. "Touch him again!"

Pegasus stopped pacing and stood watching her. He bobbed his head up and down and snorted as Emily reached her hand through the bars and stroked Chrysaor's face. Once again the stone beneath her hand grew warm.

Suddenly, from the front of the room, the pink Nirad the Gorgons called Segan made a single sound.

They both looked up as Tange left his post and approached their cage. Joel moved forward to protect Emily. "Stay back!" he cried, bravely preparing to fight the huge Nirad. "Emily told you she was sorry and didn't mean to hurt you."

Tange shook his head, grunted a few soft words, and pointed at the stone child in their cage.

"What's he want?" Joel asked.

"I think I know."

Emily crawled closer to the statue of the Nirad child and touched one of its marble arms. Instantly the stone started to warm and color rose to the surface. She released the child and looked up at the orange Nirad.

Tange's eyes went wide, and he let out an excited cry that was repeated by the three other orange guards in the room. He turned back to Segan and called out to her.

Pegasus was jumping in his cage as Emily's heart went wild with hope. "Tange, I can save the children!" she cried. She looked at Joel. "They're not dead! All those poor children can live again. If we defeat the Gorgons, I can heal everybody!"

As Emily reached for the child again, Segan made another strange sound. Tange reached into the cage and caught hold of Emily's hand. He shook his head and pointed to the doors by the thrones.

"Em, they're coming back," Joel said. He helped her move to the rear of the cage, while Tange returned to his post as if he'd never moved.

Emily sat against the bars and clutched Joel's hand. She stole a peek at Chrysaor and saw her hand marks still on his face. If the Gorgons were to look, there would be no way they could miss it.

"It is done," Stheno said. "The message has been sent. It is only a matter of time before Jupiter surrenders to us."

"We must prepare," said Euryale. She turned to the pink Nirad. "Order your men to clean this area. We have a very special guest coming, and we do not want to give him any clue as to what is happening." The Gorgon's eyes trailed over to their cage and settled on Joel.

Emily's heart nearly stopped, and she felt Joel's hand tighten on hers.

"You are awake," said Stheno as she drew near. "What is your name, boy?"

Emily could feel Joel's hand trembling as the Gorgon concentrated on him. The snakes on her head hissed and spat at him. "Joel," he answered softly, staring at the grotesque creature.

"Well, Joel," the Gorgon continued. "We brought you here because we know the Flame of Olympus cares for you. As long as she cooperates with us, you will be perfectly safe. But if she tries to use her powers against us, you will be the first to suffer." Her vicious eyes settled on Emily. "You would be wise to remember this. We used to feed on the flesh of young humans like Joel. It has been too long since I have savored such a sweet, tempting morsel as him. Mind your manners, child, or you will see horrors beyond your imagination!" As Stheno walked away, she stepped up to Tange and looked him up and down. She touched his burn and sniffed the dark green paste. Then she pointed to the stone Chrysaor. "Have that thing removed."

Tange grunted once and came forward. As he hoisted the heavy statue in his four arms, he looked at Emily and Joel and gave them a quick, almost imperceptible nod.

All around them, Nirads started to clear the room. Several moved forward to carefully lift the stone children around the dais.

"No," Euryale ordered. "Leave them here. We must ensure that your new queen understands the penalties of defiance." She looked back at the pink

Nirad. "Segan, you know how many of your children we possess. Do not make us destroy them all."

"Queen!" Joel whispered as his eyes went up to the pink Nirad. "She's their queen."

The final piece of the puzzle fell into place. Just like colonies of bees or ants, the queen controls her people—and by threatening violence against their children, the Gorgons controlled the queen. As she watched, Segan dropped her head and nodded.

Emily and Joel sat back against the bars of the cage, holding hands as the huge Nirads tidied the room. The four primary orange guards, including Tange, went about gently picking up the pieces of broken stone statues. Emily wondered, if the pieces were put back together, would she be able to heal the broken children?

Discovering that she had the power to free those turned to stone gave her some degree of hope. Somehow, they had to find a way to escape.

And when they did, they would fight to free the enslaved Nirads and face down the Gorgons once and for all.

23

TIME STOOD STILL AS EMILY AND JOEL SAT IN the cage. Across from them, Pegasus paced and kicked at his cage door. He whinnied loudly to the two Gorgons seated on their thrones.

"We will release you when Jupiter is dead," said Euryale as she rose from her throne and flew down from the dais. "But not a moment before. I will not have you trying to warn him."

Pegasus whinnied furiously. Euryale flew closer to his cage and held up a hand. "I grow tired of your constant complaints. Be silent or you shall join your brother in the stone garden."

But the stallion did not stop. As her irritation increased, the Gorgon fluttered her tiny gold wings and flew over to Emily. "For reasons beyond my comprehension, Pegasus is loyal to you. I would suggest you tell him to keep silent or I will turn him to stone."

Emily's eyes returned to the stallion. "Please, Pegs," she begged. "She'll do it. Please stop—I couldn't bear to lose you."

"Listen to the Flame, Pegasus," Euryale warned. "You know me—I will do it."

Finally, Pegasus fell silent. He looked over at Emily and snorted lightly.

"I believe I have underestimated your power over my nephew. I have never seen Pegasus surrender to anyone."

Joel stood and defiantly faced the hideous Gorgon. "It's not power that connects them. It's something you'll never understand. They care for each other."

"Foolish words." Euryale waved her hand dismissively. She flew back to her sister on the throne. "We have much to prepare. It is time we rested."

Stheno rose from her throne and turned to approach the Nirad queen. Her hand hovered threateningly before the delicate gold bars of the cage.

"Take this warning, Queen. If any of these prisoners are not in this room in the morning, we will kill you and destroy what is left of your disgusting world. Make sure they do not escape."

Segan lowered her head.

"Come, sister. The time of our exile is swiftly drawing to a close. Soon we will be free to rule."

When they were gone, Emily sat back, sighed heavily, and dropped her head. "I'm really sorry, Joel."

"Sorry for what?" he frowned.

She was unable to face him. "Sorry I got you involved in all of this. If I hadn't come to your brownstone when Pegasus first crashed on my roof, you wouldn't be here."

Joel put his arm around her and pulled her closer. "Don't be silly. You saved me that day. If it weren't for you, I probably would have ended up in prison! And even if we die here, which I know we won't, I would never regret a single moment of any of this. Don't you know what you mean to me?"

Emily looked up into his warm brown eyes.

"Emily, you're the sister I never had. Don't you

know I'd do anything for you? I'd fight those Gorgons bare-handed if I had to."

Emily felt tears rising to her eyes.

He gave her a light squeeze. "Now dry those tears before you blow us all up and ruin my plans for escape."

Emily sniffed and dabbed away her tears with Neptune's handkerchief. She looked over at Pegasus and realized Joel was right. She didn't regret a moment of her life since the stallion had entered it. She just wished she could have seen her father again. Was he safe? Was Paelen still with him? Did he know how much she really loved and missed him? Those questions haunted her as she slowly drifted off to sleep.

A short time later Emily awoke. Joel was snoring softly with his arm wrapped protectively around her. Pegasus was leaning against the bars of his cage and dozing lightly. The queen was curled in her chair, sound asleep in the gold cage. Emily looked at Tange and the other throne room guards. They were still standing at their posts. They never seemed to leave or sleep. They just kept watch over their queen.

Just as Emily was about to settle back against Joel, sounds of roaring shattered the stillness of the throne room.

Tange and the three guards stood at full attention. The guard closest to the door called out into the hall. A quick, short answer was barked back.

Up in the golden cage, Segan awoke instantly and sat up in her chair. She lifted her head and closed her eyes. To Emily, it looked like she was concentrating very hard on listening.

Joel startled and looked around wildly. "What is it?"

"I don't know," Emily said. "Something is up."

"Maybe Jupiter is here."

Pegasus nickered to the queen, who responded with a soft answer. Emily saw the stallion's reaction. He began to pace in the tight cage and paw at the floor. Whatever she had said to him upset him greatly.

"What is it, Pegs?" Emily called. "Is it Jupiter? Is he here?"

Pegasus stopped pacing and stared at her. He shook his head and snorted.

"Not Jupiter," Joel remarked. "What, then?"

The sound of the screeching Gorgons silenced Emily and everyone else in the throne room. But it didn't keep Pegasus from pacing in his cage.

The Gorgons entered and flew over to the queen. "Segan, command your men to deliver the prisoners to us at once!"

"Prisoners?" Joel said.

Emily's mind instantly flashed to her father, Paelen, and Cupid. Had they managed to find the Nirad world and been captured?

Moments ticked by slowly as they waited to see whom the Nirads had caught. Finally there were sounds in the hall outside the throne room. Emily and Joel held their breath. Their hearts sank when they saw the twins Diana and Apollo being dragged into the throne room by several gray Nirads. Deep cuts and bruises covered their arms and faces, signs of a terrible fight.

Diana's eyes flew wide when she spotted them. "Emily, Joel, what are you doing here? Are you all right?"

"They are quite unharmed," said Euryale. "Do you think we would harm children?"

"Do not tempt me to answer you, Euryale!" Diana spat as her furious eyes landed on the Gorgon. "I know all about your hideous appetites."

Apollo struggled to pull free of the Nirads holding him. "Release us, Gorgon, before I lose my temper!"

"You are not in Olympus now, Apollo," said Stheno as she flapped her tiny golden wings and flew off the dais. She landed before the Olympians. "You cannot order us around ever again. This is our world now. We rule here. Not you, not your twin sister, nor Jupiter himself! If we say bow, you will bow to us. You have no power here."

"Nor can you do anything to stop us," Euryale added. "We have waited a very long time for our vengeance. Jupiter will know our wrath for what Perseus did to our beloved sister, Medusa—"

"And for what all of you have done to us throughout the ages," Stheno finished.

"Anything we have done, you have deserved!" Apollo shouted. "You are vile, filthy creatures who have destroyed countless lives. You bring death and misery with you wherever you go. It is only through our father's generosity that you have been allowed to continue to live. But when he learns what you have done to this world and its people, there will be no escape for you."

Stheno cackled loudly. "No escape? Foolish boy! When Jupiter arrives here, he will die. Then all Olympus will be ours!"

"You cannot defeat us, Gorgons," Diana spat furiously. "That was Medusa's arrogance and fatal mistake. She tried to take us on and underestimated Jupiter's power. Remember what happened to her! You have no powers against our father."

Stheno hissed at Diana. "Your father is a coward. He did not have the courage to face Medusa himself! So he sent Perseus to murder her."

"He sent Perseus to offer Medusa a choice," Diana responded. "She refused to listen and received the justice she so richly deserved."

"The only justice will be when Jupiter dies."

"You cannot kill our father," Apollo spat. "You do not have the power."

"True," Euryale acknowledged as she stalked over to Emily's cage. "But I am not going to be the one who kills him." She pointed at Emily. "She is. It has taken us time and great effort to draw out the Flame of Olympus. But now she is ours. Emily has more than enough power to destroy Jupiter. She will do the deed, and then she will hand Olympus over to us."

Emily felt sick. How could the Gorgons expect her to kill Jupiter? They were insane. There was no way she would ever do it.

"Enough chatter! I do not care what you say—Jupiter is going to die!" Euryale screeched.

"We will stop you," Apollo challenged, struggling against the Nirads. "You will not destroy Olympus."

Euryale moved toward him. Her eyes glowed a brilliant gold. "We will do whatever we please, Apollo. Our Nirad warriors are much stronger than Olympians. However, you may rejoice in the knowledge that you and your sister will be the first of Jupiter's children to decorate our new stone garden."

Emily watched in horror as Apollo began to turn to stone. The Nirads released him and stood back as Apollo screamed in agony. In moments the spreading stone had cut off his screams and an expression of agony sealed his smooth marble face.

"Apollo!" Diana howled. She turned desperately to

the second Gorgon. "Stheno, stop your sister before it is too late."

Stheno cackled with laughter. "Too late for what, Diana? You cannot stop us. However, if you care so much for your twin brother, you will join him!"

Emily and Joel screamed helplessly as the Gorgons turned their deadly powers against Diana. Pegasus was going mad in his cage. He reared and kicked at the door again. When it was over, the Gorgons' eyes returned to normal, and they roared with laughter as they inspected the two new stone statues.

"You there," Stheno screeched as she pointed to Tange. "Have your people set these two up beside our thrones. When Jupiter gets here, I want him to see what we have done to his children."

Emily collapsed to the floor of her cage as heaving sobs escaped her. "I'll never do it," she cried. "I won't kill Jupiter and give you Olympus."

"Oh yes, you will!" Euryale shouted as she stormed up to the cage. "If you wish to keep Pegasus and Joel alive, you will. The choice is simple. You will kill Jupiter and serve us, and they will live. But if you refuse, we will kill them both and then you. With the Flame of Olympus extinguished, Jupiter will lose his powers anyway. He will be easy prey for us then. We will feast on the bones of Olympus and then your world."

"If you doubt our words, child, believe this!" Stheno crossed over to Pegasus's cage. Her eyes glowed golden as she focused her attention on the stallion's hind end.

Pegasus started screaming as his lower hind leg changed from glowing white to a cold stone marble.

"Stop it!" Emily shouted, banging her fists against the bars of her cage.

Joel was at her side. "Kill me if you must, but leave Pegasus alone!"

Stheno released Pegasus. The stallion had one marble back leg. Every time he tried to put it down it caused him so much pain, he was forced to lift the heavy stone limb in the air again. His deep whines of misery cut through Emily like a knife.

"Each time you defy us, more of your precious Pegasus will be turned to stone." Euryale laughed.

"You're sick!" Emily cried.

"No," Euryale said. "We are Gorgons!"

· · ·

As soon as the Gorgons left the throne room, Emily fell to the floor, weak and defeated. She missed her father more than ever and wished he were there to guide her. They were in so much danger she just didn't know what to do.

Joel paced. "We can't let them do it. We've got to get out of here and warn them."

"How?" Emily asked. "Even if Tange lets us out, the moment the Gorgons discover we're gone they'll kill the queen."

"Then we'll take the queen with us. We'll get her back to Olympus, where we can protect her."

Tange left his post and approached them. He pointed to the lock on the door, then up to Segan's cage, and shook his head.

"There is no lock on her door?" Joel asked as he peered up to the queen's cage.

Tange nodded.

"Then all we have to do is break her out of there," Emily said.

Once again Tange shook his head. He used his large, monstrous hands to explain that the bars of the cage were very weak. Then he clapped his hands together. With all the gold weight on the top roof, it would take very little for the thin bars to collapse and the massive weight to come crushing down on their queen.

"Then we can't take her with us," Emily stated. "But we've got to do something." Emily was certain the Gorgons would kill the queen even if Emily did as they ordered and killed Jupiter. They were far too conniving to let any of them live.

In her cage, Segan started to make strange sounds. Pegasus whinnied painfully and nodded his head. The queen seemed to reply.

"Pegasus, can you really understand her?" Joel asked.

The stallion nodded and then whinnied in pain again as he moved his stone leg.

Hearing his suffering plunged a dagger into Emily's heart. "I wish I could help you, Pegs," she called softly.

As the queen continued to make soft sounds, Tange left the throne room.

Joel helped Emily settle back against the bars of the cage. "Em, we've got to ask Tange to let us out.

You can't be here when Jupiter arrives. The Gorgons will force you to kill him."

"I won't use my powers again," Emily said firmly. "No matter what they do to any of us. The next time I try, I may not be able to stop it."

When Tange returned, he was carrying the stone body of Chrysaor. He placed the statue before their cage, unlocked the door, and motioned for Joel to help Emily get out.

From his cage, Pegasus neighed to Emily. She glanced from Pegasus to Tange and then to the queen. They were all looking at her hopefully, and she understood exactly what they wanted. They needed to reach Jupiter. Chrysaor was their only hope. But after everything he had done, could they trust him?

Joel saw her hesitation and shrugged. "Em, we don't have much choice. Do it."

He helped Emily settle on the floor beside the stone Chrysaor. She reached up and rested her hand on his snout. Beneath her fingers the temperature began to rise. Moment by moment the stone melted away, and the dark brown hair and feathers of the winged boar returned.

Soon the brown spread over his entire body. She jumped when she saw one of Chrysaor's whiskers start to twitch. After a few minutes the color poured back into his dark brown eyes. The boar suddenly took a very deep, unsteady breath and woke up.

Chrysaor jumped when he saw Emily sitting beside him. He gazed around the throne room in confusion. Behind him, Pegasus started to neigh, and Chrysaor trotted over to him. The stallion lowered his head and poked as much of his face through the bars as he could to touch him.

Watching their reunion nearly brought tears to Emily's eyes as she remembered how they had tried to kill each other back at the Red Apple. Now it appeared Chrysaor had changed and everything was forgiven. Chrysaor squealed lightly and trotted over to Emily. She looked into the boar's large brown eyes and saw so much of Pegasus there. She only hoped he had changed enough to share in his brother's compassion and sympathy for others.

"We desperately need your help, Chrysaor," she explained softly. "We can't let the Gorgons kill

Jupiter. Look at what they've done to the Nirads and what they did to you. Do you really think they won't do that to everyone else? All they want is power and destruction. They don't care who they kill to attain it."

She reached out her hand and lightly stroked the coarse hairs on Chrysaor's snout. "The Gorgons are asleep. You've got to fly back to Olympus and find Jupiter. Warn him that they are planning to make me kill him. Explain to him how they've imprisoned the Nirad queen in a fragile cage of Olympian gold. Any attempt to rescue her will kill her. And tell him how they're killing Nirad children to control her. Please, Chrysaor, you are our only hope. You must tell Jupiter to bring all his warriors here to fight the Gorgons."

Chrysaor shook his head.

"Look at him, Em, he won't do it," Joel said. "Even after you saved him, he won't help us!"

Chrysaor looked at Tange and squealed softly. Obeying him, Tange suddenly wrapped his four arms around Joel and hoisted him in the air.

"Tange, no!" Emily cried. "Let him go!"

Across from them, Pegasus whinnied softly. He was bobbing his head up and down.

"Please, Tange," Emily begged, "please don't hurt him."

The huge Nirad lifted Joel higher and grunted. Chrysaor moved and stood beneath Joel's dangling legs and opened his wings so that Tange could lower Joel onto his bare back.

It was Emily who understood first. "Joel, wait, they want you to go with them."

"What?" Joel said. "No, they don't—" Tange released him and took a step back. Joel was now seated on Chrysaor, with his legs hanging down under the boar's brown wings. When he looked back up at the huge Nirad, Tange pointed to him, then the boar, and finally to the entrance.

"Yes, he does," Emily said. "And they're right. You must go."

"There's no way I'm leaving you!" Joel tried to climb off, but Chrysaor clamped his wings tightly over Joel's legs, pinning him in place.

"You must!" Emily insisted. "Chrysaor betrayed Olympus. They won't believe him. But they'll believe you. Tell them everything you've seen here. Tell them about Diana and Apollo, and how they expect me to kill Jupiter."

"I can't leave you here," Joel said. "If the Gorgons find out, they'll kill you and the queen!"

"They'll never know. It's still early. If you go now, you can be back before they return. Just do this as fast as you can and get back here before dawn."

Joel looked uncertain. But Tange and Pegasus were nodding in encouragement. Up in the cage, the pink queen also nodded her head. "See?" Emily said. "Everyone agrees. I'll be all right. Pegasus is here, so is Tange." Emily struggled to get to her feet. Tange helped her up and led her over to Joel. She gave him a fierce hug. "Please be careful. My dad should be in Olympus by now. Find him. Tell him what's happened and that I'm waiting for him."

"I will," Joel said. "And I'll be right back—I promise."

Emily reached forward and lightly stroked the boar's head. "Please take good care of him, Chrysaor, and come back quick."

Now that she was out of the cage, Emily looked

over to Pegasus and was tempted to heal his leg but knew that she couldn't. Leaving him in pain was one of the hardest things she'd had to do, but it would be too dangerous to leave any evidence that she'd been outside. Tange carried her back into her prison and locked the door. With a final wave good-bye, she watched as the large orange Nirad escorted Joel and Chrysaor safely out of the throne room to help them escape from the palace.

OLYMPUS WAS FAR TOO QUIET. PAELEN KNEW
instantly something was terribly wrong. Flying down
into the back gardens of Jupiter's palace, he heard
and saw no one. There were birds, small animals,
and insects, but not one Olympian.

The palace itself was standing silent and
untouched. If the Nirads had conquered Olympus,
he felt certain there would have been more signs
of damage. But he searched and saw no traces of
Nirads at all.

Olympus was completely empty.

Ordering the sandals to take him in the air, Paelen
flew over the top of the palace and looked around.
Nothing moved, and he could hear no sound.

"Hello!" Paelen shouted. "Is anyone here? Please answer me!"

The gentle breeze was all he heard. As panic started to settle in on him, Paelen ordered the sandals to search for any Olympians in the area. They carried him higher. For the first time, they seemed uncertain of where to go.

But then they seemed to catch the scent of something. They turned sharply and darted forward. Paelen strained his eyes, searching for movement below. Every building, theater, and roadway was eerily quiet and empty.

The sandals carried him away from the palace and toward the Temple of the Flame. As he approached, Paelen caught movement on the ground beneath him. His eyes shot open when he saw who was there.

"Chrysaor!" Paelen shouted as he flew at the winged boar. "Where is she?" he demanded. "What have you done with Emily?"

Paelen's anger took over as he attacked the winged boar. Chrysaor was more than twice his weight, and much larger than him, but Paelen didn't care.

Chrysaor had sided with the Nirads and taken Emily and Pegasus away.

"Where are they?" he demanded as he struck the boar. Wrapping his arms around its thick neck, he fought to tackle the large animal to the ground. But despite his best efforts, Paelen was no match for Chrysaor's strength. He couldn't move him. Instead he jumped on his back, punched down on his wings, his head, and his face.

Yet despite the pounding, Chrysaor did nothing to defend himself. He stood perfectly still and let Paelen do his worst.

"Paelen, stop!" Arms wrapped around his waist and hauled him off the boar's back. "Stop it, please!"

That voice!

"Joel!" Paelen turned and screamed when he saw Joel trying to hold him back. Tears rushed to his eyes at the sight of his best friend. He threw his arms around the boy and gave him a ferocious hug. "I thought you were dead!"

"Can't breathe . . . ," Joel gasped. "Paelen, stop. . . . Can't breathe!"

Paelen released him quickly. He was shaking all

over and could hardly believe what he was seeing. "How?" he rasped. "That Nirad killed you!"

Regaining his breath, Joel rubbed his crushed ribs. "No, he just knocked me out. But listen—I can't stay here long. I've got to get back to Emily. Where are Jupiter and the others?"

"I do not know. I just arrived here."

"So did we," Joel said. "Emily's in terrible danger. We came here to raise an army, but everyone is gone."

"Where is she?" Paelen asked. "What happened? Is Pegasus with her?" Finally his eyes settled back on the winged boar, and his rage resurfaced. He pointed an accusing finger at Chrysaor. "And what are you doing with *him*? He betrayed us!"

"Yes he did, at first," Joel explained. "Now he's helping us. But we don't have a lot of time. If the Gorgons find out I'm gone, they'll kill the Nirad queen and all their children."

"Gorgons?" Paelen asked. "Are they involved in this?"

"It was never the Nirads. It is the Gorgons who are waging war on Olympus." Joel explained how the Nirads had been enslaved by the Gorgons. How they had turned Diana and Apollo to stone, but how Emily had discovered her ability to restore those turned to stone by the Gorgons.

"Why are they doing this?" Paelen asked.

"They say it's revenge for Medusa's death, but I think it's more than that. They're after power. Their plan is to force Emily to kill Jupiter. When she does, they'll take over." Joel started to walk away. "C'mon. We've got to find everyone so we can tell them what's happened."

"Joel, stop. There is no one here," Paelen insisted. "I asked the sandals to find any Olympians, and they only took me to you. The others must be using the Solar Stream to search all the other worlds for Emily."

"Then it's just us," Joel said. "We've got to stop the Gorgons." He paused and looked around. "Where are Steve and Cupid?"

"Cupid!" Paelen cried. "I almost forgot! He is still in your world and has been badly wounded. I need to take ambrosia and nectar to him and to Emily's father and Earl!"

Together they flew back to Jupiter's palace. The banquet table was still laid with untouched bowls of ambrosia, golden plates heaving with ambrosia cakes, and urns filled with nectar. They gathered as much as they could carry and raced into the back gardens of the palace.

"I will deliver this to the cabin and then meet you in the Nirad world," Paelen said.

Joel shook his head. "No, I'm going with you."

"You must not," Paelen insisted. "Joel, you must get back to Emily before the Gorgons awaken. There is no telling what they will do if they discover you have gone. Go back to her, and I will take ambrosia to Cupid and then find you."

"How will you find the Nirad world?" Joel asked. "Can your sandals track us through the Solar Stream?"

Paelen paused. "I am uncertain."

Joel caught him by the arm. "Then let's not waste any more precious time. We'll get Cupid and Steve, and then we can all go to the Nirad world together."

Paelen surrendered. "All right. If we move quickly, we may still get you back before you are missed."

They arrived at the cottage. Agent T had bandaged Cupid's wounds, but the winged Olympian was dangerously pale and still unconscious.

Within minutes of nectar being poured into his mouth, Cupid started to come around. When his eyes fluttered open, Paelen and Agent T helped him to eat the ambrosia. He feasted as though he'd never eaten before. With each bite, Cupid's strength returned.

Joel helped feed nectar to Steve and Earl. The effect was slower for the humans, but it worked. Soon Steve awoke and was able to move. Before long, he was able to sit up and feed himself. It took longer for Earl to react to the healing properties of the nectar and ambrosia, but finally his breathing steadied and his burns started to fade; he was still very weak.

"Wow, this is powerful stuff," Joel said in awe. "The myths say if mortals eats ambrosia, they become immortal. I don't know if that's true, but it's sure working wonders on Steve and Earl."

Cupid rose slowly from the coffee table. His eyes settled on Joel in shock. "I thought you were dead!"

"I could say the same about you," Joel said as he stepped closer. The Olympian was covered in bandages.

Agent T was fussing around Cupid and handed him another ambrosia cake. Cupid took a big bite and then a long drink of nectar. He held the glass up to Paelen. "You brought this?"

Paelen nodded. "It was the only way to help you. Unfortunately, we do not have time to set your wing properly, because we must get moving."

While Cupid, Steve, and Earl continued to eat, Paelen and Joel brought them up to date with everything that had happened. "The Gorgons have Emily in the Nirad world and will force her to kill Jupiter when he arrives."

Paelen saw a flash of fear on the winged Olympian's face. Cupid was still terrified at the mention of Nirads.

"Surely you are not suggesting I go with you to the Nirad world?" Cupid cried.

"You don't have to come, but I've got to go," Joel insisted. "The Nirads are on our side. It was the Gorgons who forced them to attack. It's not their fault. They want to help."

"And what if the Gorgons order them to kill us?" Cupid challenged.

"I don't think the Nirads would do it," Joel said. "They now know that Emily can restore their dead, so they won't do anything against us. And it was a Nirad called Tange who helped Chrysaor and me escape to warn Jupiter. But Olympus is empty." Joel reached for a coat. "Now, you can stay here if you want. But I've got to get back to Emily before I'm missed."

As he moved to the door, Chrysaor moved with him. He squealed lightly, and Paelen translated. "He says climb on his back. He will take you to the Nirad world."

"Wait—" Steve rose stiffly from the sofa and reached for a shirt. "Can he carry two of us? I'm going with you."

Paelen saw the look of fierce determination on Emily's father's face. He'd seen that same determination in Emily enough times to know there would be no talking him out of it, despite his wounds. "Chrysaor says he can take you both. But we must go now."

Just as they were about to leave, Cupid stepped forward. "Chrysaor is going to have to carry three of us. If you are planning to fight the Gorgons, I am going with you."

"But there are Nirads," Joel warned. "Millions of them."

"Then you had better not have lied to me, Joel. You say the Nirads are on our side? I will trust you."

"Cupid, no!" Agent T howled. "Your wing is broken, and you aren't well enough! You can't go to the Nirads, not without me!"

Cupid dropped his head and swayed on his feet. "Agent T," he said slowly, "come with me." He escorted the CRU agent over to Earl. Cupid closed his eyes and turned on his charm. Power flowed out of him, toward Agent T. "You want nothing more than to stay here and help Earl. He means more to you than I do, more than anyone. Use your CRU skills to keep him safe. Do this for me and do it for him."

Cupid turned toward Paelen. "I have never tried that before. I hope it works."

Agent T stood beside Earl's stretcher. He was looking down on Earl and stroking his hair gently. His eyes shone with brotherly love for the wounded man.

"That was kind of you, Cupid," Joel said.

"Kindness has nothing to do with it," Cupid said gruffly. "I could not have him trying to follow us and raising the alarm. At least now Earl should be safe while he recovers. So, can we please go before I change my mind?"

ON THE OTHER SIDE OF THE SOLAR STREAM, they found themselves in a cave filled with huge orange Nirads. Despite Joel's assurances, Paelen still had doubts, and Cupid was noticeably terrified.

"It's all right," Joel assured them as he, Steve, and Cupid climbed off Chrysaor. "They've been waiting for us."

The Nirads parted, and a strange creature stepped forward. He looked like a Nirad but was smaller than the others, with intelligent gray eyes and features that were fine and sharp. His skin tone was dark pink with a black marbling effect that made him stand out even more from the orange Nirads in the cave.

Chrysaor approached the pink Nirad and started

to squeal. When the pink Nirad responded, Paelen was shocked to discover he understood.

"I am Paelen," he said as he bowed to the pink Nirad.

"Who is he?" Joel asked, coming forward. "He's the same color as the queen."

"That is because he is her brother," Paelen explained. "This is Prince Toban. His sister sent him and these royal guards to help us defeat the Gorgons."

The prince closed his eyes and lifted his head. He looked back at Paelen and made several strange sounds.

"He can speak with his sister silently, just as the queen can communicate with all her people through the power of thought," Paelen explained. "That is what makes her queen. Segan says the Gorgons are still asleep but does not know for how much longer. Joel must return quickly."

Joel approached Chrysaor. "Will you take me back to the palace?"

The boar opened his wings and invited Joel to climb onto his back. "I'll tell Emily you're here," Joel told Steve. "That'll calm her down."

Steve patted Joel on the back. "Be careful. Don't

let them catch you. Tell Emily I'll be there as soon as I can and that I love her."

"I will," Joel promised. He looked over at Paelen. "Stay safe and watch out for the Gorgons. They have killer eyes!"

"You also," Paelen said as he watched Chrysaor carry his best friend to the front of the cave, spread his wings, and take off into the dull night sky.

Paelen walked out of the cave and into the dark, arid world. In the distance he could make out stone structures. There was a glow of green coming out of most of the windows, but very few Nirads were walking around the area.

Cupid emerged from the cave with an expression of doubt on his face. He looked at Toban and then at the huge Nirads surrounding them. "If you are siding with us, why did you hand over Diana and Apollo to the Gorgons? They could have helped us defeat them."

The prince sighed before he spoke. Both Paelen and Cupid nodded.

"Well?" Steve asked.

Paelen translated, shaking his head sadly. "Toban

says it was Diana's fault, not the Nirads'. When she and Apollo emerged from this cave, they started to attack the Nirads in the village. The villagers were not given a chance to explain the situation and were forced to defend themselves. The fight caused such a stir that the Gorgons were alerted. The queen had no choice but to order their capture or the Gorgons would have killed more of their people."

"Do you believe him?" Steve asked.

"With Diana's temper?" Paelen asked. "Absolutely. You have met her. She is not one for negotiating or waiting to hear details. Apollo will follow his sister in everything. Had they paused for a moment, they would not have been captured and would have been here with us."

The prince spoke again and Paelen translated. "Toban has offered to take us to a safe place until we are ready to go after the Gorgons. We cannot remain near this cave—the Gorgons have been checking it regularly since Diana and Apollo's arrival." He looked at Emily's father. "You need to rest."

"I'm all right," Steve said. "Besides, if Jupiter is coming, we should wait here to warn him."

But Paelen could see that he was far from all right. Though the ambrosia had helped greatly, Steve was still very weak and was swaying lightly on his feet. He needed more time to heal.

The prince shook his head and spoke urgently. "Toban says the Gorgons have made a fatal mistake," Cupid translated. "They are unaware of how powerful or intelligent Queen Segan really is. Once she realized Emily's abilities and that she could heal their dead, Segan called across the Solar Stream to her warriors. They have already alerted Jupiter to the danger he is facing and from whom. The Nirads are no longer bringing him here as their prisoner. Jupiter is leading them."

PAELEN WAS SEATED ON A SMOOTH ROCK IN a Nirad home, deep inside the village close to the cave. The furnishings were sparse and all made of carved, black stone. There were pots of moss scattered throughout the small room. The moss was giving off the bright, greenish glow that was the room's only light source and had been what he'd seen from the cave. In his hands was a stone bowl of foul-smelling, slimy black goo, but he couldn't bring himself to eat it.

Across from him, Steve lay on a marble slab. A different type of dark green moss was growing on the surface and worked as a kind of living mattress. A large female Nirad was applying a very smelly paste to Steve's bullet wound and tying clean bandages around his chest.

When she finished with Steve, she approached Paelen. She forced the bowl of black goo up his mouth and grunted loudly, showing a wide row of sharp, pointed teeth.

"I think you should do as she says and eat," Cupid warned as he leaned against a wall. His wing had been set and bandaged, and most of his wounds were healed.

"I am not hungry."

"It is actually not bad," Cupid said as he shoveled handfuls of the black food into his mouth. When his bowl was empty, he crossed to where a large stone barrel was stored. He refilled his bowl and continued eating.

After he downed his second helping, Cupid said, "It would not be wise to offend our host in her home. She has two children being held at the palace, and her nerves are raw with fear. It will not take much to enrage her. If she wants you to eat, you must eat."

Paelen knew the female Nirad was upset. But so was he. His two best friends were in the palace as prisoners of the murderous Gorgons, and there was no obvious way to help them. Reluctantly, he lifted the bowl to his lips and tasted the food. As she watched him, he was forced to swallow the sticky black goo. Cupid was right. Despite how bad it smelled, it really was quite good.

"Delicious," he said, smiling up at the huge female Nirad. "Thank you."

That seemed to satisfy her, as she nodded and lumbered out of the room.

When they were alone, Steve sat up slowly. "All right, everyone. Jupiter is on his way here. But Emily and Joel don't know that he's been warned. We've got to get in there to let them know. Emily must not use her powers against him."

"She would not," Paelen said. "She would never hurt Jupiter."

"Can you be so sure?" Steve asked seriously. "Paelen, you know my daughter. Answer me truthfully. Who does Emily care more for, Pegasus and Joel, or Jupiter? Who would she save if it came down to a choice?"

Paelen paused and thought back to everything he knew about Emily. She cared for Jupiter. But in truth, if their lives were at stake, there was no question who she would choose. Paelen quickly stood. "We must get in there before Emily kills Jupiter!"

"So, we are agreed?" Steve asked. "We let the Nirads capture us and take us into the throne room."

"I do not like this plan," Cupid said. "It will get us all turned to stone."

"Perhaps," Paelen said. "But we have no choice. Toban says there is only one way in and out of the palace. We must get into that throne room. If you two distract the Gorgons, I can sneak in and get the message to Emily and Joel. We must let Emily know Jupiter has been warned and that he is coming to fight the Gorgons."

"Yes, it's risky," Steve agreed. "But we don't have much choice." He stepped up to the young prince. "Toban, your sister knows the plan, right?" When the prince nodded his pink head, Steve continued. "Good. Tell her to let the Gorgons know you have just captured two more people at the cave and are bringing us in."

The prince closed his eyes. A moment later he nodded and grunted.

"Okay, boys, let's get moving."

EMILY COULDN'T KEEP HER EYES OFF THE marble statues of Diana and Apollo standing at either side of the thrones. The pain of transformation was carved into their stone faces, reminding her of the horrors yet to come.

She looked over at Pegasus, and her heart constricted. Her beloved stallion was leaning against the bars of his cage. His heavy stone leg was still raised in the air. Every few minutes he cried out as the stone hoof grazed the floor.

"It won't be long now, Pegs," she promised softly. "You'll see. Joel will let everyone know what's happening. Jupiter and the others will be here soon. Then I can heal you." Emily said the words as much to reassure herself as to help Pegasus. It seemed like ages since Joel had left. She prayed that Chrysaor hadn't betrayed them again and hurt Joel or even handed him over to the Gorgons.

Just when she thought she would go insane from waiting, Tange moved from his post. He came forward and opened the door to Emily's cage.

"What is it? Is Joel back?"

Tange nodded. He looked back to the entrance of the throne room. Emily followed his eyes and heard the sound of running footsteps. In the front cage the queen sat up and made several urgent calls.

Joel finally appeared. He dashed toward the cage. Tange held open the door and locked it after him, then returned quickly to his post.

Emily threw her arms around him as he collapsed to the floor beside her. "I was so scared," she said. "I thought Chrysaor might have betrayed you."

Joel was panting heavily and covered in a light film of sweat. "No, he didn't," he gasped. "But when we got back here, we heard the Gorgons coming down the stairs. So Chrysaor had to leave me to find my own way in here. We couldn't risk him being seen."

"Did you reach Olympus?"

Joel nodded and wiped down his face. "But everyone was gone. Olympus is deserted, and we don't know where Jupiter is." As he caught his breath, Joel quickly explained what had happened.

"So my dad is actually here in this world?" Emily asked. "Is he all right?"

"He's fine," Joel said. "He won't be running any marathons this year, but he's up and moving. So is Cupid, though his wing is still broken."

Emily sat back against the cage bars, stunned. She had always feared that her policeman father would get shot in the line of duty one day. But to hear he'd been hurt fighting the Nirads . . . It terrified her to think what could have happened to him. Now they were in the same world and facing the Gorgons.

Before she could find out more, the Gorgons flew into the throne room. Their expressions were darker and even more threatening than the day before. Their tempers were up, and they were ready to blow.

"Where are your warriors with Jupiter?" Stheno demanded as she flew over to the golden cage. "They should have been here by now!"

The queen looked up at Stheno and spoke softly.

"I do not care what he does!" Stheno spat. "Tell them to strike him. Knock him out! Tear his arms off if they must. Just get him here. This is why we chose you to fight our battles—because Jupiter's powers are useless against you."

Euryale moved closer to the braided gold bars of the queen's cage. Her bronze hands hovered threateningly before them. "Segan, you will command your warriors to get moving, or I will have more children brought in here. You will watch their suffering as we slowly turn them to stone!"

Dark tears trailed down the queen's pink cheeks. She closed her eyes and raised her head. After a time, she opened them again and spoke softly.

Stheno smiled in satisfaction. Her tiny gold wings flapped as she flew off the dais and landed before Emily and Joel's cage. "It will not be long now, Flame of Olympus. Jupiter has just entered the Solar Stream."

The tension in the throne room was intense. The Gorgons paced impatiently in front of the dais. "What is taking so long?" Euryale demanded of the queen.

"One Olympian against all your warriors should be easy to contain. What is happening?"

The queen grunted softly and held up her four arms.

"Excuses! Always excuses!" Euryale roared. "Tell them to hurry or you will feel my wrath!"

The queen closed her eyes and raised her head.

"Calm, sister," Stheno said. "Our time is nearly here. Soon Jupiter will be dead and we will rule Olympus and all the worlds along the Solar Stream. The murderers of our beloved sister will know our pain and rage. Medusa will be avenged."

"Perhaps I should go to the cave to wait," Euryale suggested.

"No, do not. I do not wish to be denied the pleasure of seeing Jupiter's face when he realizes it is we who have waged war on him. Patience, my sister, we can wait a bit longer."

As time ticked slowly by, there was a stirring in the hall outside the throne room. Soon another small pink Nirad entered. Emily could see that it was male. Was he royalty too? His sad eyes looked up at the queen in the cage before he approached the two Gorgons and bowed deeply.

"Who's that?" Emily whispered. "He looks just like the queen."

"That's her brother, Toban," Joel explained. "He was waiting in the cave for us."

The prince continued speaking with the Gorgons. Finally he lowered his head and barked out orders. All eyes in the throne room turned to the entrance. Several huge Nirads entered, escorting two people.

"Dad!" Emily cried, before she could hold it back. She struggled up to her good leg and hopped over to the bars of the cage.

"Emily!" Her father tore away from his guards and ran over to the cage. He put his arms through the bars and hugged her.

Emily clung to her father, grateful that he was alive. Suddenly everything was better. As long as he was there, she could face almost anything. But their reunion was cut short when Euryale flew forward and wrenched him away.

"More intruders!" she howled, and tossed Steve across the room. She stormed over to Cupid. "How many more Olympians are here?" she demanded. "How do you all keep finding this world? First there were Diana and Apollo and now you. How many more are coming?"

"It is just us," Cupid answered as he stood defiantly before the raging Gorgon. "Emily's father was desperate to reach her. So we followed the Nirads here."

Euryale turned furious, lethal eyes to Tange. "They followed your men! We told you to be careful! You have failed us, Nirad!"

Stheno came forward. "Sister, calm down. We ordered the Nirads to bring the Flame's father here. That he came by choice makes no difference. With Pegasus, Joel, and her father's life at stake, the Flame will have no choice but to obey us! This is a day to celebrate!"

Emily's eyes were locked on her father as Cupid helped him slowly to his feet. He was unshaven, and his hair had grown long and wild. But he'd never looked so good to her in all her life. In that moment Emily pledged that no one, not even the Gorgons, would ever separate them again.

Joel stepped up beside her and whispered tightly. "Em, look over by the entrance."

Emily reluctantly drew her eyes away from her father and nearly gasped when she saw Paelen slide into the throne room. His body was long and thin, like a large python. He was slipping past the Nirad guards, who must have known he was there but gave no warning. With the Gorgons' attention on Cupid and her father, Paelen was able to slither to the front of the room and hide behind the cage containing the queen.

"So, human," Euryale challenged as she advanced on Steve, "you wanted to see your precious daughter? There she is. Caged and defeated. Soon she will destroy Jupiter and Olympus will be ours."

"She'll never do it," Steve said. He looked over to Emily. "Don't do it, Em. Not for Pegasus, and not even for me. Do you hear me? Don't do it!"

Euryale flew into another rage and struck Steve with a crushing blow that smashed him against the bars of Pegasus's cage. The stallion screamed and started whinnying loudly.

"Dad!" Emily screeched as her father fell to the floor unconscious. "Leave him alone!" She could feel the flame starting to rumble in the pit of her stomach.

"Stop it," she cried as she raised her hands, "or the Flame will rise, and you know I can't control it!"

"Silence, Flame!" Euryale spat. She approached Steve with her hands held out and fingers bent like claws. Her eyes were glowing gold as the snakes on her head spit and hissed in anticipation. "Foolish human, now you will understand our power!"

"Sister, no!" Stheno shouted. She flew over to Euryale and placed herself in front of Emily's father. "This is what he wants! With him dead we will have no control over the Flame. Look at her—her powers are barely contained! If you kill her father now, she will lose control and destroy us all. We must not harm him yet."

"We still have Pegasus, Cupid, and the boy," Euryale challenged as her eyes continued to glow. "If she moves against us, we will kill them all."

"But this is her father!" Stheno argued. She forced her sister to look back at Emily and her raised hands. "We will not harm him—for now. Lower your hands, Flame, and contain your powers, or none of us will survive this day."

Emily was quaking with fear and rage as the

Gorgons hovered above her prone father. Finally she lowered her hands and took a deep, steadying breath. "Just don't touch him again," she warned, "or I swear I'll do it. I'll unleash it all!"

Stheno ordered Tange to move Emily's unconscious father into the cage with Pegasus. "Keep him quiet, Pegasus," she warned the stallion. "We will not hesitate to turn him to stone if we must."

Joel put a comforting arm around Emily. "Em, you've got to calm down," he whispered. "I can feel the heat coming off you. But this isn't the time to make our move."

Together they watched Tange gently carry her father into Pegasus's cage and lower him to the floor. The stallion leaned down and checked on him. He turned back to Emily, nickering softly, and nodded his head.

"Take good care of him, Pegasus," she said sadly. Emily looked up into Joel's warm brown eyes. "Maybe this is the time, Joel," she whispered. "Maybe now is the only time we'll ever have to move against them. Right now, before Jupiter arrives and I'm forced to kill him."

Her eyes trailed around the room, up to the queen in her cage, over to Cupid, who was being held by Nirads. Then they came to rest on Pegasus and her father in the cage opposite. No matter how hard she tried, she couldn't see a way out of this. With all the Olympians missing, who would come to challenge the Gorgons?

Tears rose in her eyes as hope slipped away. She automatically reached into her pocket and pulled out the green handkerchief to wipe away the tears before they could trail down her cheeks and fall to the ground. She watched as the hidden fold in the beautiful silk fabric opened and caught the volatile drops in its secret pocket.

It felt as if she had cried an ocean's worth since she had arrived in the Nirad world. She looked at the hidden pocket and pried it gently open. Deep inside was a small pool of water. These were the tears of the Flame of Olympus that contained the power of the sun.

"We'll get out of this somehow," Joel said softly.

"How?" she asked miserably. "Joel, look around you. They've got my dad, Cupid, Pegasus, and you. They'll turn you all to stone if I don't do as they tell me."

"Then you can turn them all right back again," called a high, willowy voice.

Emily turned around and saw that Paelen had crawled through the throne room and made it to the back of their cage.

Joel and Emily moved to the rear of the cage and sat down side by side to block their friend from the Gorgons' view.

"Listen to me," Paelen continued urgently. "Toban told us his sister has already warned Jupiter. Once she realized you could heal her people, she knew the Gorgons must be stopped. Jupiter knows it is them and not the Nirads who are waging war on Olympus. He is coming to face them. The Nirads will help."

"So what's the plan?" Joel asked. "What did you guys decide?"

There was a long silence.

"Paelen? Did you hear Joel?" Emily asked out of the side of her mouth. "What's the plan? What are we going to do?"

Paelen sighed. "There is no plan."

"What?" Emily whispered.

"Our plan was for your father and Cupid to distract

the Gorgons long enough for me to get in here to tell you that Jupiter has been warned about them. And to say you must not kill him."

"I wasn't going to," Emily said. "No matter what they do to me."

"Oh."

"That's it?" Joel said. "All you can say is 'Oh'? Jupiter is on his way here right now. The Gorgons are going to expect Emily to kill him. Surely Jupiter has a plan."

"If he has, he did not let the queen know," Paelen said. "All we can do now is wait."

EMILY SAT BESIDE JOEL, CLUTCHING HIS HAND as they awaited Jupiter's arrival. Paelen remained safely hidden behind them. He had made himself as small as possible. In the cage opposite, her father was standing beside Pegasus, stroking the stallion's thick neck. After strict warnings from the Gorgons, he did not try to speak to Emily again.

Emily was tormented. She was so grateful to actually see her father again and know that he was alive. But another part of her was terrified for him and wished he were still back on Earth. The Gorgons wouldn't hesitate to kill him if she didn't cooperate. Would she have the strength to defy them, with everyone she loved doomed to suffer if she did?

She had never faced such a terrible choice before. Whatever decision she made, someone would suffer. She was too young to have such a heavy responsibility thrust upon her. She should be at home in New York, her biggest worry being what to wear to school the next day or if a boy in her class liked her. Not whether she should kill the leader of Olympus in order to save those she loved or defy the Gorgons and possibly lose everyone she cared for.

The decision was too big. She wasn't up to it. Emily wished more than ever that the choice would be taken away from her. But, like it or not, she was the Flame of Olympus, and she faced a decision that would change the very existence of worlds.

After what seemed an eternity, the queen started to speak. The Gorgons were instantly on the dais and rubbed their bronze hands together excitedly. "Have your warriors bring him here immediately!" They roared in celebration.

Stheno flew to the center of the throne room and threw back her head in a screeching howl. "Jupiter, your reign is about to end!"

Emily studied the Gorgons as they awaited Jupiter's arrival. Her dread grew. She didn't have a clue what they were going to do or how this would turn out. She reached into her pocket and felt for the reassuring presence of her handkerchief. She pulled it out and checked the hidden pocket again to make sure her tears were still there. If her other powers failed, at least she had these.

"You are not planning to use those, are you?" Paelen asked softly as he reached into the cage and poked her softly in the back.

"I don't want to, but if I have to, I will," Emily whispered. "We can't let the Gorgons win."

"It wouldn't be much of a victory if we are all killed by your tears," Joel added. "But I guess it's better than letting them get control of Olympus and the Solar Stream."

Emily fell silent. They were right. Her tears would have to be the last resort. But if things got too far out of hand, she would have no choice but to use them. Outside the throne room heavy footsteps drew closer.

Emily felt Joel's hand tighten in hers. "This is it," he said softly.

As the sound increased, Emily heard heavy chains rattling and dragging on the marble floor. Soon a stream of large, gray Nirads filed into the throne room, followed by several orange-marbled Nirads. Emily spotted Jupiter at the center of them.

"Oh my God!" Joel cried. "What did they do to him?"

The leader of Olympus was wrapped in heavy chains that bowed his back and trailed along the floor. His hands were bound behind him, and he wore a heavy metal collar around his neck, with another thick chain attached to it. The lead Nirad was dragging him around like a dog on a leash.

Emily gasped. His face was badly bruised, and there was fresh blood on one eyebrow. His once-white tunic was filthy and shredded. Blood streamed down his exposed arms and legs—the result of what must have been a terrible fight.

The majestic leader of Olympus had been reduced to a bruised and battered prisoner. Had all this been a Nirad trick? Were the Nirads really on their side? Looking at Jupiter, it didn't appear so. Was this just a ploy to get her to remain in her cage and keep her from using her powers against them?

"Jupiter!" Emily called.

The leader of Olympus glanced slowly back at her with vacant eyes and appeared not to know her. After a moment he lowered his head again and was dragged forward. Pegasus also called out to Jupiter, but if he heard, he gave no indication.

"What happened to him?" Joel asked. "The Nirads are supposed to be on our side, but look what they did. They beat him up!"

"It is not possible," Paelen uttered. "I have never seen Jupiter look so defeated."

"We don't know what the Nirads did to him before the queen reached them. Maybe they really are stronger than Jupiter?" Emily suggested.

"Or maybe the Nirads really aren't on our side at all," Joel whispered.

"They must be," Paelen insisted. "We cannot defeat the Gorgons without them."

Joel turned back to Paelen. "I sure hope you're right."

Emily sat back as she watched the parade of Nirads approaching the thrones. She needed desperately to believe that the Nirads were on their side. But looking at what they did to Jupiter, she was not convinced.

When they reached the dais, Jupiter was dragged forward. The tall Nirad pushed down on Jupiter's hunched shoulders until the leader of Olympus was kneeling, defeated, before the vile Gorgons.

"Not so mighty now, are you, Jupiter," Stheno challenged.

Jupiter slowly raised his head. He gasped when his eyes fell on the stone Diana and Apollo standing on the dais beside the thrones.

"Oh, do you like them?" Euryale teased. "They shall make nice additions to our collection. I wish you could join them in our garden, but unfortunately our powers do not work on you. We do, however, have other forms of entertainment planned for you."

"What do you want, Gorgon?" Jupiter asked coldly. "Why have you waged war on Olympus?"

Jupiter may have looked defeated, but his voice was as powerful and commanding as ever. For an instant, fear rose on the Gorgons' faces. It was quickly replaced by anger.

"From you," Euryale finally spat, "we want nothing, unless you care to bring our beloved sister back to us."

"Medusa died long ago," Jupiter said. "No one can change that. Not even me. But even if I could, I would not. Medusa got what she deserved."

"Medusa did not deserve to die!" Euryale screeched. "Your son had no right to kill her!"

"Medusa was insane," Jupiter continued. "No one, not even you, could control her bloodlust. She murdered without thought. You know she had to be stopped."

"We know no such thing," Euryale replied angrily. "She was our sister. She did not deserve the punishment your son levied on her. Perseus had no right to take her head. She could have been reasoned with."

"Reason?" Jupiter responded. "What do you Gorgons know of reason? I have seen the devastation you have wrought upon this and every other world you have poisoned with your presence. You are as mad as Medusa. You must be stopped!"

Both Gorgons laughed their horrible, screeching laughs. Euryale stood and climbed down from the dais. "Stopped? You fool. We are only just getting started. You should be grateful you will not live to see our truth wrath."

She turned to one of the Nirads. "Bring Cupid over here. We shall show Jupiter what we have planned for all the people of Olympus."

Emily and Joel stood and crossed to the bars of their cage as the orange guard approached Cupid. Emily could see the terror rising on the winged Olympian's face. His worst nightmare was being realized. He was being attacked by the Nirads. As others held him in place, the orange guard caught him by the arm and hauled him forward.

"No!" Cupid screeched. "Let me go!"

"Cupid!" Emily howled.

"Emily!" Cupid cried as he opened his wings and flapped them in wild panic, desperately trying to break free of the guard's grip. But he was no match for the strength of the powerful Nirad. "Help me, please!"

"There is no one to help you, Cupid," Euryale said as Cupid was dragged forward to stand before her. The Gorgon turned to Jupiter. "Watch, Jupiter. Watch as we turn the son of Venus to stone!"

In his cage Pegasus was going mad, whinnying furiously and kicking the heavy bars with his front hoof. Emily's father stood back as the stallion raged.

"Silence, Pegasus," Stheno shouted, "or you will follow him!"

"No!" Emily howled. "Please, don't do it. Let Cupid go!"

"And you, Flame," Stheno shouted back at her, "be silent, or I will do the same to Joel and then your father."

"Em, please," Joel whispered at her side. "Calm down. You can turn Cupid back later."

"How?" Emily asked desperately. "Look at Jupiter. He can't fight them."

"Then we will," Joel insisted. "We just have to get out of this cage."

Emily and Joel gazed back to the front of the room as Cupid started to scream. Euryale's eyes were blazing gold. The snakes on her head squirmed and hissed with excitement as the Gorgon concentrated her full attention on the winged god.

"Emily, help me!" Cupid howled as the terror on his face was replaced by pain. The feathers on his open wings were the first to turn to stone. They were followed by his arms and then legs as the marble crept through his body. Finally his torso and face were frozen in a stance of pure agony.

Emily's heart constricted in pain as she saw the statue of Cupid standing at the front of the dais. He had fought for her, done everything she ever asked of him, and this is how he was to be repaid—by being tortured and turned to stone. "I'm so sorry, Cupid," she mourned softly.

Her eyes trailed over to Jupiter. She saw no reaction from the leader of Olympus. He was still on his knees looking at the floor, not at the Gorgons or Cupid. "He doesn't care," Emily muttered in haunted shock. "Look at him, Joel. Jupiter doesn't care about Cupid!"

"You are wrong," Paelen called from the floor at the back of the cage. "Jupiter cares about all of us."

"Then why doesn't he do something?" Emily challenged.

At the front of the room, Euryale screeched with delight. "Do you see, Jupiter? See the destiny awaiting all the children of Olympus?"

Stheno came forward and approached Jupiter on the floor. She slapped him violently across the face with her bronze hand. "First we will watch Olympus fall. Then we will move through the Solar Stream like a raging storm until every world knows our names and worships us!"

Jupiter looked up at the Gorgon. Finally he spoke. "And if they do not?"

"Then we will turn their worlds to stone as well!" Stheno screeched. "But you need not worry for those worlds, Jupiter. All that is will become Gorgon!"

Euryale stood before the kneeling Jupiter and caught hold of his long beard. She wrenched his head back. "You are taking your final breaths, Jupiter. Savor these moments, for the hourglass of your life runs short."

"You cannot destroy me, Euryale, and you know it," Jupiter said. "No weapon can kill me, and not even your strongest Nirad is capable of my destruction. Surrender now and I shall spare your lives."

Emily listened to the cackling laughter of the two Gorgons as they stood before the defeated leader of Olympus. They stroked his head and tugged on his beard, teasing him. "Are you so certain we cannot destroy you? If so, you are in for a big surprise."

"We've got to do something—" Emily looked back to Paelen, but he wasn't there. He was slithering behind her cage, toward the front of the throne room.

"Paelen, no," she whispered tightly. "Come back."

"Paelen," Joel added softly. "Stop, they'll kill you."

Paelen paused. "No one else is coming. It must be us who save him. Trust me: I have an idea."

Emily wanted to call to him again but feared exposing him. Instead she split her attention between him and Jupiter in the center of the throne room. She was certain the Gorgons would see him. But for now they were concentrating solely on Jupiter. Emily's eyes then went up to the queen. She was following Paelen, fear etched across her young face.

Across the room, Pegasus and her father also watched. Pegasus started to whinny, ensuring his aunt's attention was kept away from Paelen.

"Not now, Pegasus," Euryale said irritably. "Be patient. You will be out of there soon enough."

But Pegasus would not stop. He kept whinnying and pounding the floor of his cage.

"I said stop!" Euryale stormed as she flew over to Pegasus's cage. "Do not make me destroy you so close to our victory!"

"Leave him be," Stheno called to her sister. "I grow weary of all this chatter." She fluttered her tiny gold wings and flew across the room to Emily and Joel's cage. She looked at Tange. "Open the door. It is time for the Flame of Olympus to end this."

Tange looked at Emily as he unlocked and opened the door to her cage. "Child, you cannot fight your destiny," Stheno said.

Emily hopped to the back of the cage and shook her head. "I won't do it. You can't make me kill Jupiter."

"Leave her alone!" Joel moved to block Emily from the Gorgons and Tange. "Just leave her alone."

Stheno waved her hand at Tange dismissively. "Kill the boy and bring Emily out of there."

Tange stooped down and entered the cage. His mouth was working hard to try to form the word "please." There was desperation in his face.

"No! Tange, please, don't hurt Joel!" Emily begged.

"Then stop fighting us," Stheno said, "and the boy will live."

"Em, don't do it," Joel said to her. "Forget about me. Whatever happens, don't kill Jupiter!"

Emily looked at Joel, fearing it was for the last time. They had been through so much together, but now their time was at an end. This was the point where she had to make her choice, a choice where there could be no winners. She gave him a fierce hug and hoped he didn't feel her trembling.

"It'll be all right, Joel," she whispered softly, knowing full well that she was lying. She kissed his cheek, then gave him a final hug before turning to face Tange. "I'm ready."

Tange lifted her gently into the air. He carried her past Joel and out of the cage. Emily saw that Tange hadn't locked the door after her. Joel was free to leave the cage anytime he wanted. Joel had noticed this too. He moved to the door and waited.

"Please let him run when he gets the chance," she prayed silently.

Emily looked up and saw the queen sit bolt upright in her chair, anxiously. She, too, knew the end was drawing near.

When they stood in front of the thrones and faced

the kneeling Jupiter, Tange put Emily down on her good leg and helped to steady her. He wrapped one thick arm around her shoulders for support.

"Jupiter," Emily begged, "help me, please. I don't want to do this."

The leader of Olympus raised his bruised and bloodied face to her. She could see the pain and defeat in his dark eyes. Jupiter suddenly looked very old and frail. He was too tired to fight. "You will do what you must for the good of Olympus, Emily."

"That is sound advice," Stheno agreed as she moved up beside Emily. "The time has come. Your choice is simple. Summon up the power of the Flame and destroy Jupiter, or my sister over there will turn your beloved Pegasus and father to stone."

Emily glanced over at the cage. The stallion was shaking his head and snorting loudly, while her father mouthed the word "no" to her.

She looked again at Jupiter. Then back at Pegasus and her father. Her eyes trailed over to Joel, who was also frantically shaking his head no. Finally they returned to Jupiter. But the leader of Olympus had lowered his head and would not face her. Was he doing this to make the decision easier? It wasn't working. Every instinct in her body told her not to do it. But then her emotions exploded. What about her father? Pegasus and Joel? The Gorgons would kill them if she refused.

"Do not try my patience, child," Stheno warned. Emily was close enough to hear the snakes on her head hissing in wild anticipation of the violence yet to come.

In his cage Pegasus continued whinnying frantically and waving his head back and forth. She didn't need to understand him to know what he was saying. Pegasus was begging her not to do it.

"Silence, Pegasus," Euryale ordered. "You cannot tell her what to do!" The Gorgon looked at Emily. "Must I turn another of his legs to stone to prove I will not hesitate to kill him?" she asked. "How would your father look with stone legs?"

"No, please don't!" Emily cried.

"Then use your powers!" Stheno ordered. "Kill Jupiter!"

"Emily, no!" Joel shouted.

"I-I—" Emily stuttered as she faced Jupiter.

The leader of Olympus raised his head. "You know what you must do, Emily. I understand."

Emily looked around in wild desperation. She had hoped and prayed for a miracle. That somehow all the Olympians would burst into the throne room at the very last minute and rescue them. She could no longer see Paelen in the room and had no idea where he was or what he was planning. But if the others were trying to get into the palace, they were too late. The moment had come. Right or wrong, her decision was made.

Emily took a deep, unsteady breath. She closed her eyes and felt the tingling of the Flame's powers deep within. Her emotions were fanning the barely contained flames. They wanted out with or without her permission. The power was alive, rumbling and growing, moving steadily from the pit of her stomach to along her arms.

"Forgive me," she muttered as she raised her hands to Jupiter and released her power.

PAELEN WAS HIDING BEHIND ONE OF THE
Nirads. The huge creature knew he was there but
gave no alarm. Instead he opened his thick arms farther to offer him more protective cover.

He watched as Emily stood before Jupiter, wrestling with her decision. There was only one she could
make, but did she have the strength to make it?

Paelen held his breath. She wouldn't do it. Would
she? Would Emily really kill Jupiter to save the others? He watched her raise her arms. He heard her
soft plea for forgiveness. He saw her let the flames
go. . . .

Two sharp beams of deadly light flew past Jupiter's
head and burned the lock on Pegasus's cage door. The

laserlike flames shot past Pegasus and through the cage, the wall behind it, and the outer walls of the marble palace, then continued out over the land of the Nirads.

"I won't do it!" Emily shouted as her fury stopped the deadly flames before they flew out of control. She turned toward Stheno. "I won't kill Jupiter!"

Paelen cheered Emily's defiance. He saw her father burst through the melted cage door and run at Euryale, howling in fury. Whinnying in anger, Pegasus limped behind him, flapping his burned wings and dragging his heavy stone leg.

Euryale spun around, her eyes turning brilliant gold. Emily's father's agonized scream was cut short as he and the stallion turned instantly to white marble. Only then did everyone in the room understand. The Gorgons could choose how long it took for their victims to turn to stone.

"Dad, no!" Emily howled.

Emily's father was frozen beside the marble Pegasus. In the center of the room, Emily's pain-filled howls turned to roars of rage. She raised her hands to fire at Euryale.

Beside her, Stheno's eyes blazed gold as she faced Emily. "If you will not kill Jupiter, I will extinguish the Flame of Olympus myself!"

"Emily, watch out!" Paelen shouted as he burst from his cover and lunged at the Gorgon. He launched himself into the air and landed on Stheno's back.

"For Olympus!" he shouted as he wrapped his arms around the Gorgon's head and slapped both his hands over her deadly eyes. Paelen ignored the countless snakes biting painfully into his face and arms as he clung to the enraged Gorgon. Stheno screeched and howled. She spun around madly, trying to dislodge him.

"Shoot them!" Paelen called to Emily. "Do it now: Stop the Gorgons!"

Paelen clung to Stheno and felt his hands grow cold. They were becoming stiff and difficult to move. His feet and legs were frozen and unresponsive as he tried to jump away from the enraged Gorgon. Finally, his vision started to fade as his muscles seized up.

"No!" he howled.

The Gorgon beneath him screeched and screamed in fury. "You will die in agony, boy!"

Paelen suddenly realized his terrible mistake. The Gorgon's eyes did not need to be open to be deadly. The freezing in his hands spread throughout his whole body. Already he could feel his blood slowing as each cell in his body turned to stone. Paelen experienced pain he'd never known before. It was like he was freezing and burning at the same time. He could no longer move. All he knew was pain and then . . . black nothingness.

30

EMILY SCREAMED AS PAELEN TURNED TO stone. He was curled around Stheno's head like a grotesque hat. On his marble face was the pain of transformation. Stheno lifted him and screeched in rage as she tossed him aside.

Just before Emily's best friend hit the ground and shattered into a thousand pieces, Tange released Emily and dove to catch Paelen. He lowered the coiled Paelen statue safely to the floor. When he rose, Tange threw back his head and roared loud enough to shake the whole palace.

At Tange's command, the throne room erupted in fighting as the large Nirads attacked the Gorgons. But the Gorgon's deadly eyes were faster and much more powerful. No Nirad could get close without being turned to stone instantly. The throne room quickly filled with marble Nirads.

"Jupiter!" Emily cried. She hopped over to the kneeling Olympian and tried to undo the heavy chains binding him. "Please help us."

"Not yet," Jupiter replied as his wild eyes scanned the room, but he remained motionless before the thrones. "This is not the time."

"The time for what?" Emily demanded. "For all of us to die?"

"Emily!" Joel cried as he ran out of the cage.

"Go to him, child," Jupiter warned. "Leave me here and do what you must. Remember, you are the Flame of Olympus!"

Emily saw Chrysaor running into the throne room and toward Joel. The pink prince darted around the Nirad statues to join them. More warriors flooded into the throne room and joined the fight. The sound of their furious roaring was deafening, but not nearly as bad as the howls of pain that filled the room when the warriors were turned to stone by the Gorgons.

Emily reluctantly left Jupiter and joined the others as they crouched down behind a wall of stone Nirads.

"Why don't you use your powers?" Joel demanded. "You're the only one who can stop them."

"I can't," Emily cried. "Joel, you know I don't have any control. I could kill everyone in here, including Jupiter!"

Toban started to growl and pointed up to his sister locked in her cage. He caught Joel by the arm and tried to lead him up to it.

"We must save the queen!" Joel insisted. He turned frightened eyes to Emily. "It doesn't matter how much control you've got. It's the only way."

"But what if I can't? What if I kill you?"

"We're as good as dead anyway. You know we can't let them leave here to destroy other worlds!"

"But—"

"Em, look around you!" he shouted. "The Nirads can't stop the Gorgons. You're the only one who can! Look, just stay here, take a few deep breaths, and calm down. Concentrate on what you need to do. You can do it, Emily, I know you can. I'll see if we can get the queen's cage open. But be prepared to use your powers."

Emily watched Joel, the prince, and Chrysaor darting between the large stone Nirads. The room was growing crowded with statues as every Nirad who tried failed to get close enough to attack the Gorgons.

In the center of the room, Jupiter remained still. Nirad statues were falling all around him, but he refused to move. *What are you waiting for?* Emily thought. *Please, Jupiter, help us!*

Joel and the prince reached the thrones. They jumped onto the dais and moved to climb the stairs up to the queen's cage. In their determination, they did not see Stheno turn her deadly golden gaze in their direction.

But Emily did. "Joel, look out, she's right behind you! Get down!"

Joel and the prince cried out in agony as they turned instantly to stone. Halfway up the stairs to the cage, Joel was caught off balance, with one foot still raised in the air.

"Joel! No!" Emily howled as her friend teetered on the edge of the steps. Then, as if in slow motion, he fell forward and smashed into the fine braided gold bars of the queen's cage.

Beneath his heavy stone weight, the gold bars bent and crumpled. Joel tumbled, rolling down the stairs until he finally slipped off the dais and crashed to the marble floor below. On impact, his right arm exploded into hundreds of tiny stone pieces.

Emily dashed forward. But moments before she reached Joel, all the surviving Nirads in the room roared and turned toward their queen. Segan was looking up at the roof in terror as the gold bars to her cage trembled. Unable to withstand the roof's weight after the impact of the stone Joel, the top of the cage began to come down.

"No!" Emily screamed. Jupiter moved.

He rose from the floor and easily tore away all the chains wrapped around him. In three short strides, the leader of Olympus reached Segan's cage. He pushed inside and lifted the small queen from her prison chair. Jupiter wrapped his arms and powerful body around her just as the heavy gold roof collapsed down upon the two.

"Jupiter!" Emily cried.

Tange howled mournfully as he and the three other large orange throne-room Nirads charged forward. They leaped up to the dais and, each taking a corner, started to lift the heavy gold roof off Jupiter and their queen. Beneath the roof, Jupiter rose, with the queen still alive and safe within his arms.

Tange and the others howled in agony and strained to use their four arms to lift and support the gold roof. Down on the floor, Stheno raced forward. "You will all die!" she screeched.

The Gorgon directed her deadly gaze at the four Nirads and Jupiter. Tange's cries grew unbearably loud as he and the others continued to support the roof while their bodies turned to stone.

Inside the cage, Jupiter remained unaffected by the Gorgon's deadly stare. With the pink queen still wrapped in his protective embrace, he glanced over his shoulder at Stheno. "You and your sister have failed, Gorgon. You should have surrendered when you had the chance. There will be no mercy for you now."

Beside Emily, Chrysaor squealed in pain as he was turned to stone for the second time in as many days.

"You should have joined us, child," Euryale screeched as she stalked toward Emily with murder in her eyes. "We would have embraced you as our daughter."

"I had a mother," Emily cried defiantly, "and I loved her. She was enough. I would never join you."

"Then you are a fool!" Euryale shouted. "You could have ruled with us. All the worlds of the Solar Stream could have been your playground. You would have been an empress! But you made your choice. It was the wrong one!"

Euryale raised her hands as her terrible eyes blazed the brightest gold Emily had ever seen. "It is over, Flame of Olympus. You . . . are . . . extinguished!"

Emily felt searing pain in every part of her body as she stiffened. She couldn't move. Couldn't scream and couldn't breathe. Her eyes faded as the room around her blurred and turned to black. An instant later she was solid stone.

EMILY WAS AWARE. SHE COULD NOT HEAR, she could not see, and she could not feel. But she remained completely aware.

Was this what it was like for everyone else? Was her father conscious but trapped in a casing of stone? Was she alive or dead? Did her heart still pump blood through her marble body? Was this it? Was she facing an eternity as an unmoving statue while remaining fully conscious? Panic settled in as Emily struggled to move her fingers. But nothing happened. She was frozen stone.

No! Her mind raged. Emily thought of all the others she loved who were suffering the same fate around her. Was her father calling silently to be freed? But there was no one left alive to hear him. Was Pegasus suffering? Was he still feeling the pain of his burns? Emily was the only one who could heal them all. But how could she when she, too, was stone?

As Emily thought and worried for the others, her concern fed the Flame. It began to bubble within her. But trapped inside the stone casing, unable to move her arms, it had nowhere to go. For an instant, Emily feared the Flame would turn in on itself, consuming her body like a Phoenix that died in the ashes of its own fire. But she had already been burned up once. Could it happen again?

"Don't think about it, Em," she ordered. "Think only of Dad. Think of beautiful Pegasus and the pain on his face when he was turned to marble. Think of sweet Paelen, brave Joel, and handsome Cupid. Think of how they fought and suffered beside you."

Emily felt her panic subside as she thought of those she loved. Fear for her own life faded, and anger at Stheno and Euryale grew. The thought of those two vile creatures being responsible for so much pain and suffering was unbearable.

As more faces of the dead flashed in her mind,

Emily's anger boiled. No way would she let them get away with it. They could not be allowed to rule Olympus and all the other worlds along the Solar Stream. She would fight them. If it took every last bit of energy, if she had to burn herself out to stop them, she would not let the Gorgons succeed!

She concentrated on the Flame. Already boiling with her fear, she let her anger stoke the fires. If she was the Flame, so be it. Emily would finally become THE FLAME OF OLYMPUS!

A silent roar started deep within her core as Emily summoned all the powers she had been fighting so long to suppress. She fed them, called them forth, and commanded them to melt the stone shell keeping her imprisoned.

She could feel the heat rising. It was just as Vesta had told her it would be. The full power of the sun! But Emily felt no pain, only growing strength and control. As the Flame rose from her center, she was able to move again. At first just a finger, but soon more.

Her hearing returned. Emily heard the sound of the two Gorgons cackling and shouting at Jupiter.

They were taunting him and celebrating his defeat. Euryale's voice was closest. The Gorgon was standing directly beside her.

"It is over, Jupiter. See how your great Flame is nothing now but dead, cold stone. When our Nirads return to Olympus and extinguish what is left of the Flame at the temple, you will truly know defeat. Medusa is finally avenged!"

Emily felt the pressure of Euryale's bronze hand resting on her stone arm. The Gorgon was unaware of the changes raging deep inside her, oblivious to the danger standing at her side. Emily summoned up the Flame, and her hand burst free of its marble prison. Before the Gorgon could utter a word, Emily caught hold of her bronze hand and held it in a fierce grip.

"What—" Euryale cried. "Let me go!"

Emily unleashed her powers. She was a living volcano about to erupt. The stone encasing her seemed to melt and flow away from her like lava. Her temperature climbed impossibly high, yet she did not feel the heat.

Euryale, however, did. The Gorgon screeched and screamed as the bronze of her hand melted and dripped to the floor. The snakes on her foul head hissed and spat as they slowly roasted and shriveled in the intense heat.

Emily turned her head slowly and saw the Gorgon's face start to smoke and then burst into flame. Euryale's eyes went brilliant gold as she tried to fight back. But Emily did not return to stone. She was a raging inferno, untouched by the Gorgon's lethal power.

Stheno screamed in fury when she saw her sister burning. She directed her deadly golden eyes at Emily, but they had no effect. When Euryale collapsed to the floor in a melted, smoldering heap, Stheno ran over to Steve. She put her hands on his shoulders and threatened to topple him over.

"Stop now, Flame, or I will destroy your father!" she wailed.

Emily's fury renewed. She raised her hands, summoned all the power she possessed, and fired at Stheno. Unlike Euryale, who had burned, Stheno simply disappeared in a soft, soundless puff. Black ash filled the air and rained down where the Gorgon had been standing.

The Gorgons were gone.

"Emily," Jupiter called softly. "It is over, child. Call it back."

Through flaming eyes, Emily looked up at Jupiter. He was still in the cage with the queen. He lifted her lightly in the air and carried her between the bent gold bars, careful not to let the gold graze her delicate pink skin. He lowered her onto the dais and walked closer to Emily.

Jupiter raised his hands against her blazing heat. His whole body was starting to smolder. "Pull it back, Emily," he said, sounding strangely calm. "You can do it now. The powers are yours to command. Pull the Flame back."

Emily closed her eyes and concentrated on pulling the Flame back into herself. She imagined she was a giant vacuum cleaner sucking up a pile of flour from the floor. Only this wasn't flour she was collecting, but the raging power of the sun. As she concentrated harder, she felt the Flame obeying her commands. Her core temperature was dropping. The Flame was growing smaller and easier to contain. Finally it stopped completely, and Emily was herself again.

She looked around at the devastation of the room: not a living soul moved except for Jupiter and the Nirad queen. Everyone else was stone. "Jupiter?" she called softly.

Jupiter swooped in and closed his strong arms around her. He lifted her off the floor and gave Emily the biggest, most powerful hug she had ever had in her life.

"I am so very proud of you!" he cried as he kissed her cheeks. "You were magnificent!"

"I don't—don't understand," she stammered. "Jupiter, what happened?" Then she remembered how he had done nothing when the Gorgons started to attack. "Why wouldn't you help us?" she demanded. "You just knelt there while the Gorgons turned everyone to stone. They turned *me* to stone! Why didn't you stop them?"

Jupiter put her down and knelt on one knee before her. He took both her hands in his. "Forgive me, but I could not. When I came in here, my only concern was for the Nirad queen. I knew you would be safe. And anyone who was turned to stone could be healed by you. But if the queen had died in her cage, this entire Nirad society would have been destroyed."

"But, but—"

"Child, listen to me," Jupiter said softly. "This is the price I must pay as leader. Making these difficult decisions is never easy. But I could not help you no matter how much I wanted to. You had to learn to help yourself. Until this moment, you have feared and dreaded your powers. Because of that, you could not control them. It made you a danger to yourself and everyone in Olympus. But here, today, you finally embraced them. You have faced your destiny and become the Flame's master. Emily, you saved everyone and defeated the Gorgons because you are finally the Flame of Olympus. It was more than I could ever have achieved."

Emily sucked in her breath. "But—but you're Jupiter," she protested. "There's nothing you can't do."

Jupiter chuckled and rose. He kissed her on the forehead. "I appreciate your faith in me, child. But I am nothing without the power of the Flame of Olympus behind me." He reached out his hand. "May I see the handkerchief Neptune gave you? I need to check something."

Emily handed over the green fabric with the white Pegasus embroidered on it. She watched him open the hidden pocket and peer inside.

"It worked perfectly," he muttered. "I must tell my brother."

"Tell him what?"

Jupiter handed back the handkerchief. "Look inside: Your tears are gone."

Emily saw he was right. The small pocket was empty. "Where did they go?"

"Back into you—they added fuel to your fire. When Neptune had his Sirens weave this for you, he made certain that when you needed your tears back, the fabric would return them. It appears it did." Jupiter wrapped his arm around her to support her weight. "Now, Emily, I would like to properly introduce you to Segan, the queen of the Nirads."

Emily put the handkerchief back in her pocket and looked at the young queen she had spent so much time with. She bowed her head. "Your Majesty."

The queen smiled. She wrapped her four arms around Emily and embraced her tightly. She growled softly in her ear.

"Segan says thank you for your bravery and for freeing her people from the terror of the Gorgons," Jupiter explained.

Emily smiled back. "You're welcome." She looked around the room at the countless stone statues. "But you're not really free yet. We've got a lot of work ahead of us to free everyone."

Segan stepped over to the stone statue of her brother and grunted a few soft words to Jupiter. "She has asked a favor. Would you be kind enough to free her brother first?"

Emily nodded and was helped over to the pink Nirad. "I really hope this works," she said nervously as she reached out her hand and touched the prince's stone arm.

The change started immediately. Where her hand grasped the Nirad's arm, pink returned to the surface. It spread along his whole body, until he took in a deep, unsteady breath and staggered on his feet. Segan reached out to support him. Recovered, he looked at his sister and howled in joy.

Emily felt her throat constrict as she watched their noisy reunion. The queen turned to her and spoke softly.

"Segan would like you to meet her brother, Toban," Jupiter explained.

Before Emily could speak, the young prince threw his four arms around her and embraced her while growling enthusiastically in her ear.

"You're very welcome," Emily choked out when he finally released her. Leaving the pink Nirads free to continue their reunion, she looked up at Jupiter. "Will you help me get to my dad and Pegasus?"

"With pleasure," Jupiter said as he lifted her easily in his arms and carried her carefully between the marble Nirad fighters and over to the stone statues of her father and Pegasus. Emily felt a biting pain in her chest as she stared into the expressions on both of their faces.

Jupiter lowered her to the floor. Emily put her arms around her father and stood on tiptoes to kiss his stone cheek. "Come back to me, Dad."

Holding him close, Emily could feel the life flowing back into her father as the stone faded and his flesh returned. After a moment her father opened his eyes and found her in his arms.

"Em!" he cried, hoisting her in the air and giving

her a hug equaling Jupiter's. Tears rushed to his eyes, and he buried his face in her long, dark hair. "My Em, my beautiful Em!"

"Daddy!" Emily squealed, suddenly sounding like a child again. She stood, clinging to her father. It had been the longest journey of her life to get to this moment, and she didn't want it to end.

Her father put her down and looked around the room. He wiped his teary eyes. "What happened in here?"

Jupiter offered his hand. "Your daughter saved all of us. You should be very proud."

"I am," he said.

With her father at her side, Emily hopped over to Pegasus. Agony was etched on the stallion's marble face and revealed in his half-opened wings. Emily put her arms around his cold stone neck and pressed her cheek to the white marble. "Forgive me, Pegs," she whispered softly, "but I couldn't kill Jupiter to save you. Please, please forgive me. Come back. I need you."

Beneath her cheek, Emily felt the stone react. "That's it," she coaxed, "keep coming."

Soon the marble stallion warmed and became flesh again. His burns were healed, and the feathers on his wings were restored. With one heaving breath, his eyes opened and he finished the screaming whinny he'd started when Euryale had turned him and her father to stone.

"It's all right, Pegs," Emily soothed as she stroked his quivering neck. "It's over now. You're all right!"

Pegasus jumped when he saw Emily standing beside him. She started to laugh at the confused expression on his face. Pegasus looked around at all the statues in the throne room. His frightened eyes went up to the queen's cage, and he neighed loudly to Jupiter.

"The Gorgons are gone, Pegasus," Jupiter said. "Queen Segan is safe. She is with her brother, over there." He pointed at the two pink Nirads. "Soon we will heal the wounds of this world and return to Olympus."

The confused expression remained as he nickered softly. She put her arms around his neck and hugged him tightly. "I couldn't have done it without you, Pegs," she said softly.

When Pegasus neighed, Jupiter smiled and stroked his soft muzzle. "Emily did more than even I could ever have imagined. I am sure she will tell you all about it in time. For now, come, my nephew, we have a lot of work ahead of us."

With Pegasus on one side and her father on the other, Emily hopped carefully through the throne room filled with statues. She would never admit it to Jupiter, but she was frightened she wouldn't have enough power to heal everyone. But Pegasus understood. He helped her over to her best friends first.

Her father helped her down to the floor in front of Paelen. Emily stroked his head and kissed him lightly on the cheek. "Thanks for trying to save me from Stheno, Paelen," she whispered softly.

The stone beneath her lips began to warm as life quickly returned to Paelen. After a moment he took in a deep breath and screamed.

"It's all right," Emily said as she wrapped her arms tightly around him. "Paelen, you're safe. Calm down!"

Paelen looked wildly around the room and rose,

preparing to fight again. "Where are they? What happened?"

"Gone," Emily's father said as he helped her rise to her good leg.

"Gone where?"

"Well," Emily said awkwardly, "Euryale sort of melted. As for Stheno, she just evaporated. That's what is left of her, over there." Emily pointed at the dark ashes littering the floor and blowing around the throne room.

Paelen looked from the ashes back to Emily. "Did you do that?"

She shrugged. "Kinda. They turned me to stone too, and that made me really angry."

Paelen looked at her in wonder. "They made you angry, so you turned them to dust?" When Emily nodded, he whistled lightly, and his crooked grin appeared. He stepped up to Pegasus. "Pegasus, please warn me if you ever see me start to make Emily angry!"

Emily laughed and punched him lightly on the arm. "He will. Now c'mon. We've got to help Joel."

Jupiter and her father were gathering pieces of

Joel's broken stone arm at the base of the dais. The leader of Olympus looked up at her, grim faced. "I fear this may not work. Please, take this. We must see what happens." He handed Emily a small piece of stone.

The smile dropped from Emily's face when she looked and saw it was one of Joel's fingers. She enclosed it in her hand. Nothing happened. It remained a cold piece of marble. "What does this mean?"

Jupiter rose. "I am uncertain. But it may mean that once someone has been broken, not even your powers can restore them."

"Are you saying that Emily can't heal Joel?" her father asked.

Behind them, Pegasus whinnied loudly and pounded the floor. He snorted and shook his head.

"No," Emily cried. "Not Joel. I will heal him!"

Before Jupiter could stop her, Emily knelt down and touched Joel's face. It was then she noticed that part of his right ear was missing as well. "Please," she prayed as she closed her eyes. "Please, Joel, wake up! I can't go on without you here."

Finally the stone beneath her hand started to warm. "It's working!"

Paelen knelt down beside her, and Pegasus pressed in closer. Together they focused on the jagged edge of the break in the stone of his right arm.

"Come on," Paelen urged. "Grow back!"

Joel was gradually coming back to himself. His flesh returned, but they watched as the rough edge of the break folded in on itself. The wound closed and covered with healed skin. But there was no new growth. They realized that his right ear and arm were not going to grow back.

"Joel?" Emily said softly.

"Em?" Joel said as he opened his eyes. Just like Paelen, he looked wildly around the room. "The queen?" he cried as he looked back up to the cage. The four stone guardians were still holding up the roof, but the cage was empty.

"She is safe," Jupiter calmed, "thanks to your bravery."

"Joel, we've got something to tell you," Emily said.

Before she could warn him, Joel sat up and immediately noticed the change in himself. "Where's my arm?" he asked in confusion. Fear rose on his face. His left hand reached up and felt the healed stump at his right shoulder. "Emily, where's my arm?"

He looked desperately at Paelen, and his eyes flew around the room. "Tell me. Where's my arm?"

Emily quickly embraced him. "I'm so sorry," she cried as tears filled her eyes. "The Gorgons turned you to stone. You fell over, and your arm broke. I tried to fix it, but it wouldn't work. It's gone, Joel."

"Gone?" Joel said in a haunted whisper. "Gone where?"

Emily sniffed and let him go. She reached for her handkerchief to collect her tears. As she wiped them away, she watched Paelen hand over the stone finger to Joel.

"It shattered," Paelen said. "Emily tried, but—"

Joel took it in his left hand. "Is this really mine?"

Paelen nodded. "Do not worry, Joel. I promise you, Vulcan can make you a new arm, and I will help. It will be a better one. Look at the legs he built for himself."

"And my brace," Emily added. "He can do it, Joel. I know he can."

Emily's heart broke as Joel's haunted eyes lingered on his stump. He was in deep shock. "It doesn't hurt a bit," he muttered softly. "It should, but it doesn't."

"Emily's powers have healed you as much as they possibly could," Jupiter said. "I, too, am sorry she could not restore your arm. You have my word, Joel: Vulcan will have everything he needs to build you a new one."

Joel climbed awkwardly to his feet. His eyes scanned all the statues in the room. Several had been knocked over and broken in the battle. He saw a couple of Nirad statues without their heads. "What about them?" he asked.

Jupiter inhaled deeply and let it out slowly. "I am sorry to say, but most of the broken ones are dead. Perhaps some of those with lesser breaks may survive, but if Emily could not restore your arm, it is doubtful she can do anything for those who have suffered major breaks to their bodies or heads. We must all grieve their loss."

"Joel, are you all right?" Emily asked softly as she reached out to him.

He looked down at her. Tears were rimming his

eyes, but he refused to let them fall. He shook his head. "Not really." He embraced her tightly and whispered in her ear. "But I will be."

Next Emily approached Diana and Apollo. She felt a great sense of relief at the joyful and heated reunion between the twins and their father. Seeing their shining faces lightened the mood as Diana cursed and complained at not being the one to destroy the Gorgons. While his sister ranted, Apollo took Joel quietly aside and promised to teach him to fight one-armed.

The throne room was still crowded with statues. Emily's father lifted her onto Pegasus, who took her around to heal the Nirads one by one. The queen and prince were at her side, ready to reassure all the Nirads as they came back to themselves.

"Hey, do not forget fly boy over here," Paelen called as he stood beside the Cupid statue. "Personally, I believe he looks good just as he is. But Venus may not be too pleased if we leave him like this."

Emily leaned forward on Pegasus. "Pegs, I forgot all about him!"

Pegasus turned his head back to her and nickered

softly. There was a twinkle in his big brown eyes. Emily was certain the stallion was laughing at her.

"It's not funny, Pegs. How could I forget about Cupid? Please don't tell him. He'll never forgive me!"

Pegasus carried Emily over to Cupid. She reached down and touched the top of the winged Olympian's head. As Cupid returned to flesh, he panicked and cried out.

"Calm down!" Paelen said. "You are safe. Emily saved you, and the Gorgons are dust."

Cupid looked up at Emily on Pegasus. He gave the room a final check to be certain, then cleared his throat, fluttered his healed wings, and adjusted his tunic in embarrassment. "I was not panicking, Paelen," he corrected abruptly. "I was concerned that the Flame might be in danger."

Paelen started to laugh and slapped Cupid playfully on his wings. "Do not worry about my Emily. She can take care of herself!"

THE TASK OF RESTORING THE STONE NIRADS
in the throne room seemed to take forever.

"Come on, Pegs," Emily said softly. "Let's go get
Tange and the others back." She went to move toward
Tange and the three others supporting the top of the
gold cage. Segan and Toban were standing beside
Tange, their heads lowered. The queen was lightly
stroking Tange's back.

"Emily, stop," Jupiter called. He was standing with
Diana, Apollo, and several large Nirads.

"I'm just going up to help Tange."

"You cannot help him," Jupiter said. "Leave him
be, as he is."

Emily frowned and slid off Pegasus's back. She

clung to his wing as she hopped over to Jupiter. "But I can bring him back. If you and a few Nirads support the cage, no one should get hurt."

Jupiter sadly shook his head. "You must not do it."

Emily's heart started to race. "Why? Tange was the first Nirad to be kind to me! He showed me there was more to them than the monsters I thought they were. Please, Jupiter, I've got to help him!"

Diana stepped closer and put her arm around Emily. "Listen to Father, Emily. He knows what he is talking about."

Emily shook her head and pulled away. "No, he doesn't." She looked at Jupiter. "Tange is good—he really helped us. Why won't you let me help him?"

"I am not forbidding you to help him," Jupiter said kindly. "I am asking you not to. Let me explain—I think you will agree with me."

Jupiter moved closer to Emily and started to support her. With Pegasus on one side and her father on the other, he led her up to the dais. "Take a good look up there and tell me what you see."

"I see Tange," Emily said, looking up at the stone statue of the Nirad.

"Yes, and what is Tange holding?"

"The top of the cage."

"That is correct," Jupiter said patiently. "What is the cage made of?"

"Gold."

"Not just any gold," Diana added. "That is the same gold as your leg brace and our weapons."

"Olympian gold!" Paelen cried, suddenly understanding. He climbed up to the cage and pointed at the roof. "Emily, look—Tange and the others are holding the gold roof with their four bare hands. It is poisoning them."

"That is correct," Jupiter said sadly. "If you were to touch Tange or any of the others, you would certainly bring them back to life. But even your powers cannot stop the gold's poison from coursing through their systems. They will die in agony. Believe me, child, the kindest thing you can do for them now is to leave them as they are."

Emily was too stunned to speak. She looked up at Tange and saw that the marble of his four hands was black with the poison from the gold. Pain was etched on his orange marble face. That expression was there long before the Gorgons turned him to stone. Tange had known he was dying.

"They knew it would kill them, but they lifted the roof anyway," she said.

"What father would not do the same for his daughter?" Jupiter asked.

"Daughter?"

Jupiter nodded. "Tange was Segan's father. He sacrificed himself for her. The three other Nirads with him are his brothers. They were devoted to their niece. They refused to leave the throne room after Tange was ordered to travel to your world to get you."

Emily felt her throat constrict as she looked up at the four stone guardians. "Tange is really . . . dead?" she whispered. She looked at her own father. "Dad?"

Her father pulled her into a tight embrace and kissed her on the top of her head. "I'd do the same for you, Em, any day."

Segan and Toban left their father and came off the dais. Emily saw dark tears flowing down the queen's young face. She approached Emily and uttered a few soft words.

Diana stroked Emily's hair. "Tange told her how

much you reminded him of her. You share the same spirit and bravery. She says he would have died to protect you, too." Emily felt her heart breaking. As deep sobs wracked her, the pink Nirad queen put her arms around her and held her tight. Standing together, the two shared their grief.

It took several long and exhausting days to restore the lives of several thousand stone Nirads throughout the land. The Gorgon attack had been brutal and extended far beyond the palace limits.

Though still very quiet, Joel was slowly getting used to life with one arm. As Emily rode on Pegasus's back, she watched him, her father, Paelen, and Chrysaor playing a form of soccer with a group of Nirad children and Prince Toban. Chrysaor and Joel were on opposite sides, and Chrysaor snuck up behind Joel and tackled him down to the ground. The winged boar invited all the Nirad children on his team to join in the pile-on. Emily smiled as she heard Joel's shouts and, finally, laughter coming from the bottom of the pile.

"He'll be fine, Pegs," Emily said softly as she patted his neck and got back to work restoring more Nirads to life.

Jupiter, Diana, Apollo, and Cupid entered the Solar Stream to gather the other Olympians home. With so many worlds to search, they knew it would take some time to get everyone back to Olympus.

At the end of yet another seemingly endless day, Emily was relieved to restore the last Nirad. She slipped off Pegasus's back and hopped up to the lilac Nirad. With the queen at her side, she reached out and touched this final victim.

With the knowledge that this was the last statue, exhaustion pressed down on her. She had lost track of just how many there were, but it was more than she had imagined possible. She was grateful that her power to heal had been enough. As the last statue began to warm, she knew that every Nirad that could be saved had been. A sharp stab of pain pierced through her when she thought of Tange. Like the loss of her mother, his death was a pain she knew she would carry with her for the rest of her life.

The final Nirad came back to life screaming. After Segan spoke reassuringly to him, he bowed his head and knelt before his queen. Emily shared the Nirad's joy when his young children came rushing up to him and threw their tiny arms around him.

Queen Segan looked at Emily and nodded. They didn't need to speak the same language to understand. It was done. Emily smiled back. She hopped up to Pegasus's head and kissed him on the muzzle.

"We did it, Pegs," she said softly.

Emily stroked the stallion's face and looked at the strange land around her. The Nirad world was slowly coming back to life. The skies were still as dark and cloudy as ever, with the strange batlike creatures circling high overhead. There was still no plant life in sight. The earth was as black and dusty as the day she arrived. And yet, to Emily, it was beautiful.

"Em!" Joel called.

Emily looked up and saw Joel and Toban riding Chrysaor. Joel was holding on to the boar's ear with his left hand, and he was smiling. Paelen was flying beside them using his winged sandals. They touched down beside her.

"Emily, you and the queen must come back to the palace immediately," Paelen said.

"What's happening?" Emily asked.

Joel's smile grew. That alone was enough to make the day perfect for Emily. Her friend was going to be all right in the end. "Come back and see for yourselves," he said, laughing.

Emily looked over at Segan. "There's room on Pegasus for the both of us."

When Pegasus took off into the sky, the queen cried out in fear mixed with roaring excitement. Her four arms nearly squeezed the breath out of Emily as she clung to her for dear life. They flew over the bustling village and heard the calls and saw the waving of the Nirads on the ground. Finally they touched down outside the palace.

"It's in the throne room," Paelen said excitedly as he dashed up the steps into the palace. "Hurry up!"

"What is?" Emily asked.

"C'mon," Joel cried anxiously as he and Toban climbed off Chrysaor and they followed Paelen in.

Emily looked back at the queen and shrugged. "Let's go see."

Pegasus carried Emily and Segan up the steps of the palace. She hadn't been back here since the horrific battle. The scene of so much suffering and loss still disturbed her, and she hadn't been able to return. As Pegasus's golden hooves clopped on the marble floor, Emily heard voices. Lots and lots of voices.

"Hurry up, you slowpokes," her father called as he appeared at the entrance to the throne room. He was clean shaven again, and his hair had been neatly trimmed. But best of all, a broad smile spread across his face.

Emily's eyes grew large as Pegasus trotted into the throne room. The room was filled with Olympians and Nirads gathered around long banquet tables. Ambrosia and the black Nirad food sat side by side at the tables. Laughter rang out as the great celebration started.

The Gorgon thrones had gone, and there was no dais. Emily looked back at Segan. They both noticed the same thing. The golden cage with Tange and his three brothers was also missing.

At the huge head table sat Jupiter; his wife, Juno; and his brothers, Neptune and Pluto. Diana and Apollo sat at their mother's side, while several chairs remained empty between Jupiter and Pluto.

When Jupiter saw Emily, Segan, and Pegasus standing at the entrance, he stood and called the room to order. Everyone turned to face the leader of Olympus.

"Olympians and Nirads, we have gathered together to celebrate the peace between our two worlds." Jupiter held up his goblet of Nectar. "And together we mourn the loss of family and friends. We all honor our dead!"

Cheers rang out around the room as everyone raised their goblets in salute to the fallen.

Jupiter raised his cup a second time and called the room back to silence. "We are also here to thank someone very special." As he spoke, Jupiter was looking directly at Emily.

She felt her face flushing and her heart pounding. Pegasus turned his head back to her. He nodded and nickered loudly in agreement, while Segan, with her arms still around Emily's waist, gave her a light embrace and spoke softly. Paelen approached on one side of her and rested his hand on her leg; Joel and Chrysaor approached from the other. Her father reached up and took her hand and gave it a reassuring squeeze.

"None of us would be here today," Jupiter continued, "were it not for the bravery and strength of Emily Jacobs and Pegasus. My family—Olympians and Nirads—I give you the Flame of Olympus!"

Epilogue

EMILY AND PEGASUS COULDN'T HAVE BEEN any happier.

Since their return to Olympus, trade between Olympians and the Nirads had started. Nirads could often be seen walking the Olympian streets.

It wasn't long after their return that Joel had a new arm fashioned by Vulcan and his best armorers. He was proud to show it off to anyone who cared to look at it. It gave him remarkable strength, and for the first time since they met, he was able to beat Paelen at arm wrestling. Like Emily's new leg brace, it was made entirely of Olympian silver. Vulcan abandoned the use of gold because of the danger it posed to all the Nirads.

But what made Emily's life complete was having her father with her and her friends there in Olympus. She now had everything she could have dreamed of.

"Hi, Dad," she said, a smile rising to her lips as she greeted him.

"What are you smiling at?" He laughed, his dimples pinching in his cheeks.

"Nothing," Emily said. He was a sight to see in his white tunic and sandals—a far cry from his New York City Police Department uniform. He had settled in easily. "I'm just so glad to see you again."

"Me too," he said as he reached up to take her hand. "It's been a very long road for both of us, kiddo. But we've made it. Your mother would be so proud of you." His bright smile returned. "I need you and Pegasus to come with me for a moment—we have something to show you. The Nirads just delivered it."

"What is it?"

"A monument," he said. "It represents the union between the two worlds. But Jupiter says he won't have it in his garden without your approval."

"Why does Jupiter need my approval?"

"Come along, and I think you'll understand."

They moved through the beautiful, fragrant gardens at Jupiter's palace. Paelen and Joel came running up to her. "They have just finished setting it up."

Ahead of them, Emily saw a newly constructed rock garden. Huge black stones were set up to form a circle, and the ground was covered with black Nirad soil. As Pegasus approached, the crowds of Olympians and Nirads parted to let them through. Emily sucked in her breath when she saw what was at the center of the circle.

"Tange," she hushed.

Ahead of her stood the stone Tange and his three brothers. There were chains of the most beautiful Olympian flowers woven around their necks. Although pain was still etched on their faces, they no longer supported the gold roof of the queen's cage. They now held a black marble slab that supported a throne. Seated on the throne was the statue of an older pink female Nirad also surrounded by fragrant flowers.

"She was the original queen," Paelen explained softly. "When the Gorgons arrived in the Nirad world, the first thing they did was turn her to stone and smash her to bits. That was how Segan came to power. Since the Nirads do not grieve their dead the same way we do, they put the broken pieces of their queen back together and offered this to us as a way to remember the struggle that brought our two worlds together."

Beside the statue, Jupiter and Juno stood with Queen Segan and Prince Toban. They acknowledged Emily with waves and friendly nods. Jupiter stepped forward and reached up to help her climb off the stallion. Together they walked up to the monument.

"Emily, the queen and prince have given us their parents to safeguard. They want to show us their gratitude for what you did for their people. However, I explained that seeing Tange every day may cause you pain, knowing that you must never touch him or his brothers."

Emily looked at the statue of Tange, then over to Segan. She could see the anxious expression on her face. She felt her own father's reassuring presence behind her and was grateful to have everyone she cared about here, including Tange.

She walked up to the queen. "Thank you so much

for trusting us. I promise you, we will take care of your family. You and all your people are welcome to come visit them anytime." She looked over at Jupiter. "Right?"

"Of course," he agreed as he nodded. "Queen Segan, you have my word that from this day forward, Nirads will always be welcome in Olympus."

As the cheers rose and a new celebration started, Emily made her way back to Pegasus. She climbed onto the stallion's back and sat in silent contentment, watching the gathering around her. A large banquet was planned for later that evening. But for the moment, she was happy just to stay where she was.

She noticed Paelen, Joel, Toban, and Chrysaor huddled together. Paelen looked up at her and waved as a crooked grin rose to his face. Something about his expression told her they were up to more mischief, and she knew that before long, she would be invited to join in the fun with her friends.

Beside Tange's statue, her father, Diana, and the Nirad queen were speaking quietly. She smiled as her father wrapped his arm protectively around Segan's shoulders.

While he lived, Tange had treated her like his own child. He had protected her and risked his life for her. She hoped that, somehow, Tange knew her father would do the same for his daughter.

Not far away, Cupid stood with his mother, Venus. The feathers on his wings were neatly groomed, and his hair was combed perfectly into place. He was wearing a new tunic and looked impossibly handsome. She wondered if he had ever told his mother what he had done to the CRU agents at the Red Apple. Emily doubted it. After a moment Cupid felt her eyes on him, and he looked at her. He nodded his head and smiled his most radiant smile. Emily smiled back and waved. Cupid had surprised her. He had overcome his fears of the Nirads and come through for them. She was grateful to call him her friend.

Pegasus nickered and looked up at her.

"Don't worry, Pegs," she said softly, stroking the new feathers on his wings. "Cupid was just a silly crush. I'm over him." As she spoke, her eyes trailed over to Paelen and Joel, and her smile increased. She doubted if even Pegasus knew who really held her heart.

Emily looked down into the stallion's beautiful white face and laughed. "What do you say we go for a quick flight before the party gets started?"

Pegasus whinnied and turned from the crowd. He trotted into a full gallop, opened his wings, and carried Emily up into the sky.

THE ADVENTURE CONTINUES
IN BOOK 3:

The New Olympians

THE ROAR OF THE CROWD WAS DEAFENING. Olympians sprang to their feet cheering on the very first inter-Olympian soccer match. The Solar Streamers were playing Hercules's Heroes, but this was no ordinary soccer match. The scene on the field was as impressive and extraordinary as you would expect on Olympus.

When Joel first proposed the event, he was amazed by how many Olympians wanted to get involved. Now, with a full stadium of spectators cheering him on, Joel, captain of the Solar Streamers, expertly maneuvered the ball down the pitch and between the legs of a charging satyr. The half goat, half boy turned and charged after him as if his very life depended on it.

Joel broke through the defense line and passed the black-and-white ball to his Olympian teammate and friend Paelen, who dashed forward to get into position. The winged boar, Chrysaor, caught up with Joel and drove away the Hercules's Heroes defenders, Mercury and Minerva, while Pegasus flew across the field over a line of centaurs and giants and called to Paelen to pass the ball. With a quick kick, the ball was in the winged stallion's possession.

Emily sat on the sidelines beside Jupiter. She marveled at how adept Pegasus was at a sport he and the other Olympians had only just learned. Pegasus was able to keep moving forward while the ball remained in play between his four hooves.

Suddenly a satyr ducked beneath Pegasus and stole the ball away. Moving swiftly on his goat legs, he kicked it back to his teammates. But no sooner did the opposing team have the ball than a young female centaur on Joel's team made a move that caused the crowd to cheer even louder. Leaping gracefully into the air, she blocked a high kick with her brown equine body. As the ball touched down on the ground, she expertly kicked it forward to Joel.

Running toward the goal line, Joel and Paelen kept the soccer ball moving between them. Finally Joel moved into position to shoot it at the goal.

"Go for it, Joel!" Emily shouted from her seat. "Shoot!"

The opposing side's goalkeeper was a terrifying sight. The Sphinx reared on her lion's haunches, spread her arms and eagle's wings wide, and prepared to block Joel's shot.

With one quick dart away from a young Nirad defender, Joel kicked the ball. It flew in the air and then seemed to arch as if it had a life all its own. It caught the upper bar of the goalposts and flew into the net above the head of the Sphinx.

When the goalkeeper saw the ball enter her goal, she roared in fury and sprang forward, tackling Joel to the ground.

Emily's heart nearly stopped. The Sphinx had Joel pinned down with her large lion paws. She threw back her head, roaring a second time, and raised a fearsome paw in the air, as if to tear into him with her sharpened claws.

"Jupiter, stop her!" Emily cried to the leader of

Olympus standing beside her. "The Sphinx will tear him apart!"

But instead of moving to stop the attack, Jupiter cheered louder and started to applaud. He leaned closer to her. "My dear child, Alexis may be short-tempered, but she knows this is just a game. Joel is perfectly safe." Jupiter paused and looked at all the men in the stands raising their hands and cheering. "I am certain that Joel is the subject of many Olympians' envy."

Out on the field, the players on Joel's team continued to celebrate the goal, unconcerned by the goalkeeper's assault on their star player. Finally the Sphinx brushed back the hair from Joel's eyes, leaned forward, and kissed him full and long on the lips.

"Foul!" shouted Emily as she ran furiously onto the field. Pushing between the players, she shoved the goalkeeper. "Get off him!"

As the Sphinx climbed slowly off Joel, her serpent's tail swished playfully in the air. She narrowed her green eyes and smiled mischievously at Emily. "Is the Flame of Olympus jealous?"

The Sphinx may have looked ferocious and dangerous with her lion's body, eagle's wings, and serpent's tail, but she had the head and upper body of a young woman. In fact, she was breathtakingly beautiful.

Emily paused and looked from Alexis to Joel. Seeing him on the ground with his beaming smile, warm brown eyes, and handsome face, Emily was stunned to realize that she was very jealous.

"Of course not!" she shot back. "But kissing the opposing players isn't part of the game."

The smile never left the Sphinx's face as she padded lithely back to her position in front of the goal. She looked playfully over her shoulder, flicking her long raven hair. "Pity. It should be."

Paelen reached forward and, with Emily's help, lifted the stunned Joel to his feet. As they brushed him off, Paelen stole a look back at Alexis. "Wow!" he breathed. "That was some kiss. You are so lucky!"

The color in Joel's cheeks brightened further as Alexis called, "I will see you later, Joel."

"Don't count on it," Emily fired back. She ignored the soft chuckles coming from the Sphinx and returned her attention to Joel. During his time in Olympus, he had grown taller and more muscular from all the physical work in Vulcan's workshop. Joel's growth spurt was the cause of much complaint from Vulcan, as he constantly had to enlarge the silver mechanical right arm that replaced the one Joel had lost in the fight against the gorgons.

"Did Alexis hurt you?" Emily asked.

Joel looked back at the Sphinx curiously and then shook his head. "Not at all."

Paelen smiled his crooked grin, then pursed his lips in an exaggerated kiss. "Perhaps bruise your tender lips?"

"What?" Joel cried. He shoved Paelen away as his cheeks reddened deeper. "Stop that. I'm fine! Can we please get back to the match?"

As the players returned to their positions, Pegasus escorted Emily to her seat on the sidelines. The stallion nickered softly, and Emily saw an extra sparkle in his beautiful dark eyes. Pegasus was laughing.

"What are you laughing at?" she challenged.

Emily's teacher, Vesta, approached, overhearing the conversation. "Pegasus believes the Sphinx was correct. You are jealous of her."

"Jealous of Alexis? That's crazy," Emily said. "For

one, she's just an overgrown, green-eyed, flying house cat. And for two, Joel and I are friends. That's all."

The smile on Vesta's face grew. "Of course you are, dear. . . ."

"We're friends," Emily insisted as she returned to her seat. "That's all! Now, Pegs, your team is waiting for you; you'd better get back."

Pegasus let out a loud, laughing whinny before trotting back to the field of play to take his position on Joel's team.

As the match progressed, the score remained tied. While the Sphinx was the Hercules's Heroes goalkeeper, Joel's team had a huge orange Nirad called Tirk guarding their end. With his four arms, he proved a capable goalie and rarely allowed the ball into the net.

"That's quite a match going on out there. But I'm not too sure if flying up and down the field is in the rulebook."

Emily jumped at the sound of her father's voice. "Dad!" She threw her arms around his neck. "I've missed you."

He had been away from Olympus with Diana and

Apollo for what felt like ages. They were leading a small team back to Earth to determine if Jupiter's ban on visits should be lifted. The Olympians had heard about human advancements and were curious to learn more. Her father went as an adviser and guide.

When Emily released her father, she welcomed Diana with a firm hug. "I've missed you both. When did you get back?"

"Not long ago," her father said. "We went to the palace first and were told about the big match."

He looked at the pitch and whistled in amazement. "When you told me you and Joel were teaching some of the Olympians to play soccer, it never dawned on me who or what would be playing. I've never seen a more fantastic sight."

Emily looked over at the satyrs, harpies, centaurs, giants and some of the Muses out on the field playing alongside winged creatures never mentioned or even imagined in the ancient myths.

"We tried to teach Cerberus to play, but it didn't work," Emily continued. "His three heads kept fighting over the ball and tearing it to shreds. It was the same with the Cyclops. With only one eye, he kept missing the ball and got really frustrated. He even tore down the goal in a rage. Jupiter finally had to ask him to keep score. You can see him over there." She pointed to the end of the field, where the giant Cyclops was updating the scoreboard with each goal. "But most of the other Olympians seem to enjoy the game."

Their eyes were drawn back to the field, where a satyr had broken free of the giant guard and was rushing with the ball toward Joel's team's goal. As she neared the net, Paelen appeared from the left to block the kick. But the satyr was faster and ducked away from him. With a second quick dart, she kicked the ball between the Nirad's four arms, and it entered the net.

The crowd exploded with excitement and stood cheering. Emily looked around and smiled ruefully at the Olympians. She glanced back to her father. "I don't think they fully understand the concept of supporting one side or the other. Everyone celebrates when there is a goal—it doesn't matter which team made it."

Her father nodded. "Maybe they've got the right

idea. We could use more sportsmanship like that back in our world." He focused on Emily again. "You love soccer. Even with your leg brace, you can move just as well as before your leg was hurt. Why aren't you out there playing?"

Emily hesitated before answering. "I didn't feel like playing today. I wanted to watch with Jupiter so I could explain the rules. Not that anyone actually follows them."

Emily watched her father's face, relieved that he accepted her explanation without question. Emily wanted very much to play, but she couldn't. She couldn't because she couldn't trust herself.

Since her return from the Nirad world, where they'd defeated the gorgons, Emily had mastered the power of the Flame that lived deep within her. She could now control it fully. But recently more powers had surfaced. Powers that went beyond the Flame. Where objects moved by themselves, or sometimes, if she became very frustrated or upset, vanished completely. Vesta hadn't mentioned more powers. Emily wondered if her teacher even realized there were others. But too many things were happening around her. Until Emily could better understand and control them, she wasn't going to risk hurting her friends.

The match ended with Joel's team losing by one goal. A celebratory banquet was planned for later that evening. Emily walked with her father and Pegasus back to the apartment they shared with Joel and Paelen in Jupiter's palace.

"I am going to tell Jupiter that I don't think it's a good idea for Olympians to visit Earth. There are just too many dangers. Our world has changed far too much for them now. They had no idea how different or advanced it is."

"But after everything they've heard from us, they're all so anxious to visit," Emily insisted.

"I know," he agreed. "The big problem is that Olympians aren't human. Very few of them look even remotely human. Can you imagine what would happen if a centaur or even the Cyclops were to visit our world? In the past, they were accepted as gods, but today . . ." He paused and looked back to Pegasus. "Look what happened to him in New York."

Pegasus snorted and nickered loudly. Emily reached over and stroked the stallion's neck. Memories flashed to the surface of her mind. Pegasus had been shot by the secret government agency the Central Research Unit, and taken to their hidden facility on Governors Island. The sight of her beloved stallion lying prone on the floor and struggling for each breath caused a stab of pain in her heart, even now.

Emily looked back at her father and nodded. "It wasn't just Pegasus who was hurt. Look what the CRU did to Cupid. Their helicopters nearly killed him, despite Olympians being immortal. If they stop eating ambrosia, they become vulnerable, and it's too easy for them to get hurt."

"Or captured," her father added. "Personally, I don't think it's a good idea at all. I'm going to tell Jupiter this. Olympians are an amazing people, and I don't want to see anything happen to them."

As they continued to walk down the tranquil, cobbled road, the clopping sound of Pegasus's golden hooves was the only thing to disturb the calm of Olympus. After a long silence, Emily's father spoke again.

"Your aunt Maureen sends her love."

"You saw her?"

He shook his head. "There were CRU agents posted around her building; we couldn't get near her. But I did call and tell her we are fine. She asked a lot of questions, but I'm sure her line is bugged. So I told her we're in hiding but together and safe."

"I wish we could see her again," Emily said wistfully.

"Me too," her father agreed. "Maybe one day soon we can go back for a real visit. Just you and me."

Emily brightened. "That would be wonderful."

When they arrived at their apartment, Emily's eyes flew wide at the assortment of gifts her father and Diana had brought back for her, Joel, and Paelen: clothes, music, and some of Emily's favorite snacks, like salted peanuts and her real weakness, marshmallows. There was even an assortment of chocolate bars just for Paelen.

Emily noticed a stack of newspapers. She had never been interested in the news when she lived in New York, but now that she was living in Olympus permanently, she craved to learn what was happening in her city.

Top of the pile was the New York Times. A photograph on the front page caught her attention.

Was that Pegasus?

Emily immediately snatched it up, curious.

Yes, it was definitely Pegasus—but without wings!

She read the caption under the photograph.

RECORD BREAKER! TORNADO WARNING

WINS TRIPLE CROWN WITH GREATEST TIME

AND DISTANCE EVER RECORDED.

"Tornado Warning?" Emily muttered aloud as she read the article about the winning horse breaking every record in the history of horse racing.

"Look at that face," her father said lightly. "He looks just like Pegasus, doesn't he? His body and legs are darker gray, but if he were all white, it could have been Pegasus. Tornado Warning is everywhere and causing quite a stir. They haven't had a Triple Crown winner like him since Secretariat—and Tornado's even broken his records!"

Emily barely heard the knocking on the door. As her father went to answer it, she continued to scan the article.

"Pegs, you've got to see this." Emily held up the

newspaper for the stallion. "Look at his face. He really does look like you. I mean, you two could be twins!"

When Pegasus looked at the photographs, Emily could sense he was greatly disturbed. Apart from the color, Tornado Warning was identical. His size and shape were the same. All that was missing were the wings and golden hooves. Emily looked at the stallion. "How is this possible?"

"So you have seen the newspapers." Diana had entered the living room and approached Pegasus. "Is there something you wish to tell me? Did you get up to some mischief while you were in Emily's world?"

Pegasus snorted angrily and stamped a golden hoof.

Emily frowned and then shook her head. "That's not possible. Tornado couldn't be his son. Look here, the paper says Tornado Warning is three years old. But Pegasus only came to our world last year."

"But he does look just like you, my friend," Diana said softly as she stroked Pegasus's face. "What else could it be?"

Emily's father, Steve, shrugged. "Maybe he's just a

very handsome horse who happens to look a lot like Pegasus."

Emily studied her father's face and realized he didn't see Pegasus the same way she and the other Olympians did. On the surface, Pegasus could look mostly like a horse, but there was a big difference. It was something that she could plainly see, but her father couldn't. Pegasus was more than a horse, much greater than one. It was in his intelligent eyes and the way he held himself, that created the aura surrounding him that said, "I am not a mere horse."

Olympus had many horses and some, like Pegasus, had wings. But none of them were remotely like Pegasus. He was unique—until now.

"You're wrong, Dad," Emily insisted. "Tornado Warning doesn't just look like Pegasus, he's identical to him."

Diana put her arm around Emily and gave her a light squeeze. "Well, whatever it is, that horse, Tornado Warning, is in your world while we are all here in Olympus." Diana abruptly changed the subject. "Now, would you like to try on some of the new clothes that your father and I chose for you?"

Emily looked at Diana and saw there was something the tall woman was not saying aloud. A secret message that said they would speak later. She nodded. "You're right. Let's forget Tornado Warning. I want to see what you've brought back."

Molly Bigelow is NOT your average girl. She's one of an elite crew assigned the task of policing and protecting the zombie population of New York. *The Hunger Games* author Suzanne Collins says *Dead City* "breathes new life into the zombie genre."

EBOOK EDITIONS
ALSO AVAILABLE

Looking for another great book?
Find it in the middle.

in
the
middle

BOOKS

Fun, fantastic books for kids
in the in-beTWEEN age.

Inthe MiddleBooks.com

THE NEW
OLYMPIANS

Also by Kate O'Hearn

The Flame of Olympus
Olympus at War
Origins of Olympus

THE NEW OLYMPIANS

KATE O'HEARN

Aladdin

New York London Toronto Sydney New Delhi

ALADDIN

An imprint of Simon & Schuster Children's Publishing Division
1230 Avenue of the Americas, New York, NY 10020
First Aladdin paperback edition December 2014
Text copyright © 2012 by Kate O'Hearn
Cover illustration copyright © 2014 by Jason Chan
Originally published in Great Britain in 2012
Published by arrangement with Hachette UK
Also available in an Aladdin hardcover edition.
All rights reserved, including the right of reproduction in whole or in part in any form.
ALADDIN is a trademark of Simon & Schuster, Inc., and related logo
is a registered trademark of Simon & Schuster, Inc.
For information about special discounts for bulk purchases, please contact Simon & Schuster
Special Sales at 1-866-506-1949 or business@simonandschuster.com.
The Simon & Schuster Speakers Bureau can bring authors to your live event. For more
information or to book an event contact the Simon & Schuster Speakers Bureau at
1-866-248-3049 or visit our website at www.simonspeakers.com.
Cover designed by Karin Paprocki
Interior designed by Michael Rosamilia
The text of this book was set in Adobe Garamond.
Manufactured in the United States of America 0815 OFF
4 6 8 10 9 7 5 3
The Library of Congress has cataloged the hardcover edition as follows:
O'Hearn, Kate.
The new Olympians / by Kate O'Hearn. — First Aladdin hardcover edition.
pages cm. — (Pegasus ; [3])
"Originally published in Great Britain in 2012; published by arrangement with Hachette UK."
Summary: "Pegasus and Emily investigate a series of incidents back on Earth, and discover that
the CRU has been cloning Olympians"—Provided by publisher.
ISBN 978-1-4424-4415-7 (hc)
[1. Pegasus (Greek mythology)—Fiction. 2. Mythology, Greek—Fiction.
3. Cloning—Fiction. 4. Fantasy.] I. Title.
PZ7.O4137New 2014
[Fic]—dc23
2012051367
ISBN 978-1-4424-4416-4 (pbk)
ISBN 978-1-4424-4417-1 (eBook)

*For Charlie, a white fifteen-year-old carriage horse
that collapsed and died on the streets of New York City,
October 2011. He soars with Pegasus now.*

*It is for Charlie and other abused horses like him
that we will keep fighting and shouting until our voices
are finally heard and the suffering ends. . . .*

THE ROAR OF THE CROWD WAS DEAFENING.
Olympians sprang to their feet cheering on the very
first inter-Olympian soccer match. The Solar Streamers were playing Hercules's Heroes, but this was no
ordinary soccer match. The scene on the field was as
impressive and extraordinary as you would expect on
Olympus.

When Joel first proposed the event, he was amazed
by how many Olympians wanted to get involved. Now,
with a full stadium of spectators cheering him on,
Joel, captain of the Solar Streamers, expertly maneuvered the ball down the pitch and between the legs of
a charging satyr. The half goat, half boy turned and
charged after him as if his very life depended on it.

Joel broke through the defense line and passed the black-and-white ball to his Olympian teammate and friend Paelen, who dashed forward to get into position. The winged boar, Chrysaor, caught up with Joel and drove away the Hercules's Heroes defenders, Mercury and Minerva, while Pegasus flew across the field over a line of centaurs and giants and called to Paelen to pass the ball. With a quick kick, the ball was in the winged stallion's possession.

Emily sat on the sidelines beside Jupiter. She marveled at how adept Pegasus was at a sport he and the other Olympians had only just learned. Pegasus was able to keep moving forward while the ball remained in play between his four hooves.

Suddenly a satyr ducked beneath Pegasus and stole the ball away. Moving swiftly on his goat legs, he kicked it back to his teammates. But no sooner did the opposing team have the ball than a young female centaur on Joel's team made a move that caused the crowd to cheer even louder. Leaping gracefully into the air, she blocked a high kick with her brown equine body. As the ball touched down on the ground, she expertly kicked it forward to Joel.

Running toward the goal line, Joel and Paelen kept the soccer ball moving between them. Finally Joel moved into position to shoot it at the goal.

"Go for it, Joel!" Emily shouted from her seat. "Shoot!"

The opposing side's goalkeeper was a terrifying sight. The Sphinx reared on her lion's haunches, spread her arms and eagle's wings wide, and prepared to block Joel's shot.

With one quick dart away from a young Nirad defender, Joel kicked the ball. It flew in the air and then seemed to arch as if it had a life all its own. It caught the upper bar of the goalposts and flew into the net above the head of the Sphinx.

When the goalkeeper saw the ball enter her goal, she roared in fury and sprang forward, tackling Joel to the ground.

Emily's heart nearly stopped. The Sphinx had Joel pinned down with her large lion paws. She threw back her head, roaring a second time, and raised a fearsome paw in the air, as if to tear into him with her sharpened claws.

"Jupiter, stop her!" Emily cried to the leader of

Olympus standing beside her. "The Sphinx will tear him apart!"

But instead of moving to stop the attack, Jupiter cheered louder and started to applaud. He leaned closer to her. "My dear child, Alexis may be short-tempered, but she knows this is just a game. Joel is perfectly safe." Jupiter paused and looked at all the men in the stands raising their hands and cheering. "I am certain that Joel is the subject of many Olympians' envy."

Out on the field, the players on Joel's team continued to celebrate the goal, unconcerned by the goalkeeper's assault on their star player. Finally the Sphinx brushed back the hair from Joel's eyes, leaned forward, and kissed him full and long on the lips.

"Foul!" shouted Emily as she ran furiously onto the field. Pushing between the players, she shoved the goalkeeper. "Get off him!"

As the Sphinx climbed slowly off Joel, her serpent's tail swished playfully in the air. She narrowed her green eyes and smiled mischievously at Emily. "Is the Flame of Olympus jealous?"

The Sphinx may have looked ferocious and dangerous with her lion's body, eagle's wings, and serpent's tail, but she had the head and upper body of a young woman. In fact, she was breathtakingly beautiful.

Emily paused and looked from Alexis to Joel. Seeing him on the ground with his beaming smile, warm brown eyes, and handsome face, Emily was stunned to realize that she was very jealous.

"Of course not!" she shot back. "But kissing the opposing players isn't part of the game."

The smile never left the Sphinx's face as she padded lithely back to her position in front of the goal. She looked playfully over her shoulder, flicking her long raven hair. "Pity. It should be."

Paelen reached forward and, with Emily's help, lifted the stunned Joel to his feet. As they brushed him off, Paelen stole a look back at Alexis. "Wow!" he breathed. "That was some kiss. You are so lucky!"

The color in Joel's cheeks brightened further as Alexis called, "I will see you later, Joel."

"Don't count on it," Emily fired back. She ignored the soft chuckles coming from the Sphinx and returned her attention to Joel. During his time in

Olympus, he had grown taller and more muscular from all the physical work in Vulcan's workshop. Joel's growth spurt was the cause of much complaint from Vulcan, as he constantly had to enlarge the silver mechanical right arm that replaced the one Joel had lost in the fight against the gorgons.

"Did Alexis hurt you?" Emily asked.

Joel looked back at the Sphinx curiously and then shook his head. "Not at all."

Paelen smiled his crooked grin, then pursed his lips in an exaggerated kiss. "Perhaps bruise your tender lips?"

"What?" Joel cried. He shoved Paelen away as his cheeks reddened deeper. "Stop that. I'm fine! Can we please get back to the match?"

As the players returned to their positions, Pegasus escorted Emily to her seat on the sidelines. The stallion nickered softly, and Emily saw an extra sparkle in his beautiful dark eyes. Pegasus was laughing.

"What are you laughing at?" she challenged.

Emily's teacher, Vesta, approached, overhearing the conversation. "Pegasus believes the Sphinx was correct. You are jealous of her."

"Jealous of Alexis? That's crazy," Emily said. "For one, she's just an overgrown, green-eyed, flying house cat. And for two, Joel and I are friends. That's all."

The smile on Vesta's face grew. "Of course you are, dear. . . ."

"We're friends," Emily insisted as she returned to her seat. "That's all! Now, Pegs, your team is waiting for you; you'd better get back."

Pegasus let out a loud, laughing whinny before trotting back to the field of play to take his position on Joel's team.

As the match progressed, the score remained tied. While the Sphinx was the Hercules's Heroes goalkeeper, Joel's team had a huge orange Nirad called Tirk guarding their end. With his four arms, he proved a capable goalie and rarely allowed the ball into the net.

"That's quite a match going on out there. But I'm not too sure if flying up and down the field is in the rulebook."

Emily jumped at the sound of her father's voice. "Dad!" She threw her arms around his neck. "I've missed you."

He had been away from Olympus with Diana and Apollo for what felt like ages. They were leading a small team back to Earth to determine if Jupiter's ban on visits should be lifted. The Olympians had heard about human advancements and were curious to learn more. Her father went as an adviser and guide.

When Emily released her father, she welcomed Diana with a firm hug. "I've missed you both. When did you get back?"

"Not long ago," her father said. "We went to the palace first and were told about the big match."

He looked at the pitch and whistled in amazement. "When you told me you and Joel were teaching some of the Olympians to play soccer, it never dawned on me who or what would be playing. I've never seen a more fantastic sight."

Emily looked over at the satyrs, harpies, centaurs, giants and some of the Muses out on the field playing alongside winged creatures never mentioned or even imagined in the ancient myths.

"We tried to teach Cerberus to play, but it didn't work," Emily continued. "His three heads kept fighting over the ball and tearing it to shreds. It was the same with the Cyclops. With only one eye, he kept missing the ball and got really frustrated. He even tore down the goal in a rage. Jupiter finally had to ask him to keep score. You can see him over there." She pointed to the end of the field, where the giant Cyclops was updating the scoreboard with each goal. "But most of the other Olympians seem to enjoy the game."

Their eyes were drawn back to the field, where a satyr had broken free of the giant guard and was rushing with the ball toward Joel's team's goal. As she neared the net, Paelen appeared from the left to block the kick. But the satyr was faster and she easily got away from him. With a second quick dart, she kicked the ball between the Nirad's four arms, and it entered the net.

The crowd exploded with excitement and stood cheering. Emily looked around and smiled ruefully at the Olympians. She glanced back to her father. "I don't think they fully understand the concept of supporting one side or the other. Everyone celebrates when there is a goal—it doesn't matter which team made it."

Her father nodded. "Maybe they've got the right idea. We could use more sportsmanship like that back in our world." He focused on Emily again. "You love soccer. Even with your leg brace, you can move just as well as before your leg was hurt. Why aren't you out there playing?"

Emily hesitated before answering. "I didn't feel like playing today. I wanted to watch with Jupiter so I could explain the rules. Not that anyone actually follows them."

Emily watched her father's face, relieved that he accepted her explanation without question. Emily wanted very much to play, but she couldn't. She couldn't because she couldn't trust herself.

Since her return from the Nirad world, where they'd defeated the gorgons, Emily had mastered the power of the Flame that lived deep within her. She could now control it fully. But recently more powers had surfaced. Powers that went beyond the Flame. Where objects moved by themselves, or sometimes, if she became very frustrated or upset, vanished completely. Vesta hadn't mentioned more powers. Emily wondered if her teacher even realized there were others. But too many things were happening around her. Until Emily could better understand and control them, she wasn't going to risk hurting her friends.

The match ended with Joel's team losing by one goal. A celebratory banquet was planned for later that evening. Emily walked with her father and Pegasus back to the apartment they shared with Joel and Paelen in Jupiter's palace.

"I am going to tell Jupiter that I don't think it's a good idea for Olympians to visit Earth. There are just too many dangers. Our world has changed far too much for them now. They had no idea how different or advanced it is."

"But after everything they've heard from us, they're all so anxious to visit," Emily insisted.

"I know," he agreed. "The big problem is that Olympians aren't human. Very few of them look even remotely human. Can you imagine what would happen if a centaur or even the Cyclops were to visit our world? In the past, they were accepted as gods, but today . . ." He paused and looked back to Pegasus. "Look what happened to him in New York."

Pegasus snorted and nickered loudly. Emily

reached over and stroked the stallion's neck. Memories flashed to the surface of her mind. Pegasus had been shot by the secret government agency the Central Research Unit, and taken to their hidden facility on Governors Island. The sight of her beloved stallion lying prone on the floor and struggling for each breath caused a stab of pain in her heart, even now.

Emily looked back at her father and nodded. "It wasn't just Pegasus who was hurt. Look what the CRU did to Cupid. Their helicopters nearly killed him, despite Olympians being immortal. If they stop eating ambrosia, they become vulnerable, and it's too easy for them to get hurt."

"Or captured," her father added. "Personally, I don't think it's a good idea at all. I'm going to tell Jupiter this. Olympians are an amazing people, and I don't want to see anything happen to them."

As they continued to walk down the tranquil, cobbled road, the clopping sound of Pegasus's golden hooves was the only thing to disturb the calm of Olympus. After a long silence, Emily's father spoke again.

"Your aunt Maureen sends her love."

"You saw her?"

He shook his head. "There were CRU agents posted around her building; we couldn't get near her. But I did call and tell her we are fine. She asked a lot of questions, but I'm sure her line is bugged. So I told her we're in hiding but together and safe."

"I wish we could see her again," Emily said wistfully.

"Me too," her father agreed. "Maybe one day soon we can go back for a real visit. Just you and me."

Emily brightened. "That would be wonderful."

When they arrived at their apartment, Emily's eyes flew wide at the assortment of gifts her father and Diana had brought back for her, Joel, and Paelen: clothes, music, and some of Emily's favorite snacks, like salted peanuts and her real weakness, marshmallows. There was even an assortment of chocolate bars just for Paelen.

Emily noticed a stack of newspapers. She had never been interested in the news when she lived in New York, but now that she was living in Olympus permanently, she craved to learn what was happening in her city.

Top of the pile was the *New York Times*. A photograph on the front page caught her attention.

Was that Pegasus?

Emily immediately snatched it up, curious.

Yes, it was definitely Pegasus—but without wings!

She read the caption under the photograph.

Record Breaker! Tornado Warning wins Triple
Crown with greatest time and distance ever
recorded.

"Tornado Warning?" Emily muttered aloud as she
read the article about the winning horse breaking
every record in the history of horse racing.

"Look at that face," her father said lightly. "He
looks just like Pegasus, doesn't he? His body and legs
are darker gray, but if he were all white, it could have
been Pegasus. Tornado Warning is everywhere and
causing quite a stir. They haven't had a Triple Crown
winner like him since Secretariat—and Tornado's
even broken his records!"

Emily barely heard the knocking on the door. As
her father went to answer it, she continued to scan
the article.

"Pegs, you've got to see this." Emily held up the

newspaper for the stallion. "Look at his face. He really does look like you. I mean, you two could be twins!"

When Pegasus looked at the photographs, Emily could sense he was greatly disturbed. Apart from the color, Tornado Warning was identical. His size and shape were the same. All that was missing were the wings and golden hooves. Emily looked at the stallion. "How is this possible?"

"So you have seen the newspapers." Diana had entered the living room and approached Pegasus. "Is there something you wish to tell me? Did you get up to some mischief while you were in Emily's world?"

Pegasus snorted angrily and stamped a golden hoof.

Emily frowned and then shook her head. "That's not possible. Tornado couldn't be his son. Look here, the paper says Tornado Warning is three years old. But Pegasus only came to our world last year."

"But he does look just like you, my friend," Diana said softly as she stroked Pegasus's face. "What else could it be?"

Emily's father, Steve, shrugged. "Maybe he's just a

very handsome horse who happens to look a lot like Pegasus."

Emily studied her father's face and realized he didn't see Pegasus the same way she and the other Olympians did. On the surface, Pegasus could look mostly like a horse, but there was a big difference. It was something that she could plainly see, but her father couldn't. Pegasus was more than a horse, much greater than one. It was in his intelligent eyes and the way he held himself, that created the aura surrounding him that said, *I am not a mere horse.*

Olympus had many horses and some, like Pegasus, had wings. But none of them were remotely like Pegasus. He was unique—until now.

"You're wrong, Dad," Emily insisted. "Tornado Warning doesn't just look like Pegasus, he's identical to him."

Diana put her arm around Emily and gave her a light squeeze. "Well, whatever it is, that horse, Tornado Warning, is in your world while we are all here in Olympus." Diana abruptly changed the subject. "Now, would you like to try on some of the new clothes that your father and I chose for you?"

Emily looked at Diana and saw there was something the tall woman was not saying aloud. A secret message that said they would speak later. She nodded. "You're right. Let's forget Tornado Warning. I want to see what you've brought back."

WHILE EXCITED PREPARATIONS WERE BEING made to celebrate the closing of Olympus's first official soccer match, Emily and Pegasus walked through the fragrant gardens at the back of Jupiter's palace. The air was warm, sweet, and still, and the sun was welcoming but not too hot. Birds chirped in the sky and called a greeting at Emily and Pegasus's approach.

Up ahead lay Jupiter's maze. This was still the best place for Emily and her friends to meet and talk without being seen or disturbed by the other Olympians.

When they reached the center, they didn't have long to wait before Joel, Paelen, and Pegasus's brother Chrysaor appeared. Joel's hair was wet from bathing after the game, slicked back in an effortlessly cool look. Paelen had also bathed to remove the mud and grass stains from the match, but as always his dark hair was unkempt and standing up at odd angles. He was still wearing his winged sandals and had a big grin on his face as he drew near.

"What's up?" Joel asked. "What's the emergency?"

Emily offered the newspapers around. "I couldn't show you these earlier because Dad was in the apartment and doesn't see the problem. Look at the picture and read the headline."

Paelen looked from the front page of one of the newspapers over to Pegasus. His mouth fell open. "He looks just like you! What does this say?"

A frown wrinkled Joel's brow as he read the article. "It's talking about a racehorse, Tornado Warning. He's just won the Triple Crown."

"What is the Triple Crown?" Paelen asked.

Joel continued. "My father was really into horse racing." He looked over to Pegasus wistfully. "I sure wish he could have met you." Joel sighed. "He and I used to bet on the Triple Crown. It's a series of three big horse races that are close together: the Kentucky

Derby, the Preakness Stakes, and then finally the Belmont Stakes. It's really rare for the same horse to win all three. I think the last time was in the 1970s. But Tornado Warning not only won all three races, he's beaten all the records." Joel paused and looked at Emily. "Something doesn't feel right here. Look at these stats." He held up another paper.

Emily peered over and saw a lot of figures she didn't understand. "What's all that mean?"

"It means this is impossible. Look at these racing times. He's got to be the fastest racehorse in history. No horse could run like this."

"But he just did," Paelen insisted.

Beside them, Chrysaor squealed softly, and Paelen lowered his paper so the winged boar could look at the photograph. He grunted and squealed again.

"I do not understand," Paelen asked. "How could this racehorse look so much like Pegasus, run as fast as Pegasus, and yet not be Pegasus?"

Joel shrugged. "If I didn't know better, I'd swear he was a—" A sudden shocked expression appeared on his face, and he shook his head. "No, it's not possible. Are you thinking what I'm thinking?"

Emily was already frightened. The idea had come to her much earlier and left her chilled to the bone. But it was still the only thing that made any sense.

"I'm trying really hard not to," she said. "I asked my dad, and he didn't think so. He said if it were true, Tornado Warning would be white and not gray."

"What?" Paelen asked. "What are you both talking about?"

Emily leaned her head against Pegasus and stroked his neck. "We're thinking that the CRU may have had something to do with this."

Paelen's jaw dropped. "The CRU? How?"

Joel stepped closer to Emily. "It's impossible, isn't it?"

"I just don't know," she said. "But what else could it be?"

"We've got to go back there to find out," Joel finished. "Em, if they can actually do it, we're all in a lot of trouble."

"Enough!" shouted Paelen in frustration. "You are both speaking in riddles, and it is driving me mad! What you are talking about?"

Joel looked at Paelen. "This is going to sound

impossible. But we're thinking that Tornado Warning might be some kind of clone."

Paelen's expression didn't change. Emily realized he didn't understand. "In our world, science is constantly advancing. They are doing amazing things with genetically modifying plants and stuff. What Joel is saying is that while you, Pegasus, and Diana were prisoners of the CRU, they tested you and did experiments. They took samples from you."

Paelen shivered visibly. "It was terrible," he said softly. "They put me in machines, and kept taking my blood, my hair, and who knows what else."

"Exactly," Joel said. "And what I'm afraid of is that they have somehow used those samples to create some kind of clone. A clone is something that is identical to you, created from you, but not you. It's kind of like a twin, but you weren't born together." He crossed over to the stallion and stroked his face. "Tornado Warning looks exactly like Pegasus because he might have been created using cells they took from Pegasus."

Emily's face went pale. "That's crazy, like something out of a fantasy! But if he's a clone, shouldn't he be white like Pegasus?"

"We dyed Pegasus black and brown, remember? What if they are dyeing Tornado Warning gray?" Joel suggested. "I don't know if or how they could have done it, but we've got to find out. Em, we're talking about the CRU. We've seen their facilities. I'm sure they have the capabilities to do it."

Emily shook her head. "But it doesn't make any sense. Even if it is possible, why would they race him and risk exposing their experiments? Besides, the newspapers say Tornado Warning is three years old."

"I can't explain it," Joel said. "But look at those photographs. It's like Pegasus himself was in those races. Those aren't the stats of an ordinary horse."

Pegasus snorted and started to cut deep trenches in the ground. Beside him, Paelen shook his head madly. "No, no, no. This is not possible. You cannot suggest that this racehorse comes from Pegasus. It is unnatural and impossible!"

He stomped up to Emily and pointed at the stallion in one of the photographs. "Pegasus has wings. This racehorse does not. If he was created from Pegasus, surely he should have wings!"

Emily nodded. "I thought the same thing until I

saw this." She lowered herself to the soft grass in the maze and started to search through the newspapers. "Here." She pointed at a close-up color photograph of Tornado Warning in the winner's circle. The jockey was still on his back. Beneath the jockey's right knee, there was a trace of a large scar on Tornado's pale-gray shoulder. "Look at that scar. That could be where they removed his wing."

"That is a crease in the paper, nothing more," Paelen insisted. "It does not prove anything."

Joel picked up the paper and studied the image. He shook his head. "This isn't any crease, Paelen—it's a scar. And it proves one thing. We've got to go back there and see that racehorse for ourselves. If the CRU are capable of creating clones, just think of what they could do with your and Diana's DNA."

The enormity of the situation struck Emily like a brick. She looked up at Joel. "Not only Olympian DNA, Joel. Remember, the CRU had captured Nirads as well!"

3

AS THE SUN STARTED TO SET IN OLYMPUS, the soccer pitch had been turned into a huge party ground. Tables were laden with fruit, ambrosia, and nectar as thousands of Olympians gathered to celebrate the game. Torches were lit and shining brightly on the gathering, while the Muses danced and sang for the entertainment of the crowd.

Above the pitch, Cupid led a group of winged Olympians carrying flags and banners. They rose and dipped in the sky, sometimes so low they touched the tops of the heads of those below on the ground.

Cupid spied Emily entering the stadium and swooped down. Folding his large wings neatly on his back, he bowed before her. "Hello, Flame, would you like to come for a short flight with me?"

"Her name is Emily!" challenged Paelen, as he had done hundreds of times before. "When will you finally learn that?"

Cupid smiled radiantly at Emily. "When she tells me so."

Emily held up a calming hand to Paelen and then looked back at the winged Olympian. Nothing remained of the crush she once felt for him. Cupid was just as handsome as ever, but her heart was elsewhere now.

"Thank you anyway, Cupid, but I'd rather stay on the ground for the moment. Perhaps later."

"Of course, Flame," Cupid said, shooting a teasing look at Paelen. "You need only to ask." He kissed Emily's cheek and then leaped confidently into the sky.

"I keep telling you, Emily," Paelen said, "you should have left him as a stone statue in the Nirad world. It would have solved all our problems."

"I thought you two were becoming friends," Joel offered.

"Cupid and me?" Paelen said. "Hardly. I mean yes,

he did help us defeat the gorgons and overcame his fear of the Nirads. But Cupid is still Cupid. He is an arrogant mischief-maker."

Diana joined the group and faced Paelen, her expression stern. "Not too long ago people were saying the same thing about you, little thief."

Paelen shrugged. "Perhaps. But I have changed. Cupid has not."

"Really?" Diana said. "It is said that once a thief, forever a thief. I know there are several Olympians who still count their coins and jewels after you leave."

Paelen's face dropped. Despite everything he had done to help Olympus, there were a great number of Olympians who believed he hadn't changed his thieving ways.

Emily felt for him. What would it take to get them to believe he was different? She also knew that despite his wounded feelings, Paelen was smart enough not to rise to the comment. Diana's temper was legendary. It was better to let the remark rest than say something that would anger her.

Always the policeman, Emily's father came forward to calm the situation. He put his arm around Paelen and then indicated the gathering Olympians on the field. "Look at this place, this is insane! Any excuse for a party. C'mon, everyone, let's have some fun."

Emily wasn't in much of a mood to join in the celebrations around her. Neither were Joel or Paelen. A dark shadow was resting heavily over them. They weren't alone in their worry. Both Pegasus and Chrysaor were showing signs of profound disquiet.

While her father left to gather drinks for everyone, Emily stood with Diana and Pegasus. Joel nudged her gently in the back and whispered, "Ask her now."

Diana's keen hearing hadn't missed the comment. She turned back and looked suspiciously at Joel. "Ask me what?"

Emily inhaled deeply. "Diana, we need to speak with you about something important, but I don't want my dad to know yet."

Diana frowned. "This is about that racehorse, is it not?"

Emily nodded. "It may be nothing. But we need to go back to our world to see if Tornado Warning is something more than a horse. We must get away without anyone knowing."

Her father was walking back to the group, carrying a tray of ambrosia cakes and goblets of nectar.

Diana leaned closer to Emily. "After the party, meet me at the base of the Temple of the Flame. We will speak then."

The party continued well into the night. When it was over, Emily said good night to her father and waited for him to return to his room. When she was sure he'd gone to bed, she left her quarters and headed into the garden to meet her friends.

Pegasus and Chrysaor were already there. After a short time, Paelen and Joel arrived. For speed, they agreed to fly to the temple. As Emily climbed onto Pegasus, Joel settled himself on the back of Chrysaor. Paelen looked down at his winged sandals and ordered them to carry him to the temple. With a quick flap of their tiny wings, they obeyed and lifted him lightly into the air.

Of all the things Emily loved about living in Olympus, the very best was flying on the back of Pegasus. Flying at night was even better. Many times, when her father thought she was in bed, she and

Pegasus would sneak out of the palace and spend a long night soaring in the skies over Olympus. Each time they went out, the bright canopy of stars never failed to take Emily's breath away. They always filled her with profound excitement, as though the stars themselves called to her and beckoned her to join them in the sky.

It was these stars that reminded her they were no longer on her world. None of the constellations she knew appeared in an Olympian's night sky. There was no moon, and the stars seemed brighter and much closer.

But this night, there was none of the usual excitement. They launched silently into the air and flew over the dark palace. On the ground below, strange-looking Olympians moved around. These were the citizens who lived their lives only by night.

Emily had learned very quickly not to fear the night dwellers. Though they looked different with their pale skin and huge dark eyes, they spoke very softly and posed no danger to her or Pegasus. She discovered that Olympus was like two worlds in one. A day world filled with sunshine and bright colors and ruled by Jupiter; and then a night world that existed only by starlight, filled with strange, silent beings overseen by Jupiter's brother, Pluto. Olympus at night was the underworld the myths so often spoke of.

Emily looked over to Joel and realized this was the first time he'd ever seen this Olympus. At any other time, he would have asked her lots of questions and insisted on flying down to meet the night creatures. Not tonight. He looked at the night dwellers with curiosity, but remained silent.

Up ahead they saw a bright glow shining in the dark night sky. It was coming from the top of the Temple of the Flame. This was the Flame that gave the Olympians their powers and strength. Without it, Olympus would fall. It was the same Flame that Emily's power fed. She had been born with the living heart of the Flame deep within her. When she sacrificed herself in the temple, her powers were released and renewed the Flame in the temple. It was her connection to the Flame that made Jupiter and all the Olympians so protective of her. Though she still didn't understand how it worked, she did know the survival of the Olympians depended on that Flame continuing to burn. And the survival of the Flame depended on her.

As Pegasus glided lower, Emily was surprised to see three dark figures standing at the base of the temple. Drawing nearer, she saw her father standing beside Diana. His hands were on his hips, and he didn't look happy.

Emily stole a look over to Joel on Chrysaor's back. He glanced back at her. "I think we might be in trouble," Joel said.

Emily was tempted to tell Pegasus to turn around and go back to the palace. But it was too late. With Pegasus glowing in the dark sky, everyone had seen them coming.

When the stallion touched down on the ground before the three figures, Emily frowned. Standing beside her father and Diana was a third figure that she didn't recognize.

Emily's father came forward to help her down from the stallion. "Isn't there something you want to tell me before you sneak away from Olympus?"

Emily's heart nearly stopped. Diana had told him everything. She dropped her head. "I'm sorry, Dad.

I wanted to tell you, but I know you'll want to stop me."

"Darn right I'm going to stop you. Emily, you can't go back there; it's too dangerous. What were you thinking?"

"It's my fault, Steve, not Emily's." Joel stepped in to defend her. "I was the one who suggested we go. We told Diana so at least someone would know what happened to us."

"This is about that stupid racehorse, isn't it?"

"Dad, listen to me, please," Emily begged. "Tornado Warning looks too much like Pegasus and runs too quickly to be an ordinary horse. You know that. If you didn't think so, you wouldn't have brought the newspapers to show us. We need to find out. If there's even a small chance he's a clone, we've got to know. Don't you see? If the CRU can clone him, they can do the same with the other Olympians."

"Or Nirads," Paelen added.

The third shadowy figure came forward. "Do you seriously believe this is possible? The CRU could create New Olympians from our blood?"

When he moved closer, Emily saw how much he

looked like Jupiter and Neptune. But his eyes were more intense and as black as the night sky. His skin was pale as parchment. This must be the third brother, Pluto. He was the owner of Cerberus and leader of the underworld. She had heard all about him, but had yet to meet him.

Emily bowed her head respectfully. "We're not sure, sir." She turned to her father. "Dad, you've seen him on TV. Can you say for sure that Tornado Warning isn't some kind of clone from Pegasus?"

Emily's father combed his fingers through his hair. He looked from Diana to Pluto. He shook his head. "No, I can't. Human science is moving so quickly, I have no idea what they can achieve."

"Don't you see?" Emily pleaded. "That's why we must go back there and see for ourselves. If Tornado Warning is just a horse, we can forget all about him. But if he is actually a clone from Pegasus, then we've got to know. What could the CRU do with an army of cloned Olympians or Nirads? They could take over the world!"

"Or maybe even challenge Olympus," Joel added.

Pluto's voice dropped. "If that horse you speak of

really has been created from Pegasus, all of Olympus will be outraged! Jupiter will go to your world to stop them." He paused before staring Emily directly in the eye. "I will join him. The development of such creatures from our blood must not be tolerated. If this is true and they have created New Olympians, we will have no recourse but to destroy Earth."

EMILY LOOKED AT PLUTO IN COMPLETE shock. Could it be true? Would the Olympians really destroy her world? Jupiter had always been so generous and treated her like a granddaughter. Would he actually do it?

"It is true." Diana looked around and started to whisper. "Should my father hear of this, he would not hesitate to destroy your world even before there was proof. I have seen him do it before. Jupiter is capable of anything if it means protecting Olympus and the order of nature."

Emily's father shook his head. "But Earth has billions of innocent people and animals. Jupiter wouldn't destroy all of that just to punish the CRU for doing something stupid."

Diana sighed heavily. "I am sorry, Steve, but he would."

"Apollo has also seen the photos," Pluto added. "He came to me quietly, voicing his concerns. I discouraged him from telling his father. But we are all loyal to Jupiter. If the CRU has done this thing, we have no recourse but to tell Jupiter and let the punishment fit the crime."

"Destroying Earth is too great a punishment!" Steve argued. "Especially if it's just a few people who have done this—and we aren't even certain that they have done anything at all!"

"Which is why we've got to go to see for ourselves," Emily added.

"Emily is correct," Pluto said. "We must let them go see if this racehorse is real or an unnatural creation of your people."

Her father started to pace the area. "All right, but I'm coming with you."

Pegasus nickered softly. He approached Diana and made a long series of sounds.

"Pegasus does not agree," she translated. "He says you must remain here. You and I are scheduled to make our full report to my father following our trip. They will only be gone a very short time. I can make excuses to my father about why Emily and the others are not here, perhaps tell them that they have gone to the Nirad world to visit the queen. But if you leave as well, it will draw my father's suspicions, especially so soon after our return. With all that is at stake, we must not risk that."

"But it's too dangerous," Steve insisted.

"Dad, please," Emily said. "We've got to go. We'll be really quick. You must keep Jupiter occupied and stop Apollo from telling him about Tornado until we figure this out."

"But how can I protect you?" her father said as he pulled her into a tight embrace and kissed the top of her head. "The CRU separated us once. I couldn't bear that to happen again."

"It won't," Joel promised. "This isn't like before. We're not breaking into a CRU facility. We're just going to go see Tornado Warning at a racetrack."

Steve sighed heavily. "I really wish I were coming with you."

"So do I," Emily agreed as she held her father. "But

38

we'll be careful. I promise. You just keep Jupiter busy so he doesn't notice we're gone."

As the sun started to rise, the meeting was called to a halt by Pluto. They agreed to meet at the temple the following evening to prepare for departure.

The next day Emily, Joel, and Paelen packed up their new clothing and a good supply of ambrosia and nectar for the trip. Emily barely got to see her father, as he spent most of the day with Jupiter, Diana, and Apollo, presenting their report. She ached to speak with him, to talk about her fears for their world if Jupiter ever found out.

Until now, everything Emily had done was to protect and defend Olympus; first from the Nirads and then from the gorgons. But now, as she checked and rechecked her backpack, she realized that she, the Flame of Olympus, might be forced to protect Earth from the Olympians.

As night arrived and Emily's father returned from a long day with Jupiter, they waited for Olympus to go to sleep before heading out to the Temple of the Flame.

For the short journey, Emily's father rode with her on the back of Pegasus. She felt his reassuring arms around her and silently wished he were coming with them. But Pegasus was right. He had to stay to keep Jupiter from getting suspicious.

Diana and Pluto were waiting at the temple. As she and her father climbed down from Pegasus, Emily noticed that Pluto was holding a package in his hands.

Diana came forward. "I have told my father that you are all going to the Nirad world to visit the queen. He has no cause to question it. But you must be swift. My father understands your need for independence and freedom, but he does not like it when the Flame of Olympus is away from here."

"I understand," Emily said grimly. "We'll be as quick as we can."

While they spoke, Pluto opened the sack he was carrying, pulled out an ornate leather helmet, and held it up.

Paelen sucked in his breath. "That is your helmet of invisibility! Are you coming with us?"

Pluto shook his head. "No, I must remain here to ensure my brother does not become suspicious. However, my helmet will be joining you on your quest."

"May I wear it?" Paelen asked.

"It is not for you," Pluto said.

"For me?" Joel asked hopefully. "I've read all about that helmet. It's amazing."

Again, Pluto shook his head and said no.

Finally Emily said, "It's for Pegasus, isn't it? So he can travel with us and not be seen."

"I am sorry, no. I wish I could give you something to keep Pegasus hidden, but I have only the one helmet to offer."

"If not us, who is going to wear it?" Paelen asked.

"I am." A voice came from behind them.

Emily turned, and her eyes flew wide at the sight of the Sphinx landing silently on the ground. She folded her eagle's wings neatly and padded forward. As she walked past Joel, she brushed against him like a cat brushing against the legs of its owner at feeding time.

"No way!" Emily cried, feeling her temper rising. "You aren't coming with us!"

"Yes, she is," Diana said sternly. "This is the price you will pay for our cooperation in this. If you insist on returning to your world to see Tornado Warning, then Alexis is coming with you. She has great skills that will keep you safe."

"But she's a—a—" Emily struggled for the right word.

"Careful, child," Alexis warned. She approached Emily and rose up on her lion's hind legs. Her serpent's tail swished in the air in annoyance as she rested her paws on Emily's shoulders. Her claws were drawn. "We are not playing now, Emily. This is very serious. I have been told what is happening. Diana has asked me to accompany you to keep you safe. This is what I intend to do."

"You're just going to spy on us," Emily challenged, forcing herself not to look at the Sphinx's claws so close to her face.

Diana moved forward. "Alexis, get down." She concentrated on Emily. "Alexis is not a spy. It is her job to keep you safe. You are the Flame of Olympus. You must be protected at all times."

"I can take care of myself," Emily replied. "I beat the gorgons. You know I can control the Flame now."

Emily's father stood with her. "Em, we all know

you can control the Flame. But our world is a dangerous place—not just from the CRU." He looked over
to Pegasus. "And I know you'll do everything you
can to keep her safe. But Alexis has special skills that
you don't. Diana tells me she can sense danger before
it comes. She can move silently and swiftly and can
read a person's intentions. She will be an asset you
can't turn down."

Alexis held up a paw. "Thank you, Steve, but
perhaps there is another way to settle this." She
approached Emily. "I will ask you a riddle. If you
answer correctly, I will not go. However, if your
answer is wrong, I will go and you will say no more
about it."

"You want to play a game?" Emily demanded.
"Now? Right before we leave?"

"This is no game," Alexis answered seriously.
"Either you will answer my riddle, or I will join you
without your permission."

"Be careful, Em," Joel warned. "Alexis is the
Sphinx."

"What's that supposed to mean?" Emily said.

Alexis looked at Joel. "Say no more, Joel. This is

between Emily and me." She concentrated on Emily. "Riddle me this . . .

My shallow hills are the faces of kings
My horizon is always near
My music sends men to the grave
My absence sends men to work.
What am I?"

Emily frowned as she tried to work out the simple riddle. Since Alexis was from Olympus, she figured the answer would have to be something Olympian. What shallow hills were in Olympus with a close horizon? None, so it was not a place. The next line was about music. But what kind of music sent men to the grave but absence sent them to work? The Muses sang beautifully, but they never killed with their songs. Who did?

Emily smiled. "I know."

"Tell me," the Sphinx demanded.

"The answer is: the Sirens."

Alexis laughed. "You are wrong."

Emily's temper flared. "No I'm not. The Sirens

send men to their graves in the water, but when they leave, the sailors can get back to work. So it's got to be the Sirens."

"You are wrong," Alexis repeated.

"So what is the answer?"

"That is for me to know and you to figure out."

"What?" Emily cried. "You're cheating. I got the answer right and you don't want to admit it!"

The hackles on Alexis's lion's back rose as the Sphinx narrowed her green eyes. "Cheat? You accuse me of cheating!" She advanced on Emily.

Emily took a step back and raised her hands. She felt the tingling of power flowing down her arms to her hands. The Flame was just a breath away.

"Alexis, enough," Pluto said. "Control yourself. Emily, you too!"

The Sphinx's furious green eyes lingered on Emily a moment longer before she turned back to Pluto. "As you command."

Emily lowered her hands but refused to take her wary eyes off the Sphinx.

Pegasus nickered softly and nodded. He stepped closer to Emily and nudged her in the back gently.

"He says Alexis never lies," Paelen translated. "If you had said the correct answer, she is bound by honor and the laws of Olympus to tell you. Your answer was wrong."

Emily started to protest further until Pluto raised his voice. "This is not open for discussion. The riddle was asked, the answer given. Alexis will go with you."

"But—" Emily cried.

Pluto shook his head. "You are the Flame of Olympus and too precious to risk. Either you will take Alexis with you, or you will not go at all."

Joel leaned over to her. "It'll be all right, Em. With Pluto's helmet, you'll never even see her. We'll just go, see Tornado Warning, and come right back."

Emily looked at Joel, then Paelen, who was nodding his head enthusiastically. It was obvious how much they both liked the Sphinx. Finally her eyes trailed over to Alexis, who was still eyeing her up dangerously. She shook her head. "I have a very bad feeling about this."

THE GROUP ENTERED THE BRIGHT, POWER-
ful light of the Solar Stream. This was the passage
the Olympians used to travel between worlds. It was
loud and filled with white energy that caused the hair
on Emily's arms to stand on end. Riding on Pegasus,
she recalled her father's fearful face as he watched
her go. She prayed she would be returning to him in
Olympus soon with good news.

Behind Emily and Pegasus was Joel on Chrysaor,
while Paelen flew beside them using his winged sandals. Emily looked back and saw Alexis at the very
rear. The Sphinx's face was grim as her large wings
beat in rhythm with Pegasus's.

When they burst free of the Solar Stream, Emily

was alarmed to feel the sunny warmth of a summer day. What her father said was true. The time between the worlds was completely different. While it was night on Olympus, it was full daylight in the skies over New York City. They had also discovered that when a day passed in Olympus, weeks had sometimes passed on her world.

They had decided to return to the New York area, where the Belmont Stakes, the last race in the Triple Crown, was run. It was the final place Tornado Warning had been seen. When they emerged from the Solar Stream, Emily looked down to see the tall antennae of the Empire State Building pass directly beneath them. She could see tourists on the observation deck. They all seemed to be looking down on the world and failed to notice them. "Pegs, we're too low! Take us higher in the sky!"

Pegasus maneuvered his wings and led the group higher in the sky as he flew uptown over the city. Emily looked back at Joel. He was shaking his head. "That was too close!" he called. "Do you think anyone saw us?"

"I hope not!" Emily called back.

Joel shouted over to Paelen. "Take the lead! Ask your sandals to find Tornado Warning. Let's just take a look at him and get the heck out of here!"

Paelen directed his sandals forward. When he was a length ahead of Pegasus, he called down to his sandals, "Take us to Tornado Warning."

Emily gripped Pegasus's mane tighter and prepared to change direction in the sky. But when she looked at Paelen and then down to his winged sandals, nothing happened. Normally when he gave a command to the sandals, the wings fluttered to let him know they had heard and were obeying.

"Tornado Warning," Paelen repeated. "Find Tornado Warning."

Paelen repeated the command several more times, but the sandals remained unchanged. He looked back at Emily and shrugged. "They do not know where he is."

By now they were moving uptown. On their left, Emily saw the George Washington Bridge. She reached forward and pointed. "Pegasus, do you see that tall bridge over there? Please follow it. It will take us to where we can land." She called forward to Paelen, "Follow us!"

Pegasus veered in the sky. Beneath them, the tall suspension bridge crossed over the Hudson River and led them deeper into New Jersey. As they passed over Fort Lee, Emily saw a large area of dense trees rising to the far right. "Take us down, Pegs. We need to talk!"

After a few minutes of searching, Pegasus found a clearing in the trees. When the stallion neatly touched down, Emily slid off his back. She approached her friends.

"What happened?" she asked Paelen. "Why can't your sandals find Tornado?"

Paelen shrugged. "I do not know. They have never failed me before."

"Are they still working?" Joel asked. "Test them. Ask them to take you to Governors Island."

Paelen nodded and looked down at his winged sandals. "Take me to Governors Island." Immediately the tiny wings flapped in acknowledgment and lifted Paelen off the ground and moved in the direction of the small island off southern Manhattan. "Stop!" Paelen ordered. "Take me back to Emily."

"So they are still working," Joel muttered.

"Perhaps they do not recognize the command,"

Alexis added as she folded her wings and padded up to them. "If Tornado Warning comes from both Pegasus and this world, it may be confusing them."

"That's dumb," Emily said.

Alexis narrowed her green eyes. "Do you have a better suggestion?"

Emily didn't. But she didn't want the Sphinx to know that. She still resented Alexis being forced on them. "If the sandals can't find Tornado, what are we supposed to do? That was the plan."

Joel rubbed his chin. "Well, we can't go back until we've seen that horse. We just have to find him another way. Let's search the Internet to find out where he's racing next."

"How?" Emily asked. "It's not like we can just walk into an Internet cafe—we don't exactly blend in!"

"I wasn't suggesting that," Joel shot back. "We need someone with a home computer. Who do we know?"

"My aunt," Emily suggested. "But she's being watched by the CRU."

"I didn't have any school friends," Joel muttered. "And my foster family didn't own a computer, so no point going back there."

"I know," Paelen offered excitedly. "What about Earl? Perhaps he can help us."

Emily thought back to Earl, the owner of their old hideout, the Red Apple. He had helped them the last time they were in this world. Even after he'd been badly hurt—when the Nirads attacked—he'd done all he could to help.

She looked at Paelen and nodded. "That's not a bad idea. Do you think your sandals could find him?"

Paelen looked down at his sandals. "Take me to Earl."

The tiny wings flapped and lifted Paelen off the ground. There was no hesitation as they carried him over the trees and higher in the sky.

"Paelen, stop!" Joel cried. "Get back here!"

Paelen returned, and Joel looked at the group. "We can't go now, in daylight; we'll be seen. Lord only knows who's seen us already. We arrived too low in the sky over the city. I think we should wait here till dark. It will be safer to fly then."

Chrysaor nudged Joel's hand. He grunted several times. Pegasus also whinnied softly.

"They both agree, Joel," Paelen translated. "It is too big a risk to go now."

"Then it's settled," Emily said. "We wait till tonight, then we find Earl."

The day passed slowly as they sat among the trees waiting for sunset. Emily jumped at every crack and sound from the woods around them. She felt exposed and vulnerable, as though a CRU agent was hiding behind every tree and waiting to burst out at them at any moment.

Every time Emily jumped, Alexis shook her head and tutted. "Did Diana not tell you I can sense danger? Is that not the reason I am here? There is no danger; we are alone in these trees. So just sit there and let me do my job."

Emily sat on the ground beside Pegasus. Joel moved to sit beside her, leaning against the resting stallion's side.

"Alexis is right, Em, just relax. Don't you know who the Sphinx is?"

"A giant cat from the Egyptian desert," Emily said flatly.

Alexis bristled and hissed at the insult. "What did you say? Egyptian? That is not I!"

Joel held up his hand to the Sphinx. "Alexis, calm down. Not everyone in this world knows the stories."

"Then educate her. I will not suffer such insults again!" Without a second glance, the Sphinx wandered into the trees.

"Watch yourself around her," Joel warned. "The Sphinx is very dangerous. The myths say she used to guard the entrance to Thebes. Anyone who approached had to answer one of her riddles. If they got it wrong, she killed them. Some legends say she even ate them."

"Oh, gross!" Emily cried. She looked to where the Sphinx had entered the trees. "Wait, how could she eat them? Okay, she does have a lion's body and claws, but she has a woman's head. How could she?"

Paelen answered. "You have not seen her teeth."

"Yes, I have," Emily said.

Paelen shook his head. "No, you have not. If you had, you would not be asking the question. Alexis has two sets of teeth: her talking teeth and her eating teeth. She has long, sharp fangs that extend down. When she is finished eating, she can retract them like claws."

"Just like a vampire," Emily muttered.

"But a lot more dangerous than a vampire," Joel said. "If the myths are true, she was sent to Thebes by Juno, Jupiter's wife. The Sphinx was only ever defeated once—when Oedipus guessed the right answer to her riddle. It's said that she killed herself when he did."

Pegasus nickered softly. Paelen translated. "No, she did not kill herself. She simply returned to Olympus. But she is one of our best guards. Pegasus knows you do not like her and that she is not particularly fond of you. But he says we are very honored to have her with us. We are in safe hands."

"That's if Emily doesn't do something stupid and drive Alexis to kill her!" Joel added.

Emily looked at Joel and felt a sting. "If she tries anything, I'll burn her up!"

Paelen's eyes flew wide. "You must not say such a thing. The Sphinx is Juno's favorite. There would be no stopping her rage if you destroyed Alexis, even if you are the Flame of Olympus. Please—"

"Calm down," Emily said. "I wasn't serious. I could never hurt Alexis, even if she does drive me crazy!" She directed her attention to Pegasus. "You know that too, right, Pegs? I won't use my powers to hurt anyone *ever*!"

"Except maybe the gorgons," Joel added as he nudged her playfully.

Emily shoved him back. "That was different. They started it and turned you all to stone. I had no choice. Apart from them, I don't want to use my powers against anyone, ever again."

Paelen relaxed visibly. "That is a relief. I would hate to see a war start between you and Juno over Alexis."

Emily said nothing. There was already a huge weight on her shoulders, knowing she might have to fight Jupiter to protect Earth. She wasn't about to pick another fight. Sitting beside Pegasus, absently stroking the feathers on his wings, she worried about the future.

As the summer sun moved steadily overhead and started to descend in the west, they changed into their "Earth" clothes. Paelen beamed as he looked down at his jeans and T-shirt. "I do look human, do I not?" he asked proudly.

Emily smiled at her friend's eagerness to blend in, despite the fact that he was wearing jeweled sandals with wings instead of sneakers. "You look great."

Emily struggled to get her jeans up over her silver leg brace. She hated that she still needed to wear it. But the damage the Nirads had done to her left her unable to walk without it.

Across the small clearing, Alexis was refusing to put on the T-shirt Emily had given her to cover up her naked front.

"I will not do it," Alexis said. "I have never had to wear anything before—even when I was last in your world. I will look ridiculous."

Emily bit her tongue. A lion-woman with eagle's wings and a serpent's tail was worrying about looking ridiculous if she wore a T-shirt?

"Things have changed," Emily grunted, struggling to fasten her jeans. She crossed to the Sphinx and then looked over at her friends. "Not to mention you are distracting Joel and Paelen, and we need them to focus."

"No," Alexis said. "I will not wear this. Not unless you answer another riddle."

Emily groaned. "Not again."

"If you insist on me wearing clothing, I will only do it when you answer correctly."

The Sphinx moved closer to Emily and narrowed her green eyes.

"Riddle me, riddle me ranty ro
My father gave me seeds to sow
The seed was black and the ground was white
If you riddle me that
You'll escape my bite."

Emily asked Alexis to repeat the riddle. Black seeds with white ground. After the last riddle, she knew the answer wouldn't be clear or easy. One thing was sure, it would have nothing to do with planting at all. White ground and black seeds . . . What made the ground white? Snow! Finally she had a thought and snapped her fingers.

"I know! It's coal in a snowman's eyes!"

Alexis smiled and threw away the T-shirt. "Incorrect. I do not need to wear this."

"What is it, then?" Emily demanded.

Alexis shook her head. "It is not my place to tell you the answer."

Emily threw up her arms in frustration and walked back to Pegasus. When she passed Joel, she shook her head. "Will you please talk to her?"

Color rose in Joel's cheeks. "Um . . . well, I . . ." He looked awkwardly over to the Sphinx. "I know you've got Pluto's helmet and all, but it might be best if you put something on."

Alexis dropped her head and pouted. "You do not like me. You think I am ugly."

Joel jumped to his feet and picked up the T-shirt. Then he approached the Sphinx. "Alexis, I think you're amazing! But in our world, we tend to cover up. Please, for me?"

Alexis looked at the shirt dubiously. "Fine, but only for you."

Emily watched Joel fawning all over the Sphinx. With her raven-black hair and large green eyes, she was strikingly beautiful. But despite what everyone said, to Emily, Alexis was still just an overgrown, flying house cat!

Emily felt the Flame within her stir. She knew she

could control it and wouldn't let it free. But at that moment she was tempted.

Pegasus gently nudged her. Emily looked back into the stallion's big brown eyes. "Thanks, Pegs," she said softly as she hugged his neck. "But why can't he see it? She's just toying with him."

When the sun had finally set, they packed up their things and prepared to leave. Emily climbed up onto Pegasus. "Okay, Paelen, lead on. Take us to Earl."

With the lights of New York City behind them and all the towns of New Jersey ahead, Emily expected to head due north, back toward Tuxedo, New York, where they'd first met Earl. But once they were higher in the sky, the sandals took them in a southern direction.

"Did Earl tell you where he lived?" Joel called to Emily.

"In Tuxedo," Emily called back. She turned on Pegasus's back and pointed in the direction they'd come from. "But that's way back there. Where do you think we're going?"

"Guess we'll find out soon enough."

As the moon rose high and full above them in a sky

filled with stars, Emily settled down on Pegasus for a long flight. The air was warm and getting warmer the farther south they traveled. Beneath them, they watched towns and city lights passing. Yet Paelen's sandals continued without a break.

After a time, the lights of civilization stopped and they passed silently over a tall, heavily wooded mountain range with only the occasional car headlights to break the solid darkness below.

"Em," Joel finally called, "do those look like the Blue Ridge Mountains to you?"

"Don't know," she admitted. "I've never traveled any farther south than New Jersey."

"Well, I've gone down to Florida, and this looks familiar."

Emily was unsure how long they had flown. But with the passing of the moon overhead, she knew it had to be most of the night. Just before dawn, with the air becoming warmer and sweeter with the fragrance of flowers and salty sea air, Paelen's sandals finally started to descend.

They were heading down toward a densely populated neighborhood filled with houses running along a canal. With the pink rays of dawn rising in the east, Emily noticed several homes with their lights already on. There was some light traffic on the roads as commuters started their journeys to work.

"I don't like this," Emily called to Joel and Paelen. "We could be seen."

Paelen looked over his shoulder. "But this is where Earl is."

Within minutes, they were gliding over a row of homes.

"Don't land in front!" Joel called. "Paelen, if it's one of these homes, land in the backyard."

Paelen repeated the order to his sandals. Soon they were touching down in the grass of a small backyard along the canal. Palm trees were blowing in the soft, warm breeze, and the sound of morning songbirds filled the soupy, humid air.

Emily looked around nervously. "I really don't like this. We're too exposed here." Pegasus was still glowing in the predawn light. She pointed to the house directly across the canal from them. "Look, their lights are on. If they look outside, they can't miss us."

"Then let's not stay out here," Joel said. He looked

at Paelen. "Are you sure this is the right place?"

"I am not, but the sandals are certain."

Alexis fluttered her wings into position and scanned the area. "I have never been here before. The air is delicious. Where are we?"

Joel looked around. "Looks and smells like Florida to me."

"Florida?" Emily repeated. "Are you saying we flew over a thousand miles in one night?"

Pegasus nickered softly, and Chrysaor squealed as they moved closer to the back of the house. "They say we should seek cover before the sun is fully up," Paelen translated.

Joel approached the sliding glass door at the rear of the house. "I hope your sandals are right," he muttered softly, "or we're about to ruin someone's day."

"Someone's whole life, you mean," Emily added.

The door was locked. But one of the benefits of having an artificial arm made in Vulcan's workshop was that Joel now possessed amazing strength in his silver right arm.

With a quick, sharp tug, the lock on the door snapped and the glass door slid open.

"Everyone inside," Joel whispered.

As the biggest, Pegasus went first. But even with the glass door fully open, the winged stallion was too large to fit through the doorway. Joel, Paelen, and Emily had to push Pegasus from behind to force his whole body and wings through the opening.

"C'mon!" Joel grunted. "One more good push should do it."

Pegasus whinnied in complaint as he was shoved painfully through the glass door. With a final effort, the stallion made it through the tight opening, but not before losing several feathers.

As Chrysaor and Alexis trailed in behind the stallion, Emily and Paelen ran around the yard gathering Pegasus's lost feathers, now blowing in the breeze. A large feather blew into the canal just as Emily reached for it.

"Go and get it," Paelen said as the feather floated on the surface.

"I'm not going in there," Emily protested. "You go get it."

Paelen shook his head. "Not me. I do not like water. You should go."

"And I don't like alligators," Emily said. "I've heard Florida canals are full of them."

Paelen looked at her in shock. "So you wish for me to be eaten by creatures in this water?"

"No, of course not, but being Olympian, I'm sure the alligators would leave you alone."

While they argued, the feather drifted farther away. Finally Emily raised her right hand. She concentrated on the feather while summoning the Flame. A tight beam of fire shot from her hand and burned up the feather. When it stopped, all that remained was steaming water.

Emily looked at Paelen and rubbed her hands together. "That's fixed. Let's catch up with the others."

When they were all gathered in the small living room, Emily stood beside Pegasus, stroking his neck to let her powers restore his lost and damaged feathers. "Sorry about that, Pegs," she said softly. "But we had to get you in here. I don't think any of us realize just how big you are until something like that happens."

Pegasus nickered softly and nodded.

Moments later Alexis raised her head and hushed Emily. "There are two humans stirring in this dwelling."

"Two?" Emily repeated.

Alexis let out a ferocious roar. In the blink of an eye, the Sphinx launched into the air, and soared over Emily's head. A strange, choked voice behind her screamed as Alexis knocked to the floor a long-haired man wearing a brown bathrobe.

Emily received her first look at Alexis's eating teeth as the Sphinx stood on the man's chest and prepared to kill him. They were a terrifying sight. Huge, sharp canines filled her mouth as her jaw unhinged to allow her to open her mouth wider than Emily had thought possible.

"Alexis, no!" Joel cried. He ran up to the Sphinx and knelt down beside her. "Please don't kill him! We know him. He can help us."

When the Sphinx looked over to Joel, Emily saw her eyes were almost as scary as her teeth. The color was gone, and all she could see were enlarged black pupils. A low, deep rumble continued from the Sphinx's throat. Emily understood what Diana meant about Alexis being a good security guard. She was terrifying.

Finally the Sphinx's pupils returned to normal and her teeth retracted. She climbed off, but remained close and poised to strike.

Joel helped the man climb shakily to his feet.

It took a moment to recognize him because he'd changed so much. His hair was long and shaggy and he had a mustache, but it was him. "Agent T!" Emily cried. "What are you doing here?"

"Me?" the CRU agent challenged. "What the hell are you doing back here? And what is that thing you've brought with you?" He pointed a shaking finger at Alexis.

"Thing?" Alexis repeated as her soft growls grew considerably louder. "Did you just call me a thing?"

It was Agent T all right. He still possessed the same arrogance and defiance that all CRU agents had. If he wasn't careful with the Sphinx, that attitude would get him killed. Emily stepped forward to stop the disaster before it started. "This is Alexis," she introduced quickly. "She is the Sphinx of Olympus."

Agent T groaned. "More damn Olympians? Not again."

A second man charged into the room. "What's going on in here?"

Emily turned and saw Earl standing in the doorway. Like Agent T, he had changed since the last time she saw him. His light hair was dyed black and his beard was gone. They were obviously trying to disguise themselves to hide from the CRU. But there was no mistaking the sparkle in his eyes. There were no traces of the severe burns he'd received at the destruction of the Red Apple rest stop.

"Earl! I'm so glad to see you!"

Earl's eyes flew open at the sight of Pegasus and the others crammed into the small room. "Emily!" He ran over and scooped her up in his arms. "I've been so darn worried about you!" His eyes went to everyone in the room. "About all of you."

"We're doing good," Joel answered. "But we really need your help."

"Help?" Earl said as he crossed to Pegasus and patted the stallion's neck. "Hiya, big fella." He turned back to Joel. "What's wrong?"

Emily looked from Earl to Agent T. "Actually, I'm glad you are here too, because we think the CRU are involved with something horrific."

Agent T stepped away from the Sphinx and approached Emily. "Whatever it is, I don't want to know about it. I haven't been with the agency since you started that mess up in Tuxedo, New York. The CRU have been searching for us ever since. Earl and I are in hiding. We've changed our names countless times and had to take awful jobs just to survive. Look at this dump. I've got multiple degrees and was a high-ranking CRU agent. What am I doing now? Because of you, I'm a janitor."

Emily bristled. "Don't go blaming us. We didn't start that mess in Tuxedo—you did, when you took my father!"

Agent T stood defiantly erect. Despite his messy long hair, tattered robe, and bare feet, he was still an imposing sight. "We wouldn't have taken your father if you hadn't caused all that trouble in New York. Do you have any idea how much chaos those Nirads caused us? We had to buy off most of the city officials and threaten the newspapers."

"That wasn't our fault either!" Emily cried.

Pegasus nickered softly. Paelen came forward and put his hand on her shoulder. "Emily, calm down. That is in the past. Pegasus says we must focus on our mission."

Emily looked back at the stallion and nodded. She took a deep, steadying breath. "You're right."

"So why are you here?" Earl asked. "What have the CRU done now?"

Joel answered. "We think they may have created a clone from Pegasus. It's that racehorse who won the Triple Crown."

"Tornado Warning?" Earl asked. "You think that there horse was created by the CRU?"

Emily nodded. "He's too much like Pegasus."

"But cloning ain't possible," Earl insisted. "I know he's broken records and all, but it can't be. Besides, Tornado is gray."

Agent T stood beside Earl. "A horse can be dyed," he said. "Look at what these kids did to Pegasus last year. And I'm afraid to say, cloning is very possible. The CRU scientists have been doing it on a small scale for years. If they had enough genetic material from Pegasus, it would be the obvious thing to do."

Earl's eyes flashed open and he snapped his fingers. "Hey, do you think them others could be—"

Agent T shook his head and flashed Earl a quick warning. "Later . . ."

Emily studied Agent T's face and Earl's reaction. Something was going on between them. Just as she was about to ask, Chrysaor came forward and knocked Agent T backward as he made several loud and angry squeals.

"Don't you squeal at me, pig!" Agent T fumed as he recovered. "I'm not the one doing it. I told you, I left the CRU."

"Chrysaor, please," Joel said. "Losing your temper isn't helping." He concentrated on Agent T. "Why would they do it?"

Agent T gave the winged boar a final threatening look before saying, "Olympians are much stronger than humans." He paused and looked at Pegasus, Chrysaor, and Alexis. "And it seems most of you can fly. Think about it. What could the CRU achieve if they had an army of laboratory-created Olympians?"

Shock tore through the room like wildfire. Pegasus

pounded the tile floor with a golden hoof while Chrysaor squealed in rage. Paelen's face went ashen, and Alexis roared and drew her claws.

"Quiet!" Agent T ordered. "Do you want the neighbors to hear? They'll call the police and we'll all be captured."

Emily stood in silence, fearing the worst. If Jupiter had heard that one comment, there would be no stopping him. "They wouldn't, would they?"

"They could and they would," Agent T insisted. "That is what the CRU do. Use new technology to create weapons to better equip our military."

Emily shook her head. "You don't understand what this means! If it's true and the CRU is building an army of cloned Olympians, it will mean the end of everything."

Earl put his arm around Emily. "Calm down, I can't hardly understand you. What do you mean the end of everythin'?"

"Your world," Paelen finally said. "If the CRU has created Olympians, Jupiter will destroy the Earth."

BEFORE LONG, EVERYONE WAS GATHERED together to eat. Though they had ambrosia, Pegasus and Paelen also ate a whole box of sugary breakfast cereal and introduced Alexis and Chrysaor to the joys of glazed doughnuts.

While they ate, they told Earl and Agent T everything that had happened since they left the cabin in the woods and had gone to the Nirad world to fight the gorgons. Earl whistled in disbelief.

"Gorgons? Them snaky-haired women from the stories? They are real? They was the cause of all that trouble?"

Emily nodded. "They wanted to take over Olympus and tried to get me to use my powers to kill Jupiter.

When I wouldn't, they turned all of us to stone."

"For real?" Earl cried. "Just like in the stories?"

Again Emily nodded.

"What happened?"

"Emily melted the stone around her," Paelen added. "Then she melted the gorgons."

"You melted the gorgons?" Earl repeated.

Emily shrugged. "I lost my temper and kinda unleashed my powers. The Flame did the rest."

"Then she used her powers to turn us back from stone," Paelen finished.

Earl whistled. "Boy, I sure woulda liked to have seen that!"

Agent T was rubbing his chin. He looked around at the odd assortment of Olympians in the room. "Tell me something. The myths, are they all true? Everything?"

Joel leaned forward. "Seem to be. They're not exactly the same, but close. From what I've learned, the Olympians used to come here all the time."

"Why?" Earl asked.

"Because you were interesting," Alexis answered. "We were studying you."

"You were studying us?" Agent T asked incredulously.

"Of course," Alexis replied. "You were a savage people, always going to war. We found you fascinating. But you were contaminating us with your violent ways, so Jupiter stopped all visits to your world. He had hoped you would learn from your mistakes and embrace peace. From what I have seen and heard, you have not."

"Who is he to judge us?" Agent T shot back. "Or to decide if we can exist or not?"

Alexis narrowed her eyes. "He is Jupiter."

Earl looked over to Joel. "What about you? What happened to your arm?"

Emily sighed. "That's my fault."

Joel shook his head. "No, it's not. The gorgons did this to me, not you." He turned to Earl. "When I was stone, I fell over and my arm smashed. Emily tried to heal me, but it wouldn't work." He held up his silver right arm and wiggled his silver fingers. "Vulcan made this for me in his forge. I don't know how it works. There are no electronic parts and if you look, you can't see any joints for the fingers. But it's better and much stronger than my real arm. The only thing is I can't feel with it. But at least it can't be hurt."

Agent T leaned closer and studied Joel's arm and hand with the kind of intensity that disturbed Emily. She'd seen that same expression when he was in the laboratory with the wounded Pegasus on Governors Island. "The CRU would love to get hold of that thing," he mused softly. "Can you take it off?"

Joel shook his head. "Nope. It's attached to me now."

"So if they wanted it, they'd have to surgically remove it from you," Agent T muttered.

"The CRU is not going to see it!" Emily shot back. "They've caused enough trouble already. If they've created clones, Jupiter is going to destroy this world."

"Don't be ridiculous," Agent T spat. "If Jupiter is so pro-peace, he wouldn't destroy this planet just because the CRU may have created a few clones. He couldn't."

"You don't know Jupiter," Joel said. "He is very protective of the Olympians."

"And the order of nature," Emily added. "It's true that in the past some of the Olympians had children with humans. But that was natural. Clones being created in a lab are different. Diana and Pluto know about this and why we're here. If it's true, they won't stop Jupiter."

"Ah, yes—Diana," Agent T said. "Interesting woman. How is she?"

"Still angry," Joel said. "Even more so now that this has happened."

Agent T shook his head. "This is insane. A few Olympians can't possibly come to Earth to destroy the whole planet. You may be powerful, but we have weapons and we will defend ourselves."

Pegasus was standing beside Emily, munching on his large bowl of cereal. He raised his head and nickered.

"You cannot defend yourselves against Jupiter," Paelen translated. "He would not even need to come to your world to destroy it."

Emily looked at Pegasus and frowned. "He wouldn't?"

Both Pegasus and Chrysaor started to make sounds.

Paelen raised his eyebrows. "I did not know this."

"What?" Emily asked. "Paelen, what did they say? How would Jupiter do it?"

"He would open the Solar Stream and turn it on Earth."

"What?" Joel cried. "The Solar Stream?"

Earl frowned. "Ain't that the special superhighway you guys use to come to here?"

Paelen nodded. "Jupiter has control of it. All he needs is to combine his powers with his brothers', and they can redirect the Solar Stream. When they are gathered together, they are called the Big Three. And collectively they have the power to shift its direction. Instead of it opening up beside your world as it does now, they would point it at your world. The energy of a billion suns would obliterate your planet in an instant."

Emily sat in stunned silence. How many times had she traveled within the Solar Stream without really thinking about what it was or how it worked? It was just a means of transport. She never imagined it could be turned into a weapon of mass destruction.

"We've traveled through the Solar Stream lots of times," she said to Earl and Agent T. "You can feel its power when you're in it."

"We've got to stop him," Earl said.

Agent T shook his head. "Wait! You are all jumping the gun. Right now, this is only speculation. There is no proof that the CRU have done anything at all. But even if they have, I am certain we could reason with Jupiter."

Alexis sat up on her haunches and rested her front paws on the table right beside Agent T. She narrowed her eyes at the ex–CRU agent. "Jupiter cannot be reasoned with when the sin is too great. If your people have created New Olympians, nothing will stop him. He can and will destroy this world."

"They are not my people anymore," Agent T said as he leaned closer to her and stared defiantly into the Sphinx's green eyes. "I am not responsible for what they are doing now."

"Once a CRU agent, always a CRU agent," Alexis growled.

Earl looked at everyone around the table. "We've got to find Tornado Warning and pray to God he's just a horse and not an Olympian clone."

"And if he is a clone?" Agent T posed.

Emily looked Agent T squarely in the eye. "Then we must stop the CRU before Jupiter finds out."

• • •

After breakfast, Agent T took Joel, Paelen, and Chrysaor into his small office to use his computer to search for Tornado Warning. Emily helped Earl clear the table.

"I was shocked to see Agent T still with you," Emily said to Earl as she washed a breakfast bowl.

"I ain't got much choice. I can't get him to leave me alone," Earl said, picking up a cloth to start drying. "Lord knows I've tried! I don't know what the heck you kids did to him. Last I saw, he was crazy for Cupid. But I wake up in the cabin and he's there and you guys are gone. He said Cupid told him he was my brother and that he's going to protect me forever. I can't hardly go to the toilet without him checkin' to see if it's safe first."

"Cupid shouldn't have done that," Emily said.

Earl sighed. "I may complain a lot. But the truth is he ain't that bad once you get to know him. I ain't never had a brother, and it's kinda nice. And he's saved my life more than once. He knows how them CRU folk work. He's kept us one step ahead of them. I'd have been a goner long before now if it weren't for him."

Emily dropped her head. "I'm really sorry about that. It would have been better if you'd never found us at the Red Apple. You'd have your old life back."

"Hey, hey, hey," Earl said softly. "Don't you go frettin' about that. I bless the day y'all came into my life. If I hadn't met that big fella out there"—Earl stepped through the door and stroked the stallion's face—"and the rest of you, my life would have been a lot emptier. Even though you left, I still felt part of you. It's kinda like you're my family that's gone on vacation but would come back one day. And look—here you are.

"And now I get to meet even more interesting people, like this pretty lady here." Earl approached Alexis. The Sphinx was sitting on her haunches and came up to just past his waist. "That Olympus must be one amazing place if folks like you are there."

Alexis's green eyes sparkled, and she smiled demurely. "Thank you, Earl. It is a pleasure to finally meet a human who appreciates true beauty." She shot a look at Emily. "Some people only regard me as a . . ." She paused. "What were the words you used, Emily? Oh yes, now I remember: an overgrown, green-eyed, flying house cat."

Emily's face reddened. She hadn't thought the Sphinx knew what she'd called her.

Earl turned to Emily in shock. "You didn't!"

Emily shrugged. "Well, I . . ."

"It is all right," Alexis said as she patted Earl's hand with her large paw. "I understand fully. She is jealous of me. She knows I am the better woman."

Emily inhaled sharply. "I am not jealous!"

Alexis looked up at Earl and nodded. "She is."

Beside them, Pegasus nickered.

"It's not funny, Pegs," Emily said.

Suddenly Joel appeared in the room. His face was ashen. "Em, you've got to see this. We have a big problem!"

Emily followed Joel into the small office.

Chrysaor was deeply troubled. The large boar was shaking his head back and forth and fluttering his coarse brown wings. Agent T was at his laptop computer, furiously tapping away on the keyboard, while Paelen was tearing through a scrapbook. Joel approached a large bulletin board on the wall. Newspaper articles were pinned all over it.

"What's that?" Emily asked.

"We've been keeping a record of Olympian sightings," Earl explained.

"What sightings?"

"Look." Joel pointed at a newspaper clipping. There was a blurry photo at the top of the article that looked like it had been taken with a security camera. The headline read: WOMAN WANTED FOR MURDER.

Emily peered closer and her jaw dropped. "That's Diana!" She looked back at Earl. "Why didn't you tell us about this earlier?"

"I started to," Earl defended himself.

"But I stopped him from mentioning it," Agent T finished.

"Why?"

"I wanted to know why you were here first." Agent T stood up and walked toward Emily. "But if this isn't the real Diana, these sightings and the clone theory must be linked."

"It can't be Diana," Emily insisted. "What's this woman done?"

"She is wanted for robbery and murder," Agent T said.

Pegasus whinnied loudly while Emily cried, "What?"

Agent T nodded. "I saw this article a few months

back and thought Diana had returned to Earth. Earl and I have been searching for any unusual stories that suggest it could be Olympians."

"Until y'all came back today, we really thought this was her," Earl added. "I ain't never met the lady myself, but Tom has. He says she's strong and mean enough to do this."

"Tom?" Emily asked.

Agent T nodded. "My real name is Thomas. I know what Diana is capable of. I was the one who supervised the tests on her when we had you at the Governors Island facility. When I saw this article, I was convinced she was back."

"We swear it wasn't her!" Joel said. "Yeah, she was here for a quick trip with Apollo and Emily's father, but there's no way that's her. They were being inconspicuous, and anyway, she just wouldn't!"

Agent T rubbed his chin. A troubled expression crossed his face. "Then this may be further evidence that the CRU have created clones. But if it's true, how are the clones on the loose? First there was Tornado Warning and now these sightings. I know for certain the CRU wouldn't be releasing them into the community. That would be too dangerous and raise far too many uncomfortable questions. The clones must be escaping somehow. But how are they getting around CRU security systems?"

Emily turned back to Pegasus, who was standing at the threshold. "It says the mysterious woman and her large accomplice broke into a jewelry store. They killed the owner and several employees and then stole a lot of jewels. The article says there was a walk-in safe at the back of the store. They don't understand how, but the heavy door was ripped off and the contents taken. It also says that there was one survivor of the massacre. He claimed that the woman's accomplice was a monster. It had four arms. Its face was covered, but it was huge and super-strong. It ripped the door right off the safe. He said he got a look at one of the creature's hands, and it was dark gray."

"That's a Nirad!" Paelen said.

Earl looked at Agent T. "I told you so! You wouldn't believe me when I said it could be a Nirad."

"When you told me, Olympus was still at war with the Nirads. It wasn't logical for Diana to be working with one. That they could be clones was never a consideration."

"But it is now," Joel said.

Emily nodded. "The article says the police think the man was in shock and didn't understand what he was seeing. They say the accomplice had been wearing a costume. There is a nationwide hunt for them going on right now."

In the doorway, Pegasus whinnied loudly. He pounded the floor with his hoof and tore a large hole in the carpet. Chrysaor squealed loudly. After their heated exchange, Paelen translated. "They believe this is confirmation of our worst fears. We know for certain that this wasn't Diana or a Nirad—they would never kill so senselessly. The only explanation is that they are creations of the CRU. This world is in even more danger. If Jupiter were to find out . . ."

"We know," Agent T shot. "He'll destroy us."

Alexis was scanning the photos in the newspaper clippings. "There have been multiple sightings of this Diana woman all over the country. The riddle is this: Is that the same woman appearing in all these different locations, or is there more than one?"

"It is not just Diana," Paelen said as he pulled a paper from the scrapbook. "It appears I have been up to mischief as well." He held up an article with a mug shot of a teenager who looked just like him. The boy was holding up a sign with a series of numbers beneath it. Though the face was Paelen's, the expression in the eyes was very different. The boy's eyes were wild and terrified.

Paelen handed the article to Emily. "What does this say?"

Emily read the story. "It seems this boy was caught after breaking into a chocolate shop. They found him on the floor, ravenously eating an entire tray of chocolates. The police caught him and took him to the station. It says the boy never spoke a single word and appeared petrified. After he was booked and photographed, he attacked the guards and managed to escape. One witness said he was superstrong and tossed everyone around like they weighed nothing. He then seemed to squeeze himself through an impossibly small window. They are still looking for him but think he's left the area."

"I thought that was you in that article," Earl said

to Paelen. "But if it ain't, then we're all in a heap of trouble."

"I swear it is not I," Paelen insisted. "Though I must admit, I do like chocolate. But had it been me, I would not have been caught."

"Emily, where did that story happen?" Joel asked.

Emily scanned the article. "Las Vegas." She looked back up to the wall and the article with the woman who looked like Diana. "Where was the jewelry store?"

"Salt Lake City, Utah," Joel read. "And this one has Diana in Denver, Colorado. And here is a sighting in Virginia."

"We've found articles about them from all over," Earl said. "If they ain't the real Diana and a Nirad, where are they coming from?" He looked at Agent T. "What CRU facility could be creating clones?"

Agent T shrugged. "I don't know. There are multiple facilities all over this country. We also have several others scattered around the world. Any one of them could be doing it."

"Just how big is the CRU?" Joel asked.

"It's massive," Agent T answered. "It's larger than the CIA, FBI, and FSA combined."

Emily sucked in her breath. "How is that possible? I don't understand how they could be so big and no one really knows about them!"

"That's the way it was set up. I was recruited into the CRU straight from college. They have been around since the 1930s. They don't answer to the president or Congress. They're completely self-governing and independent."

Silence filled the room as everyone tried to digest the new information. Until now, no one had any idea just how large and dangerous the CRU really were. Finally Alexis approached Agent T. She raised herself up on her haunches and placed her paws on his shoulders. Her claws were out as she held her furious face centimeters from his. "Tell me now. How do we find out which facility is creating these Olympians?"

"There is only one way I can think of," Agent T answered, again meeting the Sphinx's challenge without fear. "We've got to find that racehorse. If he is a clone, we'll find his owner and demand to know where he got him."

"Did you find Tornado Warning?" Emily asked.

"Yes and no," the ex–CRU agent answered. When

the Sphinx released him, he reached for the pages he'd printed. "There are countless articles about him. After the Triple Crown win, his owner reported that he's retiring him. Tornado Warning is at his home stables at the Double R Ranch in California. His owner is a man called Rip Russell. He says he's putting the stallion out to stud."

"Stud?" Emily cried. "If he is a clone of Pegasus and they start to breed him . . ."

"There could be a lot of winged horses being born," Paelen finished.

Pegasus went mad. The stallion pounded the floor and reared up in fury until his head struck and cracked the ceiling. He kicked a hole in the wall behind him and screamed before trotting down the short hall into the room, where he took his rage out on the furniture in the room.

As a coffee table shattered to splinters, Emily ran up to him. "Pegs, calm down!" she soothed. "Please, you can't let anyone hear you!"

Pegasus snorted and continued to pound the floor, shattering the white tiles beneath him. Chrysaor ran up to the stallion, trying to calm him down.

"I promise you we won't let that happen," Emily said. "We'll go out there and stop them."

"We will," Joel agreed as he and the others followed. "We won't let them do this."

Emily looked desperately to the others. "Should we go now? We could use the Solar Stream to get there."

Alexis shook her head. "That would not be wise. We have been here longer than expected already. If we enter the Solar Stream, it may arouse Jupiter's suspicions. If you wish to protect this world and remain hidden until we solve this riddle, we must travel by other means."

"But we can't fly over three thousand miles in one night," Emily said.

"No, we cannot," the Sphinx agreed. "We must avoid being seen."

"That's easy for you to say," Emily challenged. "Pluto gave you his helmet of invisibility. But that won't help Pegasus or Chrysaor."

Pegasus nickered. Paelen said, "He says we have no choice. We must find Tornado Warning before he reproduces. We can fly by night and hide during the day."

"So it's settled," Agent T said. He turned to Earl. "Pack up, we leave tonight."

Everyone turned to the ex–CRU agent.

"What are you all looking at?" Agent T challenged. "You don't expect me to sit idly by while you kids determine our planet's future, do you? I may be ex–CRU, but I still care for this world. I have skills and specialist knowledge you'll need. If the CRU really are behind this, who better to help than me?"

AFTER MUCH ARGUING, IT WAS FINALLY
agreed that taking Agent T and Earl with them
would be the best option. With the CRU still pursuing them, it was time for the two men to move
on anyway. Agent T also voiced deep concerns that
the Olympians may have been spotted in the Florida
skies before they arrived. He drew out all his weapons and prepared to fight. While Agent T guarded
the inside of the house, Alexis put on Pluto's helmet
and prepared to watch the exterior.

When she first donned the helmet, Emily feared
it didn't work. She could still see the Sphinx. But
when the others couldn't see Alexis, they concluded
that this was another one of Emily's hidden powers.

Emily watched the Sphinx go into the backyard. Alexis spread her wings wide and launched into the air and flew up to the roof of the small house. There she settled to watch for any approaching danger.

Exhausted from the long night, the others settled down for some much-needed rest. Pegasus was too upset to settle, but stood watch over Emily and the others as they slept.

At sunset, Pegasus woke Emily and Joel. Paelen was already up and eating ambrosia cakes smothered in honey, cherry jam, half a bag of sugar, and chocolate syrup. Emily was surprised to find the Sphinx working closely with Agent T. The two had laid out maps on the dining room table, and using Agent T's compass, they were plotting their course to Ramona, California, where the Double R Ranch was located.

As she rose from the sofa and stretched, Emily studied Pegasus. The stallion had calmed some, but his eyes were still too bright and alert. The news of Tornado Warning going out to stud had badly affected him.

"Are you all right, Pegs?" she asked softly as she stroked the stallion's neck.

Pegasus looked at her. Deep in his eyes she saw the vision of the two of them soaring in the night skies over Olympus. This was Pegasus's dream: to be back safely home with her.

"I wish we were back there too," Emily agreed. "I hate what the CRU might have done. But we'll stop them, Pegs. I know we will."

Pegasus nudged Emily, and she hugged his neck tightly.

"Is he all right?" Joel asked as he came up.

"He will be," Emily said, "once this is over."

Joel reached out and patted the winged stallion. "Pegasus, we could be wrong, you know. Tornado Warning could just be a very fast racehorse. And that woman the police are looking for? She may just look like Diana. Who knows, we could be back in Olympus in a day or two and laughing about this."

Emily knew Joel too well. He was saying this for Pegasus. Deep in his heart, he didn't believe it. But she was grateful to him for trying.

"Joel's right, Pegs," she agreed. "It could all be a strange coincidence."

In the dining area, Agent T was marking a course

on the map. He looked up at Emily and Joel. "Good, you're up. Earl's in the kitchen. Grab yourselves something to eat; we'll be leaving shortly. We've got a long flight ahead of us." He reached over and picked up a large sweatshirt and then a pair of gloves. "Joel, I've got these for you. Put it on and wear the gloves."

"You want me to wear a sweatshirt in this heat?"

Agent T nodded. "Unless you want the world to see that magical silver arm and hand of yours, you'll do as I say."

Emily and Joel continued into the kitchen. She looked back at Agent T. "Who put him in charge?"

Joel followed her eyes. Agent T was back in deep discussion with Alexis. As they listened, they heard the Sphinx and ex–CRU agent discussing security measures and what they would do if they were opposed. Emily was shocked to hear them not only getting along—they were in complete agreement. If anyone tried to stop them, they were prepared to kill.

She looked at Joel. "I guess that's what puts them in charge."

When they were ready to go, they filed silently into the dark backyard. Instead of forcing Pegasus through the glass door again, Earl and Agent T took it off its tracks and opened it up completely. Pegasus fitted through without a problem.

Emily invited Earl to ride with her on Pegasus, while Alexis offered to carry Agent T. As the group took to the air, they flew as high as the humans could withstand. With the light of the moon and Agent T's compass to guide them, they started the long journey west.

Earl whooped and cheered like a kid at riding Pegasus. His excitement was infectious, and he kept Emily in fits of laughter as he waved and called to Paelen and then over to Joel on Chrysaor. Even after several long hours, Earl was still enjoying the ride.

As the long night slowly passed and the sky behind them started to lighten, Agent T finally directed Alexis down lower in the sky. Passing through the clouds beneath them, they saw the streetlights of a large city below.

"If our calculations are correct, that should be Baton Rouge, Louisiana," Agent T turned back and called to them. "We're going to pass over the main city and find somewhere to stop on the other side of it. Understood?"

Everyone called their agreement. Before the dawn arrived fully, they flew down closer to the ground. Emily saw early-morning traffic on the interstate highway directly beneath them. Following its path, they came across the last motel in the area.

Alexis glided lower and finally chose a spot to land in an open field behind the two-story motel. Earl climbed off Pegasus first and helped Emily down. Joel climbed stiffly off Chrysaor and looked around. "Are we sure we want to stop at a motel? Wouldn't it be safer to find some woods or something?"

Agent T shook his head. "No. That would be a mistake. Out in the open you feel exposed and never truly rest. For what we are facing, we need to stay fresh and sharp. Alexis, Pegasus, and Chrysaor especially need to recover after two long nights of heavy flight. We need somewhere private for them to rest their wings."

Emily hated to admit it, but Agent T was right. She could see Pegasus was tired. His wings were drooping a bit and his head was down.

She looked at the others. "He's right. You need your rest."

Agent T stepped up to Earl. "Come with me—it's the usual cover story. We're two brothers who've driven all night. Our car broke down and it's in the garage. We'll get a double room at the very back and say we need to sleep all day and don't want to be disturbed."

Earl nodded and looked to the others. "Y'all stay here. We've done this before. As soon as we get the room, we'll come for you."

Emily stood beside Pegasus as they waited for Earl and Agent T to return. Joel and Paelen came up to her.

"Do you think we should trust Agent T?" Joel asked. "He was with the CRU. What if he turns us in to get his job back?"

Alexis was lounging on the ground. Her eyes were closed, and she was enjoying the fragrance of the predawn air. "He would not do that," she answered softly. Rising, the Sphinx padded closer to the group. "He may not like you," she said truthfully. "But he will not betray you. There is too much at stake."

"How can you be so certain?" Emily asked.

Alexis cocked her head to the side and narrowed

her green eyes. Emily was certain that if she could, the Sphinx would have put her hands on her hips. "Are you suggesting I do not know my job? That after all this time, I cannot read a human's intentions?"

Emily sighed. She shook her head tiredly. "I'm sorry, Alexis. I didn't mean to insult you. But you don't understand what the CRU did to us."

"Especially Agent T," Paelen added.

The Sphinx calmed and sat down. "No, I was not there and do not know what he did," she admitted. "But I do know the man who has been riding on my back all night. He is changed. Whether it was Cupid's charm or the realization of what the CRU have done, I do not know. But he is on our side. Tom will be a great ally."

Emily looked at Joel and raised an eyebrow. "Tom?"

Paelen caught Emily's arm. He shook his head. "Do not say more. She is tired and worried like the rest of us."

The arrival of Agent T cut off further conversation. "All right—we've got a double room on the ground floor, just in from the end." He concentrated on Alexis. "We'll use Pluto's helmet to get you into the room one at a time. People are starting to move around and check out. No one but Earl and I must be seen."

One by one, the helmet was used to sneak the Olympians into the cramped motel room. Once again, Pegasus had difficulty squeezing through the narrow doorway. But with help, the invisible stallion was finally shoved through.

The DO NOT DISTURB sign was hung on the door, and the two mattresses were pulled off the beds and put on the floor to create a more comfortable sleeping space for everyone. Before long, everyone had fallen into a deep, exhausted sleep.

When Emily woke up, there was still light coming from behind the curtains. She looked over and saw Pegasus was also awake. "You okay, Pegs?" she whispered softly.

The stallion pressed his muzzle to her hand. His eyes were still bright and alert. There was no mistaking it. Pegasus was scared. Despite what Joel had said before, Pegasus didn't believe it either. Deep inside, the stallion knew that somehow, Tornado Warning was part of him.

Emily rose to use the bathroom. In the tight, crowded room, she had to climb over Pegasus. Then she stepped over Joel on the other mattress. But as she put her foot down, she trod on Chrysaor. The winged boar squealed and complained loudly.

"Sorry! Go back to sleep," Emily hushed, as she gave him a light pat. She looked around to see if his squeals had awoken the others. Satisfied that they remained asleep, Emily continued her obstacle course to the bathroom. But as she entered, she found Alexis lounging on her back in an overflowing bathtub.

"Did your father not teach you to knock?" Alexis demanded.

Too stunned at the sight of the Sphinx in the bath, Emily backed out of the room and shut the door quietly behind her. Paelen was awake and smiled at her.

"She's been in there half the day," he whispered.

Irritated by the need to use the toilet, Emily muttered, "I thought cats hated water."

"I heard that, Emily!" Alexis called from the bathroom.

. . .

Hours later, everyone was up and moving around. Joel was introducing Paelen and Chrysaor to the joys of cable television. Paelen held the remote and was learning to channel surf. "Pegasus, move out of the way—you are blocking my view!" he complained as he tried to see around the large stallion. There was just so much to watch, he couldn't settle on one station for more than a minute or two. "This is amazing," he cried as he started to follow a science-fiction movie. "We must get this in Olympus!"

Chrysaor squealed loudly in protest when Paelen changed the channel again. He tried to snatch the remote from Paelen.

Joel looked at Emily. "Do you think Jupiter would go for satellite or cable TV?"

"Neither," she laughed as she watched her friends enjoying their first television experience.

On the bed behind them, Agent T was counting out his remaining money. "Earl, how much cash do you have left?" he asked.

Earl opened his wallet and pulled out two ten-dollar bills. "Twenty bucks, that's it."

Agent T looked at Emily. "Did you bring anything from Olympus we can sell?"

"No, we didn't expect to be here this long. The plan was to get a close look at Tornado Warning and then go right back."

Agent T sighed. "We have ninety-seven dollars left. That won't get us another room, let alone a lot of food."

"Well, we can't go back to Olympus for more," Emily said.

Alexis finally emerged from the bathroom. Her dark hair was up in a towel, and she was struggling to pull on a T-shirt with her paws. As Emily helped her finish getting dressed, the Sphinx's eyes settled on Paelen. "It is lucky that we have a very good thief among us."

Paelen looked up. "I am not a thief anymore," he complained. "Why will no one believe me?"

Agent T rose from the bed. "Because we need a good thief right now, and you're elected."

Paelen handed the remote to Chrysaor and came closer. "What do you need?"

"Money," Agent T said.

"And food," Earl said. "We can't all eat the ambrosia; you Olympians need that."

Paelen nodded. "I will go. How do I find money? The last time we needed it, Cupid won a costume competition. I do not know if there is another such competition around here."

"I'll come with you," Joel volunteered. "Your sandals can carry us both. And if Alexis will let me, I'll use Pluto's helmet to stay invisible while you use your talent to stretch yourself out and fit into wherever we need to go."

The Sphinx carried the helmet over to Joel. She smiled warmly. "Anything for you. You just ask and it will be my command."

Emily balled her hands into tight fists. As she did, the ceramic lamp on the table beside her exploded.

"What the hell?" Earl cried as he jumped away from the flying pieces.

"Sorry," Emily quickly said. "My hand accidentally hit it."

"That wasn't your hand," Joel challenged. "That lamp blew up!"

Emily was shaking in fear as her new powers

surfaced again. She couldn't let the others know about them. Not now, when the world was at stake. "No, Joel, it was me. I hit it. Now, are you going or not?"

He nodded but continued to inspect the remains of the lamp. "Yeah, we're going." Finally he looked at Agent T. "Do you know how much money they keep in bank machines?"

"More than enough," the ex–CRU agent said. "But they are built tough. I doubt you'll get into one before the police catch you."

"I've got this," Joel said as he held up his silver arm. "All I need to do is get it open. Paelen can do the rest by slipping in and getting the cash."

Agent T nodded. "Try it if you want, but be careful. Those things are heavily alarmed. If that doesn't work, you're going to have to go somewhere else. Try to find a pawnshop. They always have a lot of cash in them. But be warned. The owners are usually armed, and there are going to be cameras everywhere."

"That's why we're taking this." Joel held up Pluto's helmet. He looked over to Paelen. "The sun is down; let's go."

WHEN JOEL AND PAELEN LEFT, WITH LITTLE
do to but wait, Emily took a bath. As she lay back
in the tub, she was glad to finally take off her leg
brace. Though it helped her to walk, it was heavy and
rubbed her skin painfully.

She dozed in the warm water until Alexis entered
the bathroom. "Did your father not teach you to
knock?" Emily challenged, repeating the Sphinx's
words back to her.

Alexis ignored the comment. She shut the door
and approached the side of the tub. "Do you wish to
tell me what happened out there?"

Emily looked away and shook her head. "I don't
know what you're talking about."

"You may fool the others, but you cannot fool a Sphinx. You were angry at me and you caused the lamp to explode."

Emily gasped. Alexis knew everything. "I don't want to talk about it."

Alexis sat beside the tub and put her paws up on the side. "You may not wish to, but you are going to. I know you do not like me, and that is your choice. But I took an oath to protect you and this mission. If I see something wrong, I am going to act upon it. So you might just as well tell me, because I am going to find out anyway."

"Aren't you going to give me a choice?" Emily asked. "Bargain with a riddle or something? If I get the riddle wrong, I tell you, but if I get it right, you leave me alone?"

"Not this time," Alexis said. "You must tell me what happened."

Emily dropped her head and sighed. She looked into the penetrating green eyes of the Sphinx. "I have more powers, and I can't control them," she admitted. "When Vesta first told me about the Flame, she said I'd learn to control it, and I have."

Emily lifted her hand out of the water. She summoned up the Flame, and it burned brightly and painlessly in the palm of her wet hand. "I can do anything I want with the Flame now."

"But . . . ," the Sphinx prodded.

"But these new powers are unpredictable, and they really scare me. Sometimes I can move things. Sometimes items disappear and I can never find them again. And sometimes . . ."

"Sometimes they explode," the Sphinx finished. "Why haven't you told anyone? I am sure Vesta and Jupiter would be very interested to know."

"I was going to," Emily said.

The Sphinx tilted her head to the side.

"Eventually," Emily finished. "But then Dad came back with the papers, talking about Tornado Warning, and that became more important."

"More important than making things disappear or destroying them?"

"I know," Emily said. "But if I told anyone, I couldn't have come back here. And look what we've learned so far."

Alexis sat back and dropped her paws to the wet

floor. "I do understand, Emily. Your dedication to Pegasus and this world is a credit to you. But you have endangered everyone you care for by not telling Vesta and letting her try to help you control these new powers."

Tears came to Emily's eyes. Now used to the explosive danger they posed, she kept the sea-green handkerchief with the embroidered Pegasus that Neptune had given to her close. It alone had the power to contain her tears so they couldn't do any harm. She reached for it and gently dabbed her eyes and watched the tears slipping into the secret pocket. "I'm just so scared. What am I supposed to do?"

The Sphinx reached out with her large paw and stroked Emily's head. "This must be very difficult for you: to be a child and yet so powerful. I can imagine your life and Jupiter's must have been very similar. But he learned to control his powers; I am confident you will do the same. All I can suggest is that until you learn to master them, you do your best to control your temper."

Emily looked down into the water until Alexis put her paw under her chin and drew her head up. She leaned closer. "Emily, people are going to come and go in your life who you may not like and who may annoy or upset you. You must learn to tolerate them. It appears that extreme emotions trigger your powers."

Emily sniffed and nodded. "You're right. I'll try."

Alexis shook her head. "You must do better than try, Emily. You must succeed—if only to protect your friends."

The Sphinx rose and moved for the door. "I have heard it said among humans that when they are upset, they count to ten. May I suggest you try doing the same?"

As she was about to leave, Emily called to her. "Alexis, wait!" When the Sphinx paused, she continued, "Please don't tell anyone about this. I don't want my best friends to be frightened of me."

"I won't tell them," Alexis agreed. "Not unless your powers become too unpredictable. Emily, I am here to protect them, too—even if it means protecting them from you."

When Emily emerged from the bath, she found Earl and Agent T chatting softly while Pegasus, Chrysaor, and Alexis were glued to an old Elvis Presley movie on TV. Alexis was roaring with laughter.

When Elvis started to sing, Alexis sighed dreamily. "I am in love. I must find that man."

While stroking Pegasus, Emily wondered if she should tell the Sphinx that Elvis had been dead a long time. But before she could say a word, there was a soft knock on the door.

Agent T sprang from the bed. He opened the door a crack, peered out, and then let Joel and Paelen into the room.

Joel was carrying two large pizza boxes, while Paelen had other bags of groceries. Emily immediately noticed that Paelen was covered in hundreds of tiny cuts.

"What happened to you?"

Joel started to laugh. "He was eaten by a bank machine!"

Paelen shot him a dirty look. "We had some difficulty getting the money out of the machine. Joel was able to punch a hole in it, but when I stretched out and entered it, the metal cut me to pieces."

"Were you able to get any money?" Agent T asked.

Paelen handed over a thick stack of twenty-dollar bills.

While the money was counted, Emily reached out and touched Paelen. As she traced lines along his deep cuts and gashes, her powers started to heal him. Within moments, his skin was back to normal.

"Excellent," Agent T said. "This should get us safely to California." He looked around the room. "Everyone eat; we've got a long night ahead of us."

The night passed slowly as the group made their way west. Before long they had flown over Louisiana and were crossing Texas. As they finally reached New Mexico, Emily and Earl marveled at the sudden appearance of clusters of golden light from towns and cities in the seemingly endless darkness beneath them.

Eventually they landed outside an old motel. Joel was excited to discover they were on the outskirts of Roswell, New Mexico. "This place is famous! It's where they claim aliens crashed in the 1940s," he explained to Paelen.

"Aliens did crash here," Agent T confirmed. "Where do you think we get some of our modern technology and weapons from?"

"When I was first captured by the CRU, Agent J and Agent O kept calling me an alien," Paelen said.

"That was our first thought," Agent T explained. "It was easier to believe you were an alien than Olympian because we knew already that aliens existed."

"And now?" Emily asked.

"Now we know that Olympians exist as well. Though if you ask me, since Olympus is another world away from Earth, technically, you could still be called aliens."

Exhaustion from the long flight caught up with them as they piled into the small motel room. The sun rose, crossed the sky, and finally set in the west while the group slept. As the last of the daylight faded, they awoke and prepared for the final leg of the journey to California.

"I hope we are not here much longer," Paelen said as he ate his last ambrosia cake. "You know what happens when we go too long without this. Even with sugar, we become weak and vulnerable."

"With luck, we'll be going back tomorrow night," Joel said, munching on his burger and fries. "Once we see Tornado for ourselves and prove he's just a horse, we're free to go back."

"And if he really is a clone?" Emily asked.

"Then we are all in trouble," Agent T said darkly, "not just the Olympians lacking their food."

The final comment settled heavily in the air as the group used Pluto's helmet to exit the room without being seen. They gathered together behind the old motel.

"All right," Agent T said, "by my calculations, if we put on more speed, we should arrive at Ramona before dawn. That will give us time to find the Double R Ranch to see Tornado Warning for ourselves. What happens next is anyone's guess. I don't like not knowing, but we don't have much choice."

As Emily climbed on Pegasus, it felt like lead was settling heavily in her stomach. This was it. Within a few hours they would discover the truth. But even before they saw Tornado for themselves, somehow Emily already knew the answer. He wasn't a horse. Tornado Warning was a clone of her beloved Pegasus, created by the CRU.

WITH EACH POWERFUL WING BEAT, EMILY
felt her tension grow. She looked at the others flying
around her and, in the dim light of the stars, was able
to see their expressions were the same. Paelen was
leaning forward as his winged sandals carried him
onward. His arms were crossed over his chest and his
expression grim. Even Earl stopped chatting and sat
quietly behind her on the back of the stallion. They
were all sharing her fears.

As they flew over mostly desert with very little population, without the fear of being seen, Alexis directed
the group lower in the sky. Up high, the temperatures
were much colder and it was hard on Joel, Earl, and
Agent T. Emily was no longer bothered by the cold,

but for most of the trip when they traveled over populated areas, she had felt Earl shivering behind her.

Continuing through the night, the landscape beneath them changed. From the sharp cliffs and mesas of Texas, New Mexico, and then Arizona, they were entering a region of rolling mountain ranges that was the entrance to California. It was still all desert terrain, and yet it looked so different.

Ahead of them, Alexis and Agent T continued to lead the way. The ex–CRU agent was holding his compass in one hand and struggling with a map in the other. He gripped a small flashlight in his teeth. Despite how she felt about him, she was grateful he was here. It was true. He did possess skills they needed. Without him, the trip to California would have been much more difficult.

After they had been flying for several hours, Agent T directed everyone lower. They were surrounded by mountains on either side that climbed high in the sky. Though it was still dark, they could now make out shapes and structures.

Soon they came upon a small town. Most of the lights were off, and there was no traffic on the road.

But almost immediately Emily felt a change in Pegasus. The stallion was snorting and his ears flicked back.

"Are you all right?" Emily called forward.

Pegasus didn't react. Peering closer, she could see his nostrils were flared and his eyes were wide and bright. She also noticed his glow had increased. "What is it, Pegasus?"

"We are near Tornado Warning," Paelen explained as he flew closer. "Pegasus can sense him and he does not like it."

Beneath her, Pegasus started to tremble. Chrysaor flew on the other side of the stallion and started to squeal at his brother.

"What's happening?" Joel called.

"Pegasus can feel Tornado Warning. We're getting close." She leaned forward and patted his neck again. "Just take it easy, Pegs."

"I don't like this," Earl said. "He may be an Olympian, but Pegasus is still a full-blooded stallion. We may be in for a lot of trouble."

Earl voiced what Emily was trying hard not to. For the first time ever, Pegasus was starting to frighten her. Something was driving him on. If that something was Tornado, what would he do when they met?

Emily got her answer much more quickly than she expected. Pegasus sped up. He left the others far behind as he tore through the town and started to follow along a dark road. In the predawn light, Emily saw a chain-link fence surrounding a large property. They flew over a tall gate that was the entrance. Emily barely had time to read the sign, DOUBLE R RANCH.

Directly ahead were multiple paddocks. Farther in the distance, they saw several dark shapes that were buildings. But Pegasus kept going. He flew right over the top of the first set of stable blocks and outbuildings without slowing down. Finally Emily saw their destination. It was a large, squat, circular stable at the very center of the property.

Even before Pegasus landed, they heard sounds coming from inside the stables. The horses were awake and screaming. It was almost like the first time they'd visited the carriage stables in New York. But this was different, because one voice rose higher and more furious than the others.

"That's got to be Tornado," Emily said. "He knows Pegasus is here."

Pegasus hit the ground in a full gallop. Emily had to cling to his mane to keep from being thrown off. Earl wrapped his arms tightly around her waist and did his best to stay on the stallion's back.

"Stop, Pegs," Emily cried as the stallion charged forward. "Let us down!"

Pausing only long enough for Emily and Earl to dismount, Pegasus charged forward. Glowing brilliant white, the stallion ran up to the locked stable doors. He reared high in the air as his golden hooves tore through the doors like they were made of paper.

"Pegasus, stop!" Emily screamed as she watched him losing control. The stallion threw back his head and screeched in fury as the doors came free of their hinges. Without a pause, he stormed into the stable.

Emily and Earl charged in behind Pegasus just as the others landed on the ground behind them.

"Emily, wait!" Joel called. "It's too dangerous!"

But Emily had to stop Pegasus before he did something to endanger them all.

Pegasus's glow lit the darkened stable enough to see that it was a huge circle with an open center ring for training. Countless stalls lined the circular walls.

Their doors were solid on the lower half, with bars on the upper. There were horses at the front of each. Eyes bright, they were shrieking and kicking at the tall doors to get out. But despite their strength, the doors were holding. All but one.

Light blazed through the bars as its occupant glowed almost as much as Pegasus. He was kicking at the sealed door, and large cracks formed on the outside.

"It's Tornado Warning!" Emily cried. "Look, he's glowing just like Pegasus!"

Pegasus was on the outside of the stall door, kicking at the wood in fury. His eyes were wild and enraged. This was not the stallion Emily knew and loved. Pegasus had gone insane.

"Pegasus, no!" Emily cried. "Stop!"

If he heard her, he gave no sign. Within moments, the wood of the door shattered and Tornado Warning charged out of his stable. Rearing up, the two glowing stallions attacked each other with all the fury they possessed.

Pegasus's wings opened and smashed at Tornado's head, knocking him into the large open training ring.

"Pegasus, stop!" Emily howled as she ran closer.

"Emily, no!" Alexis cried. Racing forward, the Sphinx slammed Emily to the ground and pinned her down with her large paws. "They will hurt you if you go near."

"Let me up!" Emily howled. "I've got to stop them!"

"You cannot stop them!" Alexis shouted. "Not even Jupiter could!"

"I've got to try before they kill each other!"

"How?" Paelen ran up to her. "Look at them! I have never seen Pegasus fight with such fury before. Even his brother cannot stop him!"

Chrysaor was in the middle of the fight, squealing and trying to separate the two deranged stallions. But all his presence achieved was to infuriate Tornado Warning further. The gray stallion rose high in the air and came crashing down on Chrysaor with his powerful front hooves.

Driven to the ground, the winged boar squealed in pain. His cries fed Pegasus's fury as he launched a new attack on Tornado Warning and drove him away from Chrysaor.

"Joel, help me get Chrysaor," Paelen called. They dashed into the ring and dragged the boar away from the fight. Chrysaor squealed and left a trail of blood behind him.

"Please, help him," Alexis said as she let Emily up.

Emily nodded and knelt beside Chrysaor. She saw two deep gashes on his back where Tornado's hooves had cut deeply into his skin. One wing was badly damaged. The boar moaned in pain.

"It's all right," Emily soothed as she gently touched the boar's wounds. "You'll be fine in a minute."

As she healed the damage caused by Tornado, Emily realized that when Chrysaor and Pegasus had fought at the Red Apple, Pegasus had held back. Tornado hadn't. Looking at the wound, Emily understood Alexis's warning. One good kick from Tornado Warning could kill.

When she finished healing Chrysaor, Emily looked up and watched the deadly fight continue. She felt helpless to stop it as Pegasus reared up and kicked at Tornado Warning. But the gray stallion would not back down. He was also rearing and biting at Pegasus as murder flashed in his bright eyes. Each time one stallion's hooves made contact with the other, they cut deep gouges in their opponent's skin.

The furious sounds coming from the fighting

stallions were deafening in the large stable. No one heard the workers from the ranch arriving. A blast from a shotgun fired at Pegasus alerted the group.

"No!" Emily howled as a man raised his gun to fire a second time. Even before Alexis could move, Emily reacted. She raised her hands in the air. No Flame emerged, but the man was lifted over the heads of the fighting stallions and thrown to the opposite side of the stable.

A second armed man followed the first. Emily suddenly realized her powers were reacting without her command or control. She looked desperately back to her friends, who were staring at her in shock. "Stop the men," she cried, "before my powers kill them!"

With the deadly stallion fight continuing in the center ring, Joel and the others took on the men entering the stable. The ranch workers were quickly overpowered and their weapons taken away.

Tears filled Emily's eyes as she watched her beloved stallion attacking Tornado Warning.

As the minutes passed, Pegasus was steadily gaining over Tornado. Despite the racing stallion's strength, he was no match for the enraged Olympian. As Pegasus drove the rearing Tornado back, the gray stallion lost his footing. Falling backward, he hit the ground hard.

Before he could get up, Pegasus used the opportunity to finish the fight. He reared up and came crashing down on Tornado with his lethal golden hooves. Screaming in fury, Pegasus did it again.

"Pegasus, no!" Emily howled. Unable to stop herself, she ran forward. Pegasus was rearing to come down on Tornado a third time when Emily placed herself between him and the fallen racehorse. She summoned the power of the Flame in both her hands and raised them against Pegasus.

"Stop it, Pegasus!" she commanded. "Don't make me burn you!" She raised her hands higher. "Just stop!"

Pegasus's eyes were white and wild with rage. He reared above her with his deadly golden hooves hovering mere centimeters from her face.

"It's over!" Emily cried. "You won!"

Finally something changed in Pegasus's eyes. He suddenly realized what he was doing and to whom. Lowering himself to the ground, he neighed softly.

"Get back!" Emily yelled, still unsure of what he would do next. "Go on, get back!"

Pegasus pawed the sawdust floor. Finally he turned and walked to the other side of the stable.

With her heart still pounding painfully in her chest, Emily looked at the other horses in the stable as they continued to scream and kick their stall doors.

"All of you be quiet!" she shouted.

Alexis and Chrysaor approached the stalls. Their presence seemed to calm the frightened horses. Finally they all fell silent.

Earl flicked the switch that turned on the stable lights. Agent T was holding a gun on the ranch workers and ordered them deeper into the stable. In the bright light, their frightened eyes followed Alexis and Chrysaor as they made their way around the stalls. Finally they went back to Pegasus as he stood away from the others. His head was down and his wings drooped.

"Em," Joel called softly. He and Paelen knelt on the floor beside Tornado Warning.

Emily looked down on the fallen racehorse. Tornado Warning was covered in blood from the deep cuts caused by Pegasus's hooves. His eyes were closed, and he wasn't breathing.

"He's dead," Joel said. "Pegasus killed him."

FOR THE FIRST TIME EVER, EMILY WAS furious with Pegasus. She didn't think it was possible. But Pegasus knew how important this was, and yet it didn't stop him from killing Tornado Warning. She remembered his blazing eyes when he was rearing above her. If she hadn't used the Flame, would he have attacked her, too?

Pegasus hung back, away from Emily. He neighed softly to her.

Emily looked at him but raised a warning hand. "Stay back, Pegasus. You've done enough damage already."

The stallion stopped and quietly left the stable.

"That was unfair," Alexis said.

"Unfair?" Emily shot back. "You saw what he did. Pegasus knew how important it was for us to learn the truth about Tornado Warning. But does he let us see the horse? No, he kills him."

"But we did learn the truth," Alexis said. "The fact that each was driven to kill the other says so. Is it not obvious? Tornado Warning does come from Pegasus. They have the same fiery blood. Neither could tolerate the other's existence."

"Em, look," Joel said softly. "It's true. Here's where they cut off Tornado's wings."

Emily looked to where Joel pointed. She knelt down and traced her fingers along the long, deep scars at the horse's shoulders.

"I'm so sorry, Tornado," she said softly. "You shouldn't have had to die."

"He should never have existed," Paelen said angrily.

As Emily's hand rested on Tornado's side, she felt a flicker of movement. Looking down on the fallen stallion, she placed her second hand on his wounded side.

"Joel, check his eyes," Emily said. "I just felt something."

Just when Emily thought she was mistaken, she felt another movement from Tornado.

"He is Olympian," Joel breathed. "Em, you're healing him!"

As the moments ticked by, more and more life returned to Tornado Warning. It happened more slowly than with other Olympians, but it was happening just the same. Suddenly Tornado took in a deep, unsteady breath.

Pegasus appeared at the entrance to the stables and called over to Emily.

"Remain where you are, Pegasus," Alexis ordered. "Emily is healing Tornado Warning. There will be no more fighting today."

Emily sucked in her breath as Tornado Warning's old wing scars faded and stubs appeared. Then those stubs grew. Wings began to take shape. They filled in and grew feathers. The gray dye that had covered his body faded, and all his wounds were healed.

Everyone was shocked into silence. Tornado Warning was truly identical to Pegasus—including the large wings and golden hooves.

"He's a perfect clone," Joel whispered.

Tornado Warning opened his eyes. He screeched when he saw Joel and Paelen right beside him. In a move too quick to follow, he bit Paelen viciously in the leg.

Paelen howled in pain and jumped away from the stallion.

"Everyone get back!" Alexis warned as she opened her wings, drew her fangs and claws, and faced Tornado Warning. "He may come from Pegasus, but he is nothing like him."

With his eyes wide and wild, Tornado Warning climbed to his feet. He looked back at his wings and for a moment paused with confusion. When they fluttered, he whinnied in fear.

"It's all right," Emily cried. "Tornado, calm down!"

Tornado looked at Emily and stopped. He tilted his head to the side and nickered softly.

At the entrance of the stable, Pegasus neighed back.

Tornado faced Pegasus. He reared, opened his wings, and prepared to charge again.

"Tornado, stop!" Emily shouted. "No more fighting!"

Once again, the stallion's eyes came to rest on her. He dropped to the ground and took a step forward.

"Em, get back," Joel warned.

Emily matched Tornado's stare. She knew immediately he was nothing like Pegasus. But something told her he wouldn't attack her.

"It's all right, Joel," she said softly as she approached the stallion.

Pegasus whinnied loudly from across the stable.

"He says don't touch him," Paelen warned as he rubbed his leg where Tornado had bitten him. "He says Tornado Warning is dangerously insane. He is unnatural and must be destroyed."

Emily turned back to Pegasus. His eyes were bright and his nostrils flared. He was preparing to fight again. "Trust me, Pegasus. He won't hurt me."

She didn't know how she knew, but she did. Emily concentrated on Tornado Warning and stepped up to the stallion. "Easy, boy," she said softly. "You don't want to hurt anyone, do you?"

"Yes, he does!" Paelen shot. "Look what he did to me!"

Tornado took another step forward and reached out to Emily. His eyes were calmer, and he showed no signs of aggression toward her.

"That's a good boy," Emily said as she gently stroked his soft muzzle. She could see, standing before the stallion, that physically his face was identical to Pegasus's. But there was something profoundly different in his eyes and what she felt from him.

Whenever she was with Pegasus, Emily always felt a sense of peace, calm, and intense intelligence. But with Tornado Warning, it was a mix of confusion, fear, and anger. There was no intelligence or sense of peace. She could feel that although he wouldn't hurt her, it wasn't the same for others. It was true: Tornado Warning was dangerously unstable.

With the tension easing, Emily looked back at Pegasus. He was still bleeding from his wounds caused by the fight and shotgun blast. But his head was high and proud, and his eyes were bright.

"Go to him," Alexis said softly. "He needs you."

Emily didn't need to be told. Her anger with Pegasus was gone, and she could feel her connection to him calling her. Pegasus was in pain, and she couldn't bear it. He was her first priority. She looked back at Tornado Warning and held up her hand. "Stay."

But as she walked toward Pegasus, Tornado Warning started to follow. "No, Tornado." Emily stopped and held up her hand again. "I said stay."

"He cannot understand you," Paelen said as his wary eyes watched the racehorse. "He is nothing like Pegasus. He is just a flying horse that cannot communicate and lives only by confused emotion." Paelen took a cautious step toward the stallion. "You cannot understand me, can you?"

Tornado's eyes went wild again as he looked at Paelen. His ears went back, his nostrils flared, and his breathing changed. He started to quiver and paw the ground. He looked ready to attack.

"Em, you're the only one who can get near him," Joel observed, as he and Paelen took a cautious step back.

Emily looked at Tornado and frowned. "Why will he let me touch him?"

"Silly child, do you really not know?" Alexis approached. "You are the Flame of Olympus. Your powers call to him as much as they do to all of us. He is drawn to you as we all are. He does not understand his need for you, but it is there nonetheless. He will not harm you."

"Are all Olympians drawn to my power?"

Alexis nodded. "But do not think it is only your power that draws us. We are drawn to you. Though some of us may not show it, we all care for you."

Pegasus approached Emily, but his eyes remained locked on Tornado Warning. Tornado opened his wings threateningly.

"Stop it," Emily said sharply to the racehorse. "Pegasus needs help and I'm going to give it to him. Stay there and behave yourself."

The tone of her voice stopped further protests from Tornado Warning as Emily crossed the distance to Pegasus. "Oh, Pegs, what am I going to do with you?" She stroked his neck. "You know I'll always love you best. But you can't blame Tornado for being what he is. You should pity him, not try to kill him. Promise me you won't attack him again."

Pegasus reached back to Emily. He nickered softly and tugged at her shirt, drawing her to his head. Emily hugged his face and let her powers heal his many wounds. When they were finished, she kissed him softly on the muzzle. "There, all better."

Across the stable, Agent T called, "Not that this

lovefest isn't touching, but we're wasting precious time." He held up his weapon at one of the stable workers they had captured. "You there, tell me, where is Rip Russell?"

The man said nothing as he kept his eyes locked on the Olympians. Alexis walked over to him. She rose on her hind legs and rested her paws on his shoulders. "I do not have patience for your silence. Answer the man."

"*Diablo,*" he muttered as he tried to cross himself.

"Not *diablo,*" Alexis corrected. "Sphinx. And I would suggest you not call me that again."

The worker's eyes went large with terror as he looked into the face of the Sphinx. "He is there," he said fearfully, and pointed at one of the men Emily's powers had tossed across the stable. "The one with the gun."

Agent T nodded. "Fine. Alexis, would you please escort him and the others to one of the empty stalls? We don't want any heroes here."

The Sphinx nodded and directed her attention to all the workers. "You heard him," she said loudly. "All of you, into that stall. Now!"

An elderly Mexican man stepped away from the

others. "Where do you come from? What magic do you do to Tornado Warning? I have trained him all his life." The little old man touched his head. "He is *loco*— crazy. How can that girl touch him? He has killed two riders already." Emily turned to the worker. "What did you say?" The elderly man nodded. "Tornado Warning is *loco*. He has killed two riders. No one can touch him unless he is drugged."

"You keep him drugged?" Joel was shocked.

The worker nodded. "*Sí*. It is the only way to keep him calm."

"What do you give him?" Agent T demanded.

"Sedatives and sugar," the little man said. "Lots and lots of sugar. It make him more better."

Emily suddenly understood. "No wonder he's so vicious. He's starving. He needs ambrosia."

"What is ambrosia?" the little man asked.

"Never mind," Alexis said as she directed him to join the others in the stall. "Just count yourselves fortunate that I do not kill you for what you have done here. Tornado Warning should not exist." She closed and locked the stall door.

Paelen walked across the ring to where the two

men lay unconscious. He rolled over the one they knew to be the owner of Tornado Warning. He started to shake him.

"Time to wake up," he said. "We need to speak with you."

The man started to stir and come around. He gasped in shock as his eyes found Emily standing between Pegasus and Tornado Warning.

"What the hell?" he said.

"Hell has nothing to do with this," Agent T said sharply. "Are you Rip Russell, the owner of Tornado Warning?"

The man climbed shakily to his feet and looked around the stable in complete disbelief. "What are you?" he asked fearfully. "Where do you come from?"

"We ask the questions," Agent T said. "Where did you get Tornado Warning?"

The man's frightened eyes lingered on Pegasus and then went over to Tornado. "Those horses got wings!"

"Yes," Agent T said. "Now answer my question."

Rip looked wildly around the ring. "Where is that devil horse? He was fighting with the winged one."

"This is Tornado Warning," Emily answered as she stroked the winged stallion.

"No, it isn't!" Rip insisted. "Tornado doesn't have wings. But they do."

"Yes, we have established that," Agent T said calmly. "This is Pegasus and that is Tornado. Now, I won't ask you again. Where did you get Tornado Warning?"

"I won't tell you a thing," Rip said, "until you tell me how those horses can have wings."

"Wrong answer." Agent T slapped Rip across the face. "That is me playing nice. One more wrong answer and I will gladly introduce you to Alexis. She's not so patient."

"Who's Alexis?" Rip demanded.

"I am." The Sphinx opened her wings and flew the short distance to where the group was standing. She narrowed her green eyes and stalked up to the man. "I am Alexis. You will answer our questions or you will not live to see the sunrise."

Fear rose on Rip's face. "You're a lion-woman! And you got wings too!"

"You do not miss much," Alexis said sarcastically.

"But did you also notice these?" She held up her paw to show her sharp claws.

Rip held up his hands and looked over to Agent T. "All right, all right, I'll tell you anything. Just keep that thing away from me!"

"Thing? " Alexis roared.

Emily saw only the quickest flash of movement from the Sphinx. Moments later Rip Russell was on the ground, crying in pain and grasping his lower legs. His jeans were torn from Alexis's claws, and blood was rising to the surface.

"You were lucky it was only your legs," Agent T warned. "One more remark like that and I won't stop her." The ex–CRU agent knelt down beside him. "Now tell us. Where did you get Tornado Warning?"

"My cousin," Rip gasped between gritted teeth. He was clutching his bleeding legs. "My cousin gave him to me."

"Where did he get him?" Emily asked.

Rip cursed and sat up. "I just knew it! I knew this would come back to haunt me!"

"Explain," Agent T ordered.

Still grasping his legs, Rip Russell started to speak.

"Ten months ago I was living on a broken-down farm in northern California. I had a couple of racehorses but could never catch a break and win anything. One day outta nowhere, my cousin calls me. He says he's got a sure thing. All I had to do was raise a foal and then race him. He said we would split the winnings."

"And you agreed?" Agent T asked.

"Wouldn't you?" Rip answered. "So a month later, he brings this tiny white foal to me. It had bandages all over it. But even with the bandages, I could see it was quality horseflesh. So I took it. I was given instructions to keep it fed on sugars and other sweet foods. I was also told to dye the foal gray for racing, since no one races white horses."

Agent T frowned. "How could you race him? He had no papers to prove his pedigree."

"That part was easy," Rip said. "All I had to do was find a registered gray horse that we could substitute for him. It took some time, but we found one that looked a lot like him, with the same cowlicks and everything—he was called Tornado Warning. Then all I had to do was wait for the foal to grow up. Which he did superfast. So we switched him for the real Tornado Warning and by six months of age, he was winning every race we entered him in."

"What happened to the real Tornado Warning?" Emily asked.

"There couldn't be two in case we were found out. So I had him destroyed."

Emily's hand went up to her mouth. "You killed him?"

Rip shrugged. "Hey, this is horse racing. I did what I had to do."

Agent T sat back on his haunches. "That was a grave mistake. What did your cousin tell you about the foal?"

Rip shook his head. "Nothing. I was just told to race him and to keep him colored gray. That I did. And he is one amazing racehorse. Tornado Warning is the fastest horse in the world."

"He's the fastest because he isn't really a horse. He's a clone of Pegasus!" Emily shot back. "Didn't you ever wonder about the bandages? Didn't you care that they cut off his wings?"

Rip held up his hand. "Hey, I didn't know nothing about that. I just thought he'd had shoulder surgery."

"Yes!" Emily cried. "To cut off his wings!"

Her raised voice caused Tornado Warning to whinny and pound the ground furiously. His eyes went wild.

"Keep that monster back!" Rip cried.

Emily left Pegasus and stepped up to Tornado. "Easy, boy. I'm sorry I raised my voice." At her touch, Tornado Warning calmed. He even let Pegasus move closer.

She looked back at Pegasus. "See, Pegs, you don't have to fight him. He's fine."

Emily stood between the two stallions, with one hand resting on each of their wings. Beneath her fingers, Tornado was calm. But she could feel Pegasus trembling. He wasn't happy with the attention she was giving the clone.

"Where did your cousin get the foal?" Joel asked.

"I swear I don't know," Rip said. "He's an agent with the Central Research Unit. I had no idea he was working with horses."

"The CRU." Agent T nodded and looked back at Emily and the others. "That explains everything. If his cousin was working on the clone project, he'd know just how powerful Pegasus was and how powerful the clone could be. If he has a high rank, it wouldn't be impossible to smuggle a very young foal out of a facility. A clone like that could make a fortune."

"He has," Rip said. "We've made millions from Tornado. Especially after the Triple Crown win. When he goes out to stud, there is no telling what we could make."

Pegasus's ears went back, and he whinnied angrily. He pawed the ground furiously, causing Tornado to shy back and open his wings menacingly.

"Easy, Tornado," Emily calmed. "Pegs, please. We get that you're angry. But you can't upset Tornado. There's no telling what he'll do."

"Can he understand us?" Rip asked as his wide eyes watched Pegasus.

"Yes," Joel said. "And he's furious that you were putting his clone out to stud."

"I didn't know he was a clone!" Rip insisted. "I just thought he was a horse!"

Agent T reached out and squeezed the man's wounded legs. "Where can we find your cousin?"

"I—I—I don't know how to reach him. He works at Area 51!"

"Oh God, this gets worse by the moment." Agent T started to pace and combed his fingers through his long hair.

"Isn't Area 51 where they develop all the new military aircraft?" Joel asked.

Agent T nodded. "Yes, it's an air force base. But it also holds the country's largest CRU facility. That's where we have been keeping all the debris from the Roswell alien crash. That facility has the highest security of all the US locations because it's got the most developed laboratories. Governors Island was an open theme park and the facility at Tuxedo was a children's playground compared to it."

"Where is it?" Emily asked.

"The Nevada desert," Agent T said. "At a dried-up lake bed, Groom Lake. It's a good hundred miles from Vegas. I've only been there once, and that was more than enough. I couldn't wait to leave it. For as bad as we were at Governors, they are much worse there."

"So could they be the ones creating the clones?" Emily asked.

Agent T nodded. "Most likely. I should have thought of that first. The laboratories at Area 51 would be the best equipped to create and manage the clones."

"They aren't managing them that well if the clones keep escaping," Joel said.

"I've got to get in there and see just how many clones they've created," Agent T mused. "Maybe I can stop this before it goes too far."

"You mean *we've* got to get in there," Emily corrected.

Agent T shook his head. "Not the Olympians here and especially not you. You have powers far too dangerous for them to get hold of. This all started when the CRU captured Olympians. What might they achieve if they caught hold of you?"

Alexis shook her head. "No one is going there, especially the Flame of Olympus. We did not come here to enter a CRU facility. Our mission was to see Tornado Warning and then return. We have done that. Here is Tornado Warning. We now know he has been created from Pegasus by the CRU. Our mission is complete. We must now return to Olympus and report our findings to Jupiter."

"No!" Emily cried. "If we do that, Jupiter will destroy the Earth."

"This world's fate is already sealed," Alexis said darkly. "The CRU decided it the moment they created Tornado Warning."

"There must be another way!" Agent T insisted. "It can't end like this. Please, Alexis, let me try to get in there and save my world."

Emily was stunned to see Agent T begging the Sphinx. He was always so tough and hard, even around her. Now there was genuine fear and desperation in his eyes. "I was with the CRU for almost twenty years. Look how I have changed. We all can. Please, you must let me try."

"I am truly sorry for you, Tom," Alexis said. "But nothing can save this world. The CRU have committed an unforgivable crime. It is my duty to return to Olympus and tell Jupiter the truth."

A HUSH FELL OVER THE STABLES. EMILY looked at the shocked faces around her. She continued to stroke both winged stallions as she collected her thoughts.

Tornado remained oblivious to the danger he was facing, but Pegasus knew. He nickered softly and pressed his face to Emily. Chrysaor's head was bowed, and he was pawing the ground.

Finally she spoke. "I won't go back."

Everyone turned to her.

This was it, the moment of choice. For days Emily had wrestled with the dilemma. What would she do if it came down to a choice between Olympus and Earth? Faced with the terrible decision, Emily made her choice. She would choose her world over Olympus.

"You can't change my mind," she continued. "If Jupiter decides to destroy this world, he's going to have to destroy me with it."

Pegasus nickered and looked at her in shock.

"I'm sorry, Pegs. You know how much I love Olympus, and you know I would do anything to protect it. But I love this world too. I came from here. I can't let Jupiter destroy it just because a few people have done something really stupid."

Joel and Paelen stood beside Emily. Chrysaor took up a position next to Pegasus. They crossed their arms and stood defiantly before the Sphinx.

Alexis glared at the group. "You are all being unreasonable. We told Diana, Pluto, and Steve that we would be right back. We have been here too long already, and our presence in Olympus will be missed. We must return and report our findings."

"Go back if you must, Alexis," Emily said. "But I won't let Jupiter destroy this world without a fight."

Alexis huffed and her tail swished the air. "Would you please speak with her?" she told Pegasus. "Tell her this must happen. These humans must be punished for what they have done."

Emily looked at Pegasus. The time had come for him to make his choice as well. Would he stay with her? Or would he side with Olympus? She knew how tough this must be for him. But as she watched his eyes closely, she saw no hesitation. Pegasus moved closer to Emily and stood beside her. He nickered at Alexis.

"You also, Pegasus?" the Sphinx said in disbelief. "You would betray your own people for this world? They have sinned against you most! Tornado Warning was created from your stolen blood. Do you not want vengeance for that crime?"

Emily's heart flushed with emotion for the stallion. Pegasus was going to stand with her, no matter what. She pressed herself to his side and faced the Sphinx.

"Please, Alexis, help us," she continued. "This doesn't have to turn into a battle. I have the power to destroy Area 51 if I must." Emily looked at her friends. "We all do. But maybe it won't come to that. Maybe we can stop everything and save this world."

Alexis looked at the group standing with Emily, ready to fight for the world. Her eyes found Pegasus. "Is it really true, Pegasus and Chrysaor, sons of Neptune? You will turn your back on your people for this place?"

Several long nickers and squeals confirmed their decision. "They both agree they are not turning their backs on Olympus," Paelen whispered to Emily and Joel. "Pegasus believes we can stop this before it goes too far."

"Is that your final decision?" Alexis asked.

Pegasus nodded and pounded the ground.

The Sphinx started to pace before the group. Her wings were fluttering, and her tail swished back and forth. "This is bad," she said softly to herself. She kept looking at Emily. "Very, very bad indeed."

She sighed heavily and sat down.

"So be it."

Emily's heart was in her throat. "Are you going back to Olympus to tell Jupiter?"

The Sphinx sighed again. "I should. But I promised Diana I would be your guardian. I would fail in that duty if I were to abandon you here to face

Jupiter's wrath alone. Like it or not, I must remain to keep you safe."

"Thank you!" Emily cried as she ran forward and hugged the Sphinx tightly.

"Do not thank me, Emily," Alexis said gruffly. "I have sided with you against my better judgment. I have a feeling I will live to regret it."

The sun was up fully before they were ready to leave. As more and more workers arrived on the ranch, they were marched into the stallion barn. All the workers, including Rip Russell, were now locked in two large horse stalls. Alexis kept watch and warned the workers what would happen if they made a move against her or her friends.

Outside the barn, Earl and Agent T hooked up a large four-horse trailer to a brand-new white pickup truck. Agent T was still insisting that the safest thing for everyone would be for Emily to use her powers to destroy the racehorse.

Emily refused. They would take Tornado Warning with them to keep him from being turned out to stud. After they fed him a breakfast of sugary foods and heavy tranquilizers, the winged racehorse was bridled, and Emily led him into the first box in the trailer.

"Now, what are we going to do with all the men? They're going to tell the police as soon as we leave," Joel said as he closed and secured the back door to the horse trailer.

"Maybe I can convince them not to," Emily suggested. "Especially if we explain what's at stake." She walked toward the barn.

"It would be more effective to kill them," Alexis purred. "But we can try your way first if you insist." She followed Emily back into the stallion barn to see to the workers who had been locked in the stalls.

With Pegasus and Alexis standing outside the stall, Emily entered the one holding Russell and several of his men. She tried to reason with him, explaining that if the police were called and they were captured, the leader of Olympus would destroy the world. But she could see in his face that after all he had seen and heard, he didn't care. All Rip could see was them taking away his only means of making money. That and his brand-new truck and trailer.

Shaking her head in defeat, Emily turned to leave the stall. But as she did, Alexis cried a warning.

"You're not taking my horse!" Rip shouted.

Emily turned back in time to see him order his men, "Grab her!"

Rip lunged forward and knocked Emily to the ground as his men surrounded her, just as Alexis flashed into the stall. Those who followed Rip's orders were soon to learn just how strong, fast, and lethal the Sphinx of Olympus truly was.

Russell was the first to feel her wrath as Alexis tore him off Emily. The Sphinx unhinged her jaw, and her eyes went black as she drew her teeth. She barked at Emily, "Close your eyes!"

Doing as instructed, Emily put her hands over her face. She heard screams filling the air around her, mixed with the sound of Alexis roaring as the Sphinx defended her against the attacking men.

Emily curled into a tight ball and tried to block out the terrible sounds. Moments later she sensed movement. Reaching out her hand, Emily felt Pegasus's front legs before her. His back legs were behind her, while his wings were hanging down the sides. She realized he was standing over her and protecting her with his whole body.

Just then she heard Earl and Agent T running into the stall.

"Emily, are you all right?" Earl said.

She nodded. She started to move, but Earl stopped her. "Keep your eyes shut; you don't want to see this." He helped her climb out from under the stallion.

"Pegasus, take her out of here," Agent T ordered. "And keep the others out as well. We'll take care of this."

Earl guided Emily out of the stall and hoisted her up onto Pegasus's back. "Go on ahead. We'll be out in a moment."

As the stallion carried her out of the stable, she could hear the horses screaming and kicking their stall doors. When they reached the outside, Pegasus nickered softly.

"I'm okay, Pegs," Emily said shakily as she slid off his back.

"Em, what happened in there?" Joel said. He ran up to her and looked at the blood on her clothes. "Are you hurt?"

Emily shook her head and looked at herself in

shock. "It's not my blood. It's theirs. After everything they heard and saw, Russell still didn't want us to take Tornado Warning away. He and his men attacked me."

"What did you do?" Paelen asked.

"Nothing," Emily said. "I didn't have time. Alexis did it all. She told me to close my eyes and she dealt with it. It all happened so fast."

Paelen shivered. "That is the Sphinx. When she is on your side, you cannot have a better ally. Oppose her and it is at your peril."

Earl emerged from the stallion stable. He leaned heavily against the side, struggling to stand up.

"Earl," Emily cried as she and the others approached him. "Are you all right?"

He shook his head. "I ain't never seen nothin' like it. The darn fools. Didn't they realize what would happen if they tried anythin'? We warned 'em. We warned 'em all."

"Did Alexis get everyone?" Paelen asked.

He shook his head again. "Don't think so. I saw a couple huddled in the corner of the stall. It looked like they hadn't moved."

Pegasus nickered and Paelen said, "Alexis would only go after those men attacking you. If some stayed back, she would leave them unharmed."

Earl nodded. "She left the others in the second stall alone too. It was just the ones going after Emily that she got." Earl's face turned a darker shade of green. "I'll be fine in a minute," he said. "You kids get ready to go, and I'll meet you at the truck."

"C'mon," Joel said softly as he led Emily toward the vehicles. "Get changed and then we can leave."

HOURS LATER EMILY WAS STANDING IN THE
trailer beside Pegasus as it was towed across the desert
toward Nevada. Chrysaor and Alexis were in an open
stall behind them. Tornado Warning was locked in
the rear stall, now calm and still from the tranquilizers. Joel and Paelen were up front in the four-seater
pickup truck with Earl and Agent T.

Emily hadn't said a word all journey. Alexis had
emerged from the stallion barn soaking wet after
being hosed down by Agent T. No one but Pegasus, Earl, and the ex–CRU agent had seen what the
Sphinx had done, and not one word was spoken
about it.

As Alexis dozed peacefully in the clean, dry straw

of the trailer, there was no sign of the monster she had become.

Beside her, Pegasus nickered. Emily gazed into his warm brown eyes and saw the vision of the two of them soaring together in the open skies over Olympus. There was no violence, no blood. Just the sense of peace and joy they shared whenever they were alone together.

"I hope we can do that again someday, Pegs," Emily said softly as she stroked his soft muzzle. She turned and looked out the barred trailer window. The air that blew across her face was dry and blisteringly hot. Though Olympus was warm, it never became uncomfortable. The oppressive heat only made Emily feel worse.

She sat down in the straw and leaned against the wall. She was achingly tired. Pegasus bent down and licked her face. He neighed softly.

"He suggests you get some rest," Alexis translated without opening her eyes. "We have a difficult time ahead of us, and you will need it."

Emily wanted to comment on the difficult time they'd just been through, but thought better of it. The Sphinx was on their side, but barely. It wouldn't take much to drive her back to Olympus and Jupiter.

She lay down in the soft straw at Pegasus's feet. She worried about the time ahead and she worried about what the men from the stables would tell the police. Alexis had warned them that if they told the truth she would return. But would that be enough to stop them?

Despite her worries, the gentle rocking of the trailer and the sweet smell from the fresh straw lulled Emily into a deeply troubled sleep.

"Look at that! I must see this place for myself!"

Emily awoke to see a golden lion's underbelly standing over her. The Sphinx's front paws were up on the barred window frame as she and Pegasus peered out.

"What is this place?" Alexis asked breathlessly.

Emily crawled out from under the Sphinx and climbed shakily to her feet. They were driving along a highway that ran through Las Vegas. The sun was starting to set and casting a golden light on all the windows of the buildings. They were currently passing a tall black building covered in dark glass. There was a crane on the roof, and it looked like it was still under construction. Just past it was another series of brightly colored buildings. "It's Las Vegas," she answered. "Those are casinos where people gamble and see shows."

As they continued on the road, Emily watched Alexis's excited eyes trying to take in all the sights of the city. She squinted to understand a large billboard hanging down the side of a tall casino. "Elvis . . . is . . . in . . . the . . . building," she slowly read aloud. "Elvis? My Elvis! He is here. I have found him! We must stop!"

Emily hated to shatter Alexis's illusion. "Maybe when this is over, we can come back and see him."

"Wonderful idea," Alexis agreed excitedly. "It will be our reward for saving the world."

Down at the far end of the stall, Tornado Warning was coming out of the sedative daze. He kicked the stall door and whinnied. Emily went over and stroked the racehorse's white face. "How're you doing, boy? It won't be much longer."

Pegasus crept closer, his jealousy obvious. "It's all right, Pegs," Emily said softly. "He's frightened and confused. He doesn't understand what's happened to him."

Despite her comments, Pegasus continued to hover. Tornado's ears twitched back and his nostrils flared. He started to paw the trailer floor and whinny.

"Easy, boy," Emily calmed. "Please, Pegs, get back. You're upsetting him, and I don't know what he'll do here in the trailer."

Pegasus backed down. He snorted angrily and turned away from Tornado. He walked to the far end of the trailer and kept his back to Emily.

"I believe we will need to sedate Tornado Warning again." Alexis carefully approached the stall. "He is upsetting Pegasus. In these tight confines, that would not be good. Pegasus is doing his best to contain himself. But even he has his limits."

Emily agreed. She climbed the small ladder that ascended into the "granny's attic" of the trailer and crawled along the overhang that went over the truck bed. Emily started to pound on the trailer's front wall, hoping that Paelen, with his sensitive hearing, would hear her and let Agent T know they needed to stop.

The message was received. Soon the truck and trailer were pulling over to the hard shoulder of the highway. When they stopped, Emily went up to the barred window and waited for someone to appear.

"What's up?" Earl asked as he came to the window.

"Tornado Warning is coming out of the drugs and he's really upsetting Pegasus. We need to give him some more before they start fighting again."

Earl nodded. "Well, we're pretty cooked up in the truck. This place is like an oven! How people can live here is beyond me. We were all talkin' about stoppin' to pick up some supplies and something to drink. I think now would be a good time."

"Definitely," Emily agreed.

With the promise of a pit stop, Earl went back to the cab of the truck. "Did you hear that, Pegs? We're going to stop for some food. We'll also sedate Tornado again, so he won't bother you," Emily said.

The stallion's eyes were large and bright, and he was quivering. Emily put her arms around his neck. "I know this is hard for you, Pegs. But I'm asking you to stay calm for a bit longer."

Chrysaor had been lying in the straw but now approached his brother and squealed softly. Pegasus nickered back. But when Emily looked to Alexis to translate, the Sphinx simply shook her head and remained silent.

After a time, the trailer turned off the highway and they entered the suburbs of Las Vegas. Alexis remained at the barred window, curiously taking in everything and bombarding Emily with questions.

They finally turned into a shopping center with a huge supermarket. Agent T parked the trailer, and everyone climbed out. The moment Emily left the trailer, Tornado Warning started to whinny loudly and kick at his stall door. This caused Pegasus to whinny in response and paw the floor.

"You'd better stay in there with them," Joel warned. "I don't think it's safe to leave those two alone together."

"I will stay with you," Paelen volunteered quickly. "I'd rather not go in after my last supermarket visit." It had been a CRU trap. Emily could fully understand his reluctance.

"Joel and I will go." Agent T handed the truck keys to Earl. "If anything happens, get everyone away from here."

Alexis came out of the trailer wearing Pluto's helmet so only Emily could see her.

"Where are you going?" Emily asked.

"I sense no danger here and wish to see what is inside this strange place." Alexis touched the ex–CRU agent's leg. "Tom, do you mind if I join you?"

"Not at all," Agent T said, and actually smiled. "Just stay close to me."

Emily noticed a definite change whenever he was speaking with Alexis. His tone was much softer and friendlier. Had the Sphinx's charms actually warmed his cold heart?

More loud whinnies from Tornado Warning forced Emily back into the trailer. Paelen and Earl followed her in while the others went shopping.

Little was said as they waited, and they all felt the tension pressing down on them.

Agent T and Joel returned with a shopping cart full of food. An excited Alexis reported all the things she had seen, smelled, and heard at the supermarket. She was more like a child than the fearsome creature she had become at the Double R Ranch. She and Agent T laughed as they retold the story of Alexis's tail accidentally knocking over a display and the perplexed expressions on the faces of the people who couldn't see her or understand how it happened.

Tornado Warning was fed first as they put more heavy tranquilizers in his chocolate ice cream. Once he had eaten his fill, everyone else climbed into the trailer and settled down to eat.

"Well, this is it." Agent T stood. "In a couple of hours we'll be in Rachel, Nevada. That's only a few miles from Area 51 and the entrance to the CRU facility."

"Then what?" Joel asked. "Does anyone here have any suggestions about what we do next? 'Cause I sure don't, and it's driving me crazy."

Emily shook her head. "Not this time. It seemed so clear last time because we were getting my dad back. But now . . ."

"But now we've got to see how many clones the CRU have created and if we can stop them," Agent T finished.

"Exactly," Emily agreed.

"Well, we won't know until we get there," Earl said as he too stood. "And we ain't gonna get there unless we get movin'."

"Before we do . . ." Agent T said. He concentrated on Emily. "Did you see that tall, black tower-like building when we first arrived in Vegas?" When Emily nodded, he continued, "We've all agreed that we're going to use that as a meeting place if anything goes wrong. If we ever get separated, head to the top of that black tower. Understood?"

Emily nodded.

"Good, let's go."

Under a blanket of stars, they left Las Vegas and made their way along the Extraterrestrial Highway that ran deep into the desert. When they arrived in Rachel, it was a surprise to see that the place was actually considered a town. It was more like a mobile home park. There were no houses, and the only business in the area was one motel with a small restaurant. Like everything else in Rachel, it was nothing more than a series of mobile homes parked closely together.

While Earl and Agent T went inside to arrange accommodation for the night, the others gathered outside the trailer.

"Hey, Em, did you catch that name?" Joel pointed at the restaurant.

"Little A'Le'Inn." Emily read the sign. "What else would you call it this close to Area 51?"

Paelen walked over to a flying saucer mounted on a tall pole. It was surrounded by brightly colored lights. "What is this?"

"It's supposed to be a UFO." Joel explained to a confused Paelen about alien spacecraft.

"So that is what the CRU thought I came to your world in when they had me at Governors Island?" Paelen frowned and looked even more puzzled. "It is not very big. How did they think I would have fitted in there?"

Joel and Emily laughed.

"That's only a model." Emily put her arm around him. "A real spaceship would be much bigger."

Paelen didn't look convinced. "If there were aliens, surely they would use the Solar Stream and not have to come here in these things."

Agent T returned with a key to one of the mobile homes. He leaned closer and kept his voice low. "Only you Olympians use the Solar Stream. The other aliens we have captured use vehicles like these."

Emily looked at the ex–CRU agent in shock. "How many have there been?"

"Quite a few," he said cryptically, but then changed the subject. "We got a mobile home for the night and can drive the trailer right up to it. Then I want us all to go into the restaurant and behave like one big, happy family."

"But I am not hungry," Paelen said.

"It doesn't matter," Agent T said. "This is the only place to eat within fifty miles. You can bet there will be workers from Area 51 coming here. Some of those will be with the CRU. And if I am completely honest, I would suspect that some of the people who work here are with the military. What family would come to stay and not eat at the only restaurant in the area?"

Emily frowned and looked around nervously. "But why would someone from the military work here at a restaurant?"

Agent T sighed and shook his head. "After everything you have seen and learned about the CRU, you still don't understand? Emily, think. This is the only place to eat that's anywhere near Area 51. Rachel,

Nevada, attracts every kind of person, from alien fanatics to reporters and conspiracy theorists. It's only logical that the military and especially the CRU would have a plant working here to check out the people who might be coming to the base. So let's just go in there and behave like travelers passing through."

They headed into the small restaurant. Alexis, wearing Pluto's helmet, stayed close to Emily, Joel, and Paelen as they looked around at all the pictures and UFO memorabilia on the walls. There were display racks selling Area 51 T-shirts. Coffee mugs had aliens and AREA 51 written on them. Computer mouse pads had the Area 51 warning sign on them, and there were several books written about the secret base. Even the menus had little aliens on them and were offered for sale.

There were a number of people sitting at the bar and at the tables, eating and talking softly. A group of men were playing pool. Music filled the air and the mood was light.

As they settled at a large table and their orders were taken, the middle-aged waitress smiled and casually asked why they were there. "Come to see the aliens?"

she asked Joel playfully. "Maybe see the entrance gate to Area 51?"

Agent T smiled and laughed lightly. "My kids and brother want to, but we've got a schedule to keep. We're moving a couple of horses farther up north. But we thought it'd be fun to come this route. We've heard of this place and wanted to see it for ourselves."

Earl put down his menu and asked, "So have you ever seen anythin' in the sky here?"

The waitress shrugged. "I don't look."

Emily thought that was an odd answer but remained silent. She watched the waitress closely. Although she smiled and chatted in a friendly manner to all her customers, there was something troubling about her. The woman's answers were too rehearsed, and there was a hardness around her eyes. She stood like she had a pole up her back and wasn't allowed to lean or slouch.

Alexis was also suspicious. When the waitress returned to the kitchen to place the orders, the invisible Sphinx followed her in. Alexis returned several minutes later and quietly told Agent T that the waitress had gone into a room and spoken softly with someone. Though she couldn't hear everything that was said, the waitress did mention the family traveling north with a horse trailer.

"So far so good," Agent T said. He looked at the others at the table. "Just act natural."

As their food was delivered, Emily was impressed with the act Agent T put on. He was nothing like his normal self. He smiled readily, told silly jokes, and even had a sparkle in his pale-blue eyes. He acted exactly as a father should. Emily wondered what he would have been like if he had never joined the CRU and instead had had a family. She imagined her own father might have even liked him.

When they left the restaurant, everyone paused to look up at the star-studded sky. It was breathtaking and almost as beautiful as when they were flying up in it. Over to the south, they could see the glow of Las Vegas.

The temperature was noticeably cooler than in the day, and the air was filled with the sounds of the desert. Coyotes howled in the distance, while insects chirped and small animals scurried through the scrub.

As they made their way to their mobile home, they

heard other motel guests moving around and heading toward the restaurant. Dogs were barking loudly in their pen, not too far from where the trailer with Pegasus and Tornado was parked.

"I hope the dogs don't bark all night," Emily said. "I was planning to let Pegasus out of the trailer to stretch his wings. But I don't want him drawing attention to us."

"Pegasus will have to remain where he is," Agent T said darkly. "I don't want him taken out here."

Emily noticed that the ex–CRU agent seemed agitated. "Is something wrong?"

"I have a bad feeling."

"As do I," Alexis agreed. "Coming here may have been a mistake."

Emily looked around fearfully. "Should we leave and find somewhere else to stop?"

Agent T shook his head. "That would definitely draw too much attention to us. We've just got to be extra careful. Let's get to the trailer and we can talk."

Before climbing into the trailer, Earl and Joel went into the small rented mobile home and turned on the lights. They closed the curtains and made it look as if there were people settling down for the night.

Soon everyone was gathered together in the horse trailer. Tornado Warning remained locked in his stall. The lights were off, and everyone spoke softly.

"This place is crazy," Joel said. "There's no TV or telephone in the mobile home. What are you supposed to do for the night?"

"Sleep and then get out," Agent T said. "They don't want people spending any time here. Especially this close to an active military base." He looked over to the Sphinx. "Alexis, we need all your skills right now. Let me know if you hear or feel anyone approaching the trailer."

The Sphinx nodded and sat up higher. She split her attention between the meeting and listening for sounds outside.

Agent T shook his head. "This is going to be more difficult than I thought. There were a lot of military people in that restaurant tonight. The tension is high. Something big is going on at the facility."

Earl looked at his friend. "I didn't see no military folk."

"They were there," Agent T said. "You've got to

know what you're looking for. Like I told you, I visited Area 51 some years ago. Security was tight back then. But not like this. We're going to have to watch ourselves."

As the group talked, Alexis turned her head sharply. She held up a paw. "Someone is approaching."

Emily felt a flutter of fear. The power within her stirred and started to rumble, with the prickling of the Flame reaching her fingertips.

In an instant, Agent T changed his manner. He leaned closer to the group and laughed loudly. "And you know what?" he called. "Your granddaddy never found out it was us who'd put the outhouse on the barn roof!"

He laughed louder and signaled the others to join in. He nodded at Earl.

"That's right," Earl added, joining in the laughter. "Momma knew, but she never told Daddy. To this day he still believes it was the boys down the road. . . ."

As everyone laughed, Alexis waved her paw in the air, indicating they should continue. She crept closer to the side of the trailer and pointed at the wall. "He is right here," she mouthed.

Tiny flames burst from Emily's fingertips as her

fear increased. She tried to call the Flame back, but it wouldn't obey. Pegasus nudged her, trying to get her to calm down.

Joel looked at the flames as they flickered several centimeters above Emily's fingers. He laughed louder. "So, Uncle Earl, is it true what Dad told us? That you and him went fishing with dynamite?"

"Sure did," Earl agreed brightly. "That's the best darn way to get the big ones."

Suddenly there was a loud knocking on the trailer door. Agent T motioned for Pegasus and Chrysaor to hide in one of the stalls. He nodded at Emily's hands. She put them behind her back.

"Who's there?" Agent T called lightly, returning to the role of the friendly father.

A man's voice came from outside the door. "Is everything all right in there?"

Agent T went to the door. "Of course. Everything is fine," he said, opening it. "Why do you ask?"

The man was holding up a flashlight. Emily could see his face. It was hard and cold as he tried to peer in past Agent T. "Someone reported strange sounds coming from here. We keep a secure motel. I just wanted to make sure everything was fine."

Agent T swept his hand back to invite the man to enter, and Emily's heart nearly stopped. She balled her hands into tight fists to keep back the Flame.

"Of course," Agent T said. "We understand. But my horses get a little spooked if they spend too long in the trailer. So my kids and I are spending some quiet time with them before bed. Would you like to come in and see for yourself?"

Alexis was pressed back behind the door. Her eyes were bright and her claws drawn. She was poised to strike.

The man took the first step up into the trailer when a voice called him. He paused for what seemed like an eternity as they waited to see if he was going to enter. Finally he stepped back down onto the ground. "Sorry to have bothered you folks tonight. We're just being careful."

"We understand completely," Agent T said. "Have a good night." The ex–CRU agent stood at the door for a few minutes, watching the man go.

Joel looked at Emily. "You can turn that off now," he said, indicating her burning fists.

Emily calmed down and drew the Flame back into herself. "I don't like it here. Maybe we should fly to the facility right now and see what's happening and get out."

Agent T closed the door and returned to the group. He shook his head. "They're suspicious enough already. We make one move and we'll expose ourselves. We have to plan this very carefully. This base has got ground and air sensors that pick up visual, audio, and heat traces. I know for a fact that by the time anyone gets within three miles of the gate or any of Area 51's property, the authorities have seen them and know just about everything there is to know about them. This isn't Governors or Tuxedo. This place has the highest security of all the facilities in the world. Even the president of the United States can't get in here."

"What do we do?" Paelen asked.

"We use our heads and not our emotions," Agent T said coldly. His eyes rested on Emily. "And you, young lady, must control those powers of yours. We can't have you setting things alight until we're ready."

"I know," Emily said, dropping her head. "Normally I can control them. But knowing that guy was just outside, it kind of got away from me."

Agent T's penetrating blue eyes bored into her. "Just like at the hotel in Baton Rouge with the exploding lamp? And what about at the Double R Ranch? It appears your powers get away from you a great deal."

"Yeah, what happened at the stable?" Joel added. "Those two guys went flying! And you told us to stop them before your powers killed them."

Emily realized she'd been exposed. "I'm so sorry," she started. "But I think I've got more powers than just the Flame, and I can't control them. Sometimes they get away from me completely."

"Why didn't you tell us?" Joel demanded, looking hurt. "Don't you trust us?"

Emily shook her head. "That's not it and you know it! I didn't say anything because we have bigger things to worry about. I thought I could keep them hidden until we got back."

"What are these new powers?" Paelen asked. "What can you do?"

Emily hated to tell her friends about her powers. She didn't want them to discover she was even more of a freak.

"I can move things," she started. "And sometimes they kinda explode."

"Like the lamp," Joel said.

Emily nodded. "And sometimes—but not very often—objects will disappear completely and I never see them again."

"Do they turn to ash like the gorgons did?" Paelen asked.

Emily shrugged. "Not really; they just sort of disappear."

Alexis sat down beside her. "Emily will soon learn to control these new powers as she can control the Flame. In the meantime, we must all help her remain calm and focused so her powers do not escape her again."

"Which is why we *must* plan our next move very carefully," Agent T said. "We can't let Emily lose control. Agreed?"

Everyone nodded and agreed to help her. Looking at their determined faces, Emily wondered why she had been so worried about telling them.

"Back to the problem at hand," Agent T continued. "I know for certain they have taken our vehicle details down and checked us out. The fact that we are still free means that someone at the Double R Ranch followed our orders and told the authorities we're moving horses. We are safe for the moment."

"That or they're raising an army against us," Joel said.

The ex–CRU agent shook his head. "No, with the base this close, they could be here in minutes. We're safe for the time being. I think our best course of action is to take a drive out to the base's gates in the morning and see what it's like in daylight."

Emily asked. "Shouldn't we go tonight while it's dark?"

"We mustn't make rash decisions," Agent T said. "If we overreact, this could backfire on us. We have to plan very carefully. Besides, we're all tired from traveling. We need to be fresh and prepared before we move. Rest tonight, because tomorrow we move against Area 51 and the CRU."

EMILY AND EARL REMAINED IN THE TRAILER with Pegasus, Chrysaor, and Tornado Warning. With Pegasus close at her side, Emily lay in the straw and curled into him. Exhausted from the long, hot day behind her, she quickly drifted off to sleep.

A pounding on the trailer door woke Emily with a start. Pegasus was instantly on his feet, pawing the floor and whinnying. In his stall, Tornado Warning joined in and whinnied loudly. Emily looked out the trailer windows. It was still dark out, and she couldn't see anything.

"Stay back," Earl warned. "Let me get it."

Earl reached for the door and peered out. "Oh, dear Lord!" He jumped down to the ground.

Emily ran to the door and watched Earl struggling to lift Alexis. The Sphinx was collapsed on the ground and covered in blood. He carried her up the three steps into the trailer.

"Close the door and turn on the lights," he ordered as he put Alexis down in the dry straw.

The Sphinx was moaning. "It's all right, Alexis," Emily said softly as she brushed her raven hair away from her face. "You're going to be fine."

Earl ran back to the trailer door. "Stay with her. I'll get the others."

Emily concentrated on the Sphinx. With a lack of ambrosia, Alexis was weakened and vulnerable to be hurt. She looked like she'd been in a terrible fight.

"Are these gunshot wounds?" Emily gasped as she checked Alexis's body and began to heal her. "Who did this?" But the Sphinx was too weak to respond.

As Emily's powers got to work, Pegasus and Chrysaor stood near Alexis's bruised and bloodied head. Pegasus licked her face soothingly.

Joel, Paelen, and Earl crowded around the Sphinx as she stirred and slowly opened her eyes.

"Tom is gone," Earl cried. "He ain't in the room."

"We didn't hear him go," Joel added. "I thought he was still with us. What's happening here?"

With the last of the healing finished, Alexis sat up shakily. Tears were rimming her eyes. "Tom is dead," she announced. "He was killed by his own people at the CRU."

"What?" Emily cried. "How?"

Alexis ignored Emily's question and looked at Earl. "They dislocated my wings. I could not fly and had to run back here. We do not have long before they come for us. Tom told me if anything happened we should get to Las Vegas to hide at the black tower. Go now, get us moving. I can tell you what happened later."

Earl nodded. "You kids stay with Alexis and hold on tight. I'm goin' to move this trailer as fast as it can go."

Moments after Earl left the trailer, they heard the sounds of men shouting and gunfire. The trailer rocked violently as the tires were shot out beneath them, disabling the vehicle. Joel dashed to the window. "It's that guy who said he was from the motel. He and some others have captured Earl!"

Lights flashed as military vehicles poured into the parking lot of the motel. They could hear a heavy thudding in the distance. Paelen raised his head. "I know that sound. It is soldiers in their flying machines!"

"We're trapped in here!" Emily cried.

Tornado Warning was screaming in his stall and kicking the door. Pegasus's eyes were wild, and he whinnied loudly.

"He says we must flee," Paelen translated. "Emily, get the big door open and we will fly out of here."

Emily nodded and then looked back at Tornado. "We're not leaving him here for them!" Before the others could protest, she dashed to the back of the trailer and opened Tornado's stall door.

The racehorse's eyes were wide and frightened, but he let Emily lead him forward to stand beside Pegasus. The stallions' eyes met, but neither made a move against the other, as though they both realized the bigger danger.

Emily climbed up onto Pegasus. "Everyone get ready. I'm going to burn it open. Joel, get on Chrysaor." She looked at the Sphinx. "Can you fly? Or should you ride with me on Pegasus?"

"I am sufficiently healed," Alexis said. "Use your powers—get us out of here!"

Emily looked at her friends. "The moment that ramp goes down, I want you all to fly out. Pegasus, Tornado, and I will follow you. Get up into the sky. Head to Vegas. We'll meet up at the top of that tall black tower we saw on the way in."

When everyone nodded, Emily raised her hands. "Ready?"

Her fear fed the power of the Flame. In an instant, a huge burst of blinding light flew from her hands and hit the sealed trailer ramp. On impact the ramp exploded and blew out. The debris hit several soldiers charging toward the trailer.

"Go!" Emily cried.

Chrysaor was first to move. The winged boar squealed and charged through the burning opening, Joel clinging on to his back, screaming. Paelen followed, running and ordering his sandals to take him up into the sky. As he flew over the heads of the gathering soldiers, he kicked the nearest two men. "Leave us alone!"

"Alexis, go!" Emily shouted as Pegasus moved

beneath her. She looked over to Tornado. "Come on, boy, come with us. Use your wings and fly!"

Like his brother, Chrysaor, Pegasus charged out of the burning trailer, screaming. He opened his wings and leaped confidently into the air.

Emily's eyes went wide at the sight of countless military vehicles pulling into the parking area. Men were pouring out with their weapons raised. Popping sounds filled the air as they opened fire. She felt stings on her arms and back and realized they were using tranquilizer darts, just like when the CRU were after them in New York on the 59th Street Bridge. Only this time, they had no effect other than to make her angry.

She held up her hand and released the laserlike flame at the nearest military vehicle. It exploded in a brilliant blast. A second, third, and fourth vehicle followed the first as the air around them glowed with the light of the burning trucks.

Emily's eyes sought Earl. She looked back and saw him being held down on the ground by several armed men. Earl was shouting at her, but she couldn't hear what he was saying.

"Pegs, we've got to go back for Earl!"

"Emily, no," Alexis said, swooping close. "You are the Flame; you must remain free. Earl knows this. He would not wish you to risk yourself."

Emily looked down on Earl. He had done so much for them, and all they had ever given back was trouble.

As Pegasus climbed into the sky, Tornado Warning screamed. He was still on the ground and running with amazing speed to keep up with her and Pegasus. Military jeeps were chasing him, and men were tossing ropes to catch him.

"Fly, Tornado!" Emily cried. "Use your wings and fly!" But the stallion did not know how. Instead he turned his fear into rage. He stopped, spun around, and charged the soldiers who were trying to capture him. He may not have known how to fly, but Tornado Warning knew how to fight. He instinctively used his wings as weapons. He flapped them and struck the men who were trying to catch him. Others were kicked by his lethal hooves.

As more men swarmed forward, Emily watched the winged racehorse finally brought down by the countless tranquilizer darts being shot into him. Her last sight of the stallion was him collapsing to the ground.

Emily couldn't watch anymore. She looked ahead and saw that they were far from out of danger. A squadron of military helicopters was cresting the mountains surrounding Area 51 and heading straight for them.

Joel, Chrysaor, and Paelen were ahead of them in the dark sky. Emily noticed that Paelen was flying oddly, very close to Chrysaor. Then she saw why.

"Joel!" she gasped. She saw his limp body being held up by Paelen. "Pegasus, look! Joel's been shot!"

Paelen was struggling to stop him from falling off the winged boar's back.

"Paelen!" Emily cried. She pointed at the approaching helicopters. "Get Joel to Las Vegas. Pegasus and I will slow them down!"

Without waiting for a reply, Emily and Pegasus turned in the direction of the approaching military helicopters. "If they want to fight," she called to the stallion, "we'll give them a fight they'll never forget!"

"Emily, do not do this!" Alexis called, flying closely beside Pegasus. "We must flee!"

"We can't! Paelen and Chrysaor can't carry Joel very fast while he's unconscious. We've got to help them get away."

She felt the full power of the Flame rumbling through her entire body. Despite the danger she faced, Emily felt strangely calm. "Are you ready, Pegs?"

Beneath her, Pegasus put on more speed and screamed into the night sky. He was glowing brilliant white like a blazing beacon as he flew at the helicopters. Emily focused her eyes on the closest helicopter. "This is for Joel, Earl, Tornado Warning, and Agent T!" she cried. Emily raised her hands and unleashed the Flame.

PAELEN STRUGGLED TO KEEP JOEL FROM FALL-
ing. Unconscious, he was slumped across Chrysaor's
back and at risk of sliding off. But trying to keep his
large friend steady while flying with winged sandals
was proving very difficult.

Over to his right, Paelen saw the glow of Emily
and Pegasus charging through the dark sky toward
the approaching helicopters. He couldn't bear to
watch, but couldn't draw his eyes away either.

Emily and Pegasus looked so small and vulnerable
going up against the deadly flying machines. Yet as
Paelen watched, he saw his best friend use her powers
to bring down the metal monsters.

Paelen saw endless flashes in the sky from the

machine's weapons as they fired at Pegasus and Emily. It brought back terrifying memories of the night Cupid was shot down by similar machines.

But Cupid didn't have Emily's power or determination. Paelen watched machine after machine exploding brilliantly in the sky over the dark desert.

Their burning hulks crashed violently to the ground and set the dry scrub grass and plants alight. Before long, the desert floor was littered with glowing and burning debris.

Paelen shook his head in wonder. Emily was proving to be the better fighter and yet they kept coming, hoping to cut her and Pegasus down out of the sky.

He was so engrossed watching the fight that he failed to notice Joel was slipping. Suddenly Chrysaor screamed.

"Joel!" Paelen cried as his friend tumbled away from Chrysaor and free-fell into the darkness below.

"Sandals, get me to Joel!" Paelen cried in a panic.

The winged sandals reacted instantly. Paelen entered a dive as he chased after Joel. Chrysaor continued to squeal as he turned in the sky and dived down to stop Joel from crashing to the ground.

Both Paelen and Chrysaor reached Joel just a few meters before he hit the ground. Paelen caught hold of Joel's silver arm and slowed his fall just long enough for Chrysaor to fly beneath him and let Joel land on his back.

"Take us down!" Paelen panted as he and his sandals fought to support Joel's weight.

The landing wasn't neat or graceful. As Chrysaor's feet touched down on the desert floor, the unconscious Joel lunged forward on his back. Despite Paelen's best efforts, Joel's silver arm slipped free of his grasp, and Joel was thrown off the boar's back. He crashed to the ground several meters away. Paelen cringed when he realized his best friend had just landed in a cactus patch.

Paelen split his attention between Joel and the fight raging in the sky. He could no longer see Emily or Pegasus, but he did see her laser streams of Flame cutting across the dark sky. He noticed that the remaining helicopters were flying away from where they landed and realized that Emily was leading them away from him, Joel, and Chrysaor.

Be safe, Emily, he silently prayed as the fight faded into the distance.

Paelen reluctantly drew his eyes away from the sky to concentrate on Joel. He quickly discovered that Joel wasn't in just any cactus patch—it had to be the biggest and meanest cactus patch in the desert. As he entered it and tried to get near his friend, sharp needles scratched his feet between the sandal's leather straps and stuck painfully into his ankles and legs.

Paelen cried out in pain and retreated from the patch. Beside him, Chrysaor squealed and offered suggestions.

"You try walking in there, then," Paelen snapped back at the boar. "Your tough hide should be fine with those needles. But they are cutting me to pieces!"

After several more squeals, Paelen looked at Chrysaor. "Oh, I see what you mean," he said. "Good idea."

He looked down at his feet. "Sandals, lift me up in the air and flip me upside down."

The tiny wings on the sandals gave their quick flutter of understanding and then lifted him off the ground. They hovered in the air and then flipped. Paelen yelped as he was tossed upside down.

"Now take me to Joel over the patch." They moved over the cactus needles.

"Easy," Paelen said. "Just a bit more. . . . Good! Stop there!"

Paelen reached for one of Joel's hands and grabbed it securely. "Sandals, lift me up."

Paelen cried out as his hands brushed against a cactus pad that was filled with sharp, stabbing needles. His friend had been lying on that plant. Joel would be in a lot of pain once he woke up.

Paelen carried Joel over to Chrysaor. Even in the dark, they could see the thousands of tiny needles poking into his clothing.

Using his sharp teeth, Chrysaor started to pull the needles out one at a time.

"This is going to take us all night," Paelen said as he joined in.

Chrysaor squealed. "Yes," Paelen agreed, "we did pass a lake on the way here." He looked down at the tiny swollen points of blood on Joel's bare skin where the cactus needles had been removed. He looked over to Chrysaor. "Good idea. We should get him there before he wakes."

The journey to the lake was relatively short. Paelen kept a sharp eye out for more military vehicles. But after the big fight and Emily leading them away, Paelen realized they were completely alone.

They'd landed in a completely different environment. They were still in the middle of the desert, but the lake was lined with trees and lush grass. The air was cooler and fresher.

After removing the remaining cactus needles, they carried Joel into the chilly water. On contact, Joel started to stir. He moaned softly and passed out again.

Paelen remained in the water with Joel until the sun was well up. As Joel started to stir, Paelen carried him out of the lake and settled him gently on the grass beneath a large tree. The heat of the day was already pressing heavily down on them.

Joel opened his eyes, then frowned. "Where are we?" he asked groggily. "What happened?"

"You are all right," Paelen answered. "But you had a rather difficult night. First you were shot with tranquilizer darts by the CRU, then almost crash-landed into the ground, and then had a fight with a cactus plant—and lost."

"You call that difficult? I hurt all over!" Paelen

nodded. "Yes, but at least you are alive." Joel lifted his head and looked around. "Where's Emily? Is she all right?"

"I do not know," Paelen said. "The last we saw, she was leading the machines away from us. I am certain she is fine." Even Paelen didn't believe his own words. There were too many machines against Emily and Pegasus. It was unlikely that they could have escaped unharmed.

"We've got to find them." Joel panicked as he struggled to rise. But there was still tranquilizer residue in his system, and he collapsed.

"We cannot leave here," Paelen said as he stopped Joel from trying to rise again. "Look around you. It is full daylight, and we are in the middle of nowhere. We cannot leave the safe cover of this place until dark."

Chrysaor put a small hoof lightly on Joel's chest and squealed softly.

"Chrysaor agrees. We must not be seen flying during the day. It is too dangerous for all of us."

"But what about Emily?" Joel cried. "I've got to find her."

"Yes we do," Paelen agreed. "But we will not do Emily, Pegasus, or Alexis any good if we are captured. You are still weak from the drugs and the cactus needles. Take today to recover. We will leave here the moment it is dark. Then we can meet up with the others at the black tower."

Paelen could see Joel's thoughts flying like a storm. Like Paelen, Joel was devoted to Emily and hated the thought of her being out there alone. Though Pegasus and the Sphinx were with her, there was still a chance one or more of them might have been hurt in the firefight.

"What if she's dead?" Joel asked.

Paelen shook his head. "Emily is the Flame; she is strong. But we have all been without ambrosia and nectar for days. It is Pegasus and Alexis I worry most for. I hope they are all right. But for now, all we can do is wait."

"WHERE ARE THEY?"

Emily paced anxiously along the top wall of the tall black building. She looked out over Las Vegas, searching the cloudless skies for signs of Joel, Paelen, and Chrysaor. The sun was up but there was no sign of her friends.

"They will come," Alexis called softly. She and Pegasus were hiding inside a construction shed that remained on the roof. The building was unfinished, but by the looks of things, construction work had stopped some time ago. There was still an unused crane on the roof and a lot of tools. Over the side, there were several black windows missing, and on the ground, scaffolding rose high up against the side. The construction site was surrounded by a tall wooden fence.

When Emily walked back into the shed, she was more exhausted than she'd ever thought possible. Even after all the training Vesta had given her, she was still unprepared for her encounter with the military.

It had taken a lot out of her. The Flame within had done everything she commanded. But that didn't stop her other powers from surfacing. When she had opened fire on three heavily armed helicopters, instead of flame issuing from her hands, the flying vehicles vanished. But where had they gone?

She sat down against the shed's wall and took a deep breath. Her eyes landed on the Sphinx. Alexis was weeping.

"Are you all right?"

Alexis dropped her head as more tears trickled down her smooth cheeks. "I warned him," she wept softly. "I told him it was a bad idea, but he insisted."

"Agent T?" Emily asked.

Alexis nodded. "After you all went to bed, he came to me. He said getting into Area 51 was a suicide mission. Tom was frightened for everyone, but especially you. He knew what would happen if the CRU ever got their hands on you and said he could never let that happen."

Emily felt a lump form in her throat. Agent T had never shown a trace of caring. Had he been hiding it?

"Why didn't he wait for us? We could have helped."

"He could not," Alexis wept. "Emily, Tom recognized the man who checked up on us in the trailer. He was from the CRU. He was certain the man had recognized him, too. Tom asked me to take him to the facility before they made a move against us. He was hoping he could reason with them. Tell them what would happen if they did not stop cloning New Olympians."

"Did they listen?"

Alexis shook her head. "Even before we arrived, they must have known we were coming. The moment we touched down, their lights came alive and we were surrounded. I was wearing Pluto's helmet, but they still knew I was there."

The Sphinx's voice broke as she looked tearfully at Emily. "When he realized we were captured, Tom told me to get you all away from here. But then a Nirad guard came at me. . . ."

"What!"

Alexis nodded. "They have Nirads there. We knew they would, but these were not prisoners. Those Nirads were working alongside the CRU. The gray Nirads were CRU soldiers. They were the ones who attacked me and nearly tore off my wings."

Emily's hand shot to her mouth. "This is so bad."

"It is worse," Alexis said. "While I fought the Nirad soldiers, I saw more coming from an open door, so I flew at the door and entered a world of horror." Alexis couldn't continue as her sobs increased.

Emily put her arms around her. "I'm so sorry, Alexis," she soothed, holding the shaking Sphinx. "But you must tell me. What did you see in there?"

"They have Diana clones locked in cages. I also saw Paelens and Cupids. I did not see the Pegasus clones, but I could hear them and feel their fear."

"Cupids?" Emily repeated. "How is that possible? He was never a prisoner of the CRU."

The Sphinx did her best to shrug. "I do not know, but they were there. They were suffering. But I could not help them. It took all my cunning just to escape and get back to you."

Emily shook her head and whispered, "This is worse than I imagined. It's gone too far for us to do anything. We must tell Jupiter what's happening here and beg him not to destroy this world."

Alexis shook her head. "Please, no, we cannot do that."

Emily was confused. "But you were the one who wanted us to tell Jupiter."

"Yes, I was," Alexis said shakily. "You are so very young and may not understand this. But I cared a great deal for Tom. In the short time we were together, we discovered we had much in common and . . ." Alexis paused and lifted her eyes to Emily. "And how alone we both were."

"Really?"

The Sphinx nodded. "Tom made me laugh. He treated me like a person. Not the Sphinx and not an Olympian guardian, but a person."

And suddenly Emily saw that the great and powerful Sphinx was very lonely, and Agent T had ended that loneliness. "I'm so sorry, Alexis."

Alexis dropped her head. "Before we left for the CRU facility, Tom begged me to help him save this world. It was the only thing he had left to care about." She paused and looked at Emily with her tearful green eyes. "How could I refuse him?"

Emily looked away. "That doesn't sound like the Agent T I know."

"Tom was a very tragic man," Alexis continued. "He deeply regretted many of the things he has done. He joined the CRU to help serve and protect his country. Instead he lost himself. Only at the end did he realize his mistake and want to make amends for it. He told me to tell you and Pegasus he was sorry."

Tears filled Emily's eyes. She reached for her green handkerchief and carefully gathered them before they could fall and explode. "I wish he had told me," she whispered.

The sound of approaching helicopters pulled Emily back to the present. She stood and peered out of the door to the shed. "It's just a tourist helicopter," she explained. "We're safe for the moment."

Leaving Alexis to her tears, Emily stepped out into the midday heat. It was almost unbearable. The tarmac beneath her feet was soft and starting to melt. Approaching the edge, she looked over Las Vegas.

Brightly colored casinos lined the famous strip, and thousands of people were moving around below. None of them were aware of the danger they faced. It sounded as if the CRU had created an army of Nirad soldiers. With fighters like that, they could easily take over the world. Why else would they want to clone Nirads? Emily realized that the CRU posed almost as much danger to this world as Jupiter did.

What genetic engineering had they done to create the Nirad clones? True Nirads had telepathic links to each other. Would Queen Segan or Prince Toban be able to communicate with these new Nirads, like they did with the rest of their people?

A thought entered Emily's mind. She went back into the shed.

"Alexis, did the gray Nirad soldiers seem like the Nirads we're familiar with? Or were they different, like Tornado was different from Pegasus?"

"They appeared the same," Alexis answered. "They had four arms, black stringy hair, and three large black eyes. Their skin was marble like that of all other Nirads. But something felt different about them. I am certain they are not all Nirad but mixed with something else."

"But are they Nirad enough to be like the ones we know?" Emily mused aloud. She went over to the stallion. "Pegs, do you think Queen Segan or Prince Toban would help us? If they could communicate with those military Nirads, maybe we could turn them against the CRU."

Alexis rose to her feet and padded over to Emily. "You are not proposing we bring the Nirad queen to this world?"

"Not the queen," Emily responded. "Segan must remain on her world, but what about Prince Toban? He can speak with his people using his mind, can't he?"

Pegasus neighed softly and pawed the floor of the shed.

"He says it would be very dangerous to bring the prince here. I agree with him. If the prince were captured . . ."

Emily shook her head. "What could the CRU do to him? Nirads are practically indestructible. Only Olympian gold, Pegasus's golden hooves, and my powers can harm them. Nothing on Earth seemed to stop them last time they were here. The CRU has no Olympian gold, and I doubt they'd even know that was the Nirads' weakness. Prince Toban would be perfectly safe."

"I do not think this is a good idea," Alexis said.

"I don't like it either. But they should be told what's happening here. Those are Nirad clones—part of their people. They should know what the CRU have done. It's only fair."

Alexis looked at Pegasus. The stallion shook his head and snorted. He pressed his head closer to Emily as the Sphinx focused on her. "Pegasus believes this might work. I can think of no other reasonable solution. This seems to be the only course of action. However, there is still the issue of Joel, Paelen, and Chrysaor's absence to consider."

Worry for her friends pressed heavily down on Emily. "I will stay here and wait for them, while you and Pegasus go to the Nirad world to speak to Prince Toban."

Pegasus protested loudly, and Alexis shook her head. "You will not remain here unguarded."

"Then you stay and wait for the others, and Pegs and I can go."

Alexis shook her head. "That is also unacceptable. We will all go."

"But what about Joel and Paelen? Someone should stay here for them. You are the best one to do that."

"I am sworn to protect you, Emily. I go wherever you go."

"But—"

Alexis narrowed her eyes. "I will ask you a riddle. If you answer correctly, I will remain here. If not, we all go."

Emily groaned. They didn't have time for one of Alexis's riddles. But at the same time, she knew the Sphinx needed to do this to help get her back on even footing. "Go ahead."

"Riddle me this . . .

I am the unreachable boundary,
Yet the place you wish to go,
I run away as you approach.
But I am always there.
What am I?"

Emily repeated the riddle to herself. An unreachable boundary that runs away when you approach? She tried to think of something that she might want but could never reach. She looked out of the shed, hoping to find an answer. With the sun high in the sky, there were very few shadows or shelter from the unforgiving heat. Suddenly a thought came to her. Shadows. Like Peter Pan, you can never catch your shadow!

"You are a shadow," she said triumphantly.

As always, Emily was wrong and did not receive the correct answer from Alexis. Instead the Sphinx nodded smugly and walked back to the corner. "We shall all leave at sunset. As we have nothing to eat, drink, or do, I suggest we take this time to rest. It has been an awful night, and I am greatly fatigued."

Emily stroked Pegasus and watched Alexis curl up in the corner. She looked even more like a giant house cat with her wings pulled tight to her body and her tail wrapped around her. "Do you think we're doing the right thing bringing Prince Toban here, Pegs?"

The stallion nudged Emily and invited her to stroke him. It was the best answer he could give.

Emily sighed. "I just hope this doesn't make things worse."

PAELEN AND CHRYSAOR LOUNGED UNDER A shady tree while Joel spent most of the day in the lake. His body ached and stung from the cactus patch. Only the cool water seemed to calm his inflamed skin.

Throughout the long day, tourists had come to visit the unique lake in the middle of the desert. Picnic tables were scattered along the banks, and on more than one occasion people had waved at Joel and called greetings. When they approached, Joel ducked low in the water to hide his silver arm and shoulder.

When the sun started to set, Joel emerged from the water. Paelen stifled a laugh as he watched his friend walk up the bank. Joel was covered all over in tiny red pinpricks.

He pulled on his sweatshirt and immediately cried out in pain and pulled it off again. He threw it to the ground. "It's still full of cactus needles!"

"I have no doubt your jeans are the same," Paelen commented. "I would suggest you avoid those also."

"What am I supposed to wear now? I can't walk around naked."

"Sure you can," Paelen laughed wickedly. "I'm sure Alexis and Emily will love it!"

"It's not funny!" Joel cried. "Look at me. My arm is exposed."

"That is not all that is exposed!" Paelen roared. Rolling around on the ground, he was lost in fits of laughter. Even Chrysaor's eyes sparkled, and he snorted happily.

"When we get to the black tower, perhaps we can find you some more clothing."

"You're enjoying this way too much," Joel muttered as he sat down to wait.

When darkness fell, Joel climbed on Chrysaor and they took off into the sky. The only words spoken were those of Joel complaining about Chrysaor's coarse hair scratching his bare skin. Paelen found it difficult to fly straight as his laughter continued.

But as they got closer to Las Vegas, Paelen's laughter tapered off, and he started to worry. Had Emily, Pegasus, and Alexis made it to the black building? Were the others waiting for them?

Soon they were flying over the bright city. Paelen looked down in wonder at all the colorful lights. He could never have imagined a place like this. Not even New York lit up like Las Vegas.

"There it is," Joel called as Chrysaor flew high above the Las Vegas strip.

The tall black building loomed directly ahead of them at the far end of the strip. There were no lights shining from within, and in the dark, it was a strangely imposing sight among all the brightness around it.

They touched down on the roof of the unfinished building. After a quick search, they realized Emily and the others weren't there.

"Where are they?" Joel asked as he walked to the edge and peered over Las Vegas. "They should have been here by now!"

"Perhaps they did not make it," Paelen offered.

"How are we going to find them?" Joel asked.

"I know," Paelen said. He had been hesitant to use his sandals, for fear of discovering some awful truth. But now there was no choice. He looked at Joel and Chrysaor. "Remain here. I will be right back."

Paelen looked down at his sandals. "Take me to Emily!"

The sandals flapped acknowledgment and then shot him up straight up the air. Faster and faster the sandals carried Paelen away from Las Vegas, until he realized they were gaining speed to enter the Solar Stream. But when they entered the blindingly bright Stream, the sandals paused and seemed uncertain of where to go.

Paelen felt the drawing whoosh of the Solar Stream all around him, and he could also feel the sandals struggling to keep him still. Dark shapes of travelers sped past him, but they were moving too quickly for him to identify anyone.

"Enough," Paelen called over the roaring power of the Solar Stream. "Take me back to Joel."

The sandals obeyed immediately, and Paelen was

carried back to Las Vegas. He touched back down on the roof of the black building.

"That was fast," Joel said. "Where is she?"

Paelen shook his head. "The sandals do not know. Emily has entered the Solar Stream, but that was as far as they could take me. They cannot track her through it."

"That means she's alive!" Joel celebrated. "And Pegasus is too if he was carrying her!"

"It may have been Alexis carrying her," Paelen offered. "We must consider that Pegasus may have been hurt and captured by the CRU. Emily would do anything to protect him. Including telling Jupiter what has happened."

"Emily wouldn't do that," Joel insisted. "Not even for Pegasus! She knows what Jupiter would do if he found out."

"Perhaps she did not have a choice."

Chrysaor remained silent for most of the conversation. Suddenly the boar squealed and charged across the roof. He ran into a small construction shed. High-pitched screams filled the air.

They found Chrysaor cornering a young boy in

the shed. He looked only nine or ten years old, was dressed in filthy clothing, and had a dirty face. His eyes were bright and terrified.

"Don't eat me!" he screamed.

Paelen frowned. "Why would we eat you?"

He entered the shed, and the boy screamed even louder.

"Please stop doing that!" Paelen cried, putting his hand over his ears.

"It's all right." Joel held up his hands. "We're not going to hurt you. I promise."

"You're lying. You're going to eat me!" the boy wailed.

"No, we are not," Paelen insisted, "though I might throw you off the roof if you scream again."

"That's not helping, Paelen!" Joel knelt down beside Chrysaor and faced the boy. He offered his silver hand. "I promise you, we aren't going to hurt you. This is Chrysaor, that's Paelen, and I'm Joel. Come out of there and tell me your name."

The boy looked at Joel's hand fearfully. "You're an alien robot!"

Joel shook his head. "No, I'm not. But my arm is

made of metal. My real arm was wrecked, and now I have this."

The boy hesitantly took Joel's silver hand. "It's so cold."

"Yes, it is," Joel agreed. "What's your name?"

"Frankie," the little boy said as he walked around Chrysaor and followed Joel out of the shed.

"What are you doing here, Frankie?"

"I live here."

Joel looked around the roof. "Here?"

The boy nodded. "I live on the floor beneath this one."

"But I thought this building was abandoned," Joel said. "It's unfinished."

"It is abandoned. But I live here anyway."

"With your parents?" Paelen asked. He searched for signs of others.

Frankie shook his head. "No, they're gone."

"Gone where?"

"Just gone," Frankie said flatly. He looked back at Chrysaor. "Are you the ones the girl with the flying horse and lion-lady were looking for?"

"You have seen Emily?" Paelen demanded.

Frankie nodded.

"Where?" Joel demanded. "When?"

"Here, today."

"Where are they now?" Paelen asked.

The young boy shrugged.

"You're not big on answers, are you?" Joel said in irritation. He knelt down before the boy. "It's really important that we find our friends. Please, tell us what you know."

Again Frankie shrugged. "They were here all day and left when it got dark."

"Did you speak with them?" Paelen asked.

Frankie shook his head. "No way! I was too scared—that lion-lady would have eaten me! So I stayed hidden over there." He pointed to a large pile of building debris and rubbish.

"You seem convinced everyone is going to eat you," Paelen observed.

"'Cause that's what aliens do: they eat people," Frankie said. "Everyone knows that."

"We're not aliens," Joel insisted, "and we're not going to eat you. Did you hear what the others were talking about?"

"The lion-lady was really sad. She was crying." Frankie's eyes lingered on Chrysaor. "Can I pet your flying pig?"

"He's a boar," Joel corrected. "I don't think he'd like that."

Chrysaor stepped closer to Frankie and invited a pat. The little boy stroked his wings and the coarse hair on his snout. "It feels funny," he giggled.

"Why was the lion-lady crying?" Paelen asked. "Was she hurt?"

Frankie shrugged. "Don't know."

"What *do* you know?" Paelen said impatiently. "What were they talking about?"

"They were talking about nerds."

"Nerds," Joel repeated. "Are you sure about that?"

"I think so. I couldn't hear too good. But it sounded like nerds. They were going to get a nerd prince."

Joel sucked in his breath in understanding. "Not nerds, they were talking about Nirads! They've gone to get Prince Toban."

"What?" Paelen concentrated on Frankie. "Are you sure you heard them correctly? Did they say Nirads?"

Frankie nodded. "It sounded like that. They were

saying they needed the nerd prince to control the crew nerd soldiers."

Joel frowned and tried to decipher Frankie's words. Finally it registered, and he snapped his fingers. He looked at Paelen. "CRU—Nirad soldiers! The CRU have created Nirad clones that are serving as soldiers."

"And Emily has gone to the Nirad world to get the prince," Paelen finished. "Of course—it all makes sense now. She would not go to Jupiter if there was still a chance of saving this world. Now all we need to do is go there to join her."

Chrysaor squealed softly and then nudged Frankie to pet him some more.

"What did he say?" Joel asked.

"That we should wait here. We may miss them in the Solar Stream and lose more precious time. Entering the Solar Stream again may draw Jupiter's attention. Chrysaor believes it is safer to wait here, as they know this tower is our meeting place."

Joel looked incredulous. "You want us to sit here and wait while the CRU create more clones?"

Chrysaor squealed and grunted. Paelen sighed and nodded. "Chrysaor is correct. We are hungry and getting weaker without ambrosia. We must eat first."

"And you really should wear some clothes," Frankie added. "On my planet, we don't walk around naked."

Joel realized he was still undressed. "This *is* my planet! But my clothes were ruined."

"I've got some," Frankie offered. "But they might be too small. You're really big." He paused and tilted his head to the side. "Are you sure you're not an alien robot here to invade our planet?"

"I'm not a robot!" Joel shouted.

Frankie didn't look convinced. "You sure look like one. And your friends look exactly like aliens, especially him." He pointed at Paelen.

"Why is it always me?" Paelen shot angrily. "Why am I always the alien?"

They followed Frankie down a flight of stairs and arrived on the top floor of the black building. It was still unfinished—just one big open space with no walls and a lot of exposed steel girders and wiring. In one corner, they discovered the home that Frankie had made for himself. He had scrounged crates and boxes and created crude furniture. There was a pile of old blankets and tinned food. Frankie had blacked out all the windows so no one would see the lights he had wired up.

Frankie's housekeeping skills needed a lot of work, but he obviously knew his way around computers and the Internet. He had set up what looked like a control center with at least four working computers. There were others in the process of being built. Off to one side were extra screens and parts neatly laid out and ready to be used.

"This is my headquarters," he said proudly, showing off his computers. "I'm using these to look for aliens."

Joel and Paelen admired the boy's handiwork. He had managed to build all this from scrap he'd picked up on the street. "Wow, this is really cool," Joel said. "Have you ever looked for aliens at Area 51? Can you show us how to get in there?"

Frankie shook his head. "I look all the time, but I can't get into their system. I don't think they're on the Internet. They must be using an internal intranet system instead. I tracked down a few pictures taken from satellites. But I never saw aliens until you got here today."

"We're not aliens!" Joel protested.

"If you say so," Frankie said dubiously. He continued to show Joel his work at trying to hack into Area 51's systems.

Paelen did not understand a word Frankie was saying, but Joel was nodding his head. They looked at the photos Frankie had downloaded from Area 51. They showed the open desert, the dry Groom Lake bed, and two long landing strips with several dark, squat buildings. None of the photos showed any activity or signs of Nirads or other clones.

"Hey, that's great work," Joel said. "How old are you?"

"I'm nearly ten," Frankie answered proudly. "But I'm really smart." He stopped to pat Chrysaor again. "But I don't go to school now. I just like to play with my computers."

"And you live here alone?" Paelen asked.

Frankie shook his head and pointed at the pile of blankets. "No, my friend John lives with me."

They all concentrated on the pile that they'd thought was rags. It was breathing.

"Don't worry about John," Frankie said. "He's

drunk most of the time. But he does help me live. He's taught me how to scrounge stuff and sneak into places. Without John, I don't know what I would have done."

"What about your family?" Joel pressed.

"I told you, they're gone," Frankie said quickly. "I live here with John."

"So it is just the two of you in this building?" Paelen asked.

Frankie shook his head. "No, there are others. But they're on the lower floors. Everyone knows John and I live up here. We help get them money, so they leave us alone."

"Money?" Paelen said as his interest was piqued. "How do you get money? Do you steal it?"

"Not really," Frankie said hesitantly. "I'm really good with numbers, so we go to casinos and I count cards for John. I can tell him what's coming. But we can only do it in the really small casinos. The big ones have rules and won't let kids in—but some of the smaller ones do as long as they're with adults."

Paelen frowned. "What is counting cards?"

Joel explained. "It's a way of cheating. Some

people can look at multiple decks of cards and calculate what cards are coming next. Then they know if they should bet or not. Casinos don't like it and stop card counters."

"But they don't stop me," Frankie said, "'cause they don't think I can do it. But I can."

In the light, Paelen was able to get a good look at Frankie. He was very small and very round, and appeared to be young, with bright-red curly hair. He had huge brown eyes and a freckled face. There was something about him that reminded Paelen of himself when he was younger. Perhaps it was how the kid had been living off his wits outside of society, just as Paelen had on Olympus.

Frankie walked over to a box of clothing. "This is John's stuff. I don't think he'd mind if you borrowed some." He rifled through the box and managed to find a clean but badly mismatched polyester checked suit. "This is John's best suit. He's saving it for a special occasion."

Joel looked at the hideous outfit and shook his head. He could only fit his silver arm through a bold-patterned short-sleeved shirt that clashed badly with the checked suit trousers. He used a T-shirt to fashion a crude sling to help hide his arm. "Well?" he asked. "How do I look?"

Paelen fought to keep back laughter, but failed. "Fine!" he struggled to say before bursting out laughing. "Though I would not let anyone from Olympus see you in that. Not if you hope to live there again!"

Joel looked down at himself and groaned. "I look like a used-car salesman!"

Frankie smiled brightly. "It's better than being naked."

"I guess so," Joel sighed. "Hey, do you have any money?"

Frankie hesitated and then nodded. "John and me split our winnings even Steven. He buys drink with his, but I buy computer parts. I've got all I need now and was saving my money for emergencies."

Paelen looked around and wondered what the boy thought an emergency was. He had no family and he was living wild in Las Vegas with a devotee of Bacchus. How much worse could it get?

"Frankie," Joel said softly, "we haven't eaten in a very long time, and we're really hungry. Look at poor

Chrysaor: He's starving. Can we borrow some money? I promise we'll pay you back."

Frankie stroked Chrysaor's wings again and nodded.

He walked over to a pile of construction debris. After checking to see that John was still sleeping, he put his small hand in and withdrew a used mayonnaise jar filled with money. "Take it. Get food for . . ." He struggled with Chrysaor's name. "Get food for Chrysler."

The winged boar came up to Frankie and gently licked his hand.

"Thanks, Frankie," Joel said. He counted out fifty dollars. "That will get us started."

THE JOURNEY THROUGH THE SOLAR STREAM seemed to go on forever as Emily impatiently waited to get to the Nirad world. She hated leaving Las Vegas without knowing what had happened to her friends. But with Alexis refusing to wait for them on the rooftop, her plan was to get there, convince the prince to join them, and get right back to Vegas before the sunrise.

They emerged from the Solar Stream into a dark cave. This was the entrance to the Nirad world. Since the fight with the gorgons, Emily hadn't returned, although she had been invited many times. But the memory was still too fresh and the pain of losing her Nirad friend, Tange, too great.

They emerged from the cave into daylight. Or what passed for daylight in the Nirad world. The sky was still filled with dark, scudding storm clouds, but the air was dry and arid. The black ground was dusty and swirled around their feet in the light, warm wind.

Outside the cave, they approached lilac guards at the entrance. When the guards spotted Emily and Pegasus, they roared excitedly and bowed. Emily slid off Pegasus's back and greeted them.

As the Nirads were a telepathic race, it wasn't long before others arrived. The ground rumbled as the heavy marblelike people gathered around to greet the heroes of their world.

From the back of the gathering, Emily heard a high-pitched, familiar roar. The crowds parted and bowed as a figure approached.

"Segan!" Emily cried as she ran forward to greet the Nirad queen. It hadn't been that long since Emily had seen her on Olympus, but Segan had grown taller and looked older. Yet for her Nirad size, she still remained delicate and elegant in her long pink gown.

Segan called out a sound that was as close to Emily's name as her mouth and tongue would allow.

She ran forward and scooped Emily up in her four arms. As the two friends embraced, Pegasus neighed excitedly.

Emily took one of Segan's hands and directed her over to Alexis.

The Sphinx bowed deeply. "Your Majesty, it is a great honor to finally meet you."

Queen Segan knelt before Alexis and touched the Sphinx's shoulder. She made several soft growls. The smile on Alexis's face told Emily that the queen had made her welcome.

Segan rose and turned to her people. She raised her four hands high in the air and made a long series of growls.

Alexis moved closer to Emily. "They are going to prepare a great banquet in honor of us to celebrate your return to the Nirad world."

Emily shook her head. "But we don't have time. We've got to get Prince Toban and go. We have to find Joel, Paelen, and Chrysaor."

Alexis narrowed her eyes. "I have met your father, Emily, and I know he raised you better than this. This is your first visit back to the Nirad world after the gorgon defeat. Their queen has ordered a banquet and celebration in your honor. You will attend the banquet and you will show your gratitude."

"But—"

Pegasus nickered softly beside her.

"Pegasus agrees," Alexis continued. "We are going to ask them to help us with a very dangerous situation. The least we could do is accept their hospitality. We will attend their banquet, and then approach Queen Segan and Prince Toban and seek their assistance."

Emily looked over to her host. Queen Segan's face was beaming.

She patted Pegasus's neck. "I'm sorry. You're both right. I'm just so worried about the others, and we don't have much time to spare."

"I am certain the others are fine," Alexis said. "Paelen is clever and crafty, and Joel knows your world well. They will find somewhere to hide until we return. Right now, we must concentrate on how much to tell the Nirads."

They sat around a huge banquet table filled with equal amounts of ambrosia and Nirad moss. Since the union of the two worlds, Nirads had acquired a taste for the Olympian food and always had plenty around. As they dined, Emily, Pegasus, and Alexis watched Nirad musicians beat large drums as dancers performed for the group. Emily never knew they could dance. But despite their massive size, the performers moved with a light foot and graceful movement. Emily did notice that it was only lilac and orange Nirads who danced. The grays sat at their tables, clapping their four hands and growling loudly.

Alexis sighed sadly. "I wish Tom could have seen this. He would have enjoyed himself greatly."

Emily studied the Sphinx but remained silent. She knew Alexis was grieving more than she let on. Had the Olympian Sphinx really fallen in love with an ex–CRU agent?

As the evening progressed, Emily felt more and more anxious. They shouldn't be celebrating when so much was at stake on her world. Worry for her friends only added to her stress level, and she was desperate to get moving.

Just before the celebration ended, Emily noticed

that Alexis had slipped silently away from the banquet table. She stood and spotted the Sphinx speaking with Queen Segan and Prince Toban.

"I am sorry that I could not wait for you," the Sphinx said when Emily and Pegasus approached. "But I heard that Prince Toban was planning to leave for Olympus shortly. I had to stop him."

The queen reached for Emily's hands and motioned her to sit down and join them.

"How much did you tell them?" Emily asked.

"Everything," Alexis said. "They know all about the clones. Though they do not understand fully what they are, they do understand how important this is, and what it could mean for your world if Jupiter were to find out. They will help us."

Prince Toban started to growl softly.

"He says he will come with us to rescue the children of Nirads."

"But they're not children," Emily frowned. "They are big, fully grown gray Nirads."

"He understands," Alexis said. "But there is no word in their language for clone. The closest is child or children."

"I am so sorry this has happened to your people," Emily said sincerely. "I promise we will do all we can to stop the CRU from creating more."

Prince Toban made a long series of sounds.

"The prince says he will go with you and gather the children together. He will bring them home where they belong. The children will be made welcome and cared for."

"Thank you, Toban," Emily said. "But I have to warn you. I don't know what the clones—I mean children—will be like. They could be very dangerous. They come from gray Nirads only. The child of Pegasus was wild and deadly. They may not know you as their prince and may try to hurt you."

Once again Prince Toban made a series of sounds.

"They will know him," Alexis said. "He is convinced. He also said not to fear for his safety. He will not be coming alone."

An orange Nirad approached. Emily immediately recognized him as the goalkeeper from Joel's soccer team. Tirk bowed formally to the queen before moving to stand behind the prince.

"Tirk is coming with us?" Emily said, looking at

the huge Nirad. Up close he was even bigger than Tange and twice as strong. His arm muscles seemed to pulse with barely contained strength.

The prince nodded and spoke softly.

Alexis translated. "Tirk will be Toban's royal guard. The prince will not go without him."

A royal guard would definitely help. If he was anything like Tange, he alone should be able to control the gray Nirads. "That's great," Emily said. She stood up and prepared to leave. "Can we go now, please?"

Alexis shook her head. "That would not be wise. We are all tired from the day's events and must rest. We will leave in the morning."

"But what about Joel, Paelen, and Chrysaor? We've got to get back to them!"

"Yes, we do," Alexis agreed. "In the morning. Now I will hear no more about it." The Sphinx stood and nodded respectfully to the queen and prince before trotting away.

BACK AT THE BLACK TOWER, JOEL, PAELEN, AND
Chrysaor settled down for their first meal in a long time.

Frankie took a sip of his drink and held the can
out to Joel. "Do you drink soda on your planet?"

"This *is* my planet!" Joel insisted. "How many times
do I have to tell you that? I'm human, just like you!"

Frankie shook his head. "Nah-uh, humans don't
have arms like yours. They can't fly with shoes, and
their pet pigs don't have wings."

"He's a boar," Joel corrected. "And he's not my pet.
He's my friend."

"Do you think he could be my friend?" Frankie
asked as he stroked Chrysaor's wings.

"Ask him yourself," Joel said irritably. "I'm going

up to the roof to wait for Emily." He stormed out of the area and made his way to the stairs.

"Why is Joel mad at me?"

Paelen looked at the little boy. Little Frankie seemed so lost and alone. "He is not mad at you. He is just very worried about our other friends."

Frankie nodded and continued to pet Chrysaor.

"Where is your family?" Paelen pressed. "Do you not wish to go home?"

Frankie remained silent a very long time before looking up at Paelen. Tears rimmed his eyes. "This is my home. I never had a dad, and my mom ran away. Now it's just me and John."

Paelen looked over to the pile of rags. The person under that pile hadn't stirred since they arrived. It appeared that Frankie did more for the man than he did for the boy.

"How long have you two been together?"

Frankie shrugged. "I'm not sure—longer than a year. John found me on the street when I was looking for my mom. He tried to help me find her, but we couldn't. Then we moved in here. He says when we make enough money with gambling, we're going to buy a real house. But . . ."

"But what?" Paelen asked.

"But John keeps drinking, so we can't go out to gamble much."

Paelen looked around at the home of the young boy. He felt great sympathy for him. His life was so much harder than Paelen's had ever been. Harder even than Joel's after his parents had died.

"Perhaps we can help you."

Paelen heard himself make the comment and shivered. Had he really just offered to help a human boy? He'd spent too much time with Emily and Joel. He would never have offered to help before. He had always lived only for himself. Now he was offering help to a stranger?

He stood up and stepped over to Chrysaor. "I am going up to check on Joel. Would you keep an eye on things here?"

Chrysaor grunted and remained with Frankie.

Paelen found Joel standing at the edge of the roof, looking up into the sky. "Are you all right?"

Joel shrugged. "I'm worried about Em, and what's going to happen when she gets back. What are we supposed to do? That facility is the most guarded of all of them. We can't exactly sneak in like we did last time."

"I do not know," Paelen agreed. His eyes looked out over the strip. The ground below was teeming with people despite the late hour. "But until they get back here, I suggest you and I go down there and see what is happening."

"You want to go out tonight?"

Paelen nodded. "Why not? It could be a few days before Emily returns. We don't know what horrors we will face with the CRU. This might be our last opportunity to have some fun."

Joel shook his head. "But won't she be back soon?"

"Time moves differently along the Solar Stream. A day there could be several here. We could be sitting up here for some time waiting for Emily to return. And I for one do not want to miss this chance to go exploring this strange and amazing place. Especially if it's about to be destroyed. I want to see as much of it as I can before that happens."

Joel looked longingly back down to the strip. "Well, I've never been to Las Vegas before."

"Exactly! We will not be out for long, so what can go wrong?"

IT WAS EARLY THE NEXT MORNING IN THE
Nirad world. After another large meal of ambrosia,
nectar, and black Nirad moss, extra supplies were
packed up for the other Olympians on Earth. Soon a
crowd gathered outside the cave of the Solar Stream.
The crowd had no idea where their prince was going
or the danger he faced. They just knew he was leaving, and offered their farewells and good wishes.

Emily watched the masses of Nirad people in
amazement. For all their size and fierceness, they
were a gentle and caring race, bound together by
Queen Segan and Prince Toban. She worried what
would happen to these people if something were to
go wrong and they lost Toban. Perhaps this wasn't

such a good idea after all. These people needed their prince.

As if reading her mind, Alexis padded up to Emily. "It will be all right. Tirk will not let anything happen to Toban." The Sphinx looked at the young prince and his sister as they embraced and said their good-byes. "Even if we changed our minds about him coming, we could not stop him. He is bound by blood to protect his people, even if they are just clones."

After the two royals parted, Emily approached the queen. "I promise to use all my powers to protect your brother. I know what he means to you and your people. I won't let anyone hurt him or Tirk."

Small dark tears were forming in the young queen's eyes. She growled softly and embraced Emily. She then stroked Pegasus and kissed him softly on the muzzle. Emily didn't need an interpreter to understand the messages between the two.

20

THE NIGHT AIR WAS COOL AS FRANKIE LED
Joel and Paelen on a tour of Las Vegas. Despite his
young age, Frankie was very familiar with Las Vegas
at night and knew all the interesting places to visit.

As they walked along the famous strip, Paelen's
eyes were bright and his mouth hung open as he tried
to take in all the sights and sounds around him.

"That's Circus Circus," Frankie explained as he
pointed at the large red casino across the street. "They
allow kids in there. But John and me never go in."

Joel added, "I've seen it on TV. Let's go in."

Paelen put his hand on Joel's arm. "Not there."

"Why?"

Paelen looked up to the black building beside them.

"It is too close to where we are staying. You never steal where you are living. It may lead people back to you. Trust me. I know what I am talking about."

Joel frowned. "What do you mean, steal? I thought we were playing tourist tonight."

"We are," Paelen agreed. "But we also need money for food." He looked down at little Frankie beside them. "And we promised to return what we took from you. I never break a promise." He glanced back to Joel. "To get money, we will need to steal it."

"We could always find another bank machine."

Paelen shook his head wildly. "I did that once—never again! Those machines eat people. I will not be their next meal! No, we will find some other way."

As they continued, Paelen felt his thief's senses taking over. He hadn't used them much since he met Emily and Joel. But now he needed them more than ever. Down the strip they walked, past casino after casino. The road was jammed with slow-moving traffic, and the pavement was crowded with people. Men handed out discount vouchers offering cheap tickets to shows, while casino doormen tried to attract the attention of passersby and invite them inside.

A man handed a voucher to Paelen and said, "Cool shoes, dude!"

Paelen frowned. "They are sandals, but thank you," he corrected the man as they continued walking. He looked at the voucher in his hand. On it were several showgirls in brightly colored, glittering costumes with tall feather headdresses. Paelen raised his eyebrows in appreciation. "Look at this!"

Joel studied the card and smiled brightly. "Welcome to Las Vegas! I'd love to see a show."

"Then we will," Paelen agreed.

Joel shook his head. "We can't. One, we need money to get in, and two, we are all underage."

Paelen laughed and put his arm around his tall friend. "Joel, do you forget who you are with? There is not a door, wall, or lock that can stop me. If you wish to see a show, we shall all see a show."

They continued strolling along the strip and came upon a free outdoor show.

"See." Paelen directed them toward the entrance. "I never break a promise."

They found seats and watched a husband-and-wife team working with their performing parrots.

The intelligent birds did tricks and talked to the glamorous wife. Frankie was the youngest person in the audience. When the wife spied him, she called him up to the stage to help with a trick. Paelen smiled as their young friend participated in the bird show.

At the end of the trick, the audience applauded and a beaming Frankie returned to his seat. "This is the best night ever! Did you see me with that big red bird? It was awesome!"

At the end of the show, the woman offered to take a free photograph of Frankie with the birds. Frankie insisted that Paelen and Joel joined him. Frankie proudly clutched the souvenir photograph of the three of them and the parrots as they walked away.

They continued down the strip and came upon a huge, dominating hotel casino. They couldn't help but stop and stare in awe, taking in its grandeur. Its white marble facade glowed against the dark night sky, oozing glamour and luxury and a promise of excitement within. At its entrance they spotted several familiar figures lit up under bright spotlights.

"Joel, look, it is Alexis!"

Before them was a set of Olympian Sphinxes cast

in bronze. They looked remarkably like Alexis, with a human torso, wings, and lion body.

"This is Caesar's Palace," Frankie explained. "There's lots of statues inside. There's even a big fountain with flying horses just like Emily's horse. Want to see?"

Paelen grinned at Joel. "Well, if they have flying horses, we must go in!"

When they entered the casino, Paelen's attention was captured by more beautiful statues, all familiar faces from Olympus. They encountered a giant griffin near the staircases, and deeper in the casino, Frankie led them to the magnificent fountain where a marble Pegasus flew out of each side. At the very top of the fountain stood Jupiter. Holding his lightning bolts in hand, he looked powerful and majestic as he gazed down at the crowds below. A Diana statue with a hawk on one arm and her bow in the other stood at one side of the fountain, as did Neptune with his large trident.

"Jupiter would love this," Paelen said, admiring the large fountain.

"But let's hope he never sees it," Joel finished.

When they entered the main casino, they were immediately struck by the sights and sounds. Frankie warned Paelen and Joel to keep a watch for security. If they were spotted, they could be ordered to leave.

Everywhere they looked, people were sitting at slot machines pressing buttons. Their faces were grim as they concentrated on their games.

"Is this supposed to be fun?" Paelen asked.

Joel nodded. "That's what they say. But it doesn't look like much fun to me."

As they moved deeper into the casino and entered a different area, the slot machines were replaced by gaming tables surrounded by groups of seated people. There was a soft murmur in the air as they played cards. Paelen stopped and watched a woman behind one of the tables dealing the cards.

Frankie leaned closer to Paelen. "They're playing blackjack. That's the game that John and I play. The aim is to get cards adding up to twenty-one. When you do, you win."

Paelen continued to watch the dealer. When she flipped her own cards, she said, "Twenty." The other people around the table shook their heads. Their cards and chips in front of them were taken away. "Does everyone count cards?"

Frankie shook his head. "No, and the casinos don't like people doing it. If John and me were caught, we'd be banned from the casino."

Farther along was a long rectangular table with tall sides and rounded corners. There were number markings on the table's soft covered surface. At the end a man was shaking dice in his hands. He threw the dice along the table.

"I know this game," Paelen said excitedly. "We play something like this in Olympus."

They watched the players put down their chips on numbers before the dice were thrown. When the dice stopped, some of the people earned more chips, while others had their chips taken away.

"What are those strange coins they are putting on the numbers?" Paelen asked.

"Chips," Joel explained. "They're like money. The numbers on them are their value. So if you have the number twenty on a chip, it is worth twenty dollars."

"You mean, all around us, those little pieces are worth money?" Paelen asked in shock.

"Yep," Joel said.

"But look how much that man has over there!"

Joel followed Paelen's eyes to a card dealer. There were countless piles of chips in front of him.

"That's the dealer," Joel explained. "They always have a lot of chips."

"And that means they have a lot of money?"

"I guess you could say that," Joel said.

"And the same with that man?" Paelen pointed to a player sitting at the roulette wheel. Before him were several large stacks of chips.

"That's right," Joel said. "Why?"

Paelen felt his heart fluttering with excitement. His fingers itched the way they always did when he was on the hunt. "Joel, you and Frankie wait for me over there." He pointed to a group of slot machines several meters away.

"Paelen, what are you planning to do?" Joel asked nervously.

"What I do best!" Paelen grinned.

Paelen turned on all his thieving skills. He could see, hear, smell, and taste everything going on around him. It was as though the world had slowed to a standstill, and he was the only one moving. His keen Olympian eyes scanned the gambling tables. He looked for weaknesses in either the dealers or players, someone who wasn't concentrating as sharply as they should.

Then his eyes found their mark. There! He saw a drunk player who spent more time chatting up a waitress than concentrating on the game or his many stacks of chips. Taking a deep breath, Paelen made his move.

With the stealth of a lifetime spent living only by his senses, Paelen walked soundlessly toward the player. Without changing the expression on his face, he stretched out the bones in his right arm to extend it and walked smoothly past the drunk player. His long arm flashed out so quickly, no one saw the long fingers wrap around a stack of chips and pull away instantly.

Paelen moved on to his next victim. And then another. And then another! No one noticed a thing. He walked back to Joel and Frankie and without pausing, whispered, "Follow me."

When they'd reached the other side of the casino, Paelen stopped and burst out laughing. "That was just too easy! I must do it again!"

Joel was frowning. "Paelen, I was watching you. You didn't do anything."

Paelen laughed harder and held out his right hand. Opening his fingers, he showed Joel the stack of fifty- and one-hundred-dollar chips resting inside.

"Wow!" Frankie cried. "You're rich!"

Joel's eyes went wide as he counted the chips. "There's over a thousand dollars here. How did you do it? I didn't see a thing."

"That is because I am not just a thief, I am a very *good* thief!"

"But you told Diana you weren't a thief anymore."

"I lied!" Paelen's eyes were bright as his mind raced with the things he could achieve in this strange and wondrous place. His eyes scanned the crowds of the casino. Nothing had changed. No one had noticed a thing. "Wait here. I will go and get more."

Joel caught him by the arm. "No. We have more than we need right now. Let's not be greedy. We can cash them in and get going."

Paelen wasn't happy, but he agreed. The three walked through the casino toward the secured counter, where chips were cashed into money.

"This is where we're going to have trouble," Joel said.

"Why?"

"Because we're underage. You're not allowed to gamble until you're twenty-one."

Paelen frowned. "I did not gamble. I stole these chips. And I am well over twenty-one, especially if measured in the years of your world."

"How old are you?" Frankie asked.

Paelen shrugged. "Actually, I do not know. But I do know I am very old."

Joel nodded. "Maybe, but you don't look it. I look older than you, but not old enough to play here. We have to find someone to cash them in for us."

"Let me try," Frankie offered. "I do this all the time when John is too drunk. Give me the chips."

Joel looked doubtful but handed the chips over to little Frankie.

"Follow me, but stay way back," Frankie instructed. He walked away and started to study the players at the slot machines. He stopped before a man whose shaking hand was feeding money into a machine. He was in his thirties, and his rumpled clothing suggested he hadn't changed in a few days. The expression on his face was desperate.

Frankie went into his act. His eyes grew large and

"We know you're a runaway from foster care in New York City. Normally we'd be sending you to the Juvenile Center, but after you assaulted a police officer, you're staying right here with us."

A second officer drew near and studied Joel's exposed silver arm with great curiosity. "What is that? I've seen artificial limbs before—heck, my brother came back from Iraq with one. But I've never seen anything like that. Where'd you get it?"

Joel remained silent as the police officer stepped even closer. "I can't see any joints at the wrist or fingers, but you can move it. How does it work?" He reached out to touch the silver arm.

"Don't!" Joel warned as he slid down the bench away from the officer.

"So he does speak," the first officer said. "What happened at Fremont?"

Joel glared at the officer but said nothing further.

"Fine," he said. The officer concentrated on Paelen. "Just what kind of drugs are you on, kid? From what I've heard, you and your twin brother all but destroyed Fremont Street. There are crazy stories going on about how you tossed each other around like rag dolls and destroyed a hundred-thousand-dollar sports car."

"That Runt is not my brother," Paelen said indignantly. "And I will thank you to return my sandals."

The police officer raised his eyebrows. "You will thank me, eh? How about I thank you to answer our questions? What happened at Fremont Street? How did you do all that damage?"

This was too familiar to Paelen. Back on Governors Island, Agents J and O had asked a lot of questions that he did not want to answer. Paelen avoided the question. "Why do you not ask the Runt?"

The police officer laughed, but there was no humor in it. "I've had more than my share of dealings with that freaky little punk. We'll keep him chained up and leave him alone till the folks from the psych ward at the hospital come to collect him. But you, I am interested in. Who are you?"

Paelen straightened up the best his injured body would allow. "I am Paelen the Magnificent," he said proudly. "You would do well to release Joel and me before I lose my temper."

"Oh really," the officer said, smiling. "Well, how

about we give you more time to cool off and cooperate."

A serious-looking police officer arrived and called
the others outside. They closed and locked the door
behind them.

Paelen strained to listen. "We are in deep trouble.
I heard that man say there is a special warrant out for
us. We are considered dangerous and they should not
approach us."

Out in the hall, the officers looked back at them,
but moved quickly away from the cell.

Joel's eyes grew large. "It's the CRU. They could
come for us any minute. Paelen, you've got to get
out of here." Joel rose and crossed to the door and
checked to see if the hall was clear. He looked down
at his silver hand. Curling it in, he used its strength
to break the handcuff binding it to his waist chain.
Then he reached over to his left hand and freed that
as well. With his hands free, he pushed the food flap
in the door—but it was locked.

"I will not leave you," Paelen said flatly. He crossed
to the door. "With my strength and your arm, we can
force open this door. We will both go."

Joel shook his head. "No, we can't. This is a jail. We'd never make it to the end of the hall, let alone out of the building. But you can."

"I told you, I will not leave you."

"You've got to," Joel insisted. "You must get back to Emily. Tell her what's happening."

"But—"

"You can't stay. Not if the CRU have been alerted."

Paelen and Joel looked around the tiny cell. There was only the one door and no windows. There were two air vents in the white ceiling high above their heads.

"You can fit through there," Joel offered. "Just stretch out of your chains and I'll boost you up."

Paelen saw the grim determination on Joel's face. But how could he leave his best friend to face the CRU alone? He remembered what had happened to Joel at Governors Island and how he had been drugged and tortured.

"It's the only way," Joel insisted. "Get help. If the CRU do come for us, we'll disappear and no one will ever know what happened. You are Olympian. We can't let them get hold of you again."

Paelen shook his head. "I cannot leave you. If they take you to Area 51, they will cut off your arm to see how it works. Remember how Agent T was interested in it. He told you what would happen if they caught you."

Fear rose in Joel's face as he looked at his mechanical arm. It had been a part of him for so long that it was as if he'd been born with it. "If they cut it off me, you'll just have to come and get me so Vulcan can put it back on. Now go!"

Joel was right, but it didn't make it any easier for Paelen to abandon him. "Listen at the door. Let me know if anyone is coming."

Joel stood by the door as Paelen concentrated. He was still aching badly from his fight with the clone, and his head continued to pound from the bullet.

First, Paelen extended his hands until they pulled free of the cuffs chaining him to his waist. Then his whole body started to pop, snap, and stretch until he slipped out of his clothes and he was free of the chain around his waist.

"I am ready," he said in a high, reedy voice. "Help me climb up."

Joel laced his fingers together to make a stirrup and gave the snakelike Paelen a leg up.

Clutching his clothing in one hand, Paelen reached up with his free hand and pulled the vent cover away from the opening. He shoved his clothes through the hole and stretched out his body until he was thin enough to slip up into the narrow vent.

Paelen winced in pain as he felt the bullet shift in his elongated head.

He was grateful to find the ventilation shaft was wider than he'd expected. His mind kept replaying the first time he had traveled through the vent at Governors. But then he had had the sandals to help. This time he was alone.

Paelen turned and looked back down into the small cell. He saw Joel looking hopefully up at him. His large friend suddenly looked very small and vulnerable.

"I'll be fine," Joel said. "Just go and find Emily and Pegasus. Tell her what's happened."

"I will," Paelen promised as he pulled the vent cover back into position. His last sight of his best friend was Joel sitting down on the bench, all alone.

· · ·

Paelen wasn't sure how long he'd spent in the ventilation system of the Las Vegas jail. But as he crawled along a course that took him away from the holding cells, he felt the passage of time as acutely as he felt the bullet lodged in his head.

Looking through the vents along the shaft system, he soon found he was over an empty office. A desk was directly below him. Peering sideways, Paelen could see the frame of a window. If it wasn't too high off the ground, he could jump out of it.

Paelen pushed down on the vent and peeked through. He used his thief senses to listen and feel for danger. There was no one in the hall outside the closed office door. For the moment, he was safe.

He winced as he extended his body to slip through the narrow opening. Pushing his clothes ahead of him, he poured himself into the room and landed with a heavy and painful thump on the top of the desk.

Grateful to return to his normal shape, Paelen dressed quickly and crossed to the window. It was daytime, and he realized they'd been in jail longer than he'd expected. He hoped that Emily and Pegasus would be back at the black building, waiting for them.

Looking down, he saw he was at least four, perhaps five stories off the ground. Normally that wouldn't bother him. But he was weak from lack of food, and wounded. Sighing heavily, Paelen knew he had no choice. He forced open the sealed window. Checking to see that no one was below, he climbed out on the ledge and jumped.

Paelen had leaped from greater heights many times before. But that was when he was healthy. When he hit the pavement, his right ankle gave way and twisted with a loud snap. It took all his will not to cry out.

As pain pulsed and shot all the way up his leg, Paelen looked back at the tall, brown building that was the jail.

He couldn't see anyone at the windows and hoped he'd gotten away without being noticed. Paelen limped away from the jail and Joel.

WHILE PEGASUS, ALEXIS, AND THE NIRADS rested under the trees waiting for the safe cover of darkness, Emily could not relax. She stood and started to pace. Looking back, she saw Prince Toban seated beside Tirk. Their arms were crossed over their chests, and their eyes were closed as they wilted in the oppressive desert heat. Tirk's orange, marblelike skin glistened with sweat, and he was panting softly in blistering temperatures he had never known before.

Emily worried that it had been a bad idea to bring them here. They belonged on the Nirad world, where they were safe. Not out in the middle of the open desert where dangers surrounded them. As it was, she was reconsidering her plan to take them to the black building. Two Nirads in Las Vegas? Now, that would be really stupid.

But leaving them behind would be equally dangerous and stupid. Emily cursed herself for not thinking ahead. Her thoughts spun wildly out of control as anxieties pressed down on her. She still had no idea how to get into Area 51, let alone get back out again. How would the Nirad clones react to the prince? Could he reach them telepathically? Or was she leading Toban and Tirk into disaster?

The more she thought about it, the more muddled she became. There seemed no solution to the problem. No clear plan of action. Emily ached to speak with Joel and Paelen. Maybe once everyone was together again, they could come up with a decent strategy that would solve the clone problem before Jupiter found out.

Emily returned to Pegasus and sat beside the stallion, resigned to the fact that they couldn't do anything for the moment. Until everyone was reunited, all she could do was wait and worry.

25

PAELEN WAS AN OLYMPIAN LOST AND ALONE in Las Vegas. There was a large white bandage wrapped around his head, and his clothes were tattered and covered with blood. He knew he would not receive any help from the strangers he passed, looking as he did.

"Sandals, where are you when I need you?" he muttered softly as he made his way along a quiet street.

The full heat of the day pressed down on him. The sun was high and unforgiving in the blue, cloudless sky. Paelen felt weak from his wounds and lack of food. If he didn't eat some ambrosia soon, he feared he might collapse.

Over to his left he recognized the remains of Fremont

Street. The area still smoldered and was blocked off by police tape. Fire trucks remained in the area, and men wearing white protective gear sifted through the rubble.

There was no way the damage could not attract the attention of the CRU. Fighting the clone had been a terrible mistake and had put his best friend in danger.

Paelen kept to the quieter streets as he tried to find his way back to the tall black building. But Las Vegas in daylight looked nothing like it did at night. Not to mention they had traveled to Fremont Street by taxi. There was no telling how long it would take him to walk back, especially with a broken ankle.

Paelen needed help. He approached a homeless man lying in a doorway.

"And I thought I had it bad." The homeless man smiled a toothless grin.

"Please, I need your help. I am badly lost. Do you know where Circus Circus is?"

Paelen's instincts wouldn't allow him to mention the black building. Instead he remembered the name Joel had used the previous night.

The homeless man shook his head. "Boy, you sure are lost. You're walking in the wrong direction. You want the strip." The man sat up and pointed down the street and gave Paelen a series of directions. "But on that foot, it'll take you all day."

"I have no choice," Paelen said grimly. Thanking the man, he slowly limped away.

As the homeless man had warned, it took Paelen the better part of the day, but he finally made it back to the tall black building, sunburned and with heat exhaustion. Half limping and half staggering to the elevator, he took it up to the top floor. Chrysaor was waiting for him when the doors opened.

"Emily . . . ," Paelen called out, and then crumpled to the ground.

PEGASUS PROTESTED LOUDLY AS EMILY PRO-
posed her latest idea. The sun was setting and the heat
of the day finally fading—but not by much. Within
the small cluster of trees, everyone was on their feet.

"Pegs, I've thought about it all day. This is the only
way," Emily insisted.

The stallion snorted and pawed the grass beneath
his golden hoof.

"I don't want to leave them either, but Tirk is way too
heavy for you to carry. After we get the others, we'll come
right back. Toban and Tirk won't be alone for long."

Prince Toban was standing beside Emily and nodding his pink head. He let out a long series of growls
and strange sounds.

Emily looked to Alexis to translate. "The prince agrees with you," she said. The Sphinx approached Pegasus. "Emily is correct. Tirk is too heavy for you to carry for a long distance. We are closer to Area 51 than we are Las Vegas. It would be wise to leave them here for a short time, collect the others, and then gather our forces before we make our move on the CRU."

Pegasus was still arguing when the prince started to stroke the stallion. He growled a few soft words. Pegasus bowed. Again Emily looked to Alexis to translate, but the Sphinx shook her head. "That is between the two of them," she whispered.

Finally Pegasus snorted and raised his head, but his ears were twitching. Emily knew him well enough to know he was going to go along with the plan, but wasn't happy about it.

"It is agreed," Alexis said. She turned to the prince. "Your Highness, we shall only be a short while. Please remain here and wait for us. Should any human come along, please try to keep hidden."

Toban nodded. He and Tirk returned to the trees to sit down and wait.

PAELEN AWOKE TO THE SOUNDS OF CHRYSAOR squealing and a man's loud, terrified screams. When he opened his eyes, he discovered he was lying on a smelly pile of rags. His head was screaming, the skin on his face and arms was on fire, and his ankle pounded like his foot was about to fall off.

Chrysaor had cornered a man against a wall.

Paelen's thoughts were sluggish as he finally recalled what had happened to get him to this place. He lifted his head, his eyes seeking Emily and Pegasus. When he didn't see them, he called weakly, "Has Emily returned?"

Before Chrysaor could answer, the frightened man called, "Help me! Call the police, call the FBI! Call the zoo! This freaky pig won't let me move."

Chrysaor squealed with anger and trod on the man's foot, causing him to yelp in pain.

Paelen's eyes drifted over to the piles of rags where Frankie's friend John had been sleeping. The lump was gone.

"Are you John?" he asked as he tried to climb to his feet.

"Who are you?" the filthy man demanded. "How do you know my name? And why have you brought this pig to my home? What have you done with Frankie?"

"Frankie is not here?"

"No, he's not here!" John shouted angrily. "I woke up and found this creature here instead. What the hell are you?"

Chrysaor jumped on the man's foot again.

The pounding pain in Paelen's head was unbearable as he made it to his feet. But when he tried to put weight on his broken ankle, he cried in pain and fell down. Lying in the stack of smelly rags, all he wanted to do now was sleep. It was calling to him, beckoning him and promising to take him away from the pain.

Chrysaor left the man and trotted over to Paelen.

He squealed softly, then sniffed the wound on Paelen's head.

"It has all gone wrong," Paelen muttered. "Joel is in jail and the CRU are coming for him."

Chrysaor continued to sniff along Paelen's wounded body. He snorted and squealed in deep concern.

"We cannot go back to Olympus," Paelen panted. "I know I am hurt badly. But we must wait for Emily and Pegasus. The police have Joel. He is counting on me to get him out. I must not let him down."

But Chrysaor squealed again. The high pitch of his voice bored into Paelen's head like a drill. Paelen tried to beg him to stop, but his voice was gone. Soon the world around him started to spin, and darkness approached.

Paelen welcomed the coming darkness, the end of pain. But as he started to surrender himself to it, he felt overcome with a familiar nauseous feeling. The same sickness he felt in the presence of his clone. The clone was nearby, Paelen was sure of it. The clone must have escaped the police and followed him back here.

Fighting back to consciousness, Paelen heard screaming from the stairwell and then something charged toward him. Chrysaor was the first to react. The winged boar squealed and ran toward the clone. He opened his wings and tried to knock him away. But the clone was fast and agile. He leaped high into the air and soared over Chrysaor's head. He landed a short distance from Paelen.

With the drive to fight rising in the pit of his stomach, Paelen climbed up to stand on one foot. But he was too weak to fend off the clone. It caught hold of him and, screaming in rage, lifted him high above its head.

Snarling with uncontrolled hatred, it hurled Paelen at the painted window. The hardened glass shattered with the impact and sent Paelen out into the open air, sixty-nine stories above the ground. Without his winged sandals to save him, Paelen started to fall.

PEGASUS, EMILY, AND ALEXIS FLEW HIGH
above Las Vegas. As they started to descend, they saw
bright flashing lights from fire trucks lining a street
well away from the strip. The acrid smell of freshly
extinguished fire rose up to meet them.

"I wonder what's going on down there," Emily
called.

Pegasus nickered and whinnied, and Emily wished
she could understand the stallion's language. What
Pegasus said sounded important. In the distance, she
saw the black building rising dark and silent.

When they landed on the roof, Emily's heart sank
to discover that Joel, Paelen, and Chrysaor were not
there. She climbed down from Pegasus.

"Wait!" Alexis warned. "Something is very wrong. I can feel it."

Emily stopped and watched the Sphinx lifting her head and sniffing the air. The hair on the hackles along her back was high and her wings were fluttering. Her tail whipped the air.

"Get back on Pegasus," she ordered. "Now!"

Just as Emily settled on the stallion's back, the Sphinx hissed and drew her claws.

The door to the roof was flung open. A little boy of nine or ten came running forward. His clothing was in tatters, and his eyes were filled with terror. He ran at Pegasus and waved his hands in the air. "Emily, it's a trap! Fly away before they get you!"

Alexis rose on her hind legs and roared, "Men are here. Pegasus, get the Flame away!"

The Sphinx's eyes went black, her jaw unhinged, and teeth came out. As she charged the stairwell door, she looked back at Pegasus and screamed, "Go now!"

Pegasus reacted immediately. The stallion lunged forward and caught the little boy's shirt in his sharp teeth. Lifting him off the ground, without a second's pause, he galloped to the edge of the roof and leaped off. Flapping his powerful wings, he carried them high in the air.

On the roof Alexis roared as armed men poured through the door. Their screams filled the air as they were greeted by the enraged Olympian Sphinx.

"Alexis!" Emily screamed. "Leave them, come on!"

Pegasus was flying too high and too fast for Emily to see what was happening on the roof. The sound of gunfire filled the air. But were the men shooting at them or Alexis?

The little boy was screaming in terror as he hung only by his shirt from Pegasus's mouth, suspended high over Las Vegas.

A few minutes later, Pegasus landed on the roof of a casino farther down the strip. Emily slid off his back and ran to the roof edge, searching the skies for Alexis. "Come on," she cried. "Alexis, where are you?"

"Emily?" the little boy said as he carefully approached her.

His eyes were huge as he looked at her and Pegasus. "They got the lion-lady."

"Who?" Emily demanded, turning on him. "Who was it?"

"The soldiers." He started to sob. "They shot my friend John."

There was so much pain in the little boy's face. Emily put her arm around him. "Please tell us, what soldiers?" she asked softly. "Who are you and how do you know my name?"

"I'm Frankie." The little boy sniffed. He wiped his running nose on his dirty sleeve. "Joel and Paelen are my friends. So is Chrysler the pig."

Emily's heart was pounding in her chest, and it was hard to take everything in. She knelt before the boy and took both his hands. "Where are Joel and Paelen? Can you tell me?"

Tears rushed to Frankie's eyes and trailed through the grime on his face. "Paelen is dead," he wept. "He got shot in the head, and then the wild Paelen threw him out the window and he fell. Joel is in jail. Chrysler flew away and I don't know where he is."

"What?" Emily cried. "Paelen is dead?"

Frankie sniffed and nodded.

"My Paelen?" Emily cried in panic. "No, it's not possible. He had his winged sandals. They would have stopped him. He could have flown away."

"He didn't have his sandals. John says Paelen was half-dead when the wild Paelen beat him up really bad, and then threw him out the window."

Emily sat back in shock. It wasn't possible. Paelen couldn't be dead. Not after all they'd been through, all they had suffered together. She pulled out her green handkerchief to catch her uncontrollable tears.

Emily was hardly aware of Alexis's arrival. It was only when Frankie screeched in terror and begged the Sphinx not to eat him that she realized Alexis had returned.

"Emily, what is wrong?" Alexis demanded, coming closer. "Are you hurt?"

Pegasus neighed softly to explain. "The boy is mistaken." Alexis put her paw on Emily's back. "Paelen is far too resourceful to allow this to happen."

But Emily could not speak and could hardly breathe as sobs tore through her.

"You, boy," Alexis demanded. "Tell me what happened to Paelen and Joel."

Frankie filled them in on everything that happened over the last two days.

"Wait." Emily sniffed. "You didn't see Paelen die?"

Frankie shook his head. "My friend John told me what happened. He swore he would never drink again because he was seeing too many crazy things. When I asked him what, he told me what happened. John still thinks it was the drink. But I saw the broken window. When I told him that Paelen could fly with his shoes, John said he was barefoot with a broken ankle. Chrysler followed him out the window, but John didn't see Chrysler catch him."

"Then it is likely that Chrysaor reached Paelen in time," Alexis said calmly. She concentrated on Emily. "There is no evidence that Paelen is dead—just the word of this boy's friend. You must keep your hope alive."

Emily clung to Alexis's words. Chrysaor would not let Paelen fall. He just wouldn't. "You said a wild Paelen attacked our Paelen?"

The boy nodded. "At the diner. Joel said it was the clone. But when the real Paelen met the wild one, they both went crazy and wanted to kill each other."

Alexis looked up to Pegasus. "Just like you with Tornado Warning."

Pegasus snorted at the name and pawed the roof.

Alexis concentrated on Frankie again. "Who were those men on the roof?"

"Soldiers," Frankie said. "People must have seen Paelen go out the window and called the police. John tried to protect me, but they shot him." Frankie started to cry again. He lifted tearful eyes to Emily. "I've been hiding and waiting for you."

Alexis narrowed her green eyes and concentrated on the boy. "You waited for us? Knowing you were in danger by doing so? Why would you do that?"

Frankie looked at Alexis fearfully and stepped closer to Emily. "Because Joel and Paelen and Chrysler are my friends. They told me they were waiting for you to come back. I couldn't let the soldiers get you."

Alexis tilted her head approvingly. "That was very brave of you."

"I don't think so," Frankie said. "I cried when they chased me."

"I would have done the same," Alexis said gently. She winked knowingly at Pegasus.

Frankie lifted his hopeful eyes to Emily. "Do you really think Chrysler saved Paelen?"

Emily nodded. "I'm sure he would have. They are very good friends."

She could see the relief washing over the young boy as he wiped his filthy cheeks. She just prayed it was true.

"Good. I really like him," Frankie said.

"Me too," Emily agreed, drying her own eyes.

Behind her, Pegasus nickered.

"We must get moving," Alexis said. "We must not leave Prince Toban and Tirk alone for long."

Emily shook her head. "First we've got to get Joel." She concentrated on Frankie. "You said he was in jail?"

The little boy nodded. "Near Fremont Street. That's where the two Paelens fought. They caused a really big fire."

Emily recalled all the fire trucks and the smell when they'd first arrived. "Can you show me where it is?"

Pegasus stepped forward and nickered again.

"This will be the hardest thing Pegasus has ever asked you to do," Alexis translated, "but he said we must leave Joel where he is. Prince Toban and Tirk are our first priority."

Emily looked at the stallion in shock. "No way! We've got to rescue Joel before they find out who he is and call the CRU."

Alexis sighed heavily. "It is highly likely the CRU already know, which is why Paelen would have left him. He was sent to warn us, but was wounded instead."

Emily was shaking her head. She couldn't believe they were suggesting leaving Joel to the mercy of the CRU.

"Think about it," Alexis pressed. "The chances of Joel still being in their jail are remote. We must not waste precious time on an uncertainty. Prince Toban and Tirk do not belong in this world. We must return to them and get the others away from Area 51 as quickly as possible."

"But if Joel is still in their jail, I have to get him out." Emily panicked. "You don't understand. I—"

"You love him," Alexis finished gently. "Yes, I know. We all do. But we must not let our emotions rule us."

"But—"

Alexis shook her head. "I am sorry, Emily. But we

have no choice. If you really want to help him, you will leave him where he is. If he is still in their jail, he is much safer there than at Area 51. But if the CRU have been alerted, they will no doubt deliver him to Area 51 anyway."

Emily looked at Pegasus and then gazed out over Las Vegas. Was Joel out there, just a short reach from where she was? Or had he been taken to Area 51? Every instinct in her body screamed to go to the jail to see for herself. It tore at her heart to know that there was a greater need. Prince Toban and Tirk were alone and in more danger.

She stepped up to Pegasus and pressed her forehead to him. "I know we've got to go, Pegs. But what if Joel is still in jail? How can I abandon him?"

Pegasus neighed softly. There was little he could say or do to ease Emily's pain. Finally she pulled away. She climbed onto his back without a word.

"What about me?" Frankie said. "I'm coming too. I want to help with the nerds."

Alexis padded closer to him. "I am sorry, child, but you are safer here."

Frankie shook his head. "Nah-uh, I'm not. Those

men are looking for me. What if they find me? They'll take me to Area 51 with all the other aliens. They shot John and wrecked my home. I have nowhere to go."

Alexis stole a look at Emily before turning to Frankie. "All right, child. I will ask you a riddle. If you answer correctly, you may come with us and I will carry you myself. But if you get the answer wrong, you must remain here."

Frankie's eyes trailed from Emily, to Pegasus, and finally to Alexis. "Okay."

Alexis sat down before the little boy. "Riddle me this . . .

At night I come without being fetched
And by day I am lost without being stolen.
I am like a diamond,
But I am no jewel.
What am I?"

Emily watched little Frankie chew on his lower lip as he struggled with the riddle. She realized that the ferocious and deadly Sphinx of Olympus had given the boy a very easy one. Even she knew the answer.

Finally Frankie looked up to the night sky and pointed. "I know!" he cried. "It's the stars."

Alexis smiled and stroked his head with her large paw. "There is only one other person in history who has ever answered one of my riddles. You are in very good company. Your answer is correct. You may join us."

Alexis stood and offered her back to the boy.

"I hope I'm not too heavy," Frankie said earnestly as he climbed on.

The Sphinx looked up at him. "I have carried heavier." Her eyes trailed over to Emily. "Are you ready?"

Emily inhaled deeply. She gazed out over Las Vegas in the direction of Fremont Street. "Forgive me, Joel," she said softly as she looked back at Alexis. "Let's go."

EMILY'S HEART WAS SITTING HEAVY IN HER chest as Pegasus carried her away from Las Vegas and deeper into the dark desert. Joel would never have abandoned her. Would he ever forgive her?

As they approached the area where they had left the Nirads, Emily saw a glow rising from the ground. Fear knotted her stomach. Nirads didn't use fire. The closer they got to the glow, the bigger and brighter it became. Pegasus tilted his wings and glided lower in the sky.

On the ground beneath them they saw the burning debris of two destroyed military helicopters scattered around the cluster of trees where they had left the two Nirads. One of the trees was ablaze while the

grass smoldered and burned. Pegasus circled the area a few times searching for activity from below. They saw nothing. He landed a few meters from the trees.

"Toban!" Emily cried as she slid off the stallion's back and started to search the area. "Tirk! Are you here?"

Alexis joined in, but after a few minutes of calling and searching, they received no answer. Emily approached the tree where she had last seen the Nirads and found a dark stain on the ground. Her heart dropped.

Emily bent down and summoned the Flame to her hand. Lowering it down to the ground, she discovered that the liquid was bright red. It was blood. Human blood. Not far from the stain, she saw a large piece of desert camouflage fabric.

"Pegasus, Alexis, over here!" Emily pointed at the ground and held up the fabric. "That's human blood, and this is part of a uniform. Those are military helicopters."

Alexis surveyed the area. "There must have been a ferocious battle here if the Nirads could bring down two of those machines. I pray neither of them was wounded."

Emily straightened and looked at the burning helicopters. "The soldiers must have attacked them right after we left. But how did they find them?"

Frankie was still seated on Alexis's back. "They have radar," he answered softly. "I've read about it on my computer. This whole area has big radars. This is all part of the Nellis Air Force Base. They track anyone who comes here—on the ground or in the air. I bet they're tracking us, too."

As Frankie's words sank in, Emily realized the truth. "We led them into a trap!" She looked at Pegasus. "We've just handed Prince Toban and Tirk over to the CRU."

Pegasus reared up in rage and screamed into the night, while Alexis cursed and started pacing. As the full ramifications hit Emily, she felt the power of the Flame rising uncontrolled within her. Turning away from the others, she held up her hands and released the pent-up power.

Wild flames shot from both her hands and rose for hundreds of meters into the air. Emily threw back her head and howled in fury, "I have had it with the CRU!"

Emily charged over to Pegasus. "That's it! This is

war! Pegasus, ever since you first came to my world, the CRU have been hounding us and doing all they can to destroy us. They've captured us, tortured us, and taken my father away. They've created clones that just may get this world destroyed, and they killed Agent T when he was trying to warn them. No more. If they want a fight, they've got it!"

"Calm down," Alexis ordered. "You must think before you act."

"No," Emily cried, turning back to the Sphinx. "We have been thinking all along, and look where it's gotten us! They've just captured the Nirad prince. I promised Queen Segan that I would keep him safe. But I didn't! Why have I got all these powers if not to protect us from the evil that is the CRU?"

"Emily, stop!" Alexis shouted. "Remember your other powers. You have no control when you are angry."

Emily stomped up to Pegasus. "This time they've pushed me too far. You can stay here if you like, but I'm going in and demanding they release Toban and all the other Nirads. And if they don't, they are going to see just what the Flame of Olympus can do!"

The journey to the secret CRU facility at Area 51 was short. But even before they made it to the mountain range that surrounded the large base, military helicopters were rising in the air and coming to meet them.

"Emily, you must wait!" Alexis cried. "This is a dangerous approach."

But Emily clung to Pegasus's mane and told the stallion to put on more speed.

"Take Frankie away from here," she called to Alexis. "This fight is between the CRU and me!"

"No, foolish child, it is not," Alexis called. "It is between Olympians and the CRU. I was wrong not going back to Jupiter. We must return to Olympus. The others must be told what has happened here. Jupiter would be furious if he knew I allowed you to do this alone."

Emily called an answer back, but the sound of her voice was drowned out by the heavy rotors of the approaching military helicopters. As they neared, Emily felt the power of the Flame anxious to be freed.

"Be careful, Pegasus!" she called.

Emily tucked in her knees to hold on and raised her hands. The Flame was ready, but she held back on releasing it until she knew what the military intended. Within seconds, she had her answer. Without giving a warning, or the opportunity to surrender, the nearest helicopter fired at them.

There was no time to think, only to react. Emily released the Flame. Against the dark sky it shot white-hot from her hands toward the approaching helicopters. The bullets they fired melted into liquid burning metal and glowed like fireflies as they fell, harmless, to the ground.

Emily never wanted to hurt anyone. But when the helicopters continued firing, she had no choice but to turn her full powers on them. One by one, the helicopters exploded in the air and rained fire down on the dark desert floor.

Soon they were alone in the sky. Within moments, Pegasus was cresting the mountains surrounding Area 51. Up ahead, Emily saw the lights of the two superlong runways burst to life as jet fighters taxied out of their hangars and down the runways.

"Too late!" Emily shouted in a fury. She raised her

hands again and let the Flame go. Instead of hitting the jets, her target was the two long tarmac runways. When the heat of the Flame struck them, the tarmac melted instantly and burst into flames. The jets on the ground scattered and were forced onto the desert floor.

"Emily, be careful!" Alexis warned.

Emily looked over and saw Frankie clinging to the back of the Sphinx. Both his hands were gripped around Alexis's wings where they emerged from her back. His head was tucked down, and he wasn't watching the fight.

Down on the ground, all the lights of Area 51 burst to life. The place was massive! Agent T had said only part of it was the CRU facility. But what was the rest of it? There were multiple large, squat buildings with flat, corrugated-steel roofs. She could see a parking area filled with cars. There were the two large hangars the jets had emerged from and three full-size airliners parked at the side. Farther along she spied several other military helicopters still on the ground. She hoped they stayed there.

As Pegasus flew closer, she saw the white chalk bed

of the dry Groom Lake. Agent T wasn't kidding. It had once been a huge lake. Suddenly her eyes caught movement. Soldiers were emerging from the squat buildings. As she approached lower, Emily got a closer look at them and sucked in her breath. Nirads! They were wearing the desert camouflage uniforms of the military and carrying rifles. It was true. The CRU had created a Nirad army.

"Pegasus, look," she cried. "Nirad soldiers!"

Alexis swooped closer. "Why are you not firing? Look, they all have weapons!"

The easy solution would have been to burn Area 51 off the face of the Earth. But despite her fury, Emily couldn't do that. Prince Toban and Tirk could be down there somewhere.

"I can't! Not until we get the others away. Stay behind us!" Emily concentrated on Pegasus. "Take us down, Pegs, right in the middle of them. If they fire at us, I'll shoot back."

The soldiers crouched down on the ground and trained their weapons at the group. But they did not open fire.

"Don't shoot!" Emily called. "Please, don't shoot!"

Pegasus stopped flapping his large white wings and glided silently over their heads. He landed on the ground and trotted to a stop near the large group of soldiers.

"Put your hands in the air!" a human soldier demanded.

"Listen to me," Emily cried. "Earth is in terrible danger. I must speak with your commander right away!"

As she slid off Pegasus, she heard the urgent clicking sounds of soldiers preparing their weapons. Emily held up her hands. "Please, don't fire. We need to speak with your commander!"

The soldier held up his weapon. "Get down on the ground. Now!"

"You don't understand!" Emily took a step closer. "Jupiter is going to destroy this world. You can stop it!"

"Stop!" the soldier cried. "Don't move another step!"

"Please, listen to me," Emily begged, holding her hands up. "We don't want to fight. We're here to warn you."

Behind her, Pegasus was pounding the ground

and snorting. His wings fluttered. Alexis let out a soft growl. She folded her wings to cover little Frankie and warned him to keep his head down.

"Foolish humans," Alexis spat as she concentrated on the soldiers. "Listen to the child. She speaks the truth! Jupiter of Olympus will destroy this world if you do not stop creating these clones."

As the Sphinx took a step closer to Emily, one of the human soldiers panicked. He raised his weapon and fired. His reaction caused the others to do the same. Nirad soldiers roared and charged forward. They dropped their rifles and opened their four arms. Their bead-black eyes were wide and their mouths hung open, showing rows of sharp, pointed teeth.

Pegasus shoved Emily forcefully in the back and knocked her to the ground. He reared up, spread his wings, and whinnied angrily. He struck one of the Nirads in the chest with a golden hoof.

The Nirad soldier howled in pain and collapsed instantly to the ground as the gold of Pegasus's hoof poisoned it. Suddenly more Nirad soldiers ran at them. The frightened human soldiers lost control and fired their weapons.

Emily reacted instantly. She rose to her feet and summoned the Flame. As it flowed down to her hands, she turned them on the soldiers. But before she could release the Flame fully, she felt her body exploding in pain as several bullets found their mark. Thrown backward, she hit her head on the ground with an explosive impact.

Her thoughts flew at light speed. The soldiers were firing. Pegasus and Alexis were in danger. She had to save them! She sat up and raised her hands to release the Flame, but she was hit with more bullets and knocked backward just as her powers let go. There was a blinding flash and a tremendous peal of thunder.

And then they were gone.

Alexis and Pegasus had vanished!

It took Emily a moment to realize what had happened. Her hands must have been aimed toward Alexis and Pegasus when she released her powers.

"Pegasus!" she cried. "Pegasus, no!"

More bullets tore into her, and Emily howled as she realized what she had done. Suddenly her body burst into flame. She glowed brilliantly and melted the bullets within her, healing the damage done by the soldiers.

Emily's heart blazed in agony, but not from the flames.

Pegasus was *gone*!

Overwhelmed by grief, Emily welcomed the approaching darkness that always accompanied self-healing. She no longer cared what happened to her. She had destroyed the very best thing in her life. Now all she wanted, all she deserved, was death. She prayed it would come with the darkness. The CRU could do whatever they wanted to her now.

Without Pegasus, there was nothing.

30

"COME ON, SON, DRINK IT ALL UP."

Paelen awoke in terrible pain, cradled in strong arms and with a cup being pressed to his lips. He tasted the blissful sweetness of nectar and started to gulp down the healing drink. He opened his eyes to see Steve Jacobs pulling the cup away. He was lying in his bed at Jupiter's palace. Through the open windows he could smell the sweet, warm Olympian breeze.

He tried to focus on the figures standing around his bed. Diana and Apollo were standing at his left. Pluto was at the foot of the bed, his face a picture of anger. And then his eyes moved to his right and landed on Jupiter. Paelen's heart started to pound in fear. The eyes of Olympus's leader were like thunder, and his mouth was held in a thin, tight line.

Chrysaor was crouched on the ground beside Jupiter, looking downcast and defeated. The boar was terrified and wouldn't meet his gaze.

Jupiter stepped closer. His expression was dark and threatening. "Chrysaor caught you as you fell from the window. He brought you back to Olympus. But by the time I am finished with you, you will wish he had not done either."

Paelen dropped his eyes. "Forgive me, Jupiter. I deserve everything you will do to me. But before you do, I must go back to Earth. Joel is in jail, and I fear that Emily, Pegasus, and Alexis are about to take on the CRU by themselves."

There was a sharp intake of breath from everyone in the room. As Paelen devoured ambrosia and drank several more goblets of nectar, he started to speak. He told them everything that had happened, starting with the arrival on Earth to the moment his clone threw him out of the window of the tall black building.

"So you do not know where Emily is?" Jupiter

demanded incredulously. "The Flame of Olympus is on Earth and facing down the CRU alone?"

Paelen felt the furious intensity of Jupiter's stare. "She is not alone," he stammered. "Pegasus, Alexis, and—I believe—Prince Toban are with her!"

"What?" Jupiter cried. "Are you telling me the prince of the Nirad world has left the safety of his people to join this insane quest?"

When Paelen nodded, Jupiter was furious. He walked over to the window and released a lightning bolt and peal of thunder that shook Olympus to its core. "Deliver me!" he howled as he released more lightning and thunder.

With his fury spent, Jupiter returned to the bed. "How many of these creatures, these . . ." He looked to Emily's father for the word.

"Clones."

"Yes, clones," Jupiter repeated. "How many are there?"

Paelen shrugged. "I do not know for certain. But there is a Diana clone on the loose with a Nirad clone. They have killed many people. There is my clone as well, and Tornado Warning was a clone of Pegasus.

We believe there are many more, but only Alexis has been to Area 51 to see for herself. I have not seen her since the CRU attacked us outside their facility."

The leader of Olympus turned furious eyes on his daughter. "Diana, you knew of this and did not tell me?"

Diana dropped her head. "Forgive me, Father. But we only suspected. We had no proof of the clones. That Tornado Warning looked identical to Pegasus was not enough. Emily and Pegasus were determined to return to Earth to see for themselves. We sent Alexis with them for protection."

"Why did you not come to me?" Jupiter demanded. He turned on Pluto. "And you, my own brother! You did not think to tell me?"

Pluto shook his head. "Not until we knew for certain. You have a temper, brother. Emily feared you would destroy her world if you knew they were creating New Olympians."

Jupiter's eyes went black with barely contained rage. "She was right to fear for her world," he shot back. He advanced furiously on his brother. "Summon Neptune! Prepare for war. Once we have collected Emily, we will turn the Solar Stream on Earth!"

31

FOR A BLISSFUL INSTANT, EMILY FORGOT what had happened. She awoke fully from the healing sleep and looked around but couldn't see the stallion. "Pegs?"

Then it all crashed back on her. There was no Pegs. Pegasus, the magnificent stallion of Olympus, had disappeared forever. And it was all her fault.

Suddenly Emily couldn't breathe. She sat up, gulping air as she tried desperately to deny the truth. "Pegs?" she gasped.

She looked around as the full memories of the awful night returned. Pegasus was dead, and she had been captured by the CRU. Tears rushed to her eyes. Emily was so used to having her green handkerchief with her, and automatically collecting the tears, that she was stunned to discover it was gone. Instead she used the crisp white sheets from her bed to collect her tears. And if they blew up because of the power they contained, she hoped she would blow up with them.

Emily curled into a tight ball. She sobbed openly for the loss of her beloved Pegasus. Alexis and little Frankie were gone also. But it was the death of the stallion that crippled her most.

"Forgive me," she wept. "Pegs, please forgive me. . . ."

Alexis had warned her about her powers. But in her fury at the CRU, she hadn't listened. Why hadn't she listened? Why had she done it? It was all her fault! Pegasus and Alexis would be alive now if she had only listened to the Sphinx. Why hadn't she?

It seemed a lifetime ago that the gorgons had tried to get her to use her powers against Jupiter. But she wouldn't do it. Pegasus had been there and given her strength to do the right thing. Now it was those same powers that had destroyed him.

Emily didn't hear the door in her room open. It was only when a voice called her name that she become aware of someone entering.

A man was standing at the side of her bed. Two large gray Nirad soldiers in uniform stood behind him.

"Emily Jacobs," the man repeated, "I am Agent PS. I am here to speak with you."

He appeared to be in his thirties, with cropped reddish hair and eyes the color of a peat bog. He had a neatly trimmed beard, but his eyes looked tired and drawn, as though he hadn't slept.

"Go away," Emily wept.

"No," the man said coldly. "You have a lot to answer for, young lady. Do you have any idea what you have done?"

Emily's grief turned into anger. "Yes, I know what I've done. I've killed Pegasus!"

"You've done a lot more than that," he said. "Shall I tell you?"

Emily felt the Flame inside her rumbling with anger. This CRU agent was doing his best to provoke her. "I'd go away if I were you," she warned. "You don't know what I can do when I'm upset. Pegasus is gone, and I am *very* upset!"

The agent didn't seem the least bit concerned. "I

know full well what you can do, Emily. I have made it my business to learn all about you and your amazing powers. I need to talk to you about them, to understand them. You were born in New York to two very human parents. You lived an ordinary life until last year. What changed? How do you have these powers? Where do they come from?"

"You're wrong if you think I'm going to tell you anything," Emily spat.

"Why do you want to make this so difficult?" Agent PS asked. "We are on the same side. Who knows, perhaps one day you will use those powers to work with us instead of against us."

"Work with the CRU?" Emily said incredulously. She sat up. "Are you crazy? Do you have any idea what you have done by creating clones? We came here to warn you! Jupiter is going to destroy this world if you don't stop."

The man sighed. "I know all the myths, Emily. Never has it been suggested that Zeus—or Jupiter as you prefer—has the power to destroy the world."

"You're wrong," Emily said. "He does. And he doesn't even have to come here to do it. All he has to do is turn the Solar Stream on Earth and it will be destroyed in an instant."

The comment made Agent PS pause. But only for a moment. "He wouldn't do that with you here." He smiled slyly. "We have seen your powers, Emily. We know how valuable you are to him."

"I am nothing without Pegasus," she said softly. "I don't care what Jupiter does now. If he destroys the Earth, I hope he destroys me, too."

"What about the other Pegasi we have here? Surely you could find another Pegasus among them? I know you have spent a lot of time with Tornado Warning. He is here waiting for you, along with all the others."

Emily sniffed. "Pegasi? What are you talking about?"

"Pegasus may have been the original, but we have all his clones here. Collectively we call them the Pegasi."

Hearing the pluralized name made Emily explode.

"There was only one Pegasus, and he's dead! All you've got are flying horses. There is no such thing as Pegasi. Don't you dare call them that! What do you call your Diana clones? Diani?"

The agent nodded. "Exactly."

"You're sick!" she replied as her temper flared even more. The bed started to rumble and shake. Behind the agent, the two gray Nirads stepped closer.

"Call them back," Emily threatened. She raised her hand and it burst into flame, snapping and crackling the air around her. "Not a lot can kill a Nirad, but I can!"

Emily was stunned to see the two Nirads step back by themselves. Their eyes were clearly focused on her and seemed to have intelligence. "Can you understand me?"

"Of course they can understand you," the agent said. "What did you think they are? Mindless monsters?"

"But they're clones of the gray Nirads," Emily insisted. "They're not the smart ones. I don't understand. Tornado Warning was wild. So was the Paelen clone. Why aren't these?"

The agent smiled smugly as he patted one of the clone's arms. "Nirad DNA works much better when mixed with Olympian. These two were our first successes, but there have been many more. However, it's taken us much longer to perfect Olympians."

"They're not Olympians!" Emily shot.

"Of course they are," the agent said. "Would you care to meet some of them?"

"No, I don't want to meet them. Just go away and leave me alone to die."

The agent chuckled. "Well, we both know that's not going to happen, is it? You can't die."

"Yes, I can," Emily shot. "When Jupiter turns the Solar Stream on Earth, we'll all burn up."

"All right," he agreed, almost teasingly. "Don't you want to see Joel before you die?"

"Joel?"

"Yes, he's here too. He is recovering. His surgery went well."

Was Agent PS baiting her? But if they had done anything to Joel, she had to know. "What surgery?"

"You'll have to come with me if you want to find out," the agent said. At that moment, another man entered the room.

"Agent PS, the boy is waking."

"Perfect timing," Agent PS said. He turned back to Emily. "If you want to see Joel before we start our interrogation, you'd better say so."

A desperate need to see Joel rose within her. She needed him more than ever. And if the CRU really had him, he needed her, too. Should she call their bluff?

"Joel isn't here. He's in Las Vegas," she tested.

"Not anymore."

"You're not going to touch him," she threatened.

"Who's going to stop us?"

Emily sat up and slid her legs over the side. She was wearing a hospital gown, but her silver leg brace was gone. "I am," she challenged. "Where's my brace?"

"In the lab, being analyzed," Agent PS said. "You can use these instead." He collected a pair of crutches and handed them to Emily. "Or"—he indicated the Nirad soldiers—"one of these big fellows can carry you. It's your choice."

Was this a trick? She looked around the small white room. It was similar to her room at Governors Island, but there was no lock on the door, and it was kept open. Emily reached for the crutches and followed the men to the door. She paused. "No locks?"

The agent stopped. "Could any locked door ever contain you? We all know you could leave here any time you wanted and we couldn't stop you. But it is my hope that when you see what we've accomplished here, you won't want to go."

"Don't bet on it," Emily said furiously. "Just take me to Joel."

The agent chuckled as Emily followed him out of the room. The corridor was bright and spacious and filled with people in lab coats. There were other uniformed Nirad soldiers walking down the hall beside humans. As she walked past, the Nirads paused to watch her.

She turned and looked back at her Nirad escorts. They were both staring at her intently. There was something in their eyes.

"This way," Agent PS said as he turned down a second corridor. He approached a set of double doors. "We have a couple of patients in here. I think you know them both."

The two Nirads held the door open for Emily and Agent PS. As she walked past the Nirad on the left, she felt the huge clone pat her gently on the shoulder. When she looked up at him, she was convinced he was trying to tell her something.

But then Emily got the shock of her life. There

were two curtained-off areas in the room. One had the curtain drawn around it, but in the other open area was a bed with an occupant hooked up to a breathing machine and lots of tubes.

"Agent T!" Emily cried as she hopped over to the side of the bed.

The ex–CRU agent was awake and looking at her. The breathing tube in his mouth meant he couldn't speak. But as she leaned over him, tears formed in the corners of his blue eyes and trailed silently down his cheeks.

"You're alive!"

"If you call that living," Agent PS said casually. "He was shot when he and that winged cat woman attacked us. One of the bullets severed his spine. He can't move, eat, or even breathe on his own. But in time he may be able to speak. We do have a lot of questions for this traitor."

"He's not a traitor," Emily responded angrily. "He worked with us to try to warn you about Jupiter to save this world. He's a hero."

"Not to us."

Emily stroked Agent T's cheek. She wiped away

his tears. A part of her had hoped that her powers would heal him. But he was human and had never eaten ambrosia. It wouldn't work.

"I'm so sorry," Emily said, brushing back his hair from his face. "I failed all of us."

Agent T blinked his eyes slowly. He looked so weak and vulnerable lying in the bed, hooked up to all the machines. Emily leaned forward and kissed him gently on the forehead.

"Em?" a weak voice called.

"Joel?"

Emily struggled over to the long curtain that separated each treatment area. When she pushed back the curtain, she was met with an awful sight.

The crutches fell from her arms as she hopped over to the bed. "What have they done to you?" She trembled as she looked at Joel. His silver arm was gone, and his side and shoulder were covered in thick bandages. He was deathly pale.

The roller-coaster ride of emotions took another dip as fury rose to the surface. She turned on Agent PS and pointed an accusing finger at him. "You did this!"

Suddenly the CRU agent was thrown violently

across the room. He crashed against the back wall and crumpled to the ground, unconscious. Orderlies looked at Emily fearfully but ran over to the agent. They lifted him up and carried him from the room.

But Emily could only concentrate on Joel. She stroked his pale forehead and felt her powers working. His time in Olympus and all the ambrosia and nectar he'd consumed meant Joel was now more Olympian than human and her powers could heal his wounds.

She watched in relief as the color in Joel's face returned and he was fully awake. "They took my arm!" He sat up angrily. "Vulcan is going to be furious!" Then he looked at the pained expression on Emily's face.

"What's happened? How did they catch you? Where are Pegasus and Alexis? Are they here too?" Then his eyes fell on the other bed. "Agent T!"

Joel sprang up from his bed to get closer to Agent T. "Em, can't you heal him?"

Seeing Joel without his arm and Agent T lying destroyed in the bed, Emily felt herself breaking. "No. All I can do is kill."

She looked at Joel. He was going to hate her for

what she had done, but she had to tell him. "I killed Pegasus. Alexis and Frankie, too."

"What?" Joel cried.

"My powers got away from me. Now they're dead—and it's my fault," she whispered as tears rimmed her eyes.

Joel pulled Emily into a tight embrace and clung to her with his one arm. "Where's your handkerchief?" he asked softly as tears streamed down her cheeks and landed on her hospital gown.

"They took it," she wept. "But I don't care anymore. I hope my tears blow me up!"

Joel held her tighter. "If they blow us up, there's no one I'd rather go to pieces for."

Emily turned tearful eyes up to him and saw he was smiling gently. "It's not funny, Joel." Joel kissed the top of her head. "I know it's not."

Then his voice because serious. "But you listen to me, Emily Jacobs. You did not kill Pegasus. It was an accident. I know for sure Pegasus would not want you blaming yourself."

"But it was me," she said miserably.

Joel lifted her face to him. "No, it was them. The

CRU. If they hadn't created the clones, we'd never have left Olympus."

Emily was inconsolable as her mind replayed the moment of Pegasus's death. She could never forgive herself for losing control. As they clung together, the two Nirad soldiers stepped forward.

"Stay back," Joel warned. "I may only have one arm, but I can make you sorry you tried anything!"

The closest Nirad raised one of his large gray fingers to his thin lips and made a shushing sound. He looked back to the door and grunted a few times. His companion nodded and went to the door and peered out.

The first Nirad reached out and gently stroked Emily's head. His eyes were filled with compassion.

"You can understand us," Joel said in shock, "can't you?"

The Nirad nodded.

Emily removed herself from Joel's embrace. "Do you know where Toban and Tirk are?"

Once again the Nirad nodded. He struggled to form his mouth into words. After a moment, he pointed at his head and in a deep growling voice said, "Hear—our—prince."

Emily and Joel were stunned. This was the first Nirad to ever speak a language they could understand.

"How is this possible?" Joel asked.

Emily carefully wiped her eyes on her hospital gown. She looked at Joel. "He's not pure Nirad. They mixed him with Olympian DNA."

"Can others here speak?" Joel asked.

The Nirad nodded.

"Does the CRU know?"

The Nirad shook his head quickly and put his finger to his lips again. "Shhhhhh."

"This is amazing," Joel continued. "Do you have names?"

The Nirad pointed to his chest. "A-Two." Then he indicated the Nirad by the door. "A-Three."

"And you can hear Prince Toban in your head?" Emily asked.

When the Nirad nodded, she looked at Joel with pain-filled eyes. "The plan worked. Prince Toban can reach the clones. I wish Pegasus could know. He'd have been so happy." She turned back to the Nirad guard. "Do you understand why he came here?"

The Nirad nodded and again formed two words. "Going—home."

"Yes," Joel said. "If you help us, you can go home."

The large gray Nirad nodded and patted Emily again. "We—all—protect—Flame."

Joel looked at the Nirad in shock. "Em, he knows you're the Flame of Olympus!"

"Prince Toban must have told him," Emily said softly.

Joel's face brightened. "This is fantastic! If the Nirads help us, we can get out of here and stop Jupiter from destroying the Earth."

Emily should have felt relieved. But all she could feel was pain. She approached Agent T again and stroked his face. "I'm so sorry. I wish I could heal you."

Joel joined her. "If we can get out of here and get him some ambrosia, I bet it would help him." He looked down on Agent T. "I promise we won't leave you. We'll bring you back to Olympus with us."

Agent T slowly blinked his eyes again.

Joel turned back to A-Two. "Can you take us to the prince?"

The Nirad shook his head. "Not—now," he grumbled. "Night—sleep."

"When everyone is asleep?" Emily asked softly.

Again the Nirad nodded.

At the door, A-Three growled loudly. He approached A-Two and pointed to Joel and then the bed. The message was clear: *They are coming. Get back to bed.*

Joel hesitated before returning to his bed and focused all his attention on Emily. He lifted his hand gently to her chin and tilted her face up to look at him. "It will be all right, Em," he said softly. "I promise. As long as we're together, we'll be fine. I know you don't see any hope right now, but you must find a way to go on. Pegasus wouldn't want you to punish yourself. Deep down inside, you know that. He loved you and would hate to see you suffering."

"How can I go on?" Emily said miserably.

"You go on by remembering what you felt for Pegasus. How you two fought together to protect this world. How he would want you to keep fighting."

"But I can't."

Joel bent down and kissed her gently. "Yes, you can." He held her tight. "You're my Em; you can do anything."

32

EMILY WAS STANDING BESIDE JOEL'S BED when soldiers and several more CRU agents ran into the room. Joel was lying back and pretending to be asleep.

The two Nirads were standing by the door, looking like loyal military personnel who were keeping their prisoner from escaping.

A younger CRU agent approached her with his hands in the air. "Just calm down, Emily. No one is going to hurt you. I'm Agent R. Agent PS is recovering. He will be back shortly."

Emily looked at the CRU agent and felt her anger returning. Joel was right. Pegasus was dead because of them. "Why did you take Joel's arm? You could have killed him."

"That wasn't my decision," the agent said, diverting blame away from himself. "But I'm sure you must understand. There are things we could learn from that arm. It would be a revolution in prosthetics. It could bring relief to thousands of people."

"Soldiers, you mean," Emily challenged. "Nothing the CRU does is for the good of the people. All you care about is building an army. Look what you've done to these poor Nirads. You've enslaved them!"

"These Nirads are not slaves," the young agent said indignantly. "They are personnel. Just like me and just like all the human soldiers here."

"Can they leave if they want?" Emily demanded.

The young CRU agent looked at Emily with contempt. "Don't be ridiculous. If the public were ever to see these soldiers, there would be panic in the streets."

"Then why are you creating them?"

"There is a bigger picture here you are incapable of understanding, a larger goal. With an unstoppable army, we can bring order to the world. We will end human suffering and bring peace to every country on this planet. Wouldn't you want that?"

Emily stood in stunned silence as she processed

the agent's words. It was too horrible to consider. "No," she said in a hushed voice. "You're planning to use a Nirad army to take over the world! And if anyone tries to stop you?"

"There are always casualties in any regime change," he said. "But soon everyone will see that our way is the only way."

"You're all insane!" Emily cried. "You can't use these Nirads to make war on anyone who opposes you."

"It's not war, Emily; it is change. And the Nirads aren't the only ones. We have our Olympians and now we have you." He paused and stepped closer to her. "We've taken some of your blood. Before long, you will have many sisters who can do all the things you can do. You won't be alone anymore. And together we can change this world."

Emily shook her head. "I won't let you clone me."

The young agent shook his head. "Technically, you don't have any choice. We are holding Joel and we have your friend Earl as well. And I'm sure you wouldn't want anything to happen to Tornado Warning and the other Pegasus clones we have here.

Especially now that you destroyed the original."

The agent's words cut Emily to the core. "It's wrong," she whispered. "What you are doing is wrong. You can't force other people to think like you do."

"We can and we will," he said. "One world order isn't a bad thing, Emily. There will be no more borders, no more wars. Isn't that what it's like on Olympus? One language, one people, and one country? It will be the same here. The CRU are going to create Olympus on Earth."

"But Jupiter doesn't kill people who oppose him."

"Of course he does. The myths are filled with all the tales of death and destruction caused by Jupiter."

Emily felt her temper flaring. "They're just myths! Stories! They aren't all true! Jupiter is a caring man. He would do anything for his people. And the myths said that the Sphinx was a cold-blooded killer. But Alexis wasn't that way at all. She was a caring person who loved Agent T!"

The beeping heart monitor at Agent T's bed increased as he listened to Emily's words. She stepped over to him. "It's true," she said softly. "Alexis loved you."

"Now, isn't this a lovely scene!" Agent PS said as he

returned to the room. He approached Emily, rubbing the back of his head. "That's some punch you've got there." He regarded the other agent. "Agent R, did you tell her our plan and her part in it?"

The younger agent nodded. "But she's not convinced."

Agent PS smiled, but it chilled Emily to the bone. "Well then, we're just going to have to convince her."

"And this," Agent PS said proudly as they stood in front of a large picture window, "is where we create our new world fighters. It is here that we first spliced Nirad DNA with Olympian DNA. As you know, it's been a resounding success."

Emily was being given a full tour of the CRU facility. She was in a wheelchair that was being pushed by A-Two. Emily had quietly counted almost a hundred different Nirad soldiers. As she was pushed past, they all looked at her with the secret expression in their eyes. They knew who she was and were waiting for the right moment to move against the CRU.

But the expressions on the human faces she encountered was different. The soldiers and scientists all looked delusional with their glazed eyes, as if they were all drugged.

Emily looked through the window down into the lab. The scientists were all dressed in white spacesuits with breathing tubes coming out of their backs. She couldn't tell the men from the women as they worked at their large microscopes, collections of test tubes, and huge freezers that lined the walls. There were countless other large machines inside, and Emily had no idea what they did. But whatever it was, it wasn't good.

Emily was horror-struck at the sight. This was where it all started. That white, sterile laboratory was truly the place of nightmares. Somewhere down there, they were playing with her DNA, trying to create Emily clones.

Farther away from the main lab, they entered another laboratory. This one contained tall, upright tubes. The tubes were filled with thick, pale-green liquid. Emily was shocked to see that each tube held either a Nirad or Olympian clone in the process of development.

"This is where we mature our clones," Agent PS

explained proudly. "They grow exceptionally fast. It only takes a few months to reach maturity. It takes a normal human soldier a heck of a lot longer."

Emily said nothing as she was pushed past the long line of occupied growing tubes. When they stopped, she looked up at Agent PS. "This is so wrong, can't you see that? Please, listen to me. You must shut this down before it's too late. If Jupiter were to see this—"

"Don't you worry about Jupiter," Agent R said. "We are prepared and waiting for him. Can you imagine what we could create with his DNA? An army of Jupiter clones would be unstoppable."

Emily watched the scientists around her playing with Nirad and Olympian DNA as if it were some kind of game. She suddenly realized Joel was right. Despite her crippling grief over the loss of Pegasus, she had to continue the fight. The CRU had to be stopped.

Emily felt the Flame inside her rumbling and begging to be released to melt the clone factory. But this wasn't the time. She had to wait until she understood everything about the place. More than anything, she needed to find Prince Toban and Tirk.

Once they were safe, Emily promised herself she

would free the Flame and turn the lab into ash.

Emily was next taken to another level of the facility. The entire floor was made up of large gymnasiums, training areas, and sleeping dormitories. This was where the real nightmare began. This was where they kept the New Olympians.

Diana after Diana was training at the machines, lifting weights no human could ever hope to even move and running faster than the wind. Along with the Dianas, Emily's eyes landed on several Paelens. Some were practicing manipulating and stretching their bodies the way the real Paelen could, while others trained with equipment and fought each other in mock battles.

Above them flew countless Cupids near the roof of the tall gym. Some carried weapons as they performed midair acrobatics while shooting guns at targets.

"How?" she asked in horror. "Cupid was never your prisoner."

"Sadly, no. But he was wounded," Agent PS said. "We found a large pool of his blood in the snow outside Tuxedo, New York. It was frozen enough for it to still be viable. As you can see, the cloning worked perfectly."

"These are all soldiers?" Emily said.

"Not all," Agent PS responded. "As you can see, some make perfect athletes. We are going to test some of the clones at the next Olympic Games. For the first time ever, the Olympics will have real Olympians competing. It will be the perfect arena to introduce the clones to the world. And when the world sees what our athletes can do, they will realize there is no opposing us."

While they were speaking, they hadn't noticed the change in the large training area. One by one the clones stopped their training, put down the weights and weapons, and started to approach Emily.

"What's going on?" Agent PS demanded, looking around. "All of you, get back to work!"

"Back to work!" Agent R repeated, clapping his hands. "Now!"

The New Olympians ignored the order and pressed forward. The Cupids glided down from the roof and landed on the ground near Emily's wheelchair.

Emily studied them closely and saw they were identical to the real Cupid. Their wings had the same pheasantlike colors, and their faces and bodies were just as stunningly beautiful. But the expressions in their eyes were different. There was none of Cupid's arrogance or intelligence. These Cupids were like very young, innocent children. They cocked their heads to the side and smiled brilliantly at her.

Emily leaned forward in her chair and rose on her one good leg. She hopped over to the first Cupid.

"What's going on here?" Agent PS said in alarm. "What are you doing?"

Emily looked back and shot him a cold expression. "I'm going to meet my people!"

Every clone reached out to touch her, to stroke her head, and to hold her. Soon Emily was swallowed up in the large group of New Olympians. She was embraced by all the Cupids and Paelens.

As Emily looked from face to face, she was shocked by the overwhelming silence. Some grunted and made strange, soft mewing sounds, but no words came out of their mouths.

She recalled what Alexis had told her in the barn about how all the Olympians were drawn to her. They could feel her power and knew it was the source of their strength. Looking around, she realized it was the same for these New Olympians. They instinctively knew who she was.

A tall Diana came forward and offered Emily her spear. Like the Cupid clones, this Diana was like a beautiful, hopeful child.

"Thank you," Emily said.

The clone grinned broadly.

"Can you talk?" Emily asked. When the clone shook her head, Emily continued, "But you can understand me?"

The Diana clone nodded. So did all the others in the gym. Emily looked back and saw several scientists and the CRU agents watching her intently. Finally Agent PS pushed his way through the group.

"All right, the excitement is over. Everyone get back to your training. Emily will be remaining here with us. You can see her again later."

The New Olympians did as they were told. The Cupids bowed, opened their wings, and returned to the air.

"Why aren't they wild?" Emily asked as she was helped back to her wheelchair. "Tornado Warning and the Paelen clone were wild."

"They were early experiments. It was before we perfected the mix of Olympian to Nirad to alien DNA."

"Alien?" Emily cried.

The CRU agent nodded. "We've had alien bodies here for years. But we've never been able to successfully clone them. Until now. Their DNA combined perfectly with Olympian and Nirad."

Emily didn't think it was possible to be shocked by anything anymore. But with each new revelation, she found herself stunned to the core.

But Agent PS had saved the best for last. Emily was taken down to one of the lower levels of the deep facility. When the elevator doors opened, she immediately smelled straw and heard the sounds of horses' whinnies.

"It seems they know you are here," Agent PS said curiously.

At the end of the hall, the doors were pushed open, and Emily nearly passed out. There were over fifty large stalls. Each stall contained a Pegasus clone.

"You see, Emily," Agent PS said, spreading his hand out before her, "you have no need to grieve over the loss of your Pegasus, because if you join us, all of these are yours."

All the white winged stallions came to the fronts of their stalls, kicking their doors and calling to her. Although they were all nearly identical, there was one particular stallion Emily recognized immediately. Once again she climbed from her wheelchair.

"Careful, Emily," Agent PS warned. "These experiments are our big failure. We can't seem to create calm Pegasi."

Emily cringed at the name. "They are not Pegasi!" she shot back. "There was only one Pegasus. These are just winged horses."

Agent PS straightened his back. The dark expression on his face said more than his words. "If you insist. They are all dangerous monsters. The only reason we've kept them alive is for you."

Emily ignored the warning and hopped over to a stall. "Hi, Tornado," she called softly as she stroked his soft muzzle.

Tornado Warning neighed with excitement and looked at her with his big brown eyes. Emily looked deep into those eyes, but could find no trace of Pegasus. It was true, Tornado was just a beautiful winged stallion who looked like Pegasus, but was nothing like him.

"Pegs is dead," she whispered softly as she laid her head against his warm face. "But I won't let them hurt you." She looked down at all the other stalls. "Any of you. I'm here, you're safe now."

As Emily hopped from stall to stall, each white winged stallion came forward to greet her with no aggression. They knew who she was and wanted to be with her.

Finally she returned to Tornado just as one of the scientists ran into the area. He approached Agent PS and Agent R and handed over several sheets of paper. Soon all eyes turned to Emily.

The expression on Agent PS's face darkened further. "Do you want to know what these are? They are the results of your blood tests. And you know what? They say you don't exist! You have no blood cells, no DNA, and no matter! They say you are made up of nothing!" Agent PS crumpled the pages and threw them away. He stormed over to her. "Okay, the game's over. Who the hell are you? And what did you do with the real Emily Jacobs?"

33

THOUSANDS OF OLYMPIANS OF ALL SHAPES and sizes gathered to watch their leader's departure. There was no joy in their faces, and their heads hung low. It had been eons since the Big Three had turned the Solar Stream on a living world. But this time it was especially painful. They were about to destroy the Flame of Olympus's home world.

Vesta stood at the front of the crowd, weeping softly. Venus and Cupid were beside her. Cupid's wings drooped as he dropped his head in sorrow. Several Nirads in the crowd raised their heads and howled mournfully.

Paelen ran with Emily's father up to Jupiter's chariot. "Please, Jupiter," Steve begged. "You can't do this!"

The Olympus leader's expression was as dark and thundery as the lightning bolts he carried. "I can and I must. The humans must be punished for what they have done to us."

Jupiter's large golden chariot was being drawn by six fiery, winged stallions. They pawed the ground, causing flames to rise up, and chewed at their bits, anxious to get moving.

Beside Jupiter's chariot stood Pluto's own black chariot, made entirely of the bones of the most valiant stallions fallen in battle. Cerberus, the three-headed dog of Hades, was beside the leader of the night world. The chariot was being drawn by a set of six black, skeletal stallions. The stallions had not seen the light of an Olympian day for so long that Pluto had to tie dark rags over the empty eye sockets to calm them.

On the other side of Jupiter waited Neptune, clutching his war trident. His eyes were the color of a stormy sea. Beneath him, his chariot was made of coral, large colorful seashells, and beautiful pearls. It was floating on top of a contained pool of water while six large, fish-tailed sea stallions waited and whinnied, preparing to move.

Behind the Big Three, four other chariots filled with the best Olympian fighters waited to follow their leader into battle. Vulcan was riding with Hercules and was carrying his most powerful shields and weapons.

Diana approached Steve as he continued to plead with Jupiter. She was wearing full battle armor and carrying a spear and shield. Her long dark hair was tied tightly back, and her expression was grim.

"Steve, stop," she said. "Father is correct. We tried to give Emily a chance to save your world, but she has failed. Now Earth must face the consequences of their actions. I have sent Apollo to New York to fetch your sister. Maureen will be saved from destruction and given a new home here in Olympus. But there is nothing that can be done for the others. Please ride with me in my chariot."

He looked at her incredulously. "You expect me to go with you and watch you destroy my world?"

Jupiter shook his head. "No, Steve. You are the Flame's father. Emily will need you now more than ever. You must come with us to be there for her."

That comment stopped Steve's protest. Finally

he walked back to Diana's chariot and reluctantly climbed on with her.

"And you, little thief," Jupiter said darkly to Paelen, "you and my nephew, Chrysaor, will lead us to where they are holding Joel. Then we will collect Emily, Pegasus, and Alexis, and end this once and for all."

Paelen and Chrysaor had also tried to plead with Jupiter, but had received a stark warning. The furious leader had threatened to feed them to Cerberus.

Paelen dropped his head and walked up to the winged boar. He climbed on his back. "Do you think he will ever forgive us?"

Chrysaor squealed softly.

Paelen agreed. "I do not think so either."

Once everyone was gathered, Jupiter raised his fist in the air, and thunder and lightning filled the skies.

"To Earth!" he commanded.

They emerged from the Solar Stream in the middle of the dark night. Beneath them, the colorful lights of Las Vegas were shining brightly. With Chrysaor and Paelen guiding them forward, they headed down.

As they descended, Paelen looked back. The Big

Three led the way. On the left was Pluto's bone chariot, with the skeletal stallions charging forward. Their haunting screams filled the air and struck a chill in Paelen's heart. On the right was Neptune's chariot, with the sea stallions rising on the crest of the huge wave of water Neptune had created around his chariot. Then in the very center was Jupiter's golden chariot, with its flaming stallions filling the night sky with their blazing light. Together they were a terrifying sight.

Jupiter raised his lightning bolts and fired them in the air, announcing the Olympians' arrival in the sky over Las Vegas. They continued down until they were just a few meters above traffic level. Car horns blared at the sight of the flying chariots tearing down the strip, and people on the street panicked and ran for cover.

Jupiter threw back his head and roared in fury as he unleashed more lightning bolts at the unsuspecting city. They struck the tall casinos and exploded with the impact as fire and sparks rained down on the streets.

Neptune raised his trident and commanded the

water hidden deep below the city to rise up and burst through the surface. Streams of fresh water shot high into the air.

Pluto released Cerberus. The three-headed dog sprang from the chariot and ran amok in the stopped traffic. His three heads caught hold of the bumper of an empty tourist bus and lifted it in the air. Cerberus then started to shake it like a dog would shake a toy.

Las Vegas was in an uproar with the arrival of the Olympians. But the chariots did not stop. They continued to follow Paelen through the city streets until they reached the police station and jail where Paelen had been held.

When Chrysaor landed on the top step outside the jail, Jupiter called his stallions to a halt. They hovered in the air several meters off the ground. The leader of Olympus raised a lightning bolt and fired at the police station.

"Bring out Joel!" he commanded as his booming voice filled the canyons of the city. "Now!"

The doors to the station burst open as armed police poured out. Paelen had seen this all before and ducked down into the protection of Chrysaor's wings. Behind him, Jupiter continued to demand Joel's release. But the police weren't listening. They opened fire on the chariots. Unaffected by their bullets, Jupiter returned fire with his lightning bolts. Suddenly the ground beneath the police exploded as Neptune commanded water to come forth.

"My brothers, stop!" Pluto called.

When Jupiter and Neptune paused, Pluto bowed elegantly to them. "Please, allow me."

The leader of the night world stepped down from his skeletal chariot. He was dressed in his long and flowing black robes. He carried no weapon. He didn't need one. Pluto was Death.

With Diana and Hercules moving in behind him, Pluto walked slowly and calmly up the steps of the station. "Surrender now or you will be delivered to me," he called.

The nearest police officer raised his weapon and fired at Pluto. The bullets entered his robes, but had no effect. "Fool!" Pluto said softly as he swept his hand in the air. An instant later, the officer collapsed dead to the ground.

"Who is next?" Pluto demanded as his eyes trailed

over the police officers. "Who will take on Death?" His eyes landed on a young policewoman. "Perhaps you, young woman? Are you ready to end your life early?"

The young policewoman cried in terror and threw down her weapon. She fell to her knees and begged for her life.

"Granted," Pluto said as he breezed past, leaving her untouched.

The other police officers quickly threw down their weapons and fell to the ground.

Diana moved forward. She caught hold of the policewoman and hauled her to her feet. "Tell me— where is the boy, Joel? He has a silver arm and is a prisoner here."

"I swear I don't know who you're talking about," the policewoman wept. "Please, I've only just started working here today!"

Diana's eyes scanned the other officers. "Who here knows Joel?" she demanded. "Answer me now or you will know our wrath!"

"He's not here!" a large police officer called. "They took him."

Hercules trotted over to the man and lifted him high off the ground. "Who took him?" he demanded. "Where is he?"

"The CRU!" the officer cried. "They came for him two days ago. He's not here. The CRU have him!"

Hercules started to shake the man. "Are you certain? Where would they take him?"

"That is enough, Hercules," Diana called. "Put him down."

The hero of Olympus lowered the police officer to the ground. He loomed over the man, almost a foot taller, and his eyes blazed the same color as Jupiter's. "Where did they take him?" he repeated.

"I—I don't know. Maybe Area 51."

Paelen groaned at the mention of the CRU base in the desert. He looked back at Jupiter. "We know where that is. Chrysaor and I will take you there."

"Do it!" Jupiter demanded.

As Diana, Hercules, and Pluto returned to their chariots, the building beside them exploded in fire and flying debris. Above them came the heavy, thudding sound of helicopters.

Paelen groaned a second time. "It is the military!"

he cried to Jupiter. "Those are the machines they use to attack us!"

A second rocket was fired at the Olympians. Jupiter raised his arm, and the rocket shot away from the chariots and tore into the police station. The rocket exploded on impact. All the windows were blown out as the building groaned under the pressure.

Jupiter looked up at the hovering helicopters and fired powerful lightning bolts at them. They burst into flame and crashed down to the street in a heap of burning metal.

"Olympians," Jupiter called in fury, "let us show these people who we are!"

The leader of Olympus commanded his fiery stallions to lift them higher in the air. As they rose above the burning buildings, they saw that the sky was filled with hundreds of military aircraft, heading straight for them. Jets zoomed past and launched a barrage of rockets at them.

With little effort, Jupiter diverted them, and they flew wildly into more buildings. "Father," Diana roared excitedly, "if they wish to fight, let us give them a fight!"

At Jupiter's command, the Olympians launched themselves at the military. Jupiter ordered Paelen and Chrysaor to move away from the battle until it was over, as they had no weapons and no means of protecting themselves. Not waiting to be told twice, they flew away from the fighting and headed to the tall black building. Ducking and dodging between the buildings and helicopters that pursued them, they finally made it back to the relative safety of the roof of the black building. Standing together, they watched the fight raging in Las Vegas.

Not far from their roof, three military helicopters pursued Neptune's chariot on his living wave of water. They fired their guns and launched their rockets at him. But Neptune fought back. He raised his trident in the air. Water spouts rose from the ground and knocked the rockets away. They flew straight at the city's tallest golden tower. With the impact of multiple rockets, the tall tower shuddered. Finally, like a great monster defeated in battle, it tipped over and crashed violently to the ground.

"Chrysaor, look," Paelen said in hushed shock as he pointed farther up the strip. Helicopters and jets were firing at Jupiter's chariot and the one containing Diana and Emily's father. But the weapons did not strike their mark. They were deflected by the Olympians' powers and crashed into a big black pyramid-shaped building. The light at its top went out, the windows exploded, and the building burst into flame.

"The military are destroying their own city in the hopes of stopping us. Can they not see the damage they are doing to their people? The lives they are wrecking? They cannot defeat Jupiter—why are they even trying?"

Paelen couldn't understand any of it. Not everyone in this city was bad, and yet they were being destroyed. Perhaps in the past he might not have cared. But after growing to know and love Emily and Joel, he had learned how good humans could be. Watching this destruction only made it sadder.

Chrysaor squealed in horrified agreement as they stood together watching the destruction of Las Vegas.

34

EMILY SAT ALONE IN HER ROOM. SHE WAS reeling from what the doctors and scientists had said. After the strange blood results, Emily had allowed them to examine her fully. Not only was she not human anymore, she wasn't really "alive." It was true that she had blood. It was red and it was wet. But it didn't have any cells in it. And although she had internal organs and a beating heart, they were not necessary to her survival.

"What am I?" she said aloud. "Pegasus, what happened to me in the Temple of the Flame?"

Emily heard the sounds of a scuffle outside her door. She hopped over just as it was opened by a Nirad. Out in the corridor, A-Two and A-Three were lifting several unconscious human soldiers off the floor. They carried them into her room and deposited them on the bed.

"What happened?" she asked as the Nirads bound the soldiers.

"Prince—frightened—trouble—go!"

"Prince Toban is in trouble?"

A-Two nodded. "Come." Without asking, he scooped her up in two of his arms and carried her into the corridor.

Emily pushed aside her concerns for herself. At the moment her only thought was for Prince Toban. As they entered the stairwell and started down, she tried to ask the Nirads what was happening, but their single-word answers puzzled her.

After several flights, the three Nirads stopped. A-Two dropped Emily. He and the others collapsed to the floor, clutching their heads.

"Hurt—prince!" A-Two cried. "Pain!"

Fear coursed through her. "They're hurting Toban?"

A-Two nodded and howled in agony.

"Please, I know you're hurting. But you must take me to him. I can help!"

Black tears of suffering were streaming down the Nirads' faces as A-Two picked Emily up again. Other collapsed Nirads were howling in the stairwell.

"Come with us," Emily ordered. "We will free Toban!"

A-Two roared at the others. They staggered to their feet and started to follow.

The growing group continued down deeper than Emily thought possible. She realized Agent PS had been very selective in his "tour" of the CRU facility. He'd claimed it only went down a few levels. He'd lied.

At the very bottom, Emily heard growls and roars filling the corridor. She recognized Tirk's voice. But worse than that, she heard Prince Toban screaming in agony.

The closer they got to the screaming, the harder it became for her Nirad escorts to move.

A-Two collapsed to the floor. "Pain!"

Emily crawled from his arms. "I'll stop your pain. Wait here."

Without her leg brace, walking was difficult and running impossible. But then her mind went back to the scientists' horrible words. She wasn't human. She wasn't even alive. Emily pulled up her trouser leg past her knee and looked at her damaged leg. It had been hurt in her first encounter with the Nirads. But as she studied the deep scars and ruined muscles, Emily wondered if the scars were only there because she thought they should be.

Emily concentrated harder than she ever had in her life. "Your leg is whole," she ordered. "There is no damage. It is perfect!"

The screaming of her friends threatened to distract her. But Emily closed her eyes to force it away and concentrate. "Your leg is whole!" she commanded. "There is no damage."

She opened her eyes and slowly looked down. Her bare leg was healed. No more scars and no more damage. She lifted her foot and flexed her muscles. They worked perfectly. Part of her celebrated her success. But deep down, in the darkest recesses of her mind, a part of her cried in despair. It was true. Emily Jacobs was gone. And if she wasn't human or Olympian, what was she?

With two good working legs, Emily ran forward.

She pushed through a set of double doors and entered a room of horrors.

The walls were lined with large steel cages holding what looked like failed clone experiments. She saw a Diana with four Nirad arms and no legs. There were Nirads with grotesque Cupid wings. Some of the creatures had two heads and were lying on the floors of their cages in misery. Others were beyond rational description. From her place at the door, Emily could feel their pain coming at her in waves.

These were the failures Agent PS didn't want her to see. The price they paid for creating a superrace of New Olympians and Nirad fighters.

In the center of the room, Prince Toban was strapped to a table. Gold bands pinned him down and were burning into his bare pink flesh. It was Earth gold, so it wouldn't kill him. But it scalded him until his skin smoldered, opened, and bled. She watched scientists extracting fresh black blood and skin samples from the suffering young prince.

Tirk was pounding his fists against the gold bars of his cage. With each contact, he howled in pain. But his loyalty to his prince kept him at it.

Emily was so stunned she didn't know where to look next.

"What are you doing here?" Agent R demanded furiously. "You are not allowed down here."

He was standing back from the table and holding a medical mask to his face. Around him, other scientists in caps, masks, and white jackets were crowding around the prince. Their gloves were wet with the Nirad's blood.

Watching her friend being tortured was too much to bear. Emily raised her hand and fired her powers. The scientists were tossed away from the prince and landed on the floor several meters away.

Emily ran up to the table. The prince's eyes were shut as he writhed and howled in pain. The tight gold bands were cutting deep into his smoking, opened flesh. Emily saw that the scalpels and tools the scientists were using on him had also been made of gold.

She used the flame like a laser to cut away the straps keeping him pinned down. But then she saw that the entire bed of the table was also made of gold. Every part of his back was being burned.

Emily caught hold of one of the prince's hands and

started to tug. Toban was not a large Nirad, but he was heavy. Too heavy for her to lift. As he continued to howl in pain, Emily focused her powers.

"Lift!" she commanded.

Concentrating on what she needed to do, Emily felt her powers answering. Prince Toban started to rise above the table. She turned to the side and lowered him gently to the floor.

Prince Toban was awake and looking at her in misery. Emily cradled his head in her lap and started to stroke his face. "I'm so sorry, Toban," she said. "I didn't know they knew about gold. It's over now; you're safe."

As she stroked him, Toban's open wounds started to close. It was slow and not complete, but it was enough to save the Nirad's life.

Now that the prince's pain was greatly diminished, the Nirads were released from their agony too. A-Two, A-Three, and all the Nirad soldiers from outside the lab charged in. They knelt down on the floor around their prince. Toban raised his four arms and greeted his new people.

Tirk continued to pound the bars and howl. Emily

burned the lock off the gold cage door. Tirk charged out. He barked furiously and pushed through the others to get to the prince. Finally he lifted Prince Toban in his arms and hugged the young Nirad. Emily saw that his hands were burned raw from pounding the cage. But he didn't notice. All he cared about was his prince.

"Emily, stop—you don't know what you're doing!" Agent R was moving closer.

"Stay back," Emily warned. "It's over. All of this is finished. No more torture, no more clones."

Tirk's eyes flashed with uncontained fury as he looked over at Agent R. He handed the prince over to another Nirad and ran at the CRU agent. Emily turned away as Tirk punished Agent R for his part in the torture of his prince.

Emily looked around the large room at all the clones and worried. What was to become of them now? She approached one of the mutant Dianas' cages. The clone had only one arm and three Nirad legs. Her Nirad black eyes seemed to have no understanding other than the desperate need to touch Emily.

Emily reached in and cradled the creature's face in her hands. "I promise you will be free soon," she said. As her eyes panned over all the cages, her heart—whether she had a real one or not—went out to them. "You will all be free!"

Her temper rose as she charged back to Prince Toban and the Nirads. She concentrated on the Nirad soldiers. "Capture the scientists and bring them." She looked at Agent R as he struggled to rise after being struck by Tirk.

"It's over, Agent R. This all ends now!"

SIRENS BLARED AND SOLDIERS ARMED THEM-
selves as Emily stormed through the corridors of the
CRU facility at Area 51. Behind her followed an
army of Nirad soldiers. Prince Toban was being carried in the arms of Tirk as he summoned his people
together.

Soon the number of Nirads joining her outnumbered the humans at the facility. Emily looked back
at Prince Toban. With each passing moment, his
strength was returning.

"Would you please ask some of your men to find
Joel and Agent T and guard them? And we need to
locate a man called Earl. He is a friend and is here
somewhere."

"I—go," A-Three said. "Find—Earl." He called several Nirads forward. They ran ahead into the stairwell. Gunfire echoed back, but Emily knew it would not hurt the Nirads.

As they made their way through the huge facility, Emily asked the Nirad soldiers to round up all the humans and get them to the ground level. Emily kept A-Two back to help her find her way to the main lab. Halfway there, she heard a familiar and very welcome voice.

"Em!"

She turned and saw Joel running toward her, escorted by two large gray Nirads.

"You didn't think I was going to let you total Area 51 alone!" Joel grinned.

Emily felt stronger with Joel at her side. "Of course not."

Together they made their way through the chaos to the super-lab where the clones were created. Nirads were capturing scientists and agents, disarming them and leading them up to ground level.

Joel looked through the window of the super-lab and whistled. With the alarms still blaring, the night shift of scientists were busy trying to store away the cloning materials. They looked up in terror when they saw Emily and Joel standing at the large picture window.

"Can you nuke that lab without burning down the whole facility?"

"I can try," Emily said.

The Nirads tore down the secured doors to the lab and poured in. The scientists were rounded up and presented to her.

"Get them to the surface with the others," Emily ordered.

Joel and Emily now walked through the empty lab and began to destroy the equipment. With each passing moment, Emily's confidence with the Flame grew. By the time they had left the lab, Emily could look at a machine and turn it to ash in a matter of seconds.

They moved on to the secondary labs. Emily showed Joel and Prince Toban the tall tubes that contained the clones in various stages of development, from embryonic to nearly fully grown.

"What do we do with these?" Joel said.

"I don't know," Emily admitted. "We can't destroy them; they're alive."

"But we can't leave them here either. The CRU will just build more."

Emily shook her head. "Once everyone is out of here, I'm going to destroy the place."

"And these guys?"

"We're just going to have to find a way to save them. Let's get everyone else out of here first and worry about these guys later."

In another lab they came across Joel's silver arm. It was laid out on a table and had been completely dismantled and was now useless. Paelen's winged sandals were found in the same lab, and they were grateful to discover these were intact. Emily prayed that Paelen was still alive and ready to wear them again. They also found Pluto's helmet.

"Boy, am I glad to see this!" Joel said. "Pluto would have had a fit if he knew we'd lost it."

Emily dropped her head. "No, we didn't lose it. We just lost Pegasus and Alexis instead. I'm sure Pluto won't care about his helmet after that."

Prince Toban growled softly. He closed his eyes

and tilted his head back. When he opened his eyes again, he concentrated on Emily and made several sounds.

"I don't understand," Emily said desperately.

A-Two struggled to say, "Place—all—empty. Ours. No—more—people. All—prisoners. All—above."

Joel approached the prince. "So your soldiers have gathered all the people here and taken them above? There is no one left?"

Prince Toban shook his head and made several more sounds.

"Pegasuses," A-Two said. "They—stay. Children—below."

They understood that all the CRU agents, scientists, and human soldiers had been captured and taken to the surface. The facility now belonged to them.

"All right, we've got to get the New Olympians out of here and the poor clones from down below. And I've got to free all of Pegasus's clones as well."

"You've seen them?" Joel asked.

Emily nodded. "Tornado is here too. But all the

winged stallions are the same. They're as wild and dangerous as Tornado. I'm still the only person who can get near them. I'm going to have to lead them out."

"Then what?" Joel asked. "Em, what are we supposed to do with all these clones? Yes, we can destroy this place, but then where do we take them? And how? Without Pegasus, I don't even know how we're supposed to get back to Olympus or get Prince Toban and his people back to the Nirad world."

Emily hadn't thought that far ahead. Her only concern had been to stop the CRU from creating more clones. But now what? Joel was right. They were stranded on Earth with no way of getting back.

"I don't know," she said softly. "But Dad has got to know something is wrong by now. He and Diana will come for us. And Paelen, I hope. He was hurt, but I'm sure Chrysaor must have taken him back to Olympus. Paelen knows where we are. We just have to get to the surface and wait for them."

Joel didn't sound convinced. "Or wait for the military to launch a full assault on us for destroying their base here."

"We'll just have to risk it," Emily said. "We don't have any choice."

As the long night continued into dawn, Emily, Joel, and the Nirads entered the secured quarters of the New Olympians. They welcomed Emily into their midst and showed no aggression toward Joel or the Nirads.

When Emily explained the situation, the clones were excited at the prospect of going outside. They had never been to the surface before.

The sun was rising on the horizon by the time all the New Olympians emerged to the surface level. They looked at the approaching sunrise in absolute wonder. The Cupids were thrilled to leap into the air and soar in a wide-open sky.

Emily took a moment to watch them with envy. Those sweet, ignorant clones had no idea of the danger and uncertain future they now faced.

There were hundreds, maybe a thousand gathered on the dry Groom Lake bed. The heavily armed Nirad soldiers kept the Area 51 personnel apart from the clones.

"Is that my friend Emily I see?"

Emily turned at the voice and saw Earl approaching. He ran forward and embraced her tightly. "Ain't you a sight for sore eyes! Lord, I thought you'd never get here. These CRU folks ain't nice people!"

Emily clung to Earl, grateful that he was alive. There was a Nirad standing close at his side. Earl turned to introduce him. "This is my friend B-Fifteen. He got me out of my cell."

As Emily greeted the Nirad, there were sounds and cries coming from the crowd. She turned and saw them all pointing up at the sky. The Cupid clones squealed in terror and quickly landed.

Emily and Joel looked up, and their eyes went wide. "Jupiter!"

36

EMILY WATCHED JUPITER'S CHARIOT BLAZE across the dawn sky, with Pluto and Neptune beside him in their own chariots.

A chill ran through her. It took the Big Three to move the Solar Stream. And here they all were.

"That the big fella himself?" Earl asked fearfully, watching the approaching chariots.

Emily nodded. "You'd better get back." Then she turned to Joel. "You too. I said I would fight Jupiter if I have to, and I meant it. He's not going to destroy this world and all these innocent clones without a fight."

"No way," Joel said. "I started this with you. I'm going to end it with you."

Emily's heart swelled at Joel's constant support and loyalty. She reached out and took his hand. Together they walked out onto the dry Groom Lake bed and awaited Jupiter.

As the Olympians drew closer, Emily noticed someone else in the sky. "Joel, look! It's Paelen!"

Leading the Olympians was Chrysaor, carrying Paelen. He was the first to touch down on the ground, just a few meters from them. Paelen jumped off the boar's back and ran to his friends. They embraced like they hadn't seen each other in years. So much had happened since they were last together.

"Las Vegas is destroyed!" Paelen cried. "The military tried to kill us, but we fought back. Now it is all in ruin."

"Las Vegas is destroyed?" Joel repeated.

Paelen nodded and concentrated on Emily. "He is going to do it. Jupiter is going to destroy this world. He's already started with Vegas."

This only strengthened Emily's resolve. "No, he's not," she replied.

"You cannot stop him," Paelen cried. "He is Jupiter, the all-powerful."

"And I am the Flame of Olympus!" Emily shot

back. "If he wants to destroy this world, he'll have to get past me first!"

The screaming of Pluto's skeleton stallions as the chariots landed on the dry lake bed before them cut off further conversation. Emily saw Jupiter's face. It was furious. She had never seen the leader of Olympus so angry.

"Emily!" Jupiter boomed. "What have you done?" The leader of Olympus climbed down from his chariot and stormed up to her. "You have a lot of explaining to do!"

But before she could even think of how to respond, a comforting voice cried out her name.

Emily turned around and watched as her father climbed down from Diana's chariot. He ran past Jupiter and scooped her up in his arms. "Are you all right?"

Emily nodded and fought to keep control of her emotions. She turned to Jupiter. "Pegasus is dead. So is Alexis. My powers got away from me, and I killed them."

A shocked silence halted the Olympians. The only movement came from Neptune, his face a portrait of pain. "My son is dead?"

"Neptune . . ." Emily started to break. "I didn't mean to. . . . We were fighting the CRU. . . . I got shot and lost control."

"They shot you?" her father cried.

Emily nodded again. "I'm okay," she said sadly. "But Pegasus isn't."

Chrysaor started to squeal and howl in pain, breaking Emily's nonexistent heart.

"Please, Jupiter, I beg you," she cried, facing the leader. "There has been too much death already. Don't destroy my world."

The fire was gone from his eyes. But his expression was still full of anger. "The CRU have left me no choice. Their crime cannot be forgiven."

"Then punish them!" Emily's father cried. "But not the whole world!"

"No," Jupiter insisted. "There will be others just like the CRU, ready to rise up and do this again. We must not let that happen. Earth must be destroyed."

Emily stepped away from her father and approached Jupiter. "I understand you are angry," she said, suddenly very calm. "So am I. I have lost Pegasus. I have seen firsthand the horrors these people have done here. But I cannot let you destroy my world."

Jupiter stared at her and a frown darkened his brow. "Are you challenging me?"

Emily inhaled deeply. This was it. She felt the Flame rumbling inside her, but felt equally sick realizing what she was prepared to do.

"Yes, Jupiter, I am," she finally said.

A hush fell over everyone as Emily and Jupiter faced each other.

"Em, stop," her father cried.

Emily looked back at him but shook her head. She turned back to Jupiter. "You know how I feel about Olympus and how I have fought to protect it. I love you, Jupiter. But I will not allow you to destroy my world."

Pluto's and Neptune's eyes flashed from Emily back to their brother and to Emily again. "Emily, stop," Neptune warned. "You do not want to do this."

"No, I don't," she said, concentrating on him. "But to protect this world, I must." She looked back at Jupiter. "You have taught me so much. Like how to care for others outside my family, my race, and even my species. You have shown me the price you must pay and the sacrifices you have made for leadership. You have taught me to be a better person. How could you teach me all that and then expect me to allow you to destroy this world?"

"This is different," Jupiter said.

"No, it's not," Emily insisted. "Most of the people on this planet are innocent. They have no idea what the CRU have done. Why should they be made to suffer for that?"

"Do you care so much for these people that you are prepared to make war with me?" Jupiter asked incredulously.

Emily stared Jupiter in the eye. She raised both her hands as they burst into brilliant flame. The powers bubbled up from her core as she prepared to fire at the leader of Olympus. "To save Earth? Yes!"

37

EMILY CLOSED HER EYES AND COMMANDED her powers to fly. An instant before they did, a crying whinny shattered the stillness of the air around her. It was a sound she'd never thought she'd hear again. A sound she loved. The Flame in her hands went out. She turned and saw Pegasus tearing through the sky. Alexis was behind him, struggling to keep up.

"Pegasus!" she howled.

Emily ran out onto the dry lake bed. Pegasus landed and galloped toward her. His mane billowed behind him, his nostrils flared, and his golden hooves stirred a wild dust storm in the air. Pegasus was covered in foaming sweat and panting heavily as he whinnied to her.

They met in an explosive reunion.

Emily threw her arms around his neck. She squeezed him as tight as she could, just to prove he was there. "You're alive! You're alive!"

Pegasus neighed excitedly and turned his head back to embrace her as best he could. His wings were fluttering and his tail flashed behind him.

Alexis landed on the ground beside Pegasus. Her face was bright red with exertion, her hair was a matted mess, and she was panting with exhaustion. Frankie was on her back, with a huge grin on his face.

"We're back!" he cheered. He climbed off Alexis and ran over to Joel and Paelen. He threw his arms around them and hugged them tightly. "That was so awesome! We went to another planet! There were lots of big statues and it was a jungle! There were helicopters from here too. The pilots are waiting for us to come get them."

Emily was too emotional to speak. She released Pegasus and collapsed on the ground before Alexis. She hugged the Sphinx tightly. "I'm so sorry." She started to cry.

"It is all right, Emily," Alexis panted softly, patting

her on the back with a large lion's paw. "We are all right."

Neptune and Chrysaor ran over to greet Pegasus. "When Emily told me you were dead, I could not bear it." Neptune's eyes were filled with tears as he embraced his son.

Pegasus greeted his brother, but then stepped closer to Emily. He neighed for her.

She left the Sphinx and kissed his soft muzzle, his face, and finally his eye. "Oh, Pegs, I really thought I'd killed you."

"Hardly," Alexis said. "Though you did cast us to the very end of the Solar Stream."

"She did what?" Jupiter asked as he approached.

"The Flame cast us to the very end of the Solar Stream. The journey lasted the shortest blink of an eye. But it has taken us ages to fly back here." She paused and looked from Emily to Jupiter and then back to Emily again. "It appears we arrived just in time."

The Sphinx climbed stiffly to her feet and padded over to Emily. "Do you know everything you have made disappear was on this beautiful world? There are no people but many kinds of plants and wildlife. There are ancient temples and signs of a great society that must have existed there. But they are gone."

Emily was still holding on to Pegasus to prove he was really alive. "I don't understand. How could I send you there? Why would I do it?"

Alexis smiled gently. "Child, do you not remember? The soldiers were shooting at us. You had been hit. You did the only thing you could to protect us. You sent us away from the danger." The Sphinx paused and smiled. "Though, to be honest, I would have much preferred being returned to Olympus and not across the cosmos."

"I don't understand," Emily stammered. "How did I do it?"

"That is a very good question," Jupiter said as he approached her. "And one that I believe we should investigate. . . ." He stopped, and his eyes concentrated on Emily. "Together."

Emily gazed up into the face of the leader of Olympus. Her hand was wrapped around Pegasus, and she was pressed closely to him. "What about Earth?"

Jupiter dropped his head. "Perhaps I was a bit rash in ordering its destruction. I never realized how much this world still means to you. I was wrong, and I am not above admitting it."

"So you won't destroy it?"

Jupiter shook his head. "Not this time. But Emily," he warned, "these people must be punished for what they have done."

Emily nodded. "I agree. And if you will allow me, I want to turn Area 51 to dust!"

Jupiter opened a ground-level portal to the Solar Stream. He summoned Olympians to come to Earth to escort the New Olympians back home.

With his two brothers, Jupiter watched the long lines of clones heading into the Solar Stream. Diana was standing among her many clones. The new Dianas looked at the original in awe and sought to touch her. Though she was greatly disturbed by them, Diana felt no urge to fight.

Prince Toban was still covered in cuts and burns, but his strength had returned. Tirk was behind him, keeping a protective watch over him, while other

Nirad soldiers kept guard over the Area 51 employees.

As the final clones entered the Solar Stream, Emily turned to Neptune.

"There are lot of winged stallions still inside. They're clones of Pegasus and they're wild and dangerous. But we can't leave them behind. It's not their fault they exist. Would you help me get them to the Solar Stream?"

Neptune looked uncomfortable at the mention of his son's clones, but he agreed. With the Nirads on the surface guarding their prisoners, Emily spoke to Pegasus, asking him to remain with them.

"I don't want you going down there, Pegs." She kissed his muzzle. "There are a lot of clones, and I don't want them hurting you when they're released. I lost you once; I couldn't bear it again."

Pegasus snorted but finally agreed. Emily approached Alexis. "I think you should come too. There is someone you should see."

As they made their way to the facility, Jupiter, Pluto, and a large number of Olympians joined them. "We must all see," Jupiter explained. "I must understand what has happened here."

Emily feared that Jupiter might change his mind if he actually saw what the CRU had done. But as if reading her mind, he put his arm around her and reassured her. "Your world is safe, Emily," he said. "But I must still see."

The facility was eerily quiet as Emily, her father, and the Olympians journeyed down to the lowest levels, where failed clone experiments were kept. When Jupiter saw what had been done to his daughter's clones, his fury arose.

"This must not be tolerated!" He went up to the nearest cage and tore the door off. The crippled Diana clone cried as she struggled to climb out.

Jupiter knelt down to her level and stroked the clone's misshapen head. "You will come home with me, my child," he said gently. "You are safe."

He commanded the Olympians to collect every last one of the broken, tormented clones. They would all be given a home on Olympus and cared for till the end of their lives.

From there, Emily escorted them to the lab containing the tall tubes. "These are the unfinished clones," she said softly. "I don't know how to save all of them.

The younger ones need these machines to develop."

"We cannot save them all," Jupiter said sadly, "but we will do our best to release those ready for the world. Leave it to us."

With a heavy heart, Emily reluctantly left the room to wait for Jupiter and Pluto to do what they must. She knew it was a hard task and grieved for those clones who could not survive. When it was done, she led the Olympians to the level of the Pegasus clones. When she pushed open the door, the clones began kicking their stalls and trying to escape.

Emily led the group to one stall in particular. "This is Tornado Warning."

Jupiter stepped forward. Emily was frightened Tornado might bite or try to attack him, but the stallion was calmed in his presence.

"So, my young friend, you are the one who caused all this mischief."

Tornado neighed softly and invited more attention.

Jupiter and his brothers walked from stall to stall, talking to and touching all the clones. Their touch tamed the wild stallions.

Neptune raised his hands in the air. "Open!"

The stall doors flew open, releasing the winged stallions. Emily was stunned to see there was no fighting among the clones. They all pressed in close to be with her and the Olympians.

The final spot on their tour of the CRU facility was the medical center. Two Nirad guards were keeping watch over their patient.

"Tom!" Alexis sprang over to his bed and leaned over the ex–CRU agent and kissed his face.

Agent T was making strange, excited sounds as his grateful eyes filled with tears at the sight of Alexis.

The Sphinx looked anxiously to Emily. "Heal him!"

Emily felt her throat tighten. "I've tried. It won't work."

"It cannot work," Jupiter explained. "He is a human who has never consumed ambrosia. The Flame's powers cannot touch him."

"Give him some ambrosia," Alexis demanded. "Then Emily can heal him."

Jupiter looked at all the strange devices attached to Agent T. "Do these machines keep him alive?"

Emily nodded. "His spine is destroyed. He is

paralyzed and can't breathe or eat on his own."

Jupiter dropped his head and placed his hand on the Sphinx's shoulder. "I am sorry, Alexis. The damage is too great. Ambrosia will not heal him sufficiently. It would only keep him alive but in this state. That would be too cruel."

"Please, Jupiter," Alexis begged. "I have never asked anything of you in all my life. But I ask you this. Please let me have my Tom. I love him."

"But he will not survive the journey to Olympus away from these machines. His life in this form is over."

"Then change his form," Alexis pleaded desperately. "You have the power. Turn him into something that does not require a moving body to survive. A rock, a jewel, a tree? Anything, but let him live."

Jupiter approached the side of the bed. He looked down on Agent T thoughtfully. "I am sorry that I do not have the power to restore your body. But I can change it. I will do this only if you wish me to. It must be your choice."

Alexis was still standing up beside the bed. "Please, Tom, let him do it. You can come back to Olympus with me. We can be together. Tell him you wish this."

Emily watched Agent T blinking his eyes. Jupiter reached forward and placed his hand on the man's forehead. The leader of Olympus closed his eyes. Finally he nodded.

"Alexis, everyone, stand back."

Emily stood back with her father as Jupiter unhooked Agent T from the equipment keeping him alive. When his breathing tube was removed, the agent's eyes flashed open as he started to suffocate.

"Jupiter, please!" Alexis begged.

The leader of Olympus placed both his hands on Agent T's chest. He closed his eyes again and lifted his head. The air around Jupiter snapped and sparkled and seemed to be filled with stars. There was a blinding flash and a loud snap. In a moment it was over, and when the light faded, the bed was empty.

Alexis's frightened eyes looked desperately at Jupiter. "What has happened? Where is my Tom?"

Jupiter looked at the Sphinx and smiled gently. "I suggest you return to Olympus and see for yourself. He is at your home, waiting for you."

"How will I know him?"

Jupiter smiled gently. "You will know him."

Alexis didn't pause to say good-bye. She flashed past Emily and was a blur flying down the empty corridor.

Emily looked at Jupiter. "What did you do to him?"

"I asked the man what he wanted. He told me he wanted to live with Alexis. Then I asked him what he would choose to be if he could not move."

"What did he say?"

Jupiter smiled. "A willow tree. He told me his happiest childhood memories were of a tree house he had in the giant willow in his back garden. The willow is soft and forgiving and moves gently in the breeze."

"Agent T is a willow tree?"

Jupiter nodded. "A very happy one. I am sure when we return to Olympus we will find Alexis sitting quite contentedly in her Tom-tree."

With every last living being out of the facility and on the surface, Jupiter looked at Emily. "This is yours now. Proceed."

Emily stood before the squat buildings. Her mind

played back all the horrors that had occurred in this facility. Suddenly Agent PS darted away from the guards and ran up to her. "Please, Emily, don't do it. Don't destroy all that knowledge!"

Emily looked at him and felt her anger growing. "Knowledge? Is that what you call this?"

"Yes, knowledge," the agent said. "There must always be some casualties in human development. But we could achieve something amazing here. We could change the world."

"Ah, yes," Jupiter said as he cast his eyes on the CRU agent. "Everything is permissible if it is for human development. Is that what you are telling me?"

The agent suddenly realized to whom he was talking. But instead of offering respect, he straightened his back and let his arrogance show. "Yes, Jupiter, human development! The only reason you're here is because you're frightened that one day we'll be as powerful as you—and you hate that."

Jupiter shook his head sadly. "No, we are here because you stole something precious from us, and we have now taken it back." He sighed. "I have not been back to your world for a very long time. It saddens me greatly to see that your knowledge has far exceeded your wisdom to use it wisely. You are as hard and unforgiving as a Prometheus Oak."

Suddenly a sparkle came into his eyes. "Prometheus Oak. Of course, how fitting." He concentrated on Emily. "Flame, let loose your power."

Everyone but Pegasus moved back from Emily as she raised her hands in the air. She closed her eyes and summoned not only the power of the Flame, but all her other powers as well. She envisioned every room and every corridor of every level of the wretched facility. She thought of the unfortunates who had suffered and died there in the name of science. She grieved for the clones left in the tubes that they could not save.

When she was ready, Emily unleashed her full powers. Laserlike flames rushed from her hands and burned their way into the buildings. But they did not stop. From deep beneath the ground came rumblings and loud explosions. Emily felt the power of her collected tears on her hospital gown and sheets explode and add to the firestorm.

The ground started to shake like a powerful earthquake. The sounds of the groaning and crumbling facility filled the air and grew in intensity until they became almost unbearable. In one final push, Emily envisioned it all gone!

An instant later the sounds stopped. The dust settled, and where once stood the CRU facility was nothing but an impossibly large crater.

"Well done!" Jupiter cheered as he and his brothers clapped their hands.

Pegasus nickered beside her and pressed his face to hers.

"It's over, Pegs," Emily sighed tiredly as she pressed her head to his.

"Not quite," Jupiter said. "Pegasus, if you look around us, you will see the remnants of a dead lake. I believe it is time for water and life to return to it. Would you oblige me?"

Emily looked at Pegasus and frowned. "What does he mean?"

Pegasus whinnied excitedly. He reared slightly and flapped his wings. The stallion galloped away from the group until he was a safe distance away.

"Watch this," Paelen said, coming up to her. "I have not seen Pegasus do this in a very long time."

"Do what?" Joel asked.

"Use his powers," Paelen explained.

"Pegasus has powers?" Emily asked.

"Just watch," Paelen said.

Far from where they stood, Pegasus opened his wings fully. He glowed so bright, Emily could barely see his outline in the blazing light. The stallion reared up as high as he could and came crashing back down to earth with a mighty blow.

Once again the ground rumbled and quaked. Pegasus moved farther away and repeated the action. He did this several more times around the lake bed before he returned to Emily. They stood together and watched as the cracked, dry surface of the dead lake suddenly burst open and fresh water started to rise.

It filled the whole of Groom Lake and seeped into the crater Emily had created with the destruction of the CRU facility.

Over the roar of the rushing water, Jupiter caught hold of Agent PS by the scruff of the neck and hauled him over to the edge. "What lake would be complete without shady trees?"

He released the CRU agent and pointed his hands at him. "Prometheus Oak!"

Agent PS started to run from Jupiter, but just a few steps away he slowed down. He turned back and looked at Emily. His eyes were filled with defiant hatred as his body changed and stretched out. He started to scream. Suddenly his black suit tore away and branches sprang from his body.

Emily watched in shock as Agent PS was turned into a giant oak tree.

"Ouch!" Paelen said. "Jupiter really is angry."

"What do you mean?" Joel asked. "Being turned into a tree is letting him off easy. He did the same to Agent T. He's now a willow tree."

Paelen shook his head. "They are not the same at all. Agent T will never feel pain but can still experience joy. He can think, speak, and live a long and happy life with Alexis. But not Agent PS. Being turned into a Prometheus Oak is living torture. He will remain fully conscious and aware of his previous life. He will feel everything. A snapped branch will cause him to bleed. His bark is like breaking bones, and when the wind blows through his leaves, you will hear him screaming. There is no worse punishment than that."

Emily looked back at the tree that had once been Agent PS. Yet she could feel no pity for him.

Moments later Jupiter approached the gathered scientists, military personnel, and CRU agents. "You have offended all Olympus with your actions here. But I will not kill you. Instead I will give you a thousand years to consider your actions."

Once again the leader of Olympus raised his hands in the air and shouted, "Prometheus Oak!"

Agent R and the other people of Area 51 scattered and tried to run away from the punishment raining down on them. But all they succeeded in doing was spreading out enough to create the most beautiful leafy forest around the shores of the new Groom Lake.

38

EMILY AND PEGASUS STOOD IN THE COOL shade of the tree formerly known as Agent PS. Those she cared for most were with her, including Prince Toban and Tirk. They gathered together to watch the last of the Nirad soldiers enter the Solar Stream and head first to Olympus and then on to the Nirad world. Before they entered the Solar Stream A-Two and A-Three paused and waved excitedly at them. "See—you—soon!"

When they were gone, Jupiter sealed the entrance to the portal as if it had never been there.

Frankie was standing beside Joel with a big grin still painted on his face. "That was totally awesome. I knew you were aliens!"

"We're not aliens!" Joel cried. But then he looked into the boy's hopeful face. "Okay, maybe we are."

"What now?" Earl said. "Tom is gone, now you guys are going. What am I supposed to do?"

Emily frowned. She thought it was understood. "What do you mean? You're coming with us."

"Really?" Earl cried, excited. "I can finally see Olympus for myself!"

Emily's father, Diana, and Jupiter came forward. "Of course you may return with us to Olympus. It is not safe to leave you here in this desert. But you may come only for a visit," Jupiter said. "After everything the CRU have done here, I must ask if you would return to Earth to keep watch for us. We will ensure your safe return, and you will have more wealth than you could ever spend. I promise you, no one will ever find you. But we need you here working for us."

"You betcha!" Earl said excitedly. "I always wanted to see Olympus, but this is still my home. I could never leave it for long. I'd be happy to keep an eye open for y'all." His eyes settled on little Frankie, and he held out his hand. "How 'bout it, short stuff?

You fancy being an Olympian spy with me?"

Frankie grinned. "Awesome!" he said, and took Earl's outstretched hand. He turned and looked back at Jupiter. "Can I still visit Paelen, Joel, and Chrysler?"

Jupiter nodded. "Of course."

The leader of Olympus mopped his brow. "I had forgotten how hot this world can be. I think it is time we headed back."

Diana had removed most of her armor and stood in a light tunic. "Indeed, Father. I should like a nice long swim when we get back to Olympus."

"I'm with you," Emily's father agreed.

In the distance, Pluto and Neptune were climbing into their chariots. They waved at Jupiter and then launched into the air. In moments they entered the Solar Stream and were gone.

Jupiter offered a ride in his chariot to Prince Toban and Tirk. As the two Nirads approached him, he looked at little Frankie. "Would you like to ride with me?"

The boy's eyes were huge. "Cool!"

Little Frankie bounced away with Jupiter and the Nirads.

"There's room in our chariot for you," Emily's father said to Earl.

"You don't gotta ask me twice," Earl responded.

Diana and Steve stepped up to Emily, Joel, and Paelen.

"Well, you did it," Emily's father said. "I am so proud of you!"

Emily embraced him. "I'm just glad it's over."

She clung to him and put her head against his chest, listening to the strong beating of his heart. He was alive. He was human and he was wonderful. But after everything she'd learned about herself, Emily grieved to know she was not. The Emily who had been his daughter was gone. Somehow, she was just an echo of her former self. She still felt the same, but deep inside, she knew she wasn't. It would take time to figure out exactly what she was and to learn to accept it. But as long as she had her father, Joel, Pegasus, and Paelen to help her, she knew she would be all right. Whatever she was, Emily was still Emily.

"I'm proud of all of you." Steve looked over to Joel and Paelen when he released Emily. "C'mon, everyone, let's go home."

Emily stood with her best friends as her father and Diana made their way back to their chariot. She felt Joel slip his hand into hers. He smiled at her, and his brown eyes sparkled. "I don't know about you, but I could sure use a swim about now."

Emily grinned up at Joel and then over at Paelen. He was wearing his winged sandals again. "Me too," she agreed. "Last one to Olympus is a rotten egg!"

As Joel dashed over to Chrysaor, Emily climbed up on Pegasus. Paelen launched into the air first, with Joel and Chrysaor close behind.

Emily was in no hurry. She leaned forward and hugged the stallion's neck. It terrified her to think she'd almost lost him.

"I love you, Pegs," she said softly as she held him and gazed out over the beautiful new lake surrounded by tall, leafy trees. There was no hint of the facility that had once stood there. No runways, no buildings. Area 51 was truly gone.

Pegasus looked back at her and neighed softly, sensing the change in her. "It's a long story," she said. "Just promise you'll never leave me, no matter what."

Pegasus nodded and snorted. He entered into a

trot and then a full gallop as he launched himself into the sky. In the distance, they could see squadrons of jet fighters heading their way. The CRU was going to fight back.

"It's over," she said to them. She clung to Pegasus as the winged stallion gained more speed and entered the Solar Stream.

ABOUT THE AUTHOR

Kate O'Hearn was born in Canada and raised in New York City, and has traveled all over the United States. She currently resides in England. Kate is the author of four novels about Pegasus and Emily. In addition, she is the author of the Shadow of the Dragon series and a new series about a Valkyrie. Visit her at kateohearn.com.

ACKNOWLEDGMENTS

I know I always say it, but it is still true. Books are a collaborative effort—created by a bunch of people, both seen and unseen. There are my amazing agents V and Laura, and then my fabulous editors Anne and Naomi. But then there are loads of people involved with the birth of this book that I offer my heartfelt thanks to—even if I can't name you all here.

In the case of *The New Olympians*, I would also like to offer my personal thanks to my dearest friends Debbie and Mark Obarka for introducing me to the Fremont Street Experience in Las Vegas. Many thanks also to Janine McCullough of the Golden Eagle Farm in Ramona, California, who showed me how an ethical horse farm should be run. Then, of course, there are the kind folks at the Little A'Le'Inn outside the real Area 51 in the Nevada desert, who helped so much, even if they'll never know how. Thank you and Nanoo, Nanoo!

Beyond my family, who are the support I need to keep Pegasus flying, I would also like to thank

Monica Percy and Laura O'Brian for writing such great riddles for this book. You guys are the best!

And finally, I would like to thank you, my dearest reader, for taking Pegasus into your hearts and for showing me that you love him as much as I do. I am putting all my hopes on you to create a better future for horses and animals than my generation has done. Please show them you care.

THE ADVENTURE CONTINUES IN BOOK 4:

Origins of Olympus

THE LIGHT OF THE SOLAR STREAM PULSED *and flashed as she tore through it as fast as she could. She had to get home! But the faster she traveled, the longer the journey became. Obstacles blocked her path, slowed her down. Other worlds called to her. Unseen hands reached for her and pulled her down.*

"No!" she screamed. "I have to go back before it's too late. Leave me alone!"

Breaking free of their grip, she raced through the Solar Stream until at last she made it home. She arrived in the temple and hurtled along its long stone corridors. Her heart roared and her terror grew as she felt the others gathering far from the temple. They were drawing together and merging their powers. She had to reach them. Join them. She couldn't be left behind.

She emerged from the stone temple and dashed into the dense green jungle. She put on more speed as she moved along paths as old as time itself, rushing past the great statues of her people and dodging around the massive trees. This was her home. Her sanctuary. Her world. But they were all about to leave it. To go on.

They had said they would try to wait for her. But when the stars aligned, they would go with or without her.

"Please don't let me be too late . . . ," she begged. "Please! Please!"

Emily's cry woke her from the terrifying dream, and she felt a warm tongue on her cheek. She looked up and saw the magnificent winged stallion, Pegasus, standing at the side of her bed. He was glowing brightly as he stared down at her and nickered softly.

Emily's face was hot and flushed, and she was panting heavily as if she'd been in a race. "I'm okay, Pegs," she said quietly as she looked up into his large, concerned eyes.

Pegasus nickered again and pressed his face to hers.

"Em!" Her father raced into the room. "What's wrong? You were shouting and crying."

She was shaking all over. "It's just a dream," she said. "Ever since we got back from Area 51, I've had the same dream over and over again. It's like I'm someone else and trying to get home before something huge happens. I'm so scared that I'm going to miss it. But as I go through the Solar Stream, things I can't see block my path and something tries to hold me back." She looked up into his caring face. "What does it mean?"

Emily's father sat on the bed and pulled her into a tight embrace. "I don't know, honey. They say dreams come from our subconscious as it tries to work something out."

"Like what?" Emily asked.

"I'm not sure. But you've been through so much lately. Maybe your mind is trying to digest everything that's happened. Look at how our life has changed. We live here on Olympus, and you've got so many powers now. I know they scare you. Maybe that's the cause of your nightmares."

"Not night*mares*," Emily corrected. "Night*mare*.

It's always the same. I'm desperate to get home to some kind of gathering. But I always wake up before I make it there."

"Home?" he asked. "You mean New York? Do you want to go back?"

Emily frowned and shook her head. "No, not New York, and it's not Olympus, either. It's a strange place with jungle all around. I'm in a complicated stone temple surrounded by tall statues."

Pegasus snorted loudly and shook his head. He stepped closer to Emily and stared at her intently. As she gazed deep into his warm brown eyes, Emily saw a vision of a jungle world filled with tall stone statues. "That's the jungle! Have you been dreaming of it too?"

The strong white stallion shook his head again, pawed the floor, and whinnied several times. He turned his head to the door. Then he nudged Emily's father and turned to the door again.

"What is it?" her father asked. "What are you trying to tell me?"

"He wants you to go somewhere," Emily explained. "This time of night?"

After several more failed attempts to get Emily and her father to understand, Pegasus gave up and left the room. He returned moments later with a very sleepy Paelen and Joel.

"You okay, Em?" Joel asked groggily as he stepped closer to her bed. He was just wearing pajama bottoms, so she could see where his new silver arm joined his broad body. It looked exactly like the old one that Vulcan had created for him after he lost his real arm in the fight against the Gorgons. She was amazed at how quickly Vulcan had been able to build it after the Central Research Unit scientists at Area 51 had surgically removed the old one.

Emily nodded. "I'm fine. I've had that dream again. But then Pegs showed me a place exactly like the one in my dream."

Paelen yawned loudly. His hair stood at all angles and his nightclothes were twisted and unkempt. He looked at Pegasus and frowned. "You woke me because Emily was having a dream? What about me? I was having my own amazing dream featuring several water nymphs."

Pegasus whinnied and shoved Paelen.

"What!" Paelen cried. "Am I not allowed to dream?"

"Paelen, please," Emily said. "Pegasus is trying to tell me something, but I can't understand him. I think it's important."

Paelen concentrated on Pegasus. "What is it?"

The stallion nickered several times and shook his head yet again.

"This is very strange," Paelen said. "Pegasus says the world you have been describing from your dream is the world you sent him to when you were shot at the CRU facility in the Nevada desert."

Emily frowned. "How? I've never been there or even heard about it. Why would I dream of a place I've never seen? And why is it always the same dream?"

Pegasus pawed the floor and whinnied softly. Paelen looked shocked. "Really? Why have we not heard about this when it concerns Emily?"

"What concerns me?" Emily asked.

"Apparently, after we returned from Earth, Jupiter had some of his people go to the jungle world to explore it. He was curious why your powers would send things there."

Emily looked at Pegasus. "You knew about this and didn't tell me?"

The stallion dropped his head, looking very guilty.

"Pegasus only just found out. Jupiter told him to say nothing, as he feared it might upset you. After everything that happened on Earth, he wanted you to spend some quiet time on Olympus and not worry about the jungle world," Paelen explained.

"Not telling me is what upsets me!" Emily replied angrily. "Jupiter promised we were going to figure that out together. He shouldn't have sent people there without me."

Emily's father nodded. "I agree. There must be some reason why Emily's powers sent you and Alexis, the Sphinx, there. We have a right to be involved in the investigation. I'll have a chat with Jupiter in the morning and find out what's going on."

"I'm coming with you," Emily said.

"Me too," Joel added.

"And me," Paelen said.

Pegasus nickered and nodded. Emily didn't need Paelen to translate. The stallion would be there too.

Emily couldn't go back to sleep. After her latest dream she didn't really want to. Instead she and Pegasus slipped silently out of the palace and flew high in the night skies over Olympus.

The stars were shining brightly overhead and cast enough light for them to see. Emily looked down on the night dwellers as they went about their silent lives, working, living, and playing only by starlight.

Pegasus landed on their private silver beach surrounding the calm lake. No wind disturbed its surface, and it was like a giant mirror reflecting the stars from above.

Emily climbed off Pegasus and walked knee deep into the cool, still water. She no longer needed her leg brace, as her powers had healed her damaged leg back at Area 51. The revelations from her time at the CRU facility still troubled her. She had only confided in Pegasus about what the scientists had said about her. She hadn't even told Joel or Paelen, for fear of what they might think of her.

Was she really not alive? They claimed she didn't have physical matter the same way all living organisms did—even the Olympians. And although she had blood and a heart that pumped it around her body, they weren't needed to keep her going. The scientists believed it was all there because Emily thought it should be.

In her quiet moments, or when she was alone with Pegasus, Emily asked herself the same question time and time again. "What am I?" But despite his love and support of her, Pegasus had no answers.

"It's so beautiful here." She sighed as Pegasus joined her in the water. "Sometimes I wish we could stay here forever and not worry about all the other stuff. Just you and me and this silver lake."

Pegasus pressed his head to hers.

She looked up into his beautiful face and combed his long mane away from his eyes. "Something's changed. I can feel it. I've changed, and it really scares me." Emily lifted her leg. "Look, there's no trace of the scar. All I had to do was imagine it gone, and it was gone. I sent you and Alexis away without really thinking about it, and I destroyed the CRU facility at Area 51 without any effort at all. Doesn't it scare you that I can do all that?"

Pegasus snorted and shook his head, then pressed closer to her.

"Thanks, Pegs," she said gratefully. "But it scares me. What if I make a mistake? What if I really hurt someone? I just don't have enough control."

Pegasus and Emily walked along the silver beach all night. When the dawn started to rise over Olympus, she climbed on the stallion's back and they made their way home to Jupiter's palace.

After flying through her large open window, Emily barely had time to change into her tunic before there was a knock on her door.

"You ready to see Jupiter?" Joel asked as he entered her room.

The winged boar, Chrysaor, was standing beside Joel and nudged his hairy snout into Emily's hand for a pat.

"I'm ready," Emily said as she gave the boar a good-morning kiss on the head.

They met her father in the corridor and made their way along the wide marble steps leading down to the main floor.

As always, there was a lot of activity in the palace

as people came and went about their business. Bouquets of unusual, fragrant flowers were being delivered, and the statues that adorned the palace were being cleaned by a group of young male satyrs—half goat, half boy—who saw Emily and Pegasus and greeted them excitedly.

Cupid was at the base of the stairs, chatting with a young centaur. When he saw Emily, his face lit up with a bright smile.

"Oh, great," Joel muttered to Paelen. "Just what we need, Cupid here to cause trouble."

"Good morning, Flame," Cupid said brightly as he approached Emily and bowed elegantly. He reached for her hand and gave it a light kiss.

"Hi, Cupid. What brings you to the palace?"

"My mother is in a meeting with Jupiter this morning," the winged Olympian explained. "I came along hoping to see your lovely face."

Emily blushed at the compliment. Though her crush on him was long over, he still managed to charm her in an instant.

Beside her, Joel made an exaggerated gagging sound. "Give me a break, Cupid."

Paelen was standing on Emily's left. From the corner of her eye she watched him use his Olympian powers to stretch his arm. While Cupid was distracted with Emily, Paelen's elongated arm slid past her back and then Joel's until it looped around, unseen, behind Cupid.

Emily poked her elbow in Paelen's side, but his hand had already reached Cupid and caught hold of a handful of feathers from Cupid's wings. Paelen gave a mighty pull.

"Ouch!" Cupid cried as his wings flashed open. He spun around to see who had attacked him and didn't see Paelen's arm retracting. What he did see were several feathers falling to the floor.

"Paelen!" Cupid accused. "I know it was you."

Joel and Paelen were lost in fits of laughter at the rage on Cupid's face. As the Olympian charged, Paelen called down to the winged sandals at his feet. They had been a gift from Mercury, the messenger of Olympus, and now served only him. "Take me up!"

The tiny wings flashed acknowledgment and then lifted Paelen high in the air over Cupid's head.

"Come down here, you coward," Cupid roared,

jumping up and trying to reach him. "You know I can't fly indoors!"

"Come and get me, pretty boy," Paelen teased as he dropped Cupid's feathers one by one.

Emily's father stifled a grin and raised his hands to calm the room. "That's enough, boys. We've got work to do."

"But you saw what he did to me!" Cupid cried. "He pulled out my feathers."

"I did not," Paelen teased, still hovering overhead and releasing feathers.

Footsteps on the stairs behind them stopped the argument.

"Good morning, Emily, Pegasus, and everyone," Juno called as she descended the steps. Beside her, her pet peacock fanned open its large tail, and a hundred eyes blinked at them in unison.

She looked up at Paelen. "Have I missed something here?"

Paelen ordered his sandals to land. He bowed before Juno.

"No," Emily's father said, also bowing. "The boys were just having a little fun."

Emily bowed respectfully to the wife of Jupiter. "Good morning, Juno," she said. "Do you think it's possible for us to see Jupiter sometime this morning?"

Juno was much younger looking than Jupiter and stunningly beautiful. She wore a long white gown of flowing silk that had thousands of pearls woven into the fabric. There was a delicate gold belt tied at her waist, and fine sandals adorned her feet. Her eyes were dark chocolate brown, the same color as her hair, which was elegantly styled high on her head and dressed in a ring of pearls.

"Of course, child," Juno said as she led them across the foyer and into one of the large side chambers. "He is in here with his council."

Emily's father stepped forward. "If he is with the council, we don't want to disturb him."

Juno paused and smiled radiantly at Emily's father. "My husband will always have time for you, Steve. You need not ask." She pushed open the double doors to the council chamber and invited everyone in.

Behind Emily, Paelen and Joel were still chuckling at Cupid as the winged Olympian followed, muttering threats.

Jupiter was standing with his two brothers, Pluto and Neptune, as well as an odd assortment of councillors. Among them was the Big Three's half brother, Chiron, the centaur and closest adviser to Jupiter. There was also a giant—so massive in size that his head nearly touched the ceiling of the tall chamber. Despite their size, the giants in Olympus were some of the gentlest citizens. A one-eyed Cyclops stood beside the giant, talking softly.

Emily looked at the gathering in awe. After all this time in Olympus, she still marveled at the wondrous assortment of mythical creatures that now formed part of her everyday life.

Across the chamber, Diana stood beside her twin brother, Apollo. Vesta was also there, locked in deep conversation with Cupid's mother, Venus. Hercules was standing farther back with his arms crossed over his broad chest, talking to Mars, the head of the war council, and looking very disturbed.

Emily had only seen Mars on two other occasions and had never spoken with him. He was tall, handsome, and muscular like Hercules, but seemed perpetually angry, with a scowl that always darkened his fine features. Yet despite his angry exterior, Mars had many admirers among the women of Olympus and was often seen with Venus. His presence in the council room meant something big was happening.

Paelen stood beside Emily and nudged her lightly. "Vesta is not on the general council; neither is Hercules, Mars, or Venus. I wonder what they are doing here."

"Husband," Juno called as she strode in, "Emily and her family would like a word."

Jupiter looked up, and his face lit with a broad smile. "Of course, of course, come in!"

Since the events at Area 51, where Emily had been forced to challenge Jupiter for the protection of Earth, they had grown closer. It frightened everyone to realize how near they had come to fighting over the fate of the world. They now talked often, and Jupiter, Pluto, and Neptune had become more like beloved grandfathers than the most powerful leaders of Olympus.

"What may I do for you?" Jupiter asked as he put his arm around Emily.

Before anyone could speak, Pegasus started to whinny.

Jupiter's smile faded. "You have been having bad dreams?"

Emily described the recurring dream. As she spoke of the jungle world, the other council members crowded around her. When she finished, Vesta turned to Jupiter. "I believe it is time we showed her what we have found."

"Indeed," Jupiter agreed. He swept his arm wide to include everyone. "All of you, come with me."

Jupiter led them through a second set of doors into an even larger marble chamber. It was filled with artifacts. Strange items sat on tables and on the floor. But it was the large slate chalkboard in the center of the room that immediately caught Emily's attention. The board was filled with strange writing and symbols.

"There are millions of worlds along the Solar Stream," Jupiter began, "though we have only cataloged a small number of them. But recently, thanks to Emily sending both Pegasus and Alexis there, we have discovered a world at the very start of the Solar Stream."

Chiron stepped forward, his horse's hooves clicking on the marble floor. "Until now, we never knew the Solar Stream had a starting point. This is a very exciting time for us. We have much to discover."

"Are you talking about the jungle world?" Emily asked.

"Indeed we are," Jupiter said. "Around this room are just a few of the artifacts we have found there. But among the most interesting was a stone slate mounted on the wall of a large temple."

Jupiter invited Emily forward to get a closer view. "We have transcribed the words from that stone slate here. I've had my best scholars trying to decipher it, but as yet, they have failed."

Emily studied the chalkboard. There was something familiar about the symbols. As she stared at the strange writing, everything seemed to blur and swim before her eyes. Suddenly dizziness overwhelmed her, and she started to stagger back.

Joel was at her side in an instant. He put his arm around her and steadied her. "You okay, Em?"

Emily leaned heavily into him. "I—I'm fine," she said. "It's just that . . ." When she looked back at the chalkboard, she sucked in her breath. "I know this writing!"

"What?" Her father gasped.

Emily approached the board. "I can understand it. All of it." She pointed to each symbol and started to read aloud.

GENTLE TRAVELERS—WELCOME TO XANADU.

WE ASK ONLY THAT YOU VENTURE HERE WITH PEACE IN YOUR HEARTS AND RESPECT IN YOUR MINDS. FOR OURS IS THE OLDEST WORLD AND MUCH BELOVED. YET WE OFFER IT TO YOU AS REFUGE. THAT WHICH IS OURS IS NOW YOURS. BUT BE MINDFUL OF OUR HOME AND HONOR OUR LAWS.

• XANADU MUST BE RESPECTED. IT WILL FEED YOU, IF YOU DO NOT ABUSE IT.

• OUR WAYS ARE THE WAYS OF PEACE. DO NOT BREAK THAT PEACE, OR WE WILL DEFEND OUR HOME.

• ALL LIFE IS PRECIOUS. YOU WILL NOT KILL ANYTHING HERE, OR YOU WILL BE FOREVER CAST OUT.

WE ARE THE XAN, CREATORS OF THE SOLAR STREAM.

GUARDIANS OF THE UNIVERSE.

XANADU IS SANCTUARY.

Emily turned back to Jupiter. The leader of Olympus had his hand over his mouth, and his eyes were the widest she'd ever seen them. He looked at her like he was seeing a ghost.

READ MORE IN

The Origins of Olympus

COMING IN DECEMBER 2014

THE FLAME OF OLYMPUS

Also by Kate O'Hearn

Olympus at War

Pegasus

THE FLAME OF
OLYMPUS

KATE O'HEARN

Aladdin

NEW YORK LONDON TORONTO SYDNEY NEW DELHI

ALADDIN

An imprint of Simon & Schuster Children's Publishing Division
1230 Avenue of the Americas, New York, NY 10020
First Aladdin paperback edition May 2013
Copyright © 2012 by Kate O'Hearn
Originally published in Great Britain in 2011
Published by arrangement with Hachette UK
All rights reserved, including the right of reproduction in whole or in part in any form.
ALADDIN is a trademark of Simon & Schuster, Inc., and related logo
is a registered trademark of Simon & Schuster, Inc.
Also available in an Aladdin hardcover edition.
For information about special discounts for bulk purchases, please contact
Simon & Schuster Special Sales at 1-866-506-1949 or business@simonandschuster.com.
The Simon & Schuster Speakers Bureau can bring authors to your live event. For more information
or to book an event contact the Simon & Schuster Speakers Bureau at 1-866-248-3049
or visit our website at www.simonspeakers.com.
Designed by Karin Paprocki
The text of this book was set in Adobe Garamond.
Manufactured in the United States of America 0815 OFF
10 9
The Library of Congress has cataloged the hardcover edition as follows:
Kate O'Hearn.
[Pegasus and the flame of Olympus]
Pegasus / by Kate O'Hearn. — First Aladdin hardcover ed.
p. cm.
Summary: Reborn as the Flame, thirteen-year-old Emily has saved Olympus from destruction,
but when the gruesome Nirads begin a new invasion, Emily and her friends become entangled in
the conflict as old grudges are unearthed and new enemies are discovered.
ISBN 978-1-4424-4409-6 (hc)
[1. Pegasus (Greek mythology)—Fiction. 2. Diana (Roman deity)—Fiction.
3. Monsters—Fiction. 4. Mythology, Roman—Fiction. 5. Fantasy.] 1. Title.
PZ7.O4137Peg 2012
[Fic] dc23
2011052026
ISBN 978-1-4424-4410-2 (pbk)
ISBN 978-1-4424-4411-9 (eBook)

As always, without the support and love of my family,
my wonderful editors Anne and Naomi, and my fantastic agent, V,
this book would never have seen the light of day.
Thanks, guys; you're the best. (OTB will never die.)

I would also like to dedicate this book to all the horses everywhere,
especially those that suffer under poor working conditions
and horrific abuse. I wish Pegasus would come to rescue you all.
Without him, it will be up to us to make your lives better.

My dearest reader, please help whenever and wherever you can.
Abused horses everywhere await your love and assistance.

Prologue

WAR CAME TO OLYMPUS.

There was no warning. No clues that an unknown enemy was building an army against them; an army whose only goal was complete destruction. One moment there was peace, the next they were fighting for their very existence. It was bloody, brutal, and totally unexpected.

But for one Olympian, it was the perfect opportunity to fulfill a dream.

Paelen ducked behind a marble pillar and watched the best Olympian warriors gathering to take on the invaders. Jupiter was leading the attack with his thunder and lightning bolts in hand. His wife, Juno, stood on his left, grave-faced and ready. On his right,

Hercules was looking strong and prepared, as were Apollo and his twin sister Diana with her bow. Mars was there, and Vulcan with his armory full of weapons. Standing behind them in his winged sandals and helmet was Mercury, the messenger of Olympus. All preparing to fight.

Paelen's gaze trailed over to Pegasus. The stallion's eyes blazed and wings quivered as his golden hooves pounded the ground in anticipation of the upcoming battle. Farther back gathered more Olympians, all there to defend their home.

But Paelen had no intention of fighting. He wasn't a warrior. He was a thief with plans of his own, which didn't include getting killed in a battle they couldn't possibly win. War was everyone else's problem. He was too busy concentrating on how best to profit from it. With the defenders occupied in the struggle against the Nirads, a thief would be free to enter the palace of Jupiter and take whatever he wanted.

But Jupiter's treasures weren't what interested Paelen. What he desired most was the shiny gold bridle worn by Pegasus.

Everyone in Olympus knew the bridle was the

greatest treasure of all. It alone held the key to possessing the powerful winged stallion. With Pegasus under his control, Paelen could go anywhere he wanted and take whatever caught his eye. No one would be able to stand against him. This was the true prize, not the silly jewels or gold coins that could be found in the abandoned palace.

As Jupiter called his fighters forward, Paelen crept closer to listen to the god's desperate speech.

"My children," he said gravely. "We are in our darkest hour. At no other time in history have we faced such terrible danger. The Nirad fighters have breached our borders. Even now they are making for the Flame of Olympus. If they succeed in extinguishing it, all our powers, all we have ever known, will be lost. We must stop them. That Flame is our very existence. We cannot let them succeed. If we do not make our stand against them now, then everything we have known will be destroyed."

Paelen listened to the murmurs of the crowd and felt the tension growing. His eyes were still locked on Pegasus. The stallion shook his head and snorted, causing his golden bridle to give out an enchanting tinkle that no other forged gold could ever make.

Hearing the bridle's song made Paelen's fingers itch to reach out and snatch it from the stallion. But he controlled himself. This wasn't the time to make a move. His dark eyes were drawn back to their desperate leader.

"We who never die, now face our destruction," continued Jupiter. "But it is not only our world we must defend. All the other worlds we guard will fall if the Nirads defeat us. We fight for them!"

Jupiter raised his lightning bolts in the air, and their ferocious booms echoed throughout all Olympus. "Will you join me?" he cried. "Will you rise against these invaders and drive them back to where they came from?"

Paelen's eyes grew wide at the sight of all the Olympians raising their arms to Jupiter. Pegasus reared on his hind legs and opened his wings in salute. Battle cries filled the air.

"For Olympus!" howled Jupiter as he turned and led his warriors into battle.

EMILY PUT HER HAND ON THE WINDOW AND felt the glass shaking from the heavy peals of thunder cracking overhead.

All day the radio had been reporting on the unexpected violent storms raging up and down the East Coast of the United States. Where Emily lived, in the heart of New York City, the storm was at its worst. Sitting alone in the apartment she shared with her policeman father, she never imagined that a simple thunderstorm could be *this* bad.

She clutched her cell phone and felt guilty for lying to her father. He'd just called to check on her.

"All the police have been summoned into work, honey," he explained. "We're doing double and triple shifts. The city's a madhouse because of the weather, and they need everyone on duty. Do me a favor, will you? Keep away from the windows. There are lightning strikes all over the city, and our top-floor apartment is at particular risk."

Yet, despite his warning and her promise to keep away, Emily sat in the large window seat and watched the raging storm. This had always been her mother's favorite spot. She used to call it her "perch": her special place to sit and watch the world moving around twenty stories below. Since her mother's death, Emily found herself sitting there more and more often, as though it could somehow bring her closer to her mother.

But not only that; from this vantage point Emily could see the top of the Empire State Building. Her father had once told her that the building itself worked as a giant lightning rod to protect the other buildings around it. But as more and more forked lightning struck its tall antenna, she wondered how much more it could take.

Emily hugged her knees to her chest to keep from trembling. She'd never been frightened of thunder when her mother was alive. Somehow they'd always found ways of making foul weather fun and exciting. But now, all alone with her father at work, Emily felt her mother's loss as acutely as the day she died.

"I wish you were here, Mom," she whispered sadly as she gazed out the window. Emily's eyes filled with tears that trickled down her cheeks.

Suddenly there was an ever-louder peal of thunder and brilliant flash of lightning. It struck the Empire State so hard, the antenna at the top of the building exploded in a flash of electrical sparks and flying debris.

Emily could hardly believe what she had just witnessed. She wiped the tears from her blurred eyes as all the lights in the tall building blinked out. Immediately after, the lights in buildings around it went out. The darkness spread like a grape-juice stain on the carpet, as the city was hit with a blackout.

Emily followed the progression of the blackout as she peered up Broadway. Block after block was going dark. Even the street- and traffic lights were out. It wasn't long before the power outage reached her block, plunging her apartment building into darkness. She leaned farther against the glass and tried to see where the blackout ended. It didn't. The whole city was in darkness.

She jumped as her cell burst to life. With trembling hands, she flipped it open and read her father's name on the small view screen.

"Dad," she cried. "You won't believe what just happened! The top of the Empire State just blew up! Lightning hit it and it exploded. Pieces went flying everywhere!"

"I just heard," her father said anxiously. "Are you all right? Did anything hit our building?"

"No, everything's fine," Emily replied, trying to hide the fact that she was far from fine. She was actually starting to get very frightened. "But the power's gone out. From what I can see, it's dark all over the city."

Emily heard another voice in the background. Her father cursed before speaking to her again.

"We're getting reports that the blackout has spread to all the boroughs and is hitting New Jersey. This is a big one, Em. And from what I've just been told, it's not going to be fixed anytime soon. I need you to go into the bathroom and fill the tub with water. Then fill whatever you can in the kitchen. We don't know how long this is going to last, and we'll need that water."

"I will," she promised. Then, before she could stop herself, Emily asked weakly, "Dad, when are you coming home?"

"I don't know, honey," he answered. "Hopefully soon. Look, do you want me to call Aunt Maureen and ask her to come over and stay with you?"

Emily loved her aunt, but she didn't want to sound like a baby. She was old enough to take care of herself. "No thanks, Dad, I'm fine."

"You're sure?" her father asked. "I bet she could use the company."

"Yeah, I'm sure," Emily said. "The storm's just got me a bit freaked. But I've got lots to do here. Besides, it's too dangerous for Maureen to come over in all this and then have to climb twenty flights of stairs. Really, I'm fine."

There was a hesitation in her father's voice before he said, "All right. But if you need me or anything at all, I'm just a phone call away. Understand?"

"I do. Thanks, Dad," Emily said. "Now I'd better go before the water shuts down."

Emily ended the call and used the light from her cell-phone screen to guide her into the kitchen. She quickly found the emergency flashlight and crossed to the bathroom.

This was the standard operating procedure for blackouts. Fill the bathtub and every other container with water. One of the downsides of living in a tall building during a blackout was the pumps sending water up to the apartments soon stopped. If they didn't store all the water they could, they would quickly find themselves in a lot of trouble.

She began to fill the bathtub, and then the pots and pans in the kitchen. Just as she finished filling the last big soup pot, the pressure behind the water flow started to weaken. It wouldn't be long before it stopped completely.

"Well, it's better than nothing," she sighed aloud as she shut off all the faucets.

While she worked, Emily had managed to forget about the storm for a few minutes. But with the water off, the sound of the rumbling thunder and police and fire sirens from the city were the only sounds in the apartment.

Just outside the bathroom window, Emily saw another burst of lightning and heard more thunder. The lightning was so bright it left her seeing flashes, even after she closed her eyes. There was no pause between the light and sound, which meant this latest strike was very close.

As the thunder rumbled angrily, Emily moved away from the window. This time she would follow her father's advice and stay well clear of all the windows. The storm was directly overhead—and getting worse by the minute.

PAELEN STARED IN SHOCK AT THE DESTRUC-
tion around him. He had never seen anything like it
before. The palace lay in ruins, as did every other
building around it.

He had tried to keep up with the defenders, but
they had left him behind. Now, in the far distance, he
heard the constant booming of Jupiter's thunderbolts
and saw the flashes of lightning in the sky. The violent
battle was raging, but far from this area of devastation.

Paelen's heart lurched as he saw Mercury on the
ground. The messenger was lying on his side, a spear
sticking out of his chest. Blood matted his fair hair,
and his face was covered with bruises. Paelen bent
down to see if he was still alive.

Mercury weakly opened his pale blue eyes. "Paelen," he gasped, "Is it over? Have they extinguished the Flame?"

Paelen wondered if he should call for help. But there was no one left to call. From what he could see, everyone around him was either dead or dying. "I believe it is still lit. I saw the others heading toward the temple."

"We must stop the Nirads!" Mercury reached for Paelen's arm and tried to rise. "Help me up."

Paelen helped Mercury get to his feet. As he stood, the messenger pulled the spear from his chest. His wound opened and the bleeding increased. His legs gave out, and he crumpled weakly back to the ground.

"The war is over for me. I am finished," Mercury gasped.

"No, you are wrong," Paelen said fearfully as he knelt beside the messenger and cradled him in his lap. "Mercury, you must get up."

The messenger shook his head. "It is too late—"

He started to cough. Blood pooled in the corners of his mouth. "Listen to me, Paelen," he panted. "You must join the fight. The Nirads must not extinguish the Flame."

"Me? Fight?" Paelen repeated. He shook his head. "I cannot. Look at me, Mercury. I have no real powers of my own. I am not big and strong like Hercules, and I cannot fight like Apollo. I do not know how to use weapons and I am not fast like you. All I am is a thief. My only skill is to stretch my body to escape prisons and squeeze into tight spaces. And you know how I hate doing that, because it hurts too much. I am a coward—nothing more."

Mercury reached for Paelen's hand and drew him closer. "Listen to me, Paelen. I know you are still very young," he gasped. "And I know you are not as big as the rest of us or as strong. But you are clever and much braver than you think. It lies in you to make a difference."

Again Paelen shook his head. "You are asking too much of me! I am not the person you think I am. I am nothing."

Mercury squeezed Paelen's hand as he struggled to speak. "You are special, Paelen. This may be the only chance you will ever have to prove it. I know you have never considered yourself a true Olympian. But you are one—and you carry it within you to be great.

This is the time to join your people and defend your home. Show me, Paelen." Mercury coughed. "Show all of us what you can do."

"But I—I—," Paelen stammered.

"Please," Mercury begged. "Help us."

The approaching battle cry of rampaging Nirads filled the air. It wouldn't be long before they arrived.

"A second wave of fighters is coming," Mercury continued weakly. "You must get away from here. Take my winged sandals. My helmet is lost, but you can still fly with the sandals. Take them and join the fight."

"Your sandals?" Paelen cried. "I cannot! They only work for you!"

Another choking cough came from the fallen messenger. His eyes started to glaze over. "I am dying, Paelen," Mercury said softly. "I give them to you. You are their master now. They will obey your commands."

With a final agonized cry, Mercury closed his eyes and was still.

Paelen couldn't believe the messenger was dead. Somehow the invading Nirads could kill the most powerful Olympians. If Mercury could die, so could everyone else.

He lay Mercury down gently on the ground and wrestled with himself as he thought of the messenger's final words. Part of him still wanted to steal the bridle from Pegasus and flee. But another part of him wondered if Mercury was right. Was there more to him than he realized? Did he really have the courage to join the fight? A thief was all he'd ever been. It was all he knew how to do. He did not have the powers of the other Olympians. If they were being defeated by the Nirads, what chance did he have?

Paelen finally decided escape was the only option. Why should he sacrifice his own life if the war was already lost? If Pegasus hadn't already fallen in battle, this was the time to make his move and capture the stallion.

"I am sorry, Mercury," he said sadly. "But you were wrong. I am not the person you thought I was."

Reaching down, he carefully removed the messenger's winged sandals and put them on his feet, hoping at least that Mercury had been right about them working for him.

Paelen heard roaring and grunting behind him. His eyes flew wide in terror as countless Nirad warriors approached. He'd never seen a Nirad up close before. They were massive. Their skin was gray marble and hard as stone. Each of their four arms waved a weapon in the air, and their eyes blazed with murderous hatred. These creatures had no intention of negotiating. No plans for taking prisoners. All Paelen could see in their bead-black eyes was the desire to kill. Seeing the invaders up close, he understood what everyone was up against. They didn't stand a chance. Olympus was doomed.

He quickly looked back down at the sandals.

"Fly, for Jupiter's sake, fly!" he shouted.

The tiny wings started flapping. He was lifted into the air just as the first Nirad warriors arrived. Panic-stricken, Paelen yelled, "Sandals, go! I do not care where. Just go!"

Mercury's sandals obeyed, and Paelen was carried away from the rampaging Nirads. He heard their angry roars at losing their prey.

With the immediate danger now well behind him, Paelen looked ahead. "Stop!" he ordered.

The sandals obeyed his command, and he hovered in midair. He looked in stunned disbelief at the devastation beneath him. He was sick to see that there wasn't one building left untouched, or one statue unbroken. The Nirads were destroying everything.

"Go," he finally said. "Take me to the Temple of the Flame. I need to find Pegasus."

As the sandals carried him to the temple, the sounds of Jupiter's thunderbolts grew more intense, and bright flashes lit the area. The battle was still raging, but it had now reached the base of the Temple of the Flame.

Paelen saw more fallen Olympians. Yet among the dead and dying, he saw no dead or wounded Nirads. Not one. It was as though the invaders couldn't be killed.

He glanced forward and saw smoke rising in the distance. The Flame at the temple was still lit. But as he approached the heart of the battle, Paelen saw Apollo and Diana crouching back-to-back. They were surrounded by Nirads. Diana was using her bow, but every arrow she fired glanced off the gray invaders without causing any damage at all. Apollo was using his spear but was having as little luck as his sister.

A Nirad warrior lunged forward and knocked Apollo's legs out from under him. More followed as Diana fought bravely to save her twin brother. But she was driven away quickly. As Paelen passed silently overhead, he heard her anguished cries filling the air as Apollo was killed by the invaders.

Pegasus. He had to find Pegasus.

The sandals drew him away from the horrible scene. Closer to the Temple of the Flame, he saw Jupiter fighting at its base. Roaring in rage, the leader of Olympus was shooting lightning bolts and thunder at the Nirads, to no effect. The invaders were steadily advancing up the tall marble steps.

Paelen finally saw Pegasus. The stallion was rearing on his hind legs and kicking out at the invaders. He was covered in blood from countless stab wounds as the Nirads used their vicious weapons to bring down the powerful stallion. A Nirad pounced and stabbed his spear deep into the flanks of the rearing stallion. Pegasus shrieked in pain and dropped back down to all fours, viciously kicking the Nirad with his golden hoof. But even as the wounded warrior crawled away, others moved in for the kill. They caught hold of the stallion's wings and were trying to tear them off.

Pegasus continued to fight but was quickly over-powered. As more and more Nirads attacked, the stallion was knocked to the ground. As he fell, the spear in his side broke and was driven deeper into his flanks.

Paelen watched in horror as Pegasus was swamped with Nirad warriors. There was no way the stallion would survive the attack.

Diana arrived. Shouting her battle cry, she attacked the Nirads tying to kill Pegasus. Stabbing at them with her brother's spear, her grief transformed to rage as she used all her strength against them.

One Nirad shoved past her and made for the stallion's head. But when its four hands made contact with the golden bridle, it howled in agony. Diana turned on the attacker and lunged forward with her brother's spear. Unlike all the other attempts to stop the Nirads, this time the spear worked, and she managed to kill her first invader. With Diana's help, Pegasus got back on his feet. But that was one small victory in a losing battle.

"Paelen!"

Jupiter was surrounded by Nirad fighters, but he was pointing at the temple. "Quickly," he shouted. "Stop them!"

Paelen turned to the temple and saw other Nirads cutting through the defenders and advancing farther up the marble steps.

"Stop them, Paelen!" Jupiter ordered again. "They must not extinguish the Flame!"

Paelen knew the moment the Flame went out, the war would be over and Olympus would fall. But if Jupiter himself couldn't stop the invaders, what could a thief possibly do?

In the time it took for him to decide whether or not to join the fight, the battle was lost.

Nirad warriors tore down the entrance gates to the temple and tossed them down the steps. They poured into the temple, howling in rage. Moments later there was the sickening sound of the plinth that held the Flame being knocked over. Guttural roars of triumph filled the air as the invaders went to work extinguishing the Flame.

Soon more and more Nirads abandoned the battleground and rushed up the steps to join in the destruction. The survivors of Olympus could do little more than watch in terror as their world ended.

Paelen saw Jupiter run over to Pegasus. Catching hold of the wounded stallion, Jupiter pointed in the air and shouted something. Pegasus snorted and nodded his head.

The few survivors parted to give Pegasus room to spread his wings. With a shriek, the stallion launched himself into the air.

Paelen's heart leaped with excitement. This was his moment! Finally, an opportunity to seize the bridle and control the fleeing stallion.

"Go after Pegasus!" Paelen ordered his sandals. "Get me to the stallion!"

3

EMILY MADE HER WAY BACK TO HER BED-
room, having finished collecting water. Without
electricity, there would be no TV, no radio, and no
lights. With nothing more to do, she got into bed.

She knew she wouldn't sleep. Even if the storm
hadn't been so noisy, she would be on edge. She just
wished she weren't alone. Her mother would have
known what to do. But her mother was dead, and
nothing Emily could do would ever change that. She
was alone. She started to regret not asking her aunt
Maureen to come over.

Outside the window there was another blinding
flash of lightning and a terrible explosion of thunder. Emily felt the whole building shake. But as she

listened, she heard more than thunder. Directly above her head was the sound of something very big, very heavy hitting the roof.

Living in the top-floor apartment, the only thing above them was the flat roof. Emily's family paid extra to have access to it, and her mother had planted a large flower and vegetable garden. But no one had been up there since her mother got sick and died. Emily worried that a piece of the Empire State's antenna might have just hit her building. Or maybe lightning had struck her mother's garden shed and knocked it over.

She considered calling her father to ask him what to do. Would lightning start a fire? Was her building about to burn down? The rain outside was coming down in heavy sheets, but would it put out a fire if it had started? As more and more questions and fears built up within her, Emily's heart practically stopped.

There were more sounds from above.

It was almost as though someone or something was kicking the roof.

Raising the flashlight, Emily sucked in her breath when the beam of light revealed a huge crack in the ceiling plaster. The overhead light was swinging on its cord. Small chips of paint and plaster were starting to fall.

Emily reached for her cell. But even before she used the speed dial, she closed it again. What was she going to tell her father? That something big had hit the roof and cracked her bedroom ceiling? Maybe he'd tell her to get out of the building. But that would mean going out in the dark hallway and finding her way to the stairwell. Then she'd have to walk down twenty flights of stairs, just to arrive on the street where it was pouring with rain.

"No, Em," she told herself. "There's nothing up there. It's just the garden shed fallen over and the door banging in the wind."

Long before Emily could convince herself it was nothing serious, the thumping from above started again.

"This is crazy!" she said. Even as she spoke, she was climbing out of bed. "You're not going up there. . . ."

But it was as though her body and mind weren't speaking to each other. The more Emily's mind tried to stop herself, the more determined her body was to investigate the strange sounds coming from the roof.

Emily drew on her long raincoat, reached for the apartment keys, and made for the door. As a quick afterthought, she grabbed her dad's baseball bat from a closet beside the door.

With only the single beam from the flashlight to show her the way, Emily climbed the stairs. She heard hushed sounds of footsteps and chattering voices as more of the building's occupants used the stairwell to get to their homes.

"This isn't smart, Em. There's lightning up there," she warned herself. Once again, part of her wasn't listening.

She made it to the top of the access stairs and faced the locked door that led directly out to the roof. Clutching the bat in one hand and with the flashlight tucked under her arm, Emily struggled to get the key in the lock. When she managed to turn it, the door opened a fraction. Suddenly the wind caught hold and wrenched the door from her hand. It flew open wildly and made a terrible crashing sound as it was nearly torn off its hinges.

"So much for being quiet," she chastised herself.

Emily stepped into the blowing rain and started passing the beam of light over the rooftop, searching for fire. It had been almost a year since she'd been up here. The whole area was badly overgrown. Strange vines had taken hold, covering the once lovingly tended flower beds.

The vegetable patch was unrecognizable. In the dark, with the storm at its peak, this was no longer the garden Emily knew. Instead it was a dark and frightening place filled with mystery and danger.

Through the noise of the pounding rain, Emily heard other sounds. It was the thumping again. Only this time, there was more. As she strained to listen above the terrible weather, she was sure she could hear whining, or the sound of someone or something crying out in pain.

Creeping forward, she passed the beam of light over the wild garden. To Emily's right was the large rose patch. This had been her mother's pride and joy. Every summer without fail, their apartment had been filled with the fragrance of the fresh-cut flowers her mother had grown here. Now the rosebushes had run wild and were spilling out over the roof.

A sudden movement in the roses caught Emily's attention. Directing the light back, she thought she saw the glint of gold. She inched closer and kept the light trained on the bushes. There! The flash of gold again. Taking another nervous step, Emily held up the bat.

"Whoever you are, come out of there!"

As she took another tentative step, a blinding bolt of lightning cracked in the sky. The entire roof was bathed in light. And what Emily saw in the rose garden was impossible.

She stumbled backward, lost her footing, and fell hard to the ground.

"It's not real!" she told herself. Rising to her hands and knees, she reached for the flashlight. "You didn't see what you just saw. It's just the storm playing tricks on you. That's all!"

Shining the light once again in the direction of the rosebushes, her heart was pounding so badly she thought she might pass out. Climbing unsteadily to her feet, she crept forward.

"It's not real, Em, it's not real," she repeated over

and over again as she drew near. "You didn't see anything!"

But when the light found its mark, she couldn't deny the truth.

It was very real.

A huge white horse was lying on its side in the middle of the rose garden. What had glinted in the beam of the flashlight was one of the horse's hooves. As Emily looked, she sucked in her breath. It was gold. Raising the flashlight, she received an even greater shock. A wing! Massive in size, it was covered in mud, leaves, and rose petals, but unmistakable with its long white feathers.

"No!" Emily cried. "This is impossible!"

More lightning lit the rooftop, confirming what Emily was trying so hard to deny.

A white horse with golden hooves and a vast white wing was lying on its side in the middle of her mother's rose garden.

Unable to move, barely breathing, Emily stared at the animal in disbelief.

As she watched, the wing on the horse's side stirred, followed by a terrible shriek of pain. The sound tore at Emily's heart. The animal was in agony. Racing forward and heedless of the sharp thorns that tore into her flesh, Emily entered the bushes and started to shove them away from the stricken horse.

She worked her way along the animal's side, toward its head. Lying flat on the ground, it was completely trapped within the rosebushes as the vicious thorns tore into its tender skin.

Thorns dug into Emily's flesh causing her to cry out in pain as she tried to free the horse's head from the bushes. It was awake, and looking at her with a huge, dark eye.

"It's all right. I won't hurt you," she soothed. "I'll get you free in a moment. Then maybe you can stand up if you're not too hurt."

When most of the horse's head was free, it tried to rise. It screamed in agony as the wing on its side moved.

"Wait, stop!" Emily reached out and stroked the horse's quivering neck. "Don't move. Let me see what's wrong."

Emily continued to stroke the strong, warm neck as she raised the flashlight and trailed the beam down along the horse's body. She could see one wing resting on the side, but she couldn't see the other.

"I don't suppose you've only got the one wing?"

The animal raised its head and looked at her with imploring eyes that begged for help.

"No," she sighed. "I guess not."

Emily soon freed the horse from the bushes. As she held up the flashlight, she glimpsed the upper edge of the other wing. Only it was at an odd angle, pinned beneath the weight of the horse's body.

"Your other wing is trapped beneath you," she explained. "But I guess you already know that."

With the last of the bushes gone, she moved back to its head.

"I've done all I can, but we have to get you off that wing. If I go around to your back and push, will you try to get up?"

As if in answer to her question, the horse seemed to nod its head.

"You really are going crazy, Em," she muttered. "He's a horse. He can't understand you."

She knelt down in the slippery mud and stroked the horse's side. "Okay, I'm sorry, but this is probably going to hurt. When I start pushing, I want you to try to get up."

Placing her hands firmly on its back, Emily leaned forward and started to push with all her strength. "Now!" she grunted. "Get up now!"

Emily could feel the horse's back muscles tensing beneath her hands as it struggled to rise.

"That's it!" Pushing and straining, Emily felt her knees starting to slip beneath her. "Keep going, you can do it!"

Putting all her weight against the horse, Emily felt it move. But as it rolled forward, the trapped wing sprang free and hit her squarely in the face. Emily cried out as she was knocked backward into the rose-bushes. As she fell into the center of the patch, the vicious thorns tore large holes in her jeans and rain-coat and pierced right through to her skin.

But the fresh pain from the thorns was quickly forgotten when lightning flashes revealed the horse now standing on its feet and facing her. Despite the filth from the mud and leaves that covered its body and matted its mane, and ignoring the countless cuts and gashes from the thorns, Emily was awestruck.

She'd never seen anything so amazing in her whole life.

From the moment she'd discovered the horse on the roof and seen its wing, a name had sprung to mind. A name long forgotten from an old book of myths her mother used to read to her. Now the name came flooding back. Stepping clear of the bushes, Emily approached. As she did, the stallion moved toward her.

"It's really you, isn't it?" she whispered softly as she stroked the soft muzzle. "You're Pegasus, aren't you? I mean the really real Pegasus."

The stallion seemed to pause for a moment. Then he nudged her hand, inviting another stroke. In that one rain-drenched instant, Emily felt her world changing.

Forever.

PAELEN AWOKE, STIFF AND IN A LOT OF PAIN. His back felt like it was on fire, and every muscle in his body cried out in protest.

Around him he could hear the soft sound of voices. Keeping his eyes shut, he took a moment to remember what had happened to him. The last thing he recalled was finally catching up with Pegasus and reaching for the golden bridle. He remembered tearing it away from the stallion and feeling its weight in his hand. Then there had been a blinding flash. . . .

After that, everything went blank.

Opening his eyes, Paelen discovered he was in bed in a very strange room. The walls were white with no decorations, and it smelled very odd. Over to his right was another bed, but it was empty. Outside the large window, the storm was still raging. It shocked Paelen to see the flashes of lightning and hear the roaring thunder. The way the battle had been going, he thought it would all be over by now.

Paelen turned away from the window. He saw a strange assortment of devices with beeping sounds and blinking lights. Above him, he was alarmed to see clear bags of fluid dripping down tubes that actually *entered* his left arm.

"Doctor, he's awake," said a woman from beside the bed.

Paelen focused his eyes on a man in a long white coat approaching the bed.

"Welcome back to the land of the living, young man. I'm Dr. Bernstein and you are in Bellevue Hospital. We thought we were going to lose you there for a bit. That was a rather nasty fall you took."

Paelen said nothing as the man leaned forward and shone a bright light in his eyes. When he finished, he straightened again and whistled. "I'll be darned if I know how you're doing it, but you are healing faster than anyone I've ever treated before. At this rate, those broken bones of yours will be knitted together in no time. As it is, that burn on your back is healing even as we watch."

Switching off the light, he put it in his pocket. "Now, can you tell me your name?"

As Paelen opened his mouth to speak, the lights in the room flickered and dimmed.

"I hope the generators keep working," said the woman as she looked up at the lights. "I've heard the blackout hit the whole city. They're saying it's as bad as the one in seventy-seven."

Paelen understood the words, but not their meaning. What was a "blackout"? Seventy-seven what? What did it all mean?

"The generators are fine, Mary," said Dr. Bernstein. He reached out to touch Paelen's arm reassuringly. "The hospital has spent a fortune keeping the backup generators serviced. So don't you worry about a thing, we have plenty of electricity, and you are perfectly safe."

Paelen was about to ask where he was when a new person entered the room. Dressed in dark clothing, the man drew up to the side of the bed.

"I'm Officer Jacobs from the Fourteenth Precinct,"

said the man, holding up his police badge. "I've been called in to take the details on your mystery patient. So, is this the young man who fell from the sky?"

The doctor and nurse nodded.

"I'm Dr. Bernstein," the doctor said, offering his hand. "This is Nurse Johnston. As for my patient, well, I don't know his name. But I was just about to ask."

Officer Jacobs opened his notebook. "Allow me." He turned his attention to Paelen. "So, young man, can you give us your name?"

Inhaling deeply, Paelen raised his hand in a flourish and bowed as best he could in the bed. "I am Paelen the Magnificent, at your service."

"Paelen the Magnificent?" Dr. Bernstein repeated as his eyebrows rose. "Paelen the Lucky, more like." He turned to the police officer. "This young man was found in the middle of Twenty-sixth Street and Broadway. The paramedics think he was at a costume party, stood too close to a window, and was struck by lightning. He might have fallen out. We've been treating lightning burns and electrocutions like his all night. Though I must admit, most of the others haven't been so lucky."

"Were you hit by lightning?" Officer Jacobs asked Paelen.

Paelen thought back to the last thing he remembered and frowned. "Perhaps, but I am uncertain."

Officer Jacobs started to write. "All right then, Paelen, can you give me your last name? Where do you come from? Where do you live, so we can notify your family and tell them you are here?"

Paelen looked at both men, then at the strange room again. Suddenly his thief's instinct took over and told him not to say anything more about himself or where he came from. "I—I do not remember."

"Don't remember?" Dr. Bernstein repeated. "Well, you did have a rather nasty knock on your head. Though I'm sure the memory loss is only temporary. Maybe this will help. . . ." He crossed over to the small cupboard against the far wall. He pulled out a bag and poured out the contents onto the bed.

"When you were found, this was all you were wearing: this tunic and this pair of winged sandals. You were clutching this horse's bridle. We had a nightmare of a time prying it out of your hands."

"Those are mine," Paelen protested as he tried to grab the items. "I want them back!"

"Hey, that looks like real gold," the police officer said as he reached for the bridle. Feeling its heavy weight, he frowned. "Feels like real gold, too."

"You cannot have that!" Paelen cried as he snatched at the bridle. He winced when the movement pulled at his broken ribs. "I told you it is mine."

"Where did you get it?" Officer Jacobs demanded.

"Get it?" Paelen repeated. "I—I—" He paused as he tried to outthink these strange people. Finally a solution came to him. "It was a gift."

"A gift?" the officer repeated curiously. "You're telling me that you can't remember your full name or where you came from, but you can remember that this was a gift?"

"Yes," Paelen said confidently. "That is correct. It was a gift."

Officer Jacobs moved closer to the bed and frowned. "Well, Paelen, shall I tell you what I think?" Not waiting for an answer, he continued. "I don't think this was a gift at all. In fact, I don't believe you fell out any window. I think you were pushed." He held up the bridle. "If this is real gold, which I think it is, then it's got to be worth a fortune. I'm sure someone your age wouldn't be getting it as a gift. Tell me, how old are you? Sixteen? Seventeen maybe? So I'll ask you again, where did you get it?"

Paelen wasn't about to tell them how old he was or that he hadn't been pushed out any window. He especially couldn't tell them about the bridle or from whom he'd taken it. Instead he shrugged. "I cannot remember."

"That's a very convenient memory of yours," suggested Officer Jacobs. "You say this was a gift, but you won't say who gave it to you."

He next turned his attention to the beautifully tooled winged sandals. Fine, colorful feathers adorned the tiny wings, and beautiful cut diamonds, sapphires, and rubies had been sewn into the soft leather.

"What can you tell me about these? They also look very valuable." Officer Jacobs winked at the doctor before he chuckled and said, "Or do you want to tell us that Mercury, messenger of the gods, gave them to you?"

"That is correct," Paelen answered simply.

"What's correct?" Officer Jacobs said, suddenly confused.

"They were a gift from Mercury." Paelen dropped his eyes and felt his throat tighten. "He gave them to me before he died."

Officer Jacobs frowned and shook his head. "What? Who died? Paelen, tell me, who gave you these sandals before they died?"

Paelen felt the conversation turning in the wrong direction. "No one. I told you, they were a gift."

"No, you just said someone died. I know it wasn't Mercury. So who was it? Where are they now?"

"I was wrong," Paelen said defensively. "Mercury did not die. The Nirads are not invading Olympus, and there is no war. Everyone is fine and happy."

"Nirads? Olympus?" Officer Jacobs repeated. "What are you talking about?"

Paelen realized he'd said too much. "I—I don't remember. My head hurts."

He was grateful when Dr. Bernstein stepped forward. "I think that's enough for now, Officer. This young man has obviously been through a terrible ordeal. It's best if we let him rest."

The police officer kept his sharp eyes on Paelen, but finally nodded. "All right, we'll leave it there for the moment." He started to put the bridle, sandals, and toga back in the hospital bag. "But in the meantime, I think I'll hold on to these until we can figure out who they belong to."

Paelen started to panic. He'd fought very hard to get that bridle from Pegasus and didn't want this man to take it from him. Throwing back the covers, he tried to climb from the bed but found the heavy casts on his legs stopping him. "Please, those are mine. You cannot take them."

"Paelen, calm down." Dr. Bernstein gently pushed Paelen back against the pillows. "You can't walk. Both your legs are broken, as are most of your ribs. You need rest. Officer Jacobs won't be taking your things far. He'll just keep them safe until we can figure out who they belong to."

"But they belong to me!" Paelen insisted.

"Doctor?"

A nurse had entered the room. She was holding a patient chart in her shaking hands. The color had drained from her face, and she appeared to be very frightened as she studied Paelen. With a tremble in her voice, she said, "The blood tests on your patient just came back."

The nurse handed over the chart as though it were burning her hands. Without waiting for a response, her eyes shot over to Paelen a final time before she raced out of the room.

Dr. Bernstein opened the chart and read the test results. His expression changed as his eyes darted from the chart to Paelen and then back to the chart again.

"What is it?" Officer Jacobs asked.

Saying nothing, Dr. Bernstein shuffled through the papers and checked and rechecked the results. When he finished, he closed the chart and concentrated on Paelen.

"Who, or should I say, *what* are you?"

EMILY WAS STILL ON THE ROOF WITH PEGASUS.

Sometime during the seemingly endless night, the storm had ended just as abruptly as it had begun. The rain stopped and the skies cleared. With the city still in total darkness from the power outage, for the first time in her life Emily was able to see stars sparkling in the midnight sky over New York City. She peered up Broadway and listened to the eerie silence. There was some traffic on the wide road, but not much. Only the occasional sounds of a car horn or police siren shattered the overwhelming stillness.

Pegasus was standing close beside her as she looked down to the world below. Her hand was absently stroking the stallion's muscled neck.

"It looks so strange down there," she said softly. "It feels like we're the only ones left alive in the whole city."

Looking at the stallion, Emily still couldn't believe her eyes. Even touching him didn't seem to help. It was just so hard to accept that the real Pegasus was actually here in New York City, standing beside her on the roof of her apartment building.

But as the sun started to rise, she was finally able to see him clearly. The rain had washed most of the mud away and returned his color to white. Walking around his side, she saw his left wing was hanging at an odd angle. Without knowing anything about horses, or birds for that matter, she immediately knew the wing was badly broken.

Farther down his back, she was shocked to discover a terrible burn she hadn't noticed before. She could see the singed hair and open, weeping wound.

"Were you struck by lightning?"

Pegasus turned his head back to her. As Emily looked into his dark, intelligent eyes, she felt perhaps he *could* understand her. But he gave no response.

"Well, it must have been the lightning, considering

how bad it was last night." She sighed before she continued, "You poor thing, that must have really hurt."

As the light increased, further inspection of the horse's body revealed that what Emily had first thought was simply mud, from the rose patch covering his body, turned out to be blood. A lot of it. Working her way around the stallion, Emily quickly discovered that most of Pegasus's wounds were not caused by the lightning strike or thorn cuts from the rosebushes.

"You've been in a fight!" she cried as she inspected deep gashes cutting into the stallion's back and legs. "With who? Who'd want to hurt you?"

Pegasus gave no answer. Instead he opened his unbroken wing, inviting her to peer beneath. As Emily did, she gasped. Hidden under the fold of the wing was the exposed end of a broken spear. The other end went deep into Pegasus's rear flank.

"You've been stabbed!"

With trembling hands, Emily felt around the spear wound.

"It goes in so deep," she said. "I have to do something. Maybe call a vet."

Pegasus whinnied and shook his head wildly. Emily didn't need to speak his language to know he didn't want her contacting anyone else.

"But you're hurt!" she insisted. "And I don't know what to do to help you."

Once again, Pegasus snorted, pawed the tarmac roof, and shook his head. He then turned back to her and nuzzled her hand. Emily stroked his soft muzzle and rested her forehead against him. It had been an endless night and exhaustion was taking hold.

"You need help, Pegasus," she said softly. "More help than I can give you."

To the east, the sun finally climbed over the top of a tall building. It shone golden light on the rooftop garden and felt wonderful on Emily's tired face. It also made her realize that anyone in a building taller than hers would now be able to see Pegasus on the roof.

"We've got to get you under cover," she warned. "If anyone sees you, they might call someone who'll take you away."

Pegasus quickly shook his head, snorted, and started pawing the tarmac roof with his sharp hoof again.

"Don't worry. I won't let that happen," Emily promised. "We'll just have to find somewhere to hide you until that wing heals."

Her first thought had been to take Pegasus down to her apartment. Then her father could come and help figure things out. But that thought was quickly dismissed. Even though the freight elevator made it up to the roof, it wasn't working with the power off. The stairs were not an option either. If she were to hide Pegasus, it would have to be up here.

Then her eyes landed on her mother's large garden shed. "That will have to do. I know it's probably not what you are used to, but for now, it's all we've got."

With Pegasus patiently watching, Emily quickly emptied the shed of all the garden furniture and pot-ting supplies. When she finished, she was surprised by how much room there was inside.

"Well, it's not fancy," she said as she brushed dirt off her hands and invited Pegasus in. "But at least it will keep you hidden until we figure this out. Is that all right with you?"

Pegasus stepped forward and entered the shed.

With the immediate problem solved, Emily put her

hands on her hips and looked at the stallion. "Next, we should get those wounds of yours cleaned. We can't let them get infected. So if you stay here, I'll go down to my apartment and get some water and clean cloths."

As she drew away, the stallion began to follow her. Emily shook her head and smiled. "You have to stay here, Pegasus. You won't make it down the stairs, and the elevator isn't working. I promise I'll be right back."

Back in her apartment, Emily raced into the bathroom. She caught sight of her reflection in the mirror and received quite a shock. She was a mess. Rose leaves and petals were tangled in her hair, and her face and arms were covered in dried mud and blood from the thorns. But most shocking of all was the huge black eye. As she prodded the tender area, she found the entire right side of her face was bruised and painfully swollen from where Pegasus's wing had struck her.

"Great," she muttered to herself. "What are you going to tell Dad about that?"

She decided to worry about that later. Instead she opened the medicine cabinet. It was still filled with all the medicated cream they'd used to treat her mother's sores when her illness had confined her to bed. Neither she nor her father had had the heart to throw them out. For once, she was grateful.

Grabbing all she could, Emily then went into the kitchen. There she gathered together clean dish towels, disinfectant soap, and one of the large pots of collected water.

As she packed the items into bags, she noticed a pool of water on the tile floor in front of the refrigerator. Without power, the freezer section was starting to defrost. Pulling open the door, she saw two tubs of ice cream mixed in with the thawing bags of frozen vegetables. She suddenly felt very hungry. She hadn't eaten anything since lunch the previous day.

Emily reached for one of the tubs, grabbed a spoon, and put them in her bag of supplies for the roof. She then thought to take some carrots, fresh green beans, and a few apples for Pegasus.

She caught hold of the flashlight and headed back up to the roof.

The sun was steadily climbing higher in the sky. But as she stepped out on the roof, Emily still found the city was unnervingly quiet. It was Wednesday. Usually the garbage trucks were out early, making all the noise they possibly could. But not today. With the blackout, Emily figured they would have the day off. She also assumed her school would be closed. Even if it wasn't, she wasn't going in. Pegasus needed her, school didn't.

"I'm back," she called as she walked up to the garden shed. Part of her expected to find nothing there; as though everything that had happened the previous night had been some kind of strange dream. But as she approached, she heard the sound of hooves moving on the shed floorboards.

Pegasus poked his white head out and nickered softly to her.

"Told you I wouldn't be long," Emily said as she started to unpack the bags. "Okay, I've got some water here, a bit of disinfectant soap, and some medicated cream we used to treat my mom's bedsores. The package says it's good for burns, too. So I thought it might help you."

Pegasus peered into the bags as she unpacked them. Emily giggled as his long mane tickled her face. He soon found the tub of ice cream and pulled it out of the bag.

"Hey, that's for me," Emily complained as she tried to reach for the tub. "I've got some apples and vegetables for you."

But the stallion ignored her. Putting the tub on the ground, Pegasus used his hoof to hold it still while his sharp teeth tore off the top. His long tongue started to lick the melting chocolate ice cream.

"I don't know if you should be eating that," Emily warned. "Chocolate isn't good for dogs; maybe it's the same for horses."

Pegasus stopped and looked at Emily. The expression on his face gave her the impression that he didn't much care for being called a horse.

"Well, I'm sorry," Emily said. "I just don't want you to get sick. You've got enough problems already."

Pegasus stared at her a moment longer before going back to the ice cream.

"Fine, suit yourself," she said as she unfolded a deck chair and sat down to eat the fruit and vegetables that Pegasus had refused.

· · ·

As the morning passed, Emily did her best to clean and treat Pegasus's many wounds. While working on his neck, her cell phone went off.

"Hi, Dad," she said, reading his name on the screen.

"Hey, kiddo, you all right?"

Emily looked at the cuts on her arms, then over to Pegasus. "Sure, everything's fine. You wouldn't believe what happened last night! There was this big crash on our roof—"

Before Emily could say more, Pegasus nudged her and pounded the floor with his hoof. He shook his head and snorted. Emily looked at him and knew he didn't want her to tell her father.

"What happened?" her father repeated. "Emily, did something happen?"

"Um, no, Dad. It was just the garden shed. The wind blew it over. But there are no problems here at all apart from the power being out. What about you?"

Her father sighed. "I've been held up a bit, so I'm going to be late getting home. I'm at Bellevue Hospital at the moment, trying to do a report on this kid who fell out a window. Things have gone from weird to really, really weird."

Emily was looking at Pegasus. He was still staring at her intently, as though he was listening to her every word.

"Em, you still there?" her father called.

"Sure, Dad," she quickly answered. "Sorry. What's so weird about the kid?"

"I can't get into it right now. I'll tell you when I get home later. Should be sometime before dinner. Just take it easy today."

"I will," she promised.

After she hung up, Emily looked at the stallion. "You didn't want me to tell my father about you, did you?"

Pegasus shook his head and snorted. Again, Emily had the strange feeling he knew exactly what she meant.

"I don't understand. My dad's a good man. He's a police officer and would help you. He'd never hurt you or turn you in."

Pegasus shook his head and stomped his hoof.

"I sure wish you could tell me what's wrong." Emily

sighed. "Well, if you don't want my dad to know, I'll do as you wish. But I need help. I can't get that spear out of you on my own, and your wing needs to be set properly. I'm not strong enough to do it all alone."

Pegasus moved his head closer to Emily and gently nuzzled her hand. She leaned against his thick neck as she tried to think.

Finally someone else came to mind. Someone from her school who would be strong enough to pull out the spear. Someone who was always sketching pictures of winged horses on his textbooks. The trouble was, he was the meanest boy in Emily's class. He was probably the meanest boy in the whole school.

Joel DeSilva had joined Emily's class only a couple of months ago, but he'd already been in several fights. He never talked to anyone and didn't have any friends. Most of the kids in her class were terrified of him and left him alone. Joel DeSilva was the last person in the world Emily wanted to talk to. But he was the only person she could think of.

"Pegs, I think I know one boy you might let me ask," Emily said. "He's from my school. His name is Joel. He's really big and strong. And I know he already loves you, because he's always drawing your picture on all his books. The teachers yell at him about it, but he doesn't care. He lives across the street from the school, so I could go ask him to come and help. Will you please let me do it?"

The stallion considered her words. He neighed softly.

"Thank you," Emily said, patting him. "If I leave to get him now, I should be back soon. With Joel's help, we can get that spear out of your side and set your wing."

She pulled out her cell phone and stepped up to his side. "I'm going to take your picture. It might be easier then to convince Joel that you're really here." Getting his wing in the shot, she took the stallion's picture.

"Perfect. Okay, I'm going now. You've got extra water for drinking, and there are still some carrots and beans left if you get hungry. I really shouldn't be too long. But even if I am, please keep hidden in this shed. I don't want anyone to see you and take you away from me."

Emily wondered if she should lock him in the

shed. But then she thought better of it. If Pegasus were to get frightened, he might break down the door or even destroy the shed. Then there would be no place to hide him. Instead she left the door open and hoped the stallion would remain inside.

"I'll be back soon," she finally called as she turned on the flashlight and entered the stairwell.

Emily was surprised by how many people there were on the stairs. Some, like her, had flashlights; others used lighters or candles. Everyone seemed in bright spirits. Neighbors who usually never spoke to each other laughed and chatted as they slowly descended or climbed the stairs.

It took ages getting down to the ground. But as Emily stepped into the lobby, she realized that going down was a heck of a lot easier than climbing back up was going to be. She only hoped she could get Joel to come back with her.

Once outside, Emily was struck again by the eerie silence of the city. There were people on the sidewalk, but very little traffic. All the shops and wholesalers were closed. It was like some strange holiday.

Emily ignored the stares of the people she passed

along the way. She'd forgotten to comb her hair or even wash her face. She knew she looked even worse than Pegasus.

The journey seemed endless, but as she arrived at 21st Street and Second Avenue, she looked at the line of brownstones across from the school. Which one was Joel's?

She considered calling out his name in the hopes that someone would hear and tell her where he lived. But as she walked down the street, she saw a boy sitting on the front stoop of one of the buildings. His wide shoulders were slumped, and his head of wavy black hair drooped. As she drew near, she saw that it was Joel.

Then the nerves started.

Emily wasn't sure how she should approach him. His expression was as threatening as the storm from the previous night. She took a deep breath and climbed the few steps to the stoop.

"Hi, Joel."

Joel looked her up and down.

"I'm Emily Jacobs," she pressed on. "We both have the same homeroom and math class."

Her comment received only a blank stare.

"That was some storm last night, wasn't it?" she said with forced cheerfulness. "I saw the lightning hit the Empire and blow the top right off. It did more damage than King Kong!"

Joel looked at her blankly. Finally he broke his silence. "Go away."

At that moment, seeing his angry, unwelcoming face, there was nothing on earth Emily would have rather done. But thoughts of the spear in Pegasus kept her feet locked on the spot.

"Look, Joel, I know we've never talked before, but I really need your help—"

His dark eyes flashed. "Are you deaf or just plain stupid? I said go away!"

"I would love to, but I can't," Emily said desperately. "Something happened last night, and you're the only person I can think of to help me. Please, will you talk to me for a minute? Then if you still feel the same, I'll go."

"What do you want?" Joel demanded. "What's so important that you had to come here? Have you looked at yourself in the mirror lately? You're a mess."

Emily's temper flared. The pain from her swollen

eye and scratches told her exactly what she looked like. But she also knew that Pegasus was her only priority. He needed her.

"You really want to know what's so important?" she finally shot back. "Why I would come here and try to talk to you when I know for sure you hate the whole world? Pegasus, that's why. He's what's so important!"

Joel's expression changed for the briefest of moments. In that instant, Emily saw a flicker of interest. But just as quickly, the veil of anger came crashing down again.

"What about him?" he challenged.

Emily advanced. "I've seen the pictures you've done on your books. He's all you ever draw."

"So?" Joel demanded.

Emily looked up to the sky, not knowing what to do. Did she dare risk telling him her secret? Did she really have a choice?

"What if he were real?" she started. "I mean, if he was, and he was hurt, would you want to help him?"

Anger flashed again in Joel's chocolate-brown eyes. He stood quickly, looming over her. "What kind of dumb question is that? Are you making fun of me because I like Pegasus? If you are, I swear I'll thump you!"

"No, I'm not making fun of you!" Emily said, just as quick and just as angry. "Joel, listen to me. Please . . ."

She reached into her pocket and fished out her cell. Opening it, she held up the photograph of the winged stallion.

"You may not believe me, but last night Pegasus, the *real* Pegasus, wings and all, was struck by lightning and crashed on my roof. He's there right now, and he's badly hurt. I've done all I can, but one of his wings is broken and I don't know how to set it. If you really care about him like I think you do, you'll come with me and help him!"

Emily's hands were shaking too much to allow Joel to see the photograph on the small screen. He reached out and took hold of the cell.

"He landed in my mother's rose garden. That's why I'm such a mess. Then when I tried to help him stand up again, his broken wing hit me in the face and gave me this black eye."

Suddenly the exhaustion of the long night caught

hold of her, and she sat down. "Please," she begged. "He's in so much pain. I don't know what to do for him."

Joel was still clutching the cell as he cautiously sat down beside her. "Go on, I'm listening."

"Pegasus is hurt. He's hurt really bad," Emily explained, relieved that Joel was listening. "He's also been in a terrible fight. He can't tell me why or with whom. But he's cut all over, and there's a big spear that's still in him. I'm not strong enough to pull it out on my own. That's why I thought of you."

"Why? Because I'm so big?" Joel challenged, suddenly growing angry and defensive again. "Just a big dumb Italian?"

Emily shook her head. "No, that's not it at all. Listen to me. Pegasus is hurt! I came here because I thought you cared and wouldn't want to see him captured."

Joel hesitated. There was now an expression of doubt rising on his face. "How do I know it's not a trick? Or some kind of stupid joke?"

Emily shook her head and stood again. "Look at me," she said wearily. "Do I look like I'm joking?

Does this black eye look like makeup? You think I gave myself all these cuts just so I could come here to cause trouble for you? This isn't a trick, Joel, I swear on my mother's soul. Pegasus needs our help!"

Joel was silent for so long that Emily almost gave up.

Starting to descend the stairs again, Emily looked up at him. "I can't leave him alone too long. It's a simple question. Are you coming or not?"

Joel looked from Emily up to the doors of the brownstone, then back at Emily again.

Finally he started to descend the stairs. "All right, I'm coming."

When he reached the pavement, he stood before her. "But if this is a joke, I don't care if you are a girl. I swear I'll knock your head off!"

LITTLE WAS SAID BETWEEN EMILY AND JOEL as they made their way back to her corner apartment building. When they arrived, Joel stopped before the lobby doors.

"How high is it?" he said, looking up.

"Twenty stories," Emily said. "I live on the top floor. Pegasus is on the roof above that."

"What? Twenty stories?" Joel complained. "You expect me to climb twenty flights of stairs?"

"I told you, Pegasus is on the roof."

When Joel hesitated, Emily sighed. "Look, you've come all this way. Are you going to go back now just because you've got to climb a few stairs?"

"Twenty flights aren't a few stairs!" he complained. "It's a marathon!"

Too tired to fight anymore, Emily shook her head. "Fine, Joel, go home. I guess I was wrong when I thought you liked Pegasus. Just do me a favor, will you? Keep your mouth shut. You may not believe he's here, but others might."

Emily said nothing more and pulled out her flashlight. She entered the lobby and walked toward the stairs. As she pulled open the heavy metal stairwell door, she heard footsteps behind her. Looking back, she saw Joel.

"It's still going to be twenty flights," she warned.

Joel shrugged. "I know. But I haven't got anything better to do."

Climbing the first five flights was easy. Making it to ten was tiring. By the fifteenth floor, Emily and Joel were out of breath and feeling nauseous. Taking a break, they both sat down on a stair.

"I didn't think it would be this hard," Emily panted. "I thought walking to school was enough exercise. But I'm really out of shape."

"Me too," Joel agreed between breaths. "I used to live in Connecticut and played football in school. But it's been too long."

In the dim light from the flashlight, Emily looked at him. "So you're from Connecticut?"

Joel shook his head. "I'm from Rome. You know, Italy. But when I was a kid, my father got a job at the United Nations. So we moved to the United States and found a house in Connecticut. My parents commuted into the city every day for work."

Emily was surprised. Joel didn't have any trace of an accent. She'd have never guessed he was foreign. For as long as he'd been in her class, she'd never known anything about him. Just that he was a troublemaker. "So then you moved into the city and now live in that brownstone?"

"Not exactly . . . ," he started. He paused. Suddenly his mood changed. He stood up abruptly. "I don't want to talk about it anymore," he said. "Are we going up or what?"

Without waiting for her, he charged forward into the darkness of the stairwell.

The final five flights were climbed in silence.

When they reached the top, Emily took the keys to the roof door from her pocket and stepped up beside him.

"He knows you are coming, but I don't think he's too happy about it. So take it easy on him. You can get as mad at me as you like. But I don't want you yelling at him. You got it?"

"I didn't yell at you," Joel challenged.

"Well, whatever you call it," Emily responded as she inserted the key and turned the lock. "I don't want you doing it to Pegasus. He's hurt and in pain. You're going to be nice to him or I swear I'll push you off the roof."

Joel looked shocked by the sudden change in her. "If he's really here, I promise I won't do anything wrong."

"Oh, he's here, all right."

Emily shoved open the door and stepped out onto the tarmac roof. "He's in that shed over there."

Walking forward, Emily called out, "You still here, Pegs?"

A soft nicker came from the shed. Joel's expression changed from doubt to absolute wonder.

"Remember"—Emily held up a warning finger—
"be nice or you'd better learn to fly real fast!"

She drew Joel toward the shed.

"Did you miss me?" she asked as Pegasus came
forward to greet her. She stepped up to his head
and started to stroke his smooth white face. A sharp
intake of breath was all Emily heard from Joel. She
turned back and saw his disbelieving expression.

"Pegasus, I would like you to meet Joel." She beckoned Joel forward. "Joel, this is Pegasus."

Joel entered the shed and stood before the stallion
a full minute before he was able to move or speak.
Finally he shook his head and raised a hand tentatively to reach out and stroke Pegasus's head.

"I can't believe it. Pegasus is real! And he's really
here!" Joel's eyes were beaming.

Emily watched his thick armor of anger melting
away.

"He sure is. But he's also very hurt." She led him
to the broken wing. "This needs to be set, but I don't
know how."

She then directed him around to the other side.
"Pegs?" she said, speaking softly. "Would you lift

your good wing so I can show Joel the spear? He's going to help me get it out of you."

Without hesitation, the stallion lifted his wing to reveal several centimeters of broken spear sticking out of his side. "Oh man," Joel cried as he inspected the spear. "Who did this to him?"

Emily shrugged. "I don't know. All I do know is he needs our help before someone finds him and takes him away."

As she spoke, Emily started to frown. It seemed that a lot of the deeper cuts and scratches were much smaller than they had been earlier. Further inspection revealed that the lightning burn had also shrunk and was less angry. As for the thorn scratches, they were all gone.

Emily gasped. "You're healing so fast." She looked at Joel. "This morning these cuts were much deeper. You see all these scratches on me? They were ten times worse on him. But all the thorn marks are gone."

"I'm not surprised." Joel continued to inspect the stallion's side. "Pegasus is an Olympian. He's immortal. Of course he would heal quickly."

"What's being Olympian got to do with it?" Emily

asked. "He's still a living being, just like you and me. And we sure don't heal this quickly!"

"Yes, he's a living being," Joel explained. "But he's also very different from us. If you'd asked me before, I wouldn't have thought he could be hurt at all."

"If I'd asked you before, you'd have bitten my head off."

Joel frowned and shot back, "I would not!"

Emily dropped the subject before it started another argument. Joel had a very short fuse and was easily provoked. "Well, Olympian or not, that spear has got to come out. I'm not even sure how to set his wing."

Joel stroked the smooth white feathers of the stallion's good wing. "In movies, all they ever do is pull the person's broken leg or arm to set it. Then they put a splint on it."

"But this isn't an arm or leg. It's a wing," said Emily. "And aren't most wing bones hollow? We could do more damage if we pull it and set it wrong."

Joel nodded. "Maybe, but we can't leave him like this, either." Suddenly he had an idea. "What if we take a really good look at his unbroken wing? We study it and learn how it works. Then if we look at the broken wing, we should be able to see the difference and know how it should be. After that, we could try to set it."

"Good idea," Emily agreed. "But where do we start? With his wing or with the spear?"

It was Pegasus who answered that question. As though he'd been listening to every word, the stallion lifted his good wing again and then whinnied and pounded the shed floor.

Emily stroked his muzzle. "You want us to pull out the spear first?"

In answer Pegasus nuzzled her hand.

Joel joined Emily at the stallion's head. "Then I guess we start with the spear," he said.

Emily and Joel went back down to her apartment to collect more supplies.

Joel looked around and whistled. "You apartment is a whole lot nicer than the dump I live in. Is it just you and your folks?"

"My mother died of cancer three months ago. Now it's just me and my dad." Emily felt the familiar lump start to form in the back of her throat. Taking a deep breath, she forced it back down before the tears arrived. "What about your place? I always heard brownstones were great. Lots of room, and you've actually got backyards."

Joel shook his head. "Not where I live. Our brownstone is small and falling apart. The plumbing doesn't work, and the paint is peeling."

Emily grabbed the last of the medicated creams and disinfectants from the medicine cabinet.

"Did your mother ever teach you how to sew?" Joel asked.

"Sew?" Emily repeated. "Why?"

"Because once we pull that spear out of Pegasus, he's going to bleed. We'll need to sew the hole closed to stop the bleeding and start the healing."

"You want me to sew Pegasus back together?"

"Do you have a better idea?" Joel asked.

"Yeah," Emily said. "Superglue. They sometimes use that stuff in microsurgery instead of stitches. They actually used it on my mother for one of her surgeries. After they told my dad, he got a supply of it for emergencies."

Joel frowned. "Really? Glue?"

Emily nodded and walked back into the kitchen to collect the glue. It was tossed in the bag of supplies. Finally she pulled open the freezer and reached for the last tub of ice cream.

"I offered Pegasus vegetables earlier, and all he wanted to eat was my ice cream. So maybe he'll want some more."

"Pegasus likes ice cream?"

When Emily nodded, Joel looked embarrassed. "Do you think I could have something to eat? I haven't had anything today and I'm starving."

Emily stopped and looked at him as though seeing him for the first time. This Joel was nothing like the angry Joel from earlier. "Sure, grab what you like. But let's take it upstairs."

Back on the roof, they unpacked the supplies. Emily had been right, the moment Pegasus smelled the ice cream he went straight for the tub. When he finished it all, he stole the box of breakfast cereal from Joel.

"Hey," Joel protested. "That was mine! You've got your own food."

"I don't think he likes anything healthy," Emily

said. "Look, he hasn't touched the apples I left for him. Or the carrots, either. All he wants are really sweet things."

"Well, he could have left me a little," Joel complained. "All that sugar can't be good for him. It's not like you can get it on Olympus. . . ."

Suddenly Joel snapped his fingers. "Of course, now I understand. It makes perfect sense."

"What does?"

"Don't you see? Pegasus needs sweet foods. That's all he eats on Olympus!"

"How do you know?" Emily asked.

"Because I've read all about it." Joel sounded more and more excited. "The Roman myths are my favorite books! All the legends say that on Olympus, the gods eat ambrosia and drink nectar. It's what keeps them immortal. That's why Pegasus wants it, to help him heal. Some say that ambrosia is very much like honey, so he wants sweet food. Do you have any honey in your kitchen?"

"Honey?" Emily repeated. "Joel, you're crazy. Those are just legends. We can't base our treatment of Pegasus on some dusty old myths."

Joel nodded. "Oh yes, we can. Pegasus is real, right?"

Emily nodded.

"And Pegasus is from myth, also true?" When Emily nodded again, he continued, "So if he exists, the others must too."

"Wait," Emily said, holding up her hand. "You're saying that Zeus and Hera, Poseidon and all the others are real?"

"Jupiter, Juno, and Neptune," Joel corrected. "Zeus is the Greek name. Since I'm Italian, I prefer the Roman myths. The leader of Olympus is Jupiter."

"Zeus or Jupiter," Emily protested, "it doesn't matter. But you can't really think all those myths are true?"

"Why not?" Joel said, jumping to his feet. "Look at him! Pegasus is standing right here, just as real as you or me. So if he's real, why not the others?"

Emily also stood. "Because if they were, why haven't they come to get him? If Zeus—"

"Jupiter," Joel corrected.

"All right," Emily said, exasperated. "If *Jupiter* is real, why doesn't he know Pegasus is hurt and come to help him?"

"I don't know," Joel admitted. "Maybe he can't. Or maybe he doesn't know yet. But I do know that if we don't help Pegasus, Jupiter is going to be really angry with us when he does get here."

"I don't care about Jupiter or any of the others," Emily said. "All I care about is Pegasus. So let's get started."

They cleaned the wounded area around the spear. Then Emily said to the stallion, "I'm really sorry, but this is going to hurt."

Standing beside Pegasus, towel at the ready, Emily helped support the heavy wing. Beside her, Joel wrapped his hands around the broken end of the spear. He braced himself against the side of the stallion. Together they counted down. "Three, two, one, go!" Using all his weight and strength, Joel started to pull.

Pegasus did his best not to buck as the spear was drawn slowly from his side.

"Hurry, Joel," Emily cried, trying to hold the stallion steady.

Pegasus's head was thrown back and was twisting in the air. His large, wild eyes revealed his agony, and his front hooves tore at the shed's floorboards. His screams tore at Emily's heart.

"Hurry, it's killing him!"

In one final, grunting heave, Joel drew the vicious barbed spear from the stallion's side. Blood flowed from the deep open wound.

"Put pressure on it!" Joel panted, trying to recover from the strain. "We've got to stop that bleeding!"

Emily pulled down the towel from her shoulder and pressed it to the wound. Beneath her hands, she could feel Pegasus trembling.

"You're all right, Pegasus," she soothed. "You're going to be all right. The worst is over, the spear is gone."

"We're not done yet," Joel said grimly as he took over applying pressure to the wound. "Go get the glue, Emily. We've got to finish this."

With Joel's help, Emily was able to squeeze the open edges of the wound together and use the glue to hold it closed. They covered it in clean bandages and taped it in place using silver duct tape.

"Well, it's not pretty, but it might just work." Joel gently patted the stallion's side. He turned to Emily. "That was a great idea about the glue. I would have never thought of that."

Emily shrugged. "I'm just glad it worked. I don't think I could have put stitches in him."

"Me either," Joel agreed. "Now, we just have to sort out that wing, and he'll be well on his way to recovery."

It was late in the afternoon when Emily and Joel finished setting Pegasus's wing. Despite Emily's concerns, it wasn't nearly as awful as removing the spear had been. Joel's idea of using the stallion's good wing as an example worked perfectly. Before long, they had pulled the broken bones into place as best they could and were applying a splint and holding it steady with bandages and duct tape.

When they finished, even before they could celebrate their success, Emily's phone started to ring.

"It's my dad. He doesn't know about you or Pegs, so try to keep quiet."

When Joel nodded, Emily answered the phone, "Hi, Dad."

"Em, where are you?" her father asked, sounding worried. "I'm home and you're not here."

Emily checked her watch and was shocked to see the time. "I'm on the roof," she explained.

"What are you doing up there?"

Emily improvised. "Well, remember I told you I heard sounds up here? I wanted to see the storm damage from last night, and I lost track of the time."

"Stay there. I'll be right up."

Emily felt a sudden rush of panic. "No, Dad, don't come up. I'm, um, I'm working on a surprise for you, and I don't want you to see it yet. I'll be right down."

Before she gave her father the opportunity to say anything further, she hung up.

"My dad's home," she explained. "I've got to get down there so he doesn't come up. Will you stay with Pegs? I promise to be back as soon as Dad goes to bed. He's been working long shifts and will be tired. When he's asleep, I'll bring up some more food for all of us."

"Don't forget the honey if you've got some," Joel called after her. "And anything else with sugar in it. Pegasus will need it if he's to heal."

"I won't," Emily promised as she walked over to the roof entrance. Turning on her flashlight, she gave Joel a wave before entering the darkened stairwell.

On her way down, Emily tried to think of what she

was going to tell her father. She worried what he would say when he saw her black eye. But whatever she said, she knew she couldn't tell him about Pegasus. She had given the stallion her word and wasn't about to break it. Even for her father.

She opened the door of her apartment. "Dad?"

"I'm in the kitchen," her father called.

Inhaling deeply, Emily made her way to the kitchen. She saw her father standing at the refrigerator in his police uniform, his back to her. He looked almost funny as he pulled out multiple items and tried to hold them all in his arms.

"What a mess," he said without turning to her. "Everything is going to spoil. We'd better eat a lot of this before it goes bad."

He turned around, saw her face, and dropped everything in his arms. Bottles of pickles and bunches of vegetables went rolling around the kitchen floor.

"What happened to you? Em, your eye is black!"

"I know," Emily said, trying to sound casual. "I tripped when I was on the roof and fell into the rosebushes. Somehow I managed to hit myself in the eye.

Actually," she corrected, "I think I *kneed* myself in the eye."

As her father inspected her face, he whistled in appreciation. "Good grief! I haven't seen a shiner like that in ages. It must hurt like the devil!"

"Kinda," Emily admitted. "But not as bad as the thorn scratches." She pushed up her sleeves to reveal the deep gashes on her arms. "I guess the roses won the first round."

"Looks like they won the whole fight," her father agreed. "We have to get those cleaned up."

Emily remembered that she and Joel had taken all the medicated creams and bandages up to the roof for Pegasus. "It's okay, Dad," she said quickly. "I already put some stuff on them. Really, I'm fine."

"All right," he said reluctantly. "But look, I don't want you going back up there alone. By the looks of things, it's become dangerous."

"But Dad," Emily protested, "I want to do something special for you. I—I'm fixing the garden! You know how much Mom loved her garden; we all did. After so long, it's gone completely wild. Please let me do this. It's really helping me deal with things."

Emily hated herself for using her mother's death as an excuse to continue to go up to the roof. But she couldn't allow her father to forbid her, not while Pegasus was still up there and in desperate need of help.

"Please, Dad, I really need to do this."

Finally he sighed. "Well, at least wait for me to help you. After the blackout, I'm owed a few days' leave. Why don't we make it our special project?"

Emily knew this was the best she could hope for with her father.

"That would be great. But if I promise not to do anything heavy, can I at least go up there to try to clean up a bit before we get to the real work?"

"Agreed," he said. "But only if you promise to be careful and keep away from the edge."

"I will." Emily quickly changed the subject before her father could change his mind. "So what are they saying about the blackout?"

"Well, it's not good," he said as he went back to work in the refrigerator. "The power company has put its entire staff on it, but it looks like we'll have no electricity for at least two days, maybe three." He paused and looked at her again. "You know what that means, don't you?"

Emily nodded. "It means you have to go back to work, doesn't it?"

"I was going to tell you that it means no school for a few days." Then he reluctantly added, "But yes, I've got to go back to work. I'm due back in at midnight. It was only because you were home alone that I was able to steal a few hours away."

Emily lifted the jug of milk out of her dad's arms. "Then you shouldn't waste this time here. Go sit down and I'll see what I can make us for dinner. Then I think you should try to get some sleep."

When her father smiled, it made his dimples appear. "Hey, who's the parent here?" he demanded, laughing.

"I am," Emily teased as she started to use as many items as she could to prepare their supper.

"Fair enough," he admitted. "This has been one strange twenty-four hours." He sighed heavily as he sat down at the kitchen table. "There's looting going on all over the city because of the power outage and security systems going down. Uptown, people are getting hysterical. Some even went into their local police stations claiming to have seen these huge, gray, four-armed creatures coming out of the sewers. They insisted these creatures were some kind of demon and this was the end of the world."

"Wow," Emily said as she pulled out a frying pan and set it on the gas stove. "That's weird."

"But that wasn't the worst of it," her father said. "Remember I called you from Bellevue? I was there to draw up a report on this mystery kid who'd been brought in. Seems he was hit by lightning and fell out a window. "

"Ouch! That had to hurt," Emily said as she started to scramble up some eggs. "Was he killed?"

"Nope," her father answered. "The doctor said he should have been. Not only did he not die, he's healing faster than anything they've ever seen before. His bones are knitting together in record time, and the burn on his back is shrinking by the minute."

Emily stopped scrambling her dad's eggs. "He's healing really quickly?" she said. "Who is he?"

Her father shrugged. "I'm not really sure. He said his name was"—he paused and stood up, then bowed at the waist and raised his hand in a flourish—"Paelen the Magnificent, at your service."

Emily couldn't help laughing as her father repeated the sweeping, formal gesture. "Where's he from?"

"I haven't got a clue," said her dad, sitting down again. "He claims he doesn't remember much, but after being a cop so long, I know a lie when I hear one." He paused as if reaching for something just beyond his grasp. "It's . . . it's really strange, Em. There is something seriously wrong with that kid, but I just can't put my finger on it."

"Like what?"

"A few things, really," her father answered. "The strange way he speaks. Real formal, you know? Then there's the way he was found, wearing only a blood-stained tunic and winged sandals studded with jewels. He'd obviously been struck by lightning, but somehow he survived that as well as the fall. When the paramedics arrived, they found him clutching this beautiful golden bridle. Between the jeweled sandals and the horse bridle, it all had to be worth a fortune. But he refused to tell me where they came from or how he got them."

Emily felt her pulse quicken. Paelen the Magnificent? Healing quickly? Wearing a tunic and sandals, and clutching a golden horse bridle? She knew it had something to do with Pegasus. She just didn't know what.

The eggs were forgotten as Emily took a seat at the table beside her father.

"So is he still at the hospital?"

"No," he answered darkly. "And that's another story all its own. When the staff saw his blood test results, they nearly had a fit. Things kind of went downhill from there."

Emily's ears were ringing. Everything her father said was shouting *Olympus*. Somehow there was another Olympian in New York! She had to tell Joel as soon as she could.

"What do you mean? What happened?" Emily finally asked.

"It seems one of the nurses called the CRU: the Central Research Unit. They deal with unexplained phenomena—UFO sightings, stuff like that. Anyway, she called them when she saw the test results. Not long after that, several of their agents arrived at the hospital to collect him. But when I challenged them on it, they called my captain. I was immediately ordered back to the station and told to forget everything. As always, it's all very government hush-hush. I have no idea where they took him or what they plan to do with him. But from what we know of the CRU, I sure wouldn't want to be in that kid's shoes. Or winged sandals either, for that matter."

PAELEN WAS SITTING UP IN BED IN A SECURE
hospital unit. Men in white coats were hooking up
a lot of strange wires to him. Several were taped to
his chest, while others were secured to his face and
head. When he tried to rip them off, two men in
white overalls rushed forward and caught hold of his
hands to restrain him. But when Paelen proved too
strong for them, more men arrived. They wrestled
his hands down until he was finally handcuffed to
the sides of the bed.

"Where am I?" Paelen demanded as he struggled
against the steel cuffs clamped on his wrists. "What
is this place? Why have you put me in chains?"

"We ask the questions," said one of the men in

overalls. "Not you. So just lie still for a moment while we finish hooking you up."

"I do not understand," Paelen said as he looked at the frightening array of machines being drawn up to the side of the bed. "What is hooking me up? What more are you doing to me?"

"Just relax," said a doctor. "We're not going to hurt you. This equipment will tell us a little bit more about you. It will record your heart rate and brain impulses. It will show me if you are very different from us."

"Of course I am different from you," Paelen said indignantly. "You are human and I, Olympian!"

The men in overalls raised their eyebrows at each other.

"Olympian, huh?" one of them said. "And I suppose you're the great Zeus himself?"

"If I were," Paelen asked, "would I receive better treatment?"

The man shrugged. "Maybe."

"Then I am he. Zeus," Paelen said quickly. "And as such, I demand you release me."

"Sorry, Zeusie old boy, no can do," the man said once he was certain Paelen's steel handcuffs were secure. "There are a lot of folks around here very interested in speaking to you. So just lie still and be patient. They'll be with you soon."

Seeing that his pleas were hopeless, Paelen lay back and became quiet. He couldn't believe what was happening to him. All he ever wanted was to get hold of Pegasus and be free. Free of Olympus and Jupiter with all his rules. Free of the Nirads and the war.

He'd never wanted to visit this world or meet any of its people. He'd heard countless stories about it when he was growing up. Of the strange people who lived here and how they worshipped the Olympians. But he'd never been curious about them or tempted to visit. They were just human. What could they possibly offer someone like him? But in following Pegasus here, he'd been struck by one of Jupiter's lightning bolts and was now trapped.

It was bad enough waking in that strange place they called Bellevue Hospital. But things had quickly gone from bad to worse when more men arrived to take him away. He had tried to fight them off, but his wounds were too great. Now here he was in this place, enduring more horrors.

Paelen was helpless to stop them from stealing more of his precious blood. They'd cut off samples of his hair and shone their bright lights in his eyes until he could no longer see. He'd been studied like youngsters in Olympus studied insects they found on the steps of Jupiter's palace. Poked and prodded and put in a strange device they called the MRI.

When they'd tired of that torture, Paelen had been brought to this room. It had no windows and was without any obvious means of escape except through a single door.

Paelen could smell the earth pressing in behind the white walls. He knew that wherever he was, it was deep beneath the ground.

He wondered if these same people had captured Pegasus. Was the great stallion somewhere in this place with him? Part of Paelen wanted to ask. But another part of him thought better of it. These were not good people. If Pegasus hadn't been captured, he wasn't about to alert them to his presence. He owed the stallion that much.

Watching the men as they buzzed around him like bees, Paelen tried to figure out how best to escape.

That had always been one of his talents in Olympus. No matter where Jupiter locked him up, he always managed to get away.

But with those heavy white things they called casts on his legs and his broken bones and deep burns, this wasn't the time to make his move. Instead he would tolerate his captors. Play with them, taunt them, and do his best to learn all their weaknesses.

Only when he had recovered and was strong again would he make his move. He would leave this place of pain and despair. And finally, he would capture Pegasus.

EMILY PICKED AT HER FOOD, UNABLE TO EAT.
The story her father had just told her was spinning
around in her head. She was convinced that Paelen
had something to do with Pegasus. But with the
stallion unable to speak, and Paelen now spirited
away by the CRU, Emily had no idea how they were
connected.

Not long after supper, Emily's father went to bed
for a few hours before his next shift. The moment he
shut his bedroom door, Emily dashed back into the
kitchen to gather together food and drinks to take up
to Joel and Pegasus.

"You're not going to believe this," Emily said as
she arrived breathlessly back on the roof. "There's

another Olympian in New York! His name is Paelen, and—"

The moment Emily said the name, Pegasus started to shriek and tear furiously at the shed's floorboards.

"Pegasus, what is it?" Emily ran over and stroked the stallion's quivering muzzle. "Do you know Paelen?"

Pegasus snorted angrily, rose on his hind legs, and came down brutally on the floorboards. His sharp hooves cut into the wood, tearing up huge splinters.

"Please, stop," Emily cried. "You've got to calm down. My father's asleep in the apartment below us. If he hears you, he'll come up and find you!"

Pegasus stopped tearing at the boards but shook his head, still snorting and whinnying. Emily looked desperately over to Joel.

"What do you think is wrong with him?"

"Easy boy, calm down," Joel soothed. He turned to Emily. "Seems that Pegasus doesn't like Paelen, whoever he is."

"Is that it?" she asked the stallion. "Don't you like Paelen?"

Pegasus became still and strangely silent. He looked Emily straight in the eye. In that moment, Emily felt a tight connection to him. Somehow she knew that Paelen was someone who had hurt Pegasus and caused a lot of trouble for him. As she stared into his large, dark eyes, strange images suddenly flooded her mind. She saw Pegasus in the dark, storm-filled sky with lightning flashing all around him. She felt his determination, his fear—and his urgent need to get somewhere, knowing it was a matter of life and death. Then she saw a boy in the sky beside the stallion. The boy was older than Joel, but not nearly as big. He was flying beside Pegasus and reaching across to the stallion. Then she saw him snatching Pegasus's golden bridle away. Suddenly there was a bright, blinding flash of lightning and terrible, searing pain—

"Emily," Joel repeated. "Emily, what's wrong?"

Breaking the connection, Emily blinked and staggered on her feet. "Joel?" she said in a soft and distant voice.

"Are you all right?"

"I'm—I'm fine, I think." Emily's head started to

clear. She concentrated on Joel, now looking anxiously at her. "I just saw the strangest thing," she said.

"What?"

Emily looked back to the stallion. "Pegasus, what I just saw? It was true, wasn't it? Paelen took the bridle from you. It was because of him you were hit by lightning."

Pegasus snorted and butted Emily gently. *Yes*.

"Please tell me," Joel pressed. "What did you see?"

"I don't know how to explain it," she said. "But it was kind of like watching television, only much more intense. When Paelen got the golden bridle off Pegasus, it attracted lightning and they were both hit."

"So now we've got to find this Paelen and get it back," Joel suggested.

"That's going to be impossible," Emily said. Stroking Pegasus, she explained about the conversation with her father and how Paelen had been taken by CRU, the secret government agency.

"I've never heard of the crew," Joel said, bewildered. "And my dad worked for the United Nations."

"Not crew," Emily corrected, "C-R-U. Central Research Unit. They just pronounce it like the word 'crew.' Not a lot of people know about them. These guys deal with weird science stuff and anything to do with aliens. My dad says, when the CRU come to get you, you're never seen or heard from again. He's had to deal with them a couple of times in his career, and each time, he was threatened and ordered to stay quiet or there'd be trouble. If the CRU ever learned about Pegasus, they would take him away and we'd never see him again."

"If they're as bad as you say," Joel said, "we'd probably disappear too, just because we've seen him."

"Exactly," Emily said. "Which is why we have to be extra careful until Pegasus's wing heals. He's got to get safely away to finish whatever it is he came here for."

"Did he show you what that was?"

"No," Emily said. "All I saw was Paelen stealing the bridle and then both of them getting hit by lightning. But it felt like life-and-death kind of stuff." She turned back to the stallion, "Isn't it, Pegasus?"

The stallion nodded and pounded the floorboards.

"So if we can't go after Paelen to get the bridle, what do we do?" Joel asked.

Emily shrugged. "I guess we just keep Pegasus safe and warm until he heals."

Joel nodded. "And to do that, he needs plenty of good food and care. Did you find any honey?"

Emily started to go through the bags she'd carried up from her kitchen. "I've got some honey, corn syrup, brown sugar and white sugar, and more sweet cereal. But I still can't believe a horse should be eating all this stuff."

Pegasus protested loudly.

"Sorry, Pegs," she said. She looked at Joel with a half smile. "He really hates being called a horse, doesn't he?"

"Wouldn't you, if you were him?" said Joel.

As Emily poured half the box of sweet cereal into a huge plastic bowl, Joel opened the can of corn syrup and poured it on top. He added several spoonfuls of brown sugar.

"Yuck!" Emily said as the stallion started to eat hungrily. "How can you do that, Pegs? After this, I don't think I'll ever eat that cereal again."

After Pegasus was fed, Joel sat down to eat the sandwiches Emily had prepared for him.

"What time do you need to get home?" she asked. Checking her watch, she saw it was just past six in the evening. The sun was still up, but had already crossed the city and would start to set in a couple of hours.

"I'm not going back," Joel said casually after taking a long drink of milk right from the carton.

"Not going back?" Emily said in alarm. "Won't your parents worry?"

Joel looked away. "My parents are dead. I'm living in a foster home. The people there hardly ever notice me, so probably not." He tried to sound indifferent, but Emily could hear the quiver in his tone fighting through the bravado. She wasn't sure what to say; she'd had no clue about Joel's past.

"I didn't know. Joel, I'm so sorr—"

"It's okay," he said almost too quickly. "It's not like I've told anyone." He looked down, avoiding her gaze, and began to speak slowly. "Three years ago I was living with my family in Connecticut. We were going away for the weekend when a drunk driver lost control of his car and crashed into us. My parents and little brother were killed instantly. I was hurt too, but somehow I survived. Though every day since it happened, I wish I hadn't."

"Oh, Joel," Emily said in a hushed voice. "It must have been terrible."

Joel said nothing for a long time. Finally he looked at her. "I've been in foster care ever since. But I hate it."

Emily was too stunned to speak. She could never have imagined this. She knew what it was to suffer the pain of losing one parent, but she couldn't imagine what it would be like to lose your entire family.

"Isn't there anyone in Italy you could go live with?"

"No," Joel said sharply. "No one wanted me. So I'm stuck here." He lifted his chin in defiance. "But not for much longer. I'm planning to run away. I'll find someplace where no one will be able to tell me where to go, what to do, or anything ever again. I'll finally be free!"

Joel stood up quickly and crossed to Pegasus. Emily watched the tension in his shoulders fade as he stroked the stallion's face. "I'm going to stay here tonight," he said, his back to Emily. "I don't like leaving Pegasus alone."

Emily stood and put her hands on her hips. He might have a tough life, but there was no need to insult her. "Gee, thanks, Joel, for the vote of confidence," she said, suddenly riled. "But for your information, in case you hadn't noticed, I'm here. So he's not alone."

"You know what I mean," Joel said. "You've got to get back down to your apartment before your father goes to work tonight. I can stay here so Pegasus doesn't get frightened."

Emily was about to say something more, but the look in his eyes stopped her.

He was nothing like the angry person she'd met this morning on his front stoop. In his eyes she suddenly saw—need. Joel needed to stay with Pegasus.

"All right," she said. "You can stay. There are some extra blankets and pillows I can bring up. But just so you know, I'm planning to stay up here too. Once my dad goes to work, we can bring everything up. It'll kind of be like camping."

"Without the marshmallows," Joel added.

"I think we might have some of those," Emily said. "But if I know Pegasus, he'll take them from me before I even open the bag!"

9

AFTER THE DOCTORS FINISHED HOOKING
Paelen up to the equipment, they went over to their
computers to check out the readings.

Paelen watched them curiously but said nothing.
Instead he concentrated on his surroundings. On the
wall behind him, high above the bed, was a small
ventilation grille. He could feel fresh air blowing gently down on him. He could also hear sounds coming
from other rooms floating through the same grille.
That meant that there was a system of tunnels up
there that he could easily slip through. Tunnels were
his specialty. There wasn't one tunnel in all Olympus he couldn't slip through, or find his way out of;
including the great labyrinth of the Minotaur. Paelen

knew that once he was free of the casts on his legs, he would be able to find his way to the surface.

Of course, there was also the issue of the handcuffs. But he'd seen that the men in the overalls had keys to the locks. If he worked it out properly, he could easily get the keys away from them. Failing that, Paelen could always use his talent for stretching out his body, though he preferred not to.

As his mind worked on the problem, Paelen heard the same strange series of beeping sounds he'd heard before. Soon after the door to the room opened, and two men entered.

One was middle-aged with salt-and-pepper hair. He was wearing a dark suit and had a grim expression on his face. The other man was much younger, with light blond hair cut short. Also wearing a dark suit, he looked equally unpleasant.

With their backs to Paelen, they started to whisper with the doctors. Paelen couldn't help but smile. They had no idea that he could clearly hear them discussing the test results and what had been learned so far. Just like they didn't know he could hear the other voices through the grille above him.

Once again, Paelen was reminded of how different he was to these humans. And even though the meaning of some of their words eluded him, he understood enough. They were discussing how extraordinary his brain patterns were. How he had superior muscle strength and density. How his bones were flexible and nothing like human bones, which partially explained how he'd survived the fall. They'd also found several organs they couldn't identify. When asked, one of the doctors suggested that Paelen was no more than seventeen years old.

That comment nearly had Paelen in fits of laughter. He had to bite his own tongue to keep from laughing out loud. If they knew the truth of his age, he was certain they would never believe him. But then again, maybe they would. That could only make things much worse for him.

Finally the two new men sat down in chairs beside Paelen's bed. The older man pulled out a small black device from his pocket and flicked a switch. He held it up to his lips and started speaking.

"CRU report, C.49.21-J. First interview. Date: June second. Time: nineteen hundred hours. Subject is male. His approximate age is seventeen. Medical tests reveal multiple injuries consistent with a lightning strike and fall from a great height.

"Further tests reveal profound physical anomalies. The subject's organs are not where they should be. We've identified several other organs whose function is as yet undetermined. These warrant further investigation. Subject has multiple broken bones, which are healing at a remarkable rate. Blood work has revealed an unknown cross-type with unfamiliar properties. Subject is physically strong despite his small size and youthful outward appearance. . . ."

Paelen watched the man speaking into the device. It sounded like he was describing some kind of monster and not him. The more he listened, the more he started to understand the degree of trouble he was in.

Finally the man finished and turned his attention to Paelen. "State your name for the record," he demanded, holding the device toward Paelen.

At first Paelen remained silent. But when the man repeated the question, he thought this would be a good time to start his own investigation. Breaking his silence, he replied, "Subject."

"That is not your name," the man said.

"Perhaps not," Paelen agreed. "However, it is the name you have given me. One name is as good as any other, is it not?"

"I didn't call you Subject."

"Yes, you did."

"I don't think so," the older man said.

"But you did," Paelen insisted. "Just now. You were speaking into that little black box and said, 'Subject has multiple broken bones, which are healing at a remarkable rate.' Then you said, 'Subject is strong despite his small size and youthful outward appearance.' So if it pleases you to call me Subject, then that shall be my name. I am Subject."

"I don't want to call you Subject," the man said, becoming irritated. "I just want to know how we address you before we start with our other questions."

Paelen noticed that this man was easily flustered. He was worse than Mercury. And Mercury was always the easiest of the Olympians to upset. Lines of frustration and anger already showed on the man's face. He lips were pressed tightly together, and his brows were knitted in a deep frown.

Paelen decided to push the man a little further to test him. "You seem confused," he said. "If this happens so easily over the simple issue of my name, I am certain you would be far too challenged to understand the answers to any questions you might pose."

The man shook his head in growing frustration. "I am not confused," he said angrily. "And I know your name isn't Subject. Subject isn't a name. It is what you are."

"And yet you still insist on calling me it." Paelen lay back against the pillows, enjoying the game. "I do not understand you. You are obviously a man of questionable intelligence. Please leave."

The man's face turned bright red. He took several deep breaths to calm himself. "Perhaps we'd better start again," he said. "Very simply, what is your name?"

"You may call me Jupiter."

"What? Did you say Jupiter?"

"Are you hard of hearing as well as ignorant?" Paelen asked. He turned his attention to the younger man. "I believe it is time you took him away. He is obviously unwell and should be restrained."

The older man stood up in a fury. "Why, you arrogant little—"

"Calm down, Agent J." The younger man grasped the older man's arm. "Sit down, and let me try."

Paelen carefully studied the relationship between the two. The older man was obviously in command. However, he seemed to accept advice from the younger one, as he calmed somewhat.

The younger man directed his attention to Paelen. "In the hospital, you told the doctor your name was Paelen the Magnificent. Which is it? Jupiter or Paelen?"

"If you insist," Paelen said, "I am Paelen the Magnificent. Now, release me."

"Or what?" the older man challenged.

"Or I shall bring the wrath of Olympus down upon you."

"The wrath of *Olympus*?" he cried.

"Must you always repeat everything I say?" Paelen asked. "It is really quite distracting."

The older man's hand shot out and gripped Paelen's wrist. "I have had enough of your games, young man. They stop right now. We're not letting you go. Not now, not ever. Now, you will tell us who you are, where you came from, and why you are here."

The grip on Paelen's wrist was tight, but certainly not enough to hurt him. Yet he could see that this was the man's intention. "I will answer your questions only after you have answered some of mine," he said. "I demand to know where I am. Who are you? And why you are holding me?"

"We ask the questions here, not you," the older man said as he tightened his grip.

"Then we have nothing further to discuss," Paelen answered, turning away from their prying eyes. "You may tell the others to bring ambrosia to me now."

"We will do no such thing," the younger man said. "Look, kid, this isn't funny. If you make my colleague much angrier, he'll break your wrist."

Paelen grew serious and sat up, ignoring the pain from his broken ribs. He looked at both men, then concentrated on the older one. "If you think you can hurt me with this baby grip of yours, you are sadly mistaken. I have faced down the wrath of the Minotaur and a Hydra. I have fought the Nirads and won. I am certainly not frightened of a human like you, or the empty threats you make."

"I assure you, my threats are not empty," the older man warned. "So don't make me do something you'll regret. Just tell us who you are and where you came from."

Paelen didn't like these men one bit. "If you insist, I am Mercury," he finally answered. "I came to your world for a visit but was wounded during a storm. When I recover, I shall return to Olympus."

"Still with the Greek myths?" Agent J said darkly.

"Mercury is from the Roman myths," the younger man corrected. "Hermes is the Greek."

Paelen watched the older man flash the younger one a withering look. "Whatever!"

He turned back to Paelen. "That isn't an answer. Tell me what I want to know."

"But I told you," Paelen insisted. "I am Mercury. You have my sandals. Surely you have seen their wings. Who else but the messenger of Olympus would use such things?"

Agent J took in a deep breath and held it. When he let it out again, he squared his shoulders and sat back. "If you continue to refuse to answer, I promise you, we can make things very uncomfortable for you."

"Things already are uncomfortable for me," Paelen said. "But I am still telling you the truth. That you refuse to believe me is not my fault."

Agent J looked at the younger man. "We're not getting anywhere with him." He checked his watch, then spoke into the black device. "Time: nineteen hundred twenty. End of interview."

Angrily, he shut off his device and looked at Paelen. "Whether we call you Mercury, Jupiter, Paelen, or Subject, it couldn't matter less. What does matter is that you belong to me. You will answer all my questions. Even if I have to rip the truth from your lips one word at a time."

Paelen saw the threat in his eyes. This man meant every word he said.

The men walked over to the small gray device beside the door. Paelen paid particular attention as the older man pressed several buttons. It made the same strange beeps he'd heard right before they entered the room.

"A sound lock," Paelen whispered softly to himself as he watched them pull open the door and leave the room. "If Jupiter could not build a prison to hold me, what makes you think you can?"

AN HOUR BEFORE MIDNIGHT, EMILY'S FATHER
was preparing for work.

"You sure you're going to be all right on your
own?" he asked.

Emily nodded and handed over his packed meal.
"I'm really tired from working in the garden today. I
bet I'll be asleep the moment my head hits the pillow."

"All right," he said as he kissed the top of her head.
"Just don't be too nervous with the power out. You've
got the flashlight and plenty of extra batteries. I'd
prefer you not to use candles, if you don't mind."

"I understand," Emily said. "What time are you
going to be home tomorrow?"

Her father sighed. "Late, I'm afraid. It's another

double shift. I won't be home until supper tomorrow night. But you've still got plenty of food, and there's lots of water left. You shouldn't have to go out anywhere. Now remember, if you need me—"

"I know, I'll call." Emily smiled and gently started to shove her father toward the front door. "Go to work, Dad. The city needs you."

"I hope you need me too," he said as he put on his cap.

"I'll always need you," Emily assured him as she rose on tiptoes to kiss his cheek. "Please be careful and come home safe."

"I will," he promised as he turned on his police flashlight and entered the dark hall. Turning back to her a final time, he said, "Lock the door after me."

"Will you please go?" Emily said, laughing.

After he had gone, Emily waited awhile before heading for the stairs. Stepping out on the open roof, she was once again struck by the beautiful star-studded night sky. "Wow!" she said. "I've never seen so many stars!"

"It's amazing, isn't it?" Joel agreed, moving away from Pegasus. "You don't even need your flashlight."

After sunset, Pegasus could leave the garden shed to freely wander the roof without the fear of being seen by curious neighbors. Emily saw the stallion standing before her father's strawberry plants. He was busily eating all the ripe berries he could find.

"He hasn't stopped eating since the sun went down," Joel said. "If it's growing and sweet, he's eating it. I'm afraid he's ruined what was left of the tomato patch."

"Tomatoes?" Emily repeated. "We didn't plant tomatoes this year. With my mother so sick, we didn't come up here at all."

"They must have grown back from last year," Joel suggested. "There's lots of stuff growing."

Emily approached Pegasus as he stood before the strawberries. "Hi, boy," she said as she stroked his folded wing.

Pegasus reached out and dropped a single ripe strawberry into Emily's hand.

"Thanks, Pegs!" Emily said in shock. She ate the berry and savored the sweet flavor.

"I can't believe you just ate that," Joel said in horror. "It's been in his mouth."

"So?"

"So, it's disgusting. It's got to be full of germs."

"Don't be silly," Emily said. "I bet we've got loads more germs than him." She turned her attention to Pegasus. "So, how are you feeling tonight?"

"He's getting better," Joel answered. "He's even been stretching out his wing to test it. I don't think it'll be too long before he's ready to go."

Emily suddenly felt a deep pang of sorrow. Pegasus couldn't be with her forever, she knew that. But after the recent loss of her mother, losing him as well seemed too much to bear.

As if the stallion knew what she was thinking, he offered her a second strawberry. The simple gesture brought tears to her eyes.

"Thank you, Pegasus," she said softly.

"Hey, are you crying?" Joel asked. "What's wrong?"

"Nothing," Emily said, furiously wiping tears away. "I'm tired. I didn't sleep last night, and we've been on the go ever since. I just need a bit of rest."

"Didn't you say we were going to camp out up here tonight?" When Emily nodded, Joel beamed. "Well, let's go back down to your apartment and get the blankets. Then we can get some sleep."

Emily nodded and sniffed back the last of her silent tears. "I promised Pegasus marshmallows. So I'll grab them, too."

Soon Emily and Joel were back on the roof with two sleeping bags, several blankets, and two pillows.

One of the blankets was draped over Pegasus to keep the stallion warm. But as Emily and Joel settled down on two long lounge chairs, they were surprised when the stallion lowered himself to the ground and rested between them.

"Why do you think he's here?" Joel asked as he lay back in the lounge chair, staring at the stars.

"I don't know," Emily said as she lay on her side and stroked Pegasus's neck. "I know it's really important, but I can't see why."

"Maybe it has to do with that other Olympian, Paelen."

"From what I saw, Pegasus was already on his way here when Paelen stole his bridle. I think he was more of a nuisance than anything else."

They settled into a comfortable silence. The evening was cool but not cold, and the stars above and silence of the city made them feel like they really were out camping.

"Joel," Emily said tentatively. "What's it like living in a foster home?"

She heard him take a deep breath and instantly regretted asking him.

"Why do you want to know?" he challenged, his voice growing hard.

"Please don't get angry again," she said. "It was just a question."

"I'm not angry," Joel fired back. "I just don't like talking about it."

"I'm sorry, I shouldn't have asked," Emily said quickly. She turned over and pulled the covers up. "Let's just forget it and go to sleep."

Joel remained silent for a long time. She could hear his heavy breathing but had no idea what he was thinking.

"Emily, I'm sorry," he said at last. "I shouldn't take it out on you. But you don't understand. After my family died, I lost everything I've ever known. Everyone I ever cared about. I've been alone ever since."

Emily turned back over to face him but did not speak.

He inhaled deeply again. "Things didn't work out too good with my first foster family. We were always fighting. So they sent me to this new one. But I really hate it. There are loads of other kids, and my foster parents are always yelling. I have to share a bedroom with four other boys. They're always stealing my stuff."

"Can't you ask to go somewhere else?" Emily asked.

"I've tried talking to my social workers, but they always say no. They say I should be grateful to have a place to live. They don't care what it's like there."

"No wonder you want to run away," Emily said thoughtfully. "I would too."

"And I will. Right after we get Pegasus healed." Joel reached out to stroke the stallion. "Maybe he'll take me away with him when he goes." He paused, and his voice became dreamy. "Pegasus and me. Now that would be a dream come true."

LONG BEFORE DAWN, THE SKIES OPENED UP
and awoke Emily and Joel with shockingly cold rain.
In the time it took them to find the flashlight and
guide Pegasus back into the garden shed, they were
both soaked to the skin and shivering.

Huddled together in the shed, they looked out at
the heavy rain beating down on the roof.

"At least there's no lightning," Emily said through
chattering teeth.

"That would be all we need," Joel agreed. When
he saw how cold Emily was, he moved closer. "I don't
think we should stay up here much longer. We're
both soaking wet and freezing."

"But I don't want to leave Pegasus alone."

"Me either," Joel said. "But we won't do him much good if we both get pneumonia."

Emily reached out and stroked the stallion's neck. His skin was warm to the touch. He wasn't shivering at all.

"You're right. I'm really freezing." Emily stepped closer to Pegasus, "We'll be back soon, Pegs," she promised.

Then she and Joel dashed across the roof and toward the stairwell door.

Back in the apartment, Emily borrowed some of her father's clothes for Joel, while she went into her own room to change. When she returned to the living room, she found Joel sound asleep on the sofa.

Pulling down a throw blanket, she covered her new friend. After a moment's hesitation, she went into her bedroom and sank into bed. Within a minute she had drifted off.

The rain continued all the next day. Despite it being almost summer, with the rain, the temperature dropped, keeping Emily and Joel from spending the entire day on the roof with Pegasus. Instead they split their time between the roof and gathering food for the stallion in the kitchen.

"We're now all out of sugar," Emily said. "And corn syrup, cereal, and honey."

"I've never seen such a big appetite," Joel agreed. "That horse doesn't stop eating!"

"Don't let him hear you calling him a horse." Emily laughed. "He hates that."

"He does, doesn't he." Joel chuckled.

Joel crossed to one of the apartment's many windows. "The rain is letting up a bit," he said. "And I can see down on the street a couple of the wholesalers are opening."

"With no power?" Emily asked as she joined him.

"Looks like it," Joel said. "Where is your nearest grocery store?"

"There's a big one a few blocks away," said Emily. "Dad and I usually go there on Saturday."

"I'll go there," Joel said. "We've drained your kitchen, and Pegasus needs more food. Besides, your dad is bound to notice everything missing."

"How are you going to manage?" Emily said. "Joel, there's no power. No elevator. If the store is open, you'll be carrying heavy bags up twenty flights of stairs. Remember how we felt the first time we did it?"

"I know, but I have to try."

"Then I'll come with you," Emily said. "That way we can carry more."

Joel shook his head. "Thanks for the offer, but I don't think you should. You know how upset Pegasus gets if you leave him for too long. You should go on the roof with him. I promise I won't be long."

Emily really wanted to help, but she knew Joel was right. As Pegasus healed, he was becoming more and more agitated. It was becoming difficult to keep him in the shed.

"You're right," she finally agreed. She went into her father's room to open the secret drawer where they kept hidden cash. "Dad keeps this here in case of emergencies," she said. "It should be enough to get everything we need."

Joel accepted the money and the offer of her father's raincoat. Taking the flashlight and some heavy-duty shopping bags Emily gave him, he guided her up to the roof. Then, as he headed back down the stairs, he smiled over his shoulder at her.

"Don't take any test flights without me!"

Emily smiled back and promised not to. She shut the stairwell door and headed over to the shed.

"He's gone to get you lots of sweet things," she explained as she adjusted the blanket over the stallion's wings. "I just hope the store is open."

As Emily stroked the stallion's neck, she felt Pegasus starting to quiver. But not from the cold rain. His blanket was clean and dry and his skin was warm to the touch. Yet he seemed to be growing even more anxious as his hooves pounded the floorboards.

"What is it, Pegs?" she asked. "What's wrong? Are you in pain?"

Worried for the stallion, Emily checked on his broken wing. She could actually feel the broken bones had somehow knitted back together. "Well, it's not your wing. What about the spear wound?" Crossing to the other side, Emily lifted Pegasus's good wing and pulled the duct tape away from his flank. She was shocked to see that the wound was completely healed.

"Wow!" she cried. "It's gone. How are you doing that? Is it all the sugar?"

Pegasus pawed the ground. His eyes were bright and alert. But there was something in them that worried her.

They watched the rain together. It was coming down heavily again, and she worried about Joel. Emily lost all track of time until she heard Joel calling her name from the stairwell.

"Are you all right?" She raced over to him.

"I will be once I throw up," he panted, leaning heavily against the stairwell door frame.

Emily reached for the bags in his hands and was shocked by the weight. "How much did you buy?"

"As much as I could. It's crazy out there. People are shopping like it's the end of the world! I had to fight an old lady for the last two bottles of honey. Don't even ask me what it was like in the cereal aisle."

In the shed, Pegasus started to neigh.

"Someone's hungry again," Joel said tiredly. He pulled out a box of colorful kids' cereal and tore it open. He held it out for Pegasus to eat.

"He's more than hungry," Emily said. "Something is really bothering him."

"Do you have any idea what it is?" Joel asked.

Emily shook her head. "Whatever it is, I have a feeling it isn't good."

After making sure Pegasus had enough to eat, they went back down to the apartment and unpacked the rest of the food.

"My dad is due home shortly," Emily said. "I don't think it's a good idea for you to meet him just yet."

"Why?" Joel asked, looking hurt. "Don't you want him to meet me?"

"Joel, my dad is a cop," Emily pointed out. "It's his nature to be suspicious. If he finds out you're in care, he'll want to contact your foster parents, and they may want to take you away. Pegasus needs both of us."

"So what are you suggesting?" Joel asked.

Emily sighed. "I really hate to lie to him. I think you should stay here, but keep hidden."

"Where?" he said, looking around at the apartment. "This place isn't that big."

"I guess you could stay in my room."

"Where will you stay?"

"In my room too," Emily said. "There's plenty of

space on the floor. Besides, we'll be spending most of our time with Pegs. It's only for when my dad is around. And with the blackout, he's working double shifts."

"I could always stay up on the roof with Pegasus," Joel suggested.

Emily shook her head. "It's still raining. You can't sleep outside, you'll freeze to death."

"But what if your dad catches me?"

"You're going to have to be careful so he doesn't," said Emily. "That's all."

Joel shrugged. "That's easier said than done."

The moment Emily's father returned from work, Joel dashed into Emily's bedroom. Despite his concerns, Joel kept hidden and actually slept well on the floor beside Emily's bed. By the time he rose the next morning, Emily was already up and her father had left for work again.

"Sleep all right?" she asked as she handed him a glass of orange juice.

"Great," he said. "I think that's probably the best night's sleep I've had in a very long time."

o o o

When they arrived back on the roof, Pegasus was in a state. He was out of the shed, snorting and pawing angrily at the ground. His sharp hooves had cut deep trenches in the tarmac. Emily realized that if they didn't stop him soon, he might make it all the way through to the apartment.

"What is it, Pegs?" Emily cried, racing over to the stallion. "What's wrong?"

"Emily, look," Joel said, pointing at the stallion's food. "He hasn't touched a thing. I wonder if all the sugar is starting to make him sick."

"I don't know." Emily stroked the stallion's neck. She could feel every nerve in his body tensing. "But he doesn't look sick. Look at his eyes, Joel. Pegasus is frightened."

"Of what?"

Emily shrugged. "Whatever it is, if it's got him frightened, it's got to be bad."

All morning Emily and Joel remained with Pegasus. Instead of calming, the stallion grew more agitated. He pawed the tarmac and succeeded in tearing a hole in the roof. Emily could now see down into her father's bedroom.

"How are we going to explain that?" she cried. "Pegs, please—you have to calm down!"

Yet no matter what they tried, there was nothing they could do to calm the stallion.

As the afternoon wore on, they heard loud, warning voices calling from the tall building across the street.

"Oh no!" Emily looked desperately over to the people standing before their open windows. They were pointing and shouting at the roof. "Joel, they've seen Pegasus!"

Joel stared at the groups of people gathering in the various windows. He could see more than curiosity on their faces. He saw fear.

"They look scared, too," he said. "Emily, look at them. They're not pointing at Pegasus. They're pointing at the side of your building."

As they listened, they heard the voices of the people across the street telling them to get off the roof and run.

"What do they mean, run?" Emily asked, as she stepped closer to the edge.

Suddenly Pegasus went mad. He stood on his hind

legs and started to scream. As his wings flew open, he hit Emily and knocked her several feet away from the edge. Pegasus reared over her. He was shrieking in rage and kicking out his front legs.

"Emily, get back!" Joel cried. "He's gone crazy!"

As Joel tried to drag Emily away, Pegasus lunged forward. Pushing past Joel, he charged the edge of the roof just as a monstrous-looking creature crested the top.

"JOEL, LOOK!" EMILY SCREAMED AND pointed. Joel turned.

Several four-armed creatures were climbing over the top edge of the roof. They were pale gray, with mottled skin like marble. Pegasus kicked the first one in the head and sent him tumbling down the side of the building. But as he went for a second creature, a third made it to the top. Letting out a ferocious roar, it lunged at the stallion.

"No!" Emily howled.

Joel raced to the stairwell, where Emily had left the baseball bat after she first discovered Pegasus. Grabbing it, he ran back over to the attacking creature.

"Get off him!" he howled. "Leave him alone!"

Joel swung the bat. Then he swung it again. But every time it made contact with the creature's back, it had no effect. The only thing that seemed to slow it down was when Pegasus kicked it with a golden hoof.

More murderous marble-skinned creatures crawled over the top edge. All focused on Pegasus. All determined to kill the stallion.

Emily's instincts took over. She ran to where she had left the contents of the garden shed and picked up a large pitchfork. Raising it in the air, she launched herself at the nearest monster trying to kill Pegasus.

But as they fought, another one of them focused on her. Leaving the stallion, it started to stalk Emily.

"Joel!" Emily cried. She struck out at the creature. As it drew near, its foul stench was almost overwhelming. Emily could see that its eyes were jet-black with no whites or color at all. Its teeth were large, sharp points, and it was drooling as it made ferocious, guttural sounds.

The horror attacking her was wearing rags tied loosely around its waist. But its upper half was bare. She could see the thick muscles rippling as it flexed its four arms, which ended in filthy hands and fingers with long, sharp claws.

Emily tried to defend herself. But wherever the three points of the pitchfork hit, nothing happened. They simply slipped off the creature's bare skin as if it were made of steel.

"Go for its eyes!" Joel shouted, running at the creature with Emily. Raising his bat, he used all his strength to hit it on the back of the head.

The blow only stunned it for an instant. But it was enough. Emily lunged forward and jammed the points of the pitchfork into its black eyes. Howling in rage, the creature fell to the ground and raised two hands to its face. Black liquid oozed between its fingers and dripped onto the tarmac. Where it hit the roof, the tar started to melt and smoke.

"Get down the stairs!" Joel cried as he raised his bat over the writhing monster.

"I'm not leaving Pegs!"

Emily ran forward to attack more of the creatures going after Pegasus. The stallion was still rearing on his back legs, kicking out at five attacking monsters. They had learned the damage Pegasus could inflict with his golden hooves and were staying out of his kicking range. Instead they lunged forward and dipped back, trying to get at the stallion's exposed underside.

"Fly away, Pegs!" Emily cried. "Get out of here!"

Instead of leaving, Pegasus shrieked in rage and crashed back down to all fours. He lowered his head and charged through the group of monsters, straight at Emily. Before she could react, he caught her by the shirt and hoisted her off the ground effortlessly. Lifting her easily over his head and wings, in one fluid motion he deposited her squarely on his back.

Next he ran at Joel. As with Emily, he caught hold of Joel's shirt. But instead of tossing him onto his back, Pegasus held Joel firmly in his teeth and ran full speed for the edge of the building. Emily saw what Pegasus was planning and reached forward to catch hold of the stallion's thick white mane. An instant later Pegasus launched himself into the air and was spreading his huge white wings.

Terrified but unable to stop herself, Emily looked down. They were over the edge and soaring twenty stories above 29th Street.

"Emily, behind you!" Joel shrieked, dangling from Pegasus's mouth.

Emily turned. She screamed. A creature had leaped off the building to follow them. But it had misjudged the distance and was barely holding on to the stallion's back legs. Pegasus kicked out, trying to dislodge it. But it was holding fast. Its sharp claws dug into the stallion's hind end, and it slowly started to climb up onto Pegasus's back. Emily could see the fury and bloodlust raging in its beady black eyes. It wanted to kill. More than that—it wanted to kill *her*.

She let go of Pegasus's mane with one hand and slid farther down the stallion's back. Emily started to kick at the creature.

"Be careful!" Joel warned, struggling to turn back to her.

She knew her only chance was to go for its eyes. But every time she kicked at it, it moved out of her reach.

Emily repositioned herself to kick again as a grotesque hand sprang forward and caught hold of her left leg. She had never known such pain as the vise-like grip tightened on her calf. The sharp claws cut through her jeans and tore right through her skin to the muscle and bone. Crying in agony, she felt the creature draw her back toward it.

"NO!" she howled.

Suddenly Pegasus veered in the sky. They were heading straight for the side of a building. In the instant before they struck, Pegasus maneuvered his wings and turned so the creature and his entire back end smashed into a large window.

The window exploded with the impact. Shards of jagged glass cut into the winged stallion's hindquarters. Soon Pegasus's blood flowed, making his back too slippery for the creature to cling to. As it recovered from the brutal impact with the window, it started to lose its grip. The monster released Emily's leg and struggled to remain on the stallion.

Seizing the moment, Emily reached back and started to pry the creature's fingers away from the stallion's flank. Raking its claws down Pegasus's legs, it came away from the stallion and fell down to the ground twenty stories below.

"Emily, are you all right?" Joel called.

Emily didn't want to tell her friend about her leg.

"I'm fine. But Pegasus is bleeding!" she shouted over the wind at Joel. "We have to land."

"Not here," Joel cried. "Look!"

In all the fear and excitement, Emily hadn't had time to think, let alone notice that Pegasus had lost a lot of height and changed direction. They were now flying up Fifth Avenue, only eight or nine stories high. Despite the blackout, there were thousands of tourists out on the famous street, most of them pointing up at the winged stallion soaring in the sky above them.

"Higher, Pegs, you've got to fly higher!" Emily cried.

Clinging to his mane, Emily could feel Pegasus trying to force more height out of his wings. But it wasn't working. They were steadily losing height.

"The park," Joel cried. "We can hide in Central Park!"

Emily was in too much pain, and far too frightened for Pegasus to have truly felt the terror of actually flying on the stallion's back. Let alone on a broken wing that had barely had the chance to heal. Now she clung to his mane, praying that they would make it to the safety of Central Park.

"Come on," Emily coaxed. She could see the rise of trees in the distance. "Just a little bit farther and we can stop!"

As Pegasus struggled to stay in the air, Emily could see they were now only a few stories off the ground. She looked over to his broken wing and could see a spread of red growing on the white feathers where the break had been. The bones were coming apart.

She glanced forward again and saw that they'd reached 59th Street. Central Park was on her left.

"Go into the park, Pegasus. We can hide in the trees!"

Pegasus veered over the park. But the strain was too much for his broken wing. As they soared over the open Sheep Meadow, his wing finally gave out. The bones snapped completely. They started to fall out of the sky.

EMILY AWOKE IN TERRIBLE PAIN. HER BACK ached, her shoulder was badly bruised, and her leg was on fire.

She heard voices and felt something wet on her face. When she opened her eyes, she saw a large pink tongue licking her cheek. She moaned weakly.

"Don't move," a man's voice said. "I'm just finishing with the bandages."

Focusing her eyes, Emily saw a young man in soldier's fatigues working with Joel on her leg. Joel was holding her ankle in the air while the soldier started to wrap pieces of cloth around the bleeding wounds. Her jeans had been cut off at the knee. She could see the deep gouges in her skin and heavy bruising from the monster's brutal grip. Behind them, a young woman was tearing up a tablecloth and handing the pieces to the soldier.

Pegasus was resting on the ground beside her. A large plaid picnic blanket was covering his wings. He licked her face again.

"I'm all right, Pegs," she said softly as she lifted her hand to stroke his muzzle.

"What happened?" she asked weakly, wincing in pain as the first knot was tied on her leg.

"We crashed," said Joel. "Carrying us both was too much for Pegasus. His wing gave out and we came down on the edge of the meadow. Lucky for us it wasn't crowded."

"Just us," the soldier said. "And I'm glad. If the park had been as crowded as normal, you'd have had a riot on your hands." He leaned forward and offered his hand to Emily. "I'm Eric, and this is my girlfriend, Carol. I've been serving as a medic in Iraq and thought I'd seen a lot of strange things. But I couldn't believe it when I saw you in the sky."

"I still can't," Carol agreed nervously. "And I'm standing right here looking at you. Part of my mind says it's real, the other part says you are hallucinations."

"We're real, all right," Joel said. "And we're in big trouble."

Eric finished tying the last knot. "Well, that will do for the moment. But we have to get you to the hospital as soon as possible. Those cuts go right to the bone. You've got some serious muscle damage there. And by the looks of things, you need antibiotics to stop the infection."

"We can't go to the hospital." Emily struggled to sit up. The pain from her leg was making her feel sick. "We have to stay with Pegasus."

Eric sat back on his heels and stared over to the stallion. "A horse with wings," he said, shaking his head. "How amazing is that? Pegasus really exists."

"Yes, he does," Joel said. "And so do the creatures that tried to kill us. If Pegasus hadn't flown off the roof, we'd all be dead now."

Joel explained to Eric and Carol the events of the past few days. To their credit, they listened without interrupting. But the more they listened, the more frightened Carol grew.

"Whatever they are," Joel finished, "those things are still out there. Nothing seems to stop them. I watched the one that fell off Pegasus. When he hit the ground, he got up again and tried to follow us."

This was news to Emily. "But he fell twenty stories! How could he get up?"

Joel shrugged. "I don't know. I also don't know how they are tracking Pegasus, but they are. They all seemed to know he was on the roof with us."

"I can hardly believe any of this," Eric said. "Pegasus in New York City? Vicious four-armed monsters?"

"It's true, I swear it!" Emily said. "And they want to kill Pegs."

"I'm not saying I *don't* believe it," Eric said. "I'm looking at Pegasus right now, and I saw the damage that thing did to your leg. But where did they come from?"

Emily recalled a comment her father had made. "The sewers!" she cried. "My dad is a cop. He said they'd been getting stories from uptown of people claiming four-armed demons were coming out of the sewers. They were being dismissed as crazies. I bet they saw those monsters!"

Eric shook his head. "If those creatures are loose in New York, we have to call the military."

"We can't!" Emily said at once. "The CRU have already captured another Olympian. If they find out about Pegasus, they'll take him away as well."

"What are the CRU?" Carol asked.

Eric shivered and took Carol's hand. "You don't want to know," he said. "They're a real nasty government bunch. Trust me, you don't want them on your trail."

"It's already too late," Joel added. "Half the city saw us flying up Fifth Avenue. If the CRU didn't already know about us, they do now."

"Then we've got to get moving," Emily said. She tried to stand up, but the pain from her leg drove her down again.

"You're not going anywhere but the hospital with that leg," Eric said.

"I told you, I can't go to the hospital," Emily insisted. She tried to stand again, but fell. Finally she looked over to Joel. "Please, leave me here and take Pegasus. Hide him in the trees. But don't let the CRU or those creatures get him."

Pegasus snorted and shook his head.

Emily turned to the stallion. "You're the one they'll be after, not me," she said. "We can't let them get you. You've got to go with Joel."

"He can understand us?" Eric asked, looking even more astonished.

Emily nodded. "Please, Pegasus," she begged, "go with Joel."

Once again, the stallion snorted and stubbornly shook his head.

"Then we all go," Joel said, making a decision. "But we've got to get out of the open and under cover, right now."

As everyone stood, Pegasus climbed to his feet. When Joel lifted Emily in his arms, the stallion nudged him.

"It's all right, Pegasus," Joel assured him. "She's coming with us."

Pegasus nudged him again.

"I've got her," Joel insisted.

But Pegasus nudged him a third time. "What do you want?" Joel turned to the stallion.

"He wants to carry me," Emily said as she looked at the way Pegasus was staring at her.

"How can he?" Joel said. "His wing is broken again, and his back end is a mess because of that monster and the glass. He might buck and throw you off."

Emily saw the promise of protection in Pegasus's eyes. "No, he won't. Please put me on his back."

Joel grunted and carried Emily over to Pegasus, muttering to himself, "I can't believe I'm being ordered around by a horse!"

This time Pegasus let the insult slide. He stood quietly while Joel settled Emily on the blanket on his back. Joel then led the group under the cover of the park's dense trees.

"Eric?" Emily asked. "If you are a medic, do you think you could set a broken wing?"

"You mean his?" Eric indicated Pegasus. "Maybe. But would he let me?"

Emily patted the stallion's strong neck. "Would you, Pegasus? That wing needs to be set again. Eric's better at it than Joel and me."

When Pegasus didn't snort or protest, they took that as permission. Emily was taken off his back and stood unsteadily at the stallion's head while Eric and

Joel got to work setting the wing. Tree branches were used as splints while Carol tore up the remaining piece of tablecloth to secure everything in place.

When they finished, Eric put his hands on his hips. "I have been trained to do a lot of strange things. But I don't think the army could ever prepare anyone for that!"

"Thank you," Emily said. "I know Pegs appreciates it."

"We all do," Joel added. "Now all we need is a lot of sugar."

Emily saw Eric's confusion and explained, "Sugar and sweet foods seem to help him heal really quickly. Joel thinks it's because sugar is close to ambrosia, which they eat on Olympus."

"We've got some chocolate cake with us," Carol offered as she held up the picnic hamper. "Do you think he'd like that?"

Emily nodded. "He liked chocolate ice cream. I bet he'd like the cake as well."

When Carol pulled the large cake from the hamper, Pegasus immediately smelled the sugar and stepped forward. She barely had time to peel back the cover before the stallion was hungrily munching the cake.

"That's a start," Joel said. "But he's going to need a lot more than that. This stallion can eat!"

"Well," Eric said, "my mother has friends who live around here. There are no shops near the park; everyone orders their food delivered. But we did see a few shops open on Third Avenue. I'll see what I can find."

"I'll come with you," Carol offered quickly. She turned back to Joel and Emily. "You stay here. We'll be right back."

As they started to walk away, Joel stepped closer to Emily. "Should we trust them? Eric is in the army. What if he calls someone the moment they leave the park?"

"I don't know," Emily said. "But what choice do we have?"

"I have an idea," said Joel.

He ran over to Eric and Carol. Emily heard him offering to go with Eric to help carry back heavy items and asking Carol to stay to keep Emily and Pegasus company. Even from a distance, Emily could see that Carol's eyes were wide and frightened.

"But what if those creatures find us?" Carol said. "Or the CRU come?"

"They were down on Twenty-Ninth Street," Joel assured her. "I'm sure they couldn't move that fast."

"Joel's right," Eric agreed. "We won't be long. You stay while Joel and I try to find more food." He looked over at Emily. "If you think that leg hurts now, wait a bit. By tonight you'll be screaming. I'll try to get you some disinfectant, bandages, and something strong for the pain."

Carol reluctantly agreed to stay behind, but her expression suggested she wasn't the least bit happy about it. Joel lifted Emily onto the stallion's back, and they all walked deeper into the trees.

"Try to keep hidden," Joel warned. "We'll be as fast as we can." He stood back and looked at Emily on Pegasus. "You know," he said, "with that blanket covering his wings and you sitting there, he almost looks like an ordinary horse."

"Except for the fact that he appears whiter than white," Eric added. "Have you noticed how he almost seems to glow?"

"I thought it was just my eyes," Joel said. "But

you're right. He's very bright. We may have to do something about that."

"Like what?" Emily asked. "Cover him with mud?"

"I'm not sure," Joel said. "Let me think about it."

When Joel and Eric left, Emily and Carol hardly spoke. Emily realized Carol was terrified. She wasn't sure if it was just the creatures that had her frightened, or if it was spending time alone with Pegasus. Carol's startled eyes were darting everywhere; she jumped at the tiniest of sounds. The scurrying of squirrels in the trees nearly had her in tears. Emily actually welcomed the ringing of her cell phone. When she flipped it open, she saw her father's name on the screen.

"Dad, I'm so glad it's you—"

"Emily!" he urgently cut in. "Thank God! Don't talk. Just listen. Don't say where you are, the CRU are probably listening to us. I know what's happened! I know about the apartment and the winged horse and your ride up Fifth! Em, they're coming for you. Wherever you are, you've got to get moving and keep moving."

"Dad, I—," Emily started as her heart pounded in her chest. "There are four-armed monsters in the city!"

"I know! Bullets can't stop them. They're making their way uptown right now. Listen to me, Em. Remember Robin. Think of him, and I'll be there!"

"What? Dad, I don't understand," Emily said in terror.

"There's no time. I'm sorry, sweetheart, but you must destroy your phone. They'll be tracking it. Destroy it now. I love you, Emily! Remember Robin!"

The call was disconnected. Emily's hands were shaking as she closed her cell. She quickly opened the back and pulled out the battery pack. Then she threw everything on the ground. "Step on it, Pcgs," she said. "You've got to destroy it!"

Pegasus immediately stomped down on the phone with a sharp hoof. By the time he'd finished, there was nothing left but a lot of little unrecognizable pieces.

"Emily, what's happening?" Carol was approaching panic.

This time Emily shared her fear. "The creatures are coming for us." She looked back in the direction Joel and Eric had gone. "I hope they hurry. My dad said the CRU are hunting us as well."

PAELEN WAS UNSURE HOW LONG HE HAD
been in this strange and terrible place. Without windows, there was no keeping track of time. But each
passing day was becoming worse than the one before.

He was taken to another lab. This time they didn't
draw any more of his blood or put him in machines
to study him. They didn't shine more lights in his
eyes, or take samples of him to test. Instead the
older man called Agent J ordered him strapped to an
uncomfortable metal chair. The chair was facing a
large white screen that seemed to shimmer like satin.

"Watch," Agent J ordered.

The lights in the room went down as the screen lit
up. The full-color image was almost like the colorful

mosaics scattered around Olympus. But not quite. As he studied the strange pictures, Paelen saw the tall buildings he'd first seen when he arrived in this strange world on the night of the storm.

"Do you recognize anything?" Agent J asked.

"It is your world," Paelen responded. He looked at Agent J curiously, trying to figure out what new torture this was going to be.

"Yes, it is. We call it New York City."

"New York City," Paelen repeated. "That is very nice. Thank you for showing it to me. May I leave now?"

"No, you may not," Agent J shot back. "Just sit there and keep watching."

Paelen turned back to the screen. He saw different images of the city. Some were taken from the air, others from the ground. Next he was shown a collection of various people he didn't know. As he watched the changing images, he became aware of everyone in the room studying him.

"Do you know what those are?" Agent J asked when the image changed again.

Paelen looked at the picture of countless pigeons

in a park. "Birds," he answered. "We have them in Olympus. It infuriates Jupiter when they mess on his statue."

"I'm sure it must," Agent J said sarcastically. "And this?"

Paelen saw the image of a dog. Then another image showing the same dog walking with its owner. "Olympus has dogs too," he answered. "We also have Cerberus. He has three heads and is particularly vicious. Do you have dogs like that here?"

"No," Agent J answered. "But recently we've discovered that we do have these."

Paelen's eyes flew wide as the picture of the dog was replaced by the image of several four-armed creatures charging through the streets of the city.

"Nirads!" he uttered.

"What did you call them?" Agent J demanded, moving closer.

"Nirads," Paelen repeated. He was in shock and unable to take his eyes away from the sight of the rampaging invaders.

"Who are they? Did they come on your starship?"

Paelen ignored the question and looked fearfully

at Agent J. "Are they really here in this world?"

"Yes," Agent J answered, "and they are wreaking havoc on the city. We've counted at least twenty, but there are reports of even more being seen. They appear to be practically unstoppable. We've managed to capture a couple of the creatures. But they are ferociously strong and can't be sedated. We've got them stored at another high-security facility. Now tell me. What are they? Can you control them?"

"Control them? Me?" Paelen cried. He shook his head. "No one can control the Nirads. They are feral creatures with killer instincts. They are indestructible! Please, you must let me go. They have followed me from Olympus. I must get away. They will kill me if they find me here." Paelen struggled in the chair, desperate to flee. "They will kill all of you as well."

"What are they?" Agent J demanded.

"They are the destroyers of Olympus!" Paelen cried.

"Enough!" Agent J howled. "We are in the middle of the worst security crisis this country has ever known, and you are still talking about Olympus!" He leaned down until his face was just centimeters from Paelen's. "Olympus doesn't exist! It's a myth! It was created by weak minds in a time of need. Now tell me. Where are you from? Where is your starship?"

"I do not understand what you want from me," Paelen cried. "I tell you I am from Olympus. But you claim it is just a myth. Why do you keep insisting I am from the stars?"

"Because aliens exist. Olympians don't," Agent J snapped.

Paelen regained control of himself. "Of course Olympus exists," he challenged indignantly. "It is where I am from. And I resent you calling it a myth. We are not myths! As for the Nirads, all I know of them is they have destroyed my home. Olympus is in ruins. Now they have followed me here, but I do not know why."

Agent J straightened up again and turned furiously to the screen. "All right, you say they are after you? If that is true, why have they left you untouched and are pursuing *them*?"

On the screen, Paelen saw the picture of Pegasus soaring through the canyons of buildings. The image was not as clear as that of the Nirads. But Paelen could see two young humans as well as the stallion. Pegasus appeared to have fresh wounds on his hind-quarters. And even though the image was unclear, Paelen knew Pegasus well enough to see the terror on his face.

"Why were they attacking that horse and those two kids?" Agent J demanded.

Paelen almost shouted, *Pegasus is not a horse!* but he bit back the comment. He realized he'd already made a terrible mistake by telling them as much as he had. Shock at seeing the Nirads in this world had made him drop his guard. He would not make that mistake again. "I do not know."

"You're lying!" Agent J shot at him. "I saw your face. You recognized them. Those kids, are they friends of yours? Are you from the same planet? What about that winged horse? How is it possible for him to fly?"

"He flies because he has wings," Paelen said sarcastically. "I would have thought even you could figure that out for yourself. Now, I have answered your questions. I do not know who they are. Please release me before the Nirads arrive."

Paelen's gaze followed Agent J as he walked over to a man in a white coat.

"Give it to him," he heard the agent say. "He's not telling us what we need to know."

Moments later the man in the white coat injected something into Paelen's arm. As the drug took effect, Paelen started to feel what it must have been like to be Medusa. His head was full of writhing, angry snakes; his veins were coursing with fire. He could no longer see clearly.

When Paelen felt at his worst, Agent J repeated all the same questions he'd asked moments before. Where did they come from? Who were the Nirads? Who were the kids on the flying horse? And why did the creatures want to kill everyone?

Despite the sensation of snakes squirming in his head, Paelen still had complete control over his thoughts. He wouldn't answer their questions. He especially wouldn't betray Pegasus. So as always, Paelen did what he did best. He lied. He told Agent J the most outrageous story he could think of.

This time, he claimed he was Hercules, son of Jupiter and hero of Olympus. Paelen went into long details of his achievements as Hercules, telling one amazing story after another and claiming all the glory for himself.

The more he talked, the angrier Agent J became.

Driven to fury, the older man started to slap Paelen violently across the face. But instead of hurting, the blows helped to clear away the snakes and fire raging through him. As before, human strength was nothing compared to the pounding the real Hercules had once given Paelen for stealing from him.

As others crowded forward to pull Agent J off, Paelen slipped a hand into an orderly's pocket and retrieved the keys to the handcuffs. With the keys clenched tightly in his fist, Paelen pretended to pass out.

He heard Agent J's heavy panting as the older man was pulled away.

"We're done for the day," the agent spat. "Take him away before I kill him!"

Paelen remained perfectly still with his eyes closed. Two orderlies lifted him onto a gurney and transported him back to his room. They transferred him to the bed and handcuffed him to the side bars.

"Stupid idiot kid," Paelen heard one mutter. "If he keeps pressing Agent J like that, the man will have him sliced and diced and poured into Mason jars."

"Better him than us," the other orderly said. "Where do *you* think he comes from?"

"Don't know, don't care."

"What do you think they'll do to him?"

"I guess they'll wait till they catch all the other freaks out there. Then they'll question the lot of them until they spill their guts. Then, when there's nothing left to say, they'll do what they always do. Ice the lot of them."

"Shame," the second orderly said. "I kinda like this kid. He's got a real fire in his belly. He's the first one I ever saw get the better of Agent J. Let's face it, the man needs an attitude adjustment. This kid's just the one to do it."

"That's if he lives long enough."

When they'd finished securing him, Paelen heard both men cross to the door.

"Well, that's my shift over, I'm outta here," one of them said. "Want to join me and the boys for a beer later?"

Paelen heard the beeping of the sound lock. When the door closed after the men, he remained still for a moment more. Finally he opened his eyes and looked around. He was alone.

He still couldn't believe there were Nirads in this world. Agent J had been right about one thing. The Nirads were after Pegasus, not him. As he tried to slow his racing heart, Paelen recalled the last thing he'd seen on Olympus. How the Nirads were specifically going after Pegasus. If Diana hadn't come forward, they surely would have killed him.

But why did the Nirads want Pegasus dead? And why were there two humans with him?

Paelen realized the answers were not to be found in this strange and horrible place. He needed to get out.

He recalled Mercury's last dying words, begging him to join the struggle for Olympus. Much to his own shame, Paelen had turned his back on his people and fled the fight. But now the fight had followed him here. He could not turn his back again. He would escape from these humans and find Pegasus.

Then he would finally join the battle.

EMILY FELT TERROR BUILDING UP INSIDE HER as she sat waiting for the others on Pegasus's back. It seemed like hours since Joel and Eric had left. But finally there was movement in the trees around them, and Emily heard Joel softly call out her name.

"Over here," Emily called back. "Hurry."

Moments later Joel and Eric reappeared. "We've got big trouble," Eric said as he put down the shopping bags and hugged his girlfriend. "All military leave has just been canceled. I've been ordered to meet up with my unit not too far from here. It seems there's an emergency in the city."

"The emergency's us," Emily said. "My dad called. The police know about Pegasus and our flight up

Fifth Avenue. They know about the creatures, too. He said the CRU are after us."

Eric nodded. "And they're calling us in to help find you. I'm so sorry, but I've got to go."

"You're not going to tell them where we are, are you?" Emily asked fearfully.

"Of course not!" Eric answered. "I'll do everything I can to lead them away from you. But it's not just you they're after. There are those creatures out there as well. Those I *will* try to stop."

"You can't," Emily said. "My dad said bullets won't even stop them."

"Yeah," Joel added. "When I hit one on the head with a baseball bat, it only stopped him for a moment. Even the fall from Pegasus didn't slow it down."

"That being the case, the city has more to worry about than Pegasus," Eric said. He took Carol's hand. "We've got to go. I want you out of the city as soon as possible."

Carol smiled weakly. She turned to Emily and shrugged. "I'm so sorry you kids are in trouble. But I just don't have the stomach for this."

"I understand," Emily said softly. If she had a

choice, she'd love to run away too. But she couldn't. Pegasus still needed her.

Eric jotted down two names and telephone numbers on a piece of paper he pulled out of his pocket. "Memorize these if you can," he said, handing the numbers to Emily. "They're my brother in Brooklyn and my parents in New Jersey. Call either of them if you really get stuck. My dad is ex-military. You tell them I told you to call, and they'll help you. I wish I could do more. But all hell is breaking loose in the city, and I've got to go."

As he and Carol started to move away, Eric called back, "You've got bandages and antiseptic in the bags. Get that leg cleaned up as soon as you can. And remember, memorize those phone numbers. You might need them."

"I will," Emily promised softly. "Thank you so much for everything."

"Good luck, kids," Eric said with a wave as he and Carol slipped away through the trees.

When they had gone, Emily started to shake.

"What are we going to do, Joel? The CRU are after us."

Joel shrugged. "I really don't know. But we can't do anything until it gets darker." He started going through the shopping bags. "If we have any luck at all, the CRU and military will concentrate on finding the creatures before they come after us. In the meantime, let's get Pegasus fed and that leg of yours cleaned up."

As the sun started to set, Emily and Joel cleaned and treated the deep cuts on the stallion's hind end. They had already cleaned and bandaged Emily's leg. The painkillers were working, and Emily was feeling much better.

"At least we now know who stabbed Pegasus with the spear," Emily said as she gently rubbed disinfectant cream into a deep wound on the stallion's hind leg.

"The real question is why?" Joel asked.

Emily gave Pegasus a soft kiss on the muzzle, then sat down on the ground and reached for an apple. But before the fruit reached her lips, her eyes flew open wide.

"Robin!" she cried.

"What?" Joel said. "What's wrong?"

"The last thing my dad said to me was to remember Robin!" Emily caught hold of Joel's hands and painfully climbed to her feet. "I didn't understand what he meant. He was talking in code in case the CRU were listening. But now I remember!"

"Remember what? Emily, what are you talking about?"

As she spoke, Emily started to pack their supplies into Eric and Carol's picnic basket. "When I was really young, my mom and dad used to bring me up to the park. We'd go to this really hidden area at the upper end. Dad would pretend to be the Sheriff of Nottingham. Mom would be Maid Marian, and I'd be Robin Hood! Every Sunday we'd come and play sword fights."

"I still don't understand," Joel said helplessly.

"Before he hung up, my dad said 'remember Robin.' He said he'd be there. Don't you see, Joel? Dad told me to take you and Pegasus to where we used to play Robin Hood. It's really private. No one will find us there. We could hide for a bit and plan our next move."

"Then what are we waiting for?" Joel cried. "Let's get you on Pegasus and get moving!"

Remaining in the safe cover of trees, they traveled north. The sun finally set, and they walked for much of the way in complete darkness. As they traveled, they heard the sound of multiple helicopters arriving in the sky over Central Park. Peering up through the trees, they saw bright searchlights shining down.

"They're looking for us," Joel said darkly.

Emily looked down at Pegasus and saw that in the dark, he appeared even whiter than before. He no longer looked like an ordinary horse. There was no mistaking that he was different. If the beam of a searchlight were to touch him, there would be no escape.

"Joel, wait, we've got to stop. Please help me down."

"We can't. We're meeting your dad at the play area—" Joel stopped when he saw Emily struggling to get down off Pegasus. "What is it?" he said, helping her. "What's wrong?"

"Pegs, you are just so brilliant white! We've got

to do something about your color." Emily turned to Joel. "He wasn't like this when I first found him on the roof. Even last night he wasn't this white. But look at him now! It's like he's becoming brighter by the minute."

"You're right. He's really starting to glow."

Joel put the picnic hamper down on the ground and started to dig through their supplies. "While we were out shopping, I had an idea. We bought all we could."

"What did you get?" Emily asked.

Joel held up a package, but in the dark, Emily couldn't see what it was.

"What is that?"

"Hair dye," Joel explained. "We got ten packages. But there was one little problem: They aren't all the same color. We got dark brown and black." He paused and added, "They're not the same brands, either. Do you think that could cause a problem?"

Emily shrugged. "I don't know. I used to help my mom color her hair, but she always used the same kind. I don't even know if this will work on a horse."

Once again, Pegasus complained at the *H* word.

"I'm sorry, Pegs." Emily reached out to stroke his face. "But you know what I mean. This is meant for people. I just hope it doesn't hurt you."

"We've got to try," Joel said. "He's shining like a star. It won't take long for the CRU to find us if he stays like that. It's not so bad in daylight, but now he's glowing like a beacon."

They decided to use the hair dye before they went much farther. They picked their way through the trees until they came to one of Central Park's many ponds. The major work would be done under the cover of the trees, and they would only risk exposing themselves once it was time to rinse Pegasus off.

"If you work with his head and mane, I'll start with his tail and back end. We can meet in the middle," Joel suggested. "It's too dark to read the instructions. Do you know what to do?"

Emily explained to Joel how her mother used to mix the chemicals together before applying the dye to her hair. They both put on the latex gloves that came with the packages and started to work.

"I'm so sorry, Pegs," Emily apologized as she applied the dark, smelly liquid to his beautiful white face, "but this is to help hide you. We're going to try to make you look like a regular dark horse. That way, if anyone sees you, they'll never know the truth."

Covering the entire stallion seemed to take ages and used all the dye that they had. They left his wings alone—afraid to hurt the broken one. When they finished applying the last of it, Emily pulled off her latex gloves.

"Now we wait," she said as she sat down tiredly. Her leg was really starting to hurt. "It used to take my mother thirty minutes to set the color."

"How about we give him thirty-five?" Joel said, setting his digital watch and sitting beside her.

As they waited, they listened to the sounds of the helicopters endlessly searching the park. More than once, a helicopter passed directly over their heads, but the cover of trees and new color on Pegasus kept them from being seen.

"Time's up," Joel finally said, helping Emily up.

"Let's get you rinsed off, Pegs," Emily said as she put on a fresh pair of gloves.

Leaving the protection of the trees, they looked up to check the position of the helicopters. The military were concentrating their efforts on the lower end of the park. Pegasus entered the dark water of the pond. Emily started to follow him in.

"Emily, stop." Joel held up a warning hand.

"But I can help," she protested.

"Yeah, and your leg could get really infected from this filthy water," Joel argued. "Stay on the shore and keep watch. Let me know if anyone is coming."

Emily resented being told what do to. She could do as much as he could. But deep down, she knew Joel was right. Her leg was throbbing badly. There was something seriously wrong with it. Adding dirty water would only make things worse.

"All right," she agreed. "But be as quick as you can."

Standing on the edge, Emily nervously watched the searching helicopters overhead as Joel led Pegasus into deeper water. The stallion submerged himself, and Joel quickly rubbed him down.

"Hurry," Emily cried as two of the helicopters started to veer away from the others and move toward them. "They're coming this way!"

Both helicopters were moving faster than expected.

There was no way Joel and Pegasus would have time to get out of the water before the helicopters were upon them.

"Get down!" Joel cried as he and the stallion ducked beneath the surface.

Emily barely had time to dash into the trees before the bright searchlight shone on the spot where she'd just been standing. With the blood pounding in her veins and her wounded leg throbbing, she followed the progress of the helicopters as they continued north over the park.

"All clear!" she called as she limped back to the water's edge.

Joel and Pegasus both cautiously raised their heads above the surface. With renewed urgency, Joel finished rinsing off the stallion.

Pegasus emerged from the water looking as dark as the night, though his wings were still brilliant white. As Emily covered the wings with a blanket, a new voice startled them.

"What have you done to him?"

A tall woman stormed forward. She was dressed in filthy rags but had an elegance and authority when she walked. She carried a long spear, which had a sharp point that glowed bright gold. Her eyes were electric blue and blazed in the dark.

"How dare you touch him!" she challenged, shoving Emily aside and going straight up to Pegasus. "And what is this horror you have done to him?"

She turned her attention to Pegasus. "How could you let these foolish children touch you like this?"

"Excuse me," Joel said. "But he belongs to us."

"Pegasus belongs to no one," the woman spat furiously. She turned back to the stallion, and her voice softened. "Look at you, my old friend. You look like a plow horse."

As the woman continued to inspect Pegasus, the stallion nickered with excitement. She laid her forehead against him and dropped her voice. "Pegasus, we have fallen," she said sadly. "Father is in chains. Apollo is dead, and Olympus lies in ruins. The Nirads have defeated us."

"Nirads?" Emily asked cautiously.

The woman looked down to Emily's wounded leg. "I can smell them on you, too," she said. "You have fought the Nirads? You are lucky to be alive."

"Is that what those four-armed creatures are called?" Joel asked. "Nirads?"

The woman nodded. "They murdered my brother. Killed countless others and conquered Olympus."

"You said they killed Apollo. Was he your brother?" Joel asked breathlessly. "Are—are you *Diana*?"

"That is one of my names," the tall woman answered. She studied Joel for a moment. "And you are a Roman."

The sound of the helicopters cut short further conversation.

"Please, Diana," Joel entreated. "I know you are a great warrior, but trust us—you can't stay here. Those flying machines up there will capture you. We have to hide."

"Hide?" Diana repeated in confusion. "I do not hide from a battle."

"You do now," Emily said as she moved closer to Pegasus. "Come on, Pegs. We've got to go before they see you."

Pegasus let out a soft neigh to Diana but followed Emily away from the pond.

"Pegs?" Diana repeated as she trailed behind them. "Did I just hear you call him Pegs?"

When they were safely hidden in the trees, Emily turned to her. "He doesn't seem to mind. I think it's a cute name for him."

Diana was incredulous. "Cute? Child, do you have any idea of whom you are speaking? This is Pegasus, the great stallion of Olympus. To make him suffer such indignities is beyond tolerance."

"Of course I know who Pegasus is," Emily shot back as she reached out and stroked the stallion's dark muzzle. "But he's also a friend of mine."

"Emily, stop," Joel warned fearfully. "You don't understand who you're talking to. Please, show some respect!"

"Respect?" Emily repeated. "Where's her respect for me?" She turned back to Diana. "If Pegs doesn't mind me calling him that, then why should you?"

"You insolent little nothing!" Diana cried. She stepped forward and raised her hand to strike Emily. "You have yet to learn your place—"

Pegasus quickly placed himself between Diana and Emily. He looked at Diana and let out a series of strange sounds. The expression on her face softened. The tall woman looked at Emily several times before dropping her head.

"I am sorry. My behavior is unforgivable. Pegasus has just explained to me what you have done for him and how you have helped him. Please forgive me. I have witnessed my father's defeat, my brother's murder, and my home destroyed. I am not myself."

Emily frowned. Diana could understand Pegasus? She looked at the woman with envy and more than a touch of jealousy. She secretly wished she were an Olympian too. Then she and Pegasus could actually communicate.

"I understand," Emily finally said. "I'm so sorry for your losses."

"Is Olympus really destroyed?" Joel asked, coming forward timidly. "How? You're gods. Who could defeat you?"

"The Nirads," said Diana sadly. "Soon they will destroy your world too, unless we stop them."

"Destroy our world?" Emily said in shock. "Why? What do they want?"

"We do not know," Diana said. "Until now, we

had never encountered the Nirads before. We know nothing about them or where they come from. They have made no demands on us and have taken nothing from our ruins. All they desire is destruction. And unless we find a way to stop them, all will be lost."

"How can we stop them?" Emily asked. "Nothing seems to hurt them. Even falling twenty stories doesn't slow them down."

"There is one thing we have discovered," Diana said. "In the course of battle, right before Pegasus fled to this world, I bested a Nirad. But it was only after the creature had touched Pegasus's golden bridle. He was poisoned by it. We believe he died as a result of touching the bridle and not my spear."

"You need his bridle?" Emily asked, trying to make sense of everything she was hearing.

Diana nodded. "This is why I have come here. I need it to forge new weapons to use against the Nirads. I see you have taken it off Pegasus to color him. May I have it?"

"It's not here," Emily said. "Another Olympian called Paelen stole it from Pegasus right before they were both hit by lightning. He's got the bridle. But now the CRU have taken him."

"Paelen?" Diana's face darkened. "That foul little thief! Even he would not keep the bridle if he knew what it could do for our people." She looked back to Emily. "What are the CRU who have captured him? Where do I find them?"

"You can't," Joel warned. "They're too dangerous."

"I have fought the best armies of Greece and the Romans. I do not fear these people."

"You should," Emily advised. "They're really dangerous."

Joel looked at Diana. "How long has it been since you were last here?"

Diana paused and considered. "Many ages. Your people did not have devices like those in the sky. You traveled on horseback and fought with swords."

"Then this isn't the same world you knew," said Joel. "We've changed."

"Yes," Emily agreed. "These days, people don't even believe in you."

"That's right," Joel said. "And we have new weapons that can hurt you. Look at Pegasus. He broke his wing, and even though it's healing, he needs time. If he can be hurt, so can you."

"It is not your world or those noisy flying vehicles that can wound us," Diana said, suddenly sounding very defeated. "The death of the Flame of Olympus has weakened us."

"What's the Flame of Olympus?" Emily asked curiously.

Diana looked over at Emily and sighed heavily. "The Flame is the source of all our power and strength. It has burned in Olympus since the beginning. But recently its strength has diminished. As it became weaker, we did also. The Nirads used this weakness to launch an attack on us. If the Flame had been at its full strength, we would have fought them off easily. As it is, the Nirads reached the Temple of the Flame and extinguished it completely. We all believed we would perish without it. But we haven't."

"But you've lost your powers?" Joel guessed.

Diana nodded. "My father hoped to use the gold from the bridle to defeat the Nirads and relight the Flame," she said. "Moments before he was captured, he used the last of his powers to send me here to collect the bridle and help Pegasus on his quest."

"What *is* his quest?" Emily asked. "He can't tell us."

Diana looked at Pegasus. "Why did Father send you here?"

Both Emily and Joel stood in silence as Pegasus started to nicker softly. He continued for several minutes.

"I never knew any of this," Diana said in a whisper. "None of us did. Only my Father, Vesta, and Pegasus knew."

"Knew what?" Emily asked impatiently.

"Please get off your wounded leg and sit down," Diana said as she helped Emily settle under a tree. Joel, still a little starstruck, sat beside her.

"Pegasus is on a precious quest," she started. "He says it is doomed to failure without your help. That the survival of Olympus and your world rests entirely with you."

Emily was suddenly unsure she wanted to hear this.

"Long before I was born, at the end of the Great War between the Olympians and the Titans, a Flame emerged in the heart of Olympus," Diana continued. "It was Vesta's duty to ensure that the new Flame was kept alive and strong. For its power was our power. Its life was our life. A wondrous temple was built around the Flame, and it has burned brightly in Olympus ever since."

"Vesta?" Joel said suddenly. "The Goddess of the Hearth? She used vestal virgins to keep the Flame alive at a temple in ancient Rome."

Diana nodded. "That was the symbolic Flame of Olympus. Those virgins were the servants of Vesta. The real Flame has always been in Olympus. But right from the beginning, my father worried that if this Flame were ever extinguished, we would lose our powers. So he sent Vesta to Earth with the heart of the Flame and commanded her to hide it in a human child. A girl child. This secret Daughter of Vesta would carry the heart of the Flame within her, without ever knowing it."

"But that was long ago," Emily said, frowning. "She's got to be dead by now."

"She is," said Diana. "But Vesta made certain that upon her death, the heart of the Flame would pass to another baby girl being born. It would go from generation to generation, across all the waters of the Earth."

"So out there right now," Joel said, working it out, "there is another Daughter of Vesta carrying the heart of the Flame of Olympus."

"That's crazy," Emily said. "How can a flame have a heart?"

"Emily—," Joel warned.

"No, Joel, this is getting to be too much," said Emily, cutting him off. "First Pegasus is real and crashes on my roof. Now Diana, also an Olympian, is here and telling us that a flame has a heart and that it goes from girl to girl. I can believe a lot of stuff, but this is just too crazy. How can you accept it so easily?"

"Because I've read the books!" Joel shot back. "I do more than fight, you know. I read. *The Iliad* and *The Odyssey* are my favorites. They tell some of the stories of the gods!"

"Stories, that's right," Emily challenged. "This is real life, and a flame can't have a heart!"

"Emily, I know these books," said Diana. "My father had them in his palace before the Nirads attacked. They are not lies, just retellings of certain events. Believe me. The Flame of Olympus has a living heart. And my father sent Pegasus here to find the girl who possesses it. He is charged with bringing her back to Olympus to reignite our Flame."

"Wow," Emily said softly, struggling to take it all in. "But after so many generations, how will he know who she is if she doesn't even know about herself?"

Diana smiled. "Pegasus alone can see the Flame burning within her. She will draw him to her. He won't be able to resist her, for she is the source of his strength."

Joel nodded his head in understanding. "So Pegasus came to Earth to get this girl. But he got hurt and crashed on Emily's roof instead."

"That is correct," Diana said. "With his wing broken, he has been unable to fly to her."

"Where is she?" Emily asked. "Is she even in America?"

Pegasus neighed softly.

"Pegasus says the daughter of this generation is here in this country," Diana translated. "That she is not far away. But he says something is very wrong with her because the Flame has grown weak within her. This is why it became so weak in Olympus and enabled the Nirads to attack and defeat us."

"Maybe she's sick," Emily suggested.

"Perhaps," Diana agreed. "But whoever she is, she has a great destiny to fulfill. But a tragic one. For hers must be the greatest sacrifice of all."

"What do you mean?" Joel asked.

"When the Daughter of Vesta is taken back to Olympus, she must willingly sacrifice herself to the Flame," she said. "It will consume her. But in offering herself, Olympus will be reborn and all our powers restored."

"She's got to die?" Emily asked in a whisper.

Diana nodded. "She must be willing to sacrifice herself in order for the Flame to be reborn," she said. "She cannot be forced."

"But what can we do?" Joel asked.

Diana dropped her head. "Pegasus needs you to talk to the girl when we find her. You are from this world. You can better explain it than I. You must make this child understand that her sacrifice will not only save Olympus, but this world too."

"The Daughter of Vesta is a child?" Emily asked. "And you want us to tell her she's got to die to save everyone?"

"No way," Joel said, shaking his head. "I know you guys have your own special Olympian ways. But this is too much. You can't expect us to tell a kid she's got to kill herself."

"I do not know how old she is. Nor does Pegasus," Diana explained. "He only knows that she is near. She may be an old woman nearing her natural death or a young child just starting her life. But whoever or whatever she is, ultimately, it must be her decision. None of us can force her to sacrifice herself."

"So," Emily said slowly, "we're going to knock on someone's door and ask them to commit suicide in order to save the world." She felt light-headed with shock. "What would you do if it were you, Joel?"

"I'd tell us to get lost and call the police."

"Me too," Emily agreed.

"Then all is lost and our worlds will perish," Diana said flatly. "The Nirads have enslaved the survivors of Olympus and destroyed our home. You have already seen them here in this world. They know of Pegasus's mission and will send more to kill him before he finds the Daughter of Vesta. I am here to help him any way I can."

"So will we," Emily finally said. She looked at Joel. "We haven't got a choice. If there are more of those creatures on the way, we've got to do all we can to stop them."

"Wait a minute," Joel said as an idea came to him. "What if we got the bridle back? Maybe we can make weapons to destroy the Nirads. Then when we take the Daughter of Vesta to Olympus, Jupiter will have time to figure out another way to relight the Flame without her having to die."

Emily looked at Diana. "Do you think it's possible?"

"I do not know," she said. "It might work."

"I'm willing to try," Joel said. "It's better than telling some poor girl she's got to kill herself."

"I agree," Emily said excitedly.

Joel led the group forward. "Come on, let's get moving."

PAELEN OPENED HIS FINGERS. THE KEY HE had taken from the orderly's pocket was still resting in the palm of his hand. He manipulated the key into the lock on the handcuff. With one hand free, it was little effort to open the second cuff.

Paelen knew his body was mostly healed. The burn on his back was gone, and his broken ribs no longer hurt. They had left the casts on his legs. He suspected they had done that to keep him from escaping. But as he stretched out his feet and flexed his calf muscles, he felt the plaster on the two casts crack. He felt no pain from the bones in his legs.

Paelen sat up, threw back the covers, and started to break away the casts from both his legs. Before long, his legs were free. He tested his muscles. They were a bit stiff from lack of use, but apart from that, the bones had healed.

With both legs free, Paelen climbed quietly from his bed. He pressed his ear to the metal door and heard activity in the hall. There were still a lot of people out there.

He recalled the orderlies making plans for the evening. They were going home for the night. As Paelen stood by the door listening, he heard the guards outside change. Two men were leaving. They were reporting the events of the day to the one man who would remain outside the door for the rest of the night. Paelen would wait a while longer before he made his move. He always did his best work late at night.

Paelen waited. Somehow he would always feel when it was time to move, rather than plan anything specific. As he lay back, he recalled everything he had seen of the facility so far. He knew they were deep underground. There were multiple halls, countless doors, and several levels. So far he had been taken to three different laboratories for testing. They were all two levels below this one.

Each time they took him from his room, Paelen had been careful to memorize where they went. He had been taken past a set of doors with a symbol of stairs above it. More than once, he'd seen people enter or exit at that point. That would be his escape route after he had found the lab containing Pegasus's bridle and Mercury's sandals.

Paelen now concentrated on the air vent above his bed. The sounds of people in the rooms connected by the tunnels slowly faded. Moment by moment, the facility was shutting down for the night.

When more time had passed, Paelen felt that strange tingle that told him it was time to move. He walked quietly back to the door. He heard nothing from the outside except the faint sound of paper being shuffled and a soft breath being taken. The guard was still out there. But he was alone.

As he looked at the keypad that controlled the sound lock, Paelen counted twelve buttons. To open the door, the men always pressed only four. But which four? From his angle on the bed, he had never been able to see exactly which buttons. This left only two options. To start pressing buttons until he heard the sound combination he needed, or simply use his strength to force open the door.

Neither option was particularly appealing. As pressing buttons always made sounds on both sides, any attempt he made would be heard by the guard. However, there was an equal chance of the guard hearing him force the door.

Finally Paelen chose the first option, but with a slight change. Even though the tingle in his senses told him to go, he held back. Waiting . . . waiting . . .

He eventually heard movement outside his door. The guard was saying something about leaving his post for a toilet break. A moment later another voice gave the authorization. Immediately the guard left his desk, leaving Paelen's door unattended.

Paelen looked at the buttons on the keypad. Starting with the number one, he closed his eyes and pressed the button. He listened to the distinct sound it made. It was not one he'd heard before.

One by one, Paelen pressed the twelve buttons, familiarizing himself with their sounds. When he hit the last one and heard its unique tone, he smiled. He confidently reached up and pressed the correct sequence of four buttons to open the door. A faint click immediately followed. Paelen pulled the door handle. It gave without any resistance.

Paelen saw no one. He dashed down the hall in the direction of the stairs, entered the stairwell, and descended two levels to where all the laboratories were located.

Remaining in the stairwell, Paelen lowered himself to the floor. All his senses were alert to any sounds. There were two people in the laboratory corridor. Paelen heard their voices drawing near, and then passing the doors and fading in the opposite direction.

When they had gone, he quietly entered the hall.

A series of doors lined the long corridor. Paelen recognized the first laboratory he'd been taken to. He shivered when he recalled what they'd done to him in there.

Farther along the wide, white corridor, Paelen approached a big metal box against a wall. Even before he drew near, he could smell a sweet fragrance that made his mouth water and stomach grumble. It was almost like ambrosia, but not quite.

Paelen had asked countless times for ambrosia to be brought to him. Instead he was given food that he couldn't eat. The only thing he'd managed to get any nutrition from was what the doctors had called dessert. But it was never enough.

Feeling half-starved, Paelen approached the glass front of a vending machine. Behind it he could see stacks of brightly colored items. They all smelled of that same sweet, delicious fragrance. His need for food quickly outweighed his need to get the bridle and sandals. At the side of the machine, he found a lock where a small round key should be inserted. Paelen used all his strength to tear at the lock.

He pried open the front glass door of the machine and reached for the first item. Tearing off the paper, he hungrily bit into the soft candy bar. He nearly cried out in joy as the sweet chocolate went down his throat. It was only then he realized just how hungry he was.

As he tore open another candy bar and shoved it all in his mouth, he quickly checked the hall. He was exposed and vulnerable. But he had to eat.

Pulling up the bottom of his hospital gown, Paelen made a small pouch. This he filled with as much candy as he could carry. But he was also careful to leave enough in the machine so that anyone who came by would not see that he'd been there.

When he had taken as much as he dared, Paelen closed the glass front of the vending machine and ran back to the stairwell. He crept to the back of the stairs and tucked himself under the base. It wasn't the best hiding place in the world, but it was better than nothing.

Paelen started to eat. As he tore open each package, he discovered new flavors and delights. Until this moment, there'd been nothing about this world he liked. But as he stuffed his face with candy and chocolate from the vending machine, he realized there was at least one good thing about this world: sugar.

When the last of the candy was gone, Paelen sat back and sighed with contentment. It was the first time he'd felt satisfied since he arrived. Already he could feel his strength increasing as the sugar went to work on his body, healing the last of his wounds.

Soon Paelen was ready to move again. Creeping out from his hiding place, he felt refreshed, alive, and alert. Every sense was working properly. He was himself again.

He could hear the sound of people moving around on the levels above him. But on this level, he was alone. As he moved farther along the corridor, Paelen suddenly smelled something he hadn't smelled since Olympus. It was the awful scent of rot and filth. It was the scent of—Nirads!

The odor got worse as he continued down the hall. The stench was coming from behind a locked door. He pressed his ear to the door but heard nothing. The smell told him there was a Nirad in there, but something was wrong. It didn't smell like other Nirads. This one smelled dead.

Paelen pressed the same code from his door into the sound lock, but nothing happened. He pushed hard against the door. If there was a dead Nirad in there, he needed to know how it had died, and if there was some way of defeating the awful creatures. Perhaps with that information, he could save Olympus.

With the sugar coursing through his body, Paelen

felt almost as strong as he did when he was home. No human door could withstand his Olympian might. With a grunting shove, the lock and hinges gave way and the door burst open.

Paelen found himself in another laboratory. But this was nothing like the labs he'd been in before. This room smelled of death and decay. There were similar machines in it. But there was also something else. Something awful.

In the center of the room, Paelen saw a large metal table. There was a big round light hanging above it, shining its brightness down on the table's occupant. The table had metal sides that folded up several centimeters, to keep the blood and fluids from spilling onto the floor.

Lying on the table was a dead Nirad.

Paelen could see the four arms lying limply at the sides of the creature. The stench rising from the table was so awful he had to plug his nose to keep from losing the precious food he'd just eaten. But the sight of the dead Nirad was almost enough to make him sick anyway.

The doctors of this place had clearly been cutting

the Nirad open to see what was on the inside. He didn't want to look. Instead his eyes were drawn to a deep scar burned on the folded-back skin of the Nirad's open chest.

Closer inspection revealed several other similar scars along its exposed body. There was a big one on the Nirad's bloated face. When Paelen crept closer, he immediately recognized the shape of the scars. They were caused by Pegasus's hooves.

Suddenly all the pieces of the puzzle came together. Back in Olympus, it was Pegasus and Diana who had killed the first Nirad. This Nirad here was also dead because of an encounter with the stallion. Pegasus was the only Olympian capable of killing them, and they knew it. The Nirads needed Pegasus dead before they could complete the destruction of Olympus and all the other worlds. So they had followed him to this world to kill him.

Paelen had to warn the stallion. Pegasus had to be protected. He was the Olympians' only weapon against the ferocious Nirads.

"Was that a friend of yours?"

Paelen jumped. Turning quickly, he saw Agent J

standing there, flanked by several security guards.

"You must let me go," Paelen said desperately. "Pegasus is in terrible danger. The Nirads are here to kill him."

"Pegasus?" Agent J asked.

"Yes, Pegasus," Paelen insisted. "We must help him! He is the only one who can defeat the Nirads. I must go to him."

"You aren't going anywhere," Agent J said. "You didn't think you could get away from us that easily, did you? We've been following you on the corridor cameras from the moment you left your room."

"Cameras?" Paelen repeated. "I do not understand."

"Yes, cameras." Agent J waved his hands theatrically in the air. "It is like great serpents' eyes that show us what you are doing," he said. "You were never alone. We were watching you the whole time. I must say, that was a neat little trick with the vending machine. I'm surprised you weren't sick from eating all that chocolate."

"I told you before, I needed ambrosia," Paelen insisted. "You would not provide it. That food was the closest I could find. Now please, I need to help Pegasus."

Paelen started to move, but several security guards stepped forward to block his path. "I do not wish to fight you, but I will. I must go."

"I told you, you aren't going anywhere," Agent J said. Then he looked at his men. "Take him down."

Paelen charged forward as the guards surrounded him. It was little effort for him to fight them off. He tossed them around the laboratory like they were rag dolls. When all the guards were down, Paelen shoved Agent J aside and made it to the corridor. He ran in the direction of the stairwell.

"He's running, he's running. Lock down the facility. Repeat, subject is running. Lock it down!" Agent J cried.

Loud alarms burst to life throughout the building. Paelen looked back and saw the men running toward him.

He concentrated on getting to the stairs. But as he entered the stairwell, he heard the sounds of many feet charging down the stairs in his direction.

"Stop!" a voice ordered. "Stop or we'll open fire!"

Paelen felt the sharp stinging of bees. He looked down at his chest and saw darts sticking into him. He pulled several out and threw them back at the men who'd shot him. When they struck home, the men fell to the ground, unconscious. Paelen realized the darts were intended to make him go to sleep.

Paelen continued up the stairs, using the darts against the men coming for him. But as each man fell, more replaced them. Soon the stairwell was filled with men chasing after him from below as well as above.

"Stop!" they shouted.

But Paelen couldn't stop. He needed to get to Pegasus, to warn the stallion. Charging forward, he started to fight with the guards. But even though he was much stronger than all of them, their numbers were too great. He was quickly overwhelmed.

A sudden brutal blow struck him on the back of the head. Paelen turned to see the man pulling back his weapon to hit him again. It wasn't necessary. As Paelen's world started to go dark, more men pounced on him and drove him down to the floor.

IT SEEMED TO TAKE HALF THE NIGHT TO work their way to where Emily used to play with her family in Central Park. Emily was back on Pegasus and trying to lead the group. But without a flashlight, and still no city lights to guide them, the way was dark and treacherous. The constant sound of the helicopters was a reminder of the danger they were in.

"You sure you know where you're going?" Joel asked.

"Not really," Emily admitted. "It's been years since I've been up this high in the park. But it shouldn't be much farther."

As they picked their way through the trees, Pegasus suddenly stopped. His dark ears sprang forward and he pawed the ground. Diana also stopped. She held up her hand and listened.

"There is someone moving ahead," she said softly as she raised her brother's spear and prepared to fight.

"Em?" a voice called softly. "Is that you?"

"Dad!" Emily responded. "Dad, we're here!" Weak with relief, she reached forward and patted Pegasus's neck. "It's all right, Pegs," she said. "It's my dad."

Forgetting her wounded leg, Emily slid off the stallion's back. But when her feet hit the ground, her leg gave out and she fell. Her father was at her side in an instant, taking her in his arms.

"Oh, Em, I've been so worried about you!"

Emily put her arms around him and immediately felt better. "Dad, I'm so sorry I didn't tell you what was happening."

"What *is* happening?" he asked. "Em, the city's in an uproar!" He looked at her bandaged leg. "And what happened to you?"

"Do you remember the night of the big storm?" Emily asked. "Not long after the Empire State's top blew up, Pegasus was hit by lightning. He crashed down on our roof. That's how I got my black eye.

When I went to help him, his wing accidentally hit me."

"Pegasus?" her father repeated. "That winged horse I heard about was the actual Pegasus from the Greek myths?"

"Roman," Joel corrected, stepping out of the shadows. "And they aren't myths, they're all real. I'm Joel, sir. A friend of Emily's from school."

Emily's father shook Joel's hand. Joel indicated Diana. "Officer Jacobs, I'd like to introduce you to another Olympian. This is Diana."

"Diana? The Great Hunter?" Emily's father asked as he studied the tall woman.

Diana nodded formally. "Officer Jacobs. It is an honor to meet the father of Emily."

"Call me Steve," her father said a little helplessly. He looked back to Emily. "I don't understand any of this," he said. "What's happening here? How and why are there Olympians in New York?"

Emily and Joel tried to explain as best as they could, right up to the point of being in the park.

"It's hard to accept any of this." Steve stared at Pegasus and shook his head. "I'd heard it was a white stallion you were riding today. What happened to him?"

"He was white," Emily said. "Too white. As he got better, Pegasus was starting to glow. So we dyed him black to try to hide him from the CRU."

Emily kissed the stallion softly on the muzzle. "Pegs, this is my dad," she said. "Dad? I'd like you to meet Pegasus."

Emily's father cautiously stroked Pegasus's muzzle. He lifted the edge of the blanket to see the glowing white feathers of the horse's wings resting on the dark body. "I'm seeing you, but I can't believe you're here." He patted Pegasus's strong neck. "Even touching you doesn't seem to help."

"He's real, Dad," Emily said. "And he's broken his wing again. But now there are these awful creatures after him."

"Nirads," Diana corrected.

"I—I still don't understand." Steve shook his head. "How can any of this be real? What can it all mean?"

"It means that the war in my world has come into yours," said Diana. "And unless we get the golden bridle back, neither world will survive."

Emily explained to her father about the golden bridle—how it killed Nirads—and about the history of the Flame and that Pegasus had to find the Daughter of Vesta to relight it.

Steve combed his fingers through his hair and cursed. "I held that bridle in my hands a few days ago. If only I'd kept it!" He looked at Diana. "Why don't you make more golden weapons?"

"Minerva made the bridle for Pegasus," Diana explained. "But we do not know how she created it or what other metals she used. She was one of the first captured by the Nirads. Vulcan tried forging other Olympian gold." She showed everyone the golden tip of her spear. "It can wound the Nirads, but only the special gold from the bridle can kill them. We must get it back if we are to defeat them."

"That won't be easy. I met the kid who stole it from Pegasus. The same night he arrived, the CRU were informed. They took him and everything with him away. I don't even know where they're holding him. They keep their locations quiet."

Pegasus neighed behind Diana.

"Pegasus says our main concern is the Daughter

of Vesta," said Diana. "We must get her back to Olympus."

"But we've got to wait for his wing to heal first," Emily pointed out, "which means we need somewhere safe to hide until then."

"Well, we can't stay here," Steve said. "You've seen the helicopters. By dawn, this entire park will be crawling with CRU agents and the military. We're going to have to keep moving and try to stay one step ahead."

"How do we hide a large horse in the middle of New York City?" Joel asked. "No offense, Pegasus, but you know what I mean."

The stallion remained silent as he rested his head on Emily's shoulder. She suddenly had a thought.

"I know! We hide him in plain sight! " Emily looked over to her father. "Dad, you know how they've been trying to shut down the carriage rides in the park because of that campaign for better treatment of the horses?"

"Yes," he said. He looked at Diana and explained. "Several groups aren't happy about the treatment of the horses in the city, and I agree with them, it can be awful. Finally the number of carriages is dropping."

"Exactly," Emily said excitedly. "So there are extra carriages at the stables. . . ."

"I get it!" Joel said. "You want to steal a carriage and attach Pegasus to it. We'll keep his wings covered. Then we'll simply walk right out of the city and find the Daughter of Vesta!"

"Great idea," Steve said. "Let's do it!"

Getting out of Central Park with Pegasus proved more difficult than they expected. It was well past midnight and there was still a lot of traffic on the roads. What disturbed them the most was the sheer number of police cars, running with their sirens off but lights flashing, followed by countless army vehicles traveling throughout the city.

They waited until almost two in the morning before they made their move. They exited the park on 104th Street. The closest livery was on 50th.

"We've got to walk Pegasus over fifty blocks downtown?" Joel moaned.

"Unless that wing of his is strong enough to fly,

he's got to stay on the ground like the rest of us," said Steve. "We'll head over to one of the quieter avenues and make our way downtown."

As the long night progressed, Emily felt her leg begin to swell. But she kept the information to herself. She brushed aside the feeling of nausea and concentrated on getting to the stables. Above them, helicopters broadened their search patterns, so the group kept close to the shelter of the buildings.

"Wouldn't they be after the Nirads first?" Joel asked.

"I'd imagine so," Steve answered. "I'm sure they think Pegasus is still in the park."

"I hope you are both correct," Diana said as she looked up. "I do not like those flying machines one bit."

Suddenly all around them the city burst into brilliant light as the blackout finally ended and the power came back on. Soon the air was filled with the horrendous noise of shrieking alarms as endless security systems came online again. Streetlights started to work, and Tenth Avenue was lit up like a carnival.

"It couldn't have waited just a few more minutes?"

Joel complained. "Just a few more stupid minutes! Is that really asking so much?"

"All right," Steve said tersely. "We didn't expect this. But we've only got a few more blocks to go. Let's speed up."

They had traveled no more than a block when they heard the sound of police sirens drawing near. They ducked into a large doorway just as several police cars raced past.

"They didn't even slow down to look at us," Emily commented.

More police cars rushed by.

"Something big is up," Joel said. "I have a bad feeling about this."

"Nirads are in the area," Diana warned as she sniffed the air. "I can smell them."

Beneath her, Emily could feel Pegasus quivering. "Pegs can smell them too."

"I can't," Joel added. "Where are they?"

Diana sniffed again and pointed along 58th Street toward Fifth Avenue. "Down there."

"That's the entrance to the park!" Emily said. "The Nirads have made it to Central Park?" She looked down to Pegasus. "Pegs, how are the Nirads tracking you?"

"They have tasted his blood," Diana answered. "They are using it to follow his trail. We cannot lose them. The only thing in our favor is they cannot run very fast."

"If the Nirads are only a few blocks away from us," Joel added, "they don't have to run fast to catch us."

"Come on," Steve said. "Let's get that carriage and get out of this city!"

When they reached 50th Street, Emily's father led the group to a tall gray roller door. Posted above the door was a sign: O'BRIAN'S LIVERY.

"This is it?" Joel asked. "What a dump!"

"How do we get in?" Emily asked.

"We break in," her father replied.

Emily studied her father in his police uniform and realized how difficult this must be for him, being an officer of the law.

"This isn't going to be easy." He inspected the padlock. "I can't use my gun. It'll make too much noise."

"There's another entrance here," Joel suggested as

he stood before a normal-size door beside the bigger one.

"True, but we won't get Pegasus or a carriage through that. We need to open this big one here."

"Let me try," Diana said. She reached across and easily tore both the lock and the hasp away from the door.

Everyone looked at her in shock.

"I may have lost my powers," Diana said, "but not my strength."

Steve hoisted the large roller door up on its rails. "That will come in very handy!"

Emily ducked as Pegasus stepped under the door. Steve pulled it closed again once everyone was through. As they looked around, the overwhelming smell of horses and filthy, soiled straw filled their nostrils. Up ahead, multiple carriages stood in a long row.

Above them on the upper floors, they could hear the sound of horses whinnying.

"They know we are here," Diana said as she listened to the calls of the horses. "They are suffering."

"So will we be if we don't grab a carriage and get out of here," Joel warned.

"You choose a carriage. I must see to the horses." Diana started to climb a tall ramp to reach the upper floors.

"Diana, wait! We don't have time for this!" Joel cried.

"There is always time for animals," Diana called back as she disappeared up the ramp.

Beneath her, Emily could feel Pegasus reacting to the distress calls from the horses. She looked around at the filthy walls and chipping paint. "Dad, this place is disgusting," she said.

"I know, honey. But we've got to get moving."

Emily wanted to help her father and Joel look around. But she was feeling too ill. She knew now that something was seriously wrong with her leg. Sensing her pain, Pegasus turned back to check on her.

Emily could see the question resting in his eyes. "I'm not feeling very well, Pegs," she admitted quietly. "But I can't tell them yet. We've got to get out of the city and find the Daughter of Vesta first."

She looked into his beautiful face and felt a rising twinge of jealousy. Somewhere out there was another girl who was calling to him. This stranger held the stallion's heart, not Emily. Despite all the danger they were in, Emily found herself resenting the unknown girl and the place she would hold in Pegasus's life.

"We've got something," Joel called from the back of the building. "Emily, bring Pegasus here."

Suddenly shouts and screams came from above. Emily barely had time to catch hold of Pegasus's mane before the stallion had dashed down the hall and up the ramp. At the first level, Pegasus kept moving. He was starting to race up the second ramp toward Diana when an unconscious man tumbled down from above.

"Diana!" Emily called, as a second man was also thrown forward and tumbled down the ramp.

"I am here."

Pegasus leaped over the second man and made it to the next level. He ran down the narrow hall between the tiny stalls, skidding to a stop a short distance from Diana. She was standing before the open door of a stall. Her head was down. Emily could see tears shining on her cheeks.

"What's wrong?" Emily asked. She looked into the

stall and saw a chestnut mare lying on the floor. It wasn't moving.

"She is dead," Diana said softly. "They worked her to death. But those men didn't care. I heard them cursing her. She lived a life of misery in this wretched place, and they were complaining about what it would cost them to replace her."

When Emily's father arrived, Diana charged forward, seized him by the collar, and hoisted him in the air. "What kind of world has this become where you treat your animals like this?"

"Diana, please, put him down!" Emily shouted. "Put him down! He didn't do anything!"

"Perhaps not. But he lives in a world that allows this to happen." Diana lowered Steve to the ground. "It is unforgivable."

Both Joel and Steve looked at the dead horse.

"I know it's terrible," Steve said. "I'm ashamed of what we've become and how we treat our animals. But some of us are trying to change things. To make them better."

"Then you are failing in your attempt!" Diana spat. She pointed at the dead horse. "I have been away far too long. When this is over and my world is restored, I will return. This will not be allowed to happen again. Such places as this will know my wrath."

She looked at Joel. "You said you knew of me from your books?" she said. "Then you know how I feel about animals. I will not tolerate this kind of abuse." She crossed to another stall and started to open the door. "These horses must be set free. This is no life for them."

"I agree with you completely," Steve said. He stepped over to Diana and put his hand over hers. "But we don't have time to help them all. Diana, listen to me. We don't have long before those two guys wake up or someone else notices we're here. We may have already tripped some alarms. Who do you think will be interested to hear of a break-in at a livery stable? A *livery stable*, Diana. The CRU, that's who. And who will they think of?" Without waiting for an answer, he pointed at Pegasus. "They'll think of him. We must get out of here as quickly as possible."

Pegasus stomped his foot and started to whinny.

Diana paused. Finally she calmed as she walked over to the stallion and patted his neck.

"Of course, my dear friend, you are correct."

She looked at the others. "We must get the carriage and go. I will come back to free these horses later."

Emily looked at the other sad horses in their tiny stalls, anxiously waiting for Diana to open their doors. Her heart went out to them. When this was over, she promised she would join Diana in freeing them all.

On the way down the ramp, Emily saw one of the unconscious men starting to stir. It wouldn't be long before he woke up.

When they made it back down to the main floor, Joel led the way toward the back of the building.

"We found this in their storage area," Joel explained as he pointed at a broken-down white carriage. It was resting on its side. The top canopy was torn, but its wheels and frame looked sturdy enough. "They won't notice it missing as quickly as they would one of the better ones."

"I also found us these." Steve held up two sets of

overalls. "I can't exactly go out dressed like this." He indicated his police uniform. "And Diana? You certainly can't go out in those rags."

Diana nodded. Without a word, she took the overalls and went to another area to change.

EMILY STOOD WEARILY BY PEGASUS'S HEAD as her father, Diana, and Joel did their best to hook the stallion up to the carriage. As they fought and argued how best to get the harnesses on him, Emily realized just how different the stallion was from a horse. His entire frame was much bigger, and none of the harnesses came close to fitting. The huge set of wings didn't help.

In the end, they had to piece together several parts of multiple harnesses to get the stallion roughly hooked up to the carriage. Pegasus refused to allow the leather straps to go over the top of his wings, which would bind them down to his body. He insisted that they remain unrestricted. In order to achieve this, they had to try to attach everything under his massive wings, and hope that the blanket would cover them enough not to look too suspicious in daylight.

"Forgive me for doing this to you, my old friend," Diana said softly. "You deserve better."

Emily looked at Pegasus, dyed a poor mottled dark brown and black, and tethered to the tatty old white carriage. He was covered in harnesses that didn't fit and wearing a full, heavy bridle that rested uncomfortably on his face. He looked nothing like the majestic winged stallion that had crashed on her roof a few nights ago. Emily felt terrible for having to do this to him.

"I'm sorry too, Pegs," she murmured, leaning heavily against him. "We just have to get out of the city and then we can take it all off you again."

Pegasus let out a soft nicker and licked Emily's face. His tongue lingered on her cheek for a moment. He neighed to Diana.

"Fever?" Diana looked at Emily. She raised her hand to Emily's forehead and frowned. "You do have a fever."

"What?" Steve also felt Emily's forehead and face. "Em, you're burning up!"

Emily knew Pegasus had done it for her. But his timing couldn't have been worse. "I don't feel very well," she finally admitted. "I think it's my leg."

"Let me see it," her father insisted.

Emily was helped up into the carriage. Her father started to undo the bandages covering her wounded leg. "My God," he cried when he saw the ugly wound caused by the Nirad's claws. "Why didn't you say something?"

"I couldn't. We've got to worry about keeping Pegasus safe from the CRU and the Nirads. He's got to find the Daughter of Vesta and get her back to Olympus to relight the Flame."

"Emily is correct," Diana said. "Relighting the Flame of Olympus is the only hope for both our worlds."

"We have to get her to a hospital!" Steve insisted. "Look at her. She isn't well!"

Pegasus started to whinny and pound the floor.

"Pegasus does not agree with you," Diana said. "He knows very well she is ill. But the Nirads have tasted her blood also. They can track her. If you were to take her somewhere for care, I assure you the Nirads will follow. She must stay with us so we can protect her."

Joel held up the picnic hamper. "We've got more medicated cream and fresh bandages in here," he assured Steve. "We can clean up her leg and get it wrapped again. Then when we find the Daughter of Vesta and Pegasus takes her back to Olympus, we'll get Emily to the hospital."

"Dad, it's the only way," Emily added weakly. "Keeping Pegasus safe is much more important than me. If he fails his quest, the Nirads will destroy our world. Then, whether I'm sick or not won't matter."

Steve sighed. He reluctantly lifted Emily out of the carriage and carried her over to a slop sink to thoroughly clean her wounds. He applied the last of the medicated cream and bandaged her leg again.

"That won't last long," he said as he finished.

"It won't have to," Emily said. "Just long enough for us to get Pegs out of the city—"

Suddenly Pegasus started to shriek.

"Nirads!" Diana cried as she sniffed the air. "They are coming."

"From where?" Steve asked.

"That way!" Diana picked up her spear and pointed at the tall gray metal roller door.

"That's the only way out. We're trapped!" Joel cried.

From above they heard the sound of the horses reacting to the approach of the Nirads. They were shrieking in their stalls and pounding wildly against the doors.

"I've got an idea!" Steve cried. "Joel, Diana, come with me. Em, you stay here with Pegasus. If they break down the door, make a run for it. You've got to get away."

"What are you going to do?" Emily cried.

"We're going to release the horses."

PEGASUS WAS PAWING THE GROUND AND snorting angrily as the sickening growling sounds of the Nirads drew nearer.

"What's going on here?"

Emily saw the two men Diana had attacked come stumbling down the ramp. Their faces were bruised and bloodied, and they were limping from their encounter with the enraged Olympian.

"You attacked us!" shouted one of the men. "Who are you?" His eyes fell on Pegasus, harnessed to the old white carriage. "Where did that horse come from? He's not one of ours."

"But that carriage is!" said the other man angrily.

"Please listen to me." Emily pointed at the roller

door. "There are four-armed creatures out there that are after us. They'll kill you if they see you. They don't know you're here. Just hide until we're gone!"

The men went pale as they heard the awful sounds coming from outside the stable.

"Four-armed what?" one of them said weakly.

"Creatures, monsters, demons," Emily said. "Whatever you want to call them. We're going to free the horses to distract them so we can get away. Please listen to me. You have to hide!"

From above came more sounds of shrieking horses, kicking at their doors. They were becoming frantic in their stalls.

"You aren't freeing my horses!" one of the men shouted. They both turned and started back up the ramp. "Just stay where you are. We're calling the cops!"

Everyone heard the sound of pounding on the floors above, then the rush of hooves racing down the ramp. Both men jumped aside as the first of the horses arrived. They charged the carriage wildly, panic in their eyes.

Emily was certain they would stampede and

knock it over. But Pegasus opened both his wings just in time and reared up on his hind legs. Still in the carriage, Emily was lifted high in the air. The stallion let out a shrieking whinny that stopped the terrified horses in their tracks.

"What the heck is going on here?" one of the men cried as his eyes went wide at the sight of the stallion's huge white wings. He looked back at Emily. "Who are you?"

"What are you?" demanded the other.

The Nirads began to pound at the gray door. Their snarling, growling roars promised a terrible death to everyone if they managed to get in.

"Dad!" Emily screamed up the ramp as the carriage crashed down again. "They're here!"

"We're coming!" Joel called down as more horses arrived from above. Emily could see the flared nostrils and wild terror in their eyes as the frightened animals gathered around Pegasus. The stallion was back down on all fours, but his wings were quivering and he was shaking his head with rage.

Steve, Joel, and Diana reappeared, pushing through the horses on the ramp to make it to the carriage. When Diana saw the two men, she charged forward furiously.

"You deserve the fate awaiting you behind that door for what you have done to these horses. Do not expect any help from me. You are at the mercy of the Nirads!"

"Diana, we don't have time," Steve warned. "Get upstairs and hide," he advised the terrified men. "The Nirads want us, not you. Keep hidden and you might just survive!"

Without waiting to be told twice, the men pushed through the panicked horses and dashed up the ramp.

"We're still calling the cops!"

"Go ahead," Steve called. "I *am* a cop!"

"Dad!" Emily shouted, pointing at the roller door. "They're trying to tear the door down."

The heavy metal was starting to buckle under the brutal impact of the Nirads' fists.

"That door isn't going to hold for long." Steve raced to Pegasus and snatched up the blanket from where it lay on the ground. "The moment the door goes, the horses should charge forward. With luck they'll cut a way through the Nirads for us. Pegasus, it will be up to you to get us away from here as quickly as possible."

Pegasus snorted and shook his head. His sharp hooves pounded the concrete beneath him as his wild eyes watched the roller door start to give.

Steve leaped into the carriage and snatched up the reins. Joel and Diana vaulted in behind him.

"Hold on tight, everyone," Steve warned as he took the driver's seat. He snatched up the reins. "This is going to be bumpy."

More dents were forming in the heavy metal of the gray door. It started to give at the top. The long, sharp claws of multiple Nirad fingers appeared and ripped at it.

The door finally tore free of its rails, crashing backward onto the street, trapping two Nirads beneath it.

Pegasus shrieked. The horses panicked. Wild with terror, they started to stampede. They raced over the collapsed door and crushed the Nirads beneath. Without concern for their fallen warriors, other Nirads sprang forward and tried to force their way past the charging horses.

"Pegasus, go!" Steve shouted. "Go now!"

Emily felt the carriage jerk forward as Pegasus started to run. Several Nirads fought to climb over the terrified horses and charge toward them. One of them leaped in the air, passed over the top of the panicking horses, and landed on the side of the carriage. While two arms clung to the carriage, the other two reached for Emily and started to pull at her hair. Emily screamed, clawing at the heavy, muscled arms as the Nirad drew her closer.

Joel reacted instantly. He went for the Nirad's eyes. But the Nirad fought back. It released one of its arms holding on to the carriage and swung at Joel, knocking him back with a brutal blow just as Diana raised her spear and lunged forward.

When the golden tip struck the Nirad's exposed chest, it released Emily and howled in agony, then fell away from the carriage.

"Hang on!" Emily's father cried as they approached the collapsed door.

Pegasus charged up the metal door. With the two Nirads still trapped beneath it, the broken door worked as a ramp. The carriage sailed off the end and flew several meters into the air.

Everyone screamed.

The carriage crashed down to the ground. Although the occupants were tossed down to the floor, somehow the carriage remained upright. Without pausing, Pegasus sprang forward at full speed along 50th Street.

Emily struggled to climb back up in the seat. She peered back to the livery stable and gasped. More Nirads were charging forward, raising their four arms in threat and howling with rage at losing them. They ignored the panicked horses as they concentrated on chasing the carriage.

"Go, Pegs, go!" Emily screamed.

Emily was only able to count to twelve before she lost track of how many Nirads were following them. With the two still under the door, that made at least fourteen Nirads in New York City, all hunting them.

"Emily, are you all right?" Diana anxiously checked Emily for fresh cuts. "Did they wound you?"

Emily shook her head and gingerly prodded her painful scalp. "No, I'm fine. But I think I'm going to have a bald patch where that thing ripped out my hair."

"That's nothing," Joel complained, clutching his

side. "I think I've got broken ribs! Those Nirads really pack a punch."

"They bested Hercules," Diana explained. "It is no surprise that they should defeat you."

After several more blocks, Pegasus slowed to a trot. A few blocks later and he stopped completely. Everyone climbed shakily out of the carriage.

Emily limped up to Pegasus and stroked his muzzle. "Are you all right, Pegs?"

The stallion's eyes were wide and bright with fear as his nostrils remained flared. He gently nuzzled her neck.

"That was too close," Joel said as Steve inspected the carriage for damage. "This thing was ready to break before the attack. One more flight like that and it won't last another minute."

"We were lucky back there," Steve said grimly as he tested the large wheels. "But we've got to keep ahead of the Nirads. Those four arms are lethal."

"They are," Diana said. "And with their three eyes, they have full directional vision."

"Three eyes?" Joel asked. "Really? Where's the third one?"

"In the back of their head, under all that filthy hair," Diana explained. "From what we have learned, they do not see well out of it. But it is enough that you can never take them by surprise."

"How can we ever beat them?" Emily asked. The fever flared, making her feel even more weak and tired. "They're too strong."

"We need that bridle," Diana uttered. "With it we can defeat them."

"Plus the Flame," Joel added. "Once Pegasus gets the Daughter of Vesta back to Olympus to relight the Flame, you should have your powers back. Right?"

Diana nodded. "That is correct. But we must keep away from the Nirads until Pegasus is ready to fly again. He is our only way home."

Emily was leaning heavily against Pegasus for support. Her father felt her face.

"You're getting worse," he said worriedly. "Come on. Let's get you back into the carriage. You need some sleep."

Emily didn't resist when her father lifted her into the carriage. A second blanket had been stored under the seat. He pulled it out and draped it over her. "Settle down and rest," he advised. "I'm going to try to find us somewhere to hide for the night. Then when the city starts to wake again, we can blend in with the other carriages and start to make our way off Manhattan."

As her father climbed back up into the driver's seat, Diana settled in beside her. She put her arm around Emily protectively and drew her closer. "Sleep, child," she said softly. "We will be going home soon."

When Emily awoke, the sun was up and the sounds of the city had returned to their normal noisy pitch. But there seemed to be more police sirens than usual, and the frightening sounds of the helicopters could still be heard overhead.

Diana was sitting beside her. But her father and Joel were gone.

"Where are we?" Emily asked groggily as she looked around.

They appeared to be on a building site, hidden among several large cement mixers. A large scaffold was above them, blocking them from the view of the helicopters that still flew very low over the city.

"Your father knew of this place and brought us here," Diana explained. "He said we should be safe for a while. He said it was in a place called Downtown. Though I am not certain what that means."

Emily felt relieved. "That means we're well away from the stables," she said.

Pegasus was still tethered to the carriage. He nickered gently and tried to look back at her.

"Morning, Pegs," Emily said softly.

"Sleeping Beauty wakes," her father called.

Steve and Joel were approaching through a hole in the tall fence surrounding the building site. They both carried several bags of food. At their approach, Pegasus whinnied.

"He smells the sugar," Joel said. He looked at Diana. "I bet you'll need some too. We've got lots for you both."

"And I've got more stuff for your leg," Emily's father told her as he put the bags down on the ground. He reached for her forehead. "The fever's down a bit, but not a lot. How are you feeling?"

"Not too bad," Emily lied. The truth was, she felt awful. Her head was pounding, her body ached, and her leg was throbbing painfully to each beat of her heart. "I'm fine for today. I just hope we can get out of New York before the Nirads find us again."

"We will," her father said. "Now, we've got fresh bagels and cream cheese for us. Diana, you and Pegasus can have the cereal."

"Guess what?" Joel added, reaching into one of the bags. "We made the front page of all the papers!" He handed several newspapers to Emily. "Look at the headlines. 'Flying Horse Exposed as a Hoax!' Can you believe it? Half a million people saw us soaring up Fifth Avenue and they are calling it a big hoax!"

Emily looked at the grainy images of their panicked escape flight. The pictures looked like they had been taken from a camera phone and blown up too large to clearly see any details. She could see Pegasus and his huge white wings. But she couldn't see her or Joel's faces.

She quickly scanned the article. "A movie stunt? Do they really expect the people who saw us to believe it was a stunt to promote a new movie? And look, they don't even mention the Nirads! How dumb do they think people are?"

"They don't think they're dumb at all." Steve pulled more items from the bags. "But you can bet the CRU ordered the papers to print that. I'm sure if anyone tried to challenge the story, they can expect a visit from a not-so-friendly CRU agent to set them straight. This is probably the best thing that could have happened for us. The public won't be adding to the search. Especially now that Pegasus is . . ." Her father paused and tried to think of the best possible words. Finally he said, "Now that he's not white anymore."

In the bright daylight, Emily could see that their midnight dye job on Pegasus was awful. The stallion's head and part of his neck and mane were black. But farther down his front legs, a sharp, distinct line changed to brown. Then a bit farther down his back, the color changed to medium brown. At the end of the blanket, his exposed rump and tail were black again. He looked as strange now as he had when he was glowing white.

"Let's eat and then get moving again." Steve pulled out the rest of the food. "We've got a lot to do today and not a lot of time to do it."

As expected, Pegasus was starving. The stallion

hungrily went through three large boxes of sweet, sugary cereal and several bags of brown sugar and bottles of honey before he started to slow down.

Diana was much the same. Emily watched in amazement as she ate handfuls of the cereal from the box and washed it down with honey squeezed straight from a bottle.

"This is delightful," Diana said with a mouth full of food. "What do you call it?"

"Some like to call it breakfast." Steve chuckled. "But most of us call it garbage. There's enough sugar in that cereal to keep a kid hyperactive all day."

"But it's as close to ambrosia as we could get," Joel added.

"It is very good," Diana agreed. "Different from ambrosia or nectar, but it will do nicely."

Emily watched Diana wolfing down the food and thought she was going to be sick. Her father had brought a bagel for her, but she couldn't eat it. She caught him watching her but was grateful when he didn't nag her to eat.

After the cereal, Diana and Pegasus finished off two boxes of honey-glazed doughnuts.

"Your world has changed a great deal since I was last here," Diana said as she reached for the last doughnut. "It is not all bad after all."

"Well, we do have our good points," Steve said as he began cleaning Emily's wounds and changing the bandages. Though he didn't press Emily to eat her bagel, he made sure she took the painkillers. When he finished bandaging her leg, he sat back and shook his head. "We've got to get that looked at soon. It's getting worse."

Emily didn't need her father to tell her that. She already knew it. And she suspected that Pegasus knew as well. The stallion kept looking back to check on her, whinnying softly.

"Well, it's almost seven," said Steve, checking his watch. "We'd better start making a move. The contractors will be back to work any minute. I don't want them to find us here and see what we've done to their fence."

"Isn't it too early for the other carriages to be out?" Emily asked.

"We don't have much choice," said her father. "If we take our time heading uptown, maybe no one will notice."

As the food was packed away and the stallion's wings thoroughly covered, Emily's father sat in the driver's seat again. "You ready to go, Pegasus?" Pegasus whinnied. "We've got to make it to the Fifty-Ninth Street Bridge."

"Fifty-Ninth Street?" Diana repeated. "Excuse me, Steve, but is that not where the CRU are concentrating their efforts to find us? You wish to go there?"

"We don't have much choice," he explained. "The bridge is the closest aboveground route off Manhattan." He took up the reins. "We can't take the tunnels or the ferries. Besides, with the Nirads rampaging through the city, I'm sure the CRU and military have their hands full. Hopefully, we can stay under their radar."

He looked at the stallion. "All right, Pegasus, let's get going," he said. "But nice and easy. We don't want to draw too much attention to ourselves."

Pegasus nickered once and started to move.

PAELEN WAS ONCE AGAIN HANDCUFFED TO the bed. This time there were cuffs on his ankles as well as his wrists.

The blow to the head had stunned him for only a few moments. But when he awoke and begged the men to help Pegasus, his pleas were ignored.

Agent J stood beside his bed, glaring at him. "I would suggest you reconsider speaking to us," he said. "I am authorized to use full force to get what I need from you. You have until dawn to decide. You will either tell me the truth, or I will use methods infinitely more unpleasant than you have ever known. The choice is yours."

But Paelen already knew what he planned to

do. He had no intention of cooperating. His only thoughts now were to get to Pegasus and warn him.

When Agent J and his men had gone, Paelen concentrated on the problem at hand. Getting the cuffs off wouldn't be difficult. The big problem was getting out of the facility. Agent J had claimed they had serpents' eyes watching him. The fact that they caught him on the lower level proved those words to be true. But was there anything watching him in here?

Paelen strained his eyes, carefully studying every wall and every area of his room, searching for anything that might look like a serpent's eye. He saw nothing out of the ordinary.

He was convinced the serpents' eyes were only in the corridors. With that route blocked to him, he would have to find a different way out of the facility. Once again, he looked up to the air vent above his bed. That would be his escape. He felt certain there wouldn't be any serpents' eyes in there. Decision made, Paelen turned his attention to the handcuffs and reluctantly used his one Olympian skill.

It was incredibly painful. Starting with his right wrist, he folded his thumb in tightly and started to pull. Just like all the other times he had been chained in Olympus, Paelen was able to stretch out the bones in his hand until the metal cuff slid off. He repeated the process with his left hand.

With both hands free, Paelen sat up and reached for the cuffs on his ankles. He winced in pain as the bones in his feet stretched out until the cuffs simply slid away. When he was free, he returned his shape to normal with a sigh of relief.

Paelen pressed his ear to the door and heard voices. He counted at least three men posted outside his door. They were locked in a deep conversation, talking about something called football. With their attention diverted, they would never hear him go.

Paelen climbed on his bed. Standing on his pillows, his keen eyes scanned the air vent. It would be a tight fit, even for him. But if he stretched himself out long enough, he knew he could squeeze through.

There were only four screws holding the cover to the mount. He caught hold of one of the edges and started to apply pressure. It took very little effort to pull the vent cover away from the wall. He hid it under his pillow.

Paelen stole a quick look back to the door and then reached up. He pressed his palms firmly against the inner metal walls of the duct and hauled himself up to the vent.

As he had suspected, the entrance to the air duct was brutally tight. He had to painfully stretch every bone in his body to slip through. It was only then that he realized his ribs weren't completely healed yet. As he moved, he felt sharp twinges of warning pain from the altered length of his rib cage.

Biting back the pain and wincing at every move, he entered the countless tunnels of ductwork. The ducts themselves were much larger than the entrance had been, and he was able to return his body to its normal shape.

Crawling forward on his hands and knees, Paelen used every sense to listen for danger. When he reached a T junction, he paused. To his left, he heard nothing. It was still very early in the morning, and there weren't many people in the facility yet. But to his right, he heard voices. Paelen recognized one of the voices. It was Agent J.

What he was saying wasn't clear. But Paelen was

certain he heard the word "Pegasus." Agent J was talking about the stallion!

Paelen followed the voices, moving as quickly and quietly as he could. Moment by moment, the agent's voice was getting louder. He approached a short tunnel and saw a light at the end shining through another vent. Through the vent, he heard Agent J speaking.

He approached the opening. Paelen discovered that if he moved his head just right, he could actually see through the louvered grille and down into the office.

Agent J was sitting at a large desk, his back to the vent. Two other men faced him. Paelen almost gasped aloud when he saw one of Mercury's sandals sitting on the desk before him. Agent J was waving the second one in the air while he spoke. Paelen looked at the other men and saw the younger one he knew as Agent O sitting before the desk. The third man, seated beside Agent O, was unknown to him.

"So, what do you think?" Agent J asked.

Agent O shrugged. "I just don't know. But there are too many coincidences for it not to be true. The kid's test results and the way he sticks to the same story over and over again. Those sandals and that winged horse, Pegasus? What about those creatures in the city? I hate to admit it, but I'm beginning to believe him. I think we might actually be dealing with a bunch of Olympians and not the aliens we first thought."

Agent J turned to the other man. "What about you, Agent T?"

"I'm with Agent O," he said. "We've had hundreds of men out there combing all the boroughs for signs of a crashed or landed starship. We've contacted NORAD for satellite detection. There just aren't any traces or sightings of anything coming in from space."

Agent J cursed. "How am I going to explain this?" he demanded. "Command is obsessed with finding extraterrestrials. More importantly, their technology. Look at all the weapons developed through findings from the Roswell incident! Not to mention the more recent captures. Alien technology is invaluable, and Command expects us to deliver information!"

"Calm down, sir," Agent O said. "You'll give yourself a stroke!"

Agent J held up a warning finger. "Don't tell me to calm down! We are the most powerful nation on the planet! Why? Because we have the biggest weapons developed from off-world technology. How will I explain that this kid and that flying horse aren't from outside of Earth, but a bunch of old myths coming true? What's next? Vampires? Werewolves? How about some sweet little fairies riding a unicorn?"

"I know it's hard to digest," Agent O said. "But we'd be foolish not to consider it a possibility."

"What about all the others?" Agent J demanded. "Jupiter, Apollo, Cupid, and all those other mythical characters? Are you suggesting they exist too? And if so, why haven't we heard from them before now?"

Paelen watched Agent O shrug. "I don't know. Maybe they wanted to keep a low profile," he said. "Stay hidden in our modern world. But the myths do say that Mercury traveled around in winged sandals. Look at what you're holding. What do our scientists say about them?"

"Nothing," Agent J spat furiously. "The materials are untraceable! They say these are real diamonds, rubies, and sapphires sewn onto the sides. But the feathers on the wings aren't from any known bird species on Earth. Neither is the leather. They just can't tell us where they came from."

"So our kid could in fact be Mercury?" Agent T asked.

Agent O nodded. "He claimed that was one of his names."

Agent J snorted. "He also claimed to be Hercules, Jupiter, and Paelen the Magnificent. I wouldn't put much stock in what he's told us so far."

"What about the bridle?" Agent T asked.

"Same as the sandals," Agent J answered sourly. "Untraceable materials. Yes, it's real gold. But there's a lot more mixed in with it. They found saliva on it too. The DNA doesn't match any kind of known horse. In fact, it doesn't match anything living on this planet. Just like the kid and that creature we have down on the slab."

"So it could belong to the real Pegasus?" said Agent O.

Agent J sighed heavily. "I hope not. We're here to find extraterrestrials, not Olympians! But we won't know for sure until they get here and we can test the stallion for ourselves."

Paelen almost jumped from his skin. Had they found Pegasus?

"When should that be?" Agent O asked.

He saw Agent J look at a small device on his wrist. "Based on their current movements, I would imagine we'll have them captured and delivered here before noon today," he said.

"How did you find them?" Agent T asked. "Last I heard they were hidden in the park."

"They left the park hours ago," said Agent J. "We just brought in two guys from a livery on Fiftieth. They called the police and claimed that four people with a winged stallion broke into their stables and stole a carriage. With that, it wasn't too hard for us to locate the carriage and keep an eye on it."

"Four people?" Agent O repeated. "There were only two kids in the photo with Pegasus. Who are the other two?"

"The guys from the livery said one of them was a tall, superstrong woman the others called Diana. They said she carried a spear and beat them both senseless because of the way they treated their horses."

Paelen had to cover his mouth to keep silent. Diana was in this world! If Pegasus ever told her about him stealing the bridle, he knew there would be no escaping her wrath. But to hear these people were going to bring Jupiter's daughter to this facility with Pegasus was almost too much to bear.

"The other adult with them is a New York City cop, Steve Jacobs. The girl from the picture is his daughter. What we don't know is how or why they got involved. Nor do we know who the other kid is. He may be like our Mercury, or he may be human. The owners of the stable said that the monsters arrived not long after they broke into the place. I've just seen the photos our guys took of the livery. Those creatures tore through the door like it was butter."

"What were they after?" Agent O asked.

"The stallion," Agent J said. "At least that's what the guys said."

"What if these monsters get to them before we do?" Agent T asked.

"They won't," said Agent J confidently. "We've

already got our people in position. Pegasus and the carriage are completely surrounded on all sides. They can't make a move without us knowing it. We've got the Fifty-Ninth Street Bridge locked down and secure. We're just waiting for our prey to enter the trap."

Agent O shook his head. "Sounds a little risky to me. If we know where they are, why don't we move in now and grab them? How can you be so certain they'll try for the bridge?"

Agent J stood up. He yawned and stretched. "Because that's what I'd do if I were them," he said. "Look, if we try to take them out in the open, there's a chance that stallion will fly away. We need to get them where he can't use his wings. The center lanes of the bridge are perfect for that. The bridge itself will work as a giant cage."

"And you're sure they are going to try to leave the city?" Agent O checked.

Agent J nodded. "They have to get out of the city before those creatures find them again. That bridge is the closest route off Manhattan. They can't afford to waste time heading farther uptown to one of the other bridges. Besides, we've got those covered too. New York City is secure. There is no way off."

He put down the sandal. "We've got a few hours left before we close the net. It's been a long night. I'm going to go get some rest. If they arrive here early, make sure they're all separated. I want to talk to each of them alone. Especially the kids. I have a feeling that woman with them isn't human. If she's anything like our Mercury, she won't talk. But I'm pretty certain the kids will."

Agent T looked unconvinced. "If Mercury hasn't talked, what makes you so sure about those kids?"

"I'm sure because we know at least one of them is human," said Agent J. "And unlike our strange alien or Olympian friend, I'm sure she will prove more susceptible to the persuasive powers of pain."

Paelen listened in shock. They were planning to torture the human girl he'd seen in the picture with Pegasus. She was just a child! Yet they didn't seem to care.

The men finally left the office, closing the door behind them. Paelen waited awhile to make sure they weren't coming back. When he was certain, he reached forward and applied pressure to one side of the vent. The screws gave easily. But this time Paelen was more careful. Instead of pushing the grate off completely, he only bent it a bit. When there was enough space, he winced in pain as he forced his bones to stretch out again.

Bit by bit, Paelen manipulated his body until he was able to pour himself into Agent J's office. He landed softly on the floor. Without returning his body to its natural shape, he reached for Mercury's sandals. Throwing them up into the vent, Paelen quickly climbed back in after them. He secured the vent again, caught hold of the sandals, and returned to his normal shape. He quickly took the tunnels back to his own quarters.

Paelen left the sandals in the vent outside his room. With another painful shape change, he slid back into his room and replaced the cover. Once he was satisfied that everything looked normal, he lay back down on the bed. He put the cuffs back on his ankles and wrists and returned to his natural shape.

It had been his plan to escape and find Pegasus. But he knew that his chances of finding the stallion in this strange world were remote at best. Hearing Agent J talking about how they were going to capture Pegasus and Diana and deliver them both to the very same facility, Paelen knew what he had to do. Nothing.

He would suffer their torture and whatever else they planned to do to him. He would not fight them. He would not try to leave. He would wait until the others were here. Then, when the time was right, he would take Mercury's sandals and help Pegasus and Diana escape.

Together they would return to the remains of Olympus.

AS THE CARRIAGE TRAVELED SLOWLY along 18th Street, Emily was grateful that no one was paying them much attention. Apart from the helicopters circling the city and the rotten way she was feeling, on any other day she would have enjoyed the ride. She struggled to keep her eyes open. She felt very hot and knew her fever was spiking. Diana still had her arm wrapped around her and was constantly checking her forehead.

"Hold on, child," she coaxed. "It will not be much longer."

In her fevered state, Emily thought she heard her mother's voice speaking gently to her, encouraging her to go on. "I will, Mom," she mumbled.

Diana gave her a gentle squeeze. Dimly, Emily heard Diana speaking to her dad.

"Steve, where is Emily's mother?"

"She died three months ago," he said sadly. "It hit Em really hard. She and her mother were very close."

Emily heard her father's response and felt her throat tighten. Her mother would have loved Pegasus and would have been right there fighting alongside them.

"So you are grieving," Diana said gently. She gave Emily a comforting squeeze. "My poor, poor child. Now I understand."

Struggling to keep awake, Emily watched the streets going by. Soon they were passing the United Nations buildings. As each block passed, Emily half expected to see Nirads charging at them. But so far, it had been a blissfully quiet trip.

"Steve, do they allow carriages on the bridge?" Joel asked quietly.

"No," he answered. "But I've got my badge with me if anyone tries to stop us."

Soon they were on the entrance ramp to the 59th Street Bridge.

"Here we go," Steve called. "Do we want to follow the route that goes under the framework of the bridge, or stay on the uncovered outside lane?"

Pegasus nickered several times and snorted.

Diana leaned forward to translate. "He says he much prefers to stay in the open in case something should go wrong. He says his wing is feeling much recovered and should be able to carry the carriage if need be."

"If he's sure," Steve said. "Pegasus, stay to the right. That will take us to the outside uncovered lane."

As the carriage moved into place, they found the traffic on the bridge was particularly heavy.

"It seems like a lot of other people had the same thought about leaving the city," Joel said. "The outside lane is bumper to bumper. Nothing is moving."

"That area is moving over there," Diana suggested as she pointed to the center lanes leading under the cover of the bridge. "We must go that way to keep moving."

"You heard the lady, Pegasus," Steve said. "Take us onto the bridge and away from Manhattan."

As the carriage joined with the steady flow of traffic, they listened to the strange clip-clopping sound of the stallion's sharp golden hooves on the steel grate of the bridge. The other cars slowed as they passed, but otherwise ignored the horse-drawn carriage.

When they were just over halfway, Emily saw they were passing over Roosevelt Island. She tried to recall the last time she had been here. It had been when her mother was still alive, well over a year ago. They had taken a weekend trek out of the city. She recalled the excitement of going to Long Island and Wildwood State Park. Emily remembered how happy she'd been when they had gone swimming together and—

"Uh-oh," Steve said. "This isn't good."

Drawn from her fevered memories, Emily tried to focus her attention. The traffic was slowing down to a stop.

"Look over there, it's all stopped," Joel said as he pointed to the other lanes going in the opposite direction.

Pegasus let out a warning whinny and started to shake his head. His ears were pricked forward, and he was baring his teeth.

"What is happening?" Diana asked as she sat forward and looked around.

"I have a bad feeling about this," Joel warned.

"So does Pegasus," Diana agreed.

Emily sat up and gazed around the carriage. When she looked toward the Manhattan side of the bridge, her eyes flew wide in terror. Drawing to a stop several car-lengths back were multiple military trucks. Soldiers were pouring out of the trucks and drawing their weapons.

"Dad—"

Suddenly, from both sides of the bridge, a number of armed helicopters flew down from the sky and hovered beside them. Their weapons were pointed directly at the carriage.

"It's a trap!" her father cried.

"And we're in it!" Joel shouted.

"Don't move! Stay where you are!" warned a voice from one of the helicopter's loudspeakers. "You are completely surrounded. Stay where you are!"

Without pausing, Steve jumped down from the carriage. "Joel, help me. We've got to free Pegasus!"

Emily tried to stand, but her infected leg wouldn't support her weight. She fell back down to the seat. She could no longer move. All she could do was watch as Diana stood above her and raised her spear in the air. She was preparing to take on the military.

"No, Diana!" Emily reached weakly up to catch the end of the spear. "They'll kill you. Go with Pegs. Please, get away. Save Olympus!"

"Do not speak nonsense," Diana shot back at her. "I will not allow these foolish men to hurt you. If they wish to fight, I am happy to oblige."

Everybody heard the pounding of feet on the bridge as soldiers charged at them from all directions.

"He's free!" Steve shouted as he pulled the last of the leather straps away from Pegasus. Joel tore the blanket from his wings and smacked the stallion's rump.

"Go on, Pegasus, go!" Joel roared. "Get out of here! Find the Flame and save both our worlds!"

Free of the harness, Pegasus turned and ran back to the carriage. He whinnied loudly at Emily, reached forward, and tried to catch her by the shirt to lift her up.

"No, Pegs, I can't move," Emily cried. "Please, go. Take Diana and leave here. You can't let them catch you." Tears sprang to her eyes as she shoved the stallion's head away. "Please . . . just go!"

"Stop!" Several soldiers had drawn near and raised their weapons. "Put your hands in the air and don't make a move!"

"Go, Pegs!" Emily shouted with all her remaining strength.

The air filled with strange popping sounds. At first Emily thought the soldiers were shooting bullets at them. But then she saw countless feathered darts strike Pegasus. Within moments, his hindquarters looked like a pincushion.

"What is this insanity?" Diana called in fury as she too was struck by the tranquilizer darts. She angrily pulled them from her arms and tossed them away.

Steve and Joel were both hit by the darts. Instantly they fell to the ground, unconscious.

Because of her position, Emily hadn't been hit. But as more men descended on them, Pegasus opened his wing to cover her, taking the brunt of the darts meant for her.

"Don't worry about me, Pegs," Emily cried. "Please just go!"

But Pegasus refused to leave. He reared on his hind legs, threw back his head, and shrieked in rage. His front legs cut furiously through the air and promised a violent death to any of the soldiers who tried to come closer. Diana joined in the battle cry, raising her spear and preparing to take on the soldiers.

Then Emily felt a sharp sting in her neck as a dart found its mark. She heard Pegasus's enraged cry and saw him lunging forward to attack the soldiers just as everything went black.

EMILY OPENED HER EYES. SHE WAS LYING IN a hospital bed in a clean white room. There was an IV in her arm, and countless bags of liquid feeding down tubes. Beside the bed was a lot of equipment that had wires attached to her head and chest. They beeped to the steady beating of her heart.

Her wounded leg was suspended in the air, wrapped in a thick layer of bandages. Despite the care, it was still pounding painfully.

"Good morning, Emily."

A nurse rose from a chair beside the bed. "Please don't try to move," she said. "I'll go get the doctor."

Emily struggled to remember the last thing that had happened. Then it all came flooding back. The bridge. Pegasus screaming. Diana holding a spear and preparing to fight. She remembered the dart hitting her in the neck and blotting out the rest of the world. The final realization put a cold shiver down her spine. The CRU.

Emily tried to rise from the bed. But pain and the fact that her leg was suspended stopped her. Panting heavily, she lay back down. She was in no condition to fight.

The nurse returned with two men. One was dressed as a doctor, but the other wore a dark suit and had a stern expression on his face. Both were middle-aged.

"Good morning, Emily," said the doctor, in a friendly tone that didn't match the coldness of his eyes. "How are we feeling this morning?"

The other man wasn't even pretending to be nice. Suddenly Emily understood everything her father had ever told her about the secret government agency. She was in a lot of trouble.

"We?" Emily repeated. "I don't know about you, but I'm feeling awful." She looked at the other man. "Are you the CRU?"

"I work for the Central Research Unit, yes," he said coldly. "You may call me Agent J. I have a lot of important questions for you." He looked at the doctor. "You may leave us now. Emily and I are going to have a chat."

"I really should check on my patient," the doctor said.

"And you can . . . later," Agent J said.

His tone suggested there would be no discussion, no argument. His orders were to be obeyed. Without another word, the doctor left the room.

"Where is my father?" Emily asked nervously. "Please, may I see him?"

"I'm afraid you aren't well enough for visitors," Agent J said. "You've still got a very bad infection and have suffered a lot of muscle damage. Actually, you are quite fortunate the surgeons here were able to save your leg. Though I'm sorry to say you will have trouble walking from now on."

Emily didn't feel particularly fortunate. She felt dreadful. More than that, she was terrified. Where was she? What were they doing to her father and Joel? Were they hurting Pegasus? What about Diana?

"Please tell me. Where is my father?"

"He's around." The agent moved closer to the bed. "Our first concern is taking care of you. Perhaps in time, if you cooperate, I'll let him come in and see you."

Emily saw the coldness of his pale eyes. "Cooperate?"

"Yes, cooperate," Agent J said as he sat down in the chair beside the bed. "I have a lot of questions that need answers. And you are just the young lady to give them to me."

"Me? But I don't know anything," Emily said. "I just want to see my dad."

"First you'll answer my questions. Then maybe we'll see about your father."

Agent J pulled a small tape recorder from his pocket. He flicked the switch to turn it on. "Now, I would like you to tell me what happened. Where did you find the flying horse? Where does it come from?"

"His name is Pegasus," Emily corrected. "And he's not a horse. He comes from Olympus. He was struck by lightning and crashed on my roof. That's all I know."

"I'm sure you know a bit more than that," Agent J coaxed.

"No, I don't," Emily insisted. "Where is Pegasus? Please, I must see him. He won't understand what's happening to him. He's going to be so frightened of you."

"The stallion is fine," the man said. "He gave us a great deal of trouble in the beginning and killed several of my men on the bridge. But we've managed to calm him down since then."

Emily was puzzled by his answer. But more than that, she was frightened for Pegasus. She remembered seeing the soldiers with their guns raised on the bridge. "You didn't shoot him, did you?"

"We had to," Agent J said. "He was killing my men."

"You shot Pegasus!" Emily cried. "Why? All he was doing was protecting us. How is he? Is he alive?"

"I told you, Emily, he is fine. His wounds have been treated, and he is a lot calmer than he was."

"Why couldn't you leave us alone?" Tears rose in Emily's eyes. "We weren't hurting anyone. Pegasus just wants to go home."

"Where is his home?" Agent J asked, looking alert.

"I told you already," Emily said, sniffing. "Olympus."

"Yes, you told me. But where exactly is Olympus?" the agent pressed. "How do you get there?"

"I don't know," Emily cried. "Please, can I see him?"

"Not yet. You are still too ill to move."

Emily hated to agree with him, but he was right. She really was feeling awful.

"How long have we been here?"

"Four days."

"What?" she cried.

"I told you, Emily, you have been a very sick girl." Agent J went on, "You've got a raging infection. We actually thought we were going to lose you. But you've managed to come back from the brink of death. You're a very determined young lady. So now, I'll ask you again. What do you know of the flying horse? Why is he here?"

"I told you, he's not a horse!" Emily shot back as she sat up angrily. But just as quickly she had to lie down again, as the movement threatened to make her sick. "He's Pegasus," she said softly. "And he shouldn't be here. You've got to let him and Diana go."

"Ah yes, Diana," Agent J said. "A very interesting

woman indeed. Remarkably strong. She has managed to resist all our questions. Our scientists are still trying to figure out what she is."

"She's the daughter of Jupiter," Emily said, growing angry. "That's who she is. When he finds out what you've done to her and Pegasus, he's going to be really mad!"

"Jupiter, eh?" Agent J said. "Well, if they really do come from Olympus as you claim, why hasn't Jupiter come to see us already? What's he waiting for? I would be more than happy to discuss his daughter with him."

Emily stared into his cold, prying eyes. Something inside warned her to say nothing more. If after four days he still wanted questions answered, it meant her father and Joel hadn't cooperated either. She quickly realized that the more she said, the worse it would be for the others. She closed her eyes. "I don't feel well. I'm so tired. Please, let me sleep."

"In a moment," Agent J said. "Just tell me why Pegasus and Diana are here."

"I don't know," Emily insisted. "Why don't you ask them yourself?"

Agent J shook his head angrily. "I did. Diana won't speak to me, and I would look like a fool if I tried talking to that horse."

"Pegasus isn't a horse!" Emily shouted. Her father had always taught her that violence wasn't a solution. But at that moment, she really wanted to smack Agent J right in the mouth. "He's an Olympian."

"Horse or not," Agent J said, "I want to know why they are here! You are going to tell me."

"I already told you, I don't *know* why they are here. Just that you've got to let them go. They don't belong in our world."

"What about Mercury?" Agent J asked.

"Mercury?" Emily repeated, puzzled. "The planet?"

Agent J shook his head. "No, not the planet," he said irritably. "Mercury, the messenger of Olympus. He's here as well. If their story is true, that makes at least three Olympians in my city. That doesn't even take into consideration those creatures, whatever they are called."

"Nirads," Emily answered without thinking.

She realized her mistake at once. Agent J had tricked her into telling him more than she wanted.

"Nirads," he repeated. "Why are *they* here?"

Emily didn't want to answer any more of his questions. She was feeling too ill and making too many mistakes. Instead she closed her eyes and lay back.

"I want to see my father."

"Answer my question," Agent J pressed.

Emily said nothing. With her eyes still closed, Emily could hear his breathing. He was getting angry. Suddenly she felt a searing pain in her wounded leg. Howling in agony, she opened her eyes. A cruel smile hovered on Agent J's lips as his hand pressed down on her raised leg. He was squeezing her wounds in a brutal grip.

"Why are they here?" he demanded. "Tell me!"

The pain was blinding. Emily had never known such agony. It stole the scream from her throat and drove the wind from her lungs. Stars appeared before her eyes as the sound of water rushed in her ears. A moment later she passed out.

PAELEN KEPT HIS HAND OVER HIS MOUTH AS he peered through the vent above the girl's bed. He knew the agent could be ruthless, from his own interrogations. But he would never have imagined that Agent J could do that to a child.

As he traveled back through the vent, he was grateful that she had passed out. He doubted even he could have withstood that kind of pressure on a new wound. When this was over, Paelen promised himself that Agent J would discover that hurting the girl had been a grave mistake.

Since the others had arrived at the facility, Agents J and O seemed to have lost interest in him. They were spending less and less time trying to get him to talk. He could go a full day without seeing anyone. This gave him the time to slip out of his room to go searching for Diana and Pegasus.

But as Paelen made his way through the long maze of ventilation ducts, he still had no clue where they were keeping the others from Olympus. He only managed to find Emily's room because it was just down the hall from his own, and he'd heard the doctors speaking about her through the air vent.

In the tunnel leading to his own room, Paelen saw Mercury's sandals lying just ahead of him. He pushed them aside to get past and muttered, "Diana, where are you? I have to find you."

Paelen was still touching the sandals as he spoke. The tiny wings burst to life and started to flutter and move. Paelen jumped and nearly screamed in the tight confines of the air vent as they beat against his hand. He instinctively threw them away. The wings stopped moving at once and returned to their normal quiet state. Paelen reached forward and cautiously poked the nearest one. Nothing happened. He gave it a second poke. Still nothing happened. He reached forward and picked it up. The wings remained still.

He then picked up the second sandal. Again, the wings remained quiet.

"Find Diana," he said softly.

The wings started flapping wildly again as the sandals sprang to life. Paelen clutched them tightly. But he was unprepared for the sudden twisting and bending in the tight area. If he hadn't had the talent for stretching out his body, the power of the sandals would have broken his every bone as they turned him around in the tight duct area and lunged forward to obey his command.

Biting back his cries of pain and shock, Paelen was wrenched forward. Barely able to see, he was dragged noisily and uncontrollably through the long maze of ductwork in the facility. He held on for dear life. One moment the sandals were going to the left. Then at another junction, they darted to the right. A moment later, the sandals dragged him to the edge of a long, deep drop.

"No, please wait!" Paelen cried when he saw what Mercury's sandals were intending. "Nooooo . . ."

Without pause, the sandals drew him over the edge and plunged downward. Paelen screamed and heard the echo of his terror flooding throughout the endless tunnels. But still they would not stop. Banging his elbows, shoulders, and knees on the walls of the ductwork, they were falling.

The sandals weren't obeying his command to find Diana. They were trying to kill him!

But long before they hit bottom, the sandals changed direction again. They dashed into a new series of ducts that led away from the long drop. Finally they turned down another long tunnel that ended abruptly in an exit air vent.

"Stop, please!" Paelen begged just before they smashed into the vent cover.

They immediately obeyed his command and stopped. The sandals folded their tiny wings and became still. Paelen lay unmoving as he tried to catch his breath. That had been the worst ride of his life. Worse even than the time he'd stolen the sandals from Mercury and had tried to use them. The evil winged monsters had flown him straight into a pillar and knocked him senseless. When he finally awoke, Mercury was looming above him and furious.

But even that hadn't been like this ride of terror.

As he panted heavily, Paelen was sure he was going to be sick. Rolling over onto his back, he took several deep breaths and forced his pounding heart to calm.

When he could think clearly again, he turned over onto his hands and knees. He crept forward and up to the louvered vent cover directly in front of him. He gasped when he saw Diana lying on a narrow bed. Thick, heavy chains were wrapped around her waist. Other shackles bound her wrists to her waist chains. From what he could see through the vent, her ankles were also shackled to the waist chains. These chains were then secured to the wall behind her.

"I can hear you in there. Show yourself if you dare."

Paelen paused. This was Diana, daughter of Jupiter. She was renowned for her ferocious temper. On more than one occasion, he'd seen her bring Hercules to his knees with her biting tongue and vicious strength. Even her uncle Neptune was frightened of her and did his best to stay on her good side. The only one who could control her was her twin brother, Apollo. But Paelen had watched him die in Olympus.

Paelen himself had spent most of his life trying to

avoid Diana. If she knew what he'd done to Pegasus, he doubted even those chains could restrain her.

Taking a deep breath, Paelen pushed against one edge of the vent cover. When it gave, he cautiously poked his head through. "Diana?"

"Paelen!" Diana said furiously. "I was told you were in this world. You stole Pegasus's bridle! You foul little thief! Do you have any idea what you have done?"

"Please, Diana, forgive me," Paelen pleaded as he painfully stretched out his body to fit through the small air vent. He returned to his normal shape as he knelt before Diana's bed. "I know it was wrong. I am so sorry. I just wanted to make a better life for myself."

"By stealing the bridle?"

Paelen nodded. "I thought if I took it from Pegasus, but then gave it back, he would like me. He might even let me ride him. Then everyone else in Olympus would see that I am as good as the rest of you. Perhaps you might even respect me and see me as more than a thief. I swear I meant no harm." It might not be the entire truth, but Paelen had decided a small lie was wise.

"You did that to gain our respect?" Diana said incredulously.

Paelen nodded. "I just want to be like the rest of you," he murmured.

Diana shook her head. "You foolish little boy. You did all of this just to prove that you are like the rest of us? Can you not see? Are you so blind? Paelen, you are an Olympian, just like me. Just like my father and just like my brother was. We are no better than you. But now, the damage you have done is immeasurable. You have single-handedly condemned us all."

"Me? How?" Paelen cried. "What have I done other than flee the battle and take the bridle from Pegasus?"

Diana shook her head. "We needed that bridle to fight the Nirads."

"I do not understand," Paelen said helplessly. "What can it do that Pegasus himself cannot? I have seen what his hooves did to a Nirad. They have a dead one here in this place. He died because of Pegasus, not his bridle."

"It is not the bridle itself then, but the gold," Diana explained. "I did not know that Pegasus could kill them with his hooves. But back on Olympus, we discovered that the gold of his bridle was poisonous to the Nirads. One brief touch and they are weakened. Longer contact will kill them. That bridle was our only hope to make weapons against the Nirads. But now it is gone. Olympus has fallen and my father is in chains. Perhaps now, even dead."

Paelen sat back on his heels and looked at Diana. In all their long history, he had never seen her look so defeated. As she lay there in chains, the look of despair on her face was more than he could bear.

"You are wrong, Diana. The bridle is not lost. It is here, in this strange place. I have Mercury's sandals. They can lead me to it, just as they led me to you. We can still forge those weapons and defeat the Nirads. Please, let me help. Let me prove to you and everyone else that I am more than just a thief."

Diana shook her head sadly. "It is too late. These people have Pegasus as well. They shot him. I saw him go down. He may be dead."

"He is not dead," Paelen said. He told Diana what he had heard in the vent above Emily's bed. "Agent

J insisted Pegasus is alive. I know the sandals could take me to him if we want."

"And Emily? You have actually seen Emily?"

Paelen nodded. "Her room is very close to mine. But she is gravely ill. Her leg has been badly wounded. Agent J said she almost died."

"The Nirads got her," Diana said. "She and another boy, Joel, bravely fought them to protect Pegasus."

"That human girl fought a Nirad?" Paelen repeated incredulously.

"She is a very special child," said Diana. "When we leave here, we must take her and Joel with us. We need them to save Olympus."

"I do not understand," Paelen said. "How can simple humans save our home?"

"It is too complicated to explain," Diana said. "But we need them both if we are to succeed."

Paelen shook his head. "That will be difficult. The man, Agent J, has already tortured her once to get her to answer questions about us. I have no doubt he will do more to get her to speak."

"He tortured Emily?" Diana cried. "I will kill

him!" She reared up and strained against the chains that held her. "He has no idea what he is doing. Without her and Joel, we are all doomed!"

She struggled to pull her hands free of the shackles, but they wouldn't give. "I have gone too long without ambrosia. I am weak and cannot break these chains." She looked up at Paelen. "I wish I could change my body as you do. It would be little work for you to get out of these."

Giving up, she lay back down on the bed. "Paelen, listen to me. If you are sincere in wanting to help, you can. You must use Mercury's sandals and find everyone. Tell Pegasus what has happened and that you wish to help. Tell him about Emily and what Agent J did to her. Then you must find Joel and her father, Steve, and tell them both what you know. We must leave here as soon as Emily is well enough to travel. There still may be time to save both our worlds. But Paelen, you must be careful. Use all your thieving skills. Do not get caught. If you fail, we all do."

"I will be careful," Paelen promised as he stood up. "I will do this for Olympus."

Standing proudly before Diana, Paelen stretched out his bones. He tried to hide the pain it caused him so she wouldn't see his weakness.

"I will not fail," he promised as he lifted himself back into the vent.

WHEN EMILY WOKE AGAIN, SHE WAS ALONE in her room. Her leg was pounding mercilessly from where Agent J had squeezed it. She remembered his prying questions and the cruel look in his eyes when he told her they'd shot Pegasus. Was he lying? Had Pegs really been shot? Was he dead? What about the others?

Worry weighed heavily on her. The CRU was as bad as her father had told her. Worse, even. Agent J was the evilest person she'd ever met. The last thing she remembered was the cruel smile on his face and sparkle in his eyes as his hand crushed her wound.

Emily took in her surroundings. While she had been unconscious, they had disconnected her from the heart monitor and other machines. But she was still connected to the IV as several bags of fluid fed down into her arm. Whatever was in that stuff was working. She was feeling much better. Though her leg ached, her fever was down and her head was clearer.

In the silence, she became aware of odd sounds coming from above her bed. Looking up, she jumped when she saw fingers quietly pushing through the air vent. The vent came silently away from the wall, and two strange, long hands came through.

"Hello?" she called out.

She watched, mesmerized, as two extra-long, thin arms slid out of the vent; then a mop of dark brown hair and the top of a very strangely shaped head. These were followed by painfully narrow shoulders. Moment by moment more of the snakelike thing seemed to pour itself into her room.

Emily's eyes darted to her door. She wondered if she should call out for help. Was this some new type of creature come to kill her? Had it been sent by the Nirads?

As she opened her mouth to scream, the snakelike thing spoke.

"Do not be frightened, Emily. I am here to help you."

Biting back her cry, Emily realized that the creature was wearing a hospital gown just like hers. But what was in the hospital gown was the strangest thing Emily had ever seen. It was almost human, with two arms and two legs and a head. But it was profoundly distorted.

The creature landed softly on her floor. Emily heard the sickening sound of cracking bones as the creature shrank back to a more human shape. A young man now stood beside her bed. He was almost handsome, in a strange kind of way, and had warm, smiling brown eyes. As she looked at him, Emily was certain she'd seen his face before. Then suddenly it hit her, and her eyes flew wide with recognition.

"Paelen!" she said. "You're Paelen, aren't you? I saw you steal the bridle from Pegasus. Right before you were both struck by lightning."

A look of complete shock crossed Paelen's face. "How do you know me?"

"Pegasus showed me," Emily said. Then her voice grew angry. "I saw what you did to him! He wouldn't have been hit if you hadn't stolen his bridle and attracted the lightning."

"I know. I am very sorry," Paelen said, dropping his head. "But I am trying to make up for what I did. I am here to help. Listen to me, please, as I do not have a lot of time. I have already spoken to Diana—"

"You've seen Diana?" Emily cut in. "Is she all right? What about Pegs? They said they'd shot him. Did they? Is he alive? I'm so frightened for him. What about my father? Have you seen him and Joel?"

Paelen held up his hands to silence the stream of questions. "One question at a time, please. Yes, I have seen Diana. She is here in this place with us. She appears unharmed but is in chains. I have not yet seen Pegasus, but I will find him after I leave you. Nor have I seen your father or Joel." Paelen paused and took a step closer to her. "I just came to check on you. I was hiding up there"—he pointed up to the vent—"and I saw what that agent did to your leg. He is a cruel and dangerous man. I have had more than one unfortunate encounter with him."

Paelen came closer, eager to get his message across. "Listen to me, Emily," he said. "When that man comes back in here, and believe me, he will, tell him anything but the truth. But make your claims sound reasonable. Do not refuse to answer his questions. He will hurt you again, much worse than he already has. Diana told me what you did for Pegasus and how you were wounded trying to protect him. She says you and Joel are going to help us save Olympus. But to do that, you must get well. We cannot leave until you are ready to travel."

"Diana told you that?" Emily said.

Paelen nodded. "I must now find the others. Tell them what is happening. Then we will make our plans for escape. But only after you are well enough to leave."

"I'm well enough to leave right now," Emily said. She reached forward to undo the straps holding her wounded leg in the air. As she did, she started to feel dizzy.

"Stop, you are not well enough!" Paelen said.

"I'm all right," Emily insisted as she forced herself to move.

"No, you are not," Paelen said as he caught hold of her shoulders and gently made her lie down again.

"You need a bit more time to recover. I still need to find the others before we do anything. If Pegasus truly has been shot, then he, too, may need time to recover."

Emily surrendered. Paelen was right. She really wasn't up to moving around just yet. "He'll need sugar," Emily said. "Pegs won't eat food for horses. He needs sweet things."

"I know." A charming, crooked smile crossed Paelen's face. "I am exactly the same. I do rather like chocolate."

"Me too," Emily agreed. "But the people here think Pegs is a horse. They won't give him what he needs."

"Then I will," Paelen said. "I promise you, Emily, Pegasus will have everything he needs to recover his strength. But what we all need right now is for you to rest. Then we can make our move."

Emily nodded and lay back into the pillows. "I guess you're right. But there is one thing that may change all our plans," she said.

"What is that?" Paelen asked.

"The Nirads. They are tracking Pegasus and me.

Diana says it's because they've tasted our blood. They've been able to follow us everywhere we go," Emily explained. "If we've been here four days already, they might be getting really close. Because I don't know where we are, I don't know how far away they could be."

Paelen nodded and seemed to consider her words. He rubbed his chin, thinking. "When I was at the place they called Bellevue Hospital," he said, "the men came to get me. They chained me down to a narrow bed and then carried me in a strange flying machine. We journeyed a short distance, to a tiny island across the water from where we were. This place is deep beneath the ground of that island. But I do not know how deep."

"A tiny island?" Emily repeated. "We're on an island just off Manhattan?"

Paelen shrugged. "I guess. There was a tall statue in the water of a green woman holding a torch," Paelen went on. "She was looking at us."

"A statue of a green woman?" Emily mused. Then she snapped her fingers. "Wait, you're talking about the Statue of Liberty! So where could we be?

Roosevelt Island, maybe?" Then she shook her head. "No, wait, that's on the other side of Manhattan. Maybe Ellis Island? But does the Statue of Liberty face Ellis Island?"

Paelen looked confused. "This is your world, not mine," he said.

Emily nodded. "Yes, it is. But from what I can remember, I don't think Lady Liberty faces Ellis Island." Then finally it struck Emily. *Governors Island.* When she was younger, the coast guard kids at her school had lived there until they were all moved off and relocated. As far as anyone knew, Governors Island was now empty. What better place to hide a secret government facility than on an empty government island?

"Paelen, I know where we are."

"That is good."

"No, it's not!" Emily reached out to take Paelen's hand. "You don't understand. We're on Governors Island. It's too close to Manhattan. If the Nirads can swim, it's just a quick trip across the water and they're here." She looked intently at him. "Can Nirads swim?"

Paelen shook his head. "No. They sink in water.

In Olympus, it was the rivers that slowed them down until they discovered other ways of getting across."

"Can they use boats?" Emily asked anxiously.

Paelen shrugged. "I do not know. The truth is, I know very little about the Nirads. Until they attacked Olympus, I had never heard of them."

"We have got to get out of here as quickly as possible. We're so close to the city. I've counted at least fourteen Nirads after us. If they steal boats at the harbor, they could sail over here. Even if we are deep beneath the ground, they are strong enough to reach us."

"I must tell Pegasus," Paelen said. "And you must concentrate on getting better. If it is as you say and the Nirads are close, we must leave here soon."

"I will," Emily agreed. "Just find Pegs and tell him what you know. Then please find my father and Joel. They've got to know too."

"Yes, of course." Paelen stepped back from the bed. Emily watched in gruesome fascination as he started to manipulate his body again.

"Does that hurt?" she asked, cringing at the sounds of his cracking bones.

"Yes, actually it does. Rather a lot," Paelen answered as he finished stretching himself out. "But it allows me to fit through tiny spaces that no one else can get past. It infuriated Jupiter when I got away from his prison."

"Jupiter put you in prison?" Emily asked.

Paelen's snakelike head nodded. "He caught me in his palace stealing and had me put in prison, but I got away. Perhaps if we survive this, he will forgive me and let me remain free."

"If we manage to survive this and save Olympus, I'm sure he'll do more than forgive you," said Emily. "He'll make you a hero."

Paelen smiled brightly. "Do you think he might?"

In his snakelike form, Paelen's smile was horrible to see. Emily averted her eyes to keep from being sick. "I'm sure he would," she said.

"Then I will do my best for all of us."

When Paelen had squirmed through the vent, Emily settled back in her bed. Everything was happening so quickly she could hardly keep her thoughts straight. They were deep underground on Governors Island. Pegasus might have been shot, and Diana was in chains. Her father and Joel were hidden some-where she didn't know, and Nirads were only a short boat ride away.

Emily prayed that Paelen was telling the truth about wanting to help them. Otherwise, she couldn't see how they could get away. As she tried to figure out the best way ahead, sleep tugged at her exhausted body. Before long, she surrendered to its draw and drifted away.

PAELEN LAY IN THE VENT, WONDERING where he should go next. He knew it was late in the evening, as the guards had changed outside his door and activity in the building had slowed down.

He had time. No one would return to his quarters until the next morning. So, should he go to Emily's father? Joel? Or to the one he was dreading most, Pegasus? Facing Diana had been tough, but in the end, she could be reasoned with. But Pegasus would be different. There was no escaping the fact that Paelen had stolen his bridle and had intended to enslave the stallion.

He knew it, and Pegasus knew it. Would he be able to convince Pegasus that he had changed and that he wanted to help? He had to face the stallion sometime. It might as well be now.

"Take me to Pegasus," Paelen ordered.

Immediately the sandals' wings started to flap. Despite Paelen's attempts to prepare himself to be dragged painfully through the ductwork maze again, it was still a rough and bruising experience.

Pegasus was being held in the very deepest part of the facility, down on the lowest level where they were holding the dead Nirad. As the sandals drew Paelen through the ventilation system, he smelled the tunnel leading to the laboratory where they were cutting up the Nirad. He was relieved that the sandals kept moving.

Finally they started to slow down and made a turn down a duct that ended in a vent. Long before he reached the vent, Paelen smelled the sweet scent of the stallion.

"Stop," he ordered.

He put the sandals aside and crawled the rest of the distance toward the vent. He peered through the louvers and sucked in his breath when he got his first glimpse of the stallion.

Pegasus was unrecognizable. The only remotely familiar thing about him was his wings. Those were still white, while the rest of him was a terrible combination of dull brown and black. But worse still than his color was the state of the stallion himself.

Pegasus was lying unmoving in a bed of straw. His chest and side were covered in thick bandages, and his wings were open and held at careless angles. For a moment, Paelen feared the great stallion was dead. But as he watched, he saw Pegasus's sides moving with shallow, strained breaths.

Forcing open the vent, Paelen lowered himself into the room.

"Pegasus?" he called softly.

Nothing.

Paelen called again as he carefully approached the stallion's head. "Please, it is I, Paelen. I have come to help you."

When he knelt down beside Pegasus, the stallion woke. As with Diana, Paelen had never seen such pain and despair within a pair of eyes. Tears sprang to Paelen's own eyes as he lightly stroked the stallion's face.

"I have brought this upon you," he said miserably. "Please, please forgive me. Had I known what would happen, I would gladly have faced my own destruction in Olympus rather than see you like this."

Pegasus made a long, deep, questioning sigh.

"Emily is here," Paelen answered as he sniffed. "She is alive and recovering from her wounds. But she is very worried about you. I will see her again later. But what must I tell her of you?"

Pegasus made several weak sounds.

"I will not tell her you are dead!" Paelen cried in horror. "I will not tell her because you are not dead. You cannot die. You are Pegasus. You must live."

Pegasus moaned again and tried to lift his head. He looked Paelen straight in the eye.

"Yes, I have seen Diana," Paelen responded. "She is here also and is unharmed. But she, too, is very worried about you."

Laying his head down, Pegasus made another soft sound.

"Yes, of course we will leave here," Paelen assured him. "But *all* of us will go. Together. You are not remaining here, Pegasus. I will not allow it. I know you are wounded and in terrible pain. But you will recover. You just need rest and good food."

Paelen looked around the room. Emily was right. The people here thought Pegasus was a horse. The food they had brought was not what the stallion needed. With his many wounds, without ambrosia, Pegasus was dying.

"Listen to me, Pegasus. I caused this and now I am going to mend it. Emily needs you. We all do. You will not die. I will go and get you food that will help you heal. It worked for me; it will work for you. But you must fight to live."

Paelen climbed to his feet and looked down at the fallen stallion. "Do not give up, Pegasus. Olympus needs you." As he started to walk away, he called back, "Emily cares a lot about you too. Think of her."

Pegasus raised his head and looked at Paelen pleadingly.

"You must take care of yourself," Paelen said. "If you die, you will fail her and leave her to the mercy of these cruel people. Agent J has already hurt her once. He will do so again. So please hold on, she needs you. I will return shortly."

Without further pause, Paelen folded himself into the vent. He reached for the sandals. "I surely hope you know where to go," he muttered. Lifting the sandals, he ordered, "Take me to the kitchens where they prepare our food."

Paelen had no idea how the sandals worked. But they did. Before long, they entered another tunnel. Paelen's mouth started to water at the sweet smell of sugar.

"Thank you, sandals," he said as he approached the grille. His keen "thief" sense listened and felt for any signs of life. There were none. He crawled through a large vent and into a spacious kitchen. Everything seemed to be made of metal, each surface shining brightly.

The room itself was huge. It would have taken ages for him to find what he needed. But with his own deep hunger gnawing at his stomach and his nose directing him forward, it took little time for Paelen to seek out all the sweet treasures of the kitchen. He found cupboard after cupboard of sugars, sweet syrups, and jellies, and a huge supply of cooking chocolate. Then he nearly cried with excitement when he found a freezer filled with ice cream. It would take several trips to take it all to the stallion. But with the long night spread out before him, he had time.

Paelen found a large chef's apron. When he laid it out, he was able to fill it with several items, including the first two tubs of ice cream, and tied it up into a package. Quick as he could, he climbed on the counter and shoved everything into the air vent, checking over his shoulder to ensure that he had hidden his handiwork. Satisfied that no one would notice his having been here, Paelen climbed into the vent after all the food.

"Take me back to Pegasus," he commanded the sandals, adding quickly, "But take it slower—I am carrying precious items."

The sandals obeyed. A short while later Paelen was back with Pegasus, opening the apron and pulling out the food. He pulled the lid off the first tub of ice cream.

"Here, Pegasus, eat."

Though weak and exhausted, Pegasus started to lick the ice cream from the tub. Before long, Paelen was opening a second. That too was quickly devoured.

When Pegasus had eaten all the ice cream, Paelen poured a bag of sugar mixed with honey and a bit of water into one of the tubs and offered it to the stallion. Once again, Pegasus drank with relish.

While he held the tub for the stallion, Paelen bit into a bar of cooking chocolate. It was different from what he'd taken from the vending machine, but just as good. But before he was able to finish it, Pegasus reached up to take that as well.

"Of course," Paelen said as he offered his treat to the stallion. "You need this more than I."

For half the night, Paelen worked to get as much as he could from the kitchen to Pegasus. The stallion was completely starved, and Paelen worried that it still wouldn't be enough. But finally, with less than a quarter of the supplies left, Pegasus let out a sigh and settled down in the straw.

As Paelen sat with the stallion, he apologized, once again, for being the cause of all their problems. Just before Pegasus drifted off into a deep, healing sleep, he fixed Paelen with a look that let him know that they would discuss this when he recovered.

When Pegasus finally slept, Paelen rose to his feet.

He looked down on the critically wounded stallion and felt deep regret for trying to enslave him. He realized he had been just as guilty as the humans in the facility. He'd seen Pegasus as just a winged horse and a fast way to his own riches. He'd never really seen him for the magnificent Olympian he truly was.

"Sleep well, Pegasus," Paelen said as he quietly walked away. "Sleep and heal."

BACK IN THE VENT, PAELEN HID THE REMAIN-
ing sugary items deep within the system of tunnels.
Pegasus would need more later, and soon, unless the
people here understood about their dietary require-
ments, Diana would be needing these supplies too.

As it was still night and Paelen knew he had time,
he picked up the sandals again. "Take me to Emily's
father."

When the sandals drew him forward, Paelen
quickly discovered that this was to be his worst journey yet.

It started out much the same as usual. But soon
they approached the long, vertical tunnel that connected all the levels of the huge facility. Since they

were at the bottom, Paelen looked up and could see countless levels rising above them.

The sandals entered the main tunnel and started to climb. Higher and higher. Paelen recognized the offshoot that would lead to his and Emily's rooms. The sandals quickly shot past it and kept climbing. Faster and faster they moved as they flew higher up the facility.

Paelen became aware of the curious sounds of heavy machinery. Then he heard a particularly distinctive whooping sound. Whatever it was, the sandals were drawing him straight toward it.

Paelen also noticed that the closer they came to the sound, the faster the sandals moved. Within the long, dark ventilation tunnel, Paelen couldn't clearly see where he was heading. But as he looked up, his eyes caught sight of starlight shining brightly above him.

The only trouble was, the starlight seemed to flicker as though something blocked it and then moved away again. Concentrating on it, Paelen's eyes slowly adjusted to the weak light. He sucked in his breath in terror. The sandals were drawing him toward a large, spinning fan.

This was the heart of the ventilation system. This fan drew the fresh air in from the outside world and forced it down into the deep lower levels of the facility. It was about to slice Paelen to bits.

The huge cutting fan blades were getting closer. Paelen tried to order the sandals to stop but didn't have time. They were picking up speed. All he had time to do was look up and await his death.

Closer.

Closer.

He shut his eyes and prepared for the worst. An instant later, he felt the air around him swoosh and then change abruptly. Opening his eyes, he was startled to discover that he was now outside the facility and flying higher into the night air.

"Sandals, stop!" he ordered.

Suspended in the air high above Governors Island, Paelen looked down into the wide chimney they had just flown out of. He could still see the deadly blades of the large fan turning. Somehow the sandals had carried him between them without being hit.

With a deep shiver, Paelen looked away. The lights

of Manhattan were shining brightly across the water. A little farther away, he saw the same green lady holding her torch, standing in the harbor. Lady Liberty, Emily had called her. While beneath him, Paelen received the largest shock of all.

Houses! Very pretty and very nonthreatening, houses.

As Paelen looked again at the wide chimney, he saw that it was part of a large brick house. Out front, it had beautiful, tall, white pillars, much like some of the homes in Olympus. Farther down the well-manicured, tree-lined street, Paelen saw a lovely yellow house, sitting among a group of pretty homes.

Scanning the area, Paelen couldn't take it all in. He simply couldn't understand how these lovely homes could hide such a dark and dangerous secret. There was no way anyone who looked at this pretty little island would suspect that it held such horrors as the CRU.

Now outside the facility, he wondered where Emily's father was. Just a short way away from where he was suspended, Paelen saw an ancient, squat brick building with bars on the windows. It looked just like a prison. Paelen guessed it would be as good a place as any to lock up Emily's father.

"Take me to Emily's father," he ordered, expecting the sandals to move him toward the brick building. Instead they drew him higher into the star-studded sky. They carried him over a large body of water and away from the island. When they finally passed over land again, Paelen ordered the sandals to stop.

Wherever he was being held, Emily's father was not on Governors Island.

"Take me to Joel instead."

They headed back toward Governors Island. Paelen could see boats in the water, and a few lights on in the houses on the island itself. But as he looked, he didn't see anyone moving around beneath him.

"Wait," he called. "Take me down to the ground."

The sandals settled Paelen gently down in the grass. As he ducked down, he listened for the sound of soldiers or anyone else moving around. All he heard were night insects on the island and the sounds rising from the huge city just across the water. He was alone.

Paelen scanned the area. He suddenly realized that

if he wanted, he could simply put on the sandals and tell them to take him anywhere. He could remain in this world, or go back to what was left of Olympus. For the first time in his long life, Paelen was well and truly free.

But even as he considered leaving, he recalled the horrible sight of Pegasus lying on his side. Broken, wounded, and defeated. Then there was proud Diana, chained to a wall, starved and unable to move. Finally Paelen's thoughts were drawn back to the girl, Emily, and the sounds of her agonized cries as Agent J pressed down on her wounded leg.

If he left now, he might be physically free. But he could never escape those nightmarish images. And though he might only ever be a thief, Paelen knew he couldn't live with himself if he abandoned the others to the fate of the CRU.

Standing again, Paelen lifted the sandals in the air. "Take me high enough over the island to look for Nirads."

Obeying his commands, the sandals lifted him into the air. Paelen used all his senses to look for signs of Nirads attacking the small island. After a thorough search, he was content that there were none. Perhaps they couldn't find a way over here. As he looked out over the short stretch of water that separated the island from Manhattan, he wondered if it was enough to keep the Nirads away.

"That's enough," Paelen finally said to the sandals. "Take me to Joel."

PAELEN ARRIVED AT THE VENT OUTSIDE
Joel's room, still shaking from the harrowing journey
back into the facility. Getting out through the fan
had been terrifying. Going back in was even worse.

Joel was being held on the same level as Diana.
Paelen crawled forward and peered through the louvered grille. The boy was asleep.

"Joel," Paelen called.

The boy in the bed stirred and moaned.

"Joel, wake up."

More moans rose from the bed.

Paelen knew full well how brutal Agent J was.
If he was capable of hurting Emily while she was

wounded, Paelen could only imagine what he might have done to Joel.

He forced the vent open and entered Joel's room. Standing by the bed, Paelen touched the sleeping boy's shoulder. "Wake up."

Joel opened his eyes and looked hazily at him.

"Leave me alone," he moaned.

"Please, Joel," Paelen whispered, "Emily has asked me to find you."

"Em-Emily?" Joel repeated.

"Yes, she is hurt, but recovering. I have seen Diana and Pegasus, too. Please, you must wake up."

Joel's face was bruised and swollen, his eyes bloodshot and heavy. As he pushed the covers back and struggled to sit up, Paelen saw more black bruises on the boy's neck, chest, and arms. There were also marks from where the people here had injected Joel with their drugs.

"Who are you?" Joel asked as he tried to focus.

"I am Paelen."

"Paelen!" Joel repeated. He lunged forward and caught Paelen around the neck. "You caused this," he roared as rage cleared his head. Springing from the bed, he slammed Paelen against the far wall.

"None of this would have happened if you hadn't taken the bridle. Pegasus wouldn't have been hit by lightning! Emily wouldn't have been hurt by the Nirads! I should kill you for what you've done!"

Paelen felt Joel's fingers around his neck, but there was no real pressure there. Joel was furious, but he was no murderer. Paelen also knew that Joel had every right to be angry. It was true. He had caused all this. So he did not fight the boy. Instead he let him rant and rage to get it out of his system.

Before long, Joel's energy ebbed and he released Paelen. "Why?" he demanded furiously, "why did you do it?"

Paelen saw Joel swaying on his feet. Agent J had hurt him badly. More than just the bruises showing on his arms and body, it was the way Joel was holding himself. His anger had given him strength, but the damage from their interrogation was catching up with him.

Paelen reached out and caught Joel gently by the arms. "Please, Joel, get back into bed. You are not well."

"I'm well enough to kick the stuffing out of you!"

Joel challenged, looming a full head taller than Paelen.

Paelen smiled. Despite the dire situation, he really liked the spirit of this young human. "Of course you are. But you should save your energy for the fight to come. Right now, Emily needs you."

At the mention of Emily's name, Joel calmed and let Paelen lead him back to the bed. "Where is Emily? How is she? What have they done to her?"

"She is frightened," Paelen explained. "She has cause to be. Agent J hurt her. Though I suspect he has hurt you more."

"I'm fine," Joel said defensively.

"Did they give you the drug that burns fire in your veins?"

Joel nodded, a shadow creeping across his face. "What did they do to Emily?"

"Agent J asked her a lot of questions. When Emily refused to answer, he squeezed her wounded leg. The pain was so intense, she passed out."

"I'm gonna kill him," Joel spat. "I don't care if they lock me away for life. I'm gonna kill him for hurting her."

Paelen chuckled. "I believe you are going to have to fight Diana and Pegasus for that privilege. You should be very proud of your friend. She told them nothing."

"I've tried not to talk," Joel said in a hushed whisper. "I don't think I told them about the war in Olympus, but I can't be sure. I'm so used to fighting, when they hit me, I just laughed at them. But then they used the drugs. . . ."

Joel started to shake. There was a haunted expression in his eyes. Whatever they had done to him, it would have a lasting effect.

"It is going to be all right, Joel," Paelen said softly. "We will get out of here."

"How?" Joel asked. "I don't even know where we are."

"Emily does. She said we are on Governors Island. We are deep underground, but I am free to go wherever I choose. There are serpents' eyes watching everything in the corridors, but not in the tunnels I use or in our rooms."

"Serpents' eyes?" Joel asked.

Paelen nodded. "Agent J says they can see everywhere

in here. That is how they knew when I escaped my room. I was in the corridor, and they saw me."

"You mean cameras," Joel said, finally understanding. He looked around his room. "You're right. There aren't any. I guess they don't want them in the rooms in case someone made a record of the torture they perform on their prisoners."

"Perhaps," Paelen agreed, wondering what horrors the cameras would have witnessed being done to Joel. "But that leaves me free to visit all of you as long as I use the tunnels. And when Pegasus is well enough to move, we shall escape."

"What's wrong with Pegasus?" Joel asked. "Is it his wing again?"

Paelen dropped his eyes in shame. He explained about the stallion being shot. "I have taken him all the food he needs, but it may be too late. He is gravely ill. I fear Pegasus might be dying."

Joel's hands shot out and gripped Paelen's arms. "He can't!" he cried. "If he does, we're all dead. Pegasus is the only one who can find the Daughter of Vesta!"

Paelen frowned. "What does Vesta have to do with Pegasus?"

"Hasn't Emily told you why Pegasus came here?"

When Paelen shook his head, Joel told him what he knew of the Daughter of Vesta and the Flame of Olympus.

Paelen started to pace. "So this is why we were not destroyed when the Nirads extinguished the Flame in the temple," he said. "We must get out of this place. Pegasus must complete his mission and get the Flame back to Olympus!"

"No kidding," Joel said sarcastically. "What do you think we've been trying to do all this time? But now that we're here—"

"We can get out," Paelen insisted. "We just have to ensure that Pegasus lives."

"You're an Olympian, right?" said Joel after a moment.

"I am."

"Are you strong like Diana? Can you break me out of this room so we can get to Emily?"

"I am very strong," Paelen agreed. "And I can break down this door if needed. But now is not the time to make our move. Pegasus needs time to recover, and so do you."

"I'm fine." Joel rubbed his bruised chin thoughtfully. "Okay then, here's the plan. Keep feeding Pegasus sugar, lots of it. The moment he's up again, come back here and break me out. We'll free Emily and then Diana and Steve. There should be enough of us to fight our way out of here. Then we'll go get the Daughter of Vesta, and Pegasus can take her back to Olympus."

Paelen moved back to the vent. He decided not to tell the boy that Emily's father was not at this facility. Instead he nodded. "Very good. I will see Emily later today and tell her how you are. If they come back for you, do your best to avoid their questions. It will not be long, Joel. You will be free soon."

EMILY WAS FEELING BETTER. THE ANTIBIOTICS they were using were driving away the infection from the Nirad wounds, while the painkillers took the edge off the throbbing pain from her leg. Lying in her bed, she watched the nurse changing the dressing on her wound.

The nurse kept blocking her view of the actual wound.

"How bad is it?" Emily asked.

"Bad enough," the nurse answered. "I'm afraid there was a lot of damage. The surgeons did what they could, but the infection went very deep."

Emily was almost afraid to ask, but had no choice. "Will I be able to walk again?"

The nurse stopped what she was doing and turned to Emily. "I really don't know. Possibly, but you'll need help; perhaps a cane or even a brace. But don't think about that right now. Your job is to concentrate on getting better."

"Then what?"

The nurse stared at Emily a moment longer but then returned to the task of changing the dressing on her leg. Her silence told Emily more than she really wanted to know. The answer was simple. She had no future. When the CRU had finished with her, she would simply disappear.

"Have you seen Pegasus?" Emily finally asked.

"Your winged horse?"

Emily was fed up with correcting the people here. If they wanted to call Pegasus a horse, let them. She knew the truth, and that was enough.

"I'm not allowed to see him," the nurse replied. "They've had vets in, though. But from what I've heard, it's not looking too good. I'm afraid the soldiers put a lot of bullets in him. It's doubtful he'll survive."

"Pegs is going to die?" Emily cried. She tried to climb from her bed. "I've got to see him."

"Emily, stop," the nurse warned, struggling to hold her down. "You are not strong enough. You could do more damage to your leg."

Emily began to panic. "You don't understand. I have to see him. He saved me from the Nirads. I can't lose him. Not now!"

As Emily fought with the nurse, she didn't hear the code beeping at the door. Nor did she hear the two men entering her room. All she knew was she needed to get to Pegasus.

Suddenly more arms were holding her down and keeping her from leaving the bed.

"Let me go!" Emily howled. "I have to go to Pegasus!"

"Emily, stop!" Agent J ordered.

"Leave me alone!" Emily shrieked. "I have to go to him!"

"All right!" Agent J shouted as he and the other man overpowered her and pinned her down. "All right, if you want to see him so badly, fine. Just stop struggling."

Emily was panting heavily. She looked up at the agents, her eyes blurred with tears. "Please, take me to him."

"We will. But with one condition," said Agent J. "After you've seen him, you will answer all our questions. No fighting us, no lying. If you want to see Pegasus, you promise me that you will tell us everything we want to know."

As Emily stared into his cold eyes, she recalled her conversation with Paelen and how he told her not to hold back but to tell as many lies as she could think of. She nodded. "If you take me to him right now, I promise I'll answer all your questions. But only after I've seen him."

Agent J turned to the second man. "Arrange for a wheelchair, Agent O. If Emily wants to see Pegasus, she will."

A short while later Emily was in a wheelchair, being pushed through the halls of the facility. She almost forgot the pain in her leg as fears for Pegasus overwhelmed her senses.

When they reached the elevator, she noted that Agent O had pressed the very last button. They were keeping Pegasus on the bottom floor.

Once there, they traveled down to a room at the

end of a long corridor. As Agent J stepped up to the security lock and prepared to press the code, he looked back at Emily. "I have your word? You'll see the stallion and then answer my questions?"

Saying nothing, Emily nodded.

When Agent J entered the code, he made no attempt to block the keypad. Emily could see each number he pressed and the order in which he pressed them. As the green light flashed and door clicked, she burned the code sequence into her memory.

Agent J opened the door, and Agent O pushed her wheelchair forward. Emily peered into the room, and her heart twisted in agony.

Pegasus was lying in hay in the center of the floor. He was covered in bandages and barely breathing.

"Pegs!" Emily sprang from her chair. But her wounded leg wouldn't support her, and she fell to the floor.

Agent J tried to pull her back. "Emily, stop. There's nothing you can do for him now."

Tears filled her eyes as rage filled her heart. "Don't touch me!" she shrieked viciously as she swatted his hand away. She ignored the searing pain from her leg and dragged herself over to Pegasus.

"Pegs," she said softly as her trembling hand reached out to touch the stallion's dark head. "Pegs, it's me. Please, don't die. I need you."

Emily's tears fell unchecked as she kissed his muzzle. "Please, Pegs, you can't die. You just can't."

As she lay her head down on his thick neck and wept for the beautiful stallion, Emily heard a subtle change in the stallion's breathing. She didn't know if the others could hear or see it, but she could. Pegasus took a deep, steadying breath. He knew she was there and was responding to her.

"Emily," Agent J said as he stepped closer. "I've done as I promised. I've let you see him. Now it's your turn. Come away from him and we can talk."

In that instant, Emily somehow knew that she mustn't leave him. Pegasus desperately needed her there. She could feel it. But more than that, she needed him, too.

Without looking at the agent, she said, "If you want answers to your questions, you'll get them. But I'll only answer them here. I'm not leaving Pegasus."

"That wasn't part of the deal," Agent J said threateningly.

"No," Emily answered as she glared up at him coldly. "It wasn't. But now it is. What harm can there be in letting me stay here while I answer your questions? You get what you want, and I get to stay with him."

"It's not good for you to stay here," Agent J said. "What if he dies while you're with him?"

"Then someone who loves him will be the last person with him and not you!" Emily said fiercely. "But if you try to take me back to my room, I swear I'll never speak another word, no matter what you do to me."

Anger flashed in the agent's eyes. "Fine," he said at last. "You want to stay with the dying horse while we talk, you can stay." He loomed over her. "I hope you appreciate how I am bending the rules for you, young lady. I expect the same consideration from you. You will answer *all* my questions without hesitation and with the truth. Do you understand me?"

Emily lay pressed against the stallion's neck and continued to stroke his face. "I understand perfectly."

A blanket and two chairs were brought into the

room. When the blanket was brought over to her, Emily felt Pegasus tense. He wasn't so far gone that he wasn't aware of what was happening around him. He didn't like the man coming near.

As the CRU agents settled in their chairs, Emily made herself comfortable in the straw. She was as close to Pegasus as she could get, curling neatly in the circle of his neck and head while she stroked his face and scratched his ears. Just being close to him was enough to make her feel better.

"All right, Emily," Agent J said as he switched on his recording device. "Let's take it from the very beginning. How is it you came to be with Pegasus?"

Emily took a deep breath. She knew she could never tell them why Pegasus and Diana were in New York; about the Flame or the war in Olympus. But she wanted to spend as much time as she could with the stallion. Taking Paelen's advice, Emily lied.

She began with the truth, talking about the huge storm in the city and how Pegasus was struck by lightning and crashed on her roof. But from there, the truth faded into an outrageous story that equaled the best of the Greek or Roman myths.

Agent J sat forward in his chair. "And why were they coming here?"

"Well," she started. "Diana told me that back in Olympus, a thief had stolen Pegasus's golden bridle. He escaped by using the messenger's sandals."

"So it isn't Mercury we have locked away here?"

Emily shook her head. "He's just a thief. Diana said she and Pegasus had been chasing him across the cosmos, going from world to world and through city after city. They finally ended up here in New York. She said they were hit by lightning and got separated. Pegasus crashed on my roof, and Diana fell in Central Park."

"This thief," Agent J asked. "Do you know his name?"

"I can't remember," Emily said, scratching her head. "But I think Diana said it began with the letter P."

"Paelen?" Agent O asked. "Was his name Paelen?"

"Yes!" Emily agreed. "That's it. Diana said that Paelen had also stolen a sack of gold coins from her father, Jupiter. And that she and Pegasus had come here to get it back before her father found out and lost his temper. She said when Jupiter got mad, entire worlds were destroyed."

"If he already had the coins, why did Paelen go after Pegasus's bridle?" Agent J mused.

Emily shrugged. "I guess he's greedy. Diana said Jupiter wouldn't care too much about the coins, but he would be furious if he found out about the bridle. So they were hoping to get it back before he noticed."

"Gold is gold," Agent J said lightly. "He had enough, but wanted more."

"Wait," Agent O said. "There's more to this. The myths say that whoever possesses the bridle of Pegasus can control the stallion." He concentrated on Emily. "Paelen wanted Pegasus, didn't he?"

This was the first Emily had heard of the myth. She shrugged. "I don't know. Diana never said. She just told me they needed to get everything back before her father found out. But now that the bridle and coins are lost, there's no telling what he'll do."

"The bridle isn't lost," Agent O said. "We have it here."

"You do?" Emily said. "Really? Do you have the coins, too?"

Agent O shook his head. "No coins, but we had the sandals."

"Had?" Emily said, as she continued to stroke Pegasus.

Agent J nodded. "But it seems someone has taken them."

Emily shrugged. "Maybe they flew away. Diana told me the sandals have a mind of their own. Maybe they flew back to Olympus."

"Maybe," Agent J said, not sounding convinced. "Or we could have a thief in our midst. So, tell me, where is Olympus?"

Emily shook her head and answered with the truth. "I swear I don't know." She looked down on Pegasus's closed eyes. "Diana told me that Pegasus was her only way home. If he dies, she's going to be trapped here."

"No, that's not right either," Agent O said. "The ancient myths said the gods were always coming to Earth. There was never anything written about Diana riding Pegasus. Whenever she came here, she came of her own power. What's changed?"

"I don't know." Emily shrugged. "Diana doesn't

talk to me much. I don't think she likes me. She's really mad at what Joel and I did to Pegasus when we dyed him these colors to keep him hidden from you. She nearly killed us when she saw him."

"No wonder she's mad," Agent O said. "Look at the mess you've made of her cousin."

"Pegs is her cousin?" Emily repeated in genuine surprise.

"Diana is the daughter of Jupiter, right?" said Agent O. When Emily nodded, he continued. "Well, the myths say that Pegasus came from a union between Medusa and Neptune. As everyone knows, Jupiter and Neptune are brothers. So that would make Pegasus and Diana cousins."

Emily looked at Pegasus. "Medusa and Neptune are his parents?" she repeated. "How is that possible?"

"You tell us," Agent J said. "You're the one who's claiming they all come from Olympus. You're the one who's spent time with them. Surely they must have told you this."

"Pegasus can't talk," Emily said. "All I know is what Diana told me. And like I said, that hasn't been a lot. She really hates me because of what we did to Pegs."

"From what we've seen, Diana hates everyone," Agent J finished bitterly. "But what did she tell you about the Nirads? Why are they here? And moreover, why were they trying to kill you and Pegasus?"

Emily had been dreading this question. What could she tell them that would sound reasonable? Joel was the one who knew the Roman myths, not her. But she knew that if she didn't say something, they would take her away from Pegasus, and she couldn't let that happen.

"I was hurt by accident," she finally said. "The Nirads weren't after me. They seemed to be after Pegasus. I was just in the wrong place at the wrong time, and this one Nirad got hold of my leg."

"But what are they?" Agent J pressed. "Why are they here?"

"I don't know," Emily answered honestly. "Even Diana doesn't know. All she told me was that for some reason, they were after Pegasus. Probably because he can kill them when no one else can. She said the last time the Olympians had enemies was long ago. There had been a big war with this other race. But I can't remember their names. Maybe they sent the Nirads here to get Pegasus."

"The Olympians were at war with the Titans," Agent O offered.

"Yes, that was the name Diana said," Emily quickly agreed. She looked at Agent J. "I don't know why you are asking me all these questions when he"—she pointed at Agent O—"seems to know all the answers."

"I studied the myths," Agent O responded. "That's very different from knowing the answers to these questions. If Pegasus and the others really are from Olympus, then the old tales may be true. But if that's the case, where have they been all this time?"

"Finally a question I can answer," Emily said as she offered up another plausible lie. "I asked Diana the very same thing. She said that we didn't need the Olympians any more. So they stayed in Olympus and stopped coming to our world. She said her father says it's too dangerous with all our new weapons and technology. He's actually forbidden anyone from coming here, which is why Diana and Pegasus were chasing the thief. They didn't want him captured and the secret of their existence getting out."

"Then it seems they haven't done a very good job of it, have they?" Agent J said sarcastically. "But that still doesn't answer the question of the Nirads. If Diana needs the stallion to fly, what means of transportation are the Nirads using?"

Emily paused. That was a good question. How were the Nirads getting to New York?

"I honestly don't know," she said truthfully. "Diana never told me. She said she used Pegasus and the thief used the messenger's sandals to get here. But she never did say how the Nirads were getting to New York. My dad told me that at the beginning, there were reports of four-armed demons coming out of the sewers. But that still doesn't explain how they got here or if there are more on the way. I'm really sorry, but I just don't know."

Agent O looked at his companion. "I think she's telling the truth," he said. "She really doesn't know. We have to get these answers from Diana herself."

"That woman is impossible," Agent J said, looking furious. "We stand a better chance of getting blood from a stone! Nothing works on her. Paelen's just as bad. Drugs? Torture? Threats? Nothing loosens their tongues. Emily here is our only hope of getting at the truth."

He concentrated on Emily again. "Okay, let's try this again from the top. Tell us once more what happened on the night of the blackout."

Emily finally settled back in her bed, wrung out and exhausted. She had no idea how long the agents had questioned her, but it had to have been for most of the day. They kept repeating the same things over and over again, trying to get her to make a mistake and tell them something more.

With Pegasus lying beside her and Paelen's warning ringing in her ears, Emily had been careful not to deviate from her story. She was just grateful they'd stopped when they had. She was growing increasingly fatigued and had to concentrate harder to keep all the lies straight in her head.

When the interrogation finished, Emily begged to be allowed to stay with Pegasus. But Agent J refused. She could see how much pleasure it gave him to say no.

As they tried to pull her away, Emily felt Pegasus stirring. Lying against his neck throughout the long day, she'd grown aware of his pulse getting steadily stronger beneath her. He was quickly coming back to himself. But as he did, she became frightened that he might try to move against the men. If he did anything, she felt certain Agent J would have him killed so they could dissect him to see how his wings worked.

To warn the stallion, Emily threw herself across his neck and started to wail hysterically that she didn't want to go. When two orderlies came forward to drag her away, she was able to whisper quickly in the stallion's ear, "Please don't move, Pegs. I'll be back."

Continuing with her hysterics, Emily felt him calming. He wouldn't move. She was finally pulled away from him, settled in her wheelchair, and taken back to her room.

PAELEN SPENT AS MUCH OF THE DAY AS HE could in the ductwork outside the room where they held Pegasus. He had marveled at the stories Emily told the men. The lies equaled anything he could have made up. For a human, she would have made a great thief.

When everyone had left, Paelen quietly entered the room and delivered more sweet food to the stallion. He was amazed at how much better Pegasus was. He knew it had something to do with Emily. Pegasus tried to hide it, but Paelen clearly saw the connection between the stallion and the girl.

After making sure Pegasus had everything he needed, Paelen headed back toward Emily's room.

He arrived moments before everyone else and waited silently in the air vent. Soon he heard the lock code chiming for her door. It was the same as his.

Crouching back farther in the duct, he saw the door open.

"It's been a long day," Agent J said. "I want you to rest. Then tomorrow we can take up where we left off."

As the nurse and orderly lifted her into bed, Emily looked up at Agent J. "I don't understand. I told you everything you asked me. I don't know anything more."

"Now, that's not entirely true, is it, Emily?" Agent J said suspiciously. "I'm sure there are a few bits and pieces you've been holding back."

"No, there aren't," Emily insisted. "You said I could see Pegasus if I told you the truth. I did. There's nothing more to tell."

"Emily, you spent several days with the stallion," Agent O pointed out. "And more than enough time with Diana to know what's going on and why they are really here."

As Emily started to protest, Paelen saw Agent J hold up a warning finger. "Don't bother. I know you are still holding back on us. Rest tonight, because tomorrow we're going to discuss everything again."

Without another word, they left the room. While the orderly set up her dinner tray and rolled it closer to the bed, the nurse helped Emily get her leg settled in the support strapping.

"If I were you, I'd tell them what they want to know," the nurse warned. "Those agents are not nice men."

"I've already told them everything," Emily cried. "What more do they want?"

"They want the truth. And one way or another, they are going to get it. But how they get it is up to you."

"What do you mean?"

"You can give them what they want. Or believe me, they know ways you've never imagined to get everything out of you."

Emily threw up her arms in the air. "How can I tell them what I don't know?"

"I don't know, dear. But by morning, you'd better have more to say, or tomorrow could very well be the worst day of your life."

Once Emily was in bed, the nurse and orderly left the room. Emily angrily shoved the tray table away.

"I would eat if I were you," Paelen called softly down from the vent. "You do not know when you might be fed again."

Emily's eyes shot up to the vent. "Paelen!"

The thief's fingers gently pushed the grille away from the wall. After seeing him do it yesterday, watching him stretch out his body wasn't quite as horrifying, though the sounds of his cracking bones still set her nerves on edge.

"I'm so glad you're here," Emily said. "Did you hear what the nurse said to me? They're going to torture me tomorrow."

Paelen nodded. "I also heard what you told them today when you were with Pegasus."

"You were there?" Emily said incredulously. "How? I didn't hear you in the vent. Don't they miss you when you leave your room?"

"You forget I am a thief," said Paelen. "Keeping silent is one of my special skills. They gave up checking on me once they discovered that they cannot make me speak. They leave me alone for most of the day and all night. They seem to have concentrated all their efforts on you. Though I must admit Joel has not had it easy either."

"You've seen Joel?" Emily asked anxiously. "How is he? How's my father?"

"Joel is relatively unharmed," Paelen said. "But I am sorry to say they have used violent force on him to get him to speak. Much to his credit, so far, like you, he has told them very little. But I do not know how much longer he can hold out against their torture. He is angry, but also very determined. He attacked me the first time he heard my name."

"Sorry, that was my fault," Emily said sheepishly. "I told him what you'd done to Pegasus with his bridle. But Joel is really nice once you get to know him. He's angry on the outside, but really gentle on the inside."

"He has calmed somewhat." Paelen pushed the dinner tray back to Emily. "Now, please eat. You will need your strength for what you are facing." Paelen saw the fear rising in her eyes. "Whatever happens, Emily, I will be there with you. Please don't give up."

"I won't," Emily said as she picked at her food. She reached for the bowl of chocolate pudding and handed it to him. "Here, you need this more than me."

Paelen gratefully accepted the pudding. He had been back to the kitchens several times, but most of the sugary foods he'd stolen had gone to Pegasus and Diana to build up their strength. He had kept very little for himself.

"How do you think Pegasus is doing?" Emily asked as she ate without interest.

"Recovering," Paelen said. "He is eating well, and his strength is returning."

"He looked dead when I first saw him today," Emily said. Her voice shook. "It really scared me. But then his breathing became steadier and he moved a bit."

"Pegasus cares about you," Paelen told her. "I have no doubt that seeing you today did more to help him than all the ice cream I have been taking to him."

Emily smiled, and it brightened her whole face.

"He sure does love his ice cream," she said. Then her expression fell. "We've got to get him out of here. You and Diana, too. You don't belong in this world.

If we don't go soon, I'm afraid they'll kill Pegasus just to see how he works."

"I have a similar fear," Paelen admitted. "I have pushed my luck to the limit. They are furious at me for not cooperating. If I am not careful, I am sure they will try to kill me, too."

"Okay," Emily said. "So when do we go?"

Paelen studied her in fascination. He could see the ideas spinning around in her head. "Soon," he answered.

"You must get Pegasus's bridle to Diana so she can make weapons with it to take back to Olympus," Emily said. "That's the only thing that can kill the Nirads. Then we've got to get my dad and Joel out of their rooms."

Paelen sucked in his breath and held it. Finally he let it out slowly. "Emily, there is something I must tell you. Your father is not here."

A frown creased the smooth skin between her brows. "What do you mean he's not here?" she asked. "He has to be here."

Paelen shook his head. "Mercury's sandals will take me anywhere I tell them to," he told her. "Last night I instructed them to take me to your father. They carried me out of this place and high up into the night sky. We crossed over the water and were moving away from this small island."

"Where is he? Where did the sandals take you?"

"I do not know," Paelen admitted. "I told the sandals to stop. I had them bring me back so I could help all of you."

"Wait," Emily said, puzzled. "So you were out of here? You were free?"

Paelen nodded.

"Why didn't you go? Diana said you were a thief who thought only of yourself. I don't understand."

"I could have left," Paelen said. "I must admit, I did consider it for a moment. But then I thought of Pegasus and Diana. What would happen to them? And then I thought of you. I realized I could not leave you to the mercy of these people."

"So you came back for us?"

"Yes," Paelen admitted. "I am the only one who can reach everyone. It is I who can help free all of us from this wretched place."

Paelen saw the deepening confusion in her face.

Could she really think so ill of him that she couldn't imagine he could change?

"I am so sorry I could not find your father."

Tears were rimming Emily's eyes. "Do you think he's dead?"

"I do not think so. The sandals were taking me to him," Paelen pointed out. "I doubt that they would have done so if he had died. For reasons I do not know, the CRU is holding your father elsewhere."

"But where?" Emily said. "And why? What are they doing to him?"

"I am sorry, I do not know," Paelen said softly. "But the rest of us can still get away. Then perhaps we can find your father and free him."

Emily sniffed back her tears and wiped her nose. "We still need that bridle first."

"Then I shall go get it," Paelen promised. "I will bring it back here, and then we can plan our escape."

30

WHEN PAELEN WAS GONE, EMILY LAY BACK and tried not to let fear for her father overwhelm her. But it was impossible. She had yet to meet one nice or decent CRU agent. They were all just as cruel and evil as her father had told her.

Were they torturing him right now? What were they doing? Paelen had said that they had already tortured Joel to get him to speak. What had they done to her father?

As she settled, she tried to calm herself. It wasn't completely hopeless. Paelen was free to wander the facility. He was clever and agile. But more than that, he cared. With his help, they would get back down to Pegasus. Then they could free Diana and Joel and start to look for her father.

Emily replayed the events of the day in her mind. Not the questions and not the frightening faces of the agents; she thought about Pegasus. At first he had seemed so vulnerable. But as the day progressed, she'd definitely felt him growing stronger. She knew he was pretending to be weaker than he was. Pegasus understood that if he made a move, he would put all of them in danger. So he did as she asked and played along.

But would Pegasus be strong enough to rise and escape with them? If he couldn't get up, would the four of them be strong enough to lift and carry him?

Emily was just starting to feel tired when loud, shrieking sirens burst through the silence of the facility. She sat up and listened to the sudden pounding of heavy footsteps and shouting in the hall outside her door. It seemed like countless people were running up and down the halls in a panic.

Paelen! she thought as fear gripped her heart. *He's been caught!* The thought tore through her brain like a bullet. All their plans for escape vanished in an instant. Paelen had been their only hope to get away. Now that was gone.

But just as despair threatened to crush her completely, Emily heard Paelen's voice urgently calling her name above the din of the angry alarms.

"Emily!" he cried through the vent.

Emily looked up and saw him shove the vent open. He cried out in pain as he stretched out his body faster than she'd ever seen before and poured himself through the vent. She saw the light glinting off the golden bridle he clutched in his hand.

"Paelen, they know you've escaped!" Emily cried. "You must get out of here! Get the bridle to Diana and then go to Pegs. You can't get caught now."

"It is not I who has caused this mayhem. It is the Nirads. They are here! They have come for you and Pegasus!"

"Nirads!" Emily cried. "I thought they couldn't cross water."

"It now appears they found a way," Paelen said. "I must get you out of here." He was bending down to put on a beautiful pair of sandals. They had tiny wings and were covered in jewels. Emily gasped. Mercury's sandals!

"Paelen, look at my leg," she said. "I can't walk. Leave me here. You've got to free Diana and Pegs. You're their only hope. Please save them."

"I will," Paelen promised. "But I just saw Pegasus. He is up and moving around. He said he would kill me if I did not bring you to him. I have betrayed him once. I will not do so again."

Paelen threw back her covers and went to undo the support on her leg. "I am sorry, but this may hurt."

"I don't care about that," Emily said. "Just get me free." She winced while her leg was undone from the support straps. "Have you seen the Nirads? How many are there?"

"I have not seen them," Paelen admitted. "But I can smell them. There are more than a few. The men of the facility are gathering to fight them. But they will fail. We do not have a lot of time before they reach us."

Paelen handed the golden bridle to Emily. "Here, keep hold of this. If a Nirad comes near us, hit him with it," he said. "But do not throw it at him. We will need it." He turned and offered her his back. "Climb on. These sandals can carry both of us faster than I can run."

Emily held the bridle carefully and climbed onto Paelen's back. "Am I too heavy for you?" she asked.

He turned to give her a crooked grin. "Hardly! Now hold on."

Paelen carried Emily over to the door and pressed the code to open the lock. As they entered the hall, the sounds of the alarms reached a terrifying pitch. Emily was shocked to see a mass of armed soldiers charging through the long corridor.

"You two, get back into your room," ordered one of the men as he charged past.

Paelen ignored the order. "Are you ready?" he shouted above the sirens.

"Go!" Emily shouted.

She clutched Pegasus's bridle and wrapped her arms tightly around Paelen.

"Get me to Diana as quickly as possible!" Paelen ordered. Suddenly they were jerked up into the air.

When Paelen said the sandals could move faster than he could run, Emily had had no idea just how fast that could be. She held on for dear life as the sandals darted them forward through the crowds of soldiers in the corridor. When they approached the stairwell, Paelen barely had time to hold out an arm to push the door open before the sandals drove them through.

They flew down the stairs at a terrifying pace, knocking soldiers out of the way as they went. When they reached Diana's level, the terrifying grunts and roars of Nirads could be heard from above.

"They're in the stairwell!" Emily called into Paelen's ear.

Paelen cursed. "Hold on tighter. I am going to order the sandals to move faster."

"Faster?" Emily shrieked.

In the time it would have taken for Emily to scream in terror, the sandals tore through the stairwell doors on Diana's level and flew down the corridor, coming to an abrupt stop outside a locked door.

As the area emptied of soldiers heading toward the stairwell, Paelen lowered Emily to the floor. "Stay well back. I am going to break it down."

Standing on her good leg, Emily watched Paelen

approach the door. "Diana, it is I, Paelen!" he shouted through the door over the alarms. "Get out of your chains if you can. The Nirads are here. We must go!"

He stood away from the door and looked down at the sandals. "Lift me up," he cried, "and break down the door!"

Obeying the order, the sandals lifted Paelen in the air. Then, as their tiny wings flapped at a speed too fast to see, Paelen let out a short cry. Emily wasn't sure whether it was a battle cry, or the sheer terror of flying feetfirst into a heavily secured door. Whatever it was, it rose well above the screaming alarms as he was carried forward and used as a battering ram to smash down the door like it was made of Popsicle sticks.

The door exploded under the impact of Paelen's body. Emily hopped over to the threshold and peered in. Paelen was lying in an unconscious heap in the corner.

"Emily!" Diana cried, tearing away the last of the chains restraining her. "I am so pleased to see you!" She knelt and checked Paelen for serious wounds. "Foolish little thief," she said gently. "There must have been a better way for you to open the door without knocking yourself silly."

"There wasn't time," Emily said. "The Nirads are in the stairwell. Soldiers are fighting them, but it won't take them long to get to Pegasus."

"Then we must get there first," Diana said.

She pulled Paelen into a sitting position and started to lightly slap him across the face. "Come, Paelen, wake up. Our journey is just beginning."

Paelen let out a soft moan and slowly opened his eyes. When he saw who was supporting him, his eyes opened wider. "Diana!" he cried in alarm.

"Do not fear me, little thief," Diana said. "You have earned my respect. Are you well enough to rise?"

Paelen nodded and shakily climbed to his feet. "Nirads!" he cried. "They are here."

Diana nodded. "Emily has told me. We must get to Pegasus."

"And Joel," Emily said. "We can't forget about Joel."

"Of course not," Diana agreed. "We will collect Joel first and then get to Pegasus." Diana noticed Emily carrying the golden bridle. "You have the bridle!"

Emily offered it to Diana, but she shook her head. "No, child, you keep hold of it. You may need it if the Nirads reach us."

Finally recovered, Paelen stepped to the doorway. "Joel is being held on this level as well. He is not far from here."

Diana helped Emily climb back onto Paelen's back. "How is your leg?" she asked.

"Not great," Emily admitted. "But I won't let it slow us down."

In a move that surprised Emily, Diana leaned forward and kissed her lightly on the cheek. "That is my brave girl. Come now, we must go."

Breaking down Joel's door was not quite as dramatic. With both Olympians using their superior strength, the lock couldn't hold, and before long it shattered and the door swung open.

Emily was grateful to see that Joel hadn't been chained. He was standing in the center of the room, waiting for them.

"You took your time getting back here," he complained to Paelen. Then his eyes settled on Emily, and he embraced her tightly. "I've been so worried about you!"

"Me too!" Emily agreed, hugging him back. "Joel, the Nirads are here. We've got to get to Pegs!"

Joel looked at the small group. "Where's your dad?"

Emily fought down the emotions that threatened to bring tears to her eyes. "He's not here. They've taken him somewhere else. But I don't know where."

Joel hugged her again. "Don't worry, Em, we'll find him."

"We will not be finding anyone if the Nirads get us," Paelen warned. "We must get to Pegasus and get out of here!"

Emily was once again lifted onto Paelen's back, and they made their way to the stairwell.

"They are holding Pegasus on the lowest level," Paelen said. "Though I do not like the thought of going into the stairway again. The Nirads are coming down from above."

"We have no choice." Diana pushed through the doors and led the way forward. Several levels above them, everyone heard the ferocious sounds of Nirads mixed with the sound of gunfire and screaming men.

"They are getting closer," Diana warned. "We must move swiftly."

They turned a corner—and came face-to-face with Agents J and O.

"Don't move!" Agent J ordered, drawing his weapon.

"Do not be a fool," said Diana dismissively. "The Nirads are here. They will kill you and everyone else in this place. They want Pegasus. If we move him, they will follow us. Your men need not die."

"You aren't taking that horse anywhere!" Agent J said.

"Horse?" Diana roared in a fury. "You called him a horse?"

In a move as fast as lightning, Diana charged forward. "How dare you!" she cried as she shoved both agents against the wall with the force of a freight train. "He is PEGASUS!"

The men didn't stand a chance against the enraged Olympian. The wind was driven from their chests with such strength that they were instantly knocked out and crumpled to the ground.

Diana stepped over them. "Consider yourselves fortunate," she told their unconscious forms. "Had I the time, I would show you how furious I really am for what you have done to Emily and Pegasus."

Instead she pushed through the stairwell doors with enough pressure to wrench them off their hinges.

Emily looked over to Joel. He shrugged fearfully.

They entered Pegasus's corridor, where the few soldiers they met gave them a wide berth. They had seen the stairwell doors come flying off their hinges and didn't wish to engage the angry Olympian.

"Pegasus is there at the end," Emily said, pointing at the large door she'd been taken to. When they reached it, Paelen put Emily down and prepared to force the door open with Diana.

"Wait," Emily said. "I know the code. You don't have to break it down."

Joel helped support her as she hopped over to the keypad and punched in the code she'd seen Agent J use. Immediately a tiny green light flashed, and the door opened.

Even before she entered, Emily heard the best sound of her life: a whinny from Pegasus. As she crossed the threshold, her heart swelled at the sight of the stallion standing.

"Pegs!" She threw her arms around his thick neck, feeling his strength. "Oh, Pegs," she cried. "I thought you were going to die!"

"He still might unless we get out of here," Joel warned. "Have we forgotten the Nirads? You know, four arms, long teeth, smelly. They're in the stairs. If we don't move now, they'll trap us down here!"

"He is right," Diana said. She stepped up to Emily. "May I have the bridle?"

When Emily handed it over, Diana used her amazing strength to tear the gleaming gold bridle into several large pieces. "I am sorry we do not have time to forge better weapons," she said as she handed everyone a piece. "But for the moment these will have to do. If the Nirads come near you, stab them with it. The gold will kill them. Keep hold of it. It is our only defense."

Diana handed the largest, sharpest piece to Emily.

"No, you should keep it," Emily protested. "You're a better fighter than me."

"But you are more important," Diana said.

"What?" Emily said in confusion. "No, I'm not.

You and Pegasus are. You should keep it. . . . " Emily saw something deep in Diana's eyes.

"Oh," she said softly.

Pegasus whinnied with impatience, his ears forward and his eyes wild.

"They draw near," Diana said. She turned to Paelen. "Help me get Emily on Pegasus. He will take charge of her now. The rest of us will fight if we need to."

Emily tried her best to stay quiet as they lifted her onto the stallion's back, but cried out as her wounded leg was maneuvered into position.

"I am sorry, child," Diana said gently. "When this is over, we shall take care of your leg."

Tears from the pain rose in Emily's eyes, but she said nothing as the fighters fell into position. Diana took the lead. Paelen stood a pace behind her. Then Joel. Emily could see the fear in her friend's eyes, but there was determination in his stance. He was prepared to fight and die with the Olympians.

"All right," Diana said. "When we move forward, we must make for that big metal box that will transport us to the surface."

"It's called an elevator," Emily said. "There's one at the other end of the corridor." She caught hold of the stallion's mane. "We're almost there, Pegs," she said softly.

Pegasus stole a quick glance back to her and nickered softly.

Diana led the group forward. As they ran past the stairwell entrance, Emily noticed that Agents J and O had disappeared. The loud, guttural sounds of the Nirads were getting closer. It wouldn't be long before they reached this level.

"Run!" Diana shouted. "Get to the elevator before they reach us!"

Everyone charged forward. As they reached the freight elevator, Joel pushed the button. He bounced on his feet impatiently. "I hope this thing is still working!"

"If it is not, we are all in trouble," Paelen finished.

Moments before they heard the *ping* of the elevator's arrival, the first of the Nirads reached the bottom level. They charged into the corridor and faced the group. With recognition burning in their black eyes, they charged furiously forward.

"Hurry!" Joel cried. "Please hurry!"

When the freight elevator doors opened, Emily ducked down and Pegasus entered. Joel was right behind them. But when they turned, Diana and Paelen did not follow.

"Diana, Paelen, come on!" Emily cried. "Hurry before they get here!"

Diana shook her head. "No, child, I must stay to keep the Nirads from you." She looked at Pegasus. "You know what is at stake. Do not worry about me. Get the Flame to Olympus!"

Pegasus quivered. He whinnied loudly and pounded the floor with a golden hoof.

"No, I must stay," Diana repeated. "Tell my father what has happened. Free Olympus, Pegasus. It is up to you now."

"Paelen, Diana, please," Emily begged.

Just as the door started to close, Emily saw Paelen give Diana a brutal shove. She lost her balance and fell into the elevator at Pegasus's feet. As the doors closed, Emily heard Paelen cry, "Forgive me!"

31

"PAELEN!" EMILY SHOUTED. QUICKLY SHE turned to Joel. "Open the doors! We can't let the Nirads get him!"

"No!" Diana rose to her feet and blocked Joel's path. "Paelen sacrificed himself for us. We must not dishonor him by failing."

"But they'll kill him!" Emily cried.

"Yes, they will," Diana said grimly. "But while they do, he has given us time to escape."

Emily felt her heart breaking at the thought of those terrible creatures tearing gentle Paelen to pieces. "Paelen . . . ," she whimpered as the elevator slowly rose.

When the doors opened, they were met by a

terrible sight. Dead and wounded soldiers littered the floor. The sounds of moaning and crying from the injured men added to the horrible sense of loss. Emily couldn't work out where they were.

It looked like a house; a beautiful, Southern-style house. They emerged in a large lounge. Antique furniture lined the walls, and rich, deep carpet covered the floor. Surely this couldn't still be in the facility?

"Where are we?" Joel asked in equal confusion as his eyes scanned the room.

"Governors Island," Emily said. "But I didn't know they had houses like this here."

"Come, we must move," Diana warned.

They entered a grand entranceway. To the right, an elegant stairway led upward, while around them, other halls fed into the main area. Everywhere they looked, dead soldiers lay on the fine wooden floors. A huge crystal chandelier hung from the tall ceiling. As Emily looked up at it, she shivered. There was blood splattered on the crystal teardrops.

"How many Nirads are there?" Joel asked.

"Too many," Diana said.

Suddenly Agents J and O staggered into the entrance hall.

"I told you, you aren't going anywhere!" Agent J yelled as he raised his weapon. He glared furiously at Diana. "Bullets may not stop you, but Emily and the boy are human. Unless you surrender right now, I swear I will kill one of them."

Emily felt Pegasus tense beneath her. His ears sprang forward as he threw back his head and let out a loud, ferocious shriek. The stallion rose on his hind legs and lunged forward. One golden hoof struck Agent O, leaving a deep horseshoe impression on his chest. The other hoof hit Agent J in the head with a lethal impact.

As both men fell to the ground, Pegasus turned and moved toward the front doors of the house. He reared up and kicked out at the beautiful inlaid wood of the antique doors. They both shattered under the impact of the angry stallion.

Emily was stunned to see they were now on the front porch of a large pillared house. Across the tree-lined street, by the light of the gaslights, she saw other large yellow houses, their lights were on, looking welcoming.

"My family went to Atlanta years ago," Joel said in hushed surprise. "Some of the homes looked just like this. Are you sure we're on Governors?"

Emily leaned forward on Pegasus and saw the blazing lights of Manhattan rising in the distance. "There's the city. This is Governors."

"Where we are no longer matters," Diana said sharply, helping to lead the stallion down the steep wooden steps. "It is where we are going that counts. It won't take long for the Nirads to reach the surface again. We must be gone before they do."

She looked at the stallion. "Pegasus, are you recovered enough to carry all of us, or should I stay?"

Pegasus gently nudged his cousin and let out a soft nicker.

"Of course," Diana said. She turned to Joel. "Climb on. He can carry all of us."

"What about the Daughter of Vesta?" Joel asked, as Diana helped to hoist him onto the stallion's back behind Emily. "Will there be room for her, too?"

Diana leaped up onto Pegasus, behind him. "She is already with us," she said softly.

"What?" Joel cried.

Emily turned in her seat. She looked at Diana. "It is me, isn't it? I'm the Daughter of Vesta and the Flame of Olympus."

Saying nothing, Diana nodded.

"Emily, no!" Joel cried. "It can't be you."

"It's all right, Joel," Emily said softly. "I've suspected for a while now."

"When did you know for certain, child?" Diana asked.

Emily patted the stallion's neck. "It was a few things, really. Back on the bridge, I started to wonder. You and Pegs should have escaped. If the Daughter of Vesta was really out there somewhere, Pegasus would have left me and gone to her. But he didn't; he fought the soldiers to protect me. Then, when I heard he was dying, I knew I had to get to him. That I could somehow help. And when I touched him, I felt him react. After a few hours with me, Pegasus grew much stronger. I finally knew for sure when you said I was more important. You wouldn't have said that if it wasn't me."

"That is correct," Diana confirmed. "You are more important than all of us. The Flame is burning brightly inside you now. That is why Pegasus heals so quickly when he is with you; first on your roof and then here in this place. As your feelings for him grew, so did your power to heal him. Emily, you saved Pegasus."

"And with luck, maybe I can save Olympus, too," Emily said gravely.

"No," Joel insisted. "I won't let you sacrifice yourself," he choked, staring at Emily. "You can't die."

Emily reached back to touch Joel's hand. "It's all right, Joel. Believe me, it is. If I do this, Olympus will be restored and you, my dad, and this whole world will be safe. I want to do it. Please, let me."

"But Emily—" Joel dropped his head, unable to form words. He squeezed her hand and looked away. The awful sounds of Nirads filled the air. They were on the main floor of the house and heading toward the front doors.

"They're coming," Emily said. "Pegs, take us to Olympus."

SEATED RIGHT BEHIND HIS WINGS, EMILY felt the stallion's growing strength as he trotted away from the house. When they reached an open area, he turned his head toward her and whinnied.

"He says hold on," Diana explained. "His wing is newly healed but untried. It may be a rough flight."

"You can do it, Pegs," Emily said, patting his neck. "I know you can."

As Pegasus moved from a trot to a full gallop, he spread his massive white wings. Emily clutched his mane as he leaped confidently into the air. She felt Joel tighten his grip around her waist as Pegasus rose up and over the dark water.

Manhattan lay dead ahead. As she looked at the

beautiful, sparkling lights, Emily realized this would be the last time she would ever see her home. If they made it safely to Olympus, she would die in the Temple of the Flame.

What would happen to her father? Where was he? She was going to die without his ever knowing what had happened to her. Or that she loved him and had done it for him. That pain was the worst of all.

Inhaling deeply, she looked down on New York. The city would be safe. All those millions of people in it would live and never see or hear of a Nirad again.

"Hey, wait for me!" a tiny, unsteady voice called from behind them.

"Paelen?"

Turning back, Emily and Joel saw Paelen struggling to catch up with them, limping through the dark air. Only one sandal was flapping its wings, and he was covered in blood.

"Paelen!" Emily cried. "You survived the Nirads!"

"Are you all right?" Joel called.

"No!" Paelen called back. "But I will live. Can you please slow down so I can catch up? The Nirads wounded a sandal, and only one is working."

The stallion snorted.

"Pegasus says you may hold on to his tail," Diana called back to Paelen. "He can help carry you home, but we must move faster if we are to reach Olympus."

In the night sky, it was difficult for Emily to clearly see Paelen. But as they passed over New York, the city lights revealed his deep, open wounds.

"What did they do to you?" Emily cried.

"They tried to tear me apart," Paelen called back. "But I was able to change my body so they could not do it. Though I have broken a lot of bones."

"Your bravery will not go unrewarded, Paelen," Diana promised. "My father will know what you did for us."

Before Paelen could respond, Pegasus whinnied to Diana.

"Emily, Joel," she called, "hold on. We are about to enter the Solar Stream to Olympus."

"The Solar what?" Joel started to ask.

Suddenly they were moving at an impossible speed. The starlight around them became a blur of white light. To Emily, it looked like special effects from a science fiction movie. But this was no movie. It was very, very real.

Looking back, she saw that Paelen was almost surfing the light as he struggled to cling to Pegasus's tail while the one sandal flapped its tiny wings to keep up. His terrified cries filled the air behind them.

What really surprised her was Pegasus. He was still beating his large wings. What would happen if he stopped? Emily wondered hazily. And how had Diana managed to get to Earth without wings?

As these thoughts spun through her head, Emily forgot her dark destiny for a moment. But when Pegasus slowed down and the white light faded back into simple starlight, she felt her fear return.

Not far ahead, Emily saw what looked like the top of a mountain rising in bright sunshine. They emerged from the starlight and passed into a beautiful sunny day. The sky was brilliant blue—bluer somehow than on Earth—and dotted with thick, fluffy white clouds. As Pegasus flew among them, Emily could taste their rich sweetness on her lips.

Lower and lower they went. Soon they could see lush green fields beneath them. The mountain rose from the green. Emily soon realized that they were heading toward it.

"Is that Mount Olympus?" Emily asked Diana.

"This is all Olympus, not just that mountain," Diana replied. "Though we do live at the top."

"Just like in the myths," Joel added, gazing around in wonder. "Is there a Mount Helicon here where the Muses live?"

"There is," Diana said. "That is where the Nirads first entered our world. The Muses were the first to be captured and Helicon the first to fall."

As they approached the mountain, Emily tried to take in all the sights. There were huge structures of glowing white marble. But as they drew near, she could see they had been knocked over, broken and destroyed.

"Did the Nirads do this?" she asked.

"Yes, and much worse," Diana answered.

Emily and Joel looked down on the ruins of Olympus and at last understood what they were fighting for. Before it had been destroyed by the Nirads, this world would have been the most beautiful place imaginable.

Beneath them, the amount of rubble grew in density as they entered what must have been a heavily populated area. But more than that, much to her horror, Emily started to see bodies of the dead Olympians. For as bad as seeing the men in the facility on Governors Island had been, this was so much worse. There were people of all ages, even children and strange-looking animals, lying dead on the ground.

"This is all my fault," Emily choked.

"No, it's not," Joel said, horrified. "That's crazy talk!"

"It's not crazy, Joel. If I'm the Flame, then when it became weaker in me, it became weaker here. I allowed the Nirads to attack and kill all these people."

"No, you're wrong," he protested. "I won't let you blame yourself for this. The Nirads did it, not you."

"I am sorry, Joel," Diana corrected. "Emily is not entirely wrong. She is the Flame of Olympus." Diana looked at Emily. "But she did not cause this intentionally. I now understand what did."

"What?" Emily asked weakly.

"Love," Diana answered. "The deep love you had for your mother. When she died, grief overwhelmed you. It diminished the Flame. It was not illness, as I first suspected. It was grief."

"What about now?" Emily asked in a whisper. "Is there enough Flame left in me to save Olympus and our world?"

Diana nodded. "Oh yes, child. Even I can feel it burning brightly in you now. You are recovering. I believe Pegasus had a great deal to do with it."

Pegasus snorted softly. Emily felt her heart fill with emotion for the stallion. Diana was right. Meeting Pegasus and caring for him had finally dimmed the searing pain of her mother's loss.

She looked back to Diana, "When the Temple of the Flame is lit again, will you be able to save these people? Will your brother live again?"

"I hope so," Diana said. "Without its people, there is no Olympus."

Pegasus started to glide in the clear air over the ruins.

"We are going down," Diana said. "We must all be on our guard. We are still in grave danger. Pegasus has taken us as close to the temple as he dares. But

369

legions of Nirads remain here. Their one goal will be to kill Pegasus and Emily."

"Do they know what I am?" Emily asked.

"I do not think so," Diana answered. "Because you were wounded before, they will chase you as much as they do Pegasus."

"We'll be careful," Joel said. "If we have to fight, we fight."

"I, too, am ready," Paelen said.

Emily looked back to him and could see his deep wounds and the odd angles of his arms and legs. More than just a few of his bones were broken.

Soon Pegasus landed. Emily was shocked by the stillness of the air around them.

"Is it always this quiet?"

Diana shook her head as she climbed off the stallion's back and helped Joel down. "No. Every animal, bird, and insect has fled the onslaught of the Nirads."

As Paelen touched down, Diana directed him closer to Emily. "Take her hand. She can help you heal."

Emily reached down and took Paelen's hand. As she lightly closed her fingers around his wrist, she felt the bones shift and slide, slotting back together. After a few moments, Paelen could stand better and didn't look to be in as much pain.

"I do not understand," he said as he looked at Emily in awe. "How are you doing this to me?"

Joel put his arm around Paelen's shoulders. "It's a long story, and we just don't have the time," he said. "Are you feeling well enough to fight?"

Paelen gave Emily his crooked grin. "I could take on Jupiter!" he said.

Diana actually chuckled. "Do not let my father hear you say that." Then she looked around. "We must move on. The temple is some distance away. Does everyone still have their gold?"

Emily and Joel held up their pieces of gold from Pegasus's bridle.

Paelen shook his head. "Mine is still lodged in the head of a Nirad back on Governors Island."

Diana reached up and took Emily's piece. She tore it in two, handing one part back to Emily and the other to Paelen. "Do not lose this one. We need every bit of it."

· · ·

Emily remained on Pegasus as the group slowly made their way through the rubble that once was Olympus. Several times she had to avert her eyes from the horrible casualties that littered the ground. With every nerve on edge, she strained her eyes and ears for fresh signs of the Nirads. She saw nothing but destruction and heard only the soft, empty wind. "Where are the Nirads?"

"I do not know," Diana answered, looking around. "But it worries me. There were thousands here not long ago. We must be on our guard. I do not believe they have left already."

Pressing on, they reached the spot where the worst fighting had taken place. Among all the ruins, Emily saw tall steps leading up to the remains of a temple. The heavy metal gates at the top had been torn from their hinges and cast down on the steps.

Instinctively Emily recognized this place.

"That is the Temple of the Flame, isn't it?" she asked, pointing to the ruins.

Diana nodded but said nothing. She was kneeling before the body of a fallen Olympian. She reached out and gently stroked dark hair from a bruised and bloodied face, silent tears trickling down her cheeks.

Seeing this strong, confident woman brought weeping to her knees made Emily realize all the sacrifices that had been made already.

"Is that your brother?" Joel asked softly.

Diana sniffed, and nodded. "It is Apollo. He was a brave and honorable fighter. I loved him dearly." She looked around at the other dead fighters. "They were all brave."

"He will be avenged," Paelen said, determined. "I promise you, Diana, they all will."

The horrible cries of Nirads shattered the stillness of the area. Emily looked back, and her eyes went wide at the sight of hundreds of Nirads bearing down on them from nowhere.

"We must go!" Diana cried as she rose and left her dead brother. She ran to Pegasus and Emily. "Child, it is up to you now. You are this world's only hope. Your sacrifice could save us all. I grieve at what you must now face. But I swear your name and your gift to us will not be forgotten by any Olympian!"

She pulled Emily's face closer to her and kissed her on the cheek. "Your mother will be very proud of you when she meets you in Elysium."

Tears filled Emily's eyes as she realized the time of her death had come. After only a few short years of life, it was going to end in the agony of flames in this shattered world.

"Joel, go with Pegasus and Emily. Take them to the temple," Diana ordered. "Paelen and I will do our best to hold back as many as we can." She looked back up at Emily. "Go now, child. Fulfill your destiny!"

Emily didn't even have time to say good-bye to Paelen as Pegasus darted forward. Joel struggled to keep up beside her as they ran toward the Temple of the Flame. When they reached the base of the steps, Emily looked back and saw hundreds, maybe thousands, of Nirads charging toward them. Diana threw back her head and howled the loudest battle cry Emily had ever heard. With Paelen at her side, they held up their pieces of gold bridle and charged forward into the mass of Nirads.

At the temple steps, Pegasus hesitated.

"Take me up, Pegs," Emily said softly as tears filled her eyes. "If I don't do this now, they'll kill you and Joel. Let me do it for you."

Hesitantly Pegasus started to climb the marble steps. Emily heard Joel's sniffles beside her.

"I'm not sure I can watch this," Joel whispered.

Emily looked into her friend's red, teary eyes. "It's all right, Joel. Really it is. But if you somehow survive this, please promise me you'll go back to Earth and find my dad. If the CRU still have him, get him away. Bring him back here. Don't let them hurt him."

Joel looked up at her but couldn't speak. He nodded his head weakly.

At the top of the steps, Pegasus stopped. Emily looked to Joel. "Would you help me down?"

Joel helped her climb down from Pegasus and steadied her on her undamaged leg.

"Do you want me to help you into the temple?" he whispered.

Pegasus snorted and nickered softly. Emily sniffed and shook her head. "I don't think you're allowed." As grief overwhelmed her, Emily threw her arms around Joel's neck. She hugged him tightly. "Please stay well," she wept.

"I'll try," he promised. As he broke down, he kissed Emily on the forehead. "Thank you for being my friend, Emily." Then, with a final backward glance, he drew out his gold piece and charged down the steps of the temple to join Diana and Paelen in their struggle against the Nirads.

"Joel, no!" Emily howled. But Joel gave no sign of hearing her as he ran screaming into the thick legion of Nirads.

"Oh, Pegasus," Emily wept.

Pegasus reached back and nudged her gently. She knew he was telling her it was time to go. She had a destiny to fulfill; Olympus to save. When he opened his newly healed wing, Emily used it to support herself while she hopped the final distance into the building.

The ruined temple was empty except for the huge marble bowl where the Flame of Olympus had once blazed. It had been knocked off its plinth and was badly cracked.

Pegasus slowly drew her up to the bowl. It was there that Emily knew she was about to die.

As she hopped forward, she came up to the stallion's head. Her tears were falling steadily, and she could no longer see clearly. "I'm glad it was me, Pegs," she said, her voice breaking. "I didn't want you to care for someone else. Even though I'm going to die, I know that deep in my heart, for at least a little while, you were mine. I just wish we had more time together. . . ."

Emily broke down and hugged Pegasus's head as her voice finally gave out. "I love you, Pegasus."

Letting him go, she hobbled to the large, cracked marble bowl. With a final backward glance, she saw the black-and-brown stallion with the brilliant white wings lowering his head and pawing the ground in grief.

"Please remember me, Pegs," Emily said. She looked away from him and climbed into the large marble bowl.

33

THE MOMENT EMILY STOOD UPRIGHT IN THE bowl; she felt a searing pain in her heart. She clutched at her chest and cried out in agony. This was it. Death. She was about to be burned alive.

An instant later huge brilliant flames burst out of her chest. The explosion of flame and energy filled the temple with brilliant white light and spread like huge ripples on water. Flying in every direction, it poured out of the temple and throughout all Olympus. The flames were coming from each part of her, consuming her and spilling out of her every pore.

As she stood in the center of the flames, the pain slowly ebbed and finally disappeared completely. Emily looked around. She was searching for her mother. She'd always heard that the moment you died, your family came for you. But where was her mother? Her grandfather, everyone she had ever lost?

All she saw was flame and brilliant light. She felt an increasing sense of peace washing over her.

Emily waited. For how long, she was uncertain. All she knew was that somehow, she was still herself. She could think, feel, and hold on to all the love and memories she had. She remembered everything about her life. The happy years with her mother and father in New York. Her mother's illness and, finally, death. And although there was pain at the memory, Emily knew it wasn't as bad as it had been before. But then again, she also knew her mother would be waiting for her just outside the flames.

Emily thought of Joel. Sweet, angry, hurt Joel and that first endless climb up the stairs of her building. It all seemed such a long time ago. She promised herself she would find his family and tell them what he had done for her. She recalled Paelen's crooked smile and cleverness. Then there was Diana—beautiful and strong Diana crying over the death of a New

York horse and the body of her fallen brother. But most of all, Emily remembered . . . Pegasus.

Thoughts of the stallion brought a smile to her burning lips. Of all the new friends in her life, Emily knew that in death, she would miss him the most.

After the briefest of moments, or perhaps the longest of eternities, Emily felt something change. The flames were drawing back. Soon she could see again, and somehow she knew it was time to leave the flames.

A new journey spread out before her. She felt certain her mother would be there waiting for her.

As she moved to the edge of the bowl, she could see between the flickering flames. And what she saw gave her more joy than she could imagine possible: Pegasus.

He was no longer brown and black. Pegasus was glowing brilliant white again. Not a feather stood out of place on his beautiful folded wings. Majestic and proud, he was perfect.

Emily bent down and grasped the edge of the bowl for support. When she did, she noticed that the crack in the marble was gone. Not only that, but the bowl was no longer lying on the floor of the temple. Somehow, it was back on its tall plinth.

Crawling over the top edge, Emily lowered her good leg down to the ground. When she put her wounded leg down, she felt no pain. It was true! she thought. When you died, all the pain stopped.

But when Emily added more weight, she found her leg still would not support her. Losing her balance, she fell heavily to the marble floor.

Pegasus was instantly at her side.

"Pegs?" Emily said in confusion as she looked up into his warm brown eyes and felt his tongue on her cheek. "Can you see me?"

"We all can, child," Diana called.

Emily looked over and saw Diana standing at the entrance to the temple, dressed in a stunning white tunic. Another beautiful woman stood beside her. Emily felt she should know her, but she couldn't think of her name.

Diana rushed forward and helped Emily to her feet. She handed her an Olympian robe and hugged her tightly. "We are all so proud of you."

"But I died," Emily said. "I don't understand."

"You have been reborn," said the other woman. She came forward and embraced Emily. "My beautiful child, my Flame. I am Vesta."

Emily's eyes flew wide. "You're Vesta? Really? And I'm alive?"

Both women smiled. Finally Diana nodded to Pegasus. "Ask him if you do not believe me. He never left your side. He has waited here all this time for you to return to us."

Emily turned to Pegasus, and the stallion pressed closer. She touched his glowing muzzle. "Pegs?" she said, still hardly believing the truth. Finally she threw her arms around his neck. "Pegs, I'm alive!"

"We all are," Diana said, "with grateful thanks to you. Because of what you did, your sacrifice, Olympus has been restored."

"How?" Emily asked. "What did I do?"

"Get dressed and come see for yourself."

Emily pulled on the robe and tied it at the waist. She clung to Diana and Pegasus for support as they made their way to the entrance of the temple. Behind her, the Flame continued to burn brightly on its plinth.

Emily's eyes flew wide in disbelief. Standing at the

base of the temple steps were thousands of people. When they saw her emerge from the temple with Diana, Pegasus, and Vesta, they raised their voices in cheers and salutes.

"These are your people, Emily," Diana said. "All alive because of you. My brother is down there, waiting to thank you himself. Soon my father will join us and offer his gratitude."

"Jupiter?" Emily gasped in shock.

Diana smiled and nodded.

It was almost too much to take in. But as Emily's eyes scanned the huge and endless crowd, they lit upon Joel and Paelen, standing side by side at the foot of the steps.

"Joel!" Emily cried as she started to wave frantically. "Paelen!"

Both started to race up the steps to greet her. Paelen arrived first and wrapped his arms around her and gave her a brutal embrace. Joel was right behind him. With a tight hug, he swung her around in the air.

"I don't know what the heck you did in there, or how you did it." Joel laughed as he swung Emily round again. "But it worked!"

Emily was left speechless. "I don't know either." She laughed.

Pegasus nudged Emily playfully.

"He wants you to get on his back," Diana explained. "He is going to carry you down the steps."

Joel helped Emily climb onto Pegasus. When she was settled, the stallion neighed gently.

"Pegasus, no," Vesta said sternly. "The Flame has only just emerged. She must meet her people."

Emily looked at Diana, a thousand questions in her eyes.

Diana laughed. "Pegasus says hold on tightly. He is going to show you Olympus his way."

Before Vesta could protest further, Pegasus opened his wings, reared on his hind legs, and threw back his head in an excited whinny as he leaped confidently off the top of the temple steps and into the air.

Emily's heart thrilled at the feeling of the powerful stallion beneath her. As she clung to Pegasus's mane and felt the strong beating of his wings, she was part of him. They were one. Emily threw back her own head and whooped in pure joy.

Pegasus made a full circle of the top of the temple.

Then, with Emily still safely secured on his back, he flapped his massive wings and took her away over the heads of the cheering crowd. Emily waved at the people as she passed, still hardly believing what was happening. Beneath her, the scars of the war were being healed as workers rebuilt the beautiful buildings.

There was only one thing missing: her father. He was still a prisoner of the CRU. But as she soared on the bare back of Pegasus, feeling a joy unmatched, Emily knew it wouldn't be long before he would be freed and they would be reunited. Whatever came next, as long as Pegasus was with her, Emily knew everything would be all right.

ABOUT THE AUTHOR

Kate O'Hearn was born in Canada and raised in New York City, and has traveled all over the United States. She currently resides in England. Kate is the author of Shadow of the Dragon series in addition to her books about Pegasus and Emily. Visit her at kateohearn.com

THE ADVENTURE CONTINUES
IN BOOK 2:

Olympus at War

OLYMPUS WAS UNLIKE ANYWHERE EMILY had ever been before. It was a magical fantasyland filled with people and creatures beyond imagination. A place where rain didn't fall but the lush green gardens never wilted. Flowers bloomed constantly, filling the air with their intoxicating fragrances. The air itself seemed alive. It was honey sweet and warm and enveloped you in a blanket of peace; it was rich with the sounds of singing birds and filled with insects that never stung. If a bee landed on you, it was only because it wanted to be petted.

The buildings in Olympus were as beautiful and unique as the land itself. Most were made of smooth white marble with tall, intricately carved pillars reaching high into the clear blue sky. There were open theaters where the Muses danced and sang for the entertainment of all.

The wide cobbled streets were lined with statues of the strongest fighters and heroes. There were no cars or trucks pumping pollution into the air. The Olympians walked or flew wherever they needed to go. Occasionally they would ride in a chariot drawn by magnificent horses.

Then there were the libraries, more than Emily could count, containing the texts from the many worlds the Olympians visited and guarded. Some of her favorite books were in the library at Jupiter's palace, brought in especially for her.

Emily could never have imagined a more perfect place.

But living in Olympus, amid all this splendor, Emily was miserable.

She missed her father. She spent every waking moment thinking and worrying about him. He was back in her world, a prisoner of the Central Research Unit. The CRU was a secret government agency obsessed with capturing aliens and anything out of the ordinary to use as weapons. She had been their prisoner for a short time and knew how single-minded and cruel they were. But they still had her father. What were they doing to him? Were they punishing him because of her escape? Had they killed him? So many fears and unanswered questions tore at her heart that she could never be completely happy or stop worrying about him.

Even spending time with Pegasus didn't ease the pain. Emily was desperate to get back to New York to find her father, but Jupiter wouldn't let her go. He insisted her place was here among the other Olympians. And with the invading warrior race of Nirads still posing a threat to Olympus, Jupiter couldn't risk sending any of his fighters to Emily's world on a rescue mission. No matter how much she pleaded with the god, he refused to allow her to leave.

Emily paused as she walked through the gardens of Jupiter's palace. She raised her face to the sun and felt its warm rays streaming down on her. Was this the same sun that shone in her world? Was her father allowed to see it? From her own experience as a prisoner in the CRU's deep underground facility, she doubted it.

Emily felt even more determined. If Jupiter wouldn't let her go, she had no choice but to run away and rescue her father herself. Walking along the stream that coursed through Olympus, she saw a group of beautiful water nymphs splashing on the shore. They waved and called their strange greeting. Moments later they slipped beneath the surface, and the water calmed as if they'd never been there.

Lost in thought, Emily wasn't paying attention to where she was walking and tripped over a small rock. She cursed and righted herself. On top of everything else, she was still getting used to the new gold leg brace that Vulcan, the armorer of Olympus, had made for her. He had constructed it using the same gold as Pegasus's bridle. A very special gold that was lethal to Nirads. With one brief touch they were badly poisoned. Longer contact proved fatal to the ferocious warriors. With this brace Emily could not only defend herself against the invaders, she could walk and run once again.

But learning to get around with the strange device had taken time and effort. Now she could almost move as well as she had before her leg was permanently damaged by the Nirads in New York.

She walked toward Jupiter's maze, a large labyrinth built in the middle of a garden and consisting of tall green bushes grown in complicated patterns. It took a lot of practice to navigate it, but Emily and her friends had discovered that the maze was the perfect place to hold private conversations.

Emily found her way through the labyrinth, where Pegasus was waiting for her beside the pedestal at the center. The magnificent winged stallion always stole her breath. Standing quietly in the dark of the trees, he glowed brilliant white. His head was high and proud, and his coat shiny and well groomed. There wasn't a feather out of place on his neatly folded wings.

When Pegasus saw her, he whinnied excitedly and nodded his head.

Beside the winged horse stood Emily's best friend from New York, Joel. Joel's Roman features, black hair, and warm brown eyes always reminded her of the classic Italian paintings she'd seen in the art museum. He was no longer the violent, angry boy she had first met. Spending time in Olympus had softened his outer shell of rage and hurt due to the loss of his family. Now he let others see that he had a deeply caring heart and a ready laugh. Joel spent his days working with Vulcan in the Olympus armory. He had even helped design the brace on Emily's leg.

Emily looked around. "Where's Paelen?"

"He'll be here in a few minutes. He had something to pick up." Joel reached for her elbow. "Em, you're absolutely sure you want to do this?"

"What choice have I got?" Emily answered. "Joel, all I think about is saving my dad. There's nothing else I can do. We wouldn't have to sneak around like this if Jupiter would help!" She threw her hands up in frustration. As she brought them down, brilliant flames flashed from her fingertips, hit the edge of her good foot, and scorched the ground around it. Emily howled and hopped in pain.

"Emily, calm down!" Joel warned. "You know it gets worse when you're upset."

"Nuts!" she cried. "Being the Flame of Olympus is one thing. But constantly setting myself on fire is another!"

"You've got to calm down," Joel insisted. "Remember what Vesta taught you. You can control the Flame if you remain calm."

"That's easier said than done," Emily complained as she sat down and rubbed her singed foot. Ever since she emerged from the Temple of the Flame, she was discovering powers she couldn't control. Powers that continually set things alight.

Joel sat down beside her. "We'll get your dad out of there. I promise. But you can't help him if you can't control the Flame."

"Joel's right." Paelen emerged from the trees behind them. In contrast to Joel, he was small and wiry, and he was able to get into the tiniest of spaces. Paelen had a notorious habit of getting into trouble, but with his crooked grin and dark, sparkling eyes, he always found a way to make Emily smile. "And if I were you, I would lower your voices. Half the maze can hear your conversation." He sat down beside Emily and gave her a playful shove. "Set yourself on fire again I see."

"No, I tripped," Emily answered, shoving him back.

Paelen smiled his crooked smile. "Of course you

did; which is why your sandal is charcoal and still smoldering."

In the time they'd spent in Olympus, Emily had really grown to like Paelen. Between him and Joel, she couldn't have asked for better friends. Paelen was also one of the few Olympians who understood what they'd been through as prisoners of the CRU on Governors Island.

"Speaking of sandals"—Emily changed the subject—"you didn't steal Mercury's again, did you?" She noticed the winged sandals on his feet.

"Me? Of course not," Paelen said in mock horror. "You know I'm no longer a thief. Mercury just gave them to me. He is having another set made for himself." Paelen paused and frowned. "He said the sandals prefer to stay with me. I do not understand what he means, but I'm not going to say no to such a useful gift." He petted the tiny wings on the sandals. "These flying sandals saved our lives in your world and helped us escape the CRU. There is no telling what else they can do." He leaned closer to Emily and eagerly rubbed his hands together. "So, tell me. When do we leave for New York?"

Pegasus stepped forward and started to nicker.

Paelen nodded and translated for the others. "Pegasus heard Jupiter, Mars, and Hercules talking. They are going on an expedition to see if they can discover how the Nirads entered Olympus in such large numbers without being seen. Until they know and can secure the route, we are still in danger. Pegasus suggests if we are going to go to New York to rescue your father, we should leave once they're gone."

Emily rose and kissed the stallion on his soft muzzle. "Thank you, Pegasus. That's a great idea." She turned to Joel and Paelen. "It's settled, then. The moment Jupiter leaves, we're out of here!"

Quietly they discussed their plans as they strolled through the maze. Emily rested her hand on Pegasus's neck as he walked beside her.

"We'll need some human clothes," Joel mused aloud. "We can't arrive back in New York dressed like this."

"What is wrong with these?" Paelen looked down at his tunic. "I have always dressed this way."

"You're kidding, right?" Joel smirked. "Paelen,

we look like rejects from a gladiator movie! Look at me—I'm wearing a dress!"

"It's a tunic," Emily corrected him, "and I think it suits you." She looked down at her own beautiful gown made from fine white embroidered silk with an intricate braided gold belt at her waist. The material ended above the golden brace on her damaged left leg, leaving it exposed. Emily had never felt embarrassed revealing the deep, angry scars from the Nirad wounds while she was on Olympus. The Olympians regarded them as a badge of honor. She had earned them in the service of Olympus, and she had learned to be proud of them. But as she gazed down at her leg now, she realized that the deep scars and leg brace wouldn't be viewed as positively in her world.

"Joel's right," she agreed. "I can't go back there like this either. We've got to hide this brace."

Pegasus started to neigh, and Paelen translated. "If anyone should try to steal it from you, Pegasus would defend you, as would Joel and I." A playful twinkle returned to his eyes. "Of course, should that fail, you could always set yourself on fire again. That would surely scare off any attackers!"

"Thanks, Paelen," Emily teased as she shoved him lightly. Then she patted Pegasus on the neck. "And thank you, Pegs. But I still think we will need to find other clothing."

"Other clothing for what?"

Emily looked up at the owner of the new voice. Despite all the time they'd spent in Olympus, she still couldn't get over the sight of Cupid. Seeing Pegasus's wings had been strange at the beginning. But somehow they suited him. She couldn't imagine him without them. But looking at a teenager with colorful, pheasantlike feathered wings on his back was something else.

Cupid pulled in his wings and landed neatly in the maze before them. "So, where are you going that you need new clothing?" he asked.

"None of your business," Joel shot back. "Didn't your mother ever teach you any manners? It's not polite to listen in on other people's conversation."

"Of course," Cupid said. "But she also taught me that when humans and Olympians mix, there is always trouble. And what do I see before my curious eyes? Humans mixing with Olympians."

Cupid smiled radiantly at Emily, and it set her heart fluttering. She had a terrible crush on him, and he knew it. He was the most beautiful Olympian she had ever met, with fine features, light sandy blond hair, sapphire blue eyes that sparkled, and skin like polished marble. Though Cupid was very old, he looked no more than sixteen or seventeen.

Emily stole a glance at Joel and saw his temper starting to flare. The way Cupid pronounced the word "humans" was always meant as an insult. "Get out of here, Cupid," Joel warned. "This is a private conversation, and you are *not* welcome."

"Is this true?" Cupid said slyly to Emily. "Do you really wish me to go?"

The intensity of his stare kept the words from forming on her lips. Everything about him was trouble. Joel had told her some of the myths concerning Cupid. She knew that, like a coward, he had fled the area when the Nirads first attacked and had stayed away until the danger had gone. Yet despite all this, she couldn't tell him to go.

Before the moment became awkward, Pegasus stepped forward and snorted loudly.

"Trouble?" Cupid repeated as he turned and feigned innocence to the stallion. "I am not causing trouble. I just wanted to speak with the Flame."

"Her name is Emily," Paelen said defensively. He moved to stand in front of Emily to block her from Cupid. "Do not call her Flame."

"And I told you to leave," Joel added, taking position beside Paelen and crossing his arms over his chest.

"Or what?" Cupid challenged. "What will you do to me, human?"

Once again Pegasus snorted, and he pounded the ground with a golden hoof. There was no mistaking the warning. Emily saw fear rise in Cupid's eyes. Even Paelen took a cautious step back from the stallion.

"There is no need to lose your temper, Pegasus." Cupid held up his hands in surrender. "I shall go."

His wings opened as he prepared to fly. But before leaving, Cupid plucked a colorful feather from his right wing and placed it in Emily's hair. "Something to put under your pillow to remember me by," he said as he jumped into the air and flapped his large wings. "See you later, Flame!"

Pegasus reared on his hind legs, opened his own huge wings, and shrieked into the sky after him.

As Cupid escaped, he turned and waved back at her, laughing as he went.

"I came this close to hitting him!" Joel said, balling his hands into fists.

"Me too," Paelen said.

Pegasus gently nudged Emily and nickered softly.

"You must stay away from Cupid," Paelen explained. "Pegasus says he is trouble. Even more than— What?" Paelen turned sharply to the stallion. "Me? Pegasus, how can you compare Cupid to me? We are nothing alike. I may have been a thief, but Cupid is a troublemaking coward, and I resent being compared to him. And what about you?" Paelen turned to Emily. He pulled the feather from her hair and tossed it to the ground. "You should have told him to go. Cupid would think nothing of handing you over to the Nirads if it meant saving his own skin and feathers. Stay away from him!"

Emily watched in complete confusion as Paelen stormed off into the maze and disappeared. Paelen had never shown any trace of anger or raised his voice to her before. "What did I do?"

Joel looked at her in surprise. "You really don't know?"

When she shook her head, he said, "Never mind. We've got bigger things to worry about. You must learn to control those powers of yours before we leave. You've got your training session with Vesta. Keep it and learn as much as you can."

As Joel walked away, Emily turned to Pegasus and shook her head. "You know something, Pegs? The older I get, the more confused I get. Can you please tell me what just happened here?"

Pegasus gently nudged her and led her back toward Jupiter's palace to find Vesta.

Emily spent a long afternoon back in the Temple of the Flame struggling to learn how to master her powers. Vesta tried to teach her, but every time Emily summoned the powers, they became uncontrollable.

Vesta patiently explained how to pull back the Flame, to control it. But every time Emily tried, she failed, and flames shot wildly from her hands and around the temple.

"I can't do it," Emily complained, defeated.

"Child, you must focus," Vesta scolded. "I can see your mind is elsewhere. If you are not careful, you will lose control of your powers completely and hurt yourself as you did earlier today."

Emily's eyes shot over to where Pegasus stood at the entrance of the temple. He lowered his head guiltily.

"Thanks, Pegs," she muttered.

"Do not blame Pegasus for telling me what happened," Vesta said. "He cares about you and does not wish to see you harmed." Vesta rested her hands on Emily's shoulders. "Emily, you must understand. You are the Living Flame of Olympus. Your power feeds the Flame here in this temple, and it keeps us alive. Countless generations ago, I took the heart of the Flame to your world and hid it in a child. It has passed from girl to girl throughout the ages until it finally reached you. You were born with this power. I am sorry that we have had to summon it from within you to save Olympus. But the moment you sacrificed yourself in this temple you changed. Emily, you carry the power of the sun deep within you. If you do not harness these powers soon, you may do yourself and everyone around you a great harm."

Emily looked down at her burned sandal. She already knew how dangerous her powers were. She had accidentally burned up enough items in her quarters to prove it. It was reaching the point where she was running out of secret hiding places for the singed victims of her powers.

"I'm sorry," she finally said. "I'll try harder."

Turning back to the plinth, she looked into the brightly burning flames. They were fed by her and were the only things in Olympus her powers couldn't damage.

"All right," Vesta said patiently. "Look into the flames. I want you to focus on what you intend to do. Visualize yourself doing it. Then concentrate and carefully release the power within yourself."

Emily lifted both her hands and concentrated. She imagined that she was a giant blowtorch turning on the gases. She felt prickles start in her stomach and flow up her spine and flood down her raised arms toward her hands. "Come on, Em," she muttered to herself. "You can do it."

Suddenly a wide, wild stream of fire shot out of her fingertips.

"Very good. Now concentrate," Vesta instructed. "Control the stream, Emily. Make it tighter."

Emily held her breath as the raging flames shot out of her hands. Concentrating as Vesta taught her, she pulled back and refined them until they became a narrow beam of red light. But the tighter she pulled back, the more intense it became.

The beam of light shot through the flames in the plinth and across the temple until it hit the far wall. It did not stop. It burned a narrow hole right through the thick white marble and continued out into the sky over Olympus.

"Cut if off now, Emily," Vesta warned. "Just think 'stop'!"

In her head, Emily imagined shutting off the gases to the blowtorch. But nothing happened. She mentally turned all the dials and flicked all the switches that controlled her powers. But once again, the beam would not stop.

"Cut it off, Emily," Vesta cried. "You must make it obey you!"

Emily tried again and again, but nothing happened. As her panic increased, so did the intensity of the laserlike Flame. It pulsated as it tore through the skies over Olympus.

"I CAN'T STOP IT!"

A sudden blow from behind sent her tumbling forward, and she fell to the floor. With her concentration broken, the red beam stopped. She panted heavily and studied her hands. No burns, blemishes, or pain. She looked up, and what she saw made her suck in her breath. Pegasus's whole face and neck were burned bright red. Worst of all, his soft white muzzle was black and blistering. It was Pegasus who had knocked her over and stopped the flames. But when he touched her, her power had singed his beautiful skin.

"Pegasus!" Emily ran over to him. "I'm so sorry. I swear I didn't mean to do it!"

She felt sick as she inspected his wounds. She had done this to him. "Please, forgive me!" Without thinking, Emily reached forward and gently stroked his burned face. At her touch, the skin started to heal. Soon Pegasus was completely restored.

"I can't do this, Pegs." Emily sobbed as she stepped away from him. "I just can't. I hurt you. What if I'd killed you? I'm just too dangerous to be around."

Emily dashed out of the temple. Tears rose to her eyes as she ran down the tall steps. She cringed as she replayed what happened and, worse still, what could have happened.

At the base of the steps, she looked up and saw Pegasus and Vesta emerging from the temple.

"Emily, stop!" Vesta called.

Emily turned and ran farther away. She couldn't face Pegasus again, knowing she had almost killed him. She ran past other Olympians on the street, ignoring their curious stares and concerned queries. She had to get away. Away from Pegasus and anyone else her powers could hurt. She was just too dangerous to be allowed in public.

Emily finally ran into the open amphitheater. The Muses weren't performing that day, so the thousands of seats sat empty and alone. The perfect place for someone dangerous. She ran down the steps, toward the center stage, and threw herself to the ground. It was over. Her life was over. There would be no trip back to New York, no rescue of her father.

All there was now was pain.

Sobs escaped her as she finally realized all the things she'd lost. She wished she'd never emerged from the flames at the temple. Olympus and Pegasus would have been better off without her.

Tears blinded Emily as she looked around in misery at the beautiful marble theater encircling her. She wiped them furiously away. As she flicked the tears off her fingers, there was a blinding flash and a terrible explosion.

Her world went black.